SEVEN SIX ONE

Seven Six One

G.F. Borden

BURNING GATE PRESS
LOS ANGELES

For information address:
Burning Gate Press
P. O. Box 6015
Mission Hills, CA 91395-1015
(818) 896-8780

FIRST PRINTING

Library of Congress Catalog Card Number: 91-61772

ISBN 1-878179-03-9

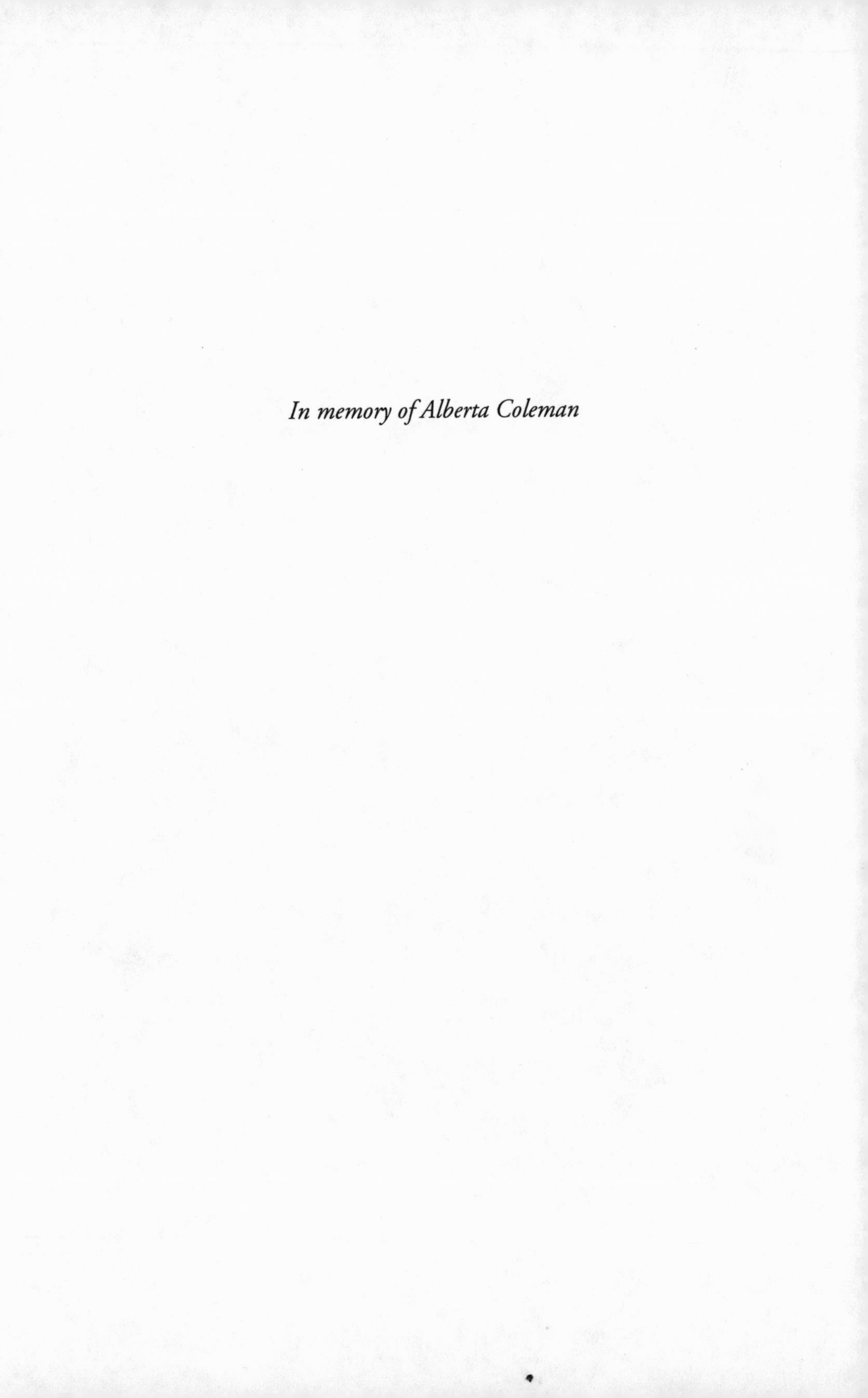

In memory of Alberta Coleman

ACKNOWLEDGEMENTS

I would not have written this novel had I not read David J. Williams's *Hit Hard* (Bantam Books, 1983) and Trezzvant W. Anderson's *Come Out Fighting* (Salzburger Drukerei und Verlag, 1945); and I could not have written it had I not studied that volume by Ulysses Lee published in 1966 as one of the Special Studies in the series entitled *United States Army in World War II* prepared by the Office of the Chief of Military History, United States Army.

Those who read these three books will understand the many general and particular debts I owe to each of them; and will note that I have taken the details of many of the events I describe from their histories. In particular, the citations I have quoted or paraphrased are set out in an appendix to *Come Out Fighting.*

My thanks to:

Captain Thomas M. Carhart (USA retired) for his careful reading of the manuscript of this novel and his generous comments about it;

Sergeant Major Dan Cragg (USA retired) for his kind and thoughtful remarks—and more for the twenty substantive changes he suggested on November 19, 1988, all but one of which I included in the manuscript on the morning of November 20, 1988; and

Margaret S. Nalle for her interest in and her kind comments about this novel—and for finding many typographical errors in the manuscript.

Al and Jo Hart of The Fox Chase Agency. Inc. cannot know how much I value their friendship. Nor can they know how much their perseverance and optimism have contributed to the writing of this novel and others.

Without Hildegard's fortitude and calm, I would not have written this book.

Author's Note

Most of the men mentioned in this novel have left their names behind them so that their praises may be reported. They are:

761st Tank Battalion:

Garland N. Adamson
Moses Ballard
Thomas E. Bruce
William E. Burroughs
L.C. Byrd
Daniel Cardell
Carlton Chapman
Ernest Chatmon
Frank C. Cochrane
Kenneth W. Coleman
George Collier
Warren G. H. Crecy
Moses E. Dade
Louis M. Daniel
Ivery Fox
Harold B. Gary
Charles A. Gates
Russell C. Geist, Jr.
George Goines
Austin C. Jackson
Otis Johnson
Harold Kingsley
Ervin Lattimore
Claude Mann
Christopher P. Navarre
Isiah Parks
Crawford Pegram
Freddie C. Reedy

Edwin W. Reynolds
Ruben Rivers
James I. Rollins
Nathaniel Simmons
Dwight Simpson
Buck A. Smith
Leonard Smith
James E. Stewart
Joseph A. Tates
Emery G. Thomas
Samuel J. Turley
David J. Williams
Harvey Woodard

In this novel I refer to the man who commanded the 761st by his rank alone. His name was Paul L. Bates.

614th Tank Destroyer Battalion (Towed):
Robert W. Harris
Beauregard King
Charles E. Parks
Frank S. Pritchard

333rd Field Artillery Group Headquarters:
Broman Williams

369th Infantry Regiment:
Henry Johnson
Needham Roberts

While I have not named any individual who served with the following units, they have left as good an inheritance as have the 761st, the 614th, the 333rd and the 369th:
57th Ordnance Ammunition Company
333rd Field Artillery Battalion
592nd Port Company
969th Field Artillery Battalion

If I have used the name of any other individual who served with the 761st Tank Battalion, that use was unintended and—except in two cases—felicitous.

"I don't care what. . .you are, so long as you go up there and kill those. . .sons of bitches!"

Lieutenant General George S.Patton, Jr., welcoming the 761st Tank Battalion to the 3rd Army near St-Nicholas-de-Port, France, on November 2,1944.

SEVEN SIX ONE

All these were honored in their generations
And were the glory of their times
There be of them
That have left a name behind them
That their praises might be reported
And some there be which have no memorial
Who are perished as though they had never been
And are become as though they had never been born
And their children after them
But these were merciful men
Whose righteousness hath not been forgotten
With their seed shall continually remain
A good inheritance
And their children are within the covenant
Their seed standeth fast
And their children for their sakes
Their seed shall remain for ever
And their glory shall not be blotted out
Their bodies are buried in peace
But their name liveth for evermore

Ecclesiasticus xliv

One

Down in the valley, beyond the stream in the unploughed winter ground, in the shadows among the pine trees at the foot of the far slope, I see bluegrey exhaust waver up and hear the grind and cough of engine start.

As the westerly wind whips the exhaust away, I see a trembling among the pines and watch bushy green branches lean against the wind. Staring through fieldglasses, I nod and nod as though I have seen an old friend: these branches have been cut from trees deeper in the forest and worked into netting drawn across a German armored fighting vehicle's hull; for in this war in northwestern Europe, only a German tank or self-propelled gun waits in ambush, engine off, until a target appears.

The driver of this camouflaged vehicle works the clutch and accelerator, hauling at the levers that brake one track and transfer power to the other. He waddles the vehicle's bulk—hardened steel, fuel, radios, weapons, machinery, electrical wiring, ammunition and men—north to south. I cannot see the vehicle behind its camouflage, but when it begins to shift left to right I know it is a self-propelled gun and not a tank: a tank does not require power to rotate its turret, while a self-propelled gun has no turret, and its main armament fixed in the sloped front of its hull can traverse through no more than twenty degrees unless the vehicle itself is shifted.

The narrow traverse of the main armament is the fault of all self-propelled guns. Yet because an SPG is turretless, it can be fitted with a more powerful gun than a tank of similar size, for the designers need not worry about the effect of recoil on the turret race, or the limited space inside a turret in which the blunt breech of the gun must fit.

These engineering details mean little: the self-propelled gun across the valley is German, and I will wager the crate of square bottles of Genever tucked under canvas in the back of the halftrack in which I stand that the narrow arc through which this SPG's gun can traverse is a design limitation for which the efficient conduct of this SPG's crew will be compensation enough.

Yet the commander of this SPG should have ordered his gunner to fire at the two B Company Shermans—Big Sam first, Bayou Queen fifty yards behind—sliding down the road on this side of the valley before he ordered the SPG's driver to start engine and shift the vehicle's position. I wonder why the SPG's commander didn't give the order. Perhaps he is as tired as we. Or perhaps he was asleep, or taking a piss, or chewing sausage, when Big Sam and Bayou Queen appeared at the top of the road on our side the valley.

It is possible this SPG's crew are children, which would account for the mistake they have made. We have seen more and more children as the fighting has approached its conclusion, and children, thank God, have a lot to learn. We have taken many of them prisoner. We have watched many more flee, and killed those who did not. But even this close to the end of the war it is unlikely this SPG's crew are young and untrained: the Germans don't have a lot of self-propelled guns left, and the crew manning this one is certain to be experienced and calm.

Still they have made an error: they shifted their position before they fired at Big Sam and Bayou Queen. However tired they may be, they have violated a rule: they should have seen Big Sam descending the road into the valley, Bayou Queen, an old M4A1 with a 75 millimeter gun in its turret, following, and shot down both Shermans before they started the SPG's engine. They didn't: and so they have been forced to shift their vehicle's position to permit their gunner to fire. And so they have shown us where they lurked in ambush.

On the other hand, though they have made a mistake, it is not serious: no mistake, even this late in the war, is serious if you're crouched inside a big enough SPG behind the breech of a seventy-five millimeter gun, or better yet, an eighty-eight.

As the SPG waddles left to right, crabbing toward the south, a clutch of branches falls from the netting its methodical crew has drawn across the elegant design of its hull. Through the fieldglasses I see the coruscations of anti-magnetic paste ridged on the sloped front of the vehicle's steel carapace, and as the SPG shifts again, more branches woven into the camouflage netting stretched over the vehicle's low bulk are dislodged and the lidded chink beside the gun's mantle from which the hull machinegun extends is disclosed. The vehicle continues to back and fill, and soon I see six feet of the guntube and the slitted fist of the muzzlebrake extended through the camouflage netting jounce and sway through short bobbing arcs with each shift of the tracks and waddle of the hull.

I note the length of the gun. As I feared, it is an eighty-eight millimeter antitank weapon. But the vehicle is not large enough to be a JagdTiger. Thus this SPG is a JagdPanther—for us, an entirely inappropriate name for an enemy armored fighting vehicle. The Hunting Panther is a Panzer V with its turret removed and its hull raised to permit the crew to service the gun. The Hunting Panther differs from the Panther in one other respect: the Panther is armed with a seventy-five millimeter gun, but the Hunting Panther's main armament is the eighty-eight.

The manual is blurry about the JagdPanther's abilities. We expect this, for all the manuals have been blurry about most of what we have done, and what has been done to us. But in this hilly country west of the Rhine the Hunting Panther is more provocative and dangerous than the Panther itself; for the Hunting Panther's style is to lurk in ambush. Its crew trains to shoot from concealment and to flee into dead ground before the havoc it has caused can be reported to tactical air and artillery.

One point in the manual about the JagdPanther is not blurry: the gun fitted into the sloped forward glacis of the Hunting Panther is an eighty-eight millimeter weapon whose barrel length is seventy-one calibers. The manual is discreet: it does not do the computation for us, but we worked it out long ago and learned that the barrel of the L71 mark of the eighty-eight is twenty feet six inches long.

The brave warm days of sweeping across the rolling plains of northern France are over. Those weeks of success, speed and fervor ended with the summer, before we arrived in Europe. Our progress has been without adulation, an isolated struggle against the jolts and shocks administered by concealed guns, tank traps, registered mortar barrages and artillery shoots. Our fight has been waged in weather deteriorating into winter. It has been a long, cold muddy slog, for another SPG, or a pair of PanzerKampfWagen IV, or a platoon of hard men armed with Panzerfaust anti-tank rockets, waited beyond each bend in the road and behind each rise in the ground. We are lucky the sky is full of heavy bombers. Day and night they drone east toward Germany. We are even luckier that our tactical Air Force has shot down most of the Luftwaffe and forced the camouflaged JagdPanthers to hide in ambush. I would hate to watch our Battalion face the Wehrmacht's tanks and SPGs in the open, without tactical air. But we have superiority in the sky, and even we, waiting near the back door, can whistle down relaxed Americans in P-47 Thunderbolts and elegant British pilots in Typhoons. Everything they fly is loaded with bombs, rockets, heavy machineguns and cannon, and even for us they will expend thousands and thousands of dollars of ordnance to destroy a single German truck.

We all pray for fine weather, for we knew last fall that winter would come, and even then, during the chilly, clear autumn days, we worried about the troubles we would have when the Germans whitewashed their vehicles and the only sound in the sky was the soughing wind full of falling wet snow.

From my position in the righthand front seat of the maintenance halftrack halted on a turnout on the crest of the ridge above the valley I see the stream in the field on the valley floor and the far woods in which the Hunting Panther readies itself to strike. The trees along the narrow road leading down and away to my right obscure the two B Company Shermans—Sam Taylor's Big Sam and Tommy Quineau's Bayou Queen—descending the road on this side of the valley and the third B Company Sherman—Eddy Stanton's Bright Lights—loitering behind, to backstop Big Sam and Bayou Queen as they trundle down the narrow road toward the valley floor.

Williston, who drives the maintenance halftrack and is my understudy, understands the meaning of the grumble of the engine reverberating in the valley and the swishing shifting in the trees half a mile away. "Jesus Christ," he says. He lifts his right fist gloved in olive drab wool toward the halftrack's windshield and says, "What about. . ?"

As Williston speaks, I picture Bright Lights loitering beyond the bend to our right. I also picture Big Sam and Bayou Queen sliding along the narrow road that descends into the shooting gallery the JagdPanther's commander has established.

Nothing can be done: I have no time, and neither do the fifteen men inside the three Shermans who may, or if this German crew is good, may not, be the first of our Battalion into this anonymous valley. Still, anything is worth a try. I drop my gloved right hand from the fieldglasses and lift the radio handset; but the Hunting Panther stops crabbing left to right, and its gunner is faster than my thumb depressing the transmitter button on the handset, faster than my voice, faster than my thoughts: he fires the JagdPanther's eighty-eight millimeter main armament.

Sooty smoke, flame at its center, spurts from the eight-eight's muzzlebrake. As the long gunbarrel recoils, the green pine branches worked into the camouflage netting fitted over the JagdPanther's hull flutter and whip in the strong wind of the muzzle blast.

An instant after the eighty-eight fires, I hear the familiar singing of stranded cable drawn tight and tighter, and the muffled clang as the Hunting Panther's eighty-eight millimeter round strikes Big Sam's armor at more than thrice the speed of sound. The eighty-eight's guntube quivers and shifts as it seeks another target, the muzzle swinging like the snout of an animal that smells putrefaction.

I imagine the loader inside the squared-off menace of the JagdPanther's carapace sliding a second round into the breech as the gunner traverses the muzzle of the gun degree by degree toward his second target: Bayou Queen.

Through the radio switched to the Company channel I hear another familiar sound: a sobbing breath drawn, a grunt like a hog coughing that lifts to a yelping bellow that keens as the last breath flees from the lungs up the throat. Williston hears this sound too, and knows it as well as I. Neither of us speaks. Neither of us says the words that would identify this single man's calvary shrieked through the radio. We can do nothing for whoever has died, and so we have nothing to say. Three months ago we might have mourned aloud; now the wind rushing through the trees around us at the top of the slope, the reverberations in the valley of the explosion of the propellant that has flung the JagdPanther's eighty-eight millimeter armor-piercing shell across the valley and through Big Sam, and the minor motion of the Hunting Panther's gunmuzzle shifting toward its second target, require no comment from us.

As the gunner in the Hunting Panther sitting to the left of the eighty-eight's breech stares through his telescopic sight and adjusts his weapon, the last reverberating echo of the strike of the eighty-eight millimeter round against Big Sam's armor diminishes. Silence returns to the valley with a long sweep of cold winter wind rustling down the slope toward the stream angling through the field of yellowgray stubble.

I lift the microphone and flick switches to call C Company Headquarters. But I do not speak: I hear Eddy Stanton, commander of Bright Lights, giving them the bad news about Big Sam. He is asking for medics, artillery fire, air support.

"Coming your way," the voice on the other end of the radio says. I listen as arrangements are made to destroy the German woods from which the JagdPanther fired.

I do not have to imagine what we will find inside Big Sam once this fight is over. I know: narrow compartments full of dead men chopped to bits. I try to think of the names of the men in Sam Taylor's crew, but I have forgotten them. This does not matter: even the ones whose names I don't remember are old friends, and I will help to do the right thing and bring Sam Taylor's men out of Big Sam into the light.

While the German gunner prepares to fire at his second target, I wait in silence. This is no time for exclamations and cluttered radios.

I imagine the commander of the JagdPanther looking across the valley through the telescopic periscope fixed in the armored hatch above his head, swinging the toe of his boot, waiting for his gunner to get on with it. After all, from his point-of-view the targets are the usual: Shermans, and not a British Firefly—a modified Sherman mounting a British 17-pounder antitank gun—among them. I understand the German's methodical unconcern. I wish we had a Firefly right up here beside our drab, utilitarian half-track full of tools, spares, grease, oil and mechanics. But we don't. It is February, 1945, and the British still can't produce enough of the modified, up-gunned Shermans to fill their own needs. We have never produced an armored fighting vehicle big enough to go up against the Hunting Panther. Furthermore, we fear we are down at the lowest end of the Army's table, and we believe that if the Army receives a batch of Fireflies, it's certain no one's going to load one on a tank transporter and hustle it up to the Seven Six One. We are a medium tank battalion and our Table of Organization and Equipment will not be upgraded. We were issued the M4A3 with the 76 millimeter gun in October in England, and we will fight in this mark of the Sherman until the end. With this Sherman we will—with the infantry, the artillery, the Air Force, the British, Canadians, Poles, French and, we understand, our new allies the Italians—beat the Germans; but we know we will not all beat them and come away safe.

The JagdPanther's gunner fires a second time, smoke and flame spurting from the muzzlebrake of the gun. Once again I hear the sound of an eighty-eight millimeter round slipping hot and slick through a Sherman's armor: Bayou Queen. In the same instant Bright Lights fires its 76 millimeter gun once, and then again, and a third time. The loader inside Bright Lights is working like a miner, flinging shells into the breech. The rounds tear past the Hunting Panther and strike among the pines low on the far slope where the German self-propelled gun lurks. Bright Lights' gunner must be upset: his shooting is wide and useless. But he is shooting down hill at an obscured target, he is angry and afraid, and I have no doubt that the men in the two Shermans farther down the road are—were—his friends.

Hidden from us beyond the trees along the road to our right, Bright Lights fires a fourth time: the round strikes the sloped carapace of the German SPG and flicks away through the dense stand of pines. Of course: nothing but the 17-pounder antitank gun fitted in the turret of the Sherman Firefly, or the weapon in the M-10 tank destroyer, or the 76 millimeter High Velocity Armor Piercing round, of which we never have enough because policy has reserved it for the use of tank destroyer battalions, can hope to pierce the tough hull of the Hunting Panther.

I hear Eddie Stanton, commander of Bright Lights, speaking on the radio, calling again for air support and fire from the Battalion's self-propelled 105 millimeter guns. He repeats the coordinates of the woods beyond the field in the valley again and again. We will destroy the woods, but it will be too late. Whoever he is, the commander of this JagdPanther knows as much as the most experienced German armored commander about our response to an ambush: he knows he should not hang around after he has shot down two Shermans.

To the right through the pines I see thick greasy smoke rising and hear the crackle of fat spitting in a hot pan. Big Sam has begun to burn, and its machinegun ammunition cooking off. The eighty-eight millimeter round must have shrugged into the Sherman behind the rear wall of the fighting compartment and ignited the fuel tanks. Had it slammed into the Sherman farther forward it would have exploded the 76 millimeter ammunition, and I would have heard the characteristic concussive ripping of a Sherman's hull torn to shreds.

But perhaps Sam Taylor and his crew have been lucky: if the eighty-eight millimeter round pierced the Sherman's fuel storage, the crew may have had instants in which to trip the fire extinguishers and to escape before the fire reached the ammunition bins and ignited the propellant in the brass butts of the shells.

What a choice for a tank's crew: some, I suppose, hope that the round that strikes their vehicle will ignite the fuel before it explodes the ammunition. Others may hope that the round will strike farther forward, piercing an ammunition bin instead of a fuel tank. Who knows? I have never heard a Sherman's crew speak of these narrow options. Rumor says fuel is more dangerous, but I have seen the inside of every one of the Shermans we have lost, and I believe the propellant in the 76 millimeter shells is more volatile than the fuel. But the crews fear to run short of ammunition, and they fill every empty space inside the fighting compartments of their Shermans with 76 millimeter rounds and boxes of .30 and .50 caliber machinegun ammunition.

As the 76 millimeter shells inside Big Sam begin to detonate with ragged knockings and muffled bangs, the grey smoke of the burning propellant in the shells displaces the greasy black smoke of burning gasoline. As Williston said, Jesus Christ.

The detonating ammunition tells me my maintenance crew will have a lot of work to do this cold windy morning. First, because the fighting must go on, we will have to determine the condition of Bayou Queen, which has not, it seems, caught fire. Then, after we bring the dead out of Big Sam, we will tip its hulk into the nearest ditch, for an intense fire destroys the integrity of the armor and renders the vehicle useless.

Bright Lights' gunner fires again, a fifth round cracking from the muzzle of his 76 millimeter weapon. This shot, like the first three, misses. One out of five. The gunner is rattled. I'm not surprised, for he knows as well as the rest of us that a Sherman cannot fight a Hunting Panther and survive. Not at this range, not in these conditions. A Sherman with a 76 millimeter gun might kill a Hunting Panther if it could fire three or four rounds of HVAP through the thin armor at the self-propelled gun's rear, or shy a round against the earth between the Hunting Panther's tracks so that it will ricochet up through the thin armor of the belly. But perhaps the gunner in Bright Lights hopes to do no more than distract the SPG's crew: so that they will not, as the Germans say, shoot down his Sherman as they have shot down Big Sam and Bayou Queen.

Down the road Big Sam's ammunition is still exploding, one ragged burst of detonating 76 millimeter shells after another. Smoke roils up through the pines and is blown away by the cold wind. More explosions, more smoke. The wind blows it all away: in ten minutes the only evidence of this vicious ambush will be Big Sam's smoldering hulk, and the damage done to Bayou Queen.

It is too bad we have to fight in Shermans. They are decent and dependable, but they're useless against the Germans' optics and guns and hot ammunition. Still we are lucky Uncle has manufactured so many of them: the one good thing about the Hunting Panther is its rarity. We have seen no more than six of them since November. Panthers, as we say, are rare in Europe. As rare as we ourselves.

"Lord Jesus," Williston says. Williston calls on the Lord in situations like this. He did so at Morville-les-Vic, and at Guebling, and now he does it again here in the hilly, befogged, dangerous terrain of Germany east of the slim last southern bit of Holland. Sitting to Williston's right in the driver's compartment of the Battalion maintenance halftrack is like attending a service back home, though Williston's services are long on hollering the name of the Lord Jesus and short on homilies. He is right to be abrupt: in Europe this winter we don't have a lot of time for homilies. The enemy is dying, and the grim paradox is that the enemy is therefore more dangerous now than he has ever been. It may be safer to fly over Germany in a B-17 than it was two years ago, when flying a Fortress to the Ruhr was an extreme risk; but the danger of driving a Sherman—or a maintenance halftrack—over a ridgeline or through the shadows along a narrow cobbled street is intense and terrifying, for a determined man, or a terrified child, may lay in wait just beyond the top of the slope, or in any doorway or window on any street between here and Berlin, a Panzerfaust clutched in his grimy hands.

I see the branches woven in the netting fastened to the Hunting Panther's hull tremble and shake as it withdraws into the pine woods. The German commander has decided he and his crew and their vicious, efficient self-propelled gun have done enough of their duty this morning.

"He's leaving," I say. "Get us out of here and down the road, Williston." I glance over my shoulder into the bed of the maintenance halftrack. Withers, whose seat is between mine and Williston's when we are travelling easy, now stands in the front center of the halftrack's bed behind our .30 caliber machinegun. Withers looks angry: he wishes he could have fired his gun. But I have instructed him in detail about the situations in which he should fire, and this is not one of them. A half-track full of mechanics armed with a single machinegun and an assortment of small arms is no match for a JagdPanther; and our job in situations like this is not to attract attention but to wait and see, and to repair the damage when the fighting stops.

Behind Withers the four men who constitute the remainder of my six-man maintenance crew—Simpson, Fellows, Franklin and Rutherford—sit on either side of the halftrack's bed, staring and staring, shoulders hunched, backs bent, helmeted heads close together as though they are conferring with one another. Rutherford holds an MP-40 Schmeisser machinepistol between his knees. Rutherford took this German weapon from the frozen hands of a German corpse in January. The other three each hold an M3 submachinegun, which is called a Grease Gun because it looks like a grease gun. The MP-40 is a better weapon than the M3, but it fires 9 millimeter rounds and it is simpler to find .45 caliber ammunition for the Greasegun. The Schmeisser presents another problem: whenever he fires the Schmeisser Rutherford runs the risk of having some G.I.—the son of some doughboy from the First World War—mistake him for a German. But Rutherford tells us he is willing to take the chance. After all, he says, he looks more like an American than anyone else in northern Europe, not counting the rest of us in the Seven Six One.

I can see that all four of them have listened to the clash down the road and understood what has happened. They cannot see into the valley from where they sit; but they have heard the rushing crack of the eighty-eight firing, the distinctive lash of its heavy, high velocity shot striking the Shermans, the milder crack of Bright Lights' 76 millimeter gun returning the Germans' fire, and the detonation of Big Sam's ammunition.

Simpson shakes his head as though Fellows, sitting across from him, has asked him a question. I know what Simpson wants: he wants this fucking war to end. But like the rest of us he will have to wait until we are listening to a Russian playing the accordion in Berlin.

Williston backs and fills the halftrack out of the turn-out and drives us down the road. The track clatters and sways as Williston swings it through the turn at the crest of the ridge. We reach for handholds. The muzzle of the .30 caliber machinegun above my head swings as the motion of the track jostles Withers from side to side.

Six hundred yards on I see the Sherman that fired at the JagdPanther: Bright Lights. It loiters, engine running, the turret rotated to port, the gun traversed, the tube depressed, the muzzlebrake pointing like a thick fist at the pine trees from which the Hunting Panther tripped its ambush. As we approach, I note the commander, Eddy Stanton, aiming with the blade sight fixed to the turret in front of his hatch. As I see him speak, his gunner fires again—another round flung into the trees across the valley.

Bright Lights' efforts are useless: the Hunting Panther is gone. Its prudent commander has ordered his driver to reverse deeper into the woods before we can retaliate. Another successful enemy defensive effort, another useless attempt to stave off the end. The outcome of this war, whatever it costs us, is obvious. We will crush them, and in the end they will have only one option: to surrender and go home.

I stand up and hold on to the armored windshield of the halftrack as we approach Bright Lights. Withers shifts the barrel of the pintle-mounted .30 caliber machinegun as I stand. I wave my right arm to attract Eddy Stanton's attention. I want him to tell his gunner not to fire while we are passing under the muzzle of his gun: concussion can blind and deafen. It can also rip the lungs right up the throat and out the mouth. Stanton glances our way, nods, waves a hand, speaks into the microphone in front of his lips. The muzzle of the 76 millimeter gun lifts. As we pass beneath the elevated gun, I smell the exhaust from Bright Lights' engine and the burned propellant of the 76 millimeter rounds it has fired into the woods across the valley where the Hunting Panther lurked. We drive on. Bright Lights jerks forward and slides after us, its turret traversing as it comes on, its gunner holding the muzzle of its 76 millimeter weapon on the woods from which the German fired.

Williston drives close to the uphill side of the road: who knows whether other SP guns, or an antitank gun and its crew, still lurk across the valley?

Williston drives us around a bend and I see Bayou Queen slouching on the road, turret traversed, guntube depressed, the drooping muzzle pointing at the woods across the valley from which the JagdPanther fired. Part of Bayou Queen's port suspension has been destroyed, and this tells me the eighty-eight millimeter round must have flashed through this elderly M4A1 on a rising track, entering below the fender. Sixty or seventy yards beyond Bayou Queen, Big Sam stands in the road, seeping smoke.

I look for the crews of these two Shermans: alive or dead, whole or dismembered, bled out or incinerated, we must account for them.

Nine men—six of them infantry who have crept from the woods—stand close by the righthand, uphill side of Bayou Queen. A tenth, who wears a helmet with red crosses stencilled on it, kneels beside an eleventh lying on the road.

The corpsman is with the infantry. I know this because I can see his pale face and the jerky movements of his hands: he's not used to the wounds inflicted on bone, blood and flesh when an armor-piercing round glows against a Sherman's armor and shrugs its way through the softened spot on the hull at fifteen hundred feet per second.

I should see five tankers from Bayou Queen. I don't. I see one down, the medic from the armored infantry, whom we call armored doughs, kneeling beside him, and three leaning against the tank. They are smoking and moving their hands.

I know the fifth man—commander, gunner, loader, driver, or bowgunner—is dead inside Bayou Queen's hull. His crew would have brought him out into the dim winter light and the bitter cold had he survived the JagdPanther's ambush.

Down the road Big Sam is slumped to port, the left track laid out behind it, the hull canted toward the valley. Tendrils of smoke seep from the turret race, the hatches, the canister air filters below the rear of the deck, and the grille over the engine. As I watch a bright yellowwhite rush of fire falls to the ground from the deck behind the turret. I see no other fire: fire consumes everything inside a Sherman—fuel, ammunition, oil, rubber, flesh, bone and blood—and once it has done so, the fire stops. Big Sam's gun droops and I see the hull and turret have been holed again and again by its own 76 millimeter ammunition. It will be difficult to identify the point at which the eighty-eight millimeter round pierced this Sherman's hull. I do not, of course, see Big Sam Taylor or any one of the four other men in his crew.

"Jesus Christ," Williston says. I glance at him. He is braking and shifting down: we are almost up to the group of men standing around the medic working on the man down on his back on the road.

"First Sergeant coming," Franklin says from the bed of the halftrack as Williston brakes to a halt. I turn in my seat and raise myself up so that I can see back over the high armored walls around the bed of the track.

First Sergeant Reardon is approaching in his jeep. No one, not even the Colonel who is our Battalion Commander, would dare drive First Sergeant Reardon's jeep without the First Sergeant's permission; and no one in the Seven Six One, not even the Colonel, has the courage to ask First Sergeant Reardon for the use of the First Sergeant's jeep. First Sergeant Reardon is a professional soldier: a transfer from the 24th Infantry. In the First World War he transferred to the 93rd Infantry Division and fought in France. We have even heard rumors that he was with Pershing in Mexico. The First Sergeant is a tall, fit man, careful with his words. He does not move his hands when he speaks and when he is spoken to he looks the speaker in the eye. First Sergeant Reardon knows what must be done in every situation and he knows how to do it. He knows the name of every single man in the Seven Six One. He also knows the contents of each personnel file carted all the way from Louisiana to Texas to here in the Headquarters two-and-a-half ton truck; and though he never speaks of those who have been killed or wounded, I have no doubt he remembers the contents of each of their files, too. The First Sergeant does not, like the rest of us, inject curses into every sentence by way of punctuation. But as Rutherford says, when the First Sergeant curse, everyone know he cursing, and everyone know what he cursing about.

Every man in the Seven Six One, from the Colonel to the last arrived out-at-the-ass buck private replacement, is cautious of First Sergeant Reardon. We are not afraid of him, but we are more than respectful. Most of all, we are grateful First Sergeant Reardon is with us, and glad that he knows what must be done and how to do it. That is why he is the Seven Six One's top kicker, and why, though we have other first sergeants in the Battalion, he is the only one every single man addresses by his rank, or by his rank and last name. The First Sergeant doesn't like familiarity, and no one calls him 'top'. No one has ever called him William, either. And no one would dare call him Bill.

I get down as the First Sergeant steers his Jeep past Bright Lights. He does not look up when he drives under the gun: no one would dare fire a 76 millimeter weapon while the First Sergeant is driving under its muzzle. He pulls around our unnamed halftrack—even if we dared give it a name, everyone in the Seven Six One would still refer to it as the 'maintenance track'—and stops the Jeep fifteen feet away. He get outs, but he leaves the engine running—who knows? we may all have to flee this place without notice. He paces toward the group of tankers and armored doughs gathered in the steel lee of Bayou Queen. I trail along in his wake.

As First Sergeant Reardon approaches the loose knot of men smoking cigarettes and watching the corpsman work, they glance at him, see the full house of chevrons and rockers enclosing the lozenge on his sleeve and drift back from the wounded man to give him room.

The wounded man is Stinson, Bayou Queen's bowgunner. His face is scrunched up, his jaws clamped shut. He is breathing through his nose as though he is running a long, uphill race. The medic has cut off his left trouser leg. I watch as the medic applies three field dressings, one overlapping the next, to the deep, straight gash running down Stinson's thigh to his knee. Between the lips of the gash I see yellow fat, purple muscle, grey sinew and white bone.

The medic tapes the layered dressings over the wound, reaches into the musette bag slung over his shoulder and brings out a Syrette of morphine and a thick chinagraph pencil. He holds the pencil between his teeth as he prepares the Syrette. Then he clenches Stinson's left arm in his fist at the elbow, looks for an appropriate vein, and, with a delicate, flowing movement of his right shoulder and arm, slides the tip of the Syrette through Stinson's skin into the vein. The medic squeezes the small tube of flexible metal, injecting the morphine into Stinson. Stinson sighs as he feels the ease of the drug coming on. The medic slides the tip of the Syrette out of Stinson's arm, and says, "Hang on two minutes. Help's on the way." Eyes closed, nostrils flared, Stinson nods. He is breathing with more ease, as though the race is over.

The medic takes the chinagraph pencil out of his mouth. He is going to write the date and the time and the dosage he has given Stinson on Stinson's forehead, so that the doctors back up the line will know, when they go to work on Stinson, how much morphine he has been given, and how long ago. The medic raises the tip of the pencil to Stinson's forehead, hesitates, and considers the problem. The medic has been working with confidence and dispatch. Everything was quite clear. Now he does not know what to do next: if he writes his message on Stinson's forehead, no one will be able to read it. He glances up. The armored doughs look at one another.

"You got a problem, Jimmy," one of the armored doughs tells the medic. He is a private with bad teeth in a wide lopsided mouth. I glance at First Sergeant Reardon and the three crewmen from Bayou Queen standing over Stinson. The gunner, Price, sucks at a cigarette. Faint tremors shift his hands this way and that. He glances at the private from the armored infantry and rolls his eyes. The doughs' sergeant grimaces and turns to look at the private. The private grins around as though he has gotten off a good one. "I mean that's a problem," he says, in case someone didn't understand him the first time.

First Sergeant Reardon stares at the private, but before he can speak the sergeant commanding the armored doughs says, "Shut up, Moore. You wouldn't recognize a problem if it bit you on the ass." Private Moore sees his sergeant's face, opens his mouth and closes it.

To the medic the First Sergeant says, "Write the date, the time and the dosage on Stinson's jacket, Corporal." I have not noticed that the medic is a corporal.

"Sorry," the medic says. "Is that his name? Stinson?"

"Yes," the First Sergeant says. "Stinson, James E. And there's nothing to be sorry about, Corporal: the Army don't issue you with no choice of pencils. You're doing fine."

The medic nods, checks his watch and prints the date, 3/7/45, and the time, 0945, and the dosage, 5, on the left breast of Stinson's jacket. Then he takes the empty malleable metal Syrette, twists it and works it through the third buttonhole of Stinson's jacket.

"We're supposed to write the information on the patient's clothes and on his forehead," the medic says. "In case the doctors don't see him before they take his clothes at the CCS."

"Stinson'll be all right with what you've written on his jacket," the First Sergeant says. "He's with us." The First Sergeant sounds as though he's talking to a headwaiter at a restaurant that requires customers to wear coats and ties.

The First Sergeant turns to the armored doughs' sergeant and says, "Thanks for helping out here, Sergeant."

"Name's Clements," the sergeant says. Then he grins at the First Sergeant and says, "No problem helping out. We knew you were on our side."

First Sergeant Reardon looks at Sergeant Clements's face for three moments before he nods and says, "You got that right, Sergeant."

"Sorry we couldn't do anything about this," the sergeant from the armored infantry says. "Before it happened, I mean. We were told there'd be recon along here and down into the valley. We were coming down through the woods"—he gestures behind him at the steep slope thick with pine trees—"when the shooting started. An SP gun. It's looks as though recon didn't show. A fuckup somewhere."

"It's war," First Sergeant Reardon says.

If anyone in the Seven Six One or anyone else, right up to the General Commanding the 79th Infantry Division, to which we have been attached since February 20, said this, the response would be guffaws, laughter and suggestions on how the motherfucker ought to fuck himself. But when First Sergeant Reardon says, "It's war," none of us says a word. Each one of us understands that the First Sergeant knows what he's talking about. So do each of the armored doughs, even though they have never seen the First Sergeant before. Perhaps they guess what we know: First Sergeant Reardon has been here before. I often wonder if it gives him an odd feeling to fight across the same ground he fought over in 1918.

Sergeant Clements nods and says, "First Sergeant, we'll be sticking around 'till someone gets all this sorted out. If there's anything we can do?"

"Thank you, Sergeant," the First Sergeant says. He turns to the three tankers standing with their backs to Bayou Queen.

"Quineau?" the First Sergeant asks. Quineau is—was—a snappy, bright New Orleans boy, commander of Bayou Queen.

"Something took him in the chest," Price says. Price is Bayou Queen's gunner. Price sucks at the cigarette in his fingers, takes it down from his mouth and nibbles a shred of tobacco from the tip of his tongue. As cold as it is, Price is sweating: he passes the back of his hand holding the cigarette across his forehead and flicks the sweat away.

As he does so, the Seven Six One's 105 millimeter self-propelled artillery arrives, a single whistling shell rising over the crest behind us. We all turn to watch the woods on the other side of the valley from which the JagdPanther ambushed Big Sam and Bayou Queen. The round whistles through the grey sky and slugs down among the pine trees. It strikes six hundred yards east of where the Hunting Panther lay in wait. White smoke rises among the pine trees. A pause. I glance over my shoulder. Eddy Stanton up in the turret of Bright Lights is speaking into his microphone. A second round of white smoke falls among the pines. This one is close enough. Stanton speaks into the microphone again. Another pause, and then high explosive shells begin to arrive, shrieking one after another through the sky. The explosions rummage among the pine trees, stripping branches and uprooting trunks. We watch as the trees topple and minor fires burn here and there.

I hear no secondary explosions and I see no sign of the JagdPanther or its crew. The artillery has accomplished nothing. The Hunting Panther has withdrawn, and will fight another day. The artillery fire stops. The fires in the cold winter woods burn themselves out. The whole useless display lasts no more than a minute.

Only Stinson has ignored the sound and light of the barrage. Floating away from the vicious gash in his leg on an iridescent shallow tide of morphia, he dreams of anything but the pain he has suffered.

When the reverberations of the last 105 millimeter shell have rolled away down the valley, First Sergeant Reardon turns to Price, and asks, "You need help with Quineau?"

"No," Price says. He throws the butt of his cigarette down into the road. "We'll get him out. Someone ought to make the call, though."

"I have," The First Sergeant says. "Medics will be here shortly with an ambulance track." The First Sergeant turns away from Price, looks at me and says, "Your men ready to look Bayou Queen over after they get Quineau out?" The First Sergeant doesn't like to see men standing around: he knows of work that needs to be done right now.

"Yes, First Sergeant," I say. I wave at the halftrack. Williston and Fellows get down and begin opening the doors on the cargo bins on the outsides of the track's bed. The other four stoop and bustle around in the bed of the halftrack, collecting toolkits and spares.

The First Sergeant looks at me and nods at Big Sam leaking smoke seventy yards down the road. The smoke is dissipating: the fires are out. "You want to come on down there with me?" the First Sergeant asks.

He has never ordered me to help him with this work, and I know I can refuse. But he and I have done this more times than either of us likes to remember, and so I nod and follow him to his Jeep. He lifts two pairs of oversize knee-high rubber boots from the back of his Jeep. They are the kind of boots gardeners wear. First Sergeant Reardon hands me one pair, and as I squirm my feet one after the other into them, he pulls the other pair on over his leather boots.

First Sergeant Reardon stamps his feet and squirms the heels of the rubber boots against the tacky ground. Then he takes an entrenching tool, a folded pair of coveralls, a pair of electrician's heavy rubber gloves and two folded blankets from the back seat. "Bring the shovel," the First Sergeant tells me. I take the shovel out of the back of the Jeep. The shovel's handle is unpainted hardwood. Its blade is straight: for the work we must do a pointed shovel is useless. I lean the shovel against the front fender of the Jeep and take three folded blankets, a pair of folded coveralls and a pair of rubber gloves from the back of the Jeep.

First Sergeant Reardon nods as though he approves of the way I have lifted the blankets, the coveralls and the electrician's gloves out of his Jeep. He turns and walks down the road toward Big Sam steaming and creaking as the cold wind leaches the heat from its hull. The entrenching tool swings in the First Sergeant's right hand and he holds the two folded brown blankets, the folded coveralls and the electrician's glove under his left arm.

I follow the First Sergeant, my rubber boots squishing and clomping. The men in my maintenance crew glance at me and at First Sergeant Reardon. Then they glance away. They know where we are going: toward the night.

The armored doughs watch us go. They are pale—paler than shit usual, Rutherford would say, hitching his Schmeisser captured from a corpse from under his right arm into his hands clenched in front of him at the level of his hips—and they shift from foot to foot, flicking looks at us from the corners of their bright eyes. These armored doughs know where we are going, too, and they know what we are going to do, and it disturbs them. Their Sergeant, Clements, stands up straighter as First Sergeant Reardon approaches. For a moment I think Sergeant Clements will salute the First Sergeant, as though he thinks the First Sergeant is an officer. But that would be improper: the First Sergeant is not an officer, and the First Sergeant's right hand clutches the entrenching tool and he clenches the two blankets, the coveralls and the rubber gloves between his left biceps and his ribs, and he cannot return a salute. To salute the First Sergeant would be improper: to do so when his hands are full would be doubly so. More important than military courtesy is the fear I feel when I think Sergeant Clements may salute: the rising, flexing movement of his right arm and hand would be, in this place and on this day, unusual and dangerous. No one salutes, and no one wishes to be saluted, this close to the Germans. Salutes are invitations to the night if the Germans are near; for here on this narrow cold road, if you salute, an SP gun might take your arm off at the shoulder and half your chest with it.

Instead of saluting, Sergeant Clements nods as First Sergeant Reardon approaches, swinging the entrenching tool in his right hand, the blankets, gloves and coveralls under his left arm. First Sergeant Reardon nods at Sergeant Clements and passes on.

It is cold for this kind of formality, and the cold wind that gusts through the cold day makes me shiver. But I am First Sergeant Reardon's acolyte and I follow him, blankets, rubber gloves and folded coverall under my left arm, shovel swinging in my right hand, and nod, as First Sergeant Reardon did, when Sergeant Clements nods at me.

I know what the First Sergeant and I will do with the blankets, the entrenching tool, the rubber gloves, the coveralls and the shovel. I also know why the First Sergeant has chosen me to help him: it has taken a lot of hard practice, but he and I have become this tank battalion's specialists in this last and most necessary of duties.

Two

CLUTCHING MY EQUIPMENT, I follow First Sergeant Reardon along the narrow, descending road toward Big Sam. The surface of the road is tacky: damp from rain and melted snow but not quite frozen, it is not quite mud. This is another seasonal problem the Army has been unable to solve: either the roads are frozen hard and our feet are cold, or the roads are muddy and our feet are wet.

The Army has had the same difficulty keeping our feet warm and dry as it has had supplying and preparing us for battle. For while the Table of Organization and Equipment of a tank battalion is an impressive list of machinery, weapons and men, even the Army has found it impossible to plan for every contingency. Thus, as no satisfactory solution for cold or wet feet has been developed, no solution to the gun-on-gun insufficiency of the Sherman has been discovered, and no orders have been written or equipment issued for the duty First Sergeant Reardon and I are about to perform inside Big Sam.

First Sergeant Reardon walks ten feet in front of me, his shoulders back, the blankets, gloves and coveralls under his left arm, the entrenching tool clenched in his right hand. His high rubber boots flex and bend and squeak as he marches forward.

I do not know where the First Sergeant got the boots we wear, but the entrenching tool, the blankets and the rubber gloves are all part of our Table of Organization and Equipment. The TO&E's list of the men, machines and weapons that constitute a tank battalion is detailed and potent: thirty-nine officers, two warrant officers, seven hundred and nine enlisted men, fifty-three Sherman medium tanks, six Shermans with 105 millimeter howitzers fitted in their turrets in place of the 76 millimeter gun, seventeen Stuart light tanks, three halftracks carrying 81mm mortars, thirty-five 2.75 inch antitank rocket launchers, twenty-six .50 caliber machineguns, eighteen .30 caliber machineguns, four hundred and forty-nine .45 caliber submachineguns, two hundred and seventy-seven .30 caliber carbines, three .45 caliber pistols, thirteen M3 halftracks, three M3 ambulance halftracks, thirty-nine 2 1/2 ton trucks, one 3/4 ton command and recon vehicle, one 3/4 ton weapons carrier, twenty-three 1/4 ton trucks, two heavy wreckers, six tank recovery vehicles, and six 81mm mortars.

Withers, who mans the .30 caliber machinegun on the pintle mounting at the front of the bed of the maintenance halftrack just behind and between my seat and Williston's, has said on more than one occasion that with all this stuff, man, that we got here, we could blow up Cincinnati in two hours. Withers comes from Nebraska and when his estimate of our potency is called into question by Fellows, our optical systems maintenance specialist, who was born in Cincinnati, Withers insists: yeah, man, Cincinnati: your home town, Fellows; and no more than two hours. Two hours tops to crunch our way right down to the river bridges.

We began our journey to Europe at Camp Hood, Texas, with fewer men than the usual battalion: thirty-six officers, two warrant officers and six hundred and seventy-six enlisted men. At Wimbourne, in England, in October, 1944, a medical team was added, and the complement rose to thirty-eight officers, three warrant officers and six hundred and eighty-seven enlisted men. We were glad to have the medical team, for we feared the treatment we might—or might not—receive without our own medics.

As we approach Big Sam squatting on the road, canted to port, track snaked out, bogeys exposed, hull holed and smeared with soot, I smell—even against the strong westerly wind—the bitter stench of all that has burned within this Sherman. It is the smell of rubber, leather, chemicals, metals and human beings churned together and incinerated. First Sergeant Reardon must smell it too, but he does not change the pace of his steady approach, and he does not turn his head or speak. He marches on, still right hand holding the entrenching tool just behind the blade as though he is marching with a rifle at trail.

At Camp Hood we were told that everything had been planned, and when we drew equipment in England our Battalion was a neat, confident package of six companies: three—A, B and C—of M4A3 Sherman medium tanks; the fourth—D—of M5 Stuart light tanks; the fifth—Headquarters—to command; and the sixth—Service—to feed the men, to arm the weapons and maintenance the vehicles, to aid and evacuate the wounded, and to pass the corpses of the killed to the rear.

Each medium tank company comprises four platoons, three of five Shermans each. The fourth, Headquarters platoon, is composed of two 76 millimeter Shermans; a single assault gun with a 105 millimeter howitzer fitted in a Sherman's turret; a maintenance halftrack and a tank recovery vehicle; a supply and mess truck; and two jeeps, one for the company first sergeant, the other for communications.

I look along the descending road at Big Sam and nod. B Company is one more Sherman short and our TO&E has been altered yet again. This does not seem to worry First Sergeant Reardon. He strides forward as though he were striding across the parade ground at Camp Hood. He also strides forward as though he knows that now the Hunting Panther has fled, no German would dare lie in ambush in the trees beyond the winter field in the valley to our left. The First Sergeant swings along as though he were back in the peacetime Army, heading for the commander's office to give him the morning report. I am less confident. I don't like the look of Big Sam. Pale smoke seeps from the seared punctures in its armor and from the grille over its engine and is swept away by the cold wind falling in waves down the slope toward the valley floor.

Our precise TO&E, like Camp Hood, is now part of our distant past. Four months in Europe have taught us that everything in life, and everything in this life in particular, suffers and changes. So we have suffered, and so we have modified the Seven Six One's Table of Organization and Equipment.

We have lost more than two hundred men killed and wounded since October, 1944. We expected casualties. At Camp Hood, and on the voyage for England, the pessimists rumbled that the Seven Six One would be thrown into the worst of the fighting to be, as they sneered, bled white. The level-headed laughed. I recalled Colonel Shaw and his men at Morris Island and withheld judgment.

The pessimists were wrong: our casualties have been no greater than most other tank battalions, and fewer than some. Yet the Army seems not to have thought we would require trained replacements. We are sent some new men from the infantry and the Services of Supply now and then; but most of them know nothing of tanks, and are incapable. Without trained men to replace our losses, we have been ground down. In the last twenty minutes we have been ground down more: we have lost Tommy Quineau killed and Stinson wounded in Bayou Queen, and Sam Taylor and the four men in his crew killed—and worse than killed—in Big Sam.

If our losses continue as they began, we will be such a slender, flexible stick by the time we clatter into Berlin that one last swipe of the whittling knife will finish us.

First Sergeant Reardon marches on as though he has not been told about our Battalion's losses. But I know he sits alone in the Headquarters halftrack when he must, writing up each dead man's file in his meticulous handwriting when his clerk is typing up requisitions. I also know he himself sorts through their personal gear before it is packed and returned to the dead man's next of kin.

Along with our killed and wounded, we have lost almost fifty Shermans since we first fought east of Nancy in November. Yet our Table of Equipment has expanded. Even we can have all the replacement tanks we can crew. The Army is as profligate with machines as it is with ammunition, now it has decided to ignore the lessons about ammunition wastage we were taught at Camp Claiborne and Camp Hood.

I glance ahead: smoke no longer slides from Big Sam's holed carcass. For lack of fuel—gasoline, propellant, rubber, fat, sinew and muscle—the fire has extinguished itself. First Sergeant Reardon carries on down the road in front of me toward Big Sam, treading without haste. The First Sergeant knows neither he nor I need hurry. No one in Big Sam requires our help; and though it is cold, and the fire has consumed itself, Big Sam's hulk needs time to cool.

First Sergeant Reardon has taught us pace: to be quick, but not too quick. Arriving early's as bad as arriving late, men. Be there when you ought to be there. You understand? We nodded as though we understood. The Germans have taught us other, harder lessons as they have tried their best to kill us all, for the Germans are the professors in this university. They are more able soldiers, and far more aggressive tankers, than we will ever be. But we have learned the lessons they have taught, and beat the sharp right angles out of the precise boxes of the Table of Organization and Equipment which, back in Texas, constituted the administrative skeleton of the Seven Six One and the basis of our tactics. Now school is out and we have become flexible and responsive. Platoons and companies are reinforced in attack: we increase the strength of our right arm, taking the chance on the weakness of our left so that we can strike them hard and harder, in the back when possible, in the side when we must. Soft vehicles are kept to the rear, armor thrust forward. The assault guns, once distributed among the companies, now travel as a distinct unit and function as Battalion artillery. We call in division and corps artillery and tactical air at the first sour scent of trouble: better a wasted, burning farmstead or a shattered village, its cobbles ploughed up and its spires blown down, than one more man dead. Above all we have learned to advance against the fire: the Germans have taught us that it is safer to go forward than to retreat.

First Sergeant Reardon walks on, ignoring the lessons the Germans have taught us. He can afford to be offhand about their instruction: he learned their lessons in the Great War. Now, twenty-seven years later, he marches forward along this narrow country road in Germany, ignoring the ascending slope thick with pine trees on his right and the slope to his left descending toward the valley; ignoring everything but the job we will do inside Big Sam up ahead of us, leaking a few last threads of smoke.

But if the First Sergeant ignores the Germans' lessons, I do not, for I remember the lessons taught in Louisiana and Texas that we disposed of in France. When we trained in Texas, the tank crews were taught to aim, to shoot, and to observe the fall of shot before shooting again. Ammunition wastage, they were told, was a sin like buggery, rape, murder or the theft of government property. They were taught to handle each round of ammunition as though it were the only round ever manufactured. Sergeants shouted and Captains lectured about ammunition wastage. Wasting ammunition, it was said, was worse than syphilis or constipation. If you wasted ammunition, you could die, or be caught short. Men wasting ammunition were told not to waste ammunition, because wasting ammunition was worse than murder, rape, theft or buggery.

Those were the lessons of 1942, absorbed when our instructors had not yet learned they were mistaken. Now when the tank commander shouts out approximate ranges his loader standing to the left of the gun flings 76 millimeter shells one after another into the ringing, smoking breech of the piece, the gunner and assistant driver drenching the area of the suspected target with fire from the main armament and the coaxial and bow machineguns. All of them work like miners paid by the ton brought to the pithead.

Squatting on the road, canted to the left, the port track laid out behind, Big Sam looks small beneath the pine trees and against the expanse of the valley beyond. The thirty ton bulk of a Sherman that has burned seems diminished, though fire cannot not destroy the shape of its armored carapace. Perhaps it seems diminished because it is: anyone seeing a burned-out Sherman knows it has shed the weight of its fuel, ammunition, coolant, fire retardant liquid and crew. Big Sam is junk, but even before it was destroyed minutes ago it seemed small and antique compared to the elegant steel monsters in which the Germans ride and fight.

First Sergeant Reardon steps up to Big Sam and places his fingers and palm flat against the starboard sponson. He does not remove his hand: the metal is cooling. I hope it is cool enough for us to go to work in safety. I worry that unexploded ammunition may still lie inside the hull, and that its temperature may still be rising.

In 1942 we were told the Sherman was big enough. Then the target was the PanzerKampfWagen III. But the PzKW III was superseded by subsequent marks of the PanzerKampfWagen: IV, V—the Panther—and VI—the Tiger. When Germany went over to the defense, the clever tank destroyer variants of the mark IV, V and VI appeared: the Sturmgeschutz, the JagdPanther, and the JagdTiger. The Sherman has been upgunned from 75 to 76 millimeters, and uparmored by the application of additional plate over sensitive spots within the hull, but it is still not big enough, and in a gun-to-gun contest the Sherman cannot destroy any German tank with impunity except the PzKw IV, and it cannot destroy the PzKW IV unless the Sherman's gunner is experienced, calm, and lucky.

So much for the wishful thinking of the theorists who sit on the Armored Board and the fixes of the mechanical experts at the Rock Island Arsenal. Yet we cannot complain: we always knew they planned in corridors and rooms, staring through the narrow prisms of their professional caste and faded experience, confident they would be permitted to repeat the methods of the conflict just past.

So we have molded the neat boxes of our Table of Organization and Equipment to fit our need, for the Germans have confirmed that they would have slaughtered us like sheep had we relied, without more, on the lessons of Camp Claiborne and Camp Hood. It was not difficult for us to discard the stolid thinking of the professional Army of 1942. It was irrelevant and we were lucky we had always been cynical of authority and suspicious of promises. Almost all of us, after all, were civilians three years ago. We had never had the protection of statutory regiments, or Uncle Sugar's patronage, or the patronizing compliments of that discreet segment of the press that recalled on occasion that we were out there somewhere.

So we have set aside staff solutions and the Armored Board's measured assessments, and as we fight toward the east we review the lessons in expedience our professors in the Wehrmacht and the SS have taught us; for we are not here to demonstrate that we have learned our lessons, or to prove the theories propounded in the antique offices of the War Department in the long afternoons of 1937. We are here to kill Germans, to end this fight and to get out of this shit alive if we can manage it, and we will take the best instruction we can find that will help us achieve our ends. So we carry private weapons and adjust the carburetors on the tanks and halftracks to make them perform beyond the specifications in the manual. In bad weather when the trucks sink into the mud and the halftracks slither on the least slope, the light tanks of D Company forsake their role as cavalry prancing on the flanks and haul supplies forward to the Shermans.

We are prodigal with ammunition: we destroy villages to save a man, and towns to save one more.

First Sergeant Reardon glances at me as I come forward. He looks at my face—to figure out if I am turning pale, I suppose—looks away, steps back from Big Sam and surveys the destroyed hulk as though he is thinking about making the owner an offer.

Big Sam's crew took a chance easing down this road with their illicit stock of ammunition laid down like strange bottles inside the hull. Had they not carried the extra rounds, one or more of the five of them might have escaped death when the JagdPanther's eighty-eight millimeter shell slid through the hull. On the other hand, they might have had to fight and might have found themselves short of ammunition. Caught between choices, they chose wrong: the explosion of the extra ammunition packed inside Big Sam's hull has killed them all. The Ordnance Department has cautioned against the improper stowage of excess ammunition. It has studied the issue, and concluded that loading excess ammunition inside the hull is the source of in-hull conflagrations. Unfortunately the Ordnance Department cannot guarantee the tank crews delivery of sufficient ammunition when they need it. So Sam Taylor and his men took a chance. And so Big Sam burned, and its crew burned with it: the eighty-eight millimeter round must have ignited the fuel, which ignited the propellant in the excess 76 millimeter rounds, which started the fire that killed the crew and incinerated their corpses.

We will never be easy with death this violent, but we adapt: we have cut and chopped and changed and gone on for three centuries more than the little motherfucker who operates Germany as an organ grinder jerks his monkey's chain to make him screech and leap. Neither Quineau's death, nor Sam Taylor's death and the deaths of his four man crew will detain us on this road for long, or prevent our descent into the valley below, or halt our long drive east. We are deterred, but we will not be prevented. Our only question is: how much this trip's ticket cost?

First Sergeant Reardon looks away from Big Sam down into the valley. He examines the pine trees on the far slope. He does not shake his head over our losses or curse or clench his fist. He looks back up the road past me, past Bayou Queen and Bright Lights. I look over my shoulder but I see nothing unusual. First Sergeant Reardon examines the valley once again, looking into the shadows among the pine trees as though he expects to see something. I wonder what it is he looks for: the JagdPanther is long gone.

When First Sergeant Reardon transferred into the Seven Six One from one of our two statutory infantry regiments, he had the experience to understand that the plans our officers laid and the lessons they taught would disintegrate when the first angry shot was fired. Yet he more than anyone demanded that we study our lessons, and distributed punishment if we did not learn. He was right to require us: the training was inapposite and dated, but it carried us enough of the way to give us a taste of what was down in the bottom of the bottle.

We studied fire discipline, military conduct, maintenance procedures, ammunition wastage, hygiene in the field, military law, tactical approaches to enemy positions, communication by flag, arm signal and radio, the proper order in which crew members were to mount and dismount vehicles, the specifications and maintenance of weapons, the tank assault by platoon, company and battalion, military courtesy, military rank, military tradition and military history.

Yet as we studied First Sergeant Reardon intimated that no one would count the shells we fired, or the vehicles we lost, when the time came. No one would want us to salute or ask us who Hiram Ulysses Grant might be. Up on the line, he said, there's none of that. And you'll learn, he said, that machines and ordnance ain't the important part. When we asked what the important part was, First Sergeant Reardon said, you'll learn that too, when the time comes.

So the First Sergeant taught us the first rule: that the rules would change when, as he said, the poor boys dance. Watching us shiver with apprehension, he ordered us to repeat the Army's antique, inapposite lessons again and again, so that we would learn how to learn.

So the First Sergeant disciplined the Seven Six One. Behind his back many called him a motherfucking motherfucker when he ordered up one more exercise to be sure we had it right. But even the most disgusted and petulant among us remembered, and remember still, that First Sergeant Reardon fought the Germans across this ground twenty-seven years ago, and wears three inverted chevrons on the right sleeve of his dress uniform four inches from the cuff, to prove they wounded him thrice but could not kill him.

In Europe, Sergeant Reardon has continued as intolerant of indiscipline as he was at Camp Claiborne and Camp Hood. He does not mind that some of us carry German weapons, so long as we keep them clean. He is also provident. He orders up from the supply train of whatever infantry division to which we are attached more of everything—food, spare parts, medical supplies, ammunition, vehicles, V-Mail blanks, weapons, fuel and trucks enough to carry it all—than we used to think we could possibly use.

First Sergeant Reardon explains his outrageous requisitions to our officers as deficiencies in our Table of Equipment. Our officers, complicit and nodding, defer to each of the First Sergeant's decisions, and sign.

First Sergeant Reardon places the equipment he has requisitioned for this job on Big Sam's rear deck. He unfolds the coveralls, shakes them out and steps into them, working the feet of his high rubber boots through the legs.

I step up beside the First Sergeant and lean the shovel against the boss of the rear element of the Sherman's suspension. Big Sam's hull smells of bitter smoke and is warm to the touch. I lay the three blankets and the rubber gloves I carry on top of the two blankets First Sergeant Reardon placed on Big Sam's rear deck. I unfold my coveralls, step into them, and button them up the front. I pick up the rubber gloves and work them between the third and fourth buttons of the coveralls. I pick up the shovel.

"Let's try the turret hatches," First Sergeant Reardon says. He does not mention my rank, or say my name. He takes his pair of heavy rubber gloves from beside the neat stack of five OD blankets and shoves them into the baggy right-rear pocket of his coveralls.

"Yes," I say. I did not call him First Sergeant the first time we did this job together, and I do not now. First Sergeant Reardon does not consider this a lapse. Perhaps he feels as I do: that when we do this work, we are not soldiers. I do not know what we are, but when we stack the blankets and pull on the coveralls and take the gloves and the shovel and the entrenching tool up onto the hull of a burned-out tank, we no longer wear the uniform or practice the etiquette the uniform requires.

I step around the First Sergeant, put the shovel on the hull in front of the turret, and walk to the front of Big Sam. I touch the metal with my fingertips. It is still warm. At least we will not have to work in the cold.

I climb and pull myself up the sloped steel front of the Sherman. This is difficult work in slippery rubber boots, but I scrabble and hoist myself up until I stand on the hatch above the bow-gunner's seat. Beane, the bow-gunner, waits for us beneath the steel hatch beneath my feet.

I bend and pick up the shovel and climb up onto the turret. The turret is rotated quarter-left: Thompson, the gunner, tried hard to face the JagdPanther's fearsome gun.

This M4A3 Sherman has two large circular hatches set into its turret. This turret is an adaptation of the turret designed for the T23 tank. We hear that the T23's development has been suspended, but we have been told that the T23's turret has been borrowed for the Sherman so that the M4A3 could be upgunned from the 75 to the 76 millimeter weapon. The

T23 turret is larger and less rounded than the turret on the previous marks of the M4. The T23 turret also has two hatches, one above the commander's position, a second above the loader's. The M4A1 Sherman had only one hatch, above the commander. In an emergency in an M4A1, the commander and gunner, who sit to the right of the breech of the gun, the commander behind and above the gunner, exited through this hatch. The driver and bow-gunner each had hatches above their heads through which they too could depart. But the loader in the M4A1 had no hatch of his own: he had to crawl beneath the breech of the 75 millimeter gun and climb up and out of the hatch above the commander's position. This maneuver required two seconds more than the loader might have to escape fire, explosion and death.

First Sergeant Reardon climbs up on the turret—he has less difficulty with his slippery boots than did I—and stands beside me. A heavy wind pushes against us and falls away toward the valley. First Sergeant Reardon squats and touches the tank commander's hatch. Sam Taylor and his gunner wait for us on the other side of this hatch. I hope the hatch has not been fused by fire or jammed by concussion.

First Sergeant Reardon glances up at me and says, "You want a see gar?"

I don't smoke cigars, and if I did I wouldn't smoke one now: the thick bitter scent of all that has burned inside Big Sam fills my nostrils. I know First Sergeant Reardon knows this; but each time we have begun one of these special jobs he has asked me this question.

When I shake my head the First Sergeant nods as though I have passed a test. I do not know why he asks me if I want a cigar. I do not tell him what I have almost said each time he has asked me if I want a cigar: that I'll give the cigar a pass, but I wouldn't mind four fingers of whiskey, hold the water. It's the truth, but it would be wrong to say such a thing at a time like this.

The commander's hatch is fitted in a cupola. Arranged in the slanted edge of the cupola are six vision blocks of armored glass. The vision blocks are cracked and opaque. First Sergeant Reardon bends, grips the handle welded to the turret hatch and pulls. The hatch does not open. First Sergeant Reardon squats and pulls at the handle as he rises. The metal screeches and the hatch opens an inch. First Sergeant Reardon works the tips of the four fingers of his right hand into the slit between hatch coaming and hatch, flexing his fingers, wriggling them into the darkness beyond. He works all four fingers into the slit and pulls again. The hatch sticks: the perfect circle of the hatchway has been pounded into an imperceptible oval.

"Hand me the entrenching tool," First Sergeant Reardon says. I step down from the turret onto the grille above the engine compartment, pick up the entrenching tool from behind the turret and hand it up to him.

First Sergeant Reardon works the tip of the tool into the groove between the hatch and the hatchring, rocking the blade back and forth, worming it into the darkness beyond the jammed hatch. When he has worked half the length of the tool's blade into the slit he leans his weight against the solid wooden handle. Just as I begin to worry that the wooden handle of the entrenching tool may snap, the hatch screeches and eases upward six inches, showing us a dark mouth that releases a puff of soot and the stench of all that has burned inside Big Sam. First Sergeant Reardon hands me the entrenching tool, sits on the loader's hatch, slides the fingers of both hands into the slit he has prised open between hatch and hatchring, grips the rim of the hatchway, places the sole of his right rubber boot against the prised-open lip of the hatch and pushes. A screech. First Sergeant Reardon pushes and goes on pushing, forcing the hatch. He pushes until the screeching circular hatch is vertical, and keeps on pushing until it is canted as far away from the hatchway as the hinges permit.

"All right then," First Sergeant Reardon says, as though he is complimenting the hatch for being tractable. His rubber boots squeak against the steel of the turret as he shifts about and kneels at the edge of the commander's hatch.

I am surprised First Sergeant Reardon has been able to open the commander's hatch. With the strike of the eighty-eight millimeter shot and the explosion of the ammunition and fuel within Big Sam, I expected all the hatches to be jammed or fused shut. I thought we would have to call for an acetylene torch, and cut our way inside. But no one knows what internal explosions will do to the many assemblies and components which, when cast, welded, bolted and slotted together, constitute an M4A3 Sherman. The only certainty about a conflagration like the one that has swept through Big Sam is that it will kill between none and five of the five man crew.

"Nothing to it," First Sergeant Reardon says. But I know he is as surprised as I am that he has forced the commander's hatch open.

The First Sergeant looks down into the darkness inside the hatchway, glances to his left as he examines the valley once again. It is mid morning, and the shadows of the trees across the valley have retreated beneath the bushy green branches of the pines. Thin high clouds are sliding from the west through the cold sky. We are going to have weather: rain, or perhaps snow.

The First Sergeant hitches himself around until he is sitting cross-legged at the rear of the opened hatch. He reaches inside his coveralls, worms his hand this way and that and slides out a rubberized olive drab flashlight. He holds it in his left armpit and slides the electrician's gloves from the right rear pocket of his coveralls and pulls them on. Now his feet and hands are encased in rubber, his uniform protected by the coverall: he is ready to go to work.

"I recall it's my turn," he says, as though he is worried he may be doing me out of an opportunity I have been expecting.

I entered first the last time we performed this duty. Then it was an M5 Stuart named Down Home. Only the driver, an Alabama boy named Bellows, had died. The other three men in the crew had been wounded: the anti-tank round that killed Bellows mangled Barker's left hand and exploded the propellant in the brass butts of three rounds of thirty-seven millimeter ammunition, blinding Tripp and breaking both of Standish's legs. No one saw the gun that did this. No one heard it fire, saw the flash of its muzzle, or felt the strike of the shot. No one, that is, except Down Home's crew, who were deafened by the fearsome clang of the armor-piercing round as it struck the hull, and sensed its flicking passage through the interior of their light tank.

Neither First Sergeant Reardon nor I do this work unless each member of a crew is dead or wounded. If one of them survives unwounded, we leave this work to the medics and the surviving crewman. Thus we have left the three unwounded members of Quineau's crew to cope with his body. They will not constitute the six pallbearers dressed in tails and the prancing New Orleans band of brass and traps hung with black crepe that Quineau might have wanted, but they will do what is important as well as anyone. Anonymous service troops will bury Quineau, and put up the regulation wooden cross stencilled with his name and serial number. When this shit of cold and killing is finished, Quineau's family will be given a choice: bring his body home to New Orleans, or let him lie in Europe among all the others who have been killed in this war. On the other hand, they may not be given a choice: the regulations, and custom, may render Quineau's burial in Europe impolitic.

For those crews who lie dead all together, leaning across one another's corpses, their guts hanging down between their knees and their throats ripped open, William S. Reardon and I pull on knee-high rubber boots, don overalls and rubber gloves and mount the warm, still steel tomb, shovels in our fists, folded blankets close at hand.

Our work is easier if the tank shot down has been consumed by fire. Fire reduces the crew to anonymity and the weight of their bodies by four-fifths. If the crew is killed and the vehicle does not burn, or does not burn enough, we must work among the liquids, smells and harrowed flesh of five—or four, if the tank is a Stuart—men. But if a conflagration has swept the narrow space in which they lived and worked and spoke to one another, recalling the details of their lives before this war began, our work is quicker, lighter, cleaner. Except, that is, for the ash oily as the crust of crackled blackened burned meat.

"All right, then," William Reardon says. "Sam Taylor first." Sergeant Taylor is right inside the open commander's hatch; or at least he should be. Big Sam Taylor might have been a problem had Big Sam not burned: Taylor was a large man, more than six feet, with heavy bones, a lot of muscle and an easy manner. But we know he weighs much less now than he did twenty minutes ago. "Then Thompson," Reardon says. Johnny Thompson was Big Sam's gunner: a sunny, friendly man, easy to get by with. A slim man, about five feet eight or so, he spoke with a New England accent. None of us will ever hear him speak the hard consonants of Massachusetts again. "Then Smith," Reardon says. Moses Smith is the loader. He waits for us beneath the loader's hatch on the lefthand side of the turret. Smith is from Indiana. He finished highschool in June, 1941 and worked six months in a foundry in Gary while he tried to figure what to do next. Then the war began and he stopped figuring and joined the Army. Now, after Louisiana, Texas, England and France, he is here, three feet from my hand, waiting for Bill Reardon and I to begin. "The way the turret's rotated I don't know if we'll be able to get at Holcomb or Beane from inside the basket." Tom Holcomb is the driver, Simon Beane the bow-gunner. Both of them are farmers, one from Ohio, the other from Alabama. I recall their debates about the climate, the soil and the crops of their respective counties. It was a debate that continued until those listening grew bored with agronomy and pork bellies and drifted away, leaving Holcomb and Beane to figure out the price of beans and the price of hogs.

The wall of the cylindrical basket hung beneath the turret from the turret race is woven steel mesh, with apertures cut into the mesh to permit access to compartments in the sponsons and to the driver's and bow-gunner's positions. The tank commander, gunner and loader work in the basket. When the main armament points straight ahead, apertures in the basket permit easy passage to the driver's and bow-gunner's positions. But when the turret is rotated, such access is narrowed, or closed. Big Sam's turret is rotated forty degrees to the left, the muzzle of the 76 millimeter gun is depressed. The angle of rotation of the turret and the depression of the gunmuzzle tell me that Sam Taylor and his crew tried to confront the enemy that killed them all from the shadows among the trees on the other side of the valley. The angle of rotation of the turret also tells me we will, as the First Sergeant says, have difficulty getting Holcomb and Beane through the basket and out of the turret. I hope the hatches above their heads are not jammed.

"Still," William Reardon says, "this isn't an M4A1. Less mesh in these M4A3s."

I nod. In older Shermans the mesh basket had fewer apertures than were designed into the basket of the M4A3. Crews in the older Shermans had difficulty reaching the ammunition stowage in the sponsons outboard of the mesh basket. Worse, they discovered that if the hatches above the driver and bow-gunner jammed and the mechanism that rotated the turret jammed and the driver and bow-gunner could not escape their positions because the apertures in the basket had slid away from the space through which they might have fled, they could do little, if the Sherman burned, except wait for the man with the white bone face to come for them.

Things are better in the M4A3: the Armored Board and the Ordnance Department considered the issue—just as they had the lack of a hatch above the loader—and the basket wall of metal mesh in the M4A3 is cut with apertures enough to give the driver and bow-gunner a decent chance to get out if the hatches above their heads jam.

"All right," Bill Reardon says. The wind rushes down the hillside across the hatch on which the First Sergeant and I sit. A crisp burned smell swirls from the hatch: the smell of cooling cinders.

Even though the day is bright, William Reardon shines his flashlight through the hatchway. I know what he sees, but I do not speak, and neither does he.

William Reardon uncrosses his legs and lowers his rubber-booted feet into the darkness. He supports his weight with his left hand against the rim of the hatch and feels with his feet. Finding a footing, he eases himself down into the turret, picking his way, following the beam of the flashlight in his right hand. I know he is trying to avoid putting his feet in certain spots on the deck of the basket. He shifts his stance, reaches inside the turret with his left hand and grips the breech of the gun with his rubber-gloved fingers. He wedges the flashlight behind the cable conduit that extends from the junction box behind the commander's seat forward along the curve of the basket.

With only his head and shoulders outside the turret hatch, Bill Reardon examines the valley to his left once again, and once again I wonder why he glances at the pines on the far slope.

I look over his shoulder as he descends into the darkness. The flashlight's dim cone of yellow light is pointed at the floor of the basket. A dark crumpled bundle the size of an infantryman's pack lies on the deck behind the gunner's seat. Another is wedged in the narrow space between the gunner's seat and the electric traverse mechanism on the curving forward wall of the basket to the right of the ammunition box container beneath the breech of the gun.

One of these bundles is Sam Taylor, the other Johnny Thompson. Desiccated and scorched black, they wait for us to bring them out into the light.

"Pass me down a blanket," Bill Reardon says. His voice is calm. I cannot remember if I sounded as calm when I went down into the darkness inside Down Home to bring Harry Bellows out into the light.

I reach down from the turret and take a blanket from the neat stack on the rear deck. As I unfold it the cold wind flowing down the slope into the valley catches it. The blanket ripples and flaps, an olive drab flag. I haul it in and pass it down into Bill Reardon's reaching hands. I hear his feet move on the deck of the basket, the rubber soles of his boots squeaking against metal.

The wind is picking up, driving grey clouds through the sky above the valley and moaning through the ragged tears in Big Sam's armor. It will rain today, or if the temperature drops it will snow. We will tip Big Sam off the road—it cannot be salvaged, and it is now nothing more than a thirty ton obstruction—and the snow will soften the sharp angles of its hull. Those coming after us tomorrow may not notice what happened here.

"Hand me the shovel," Bill Reardon says from down in the darkness inside the turret. I reach for the shovel and extend it handle first through the hatch. As Bill Reardon takes it from my hands, he mutters something I do not quite understand.

The shovel scrapes against the metal floor of the basket beneath the turret. I have heard this sound before: it is the same sound a coal shovel makes when it is thrust across concrete. The blade of the shovel in Bill Reardon's hands runs against an obstruction—the shaft of the gunner's seat to the right of the breech of the gun, perhaps, or a hinge on the battery compartment door set in the circular floor. The bright clang of metal against metal reverberates inside the turret, rises into the rising wind.

I look down into the dark pit in which Bill Reardon is working. He is crouched, his hands close to the floor. He has laid the olive drab blanket over the crumpled bundle on the deck behind the gunner's seat. He is thrusting the shovel along the metal floor beneath the lump beneath the blanket. He moves the shovel with care, each thrust of his forearms measured, each economical movement of the shovel's bright blade spaced along the length of what is left of Big Sam Taylor's body. With each thrust of the shovel, Bill Reardon works the blade right and left, separating what is left of Sam Taylor from the metal floor to which his flesh was fused by the conflagration of exploding ammunition and burning fuel.

The scraping stops. Bill Reardon hands the shovel up out of the hatch. The straight edge of the blade is crusted with a residue of fine oily ash. It reminds me of scrapings of meat burned on a grill. I lay the shovel beside the hatch above the loader's position. I think of Moses Smith, the loader who snatched 76 millimeter rounds from the ready rack and the ammunition stowage beneath the floor of the basket and flung them into the breech of the gun. He waits for us, as patient as Sam Taylor and the other three men in Big Sam.

The cold wind whips around me as I look down through the hatch. In the constricted space inside Big Sam's fighting compartment, Bill Reardon crouches with his back to the shield that protects the gunner from the recoil of the 76 millimeter gun. His left shoulder presses against the scorched back of the gunner's seat. He is working the blanket beneath the corpse he has separated from the floor of the Sherman's fighting compartment. He lifts Sam Taylor bit by bit as he edges the blanket beneath him. When he has Sam inside the blanket he slips his gloved hands beneath the bundle and lifts it. Bill Reardon does not strain as he lifts Sam Taylor. Sam Taylor was a big man, but the searing heat of the conflagration that killed him cooked the liquid out of his body and reduced him to bones and black leathery skin and tendon. Sam Taylor's body is, I see, small: fire boils moisture from flesh and shrinks tendon, draws the knees and elbows toward the center of the torso, destroys the symmetry of the body, forces the shoulders down and forward, bends the neck and spine.

Big Sam Taylor weighs no more than forty pounds now the fire has passed over him, and he is no more than four feet long. Bill Reardon lifts him up through the hatch as though he is lifting a sleeping child from its cot.

"I've got him," I say as I take the body wrapped in the olive drab blanket.

"No tags," Bill Reardon says from inside the turret.

"I'll diagram it," I say. I step down from the turret onto the scorched rear deck of the Sherman, Sam Taylor in my arms. I lay his small corpse at the rear of the deck. The cold wind ripples over the blanket, lifting the corners.

I tuck them beneath what is left of Sam Taylor. As I do so I remember him east of Nancy, in France, looking at the broken right track of Big Sam and saying, "Well, what the hell? How long to fix this here? I got to get on, rest of the Company getting away from me."

I take out my notebook, sketch the shape of a Sherman as seen from overhead, insert a rectangle at the rear of the sketch and label it 'Sam Taylor—Tank Commander.' Such he was. Such he has become.

I take a second blanket and stand back up on the turret. I look down through the hatch. Bill Reardon is waiting, looking from the darkness in which he crouches up into the light. "Clouding over," he says as he takes the blanket.

"Rain," I say. "Or maybe snow."

"Why don't you see if you can get to Beane? Or Holcomb."

"I'll see," I say. I ease over the front of the turret and stand beside the barrel of the gun. The gun is trained to the left front, but the barrel bends to the right with a perceptible warp. I consider heat so ferocious it can bend a cannon's barrel, think of Big Sam Taylor reduced to a comfortable weight wrapped in a blanket, and wonder what I will find beneath the driver and bowgunner's hatches.

I squat above Simon Beane's hatch at the right front corner of the hull. The hull in front of the hatch has been dented from the inside: when Big Sam's ammunition detonated, some of the shells pounded through the bow-gunner's compartment and struck but did not pierce the inside face of the steel glacis sloped back and up from the transmission cover to the upper deck in which the turret is fitted. I do not think about what I will find beneath Beane's hatch: whatever I find, it will be all that is left of Simon Beane.

Without optimism, for I am sure the hatch is jammed, I grasp the handle welded to the hatch inboard of the rotatable periscope. I am surprised when I pull and the hatch swings up. The inside of the hatch is scorched black and the periscope assembly is battered, the intricate parts that fit within one other pounded to bits pounded together. I look down into the bow-gunner's position beneath the open hatch.

Half of Beane leans forward in his seat. His helmeted head leans forward farther still: his chin rests against his breast, his forehead against the twisted, hammered butt of the .30 caliber machinegun he has manned since we trained in Texas. The burned leather and fiber tanker's helmet and the forward bend of his neck hide his face. His charred right arm is flexed, his clawed fist drawn tight against his right shoulder. His uniform shirt is burned away. So is the flesh across his upper back. The fire has sloped and narrowed his shoulders. His grey ribs and the blackened bones of his shoulders are collapsed. His left arm has been severed six inches below the shoulder: it lies beside his seat, the palm upward, the flesh of his hand burned away, the delicate half-clenched charred bones of his fingers exposed. His legs have been severed at his knees. They lie one on the other in front of the seat in which his torso sits.

As I look down through Beane's hatch I feel the cold wind rising from the southwest and hear the branches of the pine trees close at hand swish together.

"I see you got Beane's hatch open," Bill Reardon's muffled voice says from inside the Sherman. "You all right?"

Enough of Beane's helmet has been burned away to permit me to see the back of his head. His dark curly hair has been singed away and the skin beneath crisped. The curved grey bone of his skull is exposed.

"Fine," I say, raising my voice so that Bill Reardon will hear me. I get up. My knees ache and my face is cold. I climb over Big Sam's turret. I pick two blankets from the pile: I will need a second for Holcomb, who sits to Beane's left among the pedals and levers and dials of the driver's position, waiting for me to finish with Beane. Holcomb was a patient uncomplaining man. Now he will be patient forever. I drape his blanket, and Beane's, over my left arm.

The fifth, last blanket lies on Big Sam's scorched rear deck. Its stitched edges flutter as the cold wind gusts. I pick it up—this is Smith's blanket—and, standing at the rear of the turret, lean forward toward the hatch beneath which Bill Reardon works, and say, "You want Smith's blanket? The wind's picking up."

"Pass it on down," Reardon says. His right hand rises from the hatch. I feed a corner of the folded blanket into Bill Reardon's hand and watch as he drags it down into the Sherman's fighting compartment. I imagine him draping the rough olive drab cloth over the gunshield fitted around the breech of the 76 millimeter gun. Where else would one put it to keep it off the metal deck of the basket strewn with what the fire has left of Taylor, Thompson and Smith?

"You doing all right?" Bill Reardon asks from inside the basket beneath the turret.

"I'm all right," I say. I climb back over the turret. The rubber gloves on my hands are black with soot. My face is cold, my ears without sensation. Were this any other duty I would order up relief from the crew of men who ride with me in the maintenance halftrack. But I smell the black, crusty ash fried from the backs of five of our men, and dismiss the thought of relief.

I will go on with this until I bring Beane and Holcomb out of the darkness inside Big Sam.

I am about to reach down into Beane's hatch to lift his torso out into the light when Bill Reardon says, "I need your help."

I lay Beane's blanket, and Holcomb's, beside Beane's hatch and step the single high step up onto the turret. I kneel beside the commander's hatch. Down in the darkness, in the yellow light of the flashlight's beam, I see Bill Reardon rise from a stoop, his back against the thick curved steel mesh of the basket hung beneath the turret. He squirms past the gunner's seat as he lifts the compact bundle of Johnny Thompson's remains over the back of the seat in which Johnny Thompson rode and fought his war and, fifteen minutes ago, died. Was killed. Suffered crucifixion, that is, pinned by fire and explosion to the gunsight thrust through his chest, the gun's shield an inch from the gleaming bones of his left shoulder.

I reach down into the hatch and grasp Johnny Thompson's blanket-wrapped remains. "Take care," Bill Reardon says as he lifts Thompson. "He's in pieces." I know what he means: I have seen Simon Beane waiting in the bow-gunner's position for the pieces of himself to be wrapped in a blanket and lifted out of the dark into the cold windy light of the day.

As I lift all that remains of Johnny Thompson, I support half his weight with each hand; and as I ease what is left of him up out of the hatch, I feel the pieces of his body inside the blanket lurch and rub against one another. I cannot figure the arrangement of his limbs inside the blanket. Through the heavy rubber gantlet on my right hand I feel the sole of a boot, and the curve of a part of Johnny Thompson's skull. Through the cloth of the blanket my gloved left hand touches three sticks no larger around than the handle of an axe. The largest part of the bundle, between my hands, must be Thompson's torso; but it is not large enough to be a man's torso.

"Round took him through the chest," Bill Reardon says from inside the hatch.

"Right," I say. "Tags?" I ask.

"No tags," Bill Reardon says. I nod and nod as though Reardon can see me as I carry Johnny Thompson down off the turret. I lay him down on the rear of the M4A3's deck beside Big Sam Taylor. Now the rising wind tugs at the edges of two blankets wrapped around the remains of two-fifths of this crew. I tuck the blankets tight around each of them, to keep the wind from working open the cloth parcels in which they lie.

I take out my notebook and draw a second rectangle next to the first on the crude overhead drawing of the M4A3 I have made. I label this rectangle "Johnny Thompson-Gunner".

Seven Six One

As I go up and over the turret to go to work on Simon Beane, I hear the shovel in Bill Reardon's hands begin to grate against the floor of the basket. He is going to work on Moses Smith, separating his charred remains from the floor of the small loader's space to the left of the breech of the gun.

I shake out one of the two blankets lying beside Simon Beane's hatch, spread it on the narrow shelf between the turret and the steep slant of the glacis of armor at the front of the Sherman. Gusts of wind tug at the edges of the blanket. I kneel on the closest corner of the flapping rectangle of thick brown cloth.

Kneeling thus on Simon Beane's shroud, I reach inside the hatchway and wriggle my fingers beneath his armpits. As I do so I hear the crackling sound of burned crusted flesh separating from burned crusted flesh. As I work for a secure grip, the torso of his corpse slumps further forward against the seared, battered butt of his .30 caliber machinegun. The bones in his back are exposed half way to his waist. A heavy piece of fast-moving metal has torn through his ribs to the left of his spine, crushing bone and destroying the symmetry of his ribcage. I cannot tell whether it was an errant round of 76 millimeter ammunition that pierced him so, or part of the elevating gear, or the traverse mechanism, or a piece of the floor of the basket beneath the turret. Who knows? Who will ever know?

I grip and grip Simon Beane beneath the armpits, and as I pull this largest part of him upward my fingers inside the gantlets feel the bones in his chest shift as though he were taking a long last breath. I pull, and hear the sound of a bandage crusted with coagulated blood and fluid torn from the wound beneath. The fire has fused the muscle and fat of his buttocks to the padded leather cushion of his seat, and I rock his torso right and left as I lift to separate his flesh from the tanned leather on which he sits. With a rasping rip I free this part of Simon Beane from Big Sam and lift it out into the light. As his thighs come through the hatchway they bump against the coaming and Simon Beane's blackened face beneath the remains of his scorched fiber tanker's helmet falls forward across his chest. His torso and right arm—all of him I have been able, on this first trip, to lift into the darkening light of this late winter day—weigh no more than a large dog. Flying hot metal has eviscerated Beane and in the instant of his death fire has incinerated his stomach, lungs, heart, liver, kidneys and intestines. I look aside as I maneuver Simon Beane's head, torso and right arm, and the stumps of his left arm and legs, onto the blanket. I lay him face down on the clean brown cloth. The thickening clouds part and the pale sunlight gleams from the broken ends of his ribs and the exposed bones of his shoulders.

I flip half the blanket across this piece of Simon Beane, tuck the edges of the cloth beneath the blackened empty cavity between his broken breastbone and pelvis and turn back to the hatch. I descend feet first into the darkness and stand on Simon Beane's seat. I squat, and my right knee presses against the butt of the machinegun. The machinegun is fixed in a ball mounting in the sloped front of the hull; but the ball mounting is jammed and the machinegun does not shift when I press my knee against it. To my left, beyond the curved wall of the basket beneath the turret, William Reardon is still working with the shovel, the blade scraping across metal. The wind outside the tank whines as it swirls through the open hatchway above my head. I hear the blanket in which I have wrapped part of Simon Beane flapping as the wind swings around the turret.

As I squat on the bow-gunner's seat, the rubber boots on my feet rustle against the crust of charred fat burned from Simon Beane. I glance across the transmission into the darkness beyond: I cannot see Tom Holcomb, the driver. Perhaps he is bent forward as Beane was, parts of him distributed among the clutch and accelerator pedals and the gearshift and steering levers.

I lean forward and to the right and reach below the seat. The butt of the machinegun presses against my right shoulder as I grasp the wrist of Simon Beane's severed left arm. As I lift it from the floor I hear the distinctive sound of meat seared to a skillet prised away; and as I lift, Simon Beane's blackened fingers clawed toward his palm touch the back of my gloved hand. I stand up in the hatch and maneuver the arm between my body and the hatch-coaming. I am lucky the arm is not bent at the elbow. I lay the arm beside the hump beneath the blanket and stand up out of the hatch. I pull the edge of the blanket from beneath Simon Beane's torso and hips and place his arm beside him, his hand of blackened clawed fingers where it should be, near his waist. I tuck the blanket beneath the burned stick of Beane's severed arm and turn to the open hatch again.

I squat inside the bow-gunner's compartment again, reach my right arm down and grip one of Simon Beane's legs and maneuver it past the butt of the machinegun and out of the hatchway. I cannot tell which leg this is: the boot and foot have burned and burned, the sole of the boot has melted and lost its shape. I reach down again for his other leg. I lift it up out of the hatch. I cannot tell which boot is which. But it does not matter: he will not need his boots, or his legs, again.

I climb out of the hatch and open Simon Beane's blanket again. He lies legless face down against the brown cloth, his scorched severed arm beside him. I place his legs on his charred back and wrap the blanket tight around him, tucking the folded ends of the cloth beneath.

I stand up, my knees aching, and bend and pick up the bundle that contains all that remains of Simon Beane. Holding the blanket tight about him, I step up onto the turret and down the other side. I lay Simon Beane down on the rear deck of the Sherman beside Johnny Thompson, whom I laid beside Sam Taylor. I slide the heavy rubber gloves from my sweating hands, take out my notebook and draw a third rectangle beside the other two. I label this rectangle "Simon Beane—Bow Gunner". I hope they bury him in the rich dirt he insisted was better than the dirt Holcomb farmed in Alabama.

As I write I hear the squeak of rubber boots on metal as Bill Reardon climbs out of the commander's hatch in the turret behind me. I look over my shoulder and step out of his way as he climbs down from the turret onto the rear deck. He carries Moses Smith bundled inside a blanket folded with care about what little is left of this M4A3's loader. The bundle Bill Reardon carries is the size of the bundle in which Simon Beane is wrapped: no bigger than a five year-old child.

Bill Reardon glances at the three shapes lying on the rear deck of the Sherman and says, "That's Sam Taylor, nearest the rear there?"

"Yes," I say. "Johnny Thompson's in the middle, and Beane's at the near end."

Bill Reardon nods and places what is left of Moses Smith close to the rear of the Sherman, beside Big Sam Taylor. I draw a fourth rectangle on the crude picture in my notebook beside the one labeled "Sam Taylor—Tank Commander". I label this rectangle "Moses Smith—Loader".

When we get Tom Holcomb out of the driver's space we will have one line of three and one line of two corpses wrapped in olive drab blankets on the rear deck of this destroyed Sherman, and I will have drawn two sets of rectangles, one of three and the second of two, into the outline of the Sherman I have drawn in my notebook. Uncle's got more Shermans, but I do not know how many more men like Taylor, Thompson, Smith, Beane and Holcomb he can spare. And whatever Uncle thinks he can spare, I know we can't give up that many more.

"Smith's torn up," Bill Reardon says as he stands back up. "The ammunition in the wet-stowage on the floor went along with the rest. But it looks like the loose rounds they loaded went first."

"They worry they'll run out of ammunition," I say, to explain why the tank crews carry more ammunition than they should.

"I know that," Bill Reardon says. "Still, they ought to know they take the chance."

In the M4A3 the floor beneath the gunner and tank commander to the right of the breech of the gun is higher than the well in which the loader stands. The ammunition wet-stowed in metal containers in the floor is accessible to the loader, who stands in the well to the left of the 76 millimeter gun's breech. This is a new design. The Armored Board and the Ordnance Department determined after more than a year of live-fire tests conducted in North Africa, Sicily and Italy by German antitank guns and German antitank crews that stowage of the main armament's ammunition in the M4A1's sponsons had been a design error. Appliqué armor welded to the outside of the sponsons—two patches on the right sponson, one on the left—over the ammunition bins was found to be no more than a temporary, and unsuccessful, expedient: after a few months of further tests in the Wehrmacht's shooting gallery, everyone—the Ordnance Department, the Armored Board and the tank crews—agreed that while the raised square patches of armor on the sides of the sponsons provided more protection, they also provided distinct aiming points for antitank gunners. So the 76 millimeter ammunition stowage containers in the M4A3 were shifted into the floor of the basket beneath the turret in which the tank commander, the gunner and the loader work. Further, the ammunition in these containers was wet-stowed: each container holds ten 76 millimeter rounds and if the container's walls are pierced a mixture of water and ethylene glycol floods over the ammunition.

But tank crews stow more shells inside their vehicles than can be wet-stowed. To do so is to balance the chance of internal explosion against the chance of being caught without ammunition. Big Sam Taylor, Johnny Thompson, Moses Smith, Simon Beane and Tom Holcomb bet they could get away with it one more time. They bet wrong.

"Let's get Holcomb out," Bill Reardon says.

"Try his hatch first?"

"Yes. We'll have trouble if we have to try to get him out through the basket. There's an opening there, but it's tight."

I know what he means: worming a corpse—or as the case may be the components of a corpse—out of the driver's seat and through one of the apertures in the basket beneath the turret can be awkward. I know this and so does Bill Reardon: we tried to do it in November and it is difficult.

We climb up onto the turret. Bill Reardon waits on the turret as I step down beside the driver's hatch. Tom Holcomb sits in the dark beneath this hatch. The rotatable periscope set in the hatch is turned to the left, as though Holcomb attempted to look in the direction from which the JagdPanther fired. The thick glass is cracked and blackened: a bad sign. I grip the metal handle of the hatch and pull. The hatch swings up as though maintenance has just oiled the hinges, and I am reminded once again that it is impossible to predict the effects of an ammunition explosion inside a Sherman.

Tom Holcomb leans forward in the driver's seat, his head between his knees, his balled fists against the metal deck beside his feet drawn back from the clutch and accelerator. His shirt has burned, his back is scorched and his body has cooked, but he has not been incinerated. Something has ripped through the back of his seat, and I can see the bones of his back in the pulp of the fearsome wound between his waist and shoulder blades.

Before he died Holcomb twisted his fiber tanker's helmet from his head and dropped it on the metal deck in front of his feet. I wonder why he dropped his helmet there. I also wonder why he has not become a cinder, like Beane, Smith, Thompson and Taylor. I wonder what it was that pierced his back and killed him. But who can know? Who can ever know?

"How is he?" Bill Reardon asks from where he stands on Big Sam's turret.

"He hasn't burned," I say.

"You be all right getting him out?" Bill Reardon knows as well as I that a burned man is easier to bring out of a destroyed Sherman. An incinerated man is lighter and more anonymous than one who has not burned.

"I'll get him out," I say. After all, it's only fair: Bill Reardon brought out three: Sam Taylor, John Thompson and Moses Smith, while I have brought out only one: Simon Beane.

As usual, First Sergeant Reardon has done more than his share: as he did when he took his rifle and fought with the armored doughs at Morville-les-Vic. 'I was in infantry,' he is said to have told the doughs' Captain. Harassed, and willing to believe, the Captain said, 'Right now I can use every man who wants to join, Sergeant—First Sergeant, I mean," he said as he noted the lozenge between the chevrons and the rockers on First Sergeant Reardon's sleeve. For three hours the First Sergeant, his private '03 Springfield in his hands, a khaki cloth bandoleer of clips slung over his chest and a .45 revolver in an antique leather holster on his hip, rejoined the infantry. When he returned to Battalion Headquarters and the Colonel asked him where he'd been—even the Colonel would not dare ask the First Sergeant where the fuck he'd been—First Sergeant Reardon produced a folded sheet from a message pad on which the infantry captain had written, 'I hope transfers from your unit to mine are soon permitted. When they are, I want your First Sergeant," and had signed his name, Captain something Cunningham, and written his serial number at the foot of the note. I thought the story apocryphal until Corporal Stuart, the First Sergeant's clerk, showed me the note and pointed at Captain Cunningham's scrawled signature. Even the half-anonymous Captain Cunningham had capitalized the two words of the First Sergeant's rank.

No one has ever had quite enough nerve to ask First Sergeant Reardon what he did with the infantry on that terrible day in November when we fought in armor and he fought with the doughs before Morville-les-Vic.

I glance at Bill Reardon as he steps down from the turret. He eases Beane's hatch closed with his foot, picks up the blanket in which we will wrap Tom Holcomb, and spreads it on the narrow ledge of steel between the turret and the glacis of steel that slopes forward and down to the Sherman's transmission housing.

I reach both hands down into Holcomb's hatch and work my gloved fingers under his armpits. I pull Tom Holcomb erect in his seat. As I pull his shoulders back his intestines slide down over his knees in a slick expanding ropey heap from the wound that opened him up from his groin to his breastbone. The thick stench of his guts rises through the bitter smell of scorched metal, melted rubber, exploded ammunition, burned gasoline and charred leather.

I hold Tom Holcomb against the back of his seat with my left hand, reach up out of the hatch behind me with my right and pull the blanket toward me. I draw it down through the hatch and past Tom Holcomb's head.

"Trouble?" Bill Reardon asks as I drape a corner of the blanket over Holcomb's left shoulder.

"No trouble," I tell him. I press my left elbow against Holcomb's chest to hold him against the back of his seat as I reach down with my gloved right hand and lift as much of the sliding weight of his entrails as I can reach from between his legs into his lap. A portion of his bowels still dangles against his shins and ankles. My elbow against his chest, I hold the slick bundle of his intestines in the empty cavity below his ribs with my left hand, reach down a second time with my right and lift the rest of his viscera up into him. I shift my grip and hold him together with my right hand as I tug the blanket down with my left. I work the blanket across Holcomb's middle and withdraw my right hand from beneath it. I allow Holcomb to lean forward, draw the ends of the blanket around his back, and knot the corners of the thick brown cloth against his back.

I sit back on my heels at the edge of the hatch and say, "I'll need you to lift him while I hold the blanket and raise him up."

"I'm here," Bill Reardon says. His rubber boots squeak as he squats at the rim of the hatch.

"I'll lift him up," I say. "You take his shoulders when I've got him part way up."

"I'll do it," Reardon says.

I reach both arms down through the hatchway. I slip my left arm around Tom Holcomb's back, my right across the blanket holding his guts inside the cavity carved by the metal that killed him.

I lift, urging Tom Holcomb toward the light. He is heavy, and his dead limbs are slippery and awkward. Still I lift, pulling him up and holding his guts inside him as I lift. As I urge his shoulders up near the rim of the hatch the black rubber gantlets drawn over Bill Reardon's hands and forearms slide beneath Tom Holcomb's armpits. He lifts, and I am holding less than half of Holcomb's weight.

Bill Reardon hoists Holcomb from the hatch and I lift as I hold my right hand tight against the blanket tied over the shifting viscera beneath. Reardon lays the corpse on its back and I take my hand from the blanket that hides the terrible wound that killed Tom Holcomb. As I reach down to lift Holcomb's shins and booted feet out of the hatch I glance at Holcomb's face. His eyes are closed, his features composed. It seems he may not have known he was to become a citizen of the nation of the dead.

I stand up on Big Sam's turret as Bill Reardon swings the hatch shut, kneels beside the body and reaches both hands beneath Tom Holcomb and unties the knot I fashioned from the corners of the blanket. He spreads the blanket over Holcomb, draws it up over his face and tucks it beneath the body. When he has wrapped Holcomb in his brown winding sheet Bill Reardon slips his left hand beneath Holcomb's knees and his right beneath his shoulders and lifts. He stands and steps up onto the Sherman's turret, steps across the turret and down onto the rear deck where the other four men in Big Sam's crew wait for Holcomb to join them. Bill Reardon lays Tom Holcomb's shrouded corpse beside the small bundle that is Moses Smith and says, "Better note which one he is in your book."

I slip the electrician's gantlets from my hands and fiddle the notebook from the pocket of my coveralls. I lay the notebook on the turret and open it, take the pencil, draw a fifth rectangle and label it "Thomas Holcomb-Driver".

"You did all right," First Sergeant Reardon says. I nod, glance back up the road. My men from the maintenance halftrack are moving on and around Bayou Queen, estimating whether the work that will be required to get it back into service can be done without returning Bayou Queen to a field maintenance workshop. The armored doughs are standing and sitting at the edge of the road, talking with the three unwounded members of Bayou Queen's crew. Beyond them, and beyond Bright Lights, an ambulance halftrack marked with red crosses is approaching. It drives past Bright Lights, past the First Sergeant's Jeep and the maintenance halftrack, and stops beside Bayou Queen.

"Doc Turner's come," I tell the First Sergeant.

"I see. Let's go back." First Sergeant Reardon takes the entrenching tool and the shovel, squats beside the shrunken, shrouded shape of Moses Smith's body, places his left hand against the scorched steel of Big Sam's hull and drops to the ground.

I follow him down off Big Sam. We walk back up the muddy road together. As the First Sergeant walks along, the blade of the entrenching tool clinks against the yellow hardwood shaft of the shovel. The air is full of wind and damp: I am sure it will snow, and soon.

Doc Turner is standing up in the right front seat of the halftrack. He waves at us and raises both arms in an interrogatory gesture. First Sergeant Reardon shakes his head side-to-side. Doc Turner drops his arms, gets down from the track, walks around Bayou Queen and bends over Stinson wrapped in blankets. Someone has pulled a knitted wool olive drab cap over his head. Only his face is exposed to the cold damp wind. Beyond Stinson, Tommy Quineau lies on the road, wrapped in a blanket, his face covered.

When we come up, Doc Turner is examining the work of the armored doughs' medic. "Good job, Corporal," he tells the medic.

"Thank you, sir," the corporal says.

Doc Turner looks up at us dressed in overalls and rubber gloves, glances at the sticky sooty grit that coats the bright metal of the shovel's straight edge. "You got them out, First Sergeant?"

"Yes, sir," First Sergeant Reardon says.

"Good," Doc Turner says. He looks at me. "Good work."

"Thank you, Captain." I take out my notebook, open it and tear out the page on which I drew the crude diagram of the Sherman. I show Doc Turner the five rectangles labelled with the names of Big Sam's crew. "This identifies them, Captain. Only the driver, Tom Holcomb, has tags." I hand the sheet to Doc Turner. He takes it and looks at the five labelled boxes.

"No tags on the other four? That bad, was it?"

"That bad," First Sergeant Reardon says.

Doc Turner nods as though he has conducted laboratory tests to determine the effects of extreme heat on the base metal from which dogtags are fashioned. "We'll take care of them," he says. "Thanks again. Both of you."

"Yes, sir," First Sergeant Reardon and I say. As we walk away from the doctor, I note Williston loitering at the rear of Bayou Queen, a sheet of paper in his hand. I know what it is: the damage assessment on Bayou Queen.

"Hang on some, Williston," First Sergeant Reardon says. Williston nods. We walk past him to the First Sergeant's Jeep. The First Sergeant and I drop our gloves, high rubber boots and coveralls on the floor in the back of the Jeep. The First Sergeant puts the shovel and the entrenching tool into the back with the boots, gloves and coveralls. We put on our overcoats and button them up. The First Sergeant gets into the Jeep and lifts a canteen from under his seat.

"Want a taste?" First Sergeant Reardon asks. He shakes the canteen in his hand, sloshing the liquor. The first time we did this work together, the First Sergeant Reardon offered me his canteen when we had finished. 'Now you know,' he said as he held the canteen out to me. And I did know: I nodded and said, "Yes, I know," but I did not take a drink. It seemed the wrong thing to do.

"No, thanks, First Sergeant," I say. I do not tell him that I could have used two mouthfuls and more before we went to work inside Big Sam.

"No?" He unscrews the cap and lets it dangle from the chain. "I'll have one. Keep the cold off." He tilts the canteen into the wind—snow for sure, I think: not rain—wets his lips, takes the canteen down, screws the cap back on and lays the canteen on the seat beside him. "I want you at my tent at Headquarters tomorrow morning five o'clock. If they's no tent, look in the Headquarters track."

"First Sergeant?" I ask as he starts the Jeep's engine and puts his hand on the knob of the gear shift.

"Be there," First Sergeant Reardon says. "I got something for you to do." He looks at me but he does not enlarge on this equivocal statement.

"Yes, First Sergeant."

First Sergeant Reardon revs the engine, looks to his left down into the valley. He bends forward, puts the canteen under his seat and says, "At least we had some luck: with the hatches."

"I guess they listened when that British Major talked to us back at Camp Hood."

"Didn't do them much good, did it?" He sounds sour, as though the British Major's lesson wasn't clear enough.

"They made it easier for us, though. We didn't have to use a torch to get inside."

"There's that," First Sergeant Reardon says. He pushes the clutch pedal down with his left foot, shifts the gearshift into reverse, nods and says, "You're right about that. All right. Tomorrow morning, then. Five o'clock. You did good work. You deserve something."

The First Sergeant backs the Jeep through a tightening quarter circle, shifts into first and drives away up the road as the wind drives the first small flakes of snow down through the pinetrees.

THREE

AS THE FIRST SCATTERED flakes of snow arrive with a damp gust of wind, Williston hands me the damage assessment on Bayou Queen. I glance at the fluttering sheet of paper and know we will have to return this ancient M4A1 Sherman to a field maintenance workshop for repair. The list of Bayou Queen's hurts is impressive: the center wishbone suspension assembly pounded apart; an oval aperture punched through the hull behind the shattered suspension assembly beneath the left sponson aft of the port ammunition bin; the breech of the 76 millimeter gun wrenched and rendered inoperable by the speeding strike of the 88 millimeter round; the commander's periscope destroyed; the basket beneath the turret bent and immovable; the radio shattered; the turret's electric-hydraulic traverse mechanism punctured; total hydraulic fluid loss; the linkages of the driver's controls severed; the bow machinegun's ball mounting frozen; the electrical system's wiring shredded inside the soft metal conduit bolted to the inside of the fighting compartment; and a second ragged hole punched in the upper right hand quadrant of the Sherman's turret through which the 88 millimeter round, still traveling faster than the speed of sound, exited Bayou Queen.

Not to mention Jimmy Stinson wounded and Quineau killed. Reading the list Williston has prepared I nod and nod at the havoc a single armor-piercing 88 millimeter round can cause. Bayou Queen's crew are lucky the Hunting Panther did no more than kill Quineau and wound Stinson. Big Sam, after all, suffered only a single strike from the JagdPanther's 88 millimeter gun, and Big Sam's destruction was complete.

"Bad about Big Sam," Williston says. He scratches his two-day growth of curly beard: he reminds me of a Caribbean pirate.

"A mess," I tell him. I glance at the verge of the road, where the three unwounded members of Bayou Queen's crew sit among the armored doughs. They are smoking cigarettes and eating chocolate and passing a canteen from hand to hand. All three tankers drink, and all the armored doughs drink with them. I nod and nod: out here, with the Germans beyond every pasture and death whispering in your ear, no one has time for all that shit about glasses and cups. "I wonder what happened to recon," I say.

"Who knows," Williston says. "Got hung up, went the wrong place, not enough time. Something. Or maybe no one thought there'd be anything waiting down there in the shadows."

"There should have been some German infantry to protect the SPG," I say. "But there wasn't. There was just the single Hunting Panther."

"That JagdPanther a mean fucker."

"The worst. As I see from this list here." I tap Bayou Queen's damage assessment. "Anything else?"

"Blood inside on the floor under Quineau's seat. And Stinson's."

"I know," I say. And I do know, even though I have not been inside Bayou Queen to see the blood drying to a black crust on the metal deck beneath Quineau's seat. And Stinson's.

"You and the First Sergeant did a job," Williston says. He looks away across the valley. "Good job." I nod. I know he doesn't understand why First Sergeant Reardon and I don't leave this work to the medics, or Graves Registration. I'm not sure I understand it either. Perhaps we worry that someone may recognize our Battalion's patch on the shot-down Sherman and tip the burned tank, dead crew and all, into a ditch and let the mice gnaw at the charred bones the fire could not consume.

"Has to be done is all," I say.

"I couldn't do it, though. Go in there, bring them out. Bring out what's left of them, I mean."

"You get used to it," I say. This is a lie, and both Williston and I know it. I will never become familiar with the ritual First Sergeant Reardon and I perform: not ever. Neither, I think, will First Sergeant Reardon. But as First Sergeant Reardon said just once, in November when we collected the remains of nine men killed in and outside of their Shermans before Morville-les-Vic, it is the right thing to do.

"First Sergeant looked a little solemn?" Williston says.

"He's got a couple of doubts about the value of that British officer's advice."

"British officer?"

"Back at Camp Hood. The one who came over and lectured on tank warfare."

"Oh, him." Williston says. He rubs his hand over his bristly chin. "Yeah, I remember him. Some kind of nervous, he was."

"Who wouldn't be, after what he went through?"

"Well, if the First Sergeant think his advice poor, everybody better listen up to the First Sergeant," Williston says. He takes out a cigarette and leans down behind Bayou Queen out of the wind, cupping his hands around the cigarette and his Zippo lighter.

Where, I wonder, would we be without First Sergeant Reardon? Which one of us ignores his calm solid presence in our chancy, random travels east across Europe? When he first paced through the Battalion area at Camp Claiborne, slim and erect in his tailored uniform, shoulders back, the medals and campaign ribbons he won in the Great War set out in two rows on the left breast of his khaki shirt, all of us saw the observant flick of his eyes and the set of his narrow features in the deep shade beneath his antique campaign hat fitted with the bright blue braided cord and acorns of the infantry. Only First Sergeant Reardon, of all our sergeants and officers, wore such a hat; and only First Sergeant Reardon, chevrons and rockers on his right sleeve enclosing the lozenge that identified his First Sergeancy, could glance from beneath the wide flat round brim of his campaign hat and recognize all our sins. The first time he saw First Sergeant Reardon striding, Rutherford said, "That motherfucker gonna chew our asses every single one. And like it. And make us like it too."

Rutherford was right: First Sergeant Reardon chewed our asses every single one. Yet I know where we would be without First Sergeant Reardon. We'd be down in Italy, whimpering and pissing our drawers, retreating and pissing our drawers, praying we would be broken up and pissing our drawers, praying we could make a good story of it when we were shipped home in a scow and off-loaded at some out of the way brown-water port up a slow river in Dixie. They've got their excuses down in Italy: their officers were bad and none of their sergeants seemed to know what the hell. Still, even though *Stars and Stripes* never mentioned their derelictions, the vine runs all the way north, even up here to Germany, and we know: we've tasted the news about them, and the taste is as bitter and brown as tobacco juice.

They ought to be up here in Germany with us. First Sergeant Reardon would chew their asses every one, and tell them the iron rule in the Seven Six One: stand up and do your job. And if they did not listen, someone else would remind them of Johnny White, who refused to get into his Sherman and paid everything he had because he refused. Until the moment I die I won't forget First Sergeant Reardon; and I won't forget how Johnny White could not believe, right up to the moment he died, that the First Sergeant was going to shoot him for cowardice. First Sergeant Reardon is the rod that stiffens our spine, and the staff with which we are guided forward. When he looks at us we recall that we have escaped the embarrassment of Italy, and we remember the MPs outside the gates at Camp Claiborne swinging their sticks and grinning. We remember the sophisticated doubting slurs in the formal memoranda that circulated in Washington and were leaked to the press.

At Camp Claiborne, if we did not look First Sergeant Reardon in the eye and speak right up he turned away and we knew we had failed. Now we are in Europe and we look First Sergeant Reardon in the eye and fight our way east, wading through the black and grey tide of 2nd SS Panzer and 12th Panzer. Soon, I have no doubt, we will go up against the Siegfried Line about which we have heard so much: pillboxes, concrete tank obstacles, mine fields, registered artillery, Nebelwerfers, log, steel cable and concrete road blocks in the narrow valleys, desperate infantry dug in with Panzerfaust to defend their country; and behind them all, the long grey barrels of 88 millimeter guns peering down. Yet the terrible fighting last autumn and winter, and the heavy wastage of men in the infantry divisions, created one progressive opportunity: suitable volunteers from all branches of the service have been accepted for training as infantry replacements. This acceptance of any who volunteer and are able is gratifying, though no work is worse than the infantryman's, no duty more basic, no calvary so quintessential. Even Sam Taylor and his crew in Big Sam died a cleaner death than an infantryman dies when he is shot down and suffocates because he cannot lift his face from the muddy earth. Infantry die an arm's length from their friends, doing their best. Doing, as First Sergeant Reardon, who wears an antique, non-regulation Infantryman's campaign hat, tells us, the right thing.

"You want to go inside, look it over before you sign the list?" Williston asks. Williston stands in for me as chief damage assessor in this crew. He is precise and careful, and I know I need not check his estimates.

"Might as well," I tell him. "I know you've got it all, but I got to sign. And you know Captain Knowles."

In the Seven Six One Captain Knowles commands Service Company. He knows enough about the equipment and his men to know that our assessments of wear and damage are sound. But the Captain is nervous. He worries that the engineers and workers at the Grand Blanc Tank Arsenal and the Detroit Tank Arsenal may have taken Friday afternoon off. He worries the M4A3s issued to the 761st may suffer from latent defects. He does not believe the test equipment gives proper readings. He believes we tighten bolts and tracks too much. He also believes we do not tighten bolts and tracks enough. Because he doubts, he tries to keep watch over each nut and bolt in each assembly in each vehicle in the Battalion; and because the Captain worries, we must worry with him.

Everyone in Service Company remembers Carolina Dawn, a C Company Sherman whose engine stopped on the march at the beginning of the first week of November. Peterson, the driver, eased it to the side of the road as the engine sputtered and stalled. The Battalion clattered on and disappeared in the distance, heading for the war. We remained with Carolina Dawn to assist. We removed the Sherman's rear plate and half of Rutherford slithered inside the engine compartment. Rutherford tested the fuel and electrical systems and reported nothing wrong with the engine's components. While Rutherford lay half inside the Sherman's engine compartment, C Company's maintenance track arrived. Thomas, C Company's maintenance sergeant, got down, shifted his cigar to the other side of his mouth, mentioned he knew Carolina Dawn better than anybody from Battalion maintenance, asked me if I minded if he did his own check, coaxed Rutherford out of Carolina Dawn's guts and inserted half himself into her. Sergeant Thomas examined the engine's electrical and fuel systems and reported that Rutherford, though unfamiliar with Carolina Dawn's peculiarities, had been correct to say that the engine was, well, okay.

Fourteen specialists from Company and Battalion maintenance were standing around their two halftracks and Carolina Dawn gawking and debating the issue with the five members of the tank's crew when Captain Knowles's Jeep roared back down the road. Overweight, tense and angry, Captain Knowles leapt down from his Jeep before his driver stopped it rolling and started yelling. 'What the fuck going on here? Why this motherfucker sitting here? How many you motherfuckers I need to get one of these motherfucker's moving? Goddamnit,' he said, turning on me, 'you in charge here and you're standing around like you got a painful case of piles or a bad case of blue balls. Why in the fuck don't you do something, make this motherfucker *go*?'

Rutherford, who is a lot less cautious than the rest of us, said 'Captain, there ain't no more: this here motherfucker's fucking fucked. Ain't no one on this here road can make it go.'

'Ah,' I said, as Captain Knowles swung around and glared at Rutherford from beneath the rim of his helmet.

'What the fuck you mean speaking like that to an officer, Rutherford? And what the fuck you mean telling me this Sherman fucked? You're maintenance. You're supposed to fix the motherfucker when the motherfucker's broke. You understand me, Rutherford?'

'I understand you, Captain. All I'm saying is, it ain't going to go right now. I looked at it and Sergeant Thomas here looked at it and it don't work. Like I say: it don't fucking go.'

'Goddamnit that ain't good goddamnit enough,' Captain Knowles shouted. 'You fucking men fucking supposed to fucking know what to fucking do. Do I have to do every motherfucking thing in this outfit, snug up every fucking nut, level every gun, tighten up every motherfucking *track*? What, you want me to check the oil level in every last engine block? Maybe you'd like me to stay up nights checking for hairline cracks in the armor plate? Goddamnit, Colonel tell me: keep these machines running. And the Colonel right: if they don't fucking run, they a worthless bunch of shit.'

The Captain raged on, the proportion of obscenity in his stormy shouting rising as the logic of what he said fell. Even the cold strong wind blowing through northern France, pushing the temperature down and sweeping rain southeast from the English Channel and south from the North Sea, did not slow the Captain's tirade.

We waited in the cold slanting rain for the gale to blow over. Face dark and swollen with rage and worry, the Captain shouted louder and louder against the wind, as though no one would ever solve Carolina Dawn's problem, and the Colonel would appear and criticize Captain Knowles in front of his men. His men who, except for the war, might be fixing transmissions and changing brakepads on Chevvies back in west Cleveland and south Miami and east Houston and uptown New York.

Captain Knowles whispered a final imprecation with the last breath of air in his lungs. He breathed and breathed as his plump congested face turned from one of us to the other, the bloodshot whites of his darting eyes glinting. 'All right,' he said at last. 'All right. *I'll* fix the motherfucker. I swear, you all ought to be washing trucks and unloading ammunition back to fucking Chair Borg.'

With this, Captain Knowles got half himself inside Carolina Dawn's gaping engine compartment. Fourteen maintenance men and the five man crew of Carolina Dawn stood by, rolling their eyes, whispering to one another and trying not to look responsible for this disaster as the Captain's wide rear shifted this way and that as his short legs and small feet pushed here and there against the damp ground. He gave Carolina Dawn's engine compartment the most careful inspection it had had since it rolled out of the Grand Blanc Tank Arsenal. At last he eased backward out of the engine compartment, heaved himself erect, dusted his hands off and said, 'I apologize, Rutherford. You're right. This here Sherman is fucked for sure. Absolute write-off. I'll scratch a line through Carolina Dawn's name soon's I get back.' He turned to Carolina Dawn's crew clustered near the left front fender and said, 'Carlson. You the driver?' Carlson nodded. 'You forget something, Carlson? You forget one little thing this morning before we get going?'

'Nosir,' Carlson said.

'Nothing?'

'Nosir.'

'What about gas, Carlson? You gas up this morning?'

Carlson looked at Captain Knowles and said, 'Ah, well, Captain, I think. . . .'

'You think,' Captain Knowles shouted. 'Get the fuck up there, Carlson. Turn on the ignition and tell me what you see when you look at the gas gauge.'

Captain Knowles striding right behind him, Carlson walked to the front of Carolina Dawn, climbed up the steep steel slope and slipped down into the hatch into the driver's seat. A moment passed, and then Carlson poked the top half of his face out of the driver's hatch and said, 'It's empty, Captain.'

'No gas,' Captain Knowles said. 'No gas?' he roared. 'You motherfucker Carlson. You got fourteen men, two tracks, four tankers and a Sherman here waiting on you 'cause you such a dumb motherfucker you don't know enough to look at your fucking gas gauge? What you gonna do about this, Carlson? I mean, what you gonna do right now?'

'Get gas, Captain.'

'And where you going to get gas from, Carlson?'

'Ah, sir, maybe get a little bit of some from your maintenance people here, sir?'

'I ought to make you walk for it, Carlson. I ought to make you take a tin can and walk for it. But we ain't got time for that shit. This here isn't fucking North Carolina, Carlson. Where you from.'

'I'm from Boston, sir.'

'Huh: Boston. You seem more like North Carolina to me, Carlson. You know, kind of sleepy, kind of don't keep your mind on things, bare feet shuffling on a red dust road somewhere west of Jesusville, North Carolina. That what you seem like to me. Or maybe you seem like North Carolina, Sergeant Bellows,' Captain Knowles said, swinging around and facing the tank commander. 'What the fuck were you doing when the private here couldn't find the fucking gas gauge, Sergeant? Beating off up in the commander's seat? Thinking about down home? Thinking about the taste of country cured ham, Sergeant?'

'Nosir.'

"Nosir.' You and Carlson here got a lot of fast answers. All right, though: we'll gas you up just this one time. But lemme tell you something, Sergeant Bellows: you and Carlson here run out of gas one day when the fucking Panzers coming through the field for you, I hope to fuck you got some plan about what you gonna do. 'Cause neither me nor any my maintenance people going to come out then and gas you up. Or wipe your asses for you neither. You with me, Sergeant? You hear me talking?'

'Yessir,' the sergeant said.

'All right,' Captain Knowles said. He turned, fists on his hips, and shouted, 'Gas this fucking thing filled up and get it out of here. And the next time, before you maintenance people get the rear plate off and start poking around to see if the block's cracked or the head's blown, look at the motherfucking gas gauge.'

"Sure," Williston says. Flakes of snow fall on his helmet and on the shoulders of his coat. "I know Captain Knowles. Who don't? All these here tanks better run right all the time, even if they shot to pieces, or Captain Knowles want to know why. And he want to know right motherfucking now."

"Any news?"

"Everything a little slow," Williston says. "They say the armored doughs are going to come up and edge on down into the valley. They're waiting for their tracks to come on. Going to send three tracks and Bright Lights down to the foot of the road here where it comes out into the valley among some trees. Just as soon as everyone gets the hell off this road."

"Bayou Queen runs?"

Williston shrugs. "Nothing wrong with the engine, and the fuel system wasn't damaged. It's the stuff on the list that's the problem: the electrics are torn up and some of the control linkages too. And the weapons are useless. We can shift it, but they'll have to come from Field Maintenance and haul it out of here."

"Okay," I say.

I climb up on Bayou Queen, glance at Bright Lights behind us, up the road, its guntube still menacing the pinetrees on the other side of the valley. A jeep with red crosses on it has arrived. Two of Bayou Queen's crew are getting Stinson into it and getting his leg out in front of him up on the windshield folded down on the hood. I glance the other way along the road, toward Big Sam. Doc Turner is walking with three of his men toward Big Sam. The ambulance halftrack follows them, grinding forward, a man standing in the back inside the opened rear doors. I see the roped bundle of Quineau's body on a stretcher in the shadowed interior of the track. Doc Turner's men have placed Quineau's blanket-wrapped body well forward in the bed of the track, to make room for Big Sam Taylor and his crew. I see the stretchers on which they will be placed leaning against the right and left hand steel walls inside the track's bed. I doubt they will need five stretchers for Big Sam Taylor and his men. They will need one for Tom Holcomb; but two stretchers will be enough for Big Sam Taylor, Johnny Thompson, Moses Smith and Simon Beane. Their remains are charred lengths of bone and burned leather, and they do not take up much space. I could stuff what is left of the four of them in a gunny sack, or a mattress cover.

But I know Doc Turner, and I know he will continue the fiction of their individuality and of what they were before they burned. He will use five stretchers: each of them will lie on his own stretcher, and each of them will be buried in his own grave, and each will have his own letter written home.

I glance at Quineau's opened hatch and the smears of dried brown blood along the hatch-coaming. I descend through the loader's hatch, squatting and slipping down into the darkness inside Bayou Queen, my left foot feeling for the loader's seat.

I do not need to look at Williston's damage assessment to know what happened here: the eighty-eight millimeter round, fleeing along a rising track at three thousand two hundred feet a second, entered Bayou Queen low on the left side of the hull, flicked across the enclosed space inside the basket where commander, gunner and loader worked, struck the breech of the 76 millimeter gun and exited through the upper right quadrant of the turret. In its howling passage through the constricted space, it hammered away pieces of the assemblies inside the Sherman's turret and basket, transmogrifying them from static bits of equipment into lethal missiles flicking this way and that inside the tank. Yet I cannot figure the geometry of the flight of the debris thrown out from the strike of the shot that wrecked Bayou Queen, killed Quineau and ripped open Stinson's leg. All I know is that neither of them were struck by the eighty-eight millimeter round itself: had it touched them it would have torn them to pieces.

No wonder the three crew members who were unwounded are sitting by the road in the cold wind outside Bayou Queen, drinking Dutch gin and smoking and sweating as they remember the shrieking round of tungsten-cored steel shoulder into the narrow space within their Sherman's walls.

Except for Captain Knowles and his harrying questions—'You look yourself, or you leave it to someone? You examine the inside of this here machine? You signed this damage assessment, you better have looked to be sure someone didn't fuck up when he wrote up this paper.'—I did not need to get into Bayou Queen. Just the strike of the eighty-eight's shot against this Sherman's armor requires a trip to a field maintenance workshop. The integrity of the armor requires specialized examination when the hull is pierced, to determine whether it still protects, or whether the steel will shatter like glass if the hull is struck again.

I climb out of the turret and get down from the hull.

"You're right," I tell Williston.

"Best to check, though," he says, as though he is willing to listen to at least half of what Captain Knowles says.

"I suppose. Still: it's back to a field maintenance workshop for Bayou Queen. Let's call for a transporter."

"I called already, gave them the position," Williston says. "A Dragon Wagon is on the way. I guess they'll junk her, though. M4A1? This an old tank, and it's tight in that turret. Not up to much now. Even though everyone was glad to get them back in 1942 and such."

"Times change," I say. Williston offers me a cigarette. He holds his lighter and as I taste the smoke I think of First Sergeant Reardon looking me in the eye and saying, 'You want a see gar?' I glance through the snow falling across the westerly wind. The armored doughs have turned up the collars of their coats. One of the three crewmen—Price, Bayou Queen's gunner, gets up and approaches. "Cold," he tells us. The snowflakes are falling closer together now and the wind is dropping. "What's the story on the Queen?"

"Nothing we can do. Tank transporter coming up to haul it off. You'll ride back with them. I expect you'll get a new Sherman off the ready-for-issue line at the ordnance vehicle depot."

"Too bad," Price says. He sounds as though he likes the Queen's rounded shape and cramped quarters. But the M4A3 is a better tank, and easier to get out of in a hurry. Unless it is struck as Big Sam was struck. I glance down the road at Doc Turner helping his men get Big Sam's crew off Big Sam's rear deck and onto the stretchers they have folded opened and set down on the road.

Price sees me look and shivers. I wonder if it is the cold that makes him shiver, or the memory of the clang and rising roar of the eighty-eight millimeter round pounding through Bayou Queen's fighting compartment.

"Sorry we can't fix her for you," I say. "But it's a job for field maintenance, if they decide to repair her at all. I don't know: they might cannibalize her."

"Well, damnit," Price says. He shakes his head, steps up to Bayou Queen and loosens the ropes tied across a jumble of boxes and duffel bags on the tank's rear deck. He snakes a duffel bag from beneath the lattice of ropes and drags it behind him as he returns to the gaggle of infantry sitting with the other two members of Bayou Queen's crew. When he is half way there, he stops, turns and says, "Can you have someone call up Captain Oates and tell him we're going back with the Dragon Wagon?"

"I already did that," Williston says. "Captain said: tell them okay go on but get back quick as you can. He'll give you two men from Company Headquarters to fill out the crew. Smithers and Doan, he said."

Price says, "Okay." He turns and drags the duffel the rest of the way across the road. He opens it and pulls out two overcoats and hands them to the other two men in Bayou Queen's crew. Then he pulls out a third and shrugs into it.

Williston is a good executive: he knows what to do in a situation like this, knows which calls to make and who to make them to. He could command our maintenance section as well as I. I wonder why I am here: I would just as soon leave it to Williston and take the boat and the train back to Chicago.

Down the road Doc Turner and his men are loading the five stretchers into the ambulance halftrack.

"Look like everything about finished here. As soon as they get Big Sam off the road and Bayou Queen out the way, we can go on."

"Think they can get a dozer up here, wriggle it past Bayou Queen to shove Big Sam over the edge?" I ask. I think of a bulldozer shoving Big Sam off the road like garbage.

"Look like it to me, once Doc Turner goes back and I shift Bayou Queen a bit," Williston says. "Nothing need to be gotten out of Big Sam?"

I think of the seared interior of Big Sam blackened by fire and smoke. "No," I say. "There's nothing left. You could knock spalls of armor off the inside of the turret and hull with a claw hammer." When a tank burns, the steel weakens and becomes brittle. When a tank burns as Big Sam has burned, the armor becomes friable.

"Shit," Williston says.

"I know," I say. "There should have been better reconnaissance."

"They'll do it better the next time," Williston encourages me. "Besides, that SP gun is gone. Ain't nothing else down there." Williston peers down into the valley, looking among the shadows beneath the pines beyond the unploughed ground.

"You guarantee that?" I ask him.

"Sure do. But not enough to ride on down there without someone else go and look first. I'm in maintenance. I took my ride in a Sherman back in November. Nobody's going to get my mother's son inside one of them again. Not if someone's maybe going to shoot."

"I can understand that," I tell him. And I can: I have served as a loader three times, and once is more than enough. The claustrophobic narrowness of the space inside the M4A3 is frightening and uncomfortable. Steel angles jut and stab each time the tank lurches. The noise is terrific, and the fear that an antitank round may strike the steel inches from one's face is terrifying.

Doc Turner's men have finished loading Sam Taylor and his crew into the ambulance track. The rear doors are closed. The driver maneuvers the track, backing and filling, turning it around on the two lane road.

As the ambulance halftrack drives up the road past us, the tires judder and bounce against the road and the steel cleats of the tracks throw up damp earth. Doc Turner, sitting to the driver's right, ignores the rule that officers don't salute enlisted, raises his hand and salutes as the track grinds past. We acknowledge his salute with discreet waves. Doc Turner does not care about saluting: the Germans don't fire on ambulances. That's one good thing about the Germans. We, on the other hand, are legitimate targets.

"That was for you," Williston says, looking at the ambulance halftrack as it eases past Bright Lights, picks up speed and clatters up the road.

"What?"

"The salute. The Doc was thanking you for going in there, getting Sam Taylor and his crew out into the light."

"I wouldn't have gone without the First Sergeant." Even among ourselves we call him the First Sergeant. I have never heard anyone call him Reardon.

"Since we come over Omaha Beach in October none of us would have gone anywhere without the First Sergeant," Williston says. "But that ain't what I mean. That's beside the point. Point is, you help the First Sergeant with this kind of thing. And Doc Turner knows it."

"I guess."

"You *know*. Why you do that, anyway? Get them out? You could wait for the medics to come. But you don't. First Sergeant show up with the overalls and the rubber boots and the gloves and you and he go off and bring them out. Why you do that?"

"You've asked me that before," I tell Williston. "Who the fuck knows? Because the First Sergeant needs help with it. Because he asked me when all that happened in front of Morville-les-Vic in November. Because it seems like the thing to do, maybe."

"Okay," Williston asks. "Me, I couldn't do it. I'd think about what they were before."

"Don't you think we do?"

"I'm sure you do," Williston tells me. "I don't know about the First Sergeant. Always the same, he is. Comes up, gets himself dressed, goes in, brings what's left of them out, takes a slug out of that canteen he keeps under the seat of his Jeep, and drives off. What he say to you? Usually he don't talk at all except a couple of words. This time he said more."

"Told me to show up at his tent, or the Headquarters track, early tomorrow. Got something for me to do."

"I sure hope it's something good," Williston says. "Someone around here ought to have something good one time. Say, what are we doing here in the fucking road with the snow falling on us? Why don't we get the hell out of here?"

"I thought maybe Captain Knowles might come. You hear anything?"

"I got Fellows listening on the radio. He ain't told me anything yet."

"Maybe Captain Knowles didn't call that he was coming," I say. "Maybe he's just going to come on."

"Maybe this, maybe that," Williston says. "What I know? Why don't you get on the horn, give him a shout and ask him if he's coming or not?"

"The Captain doesn't like to be asked, Williston. You know that."

"Oh, I know." He rubs his hands together. The fall of snow is thickening. The pine woods across the valley from which the Hunting Panther fired, killing Quineau and Sam Taylor and his men, has become indistinct. It is cold, and we will be wet and uncomfortable, but the snow helps: if we cannot see the trees, no one will be able to see us, even through the best Zeiss binoculars.

"Well, what we going to do?"

"I guess I better call, see if he's going to want to come up here."

As I finish speaking Captain Knowles's Jeep comes over the top of the slope. Captain Knowles steers with his hands on either side of the wheel, his elbows up almost as high as his shoulders. The Jeep roars down the road, flashes beneath Bright Lights' gun pointed at the snow falling down into the valley, and jerks to a halt behind Bayou Queen.

As Captain Knowles heaves his two hundred and some pounds out of the Jeep he begins talking, raising his voice as he starts. The three survivors from Bayou Queen and the armored doughs sitting by the roadside glance over at the Captain and glance away. I see the canteen passing from hand to hand, rising in one man's hand and then another's. I should have taken the drink First Sergeant Reardon offered me. But I did not want a drink then. Or a see gar before.

"What the hell going on here?" Captain Knowles asks us. "Two shot down and you're standing around. What the hell you done about this?" he asks me.

"Sir, Big Sam is a write-off and Bayou Queen's got to go to field maintenance." I hand him the damage assessment on Bayou Queen.

"You checked?" he asks me, as though he expects me to tell him I haven't. "You get inside, check all this out? And what about Big Sam?" he asks before I can tell him I checked.

"Sir," Williston says, "everybody in Big Sam was killed." He jerks a thumb at me. "He and First Sergeant Reardon got them out."

Captain Knowles looks me up and down as though he is trying to do that party trick where you guess someone's height and weight. He rubs the stubble on his chin and cheeks with his right hand and says, "All right." He looks me over again and repeats what he has just said: "All right." He begins to read the damage assessment. As he reads he says, "Good work." I cannot tell whether he is referring to the paper in his hand or to my ministrations to the dead as First Sergeant Reardon's dutiful assistant.

He looks up from the paper, glances at my gloved hands, and says, "And you say Big Sam's a write-off."

"Yessir," I say. "Fuel and ammunition went. Nothing left inside worth salvaging. I didn't look in the engine compartment, but the armor's holed in a dozen places and the steel's got hairline cracks in it. Nothing left. We couldn't find tags for four of the five of them."

"Shit," Captain Knowles says. "Five of them and one more in Bayou Queen. Sam Taylor, Johnny Thompson, Moses Smith, Tom Holcomb and Simon Beane. And Tommy Quineau." I am surprised the Captain knows their names: in the past he has referred to every man in this Battalion, from the Colonel to the last replacement private, by rank alone. But perhaps this many deaths refresh his memory. "Six good men. Six more good men. Goddamnit all. All right, what else?"

"We called for a Dragon Wagon for Bayou Queen. Captain Oates says Price and the other two from Bayou Queen are supposed to go back to the ordnance vehicle depot and get another Sherman off the ready-for-use-line and come back. They took Stinson back in a Jeep."

"How is he?"

"He got a ten inch cut right down to the bone on his thigh," Williston says. "Nothing else. He's lucky."

Seven Six One

It is true that Stinson is lucky. He might have been killed outright, or suffered traumatic amputation of the leg and bled to death. Or he might not have been touched and so would have had to face the future, such as it is, with the rest of us. Stinson is, as Williston says, lucky. He will get a trip to England out of his wound; and if the doctors decree, he will go home. He may never come back to us, which he may regret when he finds out what it is like to be home and out of uniform. But whatever he finds back in California he will be better off there than he is here. There it may be bad, but here it is worse; for here is worse than anything. Here is cold, filth, discomfort, boredom, disease, fear, terror and death.

"All right, then," Captain Knowles says. "All right." He looks down the road toward Big Sam. "Here," he says, handing me the damage assessment. I take it and he says, "Take care of that. Fold it up and put it in an inside pocket." He is a captain, and I am obedient. I take off my gloves, fold the sheet, unbutton the top two buttons of my overcoat and slip the folded damage assessment into the breast pocket of my shirt beneath my sweater.

As I button up and pull on my gloves the Captain says, "All right. All right then." He pulls a package of cigarettes out of his righthand coat pocket and offers them to us. I'm surprised: Captain Knowles doesn't smoke, and I have never seen him offer anyone anything other than the side of his tongue. I shake my head and say, "Thanks, no, Captain." Williston pulls off his gloves, takes the proffered package of cigarettes, taps one out and sticks it between his lips. Captain Knowles glances at Williston's hands as he handles the package of cigarettes and takes his lighter from his pocket. "What about a dozer?" he asks.

"Coming up with the Dragon Wagon," Williston says as he pulls out his lighter, "to clear the road."

"Nothing else to do with Big Sam, I guess. It's blocking the road. Call in," he says to Williston, "and check to be sure that Dragon Wagon's on the way."

"Yes, sir," Williston says. He snaps the lighter closed and walks away through the falling snow to our halftrack, calling out to Fellows. Fellows is sitting in the bed of the track with the rest of my crew: they have nothing to do, since no repairs can be carried out on Bayou Queen here; and each of them knows more than he wants to about the mortal damage Big Sam has suffered.

Fellows looks up: he is wearing headphones. Snow has settled on the shoulders of his overcoat and on the crown of his helmet. Fellows lifts the right headphone from his ear and listens to Williston calling to him to check that the tank transporter is on the way, Captain's orders.

"Come on over here to the front of the Queen," Captain Knowles whispers. I look at him and wonder why he has whispered. He stares back at me, jerks his head toward Bayou Queen's bow. He shifts the few feet toward the front of the tank. I follow him. As I go, the snow ticks against my face. It will not, I decide, be a full bore European winter storm full of white stuff that looks pretty as it trickles down through the grey sky among the pine trees, but becomes deep resistant drifts that block the roads and halt armies. This snow will be light: it will speckle the fields and decorate, but not camouflage, the trees and the terrain.

Close to the right front fender of Bayou Queen Captain Knowles peers down the road once again at Big Sam and glances down into the valley as though he might see what caused this havoc. Then he steps closer to me, a heavy man dressed in a bulky wool coat. The Captain's face beneath his helmet is no closer shaven than ours, and it is tired and worried. I understand: since Camp Hood he has been responsible to the Colonel for the mechanical health of every single vehicle in the Seven Six One, from the Jeeps up through the trucks and halftracks to the Stuarts and Shermans. And as Captain Knowles says, the Colonel wants these motherfucking machines to go. I think Captain Knowles is terrified of the Colonel. I know he is terrified of the First Sergeant.

The Colonel is a man not unlike General McNair, who helped bring the Seven Six One into existence and encouraged us to persevere and whom our Air Force killed in Normandy before we arrived in Europe. The Colonel is another reason we have become what we are. For the Colonel is a stand-up guy, and everyone in the Seven Six One knows it. Wounded in the leg last November 7, he asked to come back to us when he was well, and we are proud of him for that. He wants to go with us right to the bloody end in the last village in the farthest corner of Germany. We all hope he makes it. We also hope we are there to see him welcome General Patton to the Seven Six One when the war is over. The General owes us a visit. The first one he made, just before we began to fight as part of 3rd Army, was short and emphatic. He was profane and encouraging, though, and we hope the Green Hornet comes again; for while we served with 3rd Army, the Seven Six One helped polish General Patton's record to an even higher luster.

Captain Knowles shifts from one foot to the other, glances this way and that and whispers, "We got a problem. I need your help."

"Sir?"

"A problem. Something bad."

"Yes, sir."

Seven Six One

"This is worse than what we got on this road here," Captain Knowles says. I look at him. What could be worse than what has happened on this road? Six men killed, one wounded, one Sherman destroyed, another wrecked, and our progress checked. And what does he mean he needs my help?

"Sir?" I say. I look at the Captain with care: he is more worried than I have seen him. This isn't valves and adjustments to gunmounts, or tensioning the tracks, or winching the guts out of a Sherman's engine compartment. This isn't even digging insubstantial, incinerated bodies out of a Sherman consumed by a fearsome conflagration.

Captain Knowles steps from one foot to the other and says, "This is bad. I need your help on this."

My help?

"We got a problem somewhere in Service Company."

"Must've been one the cooks, Cap'n," I say. At Camp Claiborne, First Sergeant Reardon asked a maintenance private named Clarence McNay why a Sherman for which he was responsible wasn't carrying a full combat load of ammunition. Mesmerized by the First Sergeant's eyes beneath the round flat brim of his infantryman's campaign hat, McNay told the First Sergeant: 'Must've been one the cooks, Cap'n.'

"That's funny most of the time," Captain Knowles says. "Today it ain't funny." He cups both ungloved hands over his mouth and blows into them. "This here is something else. Not motors. Not even the motherfuckin war."

"I don't understand, Captain."

"I'm coming to it," Captain Knowles says. He glances around and when he speaks again his whispering voice is fierce and distraught. "I'm talking about the law here. I'm talking about shit I thought we left behind us in the States. Shit that happened and was followed by more shit. You know what I'm talking about?"

How can I? "No, sir," I say. "I don't."

"Don't call me sir at a time like this." A time like this, I wonder? "Call me Jerry," the Captain says. His lips move. I think he is trying to smile, and in another time and another place he might. But something worse than the war has touched the Captain.

"Okay, Jerry. What is it?"

"Shit. That's what it is. Law and shit. Rules. Their rules. Although by Christ this time their rules are the right ones. But I don't want it to go no farther than Service Company. Or this Battalion, if it has to get out of the Company. But not outside the Battalion. You understand me?"

"This is among us, you mean."

"Yes. Among us. Something got to be dealt with right here, and right today. Something we got to do ourselves. What the First Sergeant says to do when there's nothing in the regulations that says what to do: the right thing. We got to do the right thing here."

The distance between the falling snowflakes is widening. The wind pushing the squall eastward begins to hesitate and hunt. Captain Knowles brushes his thick fingers across his wet face and says, "Any your men got an injury on the hand? Think: this is important."

"Important?" What can he mean? How can an injury to someone's hand be important here, in this place, where traumatic amputation is considered good luck?

"You don't," Captain Knowles says. "Neither does Williston. I looked. That's good. You're both good men and I wouldn't like to have found out either of you got an injury to the hand."

"No one in the maintenance track has complained about injuring themselves."

"I didn't say injuring themselves." Captain Knowles corrects me, as though he didn't use the word injury. As though he has given me all the facts and I have misunderstood.

"I don't get it, sir."

"Call me Jerry," the Captain says.

"I don't get it, Jerry."

"I told you: I want to know if anyone in your track got their hand injured any way?"

I think about it: Rutherford, both hands on his captured Schmeisser machinepistol, Withers standing up behind the pintle-mounted machine-gun behind the track's cab, both hands on the weapon, Simpson, Fellows and Johnson sitting in the back beating their cold hands against the biceps of their crossed arms.

"No, Captain. None of them have hurt their hands."

"Then it's some other motherfucker," he says. "Jesus Christ what a thing. But we got to settle this—finish it—right here among ourselves. This isn't going to the Colonel, or outside the Seven Six One. You understand me?"

"What the fuck is going on, Captain?"

"Call me Jerry. Lemme tell you what the fuck is going on. I trust you on this, and I need your advice, and the First Sergeant's too, about what we ought to do to put this right. And I need the First Sergeant's help, and you got to get it for me. You understand?"

"No."

Seven Six One

"Listen up: I don't want this official. That's why I want you to talk to the First Sergeant."

"What happened, Captain?"

Captain Knowles rubs both hands over his face. The snow falls straight down from the windless sky onto his helmet and shoulders. I wriggle my toes inside my boots and stamp my booted feet against the road. The snow has not accumulated on the road and now that the wind has dropped it must be warmer; but my feet and hands seem colder than they were twenty minutes ago. The Captain seems not to feel the cold. Perhaps his bulk—two hundred and some pounds of Army rations, French and Dutch booze and all the chocolate he can find—protects him. Or perhaps he is so nervous about whatever it is that has happened that he does not care about the temperature.

"What happened? German woman come up to Service Company Headquarters tent this morning about nine. We were east six seven miles outside that town we got to last night. Packing up, getting ready to go. Corporal Manion is getting the tent down, everybody's loading up bundles and such. Woman asks for the officer. So I spoke to her. She knew pretty good English. I guess you got to speak English or French maybe if you're brought up around here speaking German and Dutch. Who speaks German? More, who speaks Dutch? Told me this: said she was out of the house early this morning, gone two hours, trying to find something to eat. You know everything beat up around here, they can't find much of anything to eat. Told me she had to go out to one of the farms west of town to try to find something to buy. When she got back she found her daughter been raped. Whoever raped her slashed her across the face with a razor. You know anybody carries a razor? Fourteen years old, blond girl, the woman said. A child. You hear me?" he asks.

"I hear," I tell him.

"The daughter says it was someone from this Battalion done it."

"How did she know it was someone from this Battalion?"

Captain Knowles puts his heavy fists on his waist and says, "That about the dumbest thing you ever said. You fucking with me? How else you think she know?"

"I see," I say.

"You see. Woman want something done. I asked the woman why the guy cut the girl. Said because her daughter bit this sumbitch on the palm of his left hand while he was raping her. Had his hand across her mouth. Said she bit him till he bled. So he cut her from her hairline right down the side of her face almost to her throat. She gonna have a scar there right up to the day she die."

"I see," I say.

"You see. What the fuck that mean? I need you to help on this. What you mean, I see?"

"Why me?" I ask. I can't figure it out: the Captain has the authority to order inspections, to arrest, to bind over for prosecution, to take evidence and to compel testimony. And, if he wishes, as the perpetrator's commanding officer, he has the right to attend the execution by hanging which the Army prescribes for rape and attempted murder. It is obvious whoever has done this will be hanged: rape and attempted murder is a hanging offense, and no one can provide explanations which will mitigate the penalty imposed for the rape of a fourteen year old girl, even here in Germany.

"Why you?" The Captain glances over at the service track, to be sure none of my crew are approaching. "Because this is a Company matter, and you got a certain standing in Service Company. And in the Battalion. And because you're tight with the First Sergeant."

He is about to say more but I interrupt him. "No, sir," I say. "I'm not close to the First Sergeant."

"You went into Big Sam with him," Captain Knowles says. "You done that before, too. Back at Morville-les-Vic the first time. And after, right up to today." He speaks as though the fact that I have helped the First Sergeant perform the penultimate duty owed the dead means that the First Sergeant and I are buddies.

"We're not close, sir. The First Sergeant doesn't take me into his confidence. And we don't speak."

"Not even when you bring them out?" Captain Knowles's expression is quizzical.

"No, sir. We speak, but only about the details."

"The details," the Captain says, as though he cannot imagine what I am talking about.

"Yessir," I say. "Just about the details."

"Still you can talk to him about this if you have to? Am I right about that?"

"Yes, Captain. I could. But so could you, sir."

"No," Captain Knowles says. "Like I told you: if I talk to him it's official, and there's not going to be anything official about this. You understand me?"

I nod.

"I want to be sure you understand what I'm talking about here. This is between us. Among us right here. It isn't going anywhere else. Not to any military police or lawyers or whatever. This is going to end right here."

"Yes, sir," I say.

"You understand why?" Captain Knowles looks at me as though I have been his student; as though he hopes I will give the right answer to this question.

"Yes, sir," I tell him. "We don't want anybody coming in interfering here. We don't want any talk."

"You understand me, then. All right. We got to have a inspection. I want First Sergeant Reardon to hold it. I don't want to be there. If I'm there, it's official and the Colonel might ask questions. If I ain't there, and the rest of the officers ain't there, no one going's to say a thing. You understand me?"

"I understand."

"So I want you to take my Jeep back and find the First Sergeant and tell him about this and have him do the inspection. Then you come and tell me who and I'll handle it from there on."

I know what he means by 'handle it'. I am surprised: I have never seen the Captain with a weapon in his hand, but now I look Captain Knowles in the face and I see a toughness beneath his soft flesh that I had not noticed before.

"That's all you have to do," he tells me. "All I want is a name. You get me the name and then you forget about this."

"I could handle it for you, Captain," I say.

"No. Whoever this sumbitch is, he's one of mine, and I'll deal with him. You understand that?"

"I guess I do, Captain."

"Good." He sighs, as though he knows everything will turn out all right. "Okay," he says. "You take my Jeep. I'll finish up here." He pauses, glances down into the valley beyond Bayou Queen's damaged bulk. The snow has stopped falling. The pines from among which the JagdPanther fired are dusted with white. I wonder where the crew of the Hunting Panther are setting up their next ambush. "You're sure about your crew? About none of them could have been the one?"

"I'm sure," I tell him. "None of them would have done it. None of them carries a razor. And we've been on the go since six."

"All right, then. You get going. I want you to remember to get me that name. I don't care what you do, but get the First Sergeant and get me the name of that man."

"Yessir," I say.

Four

The Seven Six One's Battalion Headquarters struck its tents at dawn and is now up on wheels and tracks, parked on the verge of the road a mile back from the turn-off above the valley from which I watched the JagdPanther destroy Big Sam and wreck Bayou Queen. Far across the field south of the road the Battalion's assault gun Shermans sit in the mud, engines off, 105 millimeter guns elevated, waiting to move or to execute another fire mission. As I glance at them, a man standing behind the bustle of the turret of one of the assault guns throws a 105 millimeter shell casing down onto the ground.

The First Sergeant stands beside the Battalion's Headquarters halftrack. He seems to be waiting for orders. So does everyone else. The Colonel and his staff sit and stand in the back of the Headquarters track, listening to the crackling radios and conferring and speaking into the crackling radios. Now and then they point at a map the Colonel holds.

I suppose they are trying to figure out what to do next. I know they can do nothing more than the rest of us, and the rest of us must wait. I have looked at the map, too. We cannot move off the road through the pine trees down the precipitous slope into the valley, and the road on which the wreckage of Big Sam and Bayou Queen sits is the only road into the valley.

The Germans in the Hunting Panther planned to hold us up by blocking the road. They have succeeded, for we will have to wait until Big Sam's remains are shoved over the edge of the road and the tank transporter comes forward and winches Bayou Queen onto its trailer and carts it to the rear.

The First Sergeant sees me approaching in Captain Knowles's Jeep. He steps away from the Headquarters halftrack and waves me on down the short column that constitutes Headquarters Company's complement of vehicles. First Sergeant Reardon is a smart man: he guesses I have something to say, and he guesses it is something I will not want to say in the hearing of an officer.

I drive to the end of the Headquarters Company column and another hundred feet. The First Sergeant follows, striding along the muddy road beside the vehicles parked thirty feet apart: even now, when the Germans seem to have lost control of the air, we are concerned about air attack. The First Sergeant does not hurry and he does not saunter. He walks with the infantryman's even gait, pacing out such and such a number of paces per minute. At least that is what we think: we don't know, for none of us have served in the infantry. We have been up on wheels and tracks since we joined the Army. The men in the trucks, halftracks, weapons carriers and Jeeps in the column glance at the First Sergeant as he passes. They do not speak to him and he does not speak to them. The First Sergeant is not a chatty man, and he has never become familiar with anyone in the Seven Six One: not with the officers, not with the sergeants, and not with the men.

I get out of the Jeep and stand in the road, waiting for him to come up. The weather has passed on and though it is just after mid day the winter sun seems to be halfway down the sky. It is cold and becoming colder and I stamp my feet and beat my hands together.

The First Sergeant halts three paces away and says, "I've been waiting for you."

"First Sergeant?"

He nods as though he has already heard Captain Knowles's story. He does not speak. He does not need to speak: he knows that I will tell him the details.

I begin to describe what has happened. The First Sergeant glances across the field toward the assault guns sitting in the mud, their crews waiting for orders. He does not seem to be interested in what I am saying. Before I can give him half the details of the crime he nods and says, "I know about it."

"You do? How do you know?" The second question is impertinent and the First Sergeant looks at me as though I have forgotten to refuel his Jeep.

"Wait here." He about turns and walks the hundred and more yards back up the road to the Headquarters track. The officers are still standing up in the bed, talking and waiting for the road to be cleared so that the Seven Six One can advance into the valley. The First Sergeant stops at the rear of the track. He speaks to the Colonel. The Colonel hands the map he is holding to one of the men—a Captain: I can see his pale face between the rim of his helmet and the upturned collar of his overcoat—standing up in the back of the track. The Colonel climbs down. He and the First Sergeant walk away from the track. As the First Sergeant speaks to the Colonel, the Colonel nods and nods. The Colonel glances at his watch and nods again, speaks, gets back up in the halftrack, and speaks to a man sitting at one of the radios.

The First Sergeant walks to his Jeep parked two vehicles back from the Headquarters track. He reaches into the Jeep, takes one thing and then another out of the rear of the Jeep and puts them under his coat. I recall him taking the rubber boots, overalls, blankets and tools out of his Jeep before he and I walked down the road toward Big Sam. The First Sergeant adjusts his coat and speaks to a man in the weapons carrier parked thirty feet in front of his Jeep. The man listens and nods as the Colonel listened and nodded.

Everyone the First Sergeant addresses listens with care and nods agreement.

The First Sergeant paces back down the column. As before, he neither hurries nor dawdles. He walks around Captain Knowles's Jeep, gets into the righthand front seat and says, "Let's go." I get in and accelerate down the road. As I work my way up through the gears, First Sergeant Reardon reaches inside his coat, pulls out a canteen and tucks it under his seat. I suspect it is the same canteen he offered me after we brought Big Sam Taylor and his crew out into the light. But who knows? All canteens look the same. Maybe he's worried he won't find water anywhere in Service Company.

As I depress the accelerator down and work the clutch and gear shift, the First Sergeant says, "No need to hurry." He says it as though the war can wait.

"I'm sorry about this, First Sergeant," I say as I ease up on the gas.

"No need to be sorry," the First Sergeant says. "This sort of thing happens. When it does, it's bad for everyone, and something has to be done." He sounds as though he has had to deal with razor-wielding rapists before. Who knows? Perhaps he did, during the Great War. As everyone says, a lot of things happen during a war that no one wants to know about after and no one is going to talk about later. "There's a lot," the First Sergeant says, "in the ARs about how to deal with a thing like this." I suppose he is right: Army Regulations explain everything any soldier needs to know. Except what, in the Seven Six One, we should do about a vicious bastard who has raped a child and cut her. Army Regulations weren't written for the likes of us in a situation like this. I'm sure the ARs' authors thought their regulations applied in every situation. But we don't think so, for our situation is a little different from every other situation. "But in the Seven Six One we do what we have to," First Sergeant Reardon says. "We do the right thing. You understand me?"

I tell him I do, but I don't like the way he says 'you' and I do not ask him what the right thing is in this particular situation. I suspect I know what it is, but I do not want him to confirm my thought, and I will not speak myself, for I fear that if I speak the words, the First Sergeant will assume I am as willing to help him with this rapist as I am to help him with the corpses of those who have died alone, or all together.

The First Sergeant ignores my sensibilities. "I see," he says, "you didn't bring a weapon." I'm about to explain that as I am in maintenance, tools are more my line, but he reaches inside his coat and pulls out a .45 automatic pistol in a black leather holster with 'US' stamped into the flap. He slides the pistol out of the holster and drops the holster between the seats. He pushes the button on the left side of the pistol above and behind the trigger. The clip drops out of the butt of the pistol. He catches the clip in his left hand, glances at it and lays it in his lap. He pulls the automatic's slide back an inch, examines the chamber and allows the slide to snap forward. He picks up the clip and slides it up into the butt of the pistol until it locks with a click: even with the sound of the Jeep's engine and the rush of the wind I hear the click. He snaps the safety up, takes the pistol by the barrel and hands it to me. "Put this under your coat," he says. "Safety's on, the chamber's clear and you got six rounds in the clip."

I take the pistol by the butt. I feel the cross-hatching cut in the plastic grips. I have not handled a Colt .45 since basic training—our TO&E calls for three of them: what good is a pistol in a war?—and I have forgotten how heavy it is. I lay it in my lap and begin to unbutton my coat with my right hand, steering with my left.

"I'll steer," the First Sergeant says, "while you put that in your belt." He grips the wheel with his left hand. I take my left hand off the wheel, unbutton my coat and slide the pistol, muzzle first, beneath my belt. As I am buttoning my coat the First Sergeant says, "Here they come."

"Who?" I ask. I button the last button and look up. Two Jeeps are approaching. They are full of Service Company's officers. An officer is driving each Jeep. As we pass them Sergeant Reardon looks straight ahead. None of the officers look at us: they look straight in front of them.

"Wonder where they're going," I say.

"Must have been called up to Headquarters by the Colonel," First Sergeant says. "For a conference."

"All of them?" It is unusual for all the officers of any of our five companies to go anywhere together: they have too much work, and they do not require supervision from Headquarters to get it done. Furthermore, travelling in a group means running the risk of a group of officers being killed all together.

First Sergeant Reardon turns his head, looks at me and says, "Looked like all of them to me." He does not seem interested in Service Company's officers.

"They know, don't they?"

"Know?" Sergeant Reardon asks.

"About the rape. And the cutting."

"I don't know what they know," First Sergeant Reardon says. "I haven't talked to them. They drove right past. I don't know they know anything. I don't know anything about officers." First Sergeant Reardon turns toward me. As he does so, the acorns lying on the brim of his campaign hat swing in a small arc across the stiff felt. His face is expressionless. I suppose it takes twenty-eight years in the Army to develop this look. I can't think of another occupation in which such a smooth blank face would be useful, unless you wanted to be a professional gambler, or a killer for hire.

The First Sergeant turns his face to the front and we drive on down the road up which we fought yesterday. A mile on, the road angles toward a woods. In front of the woods are two German trucks that have been shot through and through. Their engine blocks are exposed, their tires shot away. I cannot identify the type of truck they were. Next to them in the mud is a cluster of twisted junk that was an eight-wheeled German armored car yesterday morning. We drive into the woods and out of it. Beyond the woods Service Company's trucks, halftracks, weapons carriers and Jeeps are scattered from the edge of the road out into the field. The Company's tents have been taken down and packed away. Service Company was preparing to depart when the call came through to stand fast—while, it seems, their officers attend a conference. I wonder who made the call; and then I recall First Sergeant Reardon speaking with the Colonel and the Colonel speaking to the radioman in the Headquarters track. I glance at the First Sergeant and wonder what he told the Colonel. Whatever it was, I have no doubt the First Sergeant was plausible, and the Colonel believed what he was told. As I have said more than once, everyone in the Battalion, including the Colonel, listens with care when the First Sergeant speaks. And when he speaks they nod and nod, as though they should have thought of it themselves.

"Stop short a hundred yards," the First Sergeant says.

I stop short a hundred yards. Men standing in the field and sitting in the vehicles look over at us. They are curious: they have heard rumors, and if they have not, they are still curious, for the ragged motion of Service Company's routine of repair, replacement and supply has not varied since November. The men in Service Company were trained to be soldiers, but for five months they have worked as mechanics, cooks, messengers, truckers, and stevedores.

When the First Sergeant gets down from Captain Knowles's Jeep, Service Company's sergeants raise their voices and begin harrying the men into ranks and files. As the First Sergeant strides up the road the irregular shape of Service Company's personnel divides itself into ragged groups and then into a ragged company formation. They are uneasy and awkward, shifting this way and that in ranks: they have not all stood together in formation since October in England, at Wimbourne, before we began this journey to the east.

I get down from the Jeep and follow twenty feet behind the First Sergeant. I glance over my shoulder: the clouds full of snow and wind have passed on to the east. The day is clear and the sun to the south that is as far up in the sky as it will rise this day trickles warmth down through the clear cold air the snow squall left behind. I look forward at the First Sergeant's straight back as I follow him. The cold butt of the Colt .45 presses against my stomach, the muzzle against my abdomen. The First Sergeant does not notice the weather: he would march forward with the same regular pace were we in Morocco, or the Philippines.

The First Sergeant marches down the road and through the line of vehicles into the field beyond. The waiting men look at him and glance at me trailing behind. Perhaps they think the order of our march is wrong, that I should lead the way, to announce his arrival, and he should follow. They are wrong to think so: I will never lead the First Sergeant.

The First Sergeant speaks with Cullen, the First Sergeant of Service Company. Cullen is Captain Knowles's thin counterpart: he is a stringy, nervous perfectionist and congenital worrier who shouts the orders he gives. He does not like sloppy work, and he is certain every man in Service Company intends to patch over their sloppiness with a thin layer of paint while he is not looking. Cullen is Captain Knowles's favorite soldier. The men sometimes mistake the difference in their ranks: they call Sergeant Cullen Captain Cullen, and Captain Knowles Sergeant Knowles. But not when the Captain or the Sergeant can hear.

Sergeant Cullen was a mechanic in Denver before the war. Now he is a First Sergeant standing in a muddy field in Germany, listening and nodding as the First Sergeant speaks. The movement of Sergeant Cullen's head reminds me of the Colonel listening and nodding as the First Sergeant spoke to him in the road beside the Headquarters halftrack.

Sergeant Cullen turns, walks forward and stops thirty feet in front of the center of the formation. Between him and the ranks and files of men stand the Company's sergeants. The men look past their sergeants at Sergeant Cullen. He looks back at them, glancing left and right. I see his profile: he is angry and upset. He knows what has happened and he knows something else is going to happen: what else would bring the First Sergeant to Service Company?

"Attention," Sergeant Cullen calls out. The formation comes to attention. The movement is uneven: since October we have been working and we have not had a lot of practice coming to attention. All the snap we learned at Camp Claiborne and Camp Hood and demonstrated on occasion in England has been beaten out of us by the hard, practical lessons of the war.

I walk forward and stand, like a shadow, or a bodyguard, three paces behind the First Sergeant's right shoulder.

"Stand at ease," Sergeant Cullen shouts. With a rippling ragged movement the men stand at ease. "You men will stand fast in formation until this here is finished," Sergeant Cullen shouts. The men glance at one another. Someone in the formation guffaws.

"Silence," Sergeant Cullen shouts. He looks left and right at the formation, as though he will be able to identify the man who laughed. "I don't want any talking while this here goes on," Sergeant Cullen shouts. He looks left and right at the formation again.

Deep in the ranks someone speaks.

"Shut up," Sergeant Cullen roars. "I heard you, McGraw. And I see you too. I'll talk to you later. I got my eye on you, McGraw. Now you shut up. This here is serious."

In the formation the men stand with their hands behind them, waiting for the next act of this small drama. They look as though they don't know what the hell, but I would wager most of them know what will happen next: the First Sergeant doesn't come around like this and order them into formation unless he has something specific in mind. And all of them must have heard about the rape and the cutting.

Not one of them speaks again.

"All present?" First Sergeant Reardon asks.

Sergeant Cullen swings around and says, "Yes, First Sergeant."

"How do you know that, Sergeant? The platoon sergeants didn't report."

"I counted, First Sergeant," Sergeant Cullen says. "So many in the front rank, so many ranks. And so many sergeants. They all here. Except the officers, First Sergeant. And one man, Corporal Johnson, in the maintenance truck over beyond the formation there, to guard him." He gestures at a two-and-a-half ton truck parked in the field a hundred yards beyond the ranks and files of men.

First Sergeant Reardon nods and says, "All right this time, Sergeant Cullen. Next time, have the platoon sergeants report their platoons. Do it the regular way."

"Yes, First Sergeant." Sergeant Cullen looks as though he wishes he could wring his hands with worry. "And Sergeant Peters, First Sergeant: he isn't here either. He took a Jeep and went."

"To bring the woman," the First Sergeant says. "And the child."

"Yes, First Sergeant. As you ordered."

First Sergeant Reardon nods. As the brim of his campaign hat tilts forward, a shadow falls across his face. "Okay," he says. "Keep the men in formation."

The First Sergeant sets off across the damp ground torn up by the tracks and tires of Service Company's vehicles. He walks around the end of the Company formation and across the field toward the truck Sergeant Cullen pointed out. The First Sergeant does not deviate from his course: he steps through muddy depressions and over rutted damp ground and stubbled earth as though he were walking across the pounded dust of the flat parade ground at Camp Hood, back in Texas. I follow him, three paces behind and to the right, avoiding the lower, damper places when I can.

"You stay by me," the First Sergeant says. He does not turn his head when he speaks.

"Yes, First Sergeant," I say. "You knew before I told you, didn't you, First Sergeant?"

"Yes. And I knew before Captain Knowles told you. What else?"

We walk on another ten paces before the First Sergeant says, "Stay with me until this here is over." His voice is dull, as though he has been without sleep for three days. Perhaps he has: he is our shepherd, and he is awake when we are at rest.

I pick up the pace, to catch up with him and walk by his side. As I walk beside him I wonder why he has chosen me to accompany him on this expedition, but I will not ask him why, for he would not answer: he assumes I can figure it out for myself. So I ask: "Who is he, First Sergeant?"

"He's the one with the loose cock and the bloody razor. And the teeth marks on his hand. He's the one who forgot himself."

"Who is he, though?" I ask him. I am looking ahead at the two-and-a-half ton truck in the field.

"I told you: the one who did this here thing this morning. Best unbutton your coat now." I look at the First Sergeant. He has unbuttoned his overcoat, and as he pushes the halves of the coat apart I see the antique

Bisley Colt .45 caliber revolver in the holster on his equipment belt. I take off my olive drab wool gloves, stuff them into my coat pockets and unbutton my coat. As we walk on my coat flaps against my shins below my knees and the cold seeps through the tanker's jacket and sweater I wear over my shirt. I ease the automatic pistol this way and that in my belt. I cannot find a comfortable position for it. Muzzle and butt jab against my abdomen and stomach with each step I take.

"Why the formation, First Sergeant? If you know who did it?"

"While we do this? You want them lounging around like they're sitting out on the stoop back home on a hot summer night?" the First Sergeant says. "No. They're going to stand up and watch this, so they'll know what happened here, and remember it."

We step up to the chest-high back of the truck. The tailgate is down. Inside under the canvas stretched over the metal frame, in the dark halfway to the front of the bed, a corporal—Leonard Johnson—sits on the lefthand bench seat, an M3 submachine gun across his knees, the muzzle pointed at a man sitting right up at the front of the bed on the righthand bench seat. Johnson is a large, strong man. He has long muscular arms and thick wrists and short thick legs. Before the war he worked in a foundry in Pennsylvania. Looking from the light into the dark under the canvas I cannot see the other man's face. Then my eyes adjust and I see it is Willy Thorn, a smooth, handsome private with wavy hair who has had a taste for liquor and women all across England and northern Europe—and, it now seems, a taste for rape and attempted murder. Thorn is smart, and quick. He has many opinions that he requires others to listen to and demands they accept as their own. When he talks he moves his hands to show what he means and to persuade whoever he talks at to agree with him. I wonder if he will try to persuade the First Sergeant that rape is all right, and that a little cutting doesn't mean much. I doubt it: he knows fast chatter and moving hands won't impress the First Sergeant.

Willy Thorn wears a dirty bandage on his left hand. He holds his bandaged hand in his lap, his right hand gripping his left wrist.

"Get him down, Corporal Johnson," the First Sergeant says.

Corporal Johnson gets up. He holds the M3 Grease Gun in both hands and moves the muzzle of the weapon pointed at Willy Thorn left to right. I cannot see if the M3 is on safe, but I will wager it isn't.

"Where I going?" Thorn asks. He does not whine, but I hear a nervous quaver in his voice.

"First Sergeant says to get down out of here, Thorn," Johnson says. When he speaks I realize Johnson is angry enough to shoot Thorn where he sits. "So you get down right now, you shit."

Thorn gets up and shuffles to the rear of the truck. First Sergeant Reardon and I step back three paces as Thorn squats, sits on the edge of the truck's bed and slides off onto the ground. Thorn is dressed in overalls and a tanker's jacket. He wears no overcoat. He stands at the rear of the truck, looks at First Sergeant Reardon and then at me; and then beyond us, at the Company waiting in formation for the First Sergeant and Willy Thorn to get on with it.

Corporal Johnson jumps down from the truck's bed, holding the submachinegun in his right hand. As Johnson stands up straight I note that the weapon is not on safe. This makes me nervous. I don't like people jumping down from trucks holding automatic weapons that aren't on safe. But Johnson is agile, and he knows what he is doing and I am pretty sure he is not going to shoot anyone by accident.

Holding his left hand with his right, Thorn sways as though a strong wind is blowing across this muddy field and says, "I say: where you taking me?"

"Shut the fuck up," Johnson growls. As he speaks he crouches and points the muzzle of the Grease Gun at Thorn. Johnson doesn't look like a corporal in Service Company now. He should watch himself: an aggressive display such as this could persuade the First Sergeant to transfer Johnson to one of the tank companies. Or to the infantry, now they're taking us into the infantry up here in northern Europe.

"You," First Sergeant Reardon tells Thorn. "You be silent unless I ask you a question."

"My name ain't you," Willy Thorn says. "My name's Willy Thorn."

"Not no more it ain't," Johnson growls at him as he steps forward and jabs the muzzle of the Grease Gun up under Thorn's ribs. "You shut the fuck up now and listen to what the First Sergeant tells you to do."

"What you gonna do, Johnson? Gonna shoot me right here in front of the First Sergeant? You know what, First Sergeant? While we was sitting in the truck waiting, Johnson here said he'd kill me if I moved. Said he'd like to do me right there in the truck. Said he couldn't, though, because he had to wait for you to come back."

"Those were Corporal Johnson's orders," First Sergeant Reardon says. "To guard you until we got here. And don't worry about Corporal Johnson shooting you: Corporal Johnson is not going to shoot you. Shooting you is my job."

Willy Thorn looks at the First Sergeant's face in the shadow beneath the brim of the First Sergeant's campaign hat. Willy Thorn's lips twist and his chin trembles. He has been a fast stepper and a smooth talker all the way from Camp Claiborne, dice in his hand, a razor in his back right pocket and a fast line of chatter spilling from his mouth. But right now he looks as though he is going to cry; for Willy Thorn knows that though Corporal Johnson may threaten him with death, the Corporal will not shoot, no matter how angry he becomes. But he knows the First Sergeant will keep his word. The First Sergeant has kept his word before. To Johnny White, who refused to go up, for example. After Johnny White received the First Sergeant's justice, everyone in the Seven Six One, including Willy Thorn, understood the First Sergeant's word was good.

"You ain't got no right, First Sergeant," Willy Thorn says. I listen as his voice quavers and he snuffles snot rattling in his nose and throat, and I know he does not notice the sunlight or the clear blue sky. "You ain't got the right. You got to turn me over if you think I done something. I got the right to be turned over."

"Shut the fuck up, Thorn," Corporal Johnson says. Johnson jabs Thorn in the ribs with the muzzle of the submachinegun.

"No one," the First Sergeant, "is going to turn you over to any authority outside the Battalion. We settle things like this right here. We don't like anyone coming in here saying one thing and another. Not going to be any inquiry up the line about what you did this morning. Or about what's going to happen here right now."

"You ain't got the right," Thorn shouts. His words carry across the field to the formation, but when I glance over my shoulder I do not see a single face turned toward us. When I look back I watch as Johnson punches the muzzle of the submachinegun into Thorn's ribs once, twice, a third time. Thorn twists away from the jabbing half-inch and more diameter steel cylinder and says, as though repetition were argument, "You got to turn me over."

"No," the First Sergeant says. He frowns at Thorn as though he expected more cooperation from him.

"You don't say my name. My name is Willy Thorn."

"I don't know your name," the First Sergeant says, "and I don't have any time to waste on you. We got to go on and we got no room for you. You fell out the march, and I don't have time to explain it to you. But let me tell you about what happens if I were to turn you over. MPs would take you and hold you while CID investigates. CID would find out what you and I and every other man here knows. You'd be tried and sentenced to death by hanging. Use to be, few months ago, you'd be taken back to England for the trial and execution of sentence. Now they got a travelling man with a portable gallows, comes around to do the work. You want that? To see the travelling man?"

"I'll take my chance," Willy Thorn says. "Whatever it be, I'll take my chance on a trial."

"Sure you would," the First Sergeant says. "Who wouldn't take a chance with a trial that's gonna give you six months of sitting in a cell instead of facing what's needed right here, right now? But that ain't the point. The point is, if there's a trial, you going to be all alone and they going to think bad of you and take satisfaction out of trying you and hanging you. 'See?' they'll say to one another. 'See? Dint I tell you? This here's what I told you about them.' And they aren't gonna free you: they'll put you on trial, and they'll hang you. Understand this, though: I don't care about you hanging, or whether you get a trial or not. Neither does anyone else here. You understand me? So there ain't going to be no trial and no hanging where they get to say, 'See? Dint I tell you about them?' You aren't going to get the chance to let them put a mark against this Battalion because you got a loose cock. So we're gonna finish this right here. Right now this day. In this hour right here."

"You can't, First Sergeant," Thorn says. "It ain't right to do that. I get a trial. It say so in the rules."

The First Sergeant nods and says, "Army Regulations. The law. I know the ARs. You want protection from the ARs, you should have kept yourself together. Should have done your job and kept your cock in your pants and left that razor home. You could have gone back to wherever you come from and gone to law school, maybe, and used that real quick mind of yours to do this and that. But that's gone now. So's whatever you think the ARs say. Because this here thing is among us, and whatever it might have been somewhere else, it's finished right now. Because nobody's going to look at us and remember you."

"I didn't do nothing," Thorn says. "I cut my hand working."

"Cut your hand working shit," Corporal Johnson says. Johnson is still as angry as he was when he first jumped down from the truck, and he menaces Thorn yet again with the muzzle of the submachinegun.

"We'll see," First Sergeant Reardon says, "about where you hurt your hand when Sergeant Peters gets back from town."

"Town?" Thorn asks. "What town?"

"Sergeant Peters bringing the girl and her mother out here, you bastard," Corporal Johnson says. "What you gonna say when you see her? Gonna apologize? Gonna shuffle and moan and roll your eyes?"

"I didn't go to town. I didn't do nothing."

"Take the bandage off," First Sergeant Reardon tells Thorn.

"No," Thorn says. "It hurts. It ought to be covered up, First Sergeant. That's what Silas said."

"What Silas said shit," Corporal Johnson says. "You heard the First Sergeant. Take the fucking bandage off your fucking hand. Nobody care what a fucking medic says." Johnson jabs the muzzle of the submachinegun against Thorn's ribs and holds it there. "Take it off I say," Johnson says, "or I going to end this right here right now." He probes Thorn's ribs with the muzzle of the weapon.

Thorn winces and pulls away from the submachinegun's muzzle and says, "Why you talk to me without saying my name, First Sergeant?"

"I don't know your name. Neither does anyone else here. And none of us going to know it after this morning. If you went back and went up to investigation and trial you'd have a name and they'd hang you with that name. They'd remember your name, and they'd remember ours every time they remembered yours. So no one going to remember your name after today. Now take the bandage off."

Thorn starts to say something but he closes his mouth and picks at the tape that holds the bandage against the wound on the heel of his hand. The three of us watch his clumsy movements. The First Sergeant is impassive, Johnson is furious and I am worried: worried how this is going to end, worried that Thorn is going to break up into ugly pieces, worried that Peters won't find the woman and her daughter, worried that the woman will refuse to bring her daughter out here.

"I can't get it off one-handed," Thorn says. But he goes on picking at the tape, fingertips scrabbling.

"Should have thought about that before you started in to rape that girl," Corporal Johnson says. I wish the corporal would put the Grease Gun on safe: he is angry enough to kill Thorn and tell the First Sergeant he couldn't help himself or, to be safe, that it was all a mistake.

"I didn't rape her. She asked me to. She asked me."

"You dumber than I thought, you shit," Johnson says. "First you didn't do it and you cut your hand working. Now she asked you. A child, and she ask you to fuck her? She ask you if she could bite you, too? Ask you to cut her with that razor?"

"Where's the razor?" the First Sergeant asks. He puts out his hand, pale palm upward.

Corporal Johnson holds the submachinegun in his right hand, the muzzle thrust right against the side of Thorn's chest, his right forefinger lying inside the triggerguard. He reaches into his overcoat pocket with his left hand, pulls out a folded straight razor and hands it to the First Sergeant. The First Sergeant holds the razor up and looks at it. The razor's handle into which the blade is folded is made of black plastic. Set in the plastic is a stylized silver design. I cannot make it out. The First Sergeant turns the razor and holds it so I can see. The design is of two stylized figures standing side-by-side. The figure to the right has his left arm raised, the one to the left his right arm lowered. "Zwillingswerk," the First Sergeant said. "Good German steel. From Solingen, in Germany. Henckels company trademark."

"This shit," Corporal Johnson says, waving his free hand at Thorn as though he is waving away a filthy beggar. "We got enough weapons in this Battalion to kill two cities full, and this shit need to carry a private weapon to show he something special. Ain't that right, Thorn?" Corporal Johnson jabs the muzzle of his weapon into Thorn's ribs yet again. Thorn is going to have many spreading bruises on his lower chest. But he is not going to have to worry about them for long.

First Sergeant Reardon opens the razor. The clean bright steel blade glitters as he turns it in the light.

"Why did you cut her?" the First Sergeant asks.

"I didn't do nothing." Thorn says. He is afraid, and fear has made him mulish and stupid: he is not moving his hands this way and that to persuade us of the truth of what he says. "I didn't do nothing," he says, as though repetition will make us believe.

"I thought you said she wanted it," Johnson said. "I ought to kill you right now, you shit." Thorn's mulish manner seems to increase Johnson's anger.

Willy Thorn does not answer Johnson. He hangs his head and picks at the bandage on his left hand with the trembling fingers of his right. But he does not look at his bitten hand: he stares and stares at the First Sergeant's chest, as though he is afraid to look the First Sergeant in the face, and more afraid to look at the holster on the First Sergeant's hip half-hidden by the skirt of the First Sergeant's unbuttoned overcoat.

"You shouldn't be doing this," Thorn says, as though we were raping the girl right here in front of him and he were the righteous one.

"Where'd you clean off this blade?" the First Sergeant asks. He sounds interested in Thorn's methods. "Wipe it on the girl's dress, did you? Or was she wearing a dress?"

"Nightclothes," Thorn says. As soon as he says the word he looks up at the First Sergeant's face, glances at me, at Johnson. Then he looks beyond the First Sergeant, his eyes shifting left and right. I turn to see. He is looking at the Company drawn up in formation standing with its back to us, Sergeant Cullen and the other sergeants out in front facing the formation. But though they are facing our way, Sergeant Cullen and the other sergeants do not look at us, and not a man in the formation has turned his head to look at Willy Thorn standing before us.

"You bastard shit," Johnson says. "You going over for what you done." Johnson looks at First Sergeant Reardon and says, "You tell me to and I'll do him right here and not think about what I done ten minutes from now."

"No," the First Sergeant says. "I told you: that's my work."

"Oh, Jesus," Thorn says. His eyes flick to the First Sergeant's waist, to the olive drab equipment belt from which hangs the leather holster in which the First Sergeant carries his antique .45 Bisley Colt revolver. He is said to have carried this revolver in the first war. True or not, we believe he did.

"Don't you be thinking about Jesus," Johnson says. "You not going to need Jesus for this, Willy Thorn. All you're going to need for this is some balls, if you got any left after this morning."

"Get the bandage off his hand," the First Sergeant says. I can't tell whether the First Sergeant is speaking to me or to Johnson. Then the First Sergeant turns his head to the right so that I can see his profile and says to me, "I said: get the bandage off his hand."

I step forward and stand to Thorn's left. "Hold your hand up here," I say. Without a word he lifts his left hand, holding his left wrist with his right hand. His fingers are crusted with blood, and bright red and dried brown blood stains the bandage wrapped around the palm and back of his hand. The girl must have bitten down hard and harder for Thorn's wound still to be bleeding bright red blood. I pick at the tape, worry a sticky angled corner loose, pull with care, get the tape off and drop it on the ground. My fingers are tacky with the adhesive and Thorn's blood. I lift the gauze and cotton the medic strapped to Thorn's hand. It comes away from the back of his hand but sticks against the heel of his palm.

"Pull it away," the First Sergeant says. Right, I think: better to get it over with. I jerk the bandage away from the crusted blood and congealing fluid that has seeped from the wound. I toss the bandage on the ground. Thorn's wound bleeds, but I have hurt him less than I would have had I picked the bandage away bit by bit. And I have hurt him a lot less than the bullet in one of the six chambers of the revolver in the holster on the First Sergeant's hip is going to hurt him.

"It hurts," Thorn says. "You made it bleed," he tells me.

"Stand up against it," The First Sergeant speaks as though he wants to encourage Thorn. Perhaps he does: Thorn will need a lot of encouragement to get through the rest of this.

"It ain't going to hurt at all too much longer more," Corporal Johnson shouts, his voice ringing across the field.

"Corporal," the First Sergeant tells Johnson, "everyone here knows what's going on. You don't need to tell him about it. Or anyone in the next county either."

"Okay, First Sergeant," Johnson says. He relaxes his hold on the M3 submachinegun, takes a grip on it with both hands. He breathes and breathes, as though filling his lungs with cold air will calm him.

"Hold his hand out here palm up," First Sergeant Reardon says. Thorn does not resist as I lift his left hand by the wrist and turn it palm up. Blood seeps from the semicircular mark of the girl's desperate bite in the pale flesh of the heel of Thorn's hand.

"Hurt it working huh," Corporal Johnson says. He shakes his head as though he can't believe Thorn doesn't just come out and say he raped the girl and she bit him and then he cut her.

"Why did you do it?" First Sergeant Reardon asks Thorn. The First Sergeant sounds as though he will listen to any reasonable explanation. But I don't think Thorn will be able to come up with an explanation reasonable enough to persuade the First Sergeant.

"I didn't do nothing," Thorn says. "I hurt my hand working," he says, panting as though he has just been injured in an accident and is still in shock. "I didn't do nothing."

"Working," the First Sergeant picks the word out of Thorn's sentences. "How'd you hurt it working? Tell me the details so I can look for blood where you hurt your hand working."

Thorn does not speak. He is right to be silent: nothing can explain the teeth marks bitten into the heel of his hand.

"All right, then," the First Sergeant says. He looks over his shoulder at the road angling away beyond the Company formation, as though he has heard Sergeant Peters's Jeep coming with Sergeant Peters driving and the woman and her daughter riding along.

"You got to send me back," Willy Thorn says. He tried law. Then he tried denial and deception. Now he is trying law again.

"You aren't leaving this place," the First Sergeant says. "No one sending you out of this Battalion. We aren't going to carry that much of a load. And let me tell you, if I sent you back and they hanged you we'd have to carry it. And nobody here going to do that. So nobody here going to help you. You got into this by yourself, and this here is one trip you're going to take by yourself."

"I got. . ," Thorn says. But he does not go on. He begins to weep. Long, irregular, snuffling sobs flee from his throat as tears seep from the inner corners of his eyes and slide down his cheeks. His knees wobble, his chest shudders, his hands tremble. He slumps, bending forward, hands hanging past his knees. Johnson whispers curses as he tries to hold on to the submachinegun with his right hand and to keep Thorn from sliding farther down with his left. Johnson jerks and pulls at Thorn, trying to get him up. But Thorn's knees go and he slides down onto the ground at Johnson's feet.

"Jesus Christ," Johnson says. He is disgusted and embarrassed: the vicious rapist with a razor has become a weeping, sobbing boy grovelling on the ground.

"Stand up against it," the First Sergeant admonishes Thorn. But Thorn doesn't listen: he sobs and sobs, as though he knows the pain will never end. I cringe as I watch Willy Thorn weep, cringe again as I hear him sob, and worry that he may begin to howl.

"Listen to me," First Sergeant Reardon says. "You can stand up against it or you can go down lying on the ground. Better if you stand up against it." The First Sergeant makes it sound as though standing up against it might somehow negate the filth and sadness of dying. The First Sergeant's urgings are nonsense: Thorn is not going to stand up. If the First Sergeant is going to shoot him, he's going to have to shoot him right here in the mud.

On the other hand, the First Sergeant may order Johnson and me to carry Thorn up in front of the Company, so the First Sergeant can shoot him lying down in the mud in front of Service Company's formation.

"You want it easy," Willy Thorn whispers. "You want me to be quiet and go along. Just like always. You one of them. You want me to do what I told to do even if it ain't right. Just like they do."

"We aren't debating," First Sergeant Reardon says. "I'm telling you: when you're gone and these men here talk over how you went over, what you want them to say? You want them to say you died bawling and lying on the ground? Or you want them to remember you stood up?"

"I don't want to go," Thorn says, as though we might not have understood him.

"None of us does," the First Sergeant says. "But we all go, and some went today. Six men dead this morning already, between your raping and cutting and right now. You stand up against this like Sergeant Taylor and his crew, you stand up against it like Tommy Quineau, and you be in good company. You listening to me?"

Willy Thorn snuffles and whispers, "I hear you."

"Mark what I say. You're off the march. You're going over. How you leave is for you to decide. But let me tell you: go out by yourself without someone having to hold your hand. You understand me, Goddamn you?" Johnson and I look at the First Sergeant: no one has heard him curse in anger before, not once since 1942 when he appeared in his tailored uniform on the parade ground, swinging along and measuring each one of us with his eyes looking out from the shade beneath his campaign hat. "Sam Taylor and his men and Tommy Quineau didn't have a choice how they went. They went up against it and they died hard, torn up and burned. We scraped Taylor and his men off the deck of Big Sam with a shovel, Goddamn you. They were sitting down, the five of them and Tommy Quineau too when it came for them, but let me tell you: they stood up against it. You hear me?"

Willy Thorn nods. How can he not hear? The First Sergeant stands three feet from him, and his voice is strong, his words precise.

"Okay, then," the First Sergeant says. "Let me tell you: they didn't have no choice how they went. You do. You got a choice to go one way, or the other."

"What choice?" Willy Thorn says from down on the ground, as though he hasn't heard a word the First Sergeant has said.

"I told you what choice," the First Sergeant says. "Listen up. You can either stand up and die or be dragged up in front of the Company and die lying down staring like a sheep."

"That ain't no choice," Willy Thorn whispers. "That ain't no choice," he says again, and then he begins to weep again, his face against the muddy ground. I glance over my shoulder. Some of the men in the formation are moving their feet inches one way, inches the other, shifting their shoulders this way and that. Even at the distance of a hundred paces I know they can hear the wet tearing sound of Thorn's sobs.

"Jesus Christ," Corporal Johnson says. He grips the frame stock of the Grease Gun between his right biceps and the side of his chest, his right hand holding the weapon's pistol grip. He gestures with his left hand and says, "Lookit, First Sergeant, let me do it right now. Best thing for all of us to get it over with right now."

"Shut up, Johnson," First Sergeant Reardon says. "Woman and the girl aren't here yet. And I told you: whatever happens here is my work. Not yours."

Johnson nods and relaxes his grip on the automatic weapon under his arm. "All right, First Sergeant. It's just that I thought. . . ."

"I know. But we're going to do this the right way. And that ain't here in the mud behind a truck."

"There ain't no right way for a thing like this, First Sergeant," Johnson says. "Only right way is to get it over with. To fucking do it and finish it."

"The woman and her child aren't here yet," First Sergeant Reardon says. "And he needs the chance to get himself together."

I doubt Willy Thorn will ever get himself together, but I'm not going to tell the First Sergeant that.

I hear the sound of an approaching Jeep. The First Sergeant looks over his shoulder past Service Company's uneasy formation and says, "They're here."

"About time," Johnson says, as though the cooks have been late getting lunch together.

"Get up," First Sergeant Reardon tells Thorn. "Woman and the girl coming. You want to be lying down in the dirt when they get here?" He seems almost as disgusted as Johnson.

"You don't have to do this," Thorn says. "This doesn't have to be done."

"It does," First Sergeant Reardon says, as though he has no doubts. "Get him up from down there," he tells Johnson, as though Willy Thorn were lying far down a slope.

Johnson slings the M3 Grease Gun, gets his arms around Thorn and hoists him upright.

"I don't want this," Thorn says as Johnson hauls him up.

"Goddamnit," Johnson says, "You chose, and this here what gonna happen."

"Sergeant Cullen's waving Peters this way," I say. I watch Cullen's arm swing as he gives Peters exaggerated directions to drive around the formation. Peters steers the Jeep past Cullen. It bounces and judders as it rolls across the field. The two passengers—one in the front seat, with a bandage obscuring the left half of her face, the other in the back sitting up straight—reach for handholds as the Jeep buckets along.

"You sonofabitch, Thorn, I hope your mother's dead," Johnson says as he watches the Jeep coming on. "Look what you done, Thorn: a pretty child like that."

Johnson is right. The girl is pretty, and she might have been beautiful when she grew up. But the hair on the left side of her head is pinned up and back, away from the bandage tinged with red taped to the left side of her face. Thorn's razor must have started its lashing cold passage through her flesh at her hairline. The bandage covers her left eye and I hope to Christ Thorn did not damage her sight. No one said anything about the eye: not Captain Knowles, not First Sergeant Reardon, and not Johnson, who seems to know all the details of Thorn's crime.

Beneath the arch of her hairline the right side of the girl's face is as white as milk. I wonder whether it was so white yesterday, or this morning before Thorn arrived, whistling and chatting, hips swinging, razor tucked in his back right pocket. I doubt it: no skin can be so pale. The girl must be in shock: her pale lips are pressed together and she stares and stares in front of her with her unbandaged eye.

Sergeant Peters drives straight up to us and brakes the Jeep. He gets out, nods at the First Sergeant and says, "The woman didn't want to bring her. I said she had to come. To say."

"He already told us he did it," the First Sergeant says. "But you were right to ask them both to come. The girl has to identify him."

Peters glances at Thorn and says, "He looks pretty poorly."

"Not half as poorly as he's gonna look," Johnson says.

I frown and shake my head at Corporal Johnson and the First Sergeant says, "You shut up, Johnson."

Johnson sighs as though he knows he's doing the right thing but doesn't want to argue about it any longer.

"Bring him along up to the Jeep here," the First Sergeant says. Thorn sways in Johnson's arms, leaning this way and that as though he is drunk and may fall. Johnson looks as though he would like to let Thorn try to stand up on his own. Willy Thorn does not seem to notice us: he stares and stares beyond the First Sergeant, beyond Service Company's restless formation, beyond the vehicles, the field, the road, the line of the woods beyond. I wonder what Willy Thorn thinks he sees. I fear I know.

"Bring him over here," the First Sergeant says. "But keep him four paces from the Jeep. Peters, help Johnson." Peters walks over and helps Johnson hold Willy Thorn upright. He holds Thorn around the waist with his right arm and he and Johnson urge and pull and carry Thorn forward.

The First Sergeant nods at the three of them as though they're all trying their best and he can't complain. Then he performs a smart about-turn and walks to the Jeep. He passes through a low patch in the damp field. His boots sink into the mud up to the first eyelet. He walks on. Just, I think again as I thought before, like he's back north of Austin at Camp Hood, clicking across the smooth parade ground.

I follow the First Sergeant through the damp low place. My boots stick and suck and squelch. By the time I get up behind First Sergeant Reardon he is talking to the woman in the Jeep.

"You speak English, ma'am?"

"In school." She looks at the First Sergeant as though he has jumped up out of the ground in front of her. I wonder what she thinks of him—straight back, old enough to be her older brother or even her father, gray streaks in his hair at his temples and above his ears, creases in the skin of his narrow face in the shadow beneath the brim of his campaign hat. Who knows, though? Perhaps the First Sergeant and the rest of us don't surprise her. After all, all the world is touring Europe in tracked and wheeled vehicles this year.

"And your daughter, ma'am?" The girl stares at the First Sergeant from her right eye, the white bandage on the left side of her face shifting as she glances beyond the First Sergeant at me, and beyond me at Thorn hanging between Johnson and Peters, his eyes closed tight as though he does not want to see her.

Whatever her mother thinks, I know this girl will never forget that Thorn is one of us.

"No. She knows no English. And no German after nine o'clock of this day's beginning."

Johnson and Peters urge Willy Thorn closer to the Jeep, lifting him and holding him up and pulling at him. Thorn's face rolls on his chest as though he has been drugged or beaten insensible. His boots drag furrows in the mud. Johnson and Peters drag him to within four long paces of the Jeep and prop him up between them, muttering at him as they struggle.

Thorn is pitiful. Even now, in the extreme place in which he finds himself, he should do better. I begin to see what the First Sergeant meant about standing up against it. But I doubt Willy Thorn will: right now he doesn't look as though he could stand up against a light breeze, let alone the terrible black storm bearing down on him.

"Ma'am," the First Sergeant says, "would you ask your daughter if this is the man?" The First Sergeant does not have to add, 'who raped and cut her.' Yet though he has shortened the sentence, the woman looks as though she may not have understood this many words in English. But whether she understands the Sergeant's vocabulary or not, she knows what the First Sergeant means, and what he means embarrasses her. It also embarrasses her daughter, in whose eye I see understanding, fear and, I regret, loathing for every one of us.

Just as Thorn does not want to die today, none of us want to hear the girl say what she will, and what she must. But want it or not, we must listen; and so we will, for none of us would think of walking away while the First Sergeant requires us to attend; and it is sure the First Sergeant wants every one of us to know what this child has to say.

Seven Six One

Only the First Sergeant seems unembarrassed by his request that the girl speak. I do not believe he does not care what she and her mother feel. Nor do I believe he does not care what we feel. But perhaps he has seen so much since 1916 that nothing embarrasses him now. Or perhaps he needs to hear the girl testify against Thorn before he can go on with the rest of what he is going to do here today.

"Ma'am?" the First Sergeant says.

The woman presses her ungloved hands against one another and rests them in her lap. Her face is pale, almost as pale as the gold shading to silver of her daughter's hair; but not as pale as the unstained part of the bandage that covers the left side of her daughter's shocked white face.

The woman and her daughter are wearing herringbone tweed coats. The woman's is gray, the girl's more adventurous: pale blue. It has been four years and nine months since the German army went over the border behind us into Holland, and I would have guessed all the coats in Europe would be worn at the cuffs and elbows by now; but this woman's coat, and her daughter's, are clean and pressed, and stiff with newness. Perhaps they put them away during the occupation and brought them out only on special occasions.

It is certain we have provided a special occasion for this woman and her daughter. Yesterday we liberated their town, and this morning one of us raped the girl and mutilated her smooth oval face. What occasion could be more special? I doubt this woman and her daughter will ever forget our passage from the narrow, hilly southern reach of Holland at Jabeek into this westernmost part of Germany.

"Ma'am?" the First Sergeant says. His voice is as neutral as the color of our uniforms: dull brown, without accent.

The woman nods, leans forward across the back of the seat in which her daughter sits and from which she stares at Thorn, slips an arm around the girl's shoulders and, bending close, her hair swinging across the side of her daughter's face, as though to hide what her child will say, whispers in her daughter's ear.

The woman's whisper fades and I hear the girl whisper to her mother. She speaks no more than four bright sibilant words.

The woman sits up straight in the back seat of the Jeep, her hair swinging. She grips her daughter's shoulder with her right hand and says, "My daughter says he is the one." As she says the word 'he' her daughter extends her arm, her wrist sliding thin and white from the blue herringbone cuff of her coat, the forefinger extended straight and gleaming white as bone toward Thorn's chest.

The First Sergeant looks at Johnson, Peters, Thorn sagging between them, and me. The First Sergeant nods and says, "That's it. Peters, get into this here machine and drive this woman and her daughter back up the road to where Doc Turner's lurking. Have him fix her up."

Peters drops so much of Thorn's weight as he has been supporting and comes forward. Johnson, struggling with the submachinegun, struggles to hold all of Thorn upright. But Thorn is heavy now Peters has been given leave to depart. Thorn is also uncooperative: he slides down, leaning against Johnson, to the earth, Johnson muttering and cursing at him as he goes. Thorn lies in the dirt, eyes squeezed shut, legs sprawled, holding the wrist of his bitten left hand with his right. The woman puts her hand up to her mouth. The girl stares and stares at Thorn from her single eye beside the bandage. First Sergeant Reardon looks at Thorn's sprawled limbs and looks away. He grimaces as though someone has spat three inches from his boot.

I have been trying to sympathize, but I am irritated at Thorn. He should at least stand up. He includes us all in his disgraceful spectacle.

The First Sergeant glances again at Thorn slumped on the ground and says, "And Peters," as Peters climbs into the driver's seat, "when you see Doc Turner, you got nothing to say about the girl's wound or where it come from. You understand? Not a word to him or to anyone else. Or about what else going to happen here."

Peters is fiddling with the ignition, gear shift, clutch and accelerator and does not answer right up. First Sergeant Reardon swivels his head and looks at Peters, so that Peters will know the First Sergeant is waiting.

Peters glances up, sees the First Sergeant waiting, and says, "Uh, yes, sir."

"You call me sir, Peters?" The First Sergeant tilts the brim of his campaign hat down until I cannot see his face. The First Sergeant is reinforcing an old Army tradition: he is allowing Peters to imagine the expression on the First Sergeant's face beneath the brim of the First Sergeant's campaign hat.

But when Peters first came to our Battalion, he saw the First Sergeant lower the brim of his campaign hat and wait in the threatening silent shadow beneath the brim; and so Peters says, "No, First Sergeant. I didn't. Call you sir, that is. First Sergeant."

"You're lying, Peters. But this one time here I'll let it pass. Now, what you going to tell Doc Turner?"

"Nothing, First Sergeant. Not going to tell him anything." Peters is from southwest of the Loop, as am I, and he isn't stupid. "But what if the woman says something?" he asks.

"All she knows is: she and the child were brought up here to look at him. She don't know what's going on."

"Sure, First Sergeant," Peters says. "But she's seen, ah, the prisoner here; and she can figure out the guy isn't going on no leave to Paris."

The First Sergeant nods: Peters has identified a potential complication. First Sergeant Reardon looks at the woman sitting in the back seat of the Jeep, bending forward whispering to her daughter, her right arm around the girl's shoulder. "Ma'am," the First Sergeant says. "You understand we're going to deal with this man here?"

"Deal with him, sir?" she asks.

The First Sergeant allows her the sir and says, "We're going to do the right thing here, ma'am. About this man here." I think of the First Sergeant urging Thorn to stand up against it. "You know that, ma'am?"

"That is good, sir," the woman says.

"Thank you, ma'am, for coming here. And for bringing your daughter." The daughter darts one glance after another at Thorn, at me, at the First Sergeant, at Johnson, Peters and again at Thorn. I know she will never be able to forget what Thorn has done to her; but I hope that in twenty years, say, when she is thirty-four, she will be able to put Willy Thorn aside.

The First Sergeant salutes the woman and the girl and turns away.

"He will be brought to a judge," the woman says to the First Sergeant's straight back as though she has visited the courtroom in which Thorn will be tried.

The First Sergeant turns back and says, "A judge? Yes, ma'am. Don't worry, ma'am: he'll get the justice he deserves. You can count on me." The First Sergeant has left a short space between each two words he has spoken, to permit the woman time to absorb what he is saying. "To do what's right." The First Sergeant smiles at the woman and I realize the First Sergeant is something I have not seen before: an elegant smoothy, when he wants to be. I'll bet they considered him a gentleman in the whorehouses in Juarez in the twenties, and today in family gatherings all across the country.

"I do count on you," she says. "To see that he goes to prison."

"We'll do the right thing, ma'am," the First Sergeant says. I note he does not tell her what the right thing is going to be. She might not like the idea of Thorn being killed right here, three minutes after Peters puts the Jeep in gear. It's good to know the First Sergeant can be canny, smooth, reassuring and duplicitous all in the same short sentence.

"I am glad," she says. "I knew the Americans will do what is necessary."

"We will do that, ma'am," the First Sergeant says. He nods at her, the brim of his campaign hat tipping forward over his eyes. "Go on, Peters," he says. "Take her and the girl back to Doc Turner. Then take them both home. Then get back here. We got to move on."

"Yes, First Sergeant."

"And have Major Turner's people give her and the child what they need in the way of food, blankets, fuel and such. You want me to give you a note to Major Turner?"

"I won't need a note, First Sergeant. Doc Turner doesn't know about this, but his people do. Know about the girl. And him," Peters says, turning his grim face toward Thorn, who is slumped on the ground as though he is testing the earth to see how it will feel throughout eternity.

"All right, then," the First Sergeant says, as though he has received all the reports and is ready to make a decision and issue orders. "Get on out of here, Peters. Get the girl to the medics and then get them home with whatever you think they need."

"Yes, First Sergeant." Peters starts the Jeep, puts it in gear and drives away. He circles through the field, the Jeep jouncing and bumping over the uneven ground. Peters drives past the Company formation, slows as he approaches the road, shifts down and into four wheel drive, and maneuvers the Jeep up onto the asphalt.

As he accelerates I see the girl turn her bandaged face to her mother and speak. I wonder what the girl is saying. She had not spoken, her mother said, since this morning, and she did not speak more than four words, or above a whisper, while she was here. Her mothers pats her shoulder, hugs her, smiles as she answers the girl and hugs her again as the Jeep drives away.

All of us, Thorn crouched down on the dirt with his eyes squeezed shut excepted, watch Peters accelerate down the road. We listen as he shifts up through one gear and the next. All of us except Willy Thorn, that is: Thorn does not hear, and he does not see.

"Okay," the First Sergeant says as the Jeep passes into a woods and out of sight. He looks down at Thorn and says, "Get up."

Thorn grimaces, but he does not open his eyes. He moans and draws his knees up to his chest. Returning, I think. Going back to where he came from. Back to the earth, back to his mother. Jesus Christ.

"Get him up," the First Sergeant says. "Sling that weapon, Johnson, and get him up." Johnson slings the M3 Grease Gun and begins to haul at Thorn. The First Sergeant looks at me and says, "If you'd help the Corporal get him up, I'd appreciate it." His tone is not sarcastic: I am surprised.

"Yes, First Sergeant," I say.

Corporal Johnson and I hold Thorn's arms and haul him up. My feet slide against the damp ground. Johnson whispers a vicious curse as he hauls at Thorn's limp slippery limbs. Thorn holds his knees up against his chest as we lift him. Johnson shakes his half of Thorn and whispers, "You shit, put your legs down." Thorn relaxes his legs until his boots touch the ground, but I doubt Johnson's whispered cursing instructions have persuaded Thorn: I think this rapist has just tired of holding his knees up against his chest. I am right: even with his boots touching the ground, he doesn't stand up: Johnson and I have to hold him erect. His body is limp, heavy, boneless.

"Jesus Christ," Johnson says and spits on the ground in front of Thorn.

"What is it?" I ask. But I need no answer: I see the stain spreading from Thorn's crotch down across the thighs of his pants, and as Johnson says, "Jesus Christ," and spits again, I smell the stench of excrement.

"Fouled himself, has he?" the First Sergeant asks. His tone is conversational, as though he has expected Thorn to piss his pants and shit his drawers.

"Look what this shit's done," Johnson says, as though we cannot see or smell.

"Doesn't matter," the First Sergeant says. "You going to stand up?" he asks Thorn. "Or you going to be carried?"

Willy Thorn doesn't answer. Yellowwhite snot has run out of his nose onto his upper lip and his eyelids are squeezed together. The knuckles of his bones swivel loose in their sockets. He does not want to hear, he does not want to see, he does not want to feel. He has withdrawn into the darkness inside himself, which is the same color as the darkness inside the chambers of the revolver in the holster on the First Sergeant's hip.

"Carry him, then. Bring him out in front of the Company. Here, Corporal Johnson, hand me that weapon."

Johnson hangs on to Willy Thorn with one hand and wriggles the sling of the M3 Grease Gun off his shoulder. As he holds it out to the First Sergeant he rolls his eyes at me. I know what he means: he'd just as soon the First Sergeant carried half of Thorn stinking of urine and excrement instead of the submachinegun. But the First Sergeant hasn't given Johnson or me a choice about what to carry, and we are not going to put in a request that the First Sergeant haul at least a third of Willy Thorn's limp, loose sack of a shit-stinking piss-damp body the hundred yards up to in front of Service Company's formation.

The First Sergeant slips the M3 submachinegun's sling over his shoulder. "Bring him on up," he says. He turns and walks off across the muddy field toward the formation standing fast.

Johnson and I lift and haul Thorn forward. It is going to be a long journey: a hundred yards to the formation, thirty yards more around the end of the rectangle of waiting men, and another thirty to where Sergeant Cullen waits, fists on his hips, front and center of Service Company gathered together for the first time since October. Call it near two hundred yards all in, with the shifts and lunges. A long way to carry half a man. But nowhere near as far as Willy Thorn is going.

Johnson is cursing and whispering at Thorn. "Get the fuck up, you shit," he tells Thorn. "Walk, Goddamnit: you want us to carry you all the fucking way? Stand up and walk. What, you get all tired out fucking this morning? You bastard, I'd kill you right here if the First Sergeant'd let me go at it. Save us a lot of trouble carrying you. Get the fuck up, shit. If you don't get up and walk right now, I'll kill you right here First Sergeant's orders or not."

"He isn't listening," I say. Johnson's cursing doesn't help. It won't make Willy Thorn walk and it won't get the three of us up in front of the formation any faster. Nor will it make this job any easier: carrying Thorn up in front of the formation is just another Army job that is boring, takes more time and effort than it ought to, and is, as Johnson says, unnecessary: the First Sergeant could shoot Willy Thorn right here and have done with him. We could bury him where he falls and avoid all this trouble. But the First Sergeant wants Thorn up in front of the Company, and so we will carry him there if we must. But Johnson's bitching isn't going to carry part of the weight.

On the other hand, I can understand why Johnson curses: this isn't about Willy Thorn. He's the object of the lesson the First Sergeant is going to teach, and although all of us are going to sit in the First Sergeant's class and look attentive, I know most of us would rather be somewhere else.

"It doesn't matter," I tell Johnson. "It's not far to take him." I am breathing hard. By the time we get up in front of the formation I'll be sweating and we'll be dragging Willy Thorn across the ground to get him to the place of execution the First Sergeant has chosen for him.

I don't like anything about this. I don't like touching Thorn and I don't like listening to Johnson curse and I don't like helping the First Sergeant do what he is going to do. "It'll be all right," I tell Johnson, but I doubt he believes me. I know Thorn wouldn't, if he could hear me speak.

"Be all right?" Thorn mutters.

I am surprised he has spoken: I had thought his fear had made him as deaf as he is blind and paralyzed.

"Yes," I tell him. "It'll be all right." What else am I supposed to say? "Just a little more," I say, "and everything will be fine. Ten minutes more and class is over."

"School," Thorn mutters. "Couldn't read and no one helped. No one of them."

Sad. A poor student left without encouragement or guidance. I wonder how he scored on his Army General Classification Test. Not low: he couldn't have scored low and been accepted into the Seven Six One. This Battalion accepted only those with the best AGCT scores. After all, we were an experiment, and General McNair, months in his grave in Normandy, wanted us to succeed. I wonder why the General cared?

No, I remind myself. The Seven Six One didn't get the men with the best scores. The 99th Pursuit got the men with the best scores. Of course, most of them were college graduates. Two more years and I might have been flying a P-51 Mustang and trying not to die at four hundred and fifteen miles an hour.

"Tried to study," Thorn mutters. Johnson is looking across Thorn's face at me. He shakes his head and looks away, as though Thorn is reminding him of his own days in school. "Couldn't do it," Thorn says. "Tried, though."

"Willy," I say, thinking that it never hurts to try one more time. "Willy. Before we get there, up in front of the Company, get up on your feet. Don't think about anything except standing up. Forget about school. None of us did much at school, you know?"

"I know," he says, as though he has examined all our highschool transcripts.

Thorn's feet scrabble at the ground. Johnson looks at me and raises his eyebrows as Thorn's legs begin to support a part of his weight. Johnson is surprised Thorn can try to stand at all. So am I.

"All right," Thorn says. "I'm all right. Get your hands off me. I can walk." He staggers in our arms, struggling; but he is standing up. Johnson and I take our hands off him. Willy Thorn sways, but he does not fall. I wonder what has brought his senses back. Nothing I said could have encouraged him so. Perhaps he needed nothing more than to be carried and hauled a distance.

Thorn glances at me, at Johnson, at the waiting formation, at the First Sergeant striding up the slight incline on which Sergeant Cullen stands in front of the Company. He seems to be trying to recall what has happened, to figure out where he is. He looks at me and says, "I dirtied myself."

"Don't worry about it. No one's going to say a thing about it, Willy."

"I need to change my pants," Thorn says.

"You can't," Johnson says. "No change of clothes out here, Willy." It is the first thing Johnson has said to Thorn that hasn't included a curse.

"I can't go up there in front of them like this," Thorn says. He is not refusing to go, but he doesn't want them to see he has lost control of himself.

"None of them going to say a thing." Johnson is trying to reassure him.

"I can't go up dirty." He holds his bitten left hand with his right. Both his hands are shaking, and a tremor slides through his body. His neck begins to tremble. We are nearing an impasse. If we do not move, and move now, Willy Thorn is going to be down on the ground again with his knees up against his chest and his eyes closed, hearing nothing and seeing nothing but the darkness of which he is about to become a part.

I unbutton my coat and take it off. The butt of the automatic pistol sticks up from my belt but Willy Thorn does not notice it. "Take my coat, Willy," I say. "Put it on. No one will see anything if you've got this overcoat on." I hold the coat out to Thorn, hoping he will take it and put it on and walk on with us.

"And we won't say nothing about it later, Willy," Johnson says. "Give you our word on that right here."

"Not a word," I say. "To anyone."

"What about Peters? And the First Sergeant?"

"I'll talk to Charlie Peters," Johnson says. "You know he a friend of mine. He won't say nothing. I guarantee it." Johnson sounds as though he is trying to sell Thorn a washing machine named Charlie Peters.

But I support Johnson's extension of an unlimited warranty. "You know the First Sergeant won't mention anything about it, Willy," I say. "You know what he's like. He doesn't gossip, and he won't let anyone else gossip about it in his presence." He may shoot you dead, I think, but he won't gossip about it later. And anyone who looks under the coat, if he puts it on, will think Thorn's bowels and bladder went when he was shot dead.

"I know," Willy Thorn says. "I know the First Sergeant wouldn't talk about it."

"Take the coat, Willy," I say. Cold as it is, and as much trouble as I will have talking another coat out of Sergeant Symms, the Battalion supply wizard who has everything and dispenses nothing, I hope to Christ Willy Thorn takes my coat: however much more of this everyone else standing in this German field can put up with, I've about had it. I don't like doing this. I don't like touching Willy Thorn and I don't like persuading him that it is better to die on his feet than hunched up against himself down in the dirt. Most of all, I don't like it that the First Sergeant chose me to help him with this job.

I glance ahead to where all three of us, and particularly Willy Thorn, must go: to where the First Sergeant stands with Sergeant Cullen in front of the formation, both of them at ease, their hands clasped behind their backs. I note that the First Sergeant has handed Johnson's M3 submachinegun to Sergeant Cullen, who has slung it over his shoulder.

The men in the formation are as still and sound as bricks in a thick wall now the First Sergeant is standing up in front of them. I guess none of them can believe what is going to happen, even though they know it will, and their disbelief freezes their muscles.

Willy Thorn, thank Christ, starts to edge into my coat, a piece at a time. He is awkward, as though he has regained control over no more than a part of himself. When he eases his left arm into the right sleeve of my coat Johnson holds up the back of the coat, gripping the thick cloth collar and the left shoulder. Wincing and grimacing, Willy Thorn worms his injured hand through the sleeve and out the cuff.

"I can't button it up one-handed," Willy Thorn says. As he speaks he sways as though he is trying to stand up in a gale blowing across the field. "Can't do the buttons up," he says, and raises his right arm inside the sleeve of my coat and wipes the congealed yellowwhite snot from his upper lip.

"I'll button you up," Johnson says, as a mother might to her child. He stands in front of Willy Thorn. Willy Thorn raises his chin. Johnson buttons the highest button at the base of Willy Thorn's throat, then the next, and the next, working his way down. Willy Thorn bends his head to watch Johnson button each button.

"You want gloves?" I ask when Johnson has finished with the buttons. "There're gloves in the pockets."

"Sure," Willy Thorn says. "Cold out here. Sunny day, and cold like this."

Johnson takes the gloves from the pockets of my coat. Willy Thorn holds up his right hand and slides his wriggling fingers into the glove Johnson holds open for him. When Willy Thorn edges his bitten left hand into the other glove he winces and grimaces as he did when he wormed his left hand through the left sleeve of the coat. But at last he and Johnson finish, and Willy Thorn is buttoned up, gloves on both hands, as though he is ready to go out and play in the snow.

"All covered up," Johnson says. When he looks at me his eyes glitter. Perhaps he remembers his mother buttoning him up on cold winter days.

"Shall we go on up, Willy?" I ask him.

"Sure," Willy Thorn says. "I'm ready." He looks and sounds as though he is, too. But I wonder whether he can be ready for this: who can prepare himself for the arrival of night in the middle of the day?

"Let's go on, then," Johnson says.

And so we go on, walking on either side of Willy Thorn up the faint incline toward the First Sergeant and Sergeant Cullen standing at ease in front of the Company formation standing at ease. We walk around the end of the formation. Not a man in the Company turns his head to glance at Willy Thorn and his two keepers. They face front, every single one of them looking at the sky two inches above the tip of the crown of First Sergeant Reardon's campaign hat.

"Coldern I thought," Willy Thorn murmurs as we turn the corner of the formation and walk up toward the First Sergeant and Sergeant Cullen standing with Johnson's M3 submachinegun slung on its strap over his left shoulder.

Thorn is right: it is cold, and growing colder. To the southwest clouds are forming, piling up and sliding northeast.

Johnson clears his throat and says, "It'll be all right, Willy. Little bit farther is all."

Willy Thorn nods and walks on as though he doesn't have far to go. Johnson walks to his right, I to his left. I suppose Johnson and I should be marching in step with Willy Thorn; but I cannot bring myself to say anything to Johnson, or to shuffle and slide my feet into step with Thorn's. This is not a military journey. It has nothing to do with the Army, or the war. Our long walk to where the First Sergeant waits is a private matter which concerns no one but the men in the Seven Six One.

As we begin to pace out the last thirty yards separating the three of us from the First Sergeant, and Willy Thorn from the night, the First Sergeant and Sergeant Cullen turn right and face us. Sergeant Cullen turns his face two inches to the left and flicks a glance at the formation. No man in the formation moves. Sergeant Cullen nods as though he is satisfied, at least in part, with their conduct, and turns his face to the front: to watch us coming on.

As we start walking up the last fifteen paces, First Sergeant Reardon shoves the skirt of his unbuttoned coat back and I think, Jesus Christ, he's going to shoot him right now, right here before Thorn can figure out how it's going to happen. But the First Sergeant's right hand passes over the butt of the heavy revolver in the holster on his equipment belt, slides into the right rear pocket of his pants and comes out from under the skirt of his coat holding a brown and white bone-handled pocket knife. When he levers the blade out of the handle the steel glitters and shines, as the steel blade of Willy Thorn's razor glittered and shone when the First Sergeant rotated the blade out of the razor's black plastic handle. I think of the girl's bandaged face and of the tears on Willy Thorn's cheeks.

When we are four paces from the First Sergeant, I touch Willy Thorn on the left arm above the wrist and he, and Johnson and I, halt three paces in front of First Sergeant William S. Reardon. Willy Thorn's marching days are over.

The First Sergeant nods at Johnson and me and says, "You two right and left face, forward march three paces, halt, about turn and stand at ease." Johnson and I turn our backs on Willy Thorn, walk off three paces, stop, turn around and stand with our hands clasped behind us. We face one another across a space of six or seven yards, Willy Thorn between us, the First Sergeant and Sergeant Cullen standing to my left and to Johnson's right. Johnson's face is smooth and somber. I wonder what he is thinking. The walk up here with Willy Thorn seems to have dispersed his terrific anger, but I cannot tell what thoughts have cast his anger aside and replaced the tight, infuriated cast of his features with an uncharacteristic solemnity. Perhaps he is thinking about Willy Thorn's crime, and the Seven Six One's shame. Or perhaps he is thinking about buttoning my coat over Willy Thorn's chest and helping Willy Thorn get his hands into my gloves. Thank Christ I wasn't wearing mittens. If he had had to fit mittens over Willy Thorn's hands, Johnson might be weeping right now.

The First Sergeant steps forward, the knife in his fist, and says, "Take off that coat."

Thorn looks at him. He cannot figure out what the First Sergeant wants. I can't figure it out either. I can see that Johnson is as confused as I am, and I see Sergeant Cullen's eyes flick at the First Sergeant.

"Take the coat off," the First Sergeant says.

"First Sergeant?" Thorn says.

"Take the coat off. You're not leaving with that patch on the shoulder of your uniform."

Thorn looks confused. Then he looks shocked, as though the First Sergeant has criticized him for no reason. I agree with Thorn. Our Battalion's patch depicts the head of a panther with its roaring jaws open. Beneath the panther's head are the words, "Come Out Fighting." These words, the Battalion's motto, are taken from the referee's last instruction to fighters before the first bell of the first round. The patch was issued long ago and far away in the United States, with the hope that we would live up to the panther's reputation and the motto's injunction. Every one of us is proud of the patch, and proud that we came out fighting east of Nancy, and have fought every round since. When we had the tailors sew the patch on the left shoulders of our uniform shirts we hoped for honor and feared disgrace. Now we have earned a reputation, and the patch reminds us all, as the remains of Sam Taylor and his crew incinerated inside Big Sam and Quineau's corpse laid out under a blanket on the road remind me, of the price we have paid for the reputation we have won.

"No," Willy Thorn says. "I ain't going to let you take it."

The First Sergeant says, "Get out of the coat." The First Sergeant's voice is steady and calm, as though he is explaining the rules to a man just transferred into the Seven Six One.

But the First Sergeant is wrong to take Thorn's patch. Willy Thorn was at Morville-les-Vic. I say, "First Sergeant?"

First Sergeant Reardon's head swivels and he looks at me from the corner of his right eye glittering close beneath the brim of his campaign hat.

"Thorn was at Morville-les-Vic, First Sergeant. He drove an ammunition track up during C Company's fight at the tank trap and supported the men that got out of the tanks. He fired the machinegun in the track, First Sergeant. He stood up and fired across the ditch at the bunkers and antitank guns and the German infantry."

The First Sergeant stares at me from the corner of his eye, his eyebrow arched as though he is waiting for me to go on.

"He was there, First Sergeant," I say.

"I didn't know that," the First Sergeant says.

"We were in a Jeep up behind him at the edge of the woods, First Sergeant. I saw him."

"No one told me," the First Sergeant says. He is still staring at me from the corner of his right eye. "Ammunition track, was it?"

"Yes, First Sergeant." I recall the jumble of wooden crates of 76 millimeter rounds and the steel boxes of machinegun ammunition thrown into the back of the track and into a two-wheeled trailer behind the track.

"I remember it, First Sergeant," I say. "The ammunition crates and boxes were all thrown in and jumbled up in the bed of the track and in the trailer behind."

"You remember a trailer, do you?" The brim of his campaign hat tilts forward and I can no longer see his glittering eye.

"Yes, First Sergeant."

"And he got up and fired the gun."

"Yes, First Sergeant."

"Someone was in the Jeep with you, were they?"

"Williston was driving, First Sergeant. He can speak."

The wide round brim of the First Sergeant's campaign hat lifts and I see that First Sergeant Reardon is still looking at me from the corner of his right eye. He stares at me for a moment and then he turns his head and stares at Willy Thorn. I look down at the knife in his right hand. A faint trembling in his arm and hand shakes the bright glittering blade. As though to suppress the trembling with a larger movement, he jerks his right hand up, his left rising to meet it, folds the glinting blade into the bone handle of the knife, slips his hand holding the knife beneath the skirt of his coat and puts the knife away in the rear right pocket of his pants.

"All right," First Sergeant Reardon says. He turns his head to glance at me and the brim of his campaign hat dips, dips again as he nods. He puts his hands on his hips under the unbuttoned halves of his coat and tells Willy Thorn, "I didn't know about that at Morville-les-Vic."

Standing beyond the First Sergeant and Willy Thorn, Johnson wipes his left hand across his mouth and nods at me. He seems grateful that I have spoken up about Thorn. I wonder what I could have said for Thorn had chance not let me see him at Morville-les-Vic.

"Why you don't say my name, First Sergeant?" Willy Thorn asks.

"I told you: since this morning I don't know your name." As he speaks the First Sergeant moves his right hand beneath the heavy cloth of his coat. To the handle of his revolver. What else?

"My name's Willy Thorn," Thorn says. He hangs his head, as though he knows the offer of his name will not be accepted.

"If this here were a better Army," the First Sergeant says, raising his voice so that the farthest man in the formation will hear him, "I'd send you back up. But we got a way to march here, down through this valley up ahead and up out the other side. We can't be carrying more weight than we got right now. So I'm not sending you back. You understand me?"

"I don't know," Thorn mutters. "I don't know why I did that. I should have gone another way."

"You should have," the First Sergeant says. "Kept on the march. But you didn't, Willy Thorn."

At the sound of his name, Thorn looks up at the First Sergeant as though he wants to tell the First Sergeant he might have kept up if. But before he can speak the First Sergeant slides the antique revolver from under his coat and shoots Willy Thorn in the chest. The noise of the single shot is tremendous. Willy Thorn's body is flung backward into the dirt. For two breaths I watch Willy Thorn's heels kick the ground and hear his torso thump the earth as he struggles against the mortal wound the First Sergeant has given him. One breath more and Willy Thorn's struggles end. He lies in the mud as dead as Big Sam Taylor and his men lay inside Big Sam. As dead as Quineau in Bayou Queen. Still I wish the First Sergeant had shot him in the head, to kill him outright so that I would not have had to hear him struggle; but I guess the First Sergeant did not want to kill Willy Thorn and mutilate him too.

"That's it," First Sergeant Reardon says. He is putting his revolver away. "Sergeant Cullen," he says, "pass the word Private Thorn been killed by a sniper and then dismiss the Company."

Five

THE DISMISSED COMPANY BREAKS apart. The men gather in whispering groups close to the trucks and halftracks to discuss the First Sergeant's dispensation of justice. I hope they remember to tell one another that at the end, at least, Willy Thorn stood up against it.

Two men, Price and Ridges, come forward. They do not walk in step. Price carries a sleeping bag cover. He unzips it and spreads it on the ground beside Willy Thorn's corpse. Sergeant Symms from Battalion supply will not be happy about this waste of a sleeping bag cover. I'm sure Sergeant Symms believes a mattress cover, of which I have no doubt Sergeant Symms has a sufficient supply even though none of us have seen a mattress in four months, would have been good enough for Willy Thorn's corpse. But Sergeant Symms isn't going to complain: the First Sergeant called for two men and a sleeping bag cover and Sergeant Symms is going to have to put up with the First Sergeant's willful wasteful requisition.

Price and Ridges lift Willy Thorn's corpse onto the sleeping bag cover and fold it over Willy Thorn and zip it up past his face and up over the top of his head.

So much for Willy Thorn's corpse. Now almost nothing will remain of Willy Thorn except what we remember of him: the fast talking, the smooth, confident manner, the razor in his back pocket, the girl with the bandaged face pointing a thin pale finger from the right front seat of a Jeep straight at Thorn's face. Johnson and I and the First Sergeant will also remember more intimate details: Thorn's slumped, uncooperative body, his arms sliding into the sleeves of my coat, Johnson fitting the gloves to his hands, and Thorn looking up at the First Sergeant when he heard the First Sergeant speak his name.

Price and Ridges shuffle this way and that, edging away from Willy Thorn lying inside the sleeping bag cover. They are waiting for the First Sergeant Reardon to tell them what to do.

The First Sergeant has watched Price and Ridges package Willy Thorn for the next leg of his trip. He seems satisfied with their work. "Get a Jeep," he says. "Take Thorn back to Major Turner's people and leave him. Have them tag him shot by a sniper."

"Yes, First Sergeant," Price says.

"You understand why he's to be tagged shot by a sniper?" the First Sergeant asks Price and Ridges.

The two men look at one another out of the corners of their eyes. They shake their heads. "No, First Sergeant," Price says.

"Colonel going to have to write a letter to Thorn's nextofkin. You want the Colonel to have to explain in a letter what Thorn did? You want Thorn's family to know what he did?" I hear faint outrage in the tone of the First Sergeant's voice.

"No, First Sergeant," Price says. Ridges shakes his head to show he agrees with Price.

"All right, then," First Sergeant Reardon says. "Ridges, you go get the Jeep. Price, you stay here with Thorn." Before he shot Thorn, the First Sergeant spoke of Thorn as though he were dead. Now Thorn is dead, the First Sergeant talks about him as though he still lives.

I watch Ridges hurry off to find a Jeep. I suspect he is like the rest of us: he wants this to finish.

"You," the First Sergeant says to Johnson. Johnson stands up straight and squares his shoulders. "You did all right here, Corporal Johnson. Except for a couple of comments, you handled this all right."

"Thank you, First Sergeant. I'm sorry about what I said to him." I look at Johnson's face: he is troubled, though I cannot tell whether he is troubled about what he said to Willy Thorn as Thorn was on his way to die, or about the First Sergeant's mild criticism.

"Don't matter," the First Sergeant says. He begins to button his coat. "It went all right in the end. And I understand about the remarks. I had too much mouth the first time too."

While the First Sergeant is looking down at his hands buttoning up his coat Johnson takes the chance and rolls his eyes at me as though to say, "The *first* time?" I shrug: who knows what First Sergeant Reardon may have done during his long march to this place in Germany on this March day in 1945.

The First Sergeant stops buttoning his coat, looks at me, puts his right hand out and says, "Hand me that weapon." I have forgotten about the .45 Colt the First Sergeant issued me in the Jeep. Now that I recall him sitting beside me, checking the clip and the chamber, I feel the butt and muzzle of the automatic pistol jabbing my stomach and abdomen. I pull the pistol out of my belt, hold it by the barrel and hand it butt-first to the First Sergeant. I should hand it to him with the muzzle pointed straight up in the air: that is the proper way. But I trust the First Sergeant not to shoot me. He takes the pistol, checks to be sure the safety is up, slides the weapon inside his coat into the waistband of his pants and buttons his coat over it.

"Sergeant Cullen, you get Thorn's stuff together. Go through it yourself. Be careful with it. I don't want anything getting into his package home that ought not be there."

"Right, First Sergeant," Cullen says. He hitches his thumb under the sling of Johnson's submachinegun dragging at his shoulder.

"Send it up to me when you got it done."

"Yes, First Sergeant," Cullen says.

"And get everybody ready to go, Sergeant Cullen. We're going to be moving up soon. The Colonel said that before we came down here: that we'll be moving up soon."

"I'll get them ready, First Sergeant," Cullen says. He glances left and right at the men and vehicles of Service Company. He will not have much to do to get them ready. Service Company was ready to go this morning, just before Willy Thorn decided to go into town.

"All right," the First Sergeant says. "You better go now. We got a lot to do here yet."

"Yes, First Sergeant," Cullen says. He slips the sling of the M3 Grease Gun from his shoulder and hands the weapon to Johnson. As he hands it over the clips on the ends of the sling click and tap against the submachinegun's receiver and frame stock.

"Here come Ridges with the Jeep," Price says.

"I see that," the First Sergeant says, as though he doesn't need to be told.

"I'll go, then," Cullen says.

"Yes," the First Sergeant says. "You go on."

Cullen hustles away, leaving the formality of the ceremony the First Sergeant has conducted behind him. When he is fifty feet away Cullen begins shouting and moving his arms as though the performance of every man in Service Company has been sluggish and improper all morning long. The First Sergeant looks after Cullen shouting and waving his arms and striding along. I think the First Sergeant is wondering what Cullen will remember of this morning.

Ridges drives the Jeep close up beside Willy Thorn waiting inside his sleeping bag cover. Ridges has chosen the right Jeep: this one has had its rear seats removed. He turns the engine off, gets out and lifts one end of Willy Thorn as Price lifts the other. I cannot at first tell which of them is lifting Thorn's shoulders, and which his feet; but as they lift, Thorn's body bends at the hips and knees and his corpse becomes a smaller, more distinct shape, and I see his knees and feet and head jutting against the inside of the sleeping bag cover. Ridges, I now see, is lifting Willy Thorn's legs, Price his shoulders. They get him up and lower him down onto the steel floor between the rear wheel wells in the back of the Jeep. Then they reach inside the Jeep's narrow bed and straighten Willy Thorn's legs inside the sleeping bag cover as well as they can. As they do so, the First Sergeant nods as though Price and Ridges are showing the right amount of respect.

Price and Ridges straighten up to see if the First Sergeant has anything more for them before they go.

"All right. The two of you done all right," the First Sergeant says. "Go on now and take Thorn back to Doc Turner."

Ridges and Price step up into the Jeep. Ridges starts the engine and drives away across the field, weaving among the few clumps of men which Sergeant Cullen's shouting has not yet dispersed.

"All right now," First Sergeant Reardon says. "Johnson, you go on. I'll remember you helped out here."

"Thank you, First Sergeant," Johnson says. He looks at me and nods. Then he shakes his head as though to tell me he still doesn't believe what has happened.

The First Sergeant sees him shake his head, knows what he is thinking, and says, "You'll believe it later, Johnson. Time passes, you'll believe it more than you do right now."

"'Fraid you're right about that, First Sergeant," Johnson says, as though the First Sergeant has been wrong about everything else.

"Go on, now. Get back to whatever you were doing before you were set to guarding Thorn."

"Right," Johnson says. He turns and walks off. The Grease Gun swinging from its sling over his shoulder thumps against his back with each step he takes.

"Let's get on," the First Sergeant says to me. "Like I said, this Battalion got to get down in the valley and up out the other side."

"Tank transporter hasn't come up for Bayou Queen yet, First Sergeant," I say. "Road's still blocked."

"I know that," he says, as though he was talking about going down into some other valley and out the other side. "But we got to get on."

I don't understand what he means. This is one of the many times in which we can do nothing but wait for someone else to do something so that we can then go on doing what we are supposed to be doing. The road down into the valley ahead is blocked by Bayou Queen and Big Sam, and until the burned shell of Big Sam is tipped off the road and tumbles down among the sparse pines below the narrow way, and Bayou Queen is winched up onto the Dragon Wagon and carted off, we can do nothing but wait.

Still: if the First Sergeant says we must go on, I will follow him. That is why he is the First Sergeant and I am not.

He glances at the ground where Willy Thorn's corpse lay inside the sleeping bag cover. He shakes his head as though he doesn't understand how Thorn died, or why. He raises his hand and adjusts his campaign hat, the chin strap hanging against the base of his skull. He presses the hat down, seating it on his head, as though a strong wind is rising. When he has adjusted his hat, he turns away and begins to walk across the field, marching straight toward Captain Knowles's Jeep through the vehicles and men getting ready to move on up. I catch up to him and walk beside him. It seems to me he needs someone to walk with. As we pass among the men they fall silent and glance at the First Sergeant as though they know he is troubled, or ill, or angry. When we climb up the low bank onto the road I glance back. Faces are turned toward us: Service Company is seeing the First Sergeant off. I wonder what they think of it all. The First Sergeant does not look back and I cannot tell from the single expression on the men's faces what they are thinking.

"You drive," the First Sergeant tells me, as though he, rather than I, drove us up here. He goes around the Jeep and climbs into the passenger seat.

I climb in and start the engine and back and fill on the narrow road. As I straighten the Jeep out and begin to drive forward in first gear, the First Sergeant says, "Pull over." I brake the Jeep and steer to the side of the road. "Transporter coming," he says. I look back up the road: an M26 tank recovery vehicle is coming up. The M26 is a ten-wheeled prime mover. Each of its tires stands higher than my chest. The Dragon Wagon has an angular armored cab with a pulpit-mounted .50 caliber machinegun on a rotatable ring at the back of the roof. The M26 is designed to haul a trailer that can carry a Sherman's weight and more, and haul it at forty fifty miles an hour. As this M26 pounds past us, I note that a specialized turretless Sherman is chained onto the trailer. A bulldozer blade is bolted to the front of the Sherman. The tankdozer up on the trailer has done a lot of hard work: its hull is chipped and scratched and the bulldozer blade is scoured and polished bright, as though it has been thrust again and again against steel brush and iron trees.

One of the M26's crew stands in the pulpit. He has rotated the machinegun to the left and stands with his forearms braced against the rim of the pulpit, staring down at us from under the rim of his helmet. The man's face is pale, as though he doesn't get out in the sun enough. I glimpse other pale faces inside the armored cab. The man up in the pulpit raises a hand as the huge vehicle roars past, the thick cleats of its tires pounding against the surface of the road.

"Big vehicle," the First Sergeant says. "Nothing like it before this war. Nothing like it in the infantry ever." He feels with his right hand inside his coat and eases a cigar out between the first and second buttons. The cigar is peculiar: it is not round, but triangular. The First Sergeant sees me looking at the cigar and says, "Louisiana," as though I know the cigar industry as well as he. He does not offer me one, as he did before we went to work inside Big Sam. "Lucky we have all these machines," the First Sergeant says. He puts the cigar in his mouth, nibbles the end away, pulls a box of wooden matches out of his coat pocket and lights the cigar. "Didn't have anything like all these machines in the last war."

The First Sergeant has given me an opening, for he never mentions his past. I have never heard him talk about his career with the infantry, and his sparse references to the Great War have seemed to deny the wound stripes on the right sleeve of his overcoat.

The Dragon Wagon pounds away from us down the road. I'm glad the muddy asphalt is damp, for I will bet that in dry weather the dust thrown up from the passage of an M26 can be seen for miles.

"It was all on foot, then?" I say, to test whether the First Sergeant and I are beginning a conversation.

"Had some trucks at the end, to carry us on up to the line. And the ambulances were motors. But mostly we marched, or took the train as far up as we could." He puffs at his cigar, building up the coal, the sweet smoke sliding out of his mouth and drifting southeast on the light wind. "Everything else was horses. Guns, wagons. Lot of horses killed by shellfire. Horses scream when they been hurt, you know? Worse than any man I heard scream ever. I didn't know that before the first war."

"Was it worse than this?"

"What, the first war? Worse than this here?" He takes the cigar out of his mouth, examines the leaf and says, "Maybe it was. Let's go now. But take it easy. I don't want to catch up with that M26. Big damn thing."

I put the Jeep into first, let in the clutch and accelerate. We cruise along at twenty miles an hour. I gauge that the M26 must have been roaring along at near forty.

"I don't know if it was worse," the First Sergeant says when we are moving. "It was different. We stayed weeks in the same trench, got to know the ground. Sat hours in dugouts under artillery fire waiting for the guns to stop so we could go up and over. The infantry attacked right across corn fields, wheat fields. There wasn't much movement, and not much place to hide if you tried to move. Until near the end, in August, 1918. Then we moved maybe a few miles every day. But that was nothing like the distances we're covering now. Trucks, tanks, halftracks: everything up on wheels and tracks now, running on gas and oil."

I haven't thought of this: I can't imagine marching fifteen miles, or riding to war in a horse-drawn wagon.

"You maintenance people in Service Company," the First Sergeant says, "are important. You know that? Maybe seem like a dirty job and no more, but without supply and maintenance these tank companies couldn't move. First war, supply was hardtack and water and canned meat carried up on men's backs. And hot cooked food if they risked bringing it up. Maintenance was a single ordnance sergeant who could fix a rifle or change the parts on one of those Chauchat French machineguns we were issued that weren't worth spit."

"What's it like, being here a second time?" I ask him. We drive around a bend in the road. Far ahead the Dragon Wagon is pounding toward a distant woods.

"Give me an odd feeling coming here again. One town we passed through west of Nancy I remembered I'd been there before. Changed a lot. Much smaller place in 1918. Gave me an odd feeling though, to go through it a second time like that."

"Uh, First Sergeant? Could I ask you, uh, why you gave me the pistol? When we were going back there?" I glance at my watch. It has been fifty minutes since we arrived at Service Company and looked up at Willy Thorn in the shadows in the back of the truck beyond the muzzle of the submachinegun in Corporal Johnson's hands. I am surprised: it seemed Thorn's passage out of this life required a lot more time than fifty minutes.

First Sergeant Reardon notes that I have looked at my watch and says, "Surprise you, don't it? How long it seems for a thing like that to take? When it doesn't take long at all?"

"Yes."

"I gave you the Colt because you can't know about a thing like this. I thought maybe Thorn might fight, or get his hands on a weapon. But he came on at the end no trouble at all."

"You thought I could back you up? If something happened?"

"Sure. I wouldn't have handed you the weapon to put in your belt under your coat if I hadn't thought you could." He looks at me, the cigar in his mouth, as though he is sure he can count on me. "You think you'd have hesitated?"

"I don't know," I tell him.

"You went as loader in a Sherman three times." Thus he recites my sole credential as a soldier.

"With Morgan twice. Once with Briggs."

The First Sergeant nods. "I heard you did all right."

"Not much happened."

"I heard there was a Panzer in there once on one those trips."

I nod. I recall Morgan's sharp voice barking down the intercom at his driver, Andrew Blake, and his gunner, Thomas Henry. The Sherman slid forward twenty feet as Morgan called out distance and angle to Henry. The turret rotated, Morgan said 'Halt!' and Blake threw out the levers and stopped the Sherman. I stumbled as the M4A3 lurched and struck my right shoulder against the recoil shield fitted around the breech of the gun. From beyond the gun, his face pressed to the gunsight, Henry said, 'Loader, load AP as I fire.' I reached and unclipped a round from the ready rack at the rear of the basket. I hefted the shell, the pointed tip in my left hand, the flat, circular brass butt in my right. As I lifted it Henry pressed both foot-pedal triggers, firing the coaxial machinegun and the 76 millimeter main armament. The breech of the gun recoiled, the block flicked open and flung the hot shell casing clattering down out of the rectangular framework recoil shield. I thrust the fresh round into the breech dribbling smoke. 'Loaded', I said into the intercom and Henry fired the 76 millimeter gun a second time. Morgan whooped and shouted, 'Got the bastard, Tom. Right through the buttons.'

"A Panzer four," I tell the First Sergeant. "Morgan and Tom Henry, Morgan's gunner, did the important work."

"You loaded, though," the First Sergeant said. "If you'd failed, you and Morgan and Henry and the other two in the crew might be somewhere else right now."

"This thing today with this man"—I cannot speak Willy Thorn's name—"wasn't going along as loader."

But the First Sergeant doesn't respond to what I have said. He says: "Why'd you go, anyway? With Morgan's crew? They didn't order you to go in a Sherman."

"His loader, Hill, had fever and a bad gut and they needed someone right then. So I went. And I trained as crew back at Camp Hood until they put me into maintenance."

"I remember that. I remember seeing the paper on that. Too bad, in a way. You'd do all right in a Sherman." He sounds as though he thinks I would fit right in.

"And end up like Sam Taylor, maybe," I say. "Or Johnny White."

The First Sergeant takes the cigar out of his mouth and says, "Pull over here. Go on, pull over to the side of the road." He holds the cigar in his right hand and looks at me as I brake and steer to the side of the road. I look forward: Battalion Headquarters is a long way away, parked along the road where we left it almost an hour before. The men are out of the tracks and trucks stretching and walking here and there. Far across the field the crews of the assault guns are standing near their Shermans and sitting on them.

"Listen up," the First Sergeant says. "I had my eye on you since you step up and help with them at Morville-les-Vic." I think of handling the corpses of the men killed in front of the tank trap before Morville-les Vic. "Look at me when I'm talking to you," the First Sergeant says.

I look at the First Sergeant watching me from beneath the brim of his campaign hat. He looks angry, or concerned: I cannot tell which.

"You listen up," he says. "There a difference between Sam Taylor and White. White disgraced himself, just like Thorn. White would have disgraced us if I'd turned him over. Just like Thorn would have if I'd turned him over. This ain't some Battalion in a regiment with a dozen ribbons from Shiloh to France fixed up to the top of the flagstaff. We got things to do here, and Sam Taylor did some of them. White didn't. Neither did Thorn."

"Thorn did pretty well, though."

"At the end he was all right. But that's all: a little bit at the end. But most of what he did was rape that girl and cut her, and fall down and shit his drawers and piss his pants. Tommy Quineau and Sam Taylor and the rest of them died where they were supposed to. Willy Thorn and Johnny White didn't. You see what I'm saying?"

"I think so, First Sergeant."

"You're thinking they're all dead alike, though, aren't you?" I nod. "They are. But that ain't the important part," he says. He shakes his head as though he knows he's going to have trouble with me. But I see now that he is not angry: he is concerned that I may not understand. "The important part is Taylor and Quineau and Taylor's men died doing what they came here to do. They died all right. Willy Thorn died wrong. He died a bad way. Now he's gone, no one's going to remember anything about him except what he did to that child. Maybe they'll remember he stood up a little before he died. But that's all they'll remember about him. But they'll think about Sam Taylor and Tommy Quineau and the rest of them. And when they think about them they'll remember they died doing the right thing. You understand me?"

"Yes, First Sergeant," I say.

The First Sergeant eyes me and his left eyebrow rises. "I'm not sure you do. But I think you might get a hold on what I'm saying as this here war goes on and you get more of a taste."

I don't tell him I don't like the taste I've had. I nod and say: "Yes, First Sergeant."

"I'm relying on you," the First Sergeant says. He sits back in his seat and looks ahead. "Let's get out of here. I got things to do."

I put the Jeep in gear and get us going.

"You got any questions?" First Sergeant Reardon asks. He puts the cigar between his teeth.

"About Taylor and Thorn? No."

"Well, then," the First Sergeant says, "you got any questions about anything else?"

"What do you think the woman would think?" I cannot say, 'about the way you shot Thorn.'

"She'd probably say wasn't no need to kill him. I saw she wore a crucifix up at the bottom of her throat. I expect she believes people ought not be shot without some judge saying something. But if she asked me, I'd tell her we did the right thing."

I glance at him and see the light bite of his teeth on his cigar framed by his grimacing mouth.

"Can I ask you one more question?"

"Fire away," he says.

"The Seven Six One's a tank battalion. How come you still wear the infantry cord and acorns on your hat?"

"Because I was in the infantry in the regular Army where this here cord and acorns mean something. And because no body among all you mechanics and drivers and civilians and such ever going to take it off me. You got any other questions?"

"Just one, First Sergeant. How come you wear the chin strap behind your head? Instead of under your chin?"

"Because the infantry let the fucking cavalry wear the chin strap in front so they won't lose a valuable piece of equipment when they charge around looking good up on them fucking horses. You got any more questions?"

"No, First Sergeant."

"Now you know why I won't give up this here hat or the cords and acorns. Someone want this hat he's gonna have to take it off me with a Schmeisser machinepistol. Pass that on," the First Sergeant says. "Tell anyone you want. You got anything more? You got anything to ask, go on: you're owed for this here thing with Willy Thorn. And this morning."

"I didn't do much for Thorn."

"You got him up," the First Sergeant says. "You gave him your coat and got him going. You don't have even one more question?"

"No, First Sergeant."

"I'll give you an answer anyways. I told you to come tomorrow morning five o'clock? That's changed: I got something for you to do down in Nancy. Want you to take one man of your choosing this afternoon and a weapons carrier and go see a man down in Nancy. I knew this man in the twenties at Fort Benning. Then he was in China fifteen years ago. Then he served in Hawaii, Fort Shafter I think it was. Couple years back he contracted malaria on one of these islands out to the Pacific and they give him a choice: Services of Supply or surveyed out for reasons of health. He stayed in and he's down in Nancy making inroads in a supply dump three miles square. Got anything you want down there, and he's the head man. Whatever officers he's got, they're relying on this man: I know."

"Supplies in Nancy?" I ask. Nancy is a hundred and fifty miles straight south. "Liège is thirty miles away. Why don't we resupply out of Liège?" I know this is a stupid question as soon as I ask it: if the First Sergeant is sending me to Nancy, he has a good, if to me inscrutable, reason.

"I'm running out of see gars. I checked Liège and they don't have none. And I'm short on ammunition. They don't have none of that either."

"Ammunition?" I ask. I think of the trucks and tracks in Service Company stuffed with ammunition. I consider the stacked cases and crates under canvas beneath every tree in every orchard and wood farther back, division trains and corps supply working hard to haul it up.

"I'm running short on shells for my revolver: it don't take a standard .45 cartridge." The First Sergeant nods down the road at Headquarters Company pulled over to the side of the road. "Let's get on now." I accelerate. "Got to report in to the Colonel," the First Sergeant says, "and tell him about this man killed by a stay-behind sniper. Then I got to write the letters for the Colonel. Seven letters today. Then I got to write you a letter to First Sergeant Burch and travel orders and a requisition to give to Sergeant Burch down in Nancy. Then I got to talk to Sergeant Symms, get you a weapons carrier and such and get you going." The First Sergeant puts the cigar in his mouth, grimaces and says, "You know, this here the worst damned day since Morville-les-Vic."

Six

As we rejoin the parked column of Headquarters Company's vehicles, the cold wind snatches sparks and smoke from the First Sergeant's cigar. "Draw up behind my track," the First Sergeant says. I pull in behind the M3 halftrack that serves as Headquarters Company's office and in which the First Sergeant and his clerk, Corporal Stuart, travel with the Colonel's and the First Sergeant's personal gear and the Battalion's clerical impedimenta.

"Come on with me," the First Sergeant says as he gets out of the Jeep. He takes his cigar from his mouth and throws it down on the side of the road. I follow the First Sergeant through the wind to the Headquarters track. The clicking of a typewriter ricochets against the steel sides of the track and out the open rear door. The First Sergeant climbs up into the track. I follow him. Corporal Stuart is seated before the typewriter, working the machine with all eight fingers and his right thumb. I note that he stops typing every five or six words and rubs his hands together in front of his mouth and blows into them.

"Get down, Stuart," the First Sergeant says.

Stuart stops typing and turns his face toward the First Sergeant. "I'm typing up the list of medical supplies Major Turner wanted, First Sergeant." Stuart holds his hands above the keyboard as though the First Sergeant will of course let him go on with his work, without which neither Doc Turner nor the Battalion itself can continue to function as the First Sergeant and perhaps the Colonel himself would wish.

The First Sergeant looks at him and says, "Do that later, Stuart. You got plenty time: we ain't going anywhere right now. Now get down. Take a walk, have a smoke. Make a latrine call, Stuart. Sitting there all day typing, your kidneys gonna back up on you maybe."

"Okay, First Sergeant," Stuart says as he gets up. "I just thought you'd have wanted this done right away." I think he is offended by the First Sergeant's remark about his kidneys.

"Not now I don't," the First Sergeant says. "Come back in ten minutes." Stuart nods. The First Sergeant and I block the way to the rear door of the track: Stuart turns and worms his way through and around the equipment at the front of the halftrack's bed and slips down into the driving compartment and out of the track through the righthand front door.

The First Sergeant reaches into the stowage bin between the steel wall of the track and the back of the bench seat on the lefthand side of the halftrack's bed. He pulls out a file and holds it out to me. I take it but I do not look at it. I do not have to look at the name on the tab. It is the file that describes Willy Thorn's life in the Army: his specialty, such as it was; the assignments he has performed; the commendations he may have been given; and whatever disciplinary actions may have been taken against him. All of Willy Thorn's service to his country is in this file except, I assume, the manner of his departure from Service Company of the Seven Six One.

"You take this here on up to Captain Knowles," the First Sergeant says, "and come on back here for your orders and the requisition and the letter I'm going to write."

"Captain Knowles?" I ask.

"Captain Knowles. Want you to give him that file and then come on back here. I want the Captain to know what happened to his man Willy Thorn. If he wants Cullen to process it back up the line, he can have Cullen process it. But I don't want it in here."

"You want me to tell Captain Knowles what happened, First Sergeant?"

"Tell him what happened? What you think? Don't tell him one thing. Just hand him the file."

"How's he going to know what happened to Thorn, First Sergeant?"

The First Sergeant looks at me as though I am not keeping up and says, "Open it up and read the last entry."

I open the file and read the last entry. It tells me that Willy Thorn has been killed in action by a sniper during Battalion operations near certain map coordinates in Germany.

"Oh," I say.

"That's right. That's how Thorn died. Shot by a sniper during Battalion operations. You were there. You saw it happen. You got any more questions?"

"No, First Sergeant. But there're almost a hundred and fifty men in Service Company saw what happened. And everyone else in the Battalion knows about it. Or will know about it."

"No one of them going to say a thing about it. You think they want people to know what Thorn was? What he did? You think they want people talking about us?"

"What about the officers, First Sergeant?"

First Sergeant Reardon shakes his head, looks out of the track toward the assault guns, looks back at me as though he is not sure I can carry my part of the load. "Officers?" he asks. "You think they want to have to know what Thorn did? You think they want to hear talk about Thorn? When they get together with their own kind—officers—you think they want to have to explain why one of their men rape that girl and cut her?"

"I guess not," I tell him.

"I guess not either," First Sergeant Reardon says. "And neither does any one else. Cullen can send Thorn's file up if Captain Knowles wants, and I'll write the letter to Thorn's nextofkin today for the Colonel to sign, but that's all that's going to happen about Willy Thorn."

"Okay, First Sergeant. Ah, but if Captain Knowles has the file, how're you going to write the letter to Thorn's family for the Colonel to sign? Without the address, I mean."

"I don't need some file to tell me the address I got to write to when a man in this Battalion get killed."

I hear a scrape of approaching boots. The Colonel appears at the open rear door of the track. As the Colonel steps up into the track I tuck Willy Thorn's file under my right arm and draw myself up and stand at attention. The Colonel's face is narrow, pale and intelligent. He knows what goes on in this Battalion, and is respected for what he knows about us and for what he does and doesn't do about what he knows. We appreciate his interest and his decision, although right now the enquiring look on his face makes me nervous.

The Colonel nods at me and says, "Easy. You could injure your back popping to like that." I relax. "Where's your coat?"

"I left it in the maintenance track, sir." This lie is as good as any other. The brim of the First Sergeant's campaign hat dips an inch. He agrees this lie is serviceable.

"Better keep warm," the Colonel says. "We've got some people down with flu. Keep your coat on and keep it buttoned up." I think of Johnson buttoning my coat over Willy Thorn's chest.

The Colonel turns to the First Sergeant: he doesn't have time for a lot of banter with the troops, not even when we are stalled here on a lonely country road between two villages.

"What's going on, First Sergeant?" the Colonel asks. His voice is casual and the question general: as though he knows the First Sergeant has nothing to tell him because nothing is going on. The Colonel glances across the field at the assault guns. A two-and-a-half ton truck has pulled in among the group of 105 millimeter Shermans and men are lifting yellow wooden ammunition boxes down from the back of the truck and breaking them open and sliding the shells from their cardboard containers and lifting the shells up to men standing on the assault Shermans. Other men standing up in the turrets lift the ominous tubular shapes and slide them down through the loader's hatches.

"Man got killed, Colonel," the First Sergeant says. The Colonel looks at First Sergeant Reardon. "Sniper," the First Sergeant says.

"What happened?" the Colonel asks. He sounds interested, but not too interested.

"Stay-behind sniper must have been, sir," First Sergeant Reardon says. "Shot him in the chest. Man died instantly. Sir, he didn't suffer." This is factual but it is not true. I recall Willy Thorn weeping and wiping away the snot on his upper lip with the cuff of my coat as he prepared to go up in front of the First Sergeant. "I sent the man's body back to Doc Turner, sir. He'll deal with the remains."

"A stay-behind sniper," the Colonel says, as though he has never heard of such a thing. He looks at the First Sergeant. Then he looks at me. Then he looks at the First Sergeant.

"Yes, sir," the First Sergeant says. "Surprised us all. A sniper way back there at Service Company? Surprised every one of us, sir." He speaks of Service Company's location as though the mechanics and drivers are supporting the Battalion from west Texas.

The Colonel looks us over again and says, "All right, First Sergeant. You'll write me a letter for the man's parents?"

"Yes, sir. This'll be an easy one, sir. Died in a moment. Won't be any making something up about this one. Didn't feel a thing." I think of Willy Thorn's heels kicking at the ground.

"Uh-huh," the Colonel says. He glances across the muddy field at the assault guns taking on ammunition as they wait for orders. "All right. Write the letter. And get his file finished and send it back up."

"File's right here, Colonel," First Sergeant Reardon says. The First Sergeant gestures at me standing at attention with Willy Thorn's file under my arm. "I've completed the man's file, sir. This man's taking it up to Captain Knowles for review and signature."

"Man killed, file closed," the Colonel says, as though he is talking about an insured loss. "How are you going to write the letter, First Sergeant? If Captain Knowles has the file, I mean? How'll you know the details? The man's address, for example?"

"I remember his address, sir." At least the First Sergeant does not tell the

Colonel he doesn't need some file to tell him the address he has to write to when a man in this Battalion gets himself killed.

"You remember his address," the Colonel says. He nods. "All right, First Sergeant. You write the letter and have Corporal Stuart type it up and I'll sign it."

"Yes, sir."

"And you're taking the man's file to Captain Knowles?" the Colonel asks me.

"Yes, sir." The clouds to the southwest have shifted closer, pushing the rising chilly wind before them.

"Ask the Captain if he has anything he wants to add to the letter and tell the First Sergeant here when you come back."

"Yes, sir." I cannot imagine Captain Knowles will want to add anything to a letter about Willy Thorn.

"What about the sniper?" the Colonel asks both of us. As he speaks he raises his hands and turns up the collar of his coat.

"The sniper, sir?" First Sergeant Reardon asks.

"Uh-huh," the Colonel says. "The sniper. The one that shot this man. What was the man's name?"

"Thorn, sir. Willy Thorn. They went looking for him, sir," the First Sergeant says. "For the sniper, I mean. Didn't find a thing." I recall Price and Ridges zipping the sleeping bag cover around Willy Thorn's body and farther up over Willy Thorn's face, the First Sergeant standing over them as they finished with the corpse and stood up and stood to one side to wait to be told what to do next.

"Uh-huh. Didn't find a thing," the Colonel says. "Sounds reasonable," the Colonel says.

The Colonel looks down the road as though he hopes he will see the Dragon Wagon appear with Bayou Queen loaded on its trailer. "There's usually something in the ARs about what to do, First Sergeant. Usually there is. I know sometimes there isn't. But usually there's something there about what to do in a situation."

"I know, sir."

"I'd appreciate it if you'd remember that, First Sergeant."

"Yes, sir."

"What was the man's name again?" the Colonel asks.

"Thorn, sir," First Sergeant Reardon says. "Private Willy Thorn. A driver in Service Company."

"Wasn't he the one who went up in a track and helped out at the tank trap at Morville-les-Vic?"

"Yes, sir," First Sergeant Reardon says. "I heard that too, sir."

"Went up with a load of ammunition, someone said. Stood up and fired a machinegun over the knocked out tanks across the trap at the bunkers and guns on the other side."

"Yes, sir," the First Sergeant says. "That's what I heard."

"I wasn't around then, but I heard about it when I got back," the Colonel says. The Colonel was wounded by shellfire two nights and a morning before the fight in front of the tank trap at Morville-les-Vic. "Too bad. Did that and now he's been killed. By a sniper," the Colonel adds, as though he had forgotten about the sniper.

"Yes, sir," First Sergeant Reardon says.

"All right," the Colonel says, as though he is ready to put Willy Thorn and the sniper to one side. "They'll shove Big Sam off the road and load Bayou Queen. Soon as the road's open the infantry doughs will go down and recon. To be sure there's nothing else waiting for us down there." He glances at me. "You were there, weren't you? When Taylor and the rest of them and Quineau were killed?"

"Yes, sir. We were at the turn off on the crest where the road turns and goes down along this side of the valley. I saw the SP gun fire."

"You did?"

"Yes, sir. Happened to be looking through glasses when it shifted in among the trees. Self-propelled gun, sir. A Hunting Panther."

"Fucking things," the Colonel says. He does not need to say anything more about the JagdPanther. Everyone has the same opinion of this particular tracked vehicle in the Germans' arsenal.

"Got an eighty-eight on it with a twenty foot or more barrel, sir," I say. "Fearsome thing."

"'Fearsome'. That's the word for it. There was only the one?"

I recall the camouflage worked into the netting drawn over the JagdPanther's hull as it shifted from its ambush to fire the two rounds that roared from its long barrel and killed six men. "Just the one, yes, sir," I tell the Colonel. "No other vehicles I saw. And no infantry."

"Surprising. They usually have some infantry travelling with those SP guns. For protection." The Colonel hunches his shoulders against the rising cold wind and the collar of his coat lifts up under the back of his helmet. "More snow, maybe," he says: I remember Corporal Johnson helping Willy Thorn to button up and get his gloves on before he went out into the snow.

"I didn't see any infantry, sir. The gun was across the valley. Maybe they figured if they blocked the road and got away before we laid down artillery they wouldn't need infantry protection. Maybe they thought: shoot at the first thing moving on the road and get out. I saw the Hunting Panther reverse back into the woods, sir. I figure there must have been some kind of track back in the woods."

The Colonel nods, First Sergeant Reardon nodding right along with him. "Sounds as though you may be right," the Colonel says. "Still, we'll have the armored doughs go down first and take a look. I don't want any more killed today. Seven men in a day? We don't have that many left. We can't afford seven men a day, First Sergeant," the Colonel says, as though the First Sergeant has suggested we barrel right down into the valley. Or killed the seven men himself.

"Seven's too many, all right, sir," the First Sergeant says. "One's too many."

"And we're going to get some more weather this afternoon. More snow maybe, rain for sure. We won't get any air in here if the weather closes in. And the forward observers will have a hard time spotting. So we'll let the doughs from the 79th leg it down to see before we move."

"Yes, sir," First Sergeant Reardon says.

"All right, then. Get everybody ready, First Sergeant. I figure half an hour and they'll have Bayou Queen out of there."

"What about C and D Companies, sir?" First Sergeant Reardon asks. "They going to come back around this way?"

"No. They're going north, and then east. They'll flank back of the ridge beyond the valley up ahead. We'll meet them on the other side. All but seven of us, that is."

"Yes, sir," First Sergeant Reardon says.

"You're right to think about where the companies are," the Colonel says, as though he had forgotten that his Battalion has three companies of M4A3 Shermans and one of M5 Stuarts. "Tell Cullen—and you tell Captain Knowles when you take him that file," the Colonel says to me, "C and D companies will go to the north. A and B will go through the valley. Tell Captain Knowles to call in for the coordinates so he and Cullen can get Service Company ready to resupply A and B here and C and D to the north and east."

"Yes, sir," I say. "I'll tell Captain Knowles, sir."

"Anything else, First Sergeant?"

"Just the one thing, sir. This man here and another are going down to supply in Nancy in a weapons carrier to get some periscope blocks and radio parts."

"Nancy? Hell of a long way, isn't it?"

"Yes, sir," the First Sergeant says. "But I can't find what we need any closer. None of the armored divisions up here in Ninth Army want to give up anything they got, sir. Or they say they don't have it."

"You're telling me this man's going to have to pass down out of Ninth Army's area, through First Army into Third Army's area, just to find radio parts and periscope blocks? How far you making this man go, First Sergeant?"

"No more than two hundred miles," the First Sergeant says.

"Boston to New York, say," the Colonel says. "Hell of a long way to go for periscope parts. And radio parts."

"That's where they are, sir." The First Sergeant looks forthright and concerned, as though America's industrial base has let him down.

"You checked on this?"

"Made the calls, sir. Sir, the calls are noted in the log in the communications track. The periscope parts are hard to find, sir. Lot of Shermans being shot up in around here, sir." The First Sergeant is fending the Colonel off, weaving a tight fence around himself with a sir in every sentence.

"Two hundred miles," the Colonel says. "Down through part of Belgium, Luxembourg, down into France. I don't know, First Sergeant. You think the trip's necessary?"

"Need those periscope blocks, sir. And radio parts. Third Army only place they got them."

"You know somebody down there, First Sergeant?" As we all found out long ago in Louisiana and Texas, the Colonel is not slow.

"Why, yes, sir, as a matter of fact I do," the First Sergeant says, as though he has friends in every supply dump from Cherbourg east all the way to right here on this country road. "Got an old friend down there used to be at Fort Benning says he can help out. And besides, sir, there's the movement order."

"This man here know about that?" the Colonel asks, jerking his head at me.

"No, sir."

"The movement order the First Sergeant just mentioned," the Colonel tells me, "is confidential. You're to keep it so."

"Yes, sir," I say. I won't say a word. Besides, if I'm on the road to Nancy I won't have anyone to say a word to, except Rutherford gripping his Schmeisser and glowering from the righthand front seat of the weapons carrier.

"Today the 7th of March, sir," the First Sergeant says. "We're supposed to be moved down there by the 12th. So we're all going to make the trip. This man here and the man who goes down to Nancy with him can meet up with us there. At least, that's the way I wrote the orders, sir."

"Wrote up the orders already, did you, First Sergeant?"

"Yes, sir. Seemed like the right thing to do."

"Uh-huh," the Colonel says. "You may be right. What would you have done if I didn't want to let this man go on down there, First Sergeant? With another man to go with him in the weapons carrier?"

"Tear up the orders, sir."

"Uh-huh. Right. Well, if someone can cover for him while he's gone, okay. Someone covering for you?" the Colonel asks.

"Yes, sir. My crew can handle anything I can, sir."

"Fifth wheel, are you?" The Colonel gives me a quick smile to show me he's just funnin'. "Feel the same way myself with the First Sergeant here handling everything for me. That's right, isn't it, First Sergeant? You could handle this Battalion as well as I do, couldn't you? Or better? Isn't that right?"

"No, sir. That's not right." The First Sergeant looks out from under the brim of his hat as though he expects the Colonel and me to believe this.

"I don't doubt your word, First Sergeant. But I'm not sure you're telling the truth about that." The Colonel glances around at the empty fields to the left of the road, at the assault guns squatting in the field to the right, cranes his neck and looks up at the sky full of clouds and wind, and asks me, "When you're down at Nancy are you going to go up to Morville-les-Vic?"

I had not thought about it: that is the past, and so are the men—Willy Thorn among them—who, as I suppose the First Sergeant would say, stood up against it that November day at the tank trap in front of Morville-les-Vic. I had not thought of returning to that place, but I say, "I thought I would, sir, if we find the time."

"Good. I'd like to hear how it looks now everything's passed on east." I wonder why: the Colonel was wounded two nights before the fight in front of the tank trap at Morville-les-Vic.

"I'll report to you when I come back here, sir."

"Like the Colonel said," the First Sergeant says, "you're not coming back here. You report to the Colonel when you meet the Seven Six One down southwest of Bitche, in France. That's northeast of Nancy."

"Yes, First Sergeant. Southwest of Bitche," I say. I know what southwest of Bitche means. In November, when we began, we drove on Bitche sixty miles northeast of Nancy. I suppose someone thought that we would make the sixty miles in a couple of weeks. But east of Nancy in November we found tank traps, self-propelled guns, roadblocks, artillery fire, minefields, infantry in fixed defenses. And mud, rain, cold, grunting wounded and corpses wrapped in shelter halves, mattress covers and sleeping bag covers. Since November we have driven north to Tillet, near Bastogne, in Belgium, into the flank of the German winter offensive, then east through northern Luxembourg into Germany. Now we have fought east from Belgium through Holland east into Germany. Four months ago we began driving on Bitche. Now it is March, and once again we are going to drive on the Germans' fixed defenses in front of Bitche.

"That's it," the Colonel says. "The Siegfried Line. But don't worry: it's weaker now than it was then. They used up a lot of muscle in the offensive in December. And they're fighting the Russians, and down in Italy. We ought to have an easier time of it, this time."

"I hope so, sir," I say, and I mean what I say.

"Also," the Colonel says, "the tactics are going to be different this time. Last time we went up as we were trained back home. Shermans in a wedge pounding forward. That didn't work. As we know."

I nod and the First Sergeant nods. We both recall the price C Company paid when it pounded forward on November 9. I remember the smooth lax shapes of the bodies of those killed scattered among the wrecked Shermans and on the muddy, snowy ground on which Sam Turley led his men forward, and was killed.

"But this time," the Colonel says, "we're going to slide through them. We'll be part of a Task Force and they won't stand against us. Or not for long," The Colonel pounds one gloved fist into the other and says, "All right, then. We're finished here. Send him and whoever's going with him down to Nancy, First Sergeant. For the periscope parts and the radio parts and whatever. What the hell, we're going to be on the road south tomorrow or the day after. And when you get back to the Seven Six One," the Colonel tells me, "report back to me. I want to know what it's like at Morville-les-Vic now we've passed on."

"Yes, sir," I say.

"All right, then," the Colonel says. He nods at me. Then he turns and steps down from the Headquarters track and walks away toward the communications halftrack.

"Okay," the First Sergeant says. "You're going to Nancy. Stuart will have your orders finished in an hour. Be back here with a weapons carrier then: I'll call Sergeant Symms to fix you up. We'll probably be farther up: look for us. Then you can take off. You ought to be able to make it most of the way down there before night come on."

"I'll be here, First Sergeant, with Rutherford and a weapons carrier."

"Be sure you see me. I got some things for you to take down to First Sergeant Burch. And Sergeant Symms will have some things for you to take down to Nancy too."

"I'll be here, First Sergeant."

"All right then," he says, just as the Colonel did. The First Sergeant turns away and I step to the back of the halftrack.

"Hang on a minute," the First Sergeant says. I turn back. He is standing over Stuart's typewriter, reading what Stuart has typed.

"Yes, First Sergeant?"

"You gave him your coat," the First Sergeant says. He does not turn around when he speaks.

"Yes, First Sergeant."

The First Sergeant goes on reading what Stuart has typed. "You did the right thing," he says. His head is bent forward. I see his shoulders rise and fall in one sharp motion and hear a faint sound escape his throat. He raises a hand to his face, drops it to his side and says, "You ready to go?"

"Yes, First Sergeant."

"Who'd you say you were going to take?"

"Rutherford. He's in the maintenance track with me."

"I know. Carries that Schmeisser machinepistol. I'll give you a letter to First Sergeant Burch. You and Rutherford will be alone down there. Except for Burch. And all them others lifting boxes and such." The First Sergeant doesn't seem to think much of the Services of Supply.

"Yes, First Sergeant." His face is still turned away from me: I am talking to his back. As I wait for him to speak, a shudder ripples across his shoulders.

"You said the right thing about the patch," the First Sergeant says. "I made a mistake there, thinking about taking it off him. He stood up at the tank trap. I should have known that. I shouldn't have said that about cutting his patch off."

"It doesn't matter," I tell him.

"No," the First Sergeant says. "Not now it doesn't. Not to Willy Thorn, at least. But it matters to me."

"It'll be all right," I tell him, as though he has skinned his knee and is worried about it.

"Maybe so," the First Sergeant says. "Anyhow, get on out of here and go see Captain Knowles and give him that file."

"He said he was going to deal with the man who raped the girl, First Sergeant."

"He don't have to worry about that now." Another shudder passes down his back.

"He doesn't know what's happened?"

"Not," the First Sergeant says, "unless someone's told him. And I doubt anyone's told him: he's an officer."

"You want me to tell him, First Sergeant?"

"No. Like I told you: hand him the file and let him figure it out. That's what officers are for: to figure it out."

"Yes, First Sergeant."

"Get on, now. You got to go up to Captain Knowles and get back to Service Company and get a weapons carrier and get back here, wherever we are, with Rutherford, soon as you can."

"I'm on my way," I say. I step down through the doorway at the back of the track. The First Sergeant does not turn around: he stands over Stuart's typewriter, staring at what Stuart has typed. It must, I think, be a difficult document, full of medical terms and a lot of parts numbers.

"You helped out," the First Sergeant says, "in Big Sam. And with Thorn. I want to thank you for that."

"It was nothing, First Sergeant."

"All right, then," he says. His back is still turned away from me, his head bent. "Get on out of here like I told you."

I nod at his back and as I do a third shudder passes from his shoulders down his spine. I wonder if I should say something more to the First Sergeant. But I can think of nothing. I turn and walk away toward Captain Knowles's Jeep.

Seven

As I drive past Bright Lights still threatening the quiet winter valley with its 76 millimeter gun, I note that my crew is huddled in the lee of the maintenance halftrack, sheltering from the wind and Captain Knowles's hectoring voice. The recovery crew has backed the M26 recovery vehicle and its attached trailer down the narrow road, snaking the huge bulk of the prime mover and its trailer loaded with the tankdozer past Bright Lights pulled over onto the verge. Captain Knowles is supervising the M26's crew as they prepare to winch Bayou Queen up onto the tank transporter. Captain Knowles waves his arms and points as he tells the recovery crew what to do. The recovery crew's sergeant stands up straight, nods and says yessir each time the Captain speaks. The sergeant's crew works on without reference to the Captain's orders: theirs is the specialized work of mechanical undertakers, and they do not require instruction about what must be done to get Bayou Queen out of the road and up onto the Dragon Wagon's massive trailer.

The three unwounded men from Bayou Queen's crew stand near the angular cab of the M26 primer mover, as far as they can get from Captain Knowles's interference with the tank recovery crew's efficient activity. The armored doughs have moved on. Down in the valley, I suspect, reconnoitering beneath the windy grey sky for other surprises hidden in the shadows beneath the pine trees.

Farther down the road, where First Sergeant Reardon and I worked to bring Sam Taylor and his men out of Big Sam, the worn tankdozer that was brought forward chained down to the trailer onto which the recovery crew is now winching Bayou Queen nudges Big Sam toward the edge of the road. Big Sam squeals and shrieks as the tankdozer's blade thrusts against its flank, shoving Big Sam's seared steel carcass toward the top of the steep slope that falls away from the lefthand edge of the road.

Captain Knowles hears his Jeep approaching, glances up, sees me behind the wheel, places his fists on his hips and waits for me to drive up. As I stop the Jeep and turn off the engine Captain Knowles strides forward, opening his mouth as he comes; but before he can speak, the tankdozer leans the grinding dozer blade into Big Sam's right side again and nudges half of Big Sam over the edge of the road. Big Sam's thirty tons screech as the dozer shoves. The tankdozer pushes and pushes and Big Sam topples down the slope, snapping pine trees, crushing brush and screeching against rocks. Big Sam slides and then tumbles and rolls over and over down the slope through the ruined pinetrees, exposing its belly with each roll. At last its rolling plunge ceases: Big Sam—or what is left of Big Sam—lies a hundred feet down the slope, bogeys and track in the air, belly hatch exposed. It reminds me of the dead cows we have seen in France, Belgium and Holland lying on their backs, legs extended toward the sky.

Big Sam's end is an indecorous spectacle, indecent to watch.

Captain Knowles has turned his head to watch Big Sam go. Now he turns back, and as I get out of the Jeep, he begins talking: "Where you been? Road's almost open here. These recovery men seem to know their job. You got anything for me? A name, like? Your crew did all right here without you. You ask anybody anything about replacements for Bayou Queen and Big Sam? First Sergeant say anything about getting some more crew up here?"

Who can answer all his questions? I hand Captain Knowles Willy Thorn's file.

"What's this?" he asks. He does not look at the file, and he does not ask me whose file it is.

"First Sergeant said for me to give you that file, Captain. Asked me to ask you to read the last entry."

Captain Knowles handles the edges of the file as though he may try to hand it back to me without reading it. "What's it say?" he asks, and I know he wants to ease into whatever this means.

"Closes out that matter, Captain," I tell him.

"It does?" He reads the name on the file, flips it open, glances at the last entry and said, "Jesus Christ. A sniper? Who the hell is Willy Thorn?"

"Driver in Service Company, sir," I remind Service Company's commander.

"And a sniper shot him? And that's all? What about the other thing?" By 'the other thing' I understand him to mean the rape and cutting.

"That's been taken care of, Captain," I tell him. I am not going to describe Willy Thorn dressed up in my coat, preparing to go out into the cold dark day.

"What you mean, 'taken care of'? You find out who the man with the cut hand is? You talk to First Sergeant Reardon like I told you?"

"Thorn cut his hand, Captain. Sometime this morning. Before the sniper got him. First Sergeant Reardon took care of it."

"Cut his hand? What do you mean, cut his hand?" I know the Captain skates from one thing to the next, and his orders can become contradictory and confusing, but I had not thought he was obtuse. On the other hand, I see something in his eyes: a faint nervous strain, a need to be reassured that at least one of his problems has been resolved.

"That's it, Captain. Cut his hand this morning. Then a sniper killed him. Like the file says."

"What about the man raped and cut that girl?"

I wonder how many more times we are going to go around this track. "That problem no longer exists, Captain. As I said, the First Sergeant took care of it."

Captain Knowles weighs Willy Thorn's file in his hands. Behind him the recovery crew is checking the cables they have bolted to the towing rings on the rear of Bayou Queen's hull; and beyond Bayou Queen, one of the recovery crew is directing the driver of the nicked tankdozer with hand signals. The dozer driver raises the blade, halts the left track and allows the right track to scrape and grab at the surface of the road. The man standing in the road directs the tankdozer's driver with his hands and the tankdozer turns and slides forward, halts, turns and slides forward, trundles up the road and halts twenty feet behind Bayou Queen.

"No longer exists," the Captain says. "You're telling me. . . ?" But the Captain stops speaking. He hefts the file in his right hand, glances at me, glances over his shoulder, glances down into the valley. "Okay," he says. He has figured out that he need not ask any more questions: because he is not going to get, at least from me, any answers.

"First Sergeant is writing the letter for the Colonel, sir. Colonel told me to ask you do you have anything to add to the letter?"

"Add to the letter," Captain Knowles says. "Add what? What am I gonna say that the Colonel and the First Sergeant don't know to say?" Captain Knowles demands, as though I know the answer.

"I don't know, sir." Behind the Captain's back the recovery crew has started the two winches behind the armored cab of the M26 recovery vehicle. I watch as the cables attached to the towing rings low on the rear of Bayou Queen's hull tighten. As the winches take up the slack in the cables, Bayou Queen's bulk rocks and shifts, its trackless left bogeys grinding against the road.

"You don't know," Captain Knowles says. "Uh-huh." He glances over his shoulder as the winches begin to pull Bayou Queen up the ramp at the rear of the transporter's trailer. "Well," Captain Knowles says, still glancing over this shoulder, "if you don't know, I'll leave it to the Colonel and the First Sergeant." He looks back at me and says, "Goddamnit. Goddamnit to hell. Why a man in my Company had to go and do this I'll never know." He hefts Willy Thorn's file. "Shot by a sniper," he says. "Goddamn him to hell." He takes Thorn's file in both hands and rips it across and across into four pieces. "Take this and get rid of it. I don't want to know anything more about this man."

I take the fluttering pieces of the file. I don't think the First Sergeant will care that Captain Knowles has given the record of Willy Thorn's career in the Army such a summary disposition. But I wonder how I will dispose of the last evidence of Willy Thorn's service to the nation.

"How'd he go?" the Captain asks.

"Go, sir?" I ask.

"This man who did this rape. How'd he go?"

I eye the Captain. I am not going to discuss details with Captain Knowles. He is an officer, after all, and has obligations under the law that are set out in detail in Army regulations. On the other hand, Captain Knowles is not a lawyer and he is not going to disinter Willy Thorn's corpse and make an issue of the manner in which he died.

"He did all right, sir, at the end." I recall Thorn telling the First Sergeant he would not give up his shoulder patch. "He did well. As well as anyone might, sir. Given the circumstances."

"The circumstances," Captain Knowles says. "Well Jesus Christ. And I thought I was going to have to deal with this. First Sergeant knew all about it, didn't he?"

"I think he knew all about it before anybody else, sir. But he didn't say how he knew, Captain."

"That's why he's the First Sergeant, I guess. Because he knows before anyone else." Captain Knowles removes his helmet and draws his sleeve across his forehead. Behind him Bayou Queen screeches as the winches draw it foot by foot up onto the ramp toward the bed of the trailer.

"Where's your overcoat?" he asks. "Pretty cold out here without an overcoat."

"I left it somewhere, sir," I tell him.

"No fooling? Better talk to Sergeant Symms and get another one."

"Yes, sir," I say.

"Well," Captain Knowles says. "This here has been some fucking morning, hasn't it? Big Sam, Bayou Queen and then that man and the shit he did." He gestures at the pieces of Willy Thorn's file fluttering in my hands. "Some morning. I wonder what he did it for." I cannot tell whether he is wondering about Willy Thorn's crime, or the First Sergeant's peremptory, unofficial solution of the problem Willy Thorn created for the Seven Six One.

"I don't know, sir. I'm not sure he could give you an answer either. If he could give you an answer at all, I mean. Thorn, I mean," I say, to make sure that the Captain and I are talking about Thorn, and not the First Sergeant.

"That's it, isn't it? That you can't find an answer to a thing like this. One thing happens, then another. Still I wonder what the hell he did it for? He never did anything like that before, did he?" he asks me, as though I can tell him whether Willy Thorn was a known rapist.

"I don't know, sir. I don't think so. I never heard anything about it."

"Neither did I," Captain Knowles says. "I never heard much about this man at all."

I note that the Captain does not speak Willy Thorn's name now that Thorn is dead. The First Sergeant, on the other hand, refused to speak Thorn's name until he had killed him. Perhaps this is another of those arcane, distinctive differences that separate non-commissioned officers from officers, and career soldiers from the rest of us, who are here for one day more, we hope, than the duration of hostilities.

"Well, the right thing's been done," Captain Knowles says. "I wouldn't want to have seen this man sent up for trial and sentence. You know what they'd say if he'd been sent up."

"Yes, sir."

"Nothing more here, I guess. Recovery crew seems to know what they're doing, road ought to be open in ten minutes."

"Yes, sir." Bayou Queen teeters at the top of the ramp at the back of the trailer. The cables hum as the winches pull Bayou Queen's center of gravity up to and over the top of the ramp. Half of Bayou Queen's weight slams down on the trailer. The winches pull and Bayou Queen slithers and grinds forward on the trailer. The recovery crew standing beside the rear of the trailer look bored. The man operating the winches at the back of the cab of the Dragon Wagon is smoking a cigarette.

"Well," Captain Knowles says, "This job's just about done. Pretty soon no one'll be able to tell what happened here. Just like that," he says, gesturing at the ripped up pieces of Willy Thorn's file I hold.

"Yes, sir."

"You see the girl?"

"Yes, sir."

"And?"

"She was cut down the left side of her face, sir. From the hairline right down to her lower jaw, I'd guess. I couldn't see, though: she had a bandage over her left eye and the side of her face. I couldn't tell if he cut her eye."

Captain Knowles beats his right fist into his left. "Shit. That motherfucker got what he deserved. And he raped her first. That sonofabitch. What a fucking mess he got himself into." His words are the words of anger; but I hear a certain sadness in the tone of his voice, as though his cursing is camouflage. "I wish there'd been some other way."

"Yes, sir. But there wasn't. They would have hanged him if he'd been sent back for trial. The Army executes for rape and cutting. And in his case he wouldn't have had much going for him. If you know what I mean, sir."

"I know what you mean," he says. "I know that. I've always known that. Ever since they told me when I was a boy." Behind him the recovery crew is working up on the trailer. They have removed the cables from Bayou Queen's towing rings and are chaining Bayou Queen down to the bed of the trailer. The sergeant in charge of the M26 stands beside the Dragon Wagon's rear tires. He hunches his shoulders against the wind and lights a cigar.

"Yes, sir."

"Well, you and your men get on out of here."

"Sir, the First Sergeant is sending me and Rutherford down to Nancy for supplies."

"Nancy?" The Captain frowns as though he is trying to remember where Nancy is located. "Pretty far. But okay: First Sergeant tell you to go down there, you go down like he said. It must be for something."

"Yes, sir."

"All right, then. Go on back and get ready." He gestures at Willy Thorn's torn-up file in my hands and says, "You think the First Sergeant is going to want that back?"

"I don't think so, Captain."

"Then get rid of it like I told you. I don't want that man's name associated with us. Not now, and not after."

"Yes, sir."

"All right, get on out of here."

Captain Knowles nods and turns away. He walks to the rear of the tank transporter's trailer and speaks to the sergeant. The sergeant takes the cigar out of his mouth and answers. Captain Knowles nods and nods as he listens to the sergeant speak. I unzip my jacket, shove Willy Thorn's ripped-up file inside my jacket and zip the jacket up.

As I approach the maintenance halftrack my crew stops talking. "Let's go," I say. Williston starts the engine as I climb up into the cab. Withers stands up behind the .30 caliber machinegun on the pintle mounting behind and between my seat and Williston's. Simpson, Fellows, Franklin and Rutherford sit in their places in the back of the track.

"What's going on?" Williston asks. I do not turn to look, but I know the five men in the bed of the track are listening for my answer.

"Job's finished. They'll have Bayou Queen out of here in ten minutes and we can get on."

"We know that," Williston says. "I mean, what's going on?"

"Nothing."

Williston pushes the clutch pedal to the floor and shifts into reverse. Simpson stands up in the back of the bed to call directions to Williston. As he begins to back the maintenance track, Williston says, "Where'd you go in the Captain's Jeep?"

"Back up to see First Sergeant Reardon."

"You saw him here this morning."

"Yes."

"Come on," Williston says, "something happened. I know that. Everyone else here knows it too. Knowles was about as prickly as I've seen him while you were gone. What the hell happen?"

"Left," Simpson calls from the rear of the track. Williston glances out the window and adjusts the wheel as the track backs. "Straight on back now," Simpson calls. Williston straightens the wheel and accelerates. The maintenance halftrack picks up speed, clattering up the road backward past Bright Lights. Eddy Stanton standing up out of the commander's hatch takes the fieldglasses down from his eyes and looks us over as we pass. He does not wave or nod as we pass and he looks troubled. I guess someone has radioed him and passed him the word about Willy Thorn.

"So?" Williston asks when we are past Bright Lights. "What happened?"

"Someone raped a German girl and cut her. The girl bit him on the left hand. I went back to help take care of it."

"What's that mean, help take care of it?" Williston is persistent: he wants to get to the bottom of this.

"We found out who did it and dealt with him."

"Come on, what's dealt with him mean?" Williston holds the wheel straight as the halftrack reverses up the road.

"He's dead."

"Dead? What you mean, dead? Who's dead?" Williston asks, as though he has not, even after four months of travelling with this tank Battalion, figured out what 'dead' means."

"A sniper killed him," I say. I am not going to describe First Sergeant William S. Reardon standing up in front of Willy Thorn with his hands on his hips underneath his coat, his right hand close to the butt of his revolver. Williston will have to get the fine points from someone else in Service Company. From anyone else in Service Company, that is. Except Willy Thorn, that is.

"Who was he?"

"Willy Thorn."

"Willy Thorn? You mean that smooth, genteel little fast talker drives one of the supply trucks?"

"That's him." I do not tell him that Willy Thorn was not smooth or genteel in the minutes before the First Sergeant shot him dead. Nor do I mention that Willy Thorn will no longer drive a supply truck. It would not matter if I told him how Thorn acted, but I told Thorn I would not.

"Where's your coat?" Williston asks. Everyone seems interested in my coat: the Colonel, Captain Knowles, Williston. I hope Sergeant Symms, who controls the issue of coats and decides who may or may not need an overcoat, is as interested as the rest of them.

"I lost it."

"Lost your coat?" Williston asks. "How come you lost your coat?"

"For Christ's sake, Williston," I say. "Forget it, would you? I lost the coat, that's all. If you want to know what happened to Thorn, ask anyone in Service Company. If you want to talk over the details once you find them out, talk them over with someone else. All right?"

"All right," Williston says. "All right, then. Don't get so touchy, would you?"

"It's been a long morning."

"Every morning out here's a long morning. Don't get so touchy about it. Hell, you chose to help the First Sergeant with Sam Taylor and the rest of them, and the Captain ordered you back to do something for him. I'm just asking you what is all. Besides, you oughtn't to complain. If Knowles hadn't ordered you back, you might have had to stay here and listen to him giving those guys in the recovery crew advice on how to do their job. Shit. They need advice about that like I need advice on how to drive this here track."

"Sorry," I say. After all, I should not be angry with Williston. He has done nothing. Only Willy Thorn did something that has angered me, and he's not here to get angry with. Not any more.

"No need to be sorry. I was just asking." The halftrack backs and backs up the road leading down into the valley. Looking ahead I see the crew of the M26 tank recovery vehicle mounting up. The sergeant says something to Captain Knowles, nods, puts his cigar into his mouth and climbs up into the passenger side of the Dragon Wagon's cab. Exhaust puffs from the stack behind the M26's cab. I recall the sudden puff of smoke among the shadows in the pinetrees across the valley when the JagdPanther's driver started its engine and this morning began.

"All right, then," I tell Williston, raising my voice so that the five men behind me will hear too. "If you want to know, I'll tell you so you won't hear it garbled from someone else. Knowles sent me back to try to find out who it was who raped the girl. I was supposed to get the First Sergeant to look at every left hand in Service Company, because the girl bit whoever did it on the left hand. First Sergeant already knew all about it. Knew what had happened, knew who'd done it, and knew what had to be done. He took me back to Service Company with him. Called the Company into formation. The woman and the girl came. The girl identified Thorn. The First Sergeant brought Thorn up in front of the Company and shot him once in the chest and killed him. Is that clear enough for you?"

"Sure," Williston says. As he drives the track backward up the road, listening in case Simpson calls out directions from the back of the track, he seems to consider what I have said: to be sure I have not left anything out. Then Williston nods and says, "Sure, that's clear enough."

"I gave Thorn my coat to wear," I tell him. I recall removing my coat and encouraging Willy Thorn to put it on, to cover at least part of his shame.

"What for?"

"I'm not going to tell you that. But he wasn't going to go up in front of Reardon without a coat. So I gave him my coat and he went on."

Williston nods, opens his mouth, closes it as Simpson calls out from the rear of the track, "Turn out coming up." Williston sticks his head out of the driver's side window and looks back past the left armored wall of the track as he backs into the turn-off from which I looked down into the valley and watched the Hunting Panther shoot down Big Sam and Bayou Queen.

"Okay," Williston says. "We're ready to roll. Where to?"

"Back to Service Company. They ought to be on the road by now, heading this way." Williston puts the halftrack in gear and we move off. In the distance, in the fields on either side of the road that were empty when I came up twenty minutes ago, the halftracks of the armored infantry regiment to which we are attached have gathered. As we clatter down the road, the infantrymen in the tracks glance at us. Some of them wave, or nod. I guess they have heard about Big Sam and Bayou Queen. I know they have not heard about Willy Thorn: no one outside the Seven Six One is ever going to hear about Willy Thorn.

"What happens next?"

"First Sergeant's ordered me down to Nancy. I'm taking Rutherford with me. You're going to cover here."

"Nancy?" Williston asks. "What's he sending you all the way down there for?" Everyone asks the same question. Everyone gauges Nancy to be as far away as New Guinea.

"Periscope blocks, radio parts, like that." I do not mention the First Sergeant's friend from Fort Benning who now ramrods the gigantic supply dump at Nancy.

"Periscope blocks? Radio parts? You expect anybody here to believe that? Sergeant Symms got enough periscope blocks and radio parts, you'd think he was going into the periscope and radio business after the war."

"Still, that's what the First Sergeant wants. Me and Rutherford to go down to Nancy and get a bunch of things he's got on a list."

"And that's all?"

"There's more, but you'll have to find it out later. First Sergeant and the Colonel told me not to talk about it."

"Uh-oh," Williston says. "Sounds like we're going to make another move, and down south."

"I don't know."

"You know," Williston says.

"Okay," I say. "I know. But I'm not saying."

Williston nods, shifts up, accelerates. He drives on until Headquarters Company's vehicles appear, still parked along the road. I do not wonder what they are waiting for: I know they are waiting for orders. The field beside Headquarters Company is empty: the assault guns have moved off to the southeast. We rattle past the Shermans, tracks, trucks, weapons carriers and Jeeps of Headquarters Company. I do not see First Sergeant Reardon. The Colonel is standing beside the Headquarters track talking to three officers. The Colonel looks up as we pass. Williston glances at me, but he does not speak. I point forward and Williston nods. We drive on.

Service Company's vehicles are also waiting for orders: they are lined up on the road beside the field in which Johnson and I struggled to carry Willy Thorn part of the way forward toward the First Sergeant waiting in front of the formation. I look across the field, but I cannot identify the place where Thorn stood up, at last, in front of the First Sergeant.

"There's Sergeant Symms," Williston says. Sergeant Symms is sitting in a Jeep, a two-and-a-half ton truck in front of the Jeep, a weapons carrier behind. The weapons carrier's hood is up and a mechanic whose face I cannot see is leaning over the engine. Sergeant Symms watches as we come on. Williston brakes the halftrack across the road from Sergeant Symms's Jeep. "Good luck getting that coat," he whispers to me as I get down. I nod, preparing to explain to Sergeant Symms that I require a new coat because I loaned the other one to Willy Thorn and he took it with him into the dark inside the sleeping bag cover in which he was shipped back to Doc Turner.

I walk around the halftrack. As I cross the road Sergeant Symms gets down from his Jeep. Before I can begin to explain about the coat he says, "Come on up in this here truck." Sergeant Symms is lithe and nimble, as though he works twelve hours a day shifting cases of ammunition and crates of whisky and cartons of cigarettes. He steps up onto the rear bumper of the truck parked in front of his Jeep, reaches down, grips the lower righthand corner of the canvas curtain at the back of the truck and holds it open with one hand. I climb up through the triangular opening into the truck. Sergeant Symms follows me up. He drops the canvas curtain behind him.

"First Sergeant," he says in the gloom inside the truck, "said for me to give you a coat, a weapons carrier and whatever else you need for this here trip you going on."

"Thanks, Sergeant," I say.

"No need for you to thank me. I was there with the rest of the Company and I saw. You stood up with Thorn. I thought he was better than to go and do something like that with that child." Sergeant Symms shakes his head as though he has discovered that a deal he promoted has gone sour. "You did all right getting him and the First Sergeant through that. Here's the coat," he says, gesturing to a coat folded on the righthand bench seat. I pick it up, look at the size on the tab inside the collar and slip into it. It fits.

"Gloves are in the right hand pocket," Sergeant Symms says.

"How did you know the size?" I ask.

"I called back to Doc Turner's people and asked one of them to check the size of the coat Thorn was wearing." He pauses, and then he says, "I hope you don't find that upsetting or anything. That I called, I mean. About the coat size."

"No, Sergeant," I tell him. "Not at all." He looks relieved, as though he thought maybe he had not done quite the right thing.

"Weapons carrier behind my Jeep here being checked over right now, to be sure everything all right. It's gassed up, got jerrycans up behind and six more in the bed. I had them put in cooking equipment, flashlights, sleeping bags, change of underwear and socks for you and the man going with you, Rutherford the First Sergeant said. I also put in six cartons, ten rations a carton, of Menus 1, 2 and 3. Also two cases wine—one red, one white, that's all I know about wine though Brooks say it's good wine, and I rely on Sam Brooks in D Company Headquarters when wine come up as a subject. All this under a tarpaulin in the back next the spare jerrycans. You'll also find six cartons cigarettes—two Camel, two Lucky and two Chesterfield—two boxes cigars and two bottles Scotch whisky. Officers aren't drinking a whole lot these days, and when they do they seem to take the local stuff. Let's see now, that's about it." He frowns as though he's forgotten something. "Oh, yeah. First Sergeant said I was to put in a case of this here Dutch gin in the square bottles for you to take down to his friend where you're going. I put in two cases, so you and the First Sergeant's friend won't run short. And a box of trade goods, also for his friend down where you going."

"Trade goods?" I ask him.

"You know: Lugers, rank badges, nazi flags, maps, one of them knives with the swastika on the hilt, a couple of Walther pistols and three of them iron crosses somebody took somewheres and turned in to me thinking I might need a supply for a situation just like this one here." Sergeant Symms grins as though he has enough loot to be able to share.

"Thanks for all this, Sergeant. Seems like a lot more than we'll need."

"Don't be saying that," he says. "You're going back down the line away from the Battalion and you know soon as they see your faces you're going to find it hard to find a place to get in out of the cold to eat."

I had not thought about that, but Sergeant Symms is right: I doubt any messhall between here and Nancy will give Rutherford and me a hot meal.

"Besides," Symms says. "You did all right today with all you had put on you. First Sam Taylor and his men and Tommy Quineau and then this other thing right here. First Sergeant said, fix him up. So I fix you up like he said. Though I'll tell you, I would have done just the same even if he hadn't said a word. You went a long way today, you and the First Sergeant, and whatever we got here in supply is yours."

"Thanks, Sergeant."

"Oh, and I forgot: I put in two Thompson guns and some magazines, just in case. Though there ain't nothing going on where you're going. Quiet and all. But you never know: you two going south, after all. So I put them in."

"Thanks, Sergeant."

"Like I said: no need to be thanking me. Sam Taylor was a friend of mine."

"But thanks anyway," I say.

Sergeant Symms stands in the gloom looking at me. "I could have brought the coat outside but I wanted to tell you in private you did all right today. Someone had to help the First Sergeant and he relied on you."

"I wonder why," I say. Who can say why the First Sergeant chose me to come along with him today, first into Big Sam and then to help, as everyone says, with Willy Thorn.

"I don't know," Symms says. He rubs his chin as though he has considered the question. "I don't know," he says. "Point is, First Sergeant called you up and you went. Today, and before. That's enough."

"Yes, Sergeant," I say.

"I couldn't have done it," Sergeant Symms. "Not go into Big Sam like that. And not bring Willy Thorn up front the Company." He pauses, glances this way and that in the cold gloom inside the truck. "I saw you give him your coat," he says. "You did a good thing when you did that. For him and the rest of us too. Made it easier for him, and us too. And Johnson told me how you told the First Sergeant about Willy Thorn at Morville-les-Vic." Sergeant Symms nods and nods in the gloom. "I knew about that but I forgot. When Johnson told me about it I remembered Thorn going up in that track full of ammunition. You remembering that made it go off easier when the First Sergeant went up to him to take his patch."

"I guess it helped." What else can I say? That I did it to hurry things up, to get Willy Thorn over the hump and into the dark before he had time to think about where he was going? That I guessed the First Sergeant hadn't known about Thorn standing up on our side of the tank trap at Morville-les-Vic? That Thorn, no matter what he had done, should have been left something—even if was nothing more than the Battalion's stylized patch—to take with him on his trip?

"It helped all right," Sergeant Symms says. "More than helped. Made everything go real easy." I think of the First Sergeant standing over the typewriter in the Headquarters halftrack, tremors running down his back, his face turned away from me, and wonder just how easy everything went.

"Anyhow," Sergeant Symms says, "you and Rutherford all set to go. Anything else you need?"

"I can't think of anything, Sergeant. Thanks again for all this stuff. And the help. And, ah, the words."

"Don't worry about no words. Words the easy part. You just go on down to Nancy like the First Sergeant said and we'll see you when you get back.

And don't worry about bringing any of the stuff I put in the weapons carrier back. Just like Uncle, I got more."

"Ok, Sergeant."

Sergeant Symms pushes the canvas at the back of the truck to one side and holds it open. I jump down from the back of the truck in my new overcoat. Sergeant Symms jumps down after me. He walks up to the mechanic bending over under the opened hood of the weapons carrier and says, "You got this thing all ready to go, Jenkins?"

Jenkins straightens up and says, "All set to go." He glances at me. I recall his face, but I cannot place him: he has not been in Service Company long. "This weapons carrier had a complete check no more than a week ago," Jenkins says. "Got new belts, filters, oil change, plugs, points, greased up, everything ready to go. You could drive this carrier right down to Madrid, be there in three days."

"That's good, Jenkins," Sergeant Symms says. "You did good work. Now get on out of here."

"Yes, Sergeant Symms," Jenkins says. "Of course, Sergeant Symms. Right away, Sergeant Symms."

"Get on out of here, Jenkins," Symms says. "I call you over here to check on this weapons carrier, not to give me and everyone else standing around here a bunch of lip longer than it ought to be."

"This vehicle didn't need a check," Jenkins says. "You think we don't keep these things checked, Symms?"

"Get the fuck out of here, Jenkins," Sergeant Symms says.

"I'm going. And I'm happy to go. More than happy." Jenkins turns and saunters away.

"Fucking Bolshevik," Sergeant Symms says. "Thinks he's something special 'cause he was down in Spain during the war down there. Abraham Lincoln Brigade huh. No wonder he still a private: he's one of them Bolsheviks, some kind of a communist motherfucker. Got no respect for rank at all." Sergeant Symms throws out his arm to display his chevrons. "And I don't like them communists using President Lincoln's name that way. Fucking communists."

"Wasn't he with C Company before?" I ask. Now I remember him: a tank commander in C Company.

"Sure was," Symms said. "Had to be sent back from the line. C Company Captain thought he was taking too many chances with himself and his crew. Kept pushing right up front of everybody else, trying to shoot it out with every nazi came his way. So now he's back here, checking the oil level in these here vehicles. Fucking Bolshevik, that's what he is."

"You'd think they'd want him in the tank companies," I say.

"He thinks so too. Keeps trying to get back into them. But Captain Knowles says no one in tanks wants to go with him. So he's going to stay here and check the oil level in these here engine blocks." Sergeant Symms spits onto the road, steps up to the weapons carrier and closes the hood. "Didn't even close the damned hood," he mutters.

"It'll be all right," I tell him.

"Maybe so," Sergeant Symms says. "Still, I don't like him acting like that. We got a chain of command here, after all." He breathes hard and glares at Jenkins walking away down the column of Service Company vehicles. "But all right," he says. "All right, then. I'll leave you here. You go on."

"Thanks for the help, Sergeant Symms."

He waves my words away. "Nothing," he says. "You take it easy now," he says. "You and Rutherford both. Where you're going, I mean." He sounds as concerned as if we'd been ordered to drive straight through to Berlin. He nods, nods, turns and walks away.

I look across the road. The six men in my crew in the maintenance track are looking down at me. Simpson grins and calls down, "Looks like you found a friend in the Services of Supply."

"A new coat, at least," I say. "Rutherford, come on. We're going."

"Going where?" Rutherford says. He sounds suspicious, and he hefts his Schmeisser. I recall I have not told him that he is going to Nancy with me. First Sergeant Reardon, the Colonel, Captain Knowles, Sergeant Symms and Williston know; but I have forgotten to tell Rutherford.

"We're going down to Nancy on the First Sergeant's orders," I tell him. "Get your stuff and let's get out of here."

"I'm coming," Rutherford calls. He makes his way through the bed of the track to the rear door. As he gets down he looks back up into the track and calls out, "You men keep on the job up here, now, while we go on south."

Eight

THE FIRST SERGEANT HANDS me our orders, gives Rutherford three folded maps, unfolds a fourth and spreads it over the righthand bench seat of the Headquarters halftrack. The First Sergeant shows us the route he has marked on the map. I note that he has also circled, but not labelled, two locations to the east of our route. I do not ask him what they are: I know First Sergeant Reardon will explain them to us when he is ready to do so.

"What those marks, First Sergeant?" Rutherford asks.

The First Sergeant straightens up and looks at him. "I thought I'd get to that, Rutherford. But since you're eager for information, I'll tell you now. Friendly forces," the First Sergeant says. "You'll be fine when you get to Nancy and check in with First Sergeant Burch. Most his men Services of Supply troops. Until then you'll be travelling down through the corps areas to the south. These places I've marked show you the approximate locations of units where you can go if you need to. Need to don't mean a hot shower and a mess of fried chicken, either. You get me? I haven't put the names of these units on the map because I ain't supposed to write them down. But I can tell you: this one here," he says, pointing at one of the marks, "is the 969th Field Artillery Battalion."

"Some Christmas they had," Rutherford says. The First Sergeant looks at him and nods as though he is surprised that Rutherford knows about the 969th. Trapped with the 101st Airborne Division inside the Bastogne perimeter, the 969th, into which the remains of the 333rd Field Artillery Battalion were incorporated, fired in support of the defense and was commended by the 101. Among them, from the 333rd Field Artillery Group Headquarters, was a Tech 4 named Broman Williams, who set up a kitchen and fed a thousand men a day inside the Bastogne perimeter. Since we learned about Williams's efforts, our harassed, exasperated cooks have been required to listen, when the Seven Six One's food is a little cool, to men call out, 'Bring on Broman Williams' and 'If Broman Williams were here we'd be having hot food and biscuits too. And enough to eat just one time.'

"Now, down around east of Nancy," the First Sergeant says, "you'll find the 614th Tank Destroyer Battalion. You go there, you remember one thing: they're towed." Rutherford nods and looks serious. I know what he is thinking. Crewing towed antitank guns is heavy, dangerous work: the guncrews must dismount from the halftracks in which they travel and which tow their guns, set the guns up, get them into action and stand behind them to serve them. The crews cannot operate the weapons from cover, and they cannot crouch behind armored walls: the weapon's tinny gunshield is a joke. They must stand up to load, aim, fire and reload. We have heard about the 614th Tank Destroyer Battalion (Towed). They have as good a reputation as we do, and they have paid more for that reputation than we have.

"You're all set, then," the First Sergeant says. "You get that case of gin from Sergeant Symms?" I nod. "And those souvenirs? I want First Sergeant Burch to have those. He sent me an Arisaka rifle to Texas from where he was out in the Pacific. Long damned thing with a bayonet on it eighteen, twenty inches long. You could fight the devil with that thing." He shakes his head, as though he cannot understand the Japanese arms industry. "But that's the Pacific and it's to one side. Here," the First Sergeant says. He pulls a letter out of his pocket and hands it to me. "You take this letter and give it to First Sergeant Burch when you get down to Nancy. He'll take care of you. And take this requisition for periscope blocks and radio parts: this is the reason you're going down there. But you be sure," he says, "to give First Sergeant Burch that letter. You understand? Letter's more important than this here requisition." The First Sergeant gives me a severe look as I take the requisition the First Sergeant's clerk, Stuart, has typed up. I fold it and the letter and place them in the left hand pocket of my shirt inside my coat. "Now, I want you two to drive straight down there. No side trips and no sightseeing. If something comes up, you got a radio in the weapons carrier. Last thing: when you're down there I want you to check with First Sergeant Burch on where you're to report back." He glances at Rutherford. "We're moving out of here, Rutherford," the First Sergeant says, "and you're not to mention it. Understand?"

"I understand, First Sergeant."

"All right. You got everything you need. Time to go. You ought to be able to go a good piece by this evening. Get at least down into Luxembourg."

"Right, First Sergeant," I say.

"This gonna be sort of a two three day vacation for you two. I figure a day to get down there, a day in Nancy, and a day to get up to where we all going. But be sure you ask First Sergeant Burch where we're at before you start off to find us. I know where we're going, starting late today and travelling tomorrow all day. But I ain't supposed to tell you. And even if I told you right now, that doesn't mean it's going to happen. Things change, and they might change these orders we got even after we're on the way. So check with First Sergeant Burch before you take off. You with me?"

"Yes, First Sergeant," Rutherford and I say together.

"What you going to do with that Schmeisser, Rutherford?" the First Sergeant asks. "Going to kill some these sonsofbitches, are you?"

"Take it along with me, First Sergeant. Good gun. Bettern these things they give us." Rutherford is right: the Schmeisser machinepistol is an excellent weapon. It has a very high rate of fire and has killed a lot of men.

"Just be sure you don't run out of ammunition," the First Sergeant says. "That's a problem you got with these here German weapons you all collect: ammunition." I do not mention his antique .45 pistol and his Star Gauge '03 Springfield rifle.

"Yes, First Sergeant," Rutherford says. He hooks his right thumb through the sling of the German machinepistol and hitches the weapon higher up his back.

"All right then," the First Sergeant says. "We're going to be moving, but maybe not down through that valley where we were headed this morning. Most likely we're going to be pulled back and then sent south. This the Army. They tell you, go this way and you go. Then they tell you, go this other way, and you go there too."

I think of Tommy Quineau and Sam Taylor and the four men who died with him inside Big Sam part way down the road into the valley.

"Shit," Rutherford says. "Then they in Big Sam and Bayou Queen got killed for nothing."

"That ain't the case, Rutherford," the First Sergeant says. "No one who's died in this Battalion died for nothing." The First Sergeant stares at Rutherford from beneath the brim of his campaign hat. "Sam Taylor and them might have died yesterday, or tomorrow, if they didn't today. You remember that, Rutherford. Somebody had to go down that road, and they were the ones who went. That's all there is. Are you following me, Private?"

"Yes, First Sergeant," Rutherford says. But he glowers and hitches at the sling over his shoulder. Rutherford believes that if everyone took a little more care, no one would die. He forgets that the Germans take care too.

"All right," the First Sergeant says. "You two get on out of here now."

Rutherford and I get down from the Headquarters halftrack, walk across the road to the weapons carrier and get in. I start the engine and work the gears, push the clutch to the floor and let it out. "You driven one of these here before?" Rutherford asks.

"No. But it's no different from a large automobile."

"Huh," Rutherford says. "Large automobile. Let's motor on down to Nancy, then."

I look across the road at the Headquarters track. First Sergeant Reardon waves us on. I move the gearshift lever into first and let in the clutch. We move off, west up the road toward Geilenkirchen, where the 84th Infantry Division's 333rd Infantry fought and suffered last autumn. From there we will turn south to Aachen, southwest to Verviers and south from there to Spa, in Belgium, down through Luxembourg to Thionville, in France, then on through Metz up the valley of the Moselle to Nancy.

And no side trips, as the First Sergeant said. We are strangers among strangers in a foreign land. Whatever the reputation we have earned, I understand why Sergeant Symms has issued us two Thompson submachineguns; and why Rutherford sits beside me with his Schmeisser across his knees, the muzzle, I note, pointed at my right knee.

"That thing on safe?" I ask Rutherford.

"This here weapon?" he asks. He puts the safety on and eases the muzzle away from my knee, toward the dash. "Sure it is."

"Don't shoot up the dash, will you?"

Rutherford squints at me and says, "I ain't going shoot anything I don't intend on shooting."

We drive on, past the last of Service Company still waiting in its trucks and halftracks and weapons carriers to be told where to go next, past Doc Turner's medical detachment a mile farther back beside a woods. I do not see Doc Turner. Nor do I see Willy Thorn inside his sleeping bag cover. Medical corpsmen wearing helmets with red crosses on them are standing around, waiting. One of them raises a hand as we drive past. I do not recognize him.

Soon we have left the Battalion behind, and begin to pass through the rear areas of the 79th Infantry Division, in support of which we began fighting on February 18. I drive on and we pass through the 79th Infantry Division's artillery and then through the 79th Infantry Division's supply trains. Soon we have left the war behind: we roll through Linnich and descend into the valley of the Roer river and drive up out of it on the road to Geilenkirchen. Geilenkirchen was fought over until late last November. Its houses are battered, as though a fierce storm has been blowing through its streets every day for six months. Every house we pass has been damaged. Stones displaced from the walls lie in the street, shards of plaster, glass and roofing slates litter the sidewalks. Fire seems to have gutted every third house, burning the timbers and staining the white plaster walls black beneath the eaves. Military police slouch at intersections, eying the occasional civilian passing in tattered clothes. The civilians are bereft. As they walk through the streets, they stare and stare, as though they too are strangers in this place. I suppose they did not think about what might happen when they began all this back in the thirties.

As we drive past, the military police examine us with as much care as they examine the civilians. But they do not stop us to check our orders: perhaps they recognize us, or the patch on our shoulders. More likely they, like every other American in Europe, are confident we're not German spies. As we drive out of Geilenkirchen south toward Aachen a long train of ammunition trucks approaches, led by a single Jeep with an officer sitting in the right-front seat. He glances at us without interest. The truck drivers are more animated. They wave at us as we pass, and the assistant drivers standing up in the pulpits in the roofs of the cabs behind the machineguns yell down to us. Rutherford sits up straight and waves and calls back to them, yelling something about Kansas City. I am more dignified: I raise my right hand from the wheel every now and then to show that I notice them. I hear one of the assistant drivers shout, "Go on!"

These drivers deserve our recognition, and more: where would the Seven Six One and the 79th Infantry Division and the rest of the troops slogging east into Germany get the ammunition, fuel, vehicles, food, clothing, tools, maps and spare parts if these truck crews did not set out on their long tedious journeys across France and Belgium into, at last, part of Germany? We do not see much of these soldiers, but we do not disparage what they do. Neither does General Eisenhower, who seems to understand the importance of the morale of the men in the Services of Supply: I recall a photograph of him standing beside a jumble of hawsers and loose artillery shells on the docks at Cherbourg, the side of a railroad truck behind him, grinning at a grinning ammunition handler, his hand on the private's shoulder, a grinning aide standing by.

We approach Aachen in the late afternoon. The skyline of its buildings against the southern sky is jagged and inexact. Little smoke rises from the city's chimneys, and I guess that the populace—such of the populace as is left, that is—finds coal with difficulty. Still, spring is coming, and Aachen is lucky to be here at all: in September and October of last year, the 1st Infantry Division and the 3rd Armored Division pierced two concentric rings of defenses drawn around Aachen. To help the 1st and the 3rd get forward through those defenses and into the city, Aachen was shelled and bombed and bombed and shelled. The city held out for six weeks: in the end it was more rubble than city.

Rutherford examines Aachen as we drive into its outskirts and says, "Pretty bleak."

"Yeah," I say. "Someone crunched this place from one end to the other."

"Didn't we get down there around east of Nancy just after they finished up here at the end of October?"

"That's it."

"You think we should stop here tonight?"

"Take a peek at the first map there. See if the First Sergeant indicated one of those units of ours around here." Rutherford unfolds the map that shows the area from southern Holland down beyond Aachen. He examines it as though he is planning the invasion of Germany.

"Nothing," Rutherford says. "First spot the First Sergeant marked seems to be down here south of Luxembourg. And east."

"Drive on through, then?" I ask. I know Rutherford will agree with me. Neither of us wants to look for a place to eat and sleep in a bombed and shelled German city just east of the Belgian border. Nor does either of us want to worry about the reception we will receive if we stop.

"Seems right to me," Rutherford says. "Right on down through Aachen and down into Luxembourg. We can go on till we can't any more and then pull off and sleep in the back."

We drive into Aachen. This city has suffered more than Geilenkirchen. Buildings blown down into the streets in September and October have been carted away stone by stone. The paving blocks have been gouged out of the ground and the walls of every building are cracked, scorched, pitted, holed. Street signs are missing from the poles at the corners. The bombing and shelling was indiscriminate: houses are as damaged as official buildings, sidestreets as rutted, holed and furrowed as the main arteries.

"Smell that?" Rutherford asks. "Smells like putrefaction, death and shit to me."

He is right: a stench composed of the separate sour and sweet smells of urine and excrement, slaughtered animals left to waste and wasted humans dead seeps from beneath the rubble.

"Let's get out of here into the country," I say. I accelerate south along an avenue from which rubble has been bulldozed onto the curbs on either side. We drive past soldiers walking here and there along the way bulldozed through the rubble that used to be buildings. The soldiers glance at us and away. Farther along we pass elements of a fresh armored division parked in a broad square and along the avenues leading away from the twisted stump of a statue up on a pitted granite block.

"What was that?" Rutherford asks as we drive around the square past Jeeps, shiny Shermans and brand new M10 tank destroyers. I wonder what division this is, but I do not glance at the men in the vehicles. I was taught when I was growing up never to look curious.

"Don't know," I tell him. It could not have been a statue of a human: the twisted metal left up on the granite block by the bombing and shelling is too thick to have been the lower part of a statue of a man. A group? I wonder. Some kind of animal?

We are through the square and out the other side before I can decide. I know I could stop and try to piece out the German words struck into the pitted granite plinth, but I do not. Perhaps I will come back in thirty years and try to figure out what hope this destroyed statue expressed, what allegory it recited.

"Let's get the fuck out of here," Rutherford says. I note he is gripping his Schmeisser. Looking through the windshield of the weapons carrier I see the tanks and tank destroyers parked on either side of the avenue flashing past. The crews seem to be looking at us. I agree with Rutherford: it is time to get the fuck out of here. I accelerate.

"Uh-oh," Rutherford says. Two hundred yards ahead an MP stands in the middle of the road with his arms raised. I slow the weapons carrier, bring it to a halt ten feet short of the MP. Curious tankers in new uniforms look down from their Shermans. The MP saunters up to my side of the weapons carrier.

"Orders," he says. I take out our orders and hand them to him. He is a corporal. He points his long thin nose at our orders, reads them, looks us over, hands them back and says, "You all going pretty fast in through here. You want to burn up this vehicle? No? Well, you're burning up our road here."

When I speak, my voice is neutral, but not craven. "Sorry about that," I tell him. "We were ordered to get on fast as we could might do." I modify my grammar for the corporal: he might think I am getting beyond myself and query me about whether I a college boy. I would have to tell him yeah I a college boy, and then we would have to go around again. "And Nancy a long ways down south," I tell him.

"Don't care about that," the MP says. "Nothing in your orders say you all get to exceed the speed limit in a built-up area like this here." I do not glance around at the blasted buildings.

"You're right," I say. "We'll take it easy from here on, Corporal."

"You better take it easy. We got military *po*lice all along these roads for just this reason. For people like you. We're losing a lot of vehicles and valuable equipment cause you people are speeding on these roads." When he says 'you people' I hear Rutherford's eyeballs click: but at least I do not hear the safety on his Schmeisser snap down.

Three Shermans down the line on the right hand side of the avenue a tanker wriggles up out of the commander's hatch in the turret and steps down off the turret and down the front of the tank. I can tell from the way he dances down the face plate that though this may be a fresh armored division, he is used to getting out of a Sherman in a hurry. He saunters up the road toward us. As he comes closer I see he is a Captain, which means that he commands a tank company.

"Trouble, Corporal?" he says from behind the MP's back.

The MP corporal turns, comes to attention, salutes and says, "Nosir. No trouble. Just that these men were driving pretty fast in through here and I cautioned them."

"That'll be all right, Corporal," the Captain says. "You take off. I'll handle this."

"This here is a military *po*lice matter, Captain. Ain't got nothing to do with you all in the tanks."

"That's all right, Corporal. I'll caution them for you."

"Sir, we're losing a lot of vehicles in through here," the Corporal says, as though he owned the trucking company, "cause of the way these men drive."

"Corporal? I said: I'll take care of this."

"But sir," the corporal says. I can see he doesn't understand about captains and corporals yet.

"You fresh over here, Corporal?" the Captain asks.

"Yessir. Come over last month."

"You see these bars, Corporal?"

"Yessir."

"Good. Then I'll take care of this while you take off."

The corporal looks angry and confused. He doesn't understand it: he thought he was doing the right thing cautioning the driver of this here weapons carrier. "Okay, sir, I'll leave them to you."

"You did your job, Corporal. You've done all you could. And don't worry: I'll caution them."

"All right, Captain." He hesitates, as though he has thought of something. But he thinks better of it and says, "All right, Captain, I'll leave them to you, then." He steps back, salutes, about turns and walks away. I can tell from the way he holds himself that he disapproves.

"Mayhew," the Captain introduces himself. "I saw the Battalion's number on the carrier here. You doing all right?"

"Yes, sir," I say. I note the Captain stands with most of his weight on his left leg. "But we're in Service Company, sir."

"Doesn't matter. Good to see you," he says.

"He been up twice as loader, sir," Rutherford ventures. He shifts the machinepistol in his lap, places the butt of the wire stock on the metal floor between his feet, the muzzle pointing straight toward the sky above the canvas roof.

"Schmeisser?" the Captain asks. "I know that fuck. Used to be with 6th Armored until I got nicked in the thigh south of Bastogne about thirty miles. I remember you guys from then. You were up at Tillet, weren't you?"

"Yes, sir," Rutherford says. "Coldest time I ever saw."

"Where you from?" The Captain shifts a little of his weight to his right leg as though he is testing to see if it can hold any more weight than it did the last time he tested.

"Kay See," Rutherford says. "Kansas City, that is, sir."

"I'm from Chicago," I tell him. "Thanks for helping us out here, sir."

"No problem. Problem is, you get a little behind the line and everyone has their own problems."

"You're from the midwest, sir?" I ask.

"Wisconsin. Madison, Wisconsin. And can't wait to go the hell back there. Listen. You guys ought to get on. And hold it down in these towns. MPs don't have a whole hell of a lot to do, you know. Small town cops: they'll flag anyone down. No sense of humor."

"We'll do that, sir," I tell him.

He steps back from the weapons carrier and says, "Take it easy, now."

"Yes, sir," we both say. Rutherford turns to look back and wave as I drive away.

"Decent officer," Rutherford says as he turns back. "Nice of him to get that fucking MP off of us."

"He's right about the speeding, though. You know the *po*lice, as the Corporal said."

"I know all right," Rutherford says, as though he spent every night before the war speeding through Kansas City in an eight cylinder Packard, sirens screaming in his wake. "Except that, out in Kansas City, they called the 'pleece'."

"He's got his job to do," I say.

Rutherford lifts his precious MP-40, runs his hand over the receiver and says, "Sure he does. But why the hell you think he choose us to do it on?"

"Why else?" I ask him. Rutherford nods and nods, lifts his machinepistol onto his lap. He shifts the muzzle away from my right knee when I remind him.

By six o'clock the dark is perfect and we have passed across Belgium and are in Luxembourg. I cannot see much beyond the faint yellow spread of the headlights' beams, but neither the Germans nor the Allies seem to have inflicted much damage on the towns and villages through which we drive. Yet though they are undamaged, the towns and villages seem deserted. Beside the road between two villages I stop the weapons carrier, dismount and walk into the woods. "Weak kidneys?" Rutherford calls after me. I nod and wave and go on into the woods. I unbutton my jacket and take out the pieces of Willy Thorn's file. I drop them and mash them into the ground with my boot, scrape mud and dead leaves over them with the sole, and shift bits of broken tree limbs on top of the mud and dead leaves. When I return to the weapons carrier Rutherford is standing by the side of the road urinating onto the grass at the verge. "Long way to go to take a piss," he says.

We drive on through Wemperhardt close to the Belgian border, and on south through Diekirch, Ettelbrück and Mersch, where we park at the curb in a silent main street to boil water for coffee. Rutherford rummages under the tarpaulin in the back of the weapons carrier.

"Glad Sergeant Symms put in all these rations," he says. "Wonder where we'd be without them?"

I am about to tell him that we would in cold and hungry, but as I am about to speak, I hear the sound of engines approaching through the dark streets of Mersch.

"What this here coming?" Rutherford asks from the back of the weapons carrier, as though he expects me to know.

"Who knows? But at least they're not German engines. I think."

"You think? What the hell's that mean?" He is joking, but he is concerned, too, and he is right to be so: who knows who may be driving around in the night here in north central Luxembourg?

"Maybe we ought to. . ," I say as the vehicles' lights glimmer against the walls of buildings a block behind us and around a corner. Before I can finish speaking, I hear Rutherford's machinepistol knock against metal. Something touches my shoulder. I put my hand on it: it is the smooth wooden stock of one of the two Thompson submachineguns Sergeant

Symms included in our Table of Equipment. I grip the stock and lay the weapon across my lap, feel in front of the grip and triggerguard. The magazine Rutherford has inserted up into the bottom of the breech is oily to the touch. I heft the submachinegun: I can tell from the weight that the magazine is full. I pull back the lever on the righthand side of the receiver, let it snap forward and put the weapon on safe.

"Seem like three vehicles," Rutherford says. I glance back. The hooded headlights of the vehicles glow yellow in the dark in the side street behind us, shifting this way and that as they approach. I think Rutherford is right: three vehicles. But who are they? And why are they travelling off the main road through this rural town in the dark?

The vehicles turn the corner into the street in which we have parked. The first one is a Jeep. A command car, a vehicle similar to our weapons carrier, follows it, and a second Jeep follows the command car. In the glow of their headlights I see Rutherford's helmeted head and shoulders in profile. The first Jeep drives past us. A sergeant holding a submachinegun like the one in my lap sits to the right of the driver. In the back of the Jeep a third man sits beside a pintle-mounted .30 caliber machinegun. As the Jeep passes, the driver of the command car honks and brakes. The lead and trailing Jeeps halt. In the headlights of the command car, the brass shells in the belt of ammunition swinging from the breech of the machinegun in the lead Jeep glitter. The command car halts beside us. I note a red rectangle painted on the right-front corner of the command car's hood. Two white stars are painted on the red field.

As Rutherford might say, Uh-oh.

A strong voice speaks from the rear seat of the command car: "What outfit?"

"Service Company of the Seven Hundred and Sixty First Tank Battalion travelling on orders to Nancy to obtain supplies, sir." I'm pretty good at getting out this kind of long, factual answer with a single breath.

"Seven Sixty First? What are you doing out here in the middle of the night?" It is only seven o'clock, but I am not going to correct a Major-General.

"Sir, we drove down from beyond Geilenkirchen, northeast of Aachen, starting this afternoon and we were going to stay here for the night."

"Why here?"

"Sir, we have no, ah, orders to stay anywhere along the way."

A silence. Someone in the back of the command car whispers. An aide proffering advice.

"No need for you men to stay out here. Follow me." I note he does not say, 'Follow us.' I also note he does not give us a choice. The driver of the command car honks his horn twice and the lead Jeep gets under way, the glittering brass of the shells in the belt of ammunition fed into the breech of the machinegun swinging beside the pale face of the man sitting in the back seat beside the gun. The command car moves forward. The trailing Jeep waits while I start the engine and get the weapons carrier moving. I fall into convoy twenty-five yards behind the command car. The trailing Jeep follows. I reach out of the cab and adjust the mirror so that the following Jeep's headlights do not shine in my eyes.

Rutherford slides from the bed of the weapons carrier and sits down in the seat to my right. "What the hell?" he asks.

"I don't know," I say. "But he's a Major-General: we can't tell him we'd rather camp out here instead of following him."

"Sure. But where we going, that's what I want to know."

So do I, but I don't know and it is useless to worry about it. The General leads, and we follow.

We drive on, back to the main road, and turn south. At least we are heading in the right direction. We proceed through the night at a precise forty miles an hour, Rutherford, I and our weapons carrier herded between the General's command car and the Jeep following.

"I ain't sure I like this," Rutherford says, as though he has a choice. He is holding his machinepistol across his knees again, and once again the muzzle is pointed at my right knee. I take my right hand from the wheel and push the muzzle forward. "Sorry about that," Rutherford says.

"I'll be the sorry one if you shoot my leg off. How would you explain that to the General?"

"Tell him it's just these fucking German weapons don't work right." In the faint glow from the instrument panel I see Rutherford grinning. But he shifts the weapon and places the butt of the frame stock between his boots.

"Nothing going to happen," Rutherford says. Before he was worried about where we were heading: now he is optimistic. "We got orders signed by the Colonel."

"Right," I say. "I just don't want to have to deal with a General this time of night."

"That's all? Hell, General nothing compared to, say, the Colonel. Or the First Sergeant. First Sergeant Reardon's the man to worry about."

"He's all right. Strict, by the book, all that. But he's all right."

"I know he all right. I just worry I might get on the wrong side of him."

"My advice is: don't."

"I try real hard, ever since the first time I saw him in Texas. He's the wrong man to mess with. You can get around the Colonel a little if you stand up straight and explain everything away. Colonel just says, 'Uh-huh' like he does, even though he knows you telling him a story. First Sergeant's another matter. You try to explain away anything to the First Sergeant and you be in shit right up to your neck."

"And higher," I say, thinking of Willy Thorn. On the other hand, Thorn could not have explained away what he had done even to the most gullible man in the Seven Six One. He could not get around his crime: the high wall in front of him ran left and right to the horizons.

"Well," Rutherford says, "I guess we'll see what the hell going to happen now. I mean, this here General can't do anything but look over our orders and send us on. What else could he do?"

"Nothing," I say. Rutherford nods as I reassure him. But though I am sure the General can do nothing, I know he can do anything he wants.

We drive on for half an hour. I see a sign that points the way to Luxembourg City ten kilometers to the south. Maybe, I think, the General is holding out in Luxembourg City until he gets orders from a Lieutenant-General to move on up.

Rutherford has noted the sign. "Going to the city, you think?" he asks.

"Who knows?" I say, and as I say it the lead Jeep and then the command car turn left. We follow, our headlights focussed on the back of the command car. Half a mile on the lead Jeep and the command car turn right onto a dirt track. The trailing Jeep follows us onto the dirt track. Through the trees on either side of the track I see the dim humped shapes of Shermans, tank destroyers, trucks. We pass on. Military police loiter here and there along the road, waving the General's small convoy on, saluting the General's command car as it passes and glancing at us. One MP salutes the General's flag, glances at us, does a double take and glances at us again. But we sweep on, travelling under the General's protection.

The lead Jeep and the command car turn right off the track, edge in among the trees, pass through a hedge and drive into the field beyond. We follow the command car as it bounces across the uneven ground, the headlights of the trailing Jeep jerking up and down behind us.

"We here yet?" Rutherford asks.

"Looks like it," I say. "See the tents?" Ahead, at the far edge of the field, I see the dim outline of pitched tents. They are not the small tents infantrymen form from two shelter halves. These are commodious: they are a General's tents, and this is the General's Headquarters.

The lead and trailing Jeeps wheel out of the convoy and drive around the tents. The General's command car halts in front of the largest tent. As two men get out of the back of the command car, I halt the weapons carrier and turn off the engine. Rutherford and I are standing at attention when the two dark shapes approach.

"No need for you men to sleep out in the cold," the General says. I cannot see his face. He wears a helmet and a plain soldier's overcoat without insignia on the shoulders. "You'll spend the night here and go on tomorrow morning." He asks for our names and we tell him.

"Would you like to see our orders, General?" I ask.

"What for?" he asks me. He sounds puzzled.

"I just thought the General might like to see our orders, sir."

"I don't doubt your word, soldier," the General says. He sounds offended, as though he thinks I have doubted his.

"Thank you, sir," I say.

"Paul," the General says to the man standing beside him. "See these men are fed out of the mess. Have Sergeant Milton feed them what the cooks eat. And find them a place to sleep. What time you men want to head out in the morning?"

"Early as possible, sir," I tell him. "We're supposed to get down to Nancy and pick up periscope blocks and radio parts."

"Couldn't find them up where you were?"

"Apparently not, sir," I tell him. "Our First Sergeant checked and couldn't find them."

"What's your First Sergeant's name, men?"

"Reardon, sir. First Sergeant William S. Reardon."

"First Sergeant Reardon? What's the First Sergeant doing out of the infantry?" I note that the General, like everyone else, calls the First Sergeant First Sergeant.

"Sir, does the General know the First Sergeant?"

"I was with the 369th Infantry in the first war. You know, Johnson and Roberts?"

"Sir?" I say.

"You don't know about Johnson and Roberts? They were in my company. First Sergeant Reardon was a corporal then. They were his men. You don't know about them?"

"No, sir."

"Humph. I'm going to write First Sergeant Reardon a letter tonight and you're going to take it to him. He's not keeping up with your education. But, ah, don't tell him I said that. I don't want to have him give me one of his looks."

"Yes, sir."

"Then after the war I did a year and a half with the Twenty-Fourth Infantry. First Sergeant Reardon was with them too. And now he's in tanks?"

"Yes, sir," I say, recalling the sound of the shovel in the First Sergeant's hands scraping across the floor of Big Sam's fighting compartment as the First Sergeant scraped up what the incinerating fire had left of Moses Smith, Big Sam's loader.

"Keep you moving, does he?" In the faint starlight I can see the General's teeth: he is grinning.

"Yes, *sir,*" Rutherford says.

The General laughs and says to his aide, "Hear that, Paul?" and to us, "First Sergeant's about as good as there is. Kept me out of a lot of trouble in France in '18. And in the Twenty-Fourth. He knows what to do. And let me tell you: you can rely on his judgment." I think of the First Sergeant waiting in front of Service Company's formation for us to come on up with Willy Thorn. "I expect your officers think pretty highly of him?"

"Yes, sir," I say, "They do." I recall the Colonel standing up in the back of the Headquarters halftrack saying, 'Uh-huh' again and again as the First Sergeant explained about the stay behind sniper who killed Willy Thorn with a single shot.

"Except he doesn't seem to have told you much about the history. You sure you don't know about Johnson and Roberts?"

"I'm afraid not, sir," I say. I feel as though I have let the General down.

"I'll write him an order about that. Paul," he says to his aide. "You remind me to write the First Sergeant an order before these men leave tomorrow morning."

"Yes, sir," Paul says.

"We had some problems in fourteen eighteen. Officers lacked training and were reluctant to order their men. Lot of the men were illiterate, and the Army's slow to change. But it's changing now, and by the time the next war starts, everything will be different."

The *next* war? I think. But I say, "I hope so, sir." But in a way I will regret the disappearance of the Seven Six One's individuality: we have made our reputation, and if the General is right, that reputation will become a memory rather than a foundation.

"You men thinking about staying in the Army?" The General likes to think ahead: even now he is thinking about the post-war Army.

"Sir," I say, "I think I will finish college."

"That's the right thing to do," the General says. "But think about it later:

the Army needs educated men."

"I'll think about it, sir." But I know I won't.

"Good. All right, Paul: get Sergeant Milton to feed these men and bed them down. Then come back."

"Yes, sir," the aide says.

"Sir," I say, "may we know the General's name?"

"Oh, I'm sorry," the General says. "Hillman, Arthur Kendall."

"Thank you, sir."

"The Seven Sixty First has been doing a lot of good work," he tells us.

"Thank you, sir," Rutherford says.

"More than a lot. I read about your first action. It's strange you started out down there, though. I wonder what First Sergeant Reardon thought of it."

"Sir?"

"First Sergeant Reardon and I were south of there, in Champagne and the Vosges, and then in the Oise-Aisne offensive, in the summer of 1918. I wonder if he thinks it's odd to fight over the same ground again."

"I think he's does, sir," I say.

"Let's just hope we don't have to do it a third time," the General says. "Paul, take care of these men." He turns and walks to the tent. As he opens the tent flap a faint gleam from a lantern within illuminates his face. The hair beneath the rim of his helmet is gray. He is more than six feet tall, and skinny. I wonder if he has been ill. His face is narrow and lined, as though he has been worrying since 1917. He glances back at us. His eyes are dark, set deep in the orbits in his skull. Whatever made him turn to look at us, he dismisses the thought with a nod, steps inside the tent and lets the tent flap fall behind him.

"General's been around a long time," Paul says.

"Yes, sir. Ah, we didn't get your name, sir."

"Major Paul Cleaves. I'm the General's aide and dogrobber. And I'll tell you: as he said, he's been following the Seven Six One's movements with a lot of interest. And the 969th Field Artillery. And the 614th Tank Destroyers."

"Yes, sir."

"I'm in artillery myself, and I'll say this for the 969th: you can't ask for better than what they did in December and January."

"Thank you, sir," I say on behalf of the officers and men of the 969th Field Artillery Battalion.

"Come this way," Major Cleaves says. He walks in front of us past the tent into which the General disappeared, past the next tent and the next.

He opens the flap of the fourth tent and steps inside. As he does so, he says, "General's mess." We follow him in.

A sergeant with brown hair and a wide pale face with an apron over his uniform says, "Evening, Major." He is setting out silver and napkins at four six man tables. From behind a canvas wall behind him comes kitchen clatter and the smell of cooking food.

"Hey, Harry. How's it going? Got some customers for you. Men, this is Sergeant Milton. Harry, General wants these two fed—your rations, nor ours—and bedded down for the night. You think you can find a place for them to sleep tonight?"

"Right here, if they don't mind getting up early. Like you probably know," he tells us, looking beyond the Major, "cooks get up before everybody else. If they want to sleep in later than five I could put them with Sergeant Stafford in communications."

"Men?" the Major asks me and Rutherford.

"Here's fine, sir. We have to get out early. Thanks for the help," I tell the Sergeant.

"No problem," he says, as though visitors as distinguished as we pass through the General's mess every day.

"What's for chow, Harry?" the Major asks.

"Chow, Major?" the cook says. "In the *General's mess* this evening, we'll be serving the usual rations for the officers. We, on the other hand, have the following dishes, Major: apple pie—got the apples from that farm down the lane there, lady had them in a storage bin there in the cellar—roast beef, vegetable soup, fresh beans I found at the same farm—and mashed potatoes."

"You're going to eat the dishes in that order, Harry?" Major Cleaves asks. He looks a little sour, as though he's not going to eat any of it.

"'Course not, Major. That's what there is, not the way we're going to eat it."

"Better bring the General's rations to operations on a tray. Then feed everybody else and these men all at the same time."

"Uh, these are enlisted men," Harry says. I wonder if this is what he means.

"You're kidding me," Major Cleaves says. "I thought they were field grade officers travelling incognito. General said to feed them in his mess and bed them down. You want to check back with the General?"

"No, sir. Of course not. It's just that some of the officers might wonder, these men being enlisted and all. Besides, there's the different menus. You want them to eat rations like the General's, or what I got?"

"The General said they were to eat what you're eating."

Harry says, "Whatever the General says is okay by me, sir."

"By me too," Major Cleaves says. "All right then," he says, "you two stay here until dinner. I'll be back. Your uniforms are all right. The General isn't formal." I recall the private soldier's overcoat the General was wearing. "Everybody here just digs in, and when dinner's over and Harry and his crew have cleared away you can bunk in here. Harry, they'll need blankets."

Harry nods but I say, "Sir, we brought sleeping bags with us. We don't need to trouble you or the Sergeant."

"Good," the Major says. "Then you're all set. You all set, Harry?"

"Yes, sir."

"Good. Then everybody's set. I'll be back in ten minutes. I'll be here before the other officers get here." I hope the Major is not late: I'm not very good at introducing myself to strange officers.

"Thank you, sir."

"No problem. General's orders. That's what we're all here for: General's orders." Major Cleaves turns and walks out.

"You guys want a drink before dinner?"

"A drink, Sergeant?"

"In here, you call me Harry. We got wine, scotch, bourbon and gin. If you want a drink, though, you'd better come back in the kitchen. Officers get cranky if they see anybody standing around drinking. General doesn't permit any drinking unless there's a lull. And me and the General haven't had a lull since New Guinea two years ago."

"I'd like a bourbon, Sergeant," Rutherford says. "I ain't had any bourbon since we left New York last October."

"Jimmy!" the Sergeant calls through the canvas that separates the kitchen from the General's mess.

"I'm slicing the beef, Harry," a voice from the kitchen says.

"Oh, yeah? Well, when you're finished slicing the beef, get the bourbon out—you want bourbon?" he asks me. I nod. "—and make a couple highballs for these men here. And slice the beef thin, Jimmy. You hear me?"

"Slice the beef, mix the drinks."

"Jimmy, you know that transfer to a tank company you were offered?"

"I'm slicing," Jimmy says. "I'm slicing. And mixing drinks."

"You guys go on through to the kitchen," Harry says. "Jimmy'll make you whatever you want."

I pass through the canvas wall that separates the mess from the kitchen.

Right behind me, Rutherford mutters, "Bourbon. I should have been a general. But what this about us eating the cooks' food?" I shrug: we will eat what we are served.

"How's it going?" a private says. He wears an apron like Sergeant Harry's. The private is nineteen or twenty, blond and thin. He looks like he does not eat enough of the General's food. He holds a fork and a carving knife. The roast he is carving does not seem enough for twenty-six men. "Tomasino," he says.

"Tomasino?" Rutherford asks.

"Me. I am. Tomasino. Jimmy Tomasino. Boston."

"Kansas City," Rutherford says and gives Jimmy our names. He nods at me. "Chicago," he says. Rutherford's eyes flick this way and that. Neither Rutherford nor I have seen a place as clean as this since October of last year. Or perhaps Rutherford is trying to figure out where they keep the bourbon.

"He's Fredericks," Tomasino says. "Looking into the oven. Weldon Fredericks. Midwest, huh? Fredericks here's from Canton, Ohio. Wherever in the hell that is."

"Wherever the hell it is," Fredericks says, peering into the oven, "it's better than here. Pie's about done. I think."

"You think? I thought you took the cooks' course on pastry?"

"Fell asleep during the three hours on crusts," Fredericks says. He lifts a steaming pie out of the oven, sets it on top of the oven. I expect him to reach back into the oven for more pies, but he does not. He looks over his shoulder at us watching Jimmy slice the beef and says, "Apple. Seemed a little green to me, but Harry said they'd be all right. Hope we don't get complaints."

"Am I complaining?" Jimmy asks. "It's eat this or the usual rations: Menus 1, 2, or 3. So no complaints." I glance around: cases of rations are stacked in the corners.

"Smells good," I say.

"It is," Fredericks says. "Sergeant Harry knows cooking. I know carving, and vegetables. And Fredericks here does the bread and pies, even if he did fall asleep during crusts."

From beyond the canvas curtain Sergeant Harry says, "You two working in there, or talking? We're going to have twenty-four hungry officers in here in a couple of minutes. And remember: hungry officers are cranky officers."

"I'm slicing," Jimmy says.

"And I'm doing the pie," Fredericks says.

"So you're slicing and doing. You got to get the officers' dinner ready yet. Get to work, you two. Another thing: you get those guys the drinks I told you to get them?"

"Right now," Jimmy says. Without lowering his voice he says, "You guys mind? Over there in the box next to the sink: bottles. Take what you want."

"Thanks," I say.

"Glasses in the box beside there," Jimmy says. "Water in the pitcher. If you want water. Sorry we don't have ice: this isn't the Biltmore."

"What the hell you mean this isn't the Biltmore?" Sergeant Harry says from the beyond the canvas divider.

"Sorry, sir," Jimmy says.

"You better be. You finished screwing around back there? I figure five minutes until the officers show." I glance at my watch: 7:55pm. Late for dinner, but then the General looked as though he worked himself and his staff hard.

Jimmy finishes carving the beef and sets it on top of the oven beside the pie. Rutherford glances at me as we walk across to the box. I know what he's thinking: how these guys going to feed the General and twenty-three officers and us with a medium roast and one pie and a mess of vegetables? I shrug and open the box. I reach in and lift out the plump, familiar bottle of bourbon. It is American, and annoying: on the label, two gentlemen in powdered wigs are conversing on the lawn before a mansion. A servant approaches across the lawn carrying a tray with a bottle and two glasses on the tray.

"Shit," Rutherford whispers. "That shit? I'll drink water before I'll drink that shit. Or go out and get some that gin the First Sergeant sending down to this First Sergeant in Nancy." It seems that even in Kansas City they don't drink this brand of bourbon.

"This is war." I hold up the bottle, looking from Rutherford's offended face to the offensive label.

"I know it's fucking war," Rutherford whispers. "What you think I'm doing here, touring fucking Europe? Gimme some of that scotch there."

"I agree." I replace the bourbon, lift out a bottle of scotch. On the label, a man in a kilt holds a broadsword. I take two glasses from the adjacent metal box, pour two slugs, hand a glass to Rutherford and replace the bottle.

"Water," Rutherford says. He pours water into his glass and looks at me, holding the pitcher up. I shake my head.

"Hard man," he says. "Me, I'm not so straight about scotch."

"Whatever," I tell him.

"You guys find what you want?" Jimmy asks. Beyond him Weldon Fredericks, the pastry specialist, is opening a case of rations. I see it is our old favorite, Menu No. 2.

"We're set," Rutherford tells Jimmy.

"Doing fine," I say, sipping at the bitter whiskey.

"Something I don't get," Rutherford says. Jimmy stops carving and looks at us. "How you going to feed all these here officers on what you got here?"

"You mean this roast?"

"And the one pie," Rutherford says. "And those little saucepans of beans and mashed potatoes."

"You don't get it?" Jimmy asks. "Sure. You don't get it."

"Fill 'em in, Jimmy." Sergeant Harry says from beyond the canvas.

"This roast is for us. The officers get the rations. General's orders. Officers eat the same rations as the men in the field."

"No shit?" Rutherford asks.

"Absolutely not," Jimmy says. "He doesn't care what we eat, though. So we eat the roast, and the beans and the pie."

"The officers don't care?"

Jimmy stops carving and looks at us. Weldon looks up from the box of rations. "Well. . . ," Jimmy begins.

From beyond the canvas divider Sergeant Harry says, "You guys saw the General, didn't you?"

I recall General Hillman's narrow seamed face and sunken eyes beneath his high forehead and grey hair. "For a minute," I call through the divider.

"Then you know all you need to about the General," Sergeant Harry says. Jimmy and Weldon nod. Jimmy is cleaning the carving knife and Weldon is lifting packaged rations out of the case he has opened.

"Harry," Weldon says to the canvas divider. "You want to take the General's ration over?"

"I'm coming," Sergeant Harry says. Then he says: "Major Cleaves?"

"I came over to tell you," Major Cleaves says beyond the divider, "Don't bring the General's rations to operations. He's going to mess in here tonight. He wants to eat with those men from the Seven Six One."

"Maybe he'll take a drink," Sergeant Harry says, as though he knows the General will not.

"You can try, Harry. But you know how it is."

"I know," Sergeant Harry says. I hear men—officers—entering the mess.

We finish our drinks and go into the mess and sit down to eat with the General at the General's table. It is cold and all the officers wear their overcoats: I am surprised Sergeant Harry does not have a heater going in the General's mess. But the General seems not to notice the cold, and so his officers seem not to notice it either.

The General and his officers eat the rations we have eaten since November, although the ambience is different: in the General's mess the rations are served by Harry, Jimmy and Weldon and are eaten off plates. Rutherford and I eat roast beef, beans and mashed potatoes. The General glances at our plates and says, "Looks good," but he does not look wistful, and he eats his portion of Menu No. 2 as though it is real food. While he eats, he chats with us about the Seven Six One. As we speak, I hear the distant hum of aircraft engines high in the dark night sky. The British, I think, heading east, as they have for almost six years, to burn cities and kill more people in a single night than the General's corps will kill in a month of fighting.

The faces of the other officers at our table, and at the other tables in the mess, are blank and incurious, or curious but stealthy. I suppose they wonder what we're doing here instead of out behind the kitchen. But the General has invited us to dine with him, and they're not about to get up and leave. Or perhaps our shoulder patch, the roaring panther's head, makes them more liberal about their dinner companions: perhaps they see the patch and know what it means.

The General asks us about road movement of a tank battalion, tank tactics in support of infantry and the quality of the enemy's defenses. I think of the Seven Six One's vehicles stalled beside the road, of the disastrous tactics we learned at Camp Hood, and of the JagdPanther that shot down Big Sam and Bayou Queen this morning. We try to answer the General's probing questions, but I feel like a new boy at the Command and General Staff School at Fort Leavenworth: at sea and on watch twenty-five hours out of twenty-four. The General nods and listens when we speak, squeezing what he can from our comments. I know he understands that we see events from the modest vantage of a maintenance halftrack; but I suspect that he wants to find out everything he can about what his new corps will face on the day it goes up against the Germans. The General asks me what the most important thing is. He sounds as though he is questioning a class of officers at the Infantry School at Fort Benning. I grope for an answer as I think of the Colonel who rules the Seven Six One, of First Sergeant Reardon looking out from beneath his infantryman's campaign hat, and of Sam Taylor and his crew dying in the exploding fire inside Big Sam.

I say: "To keep moving, General. Right now the Germans are doing the best they can to slow us down. They ambush us in places where a single vehicle bogged down will block the way."

Rutherford holds up a fork of mashed potatoes and says, "And fire."

"How do you mean, Rutherford?" the General asks.

"Keep firing," Rutherford says. "Lay rounds on them. Lay on more than you think you need and then lay on five more. The Germans are worse than crafty, and the best way to deal with them is to lay down everything you got, and do it right up front without asking no questions." Rutherford is right: our Shermans and Stuarts fire and fire, wearing out bores, keeping the ammunition trucks and halftracks grinding forward with fresh ammunition. "All that about firing and observing where the shot falls that we learned back in Texas? Here there ain't time for all that. Better to blow up a woods or a field than to take the chance there might be something lurking."

"Fire and move, then," the General says. "You hear that, gentlemen?" Cleaves and the two other officers—another major and a lieutenant colonel—sitting at our table nod. "That's the ticket: fire and move, move and fire. Keep moving."

"Yes, sir," Rutherford says.

"That's it, sir," I say, to show him I agree with the majority on the issue of fire and movement.

"What about German tanks?" the Lieutenant Colonel asks. He is a cavalry officer.

"Their tanks aren't very sound mechanically, sir," I say. "I went into one of their Tigers in January. Complicated machine: the one I looked at was lost because something in the powertrain went. Engines hatches were open, crew had been trying to get it going. The Sherman is more reliable."

"But," Rutherford says. He is cutting the beef on his plate. "Their armor thicker, and they guns bigger. Much bigger. Specially on them self-propelled guns. Like that fucking Hunting Panther this morning," Rutherford says to me. He glances at the General, realizes what he has said, and says, "I beg your pardon, General."

"No," the General says. "I've seen a picture of the JagdPanther. And read reports about it. You're right: it's a fucking menace."

"One thing, though," Rutherford says. "They don't seem to have that many of them."

"How do you handle them?" the Lieutenant Colonel from the cavalry asks, as though the Hunting Panther is just another tactical problem. The major sitting beside him doesn't look quite so sure.

"Go around," I say. "Chase them off, pound them with artillery. If you get in front of the muzzle of that twenty foot barrel they will cut you up. The Sherman doesn't have the armor or the gun to stand up against them." I recall the First Sergeant telling Willy Thorn to stand up against it. The proportions of threat and defense were the same: the First Sergeant's revolver was to Willy Thorn's chest as the eighty-eight millimeter gun is to the Sherman's frontal armor.

"And pass out as many HVAP rounds as you can find," Rutherford says.

"That's reserved for tank destroyer battalions," the Lieutenant Colonel says. But the major beside him nods as though we have told him at least one thing he knows is right.

"High Velocity Armor Piercing do a job easy on the Mark Four and on bunkers and such," Rutherford says. "And it can pierce the Panther's frontal armor if you're close enough. Regular armor piercing coming out the tube don't do a thing. And the 75 millimeter's only good for firing smoke."

"Major Barnes, how much HVAP do we have?" the General asks.

The Major sitting beside the Lieutenant Colonel says, "More than we're supposed to have, sir. A lot more. I read the reports about the penetration of HVAP. So I, ah, arranged to get in as much as I could find."

"Arranged, Ted?" the General asks.

"Ah, yes, sir," Major Barnes says. It appears the Major is Sergeant Symms with a commission: he files the Table of Organization and Equipment and collects what he knows he's going to need.

"I better not ask," the General says. The Major nods as though he agrees that the General better not ask.

The General finishes his dinner and stands up. As he does so he places his hand on my shoulder and says to Rutherford and me, "You two stay seated." Everyone else in the mess stands up. I note that all of them have finished eating. I struggle up under the General's hand pressing down on my shoulder. Beside me, Rutherford stands too, chewing and holding his napkin in his left hand.

"Thank you for taking us in here, General," I say.

"Nothing," the General says. "If I hadn't, I'd probably get a nasty note from First Sergeant Reardon. Good to talk to you."

"Thank you, sir," I say.

The General nods and walks out of the mess. His staff follows him.

We sit down and go on with dinner. Harry, Jimmy and Weldon join us. They ask us what it is like to be in an armored battalion. We try to explain about cold, hunger, mud, noise and stench. Rutherford tries to tell them what it is like to wait to see what will happen, and then to have to act without knowledge. As Rutherford says, it is risking it all on one long roll of the dice down the green baize on the table. They sympathize, but they do not understand the uncertainty and strain. They cannot. For that matter, neither can Rutherford or I: we are in Service Company, and I have only gone in a Sherman three times as a loader, and only once did I load the gun in anger and fear, sensing what we all know: that the thick armored walls of the Sherman are not half as thick as they ought to be.

After dinner Rutherford and I help the cooks clean up the mess. Then we spread our sleeping bags on the floor of the tent, remove our boots and slide into the bags fully dressed. It is March, and somehow Europe seems colder and more damp than any Chicago March I recall. Sergeant Harry and his two men wrap themselves in blankets on the floor of the kitchen space behind the canvas divider. They do not speak. I can understand it: they are going to get up at five in the morning, well before dawn, and work all day as they did today.

"General all right, ain't he?" Rutherford whispers.

"Lucky he knew First Sergeant Reardon. Strange, too."

"Not that strange," Rutherford whispers. "Army back in the twenties was small, you know. I bet most people knew most others. Now it's millions and nobody know anybody outside their unit."

"I suppose you're right."

"I'm right all right. Still, you got a point: finding a two-star who knew the First Sergeant twenty-some years ago is something."

I wonder what the First Sergeant is doing. I hope he is not lying in his sleeping bag thinking again and again of Willy Thorn standing before him in my overcoat. But I fear he is.

"Nancy tomorrow."

"Yes," I say. "Another old friend of the First Sergeant's."

"That's it," Rutherford says. "Still, we best not forget: we're outside the fence here, back in the United States of America."

"I haven't forgotten that," I tell him. "That's the last thing I'm going to forget."

Rutherford grunts to show he understands what I have said. Soon he is asleep, and soon I too sleep.

Before dawn we wake to a murmur from the kitchen and a clatter of pans and pots: Sergeant Harry and his crew are up and working by lantern light. I nudge Rutherford awake, slip out of my sleeping bag and into my boots, roll the fluffy bag up and tie it and take it to the weapons carrier behind the tent. The day is cold, the dark sky clear. Far to the southeast the horizon is grey. Dawn is coming and I hear aircraft humming this way and that through the sky. The grass is wet with dew and my boots are damp by the time I return to the rear of the mess tent. As I enter, Harry says, "Coffee? Or you want the latrine first?"

"The latrine."

"Straight out past where you parked. You'll see the sign. Officers latrine: shouldn't be anybody there this time of day."

I go out into the field, around our weapons carrier. A sign points the way. As I go I feel in my pocket for toilet paper. The latrine is deserted, for which I'm grateful. The proximity of officers makes my bowels and bladder seize up. I unbutton, urinate, defecate, use the paper, button up and head back to the mess. When I enter, Harry hands me a white enamel bowl, a towel and a bar of soap. I note that Harry has washed, shaved and combed his hair. "Water out back in the trailer with the white stripe on it. You got a razor? General's pretty strong on shaving every day. Says there'll be plenty of time later to wear beards. I'm not sure I like the sound of that part about later."

"Going day to day without washing," I tell him, "is one of the reasons for the stomach problems we get: dysentery, diarrhea, like that."

"Oh," Harry says: he is a cook, and I guess he is squeamish about intestinal ills. Behind him Rutherford appears with a cup of coffee in his hand.

"Better use the latrine now," I tell him, thinking of officers coming and going. "I'll bring your shaving gear from the carrier."

"Shaving gear?" Rutherford asks, as though he's on vacation and doesn't have to worry about shaving.

"Harry says the General likes everyone shaved every day."

"Sounds like the Colonel," Rutherford says. "Or more like the First Sergeant. All right, though. Latrine straight out that way, is it?" he asks. I nod. He hands me his coffee cup and goes out. I set Rutherford's cup down on a fold-up table beside the field stove. "Coffee," Sergeant Harry says, nodding to a pot on the stove. I pour and drink. "We'll be having breakfast soon. General gets here about six on a slow day. This is a slow day."

"When does he get here on a fast day?"

"Any time of the day or night. Sometimes we eat lunch three o'clock in the morning. The word is we're going east in a couple of days. I think we're going today. We'll be cooking all hours, day and night, then. But now we got time for breakfast before the General and his staff get here."

"We've got rations in the weapons carrier," I say. "We can stay out of your way."

"No problem. I got ten eggs yesterday down the road. And some bacon. Got fresh bread, too. General lets the officers eat fresh bread with their rations."

"Who gets the eggs?" I ask.

"Us. The three of us and you two. General doesn't permit fresh eggs for the staff. They eat reconstituted, same as the men. Worse than the men, actually," Harry says. "Most of the companies' cooks scrounge here and there, come up with something decent to eat out of the local market. War doesn't seem to have done much to farming here in France."

Harry is right: the industrial economy of Europe may have been diverted into the production of munitions, but agriculture in France seems to have continued much as it must have before the war. Except for the wastage of farm animals, French farmers do not seem to have suffered much.

Rutherford sticks his head through the tent flap. He is scowling. He beckons and I go out. Rutherford walks to the weapons carrier. When I come up to him he says, "Motherfucker ordered me out."

"Out of the latrine?"

"Yeah. Motherfucker."

"Did he have his pants up, or down, when he ordered you?"

"Ain't no fucking thing to laugh at. What I gonna do? Gotta shit, man. Can't just go squat behind some tree." He jerks a thumb over his shoulder. Dawn is near. Among the trees and in the fields men are moving in the grey light, stepping up onto tanks and down from tank destroyers, trucks, self-propelled guns, halftracks and weapons carriers. All the men I see are dressed and ready to go. It seems the General's corps follows the General's example and rises early.

"Lot of enlisted out there. They have to have an enlisted latrine somewhere around here."

"Ain't gonna do that, either. You know well as I do someone's gonna say something and then I'll start." I know what he means by 'start', and I'm pleased he has left his Schmeisser in the weapons carrier along with the Thompson submachineguns. On the other hand he has a trench knife in a scabbard on his belt.

"Morning, men," Major Cleaves says from behind me. Rutherford and I turn and salute as he comes out of the tent.

"Just this one time," Major Cleaves says as he returns our salute. "The General's trying to get us out of the habit of saluting. Come on. General's inside, ready for breakfast." He turns to go.

"Sir," I say. "I'm sorry to bother you, but Rutherford was. . . ," but I stop speaking when General Hillman steps out of the mess tent behind Major

Cleaves and says, "Ready for breakfast, men?"

"General," the Major says, "this man was about to tell me something."

"Go ahead," the General says. He puts his hands on his hips and listens to every word I say. I glance at Rutherford. He does not look aggrieved, or embarrassed. His face is the blank, smooth face characteristic of each one of us when we are outside the Seven Six One and back inside the United States of America.

"Well," Major Cleaves said, "I think. . ."

But the General takes a step forward and says, "Officer ordered you out of there, did he?" I think I see why General Hillman is a general.

"Yessir," Rutherford says.

"You explain you were here at my mess?"

"I tried to mention it, sir," Rutherford says.

"Uh-huh. Major, you stand fast with this man. Rutherford, you come with me." The General strides away, around our weapons carrier and across the grass, his boots flicking dew up into the strengthening light of dawn. Rutherford walks beside him.

"Uh-oh," Major Cleaves says. We watch as the General and Rutherford stride on toward the latrine. "Your commanding officer get angry sometimes?"

"Yes, sir. Every now and then."

"Lieutenant Colonel, is he?"

"Yes, sir."

"Generals are exponential. Two stars equals a lieutenant colonel to about the fourteenth power." Major Cleaves crosses his arms and watches the General and Rutherford approach the canvas screen around the latrine. The General says something to Rutherford. Rutherford halts thirty feet from the canvas wall behind which an unsuspecting officer squats in privacy. The General paces forward.

The General shoves the canvas flap aside and disappears inside. Major Cleaves and I watch without comment. Rutherford stands in the field, his back to us, at attention. I will remind Rutherford later that I have never seen anyone standing at attention in front of a latrine.

A voice calls from within the latrine.

"That's my General," Major Cleaves says. "Know that voice anywhere." I look at him. He is not smiling; but then he is not not smiling, either.

Rutherford passes through the flap into the latrine.

"This could take some time," Major Cleaves says. "General usually takes a glass of fruit juice before he turns out for the latrine. Doc says it's worry. General tells the Doc it's the lack of exercise. One of our on-going debates."

"Yes, sir." What else can I say? The small politics of the Seven Six One fill my horizon. What happens at division and corps is high above me.

"Here he comes," Major Cleaves says. A man slips from behind the canvas flap of the latrine. He is buckling his belt. I recognize him: he sat at one of the other tables last night in the mess. Then, his glasses were askew. Now, his glasses are askew and the right edge of his helmet liner rides below his right ear. "Oh, shit," Major Cleaves says. "Sterling," he explains, as though everyone knows about Sterling.

I don't ask him what he means. Sterling looks this way and that. His face is more pale than it ought to be and he does not seem to know what to do, where to go. He walks away to the right. He adjusts his helmet liner, turns around and walks to the left. When he turns he stumbles. "That's Sterling, all right," Major Cleaves says.

I nod, as though I have spent a lot of time dealing with Sterling.

"Two left feet," Major Cleaves explains.

Sterling disappears among the tents to our left.

"I guess he's going to give breakfast a pass. Oh, well, he can spend the time practicing about turns. Here they come."

Rutherford and the General come from behind the canvas screen around the latrine. Rutherford looks like his old, pre-insult-by-Sterling self. The General is grinning: even at this distance, fifty yards or more, I can see his teeth gleaming in his pale, narrow face.

When the General comes up, he says, "Sterling," as though the name explains everything.

"I saw," Major Cleaves says. He nods and says, "Sterling."

"Man's got a severe case of self-importance," the General says, "and not much to base it on."

"Reads and speaks German, though, General," Major Cleaves says.

"That's why he's here," the General says. "If he didn't read German I'd send him to an infantry battalion."

Cleaves raises his hands in protest and says, "No, General, not that. You have to think of the men in the infantry, sir."

"Precisely. Well, he's only a civilian. And he does read German. And now he's learned some manners." Rutherford rolls his eyes at me and nods. I'm not sure I would like to sit in the General's class on manners.

"We've got a lot to do this morning, Paul," the General says. "Let's go in."

The General goes into the mess tent. We follow him in and through the kitchen. In the mess everyone begins to stand up when the General enters, but he says, "Sit, gentlemen, sit," and they sit back down. "Don't wait for me, gentlemen. Don't have any time to waste."

We sit at the table at which we sat the night before. The same Lieutenant Colonel and the same Major are forking up reconstituted eggs, eating bread and drinking coffee. They are not happy about the reconstituted eggs. Jimmy serves the General and Major Cleaves as Sergeant Harry serves Rutherford and me fried eggs, bacon and toast from a platter. The Lieutenant Colonel glances at us and then at the powdered eggs on his plate. The General grins at him and says, "Thinking about the men's rations, Colonel?"

The Lieutenant Colonel shakes his head and says, "General, after serving with you, I'll never forget the men's rations."

"How're the bacon and eggs?" the General asks me. He is grinning. "Surprises me the stuff Sergeant Harry finds. Everywhere we stop, he finds food."

"Very good, sir."

"Paul," the General says, "you have that letter for First Sergeant Reardon?"

Major Cleaves's mouth is full of bread and reconstituted eggs. He swallows and swallows as he puts down his fork and takes an envelope from his coat pocket. Major Cleaves swallows a third time, says "Yes, sir," and hands the envelope to the General.

The General hands me the envelope and says, "I want you to give this to First Sergeant Reardon when you get back."

"Yes, sir. I will, sir."

"Good, good," the General says. He pushes his empty plate away and stands up. The officers in the mess push their plates away and stand up too. Rutherford and I get up. "All right then," the General says. "Good to meet you." Rutherford and I salute him. He salutes us and shakes hands with me, and then with Rutherford. "Say hello to the First Sergeant for me. And be sure to give him that envelope."

"Yes, sir," I say.

"All right then," the General says. "If you come this way again, come see me." The General turns and goes out of the mess. His officers follow him. Major Cleaves lags behind.

"Good to meet you," the Major says. "Like the General says: if you come by again, you've got a place to stay. Pass that on to the rest of your Battalion. And your First Sergeant. I think the General would get a boost out of seeing him. And the General can do with a boost."

"Thanks for everything, Major," I say.

"Nothing," the Major says.

"And thanks for the help out back," Rutherford says. He grins. So does the Major.

"Someday you'll have to tell me what happened in there."

"I will, sir."

"Don't worry about the Sterlings. Find people like them everywhere. Stand on their own importance. Or in his case, sit on it."

Rutherford guffaws.

"Sir," I say, "you're lucky to serve with the General."

"I think so. Strange: midwest farm boy, grows up and ends up here. Maybe it's not so strange: his grandfather was in the Iron Brigade in the Civil War."

I nod as though I know what he is talking about. I have never heard of the Iron Brigade, but I know about the Civil War.

"Whatever. I've got to go. Finish your breakfast. If there's anything more you need, ask Sergeant Harry. He pretty much runs this part of Headquarters."

"Thank you, sir," Rutherford and I say. Major Cleaves nods and leaves the mess.

When Major Cleaves is gone, Sergeant Harry, Jimmy and Weldon come from the kitchen behind the divider. Weldon carries a platter, Jimmy three plates, cutlery and napkins, the Sergeant three coffee cups and a coffee pot. The Sergeant and Jimmy sit down with us at the General's table. Jimmy and the Sergeant set three places. Weldon serves their bacon and eggs and toast.

"Pretty good here with the General," Rutherford says.

"You're not just kidding," the Sergeant says. "Treats everyone the same, so long as they do their job. If they don't, he gives them hell and expects them to do better. If they don't, he gets rid of them. Pretty hard guy, actually. If you don't do your job."

"Way it's got to be," Rutherford says. "This ain't no summer camp here."

"It'll get worse, too," Sergeant Harry says. "Once we go on up." Jimmy and Weldon look at Sergeant Harry.

"Harry was with the General in New Guinea," Weldon says.

"New Guinea?" Rutherford asks. "You mean way around the world there in the Pacific Ocean?"

"That's it," Jimmy says. "Harry and the General and Major Cleaves were all there."

"Quite a change," I say.

"You're not just kidding," Harry says. "I never seen anything like it in my life, and I don't want to see it again. Heat, rain, mud, insects, snakes and the fucking Japanese. And the mountains. You wouldn't believe the mountains. Me and the General had the gut for two months running. I thought we were both going to die. Now I'm all right, but the General's guts were fucked up for fair. That's why he's so thin. Hair was brown in 1942. Now it's grey. I wish this war was over and he could go home and take it easy. Hell, I wish it were over and we could all go home and take it easy."

"Won't be long now," I tell him. "The main thing now is to get through to the end without getting hurt bad. Or killed."

"You're not just kidding, brother," Sergeant Harry says. "I wish to Christ he'd eat some of this food I cook, though. But he won't. Says every officer in this Headquarters is going to eat the same rations as the troops. I think he'd do better if he ate better. I talked it over with the Doc and the Doc agrees with *me*, for Christ sake. I told the General that. Told him the Doc agreed with me. So did the Doc: tell the General the Doc agreed with me. Doc said: I agree with Sergeant Harry. General told us what to do." Sergeant Harry sounds aggrieved, as though he and the Doc were reasonable and the General should have listened.

"Won't last long now," Rutherford says. "Couple more months and that's it." He nods at me. "Like he say: main thing now is to get through and out the other end."

"Lot of men won't, though," Sergeant Harry says. "Gonna be more people killed. Here, and in Germany, too. And then, whatever anyone says, you don't forget the ones gone. General's son was killed in Sicily while we were out in the Pacific. I was there when Major Cleaves gave him the letter: a personal letter, from General Marshall. General read the letter, folded it up, put it in his pocket. He's never mentioned his son since, but I know it's part of what's happened to him. The most part of what's happened to him, I guess. I think he wishes he had been killed instead."

"How'd his boy die?" Rutherford asks.

"Gunner in a Sherman. They say an antitank round came right through the turret and killed him. This was before they came out with the applique armor on the turret outside the gunner's position and over the ammunition bins in the sponsons."

"Pretty hard," Rutherford says, "boy dying like that. And the General losing a son like that."

"Lot of sons being lost like that," Sergeant Harry says. He gets up and begins collecting dishes and cutlery. "Shit and perdition," he says. "All this shit and the General's getting thinner and more tense. Fucking war better end is all I can say." Jimmy and Weldon and Rutherford and I all nod and nod: what can we say to encourage him? The war will go on until it is finished. Then it will be over.

We get up and help Sergeant Harry clean up the mess. When we are finished and the mess is ready to move, Harry says, "Thanks, you guys. We can use all the help we can get."

"I guess we better take off," I say. "Sorry about the General. If there's anything we can do?"

"Come back and see us. Or rather, come up and see us. We're not going to be here this afternoon. And if you come, bring that First Sergeant of yours the General knew: do the General some good to see an old friend."

"I'll tell him," I say. But I know the First Sergeant will not come: not until the fighting is finished, or we are withdrawn. And we are not going to be withdrawn. We are going all the way to the heart of Germany, wherever that is.

"Didn't seem like Major Cleaves thought you were going any place today," Rutherford says.

"We're leaving: I know. General's getting ready for something, I can tell. He's working himself up for something. So: today's moving day. We'll be working out of a halftrack by dinnertime tonight."

Rutherford and I shake hands with Sergeant Harry, Jimmy and Weldon and go out the back of the mess tent to our weapons carrier.

"What about we give them couple bottles of this gin we got here?" Rutherford says. "Sergeant Symms put in two cases. Generous of him: I didn't know Symms was that generous."

"Neither did anybody else," I tell him. "But you're right: let's leave them some. First Sergeant would think it's right." Rutherford gets into the back of the weapons carrier and hands me two of the square bottles of Dutch gin. "Bring another," I tell him. He gets down from the weapons carrier with a third bottle and we go back into the mess tent. The General's mess men are sitting at a table drinking coffee.

"Brought you these here," Rutherford says. He sets down the bottle he has brought in. I set down the other two.

"Thanks for the dinner and the breakfast," I say. "And the place to sleep."

"Yeah," Rutherford says. "Hard to find a place to sleep down around in here."

Sergeant Harry picks up one of the bottles. "Gin," he says. "I can use all I find." Jimmy and Weldon nod and say, "Hey, thanks a lot." Jimmy and Weldon don't look like gin drinkers to me: they aren't twenty yet, and I think coffee is about as strong as they go. But Sergeant Harry nods and nods, and says, "Now I've got something to go with the Vermouth. If I'm crafty enough, I'll get the General to take a martini now and then."

"General drink gin, does he?" Rutherford asks.

"Used to. Haven't been able to find much of it lately. And when I do he says: no, not tonight."

"Maybe we ought to leave a bottle here for the General, too," I say.

Harry nods. "That's a thought. But if you could go over to operations and give it to him personally, I'd appreciate it. That way, I'll have an easier time getting him to take a taste now and then. Tell him he's got to have a belt, since you gave it to him. If you see what I mean?"

"I see," I say.

"Think he'll see us?" Rutherford asks.

"I don't see why not," Sergeant Harry says.

"Okay," I say. "We'll see you guys, then." We say good-bye a second time and leave the mess tent. We get into the weapons carrier. Rutherford drives around the mess tent and along the row of tents to operations. Officers are entering and leaving. Rutherford stops the weapons carrier in front of the tent. I climb into the back and take two bottles of gin out of the neat wooden case with the word 'Genever' burned into the white wood on all six sides. I note Sergeant Symms's box of 'trade goods' and ask Rutherford, "What about we give the General one of these souvenirs?"

"Seem like a good idea to me," Rutherford says.

I open the cardboard box. The contents smell of earth, gun oil, sweat and putrefaction. Sergeant Symms has given us a decent selection: a Luger pistol and two Walthers, rank badges, shoulder boards of silver thread, Iron Crosses, a folded red black and white nazi flag, SS collar tabs, and a cuff band from the Das Reich 2nd SS Panzer Division. In the German army, elite divisions wear bands around their sleeves a few inches above the cuff with the name of their division woven in gothic letters on the band. This cuff band has a smear of blood on it. I suppose that's only fair: we fought elements of the 2nd SS Panzer Division last fall, and they bloodied us. I take the cuffband and two bottles of gin and climb down out of the weapons carrier.

"Give him two bottles of gin and this cuff band?"

Rutherford nods and says, "Good idea."

We approach the tent. Officers are entering and leaving. I recognize one of the departing officers: Major Barnes, who sat at our table last night and this morning and who arranged for an illicit supply of HVAP to be distributed to the General's Shermans.

"Major Barnes?" I ask.

"How's it going? Anything I can do for you?"

"Do you think we could see the General, sir? Got a couple of things here we want to give him."

Major Barnes eyes the bottles of gin and the cuffband in my hands. "Absolutely. Gin, is it? Come on."

We follow Major Barnes into the tent. Sergeants and corporals sit in front of typewriters and radios. The General is standing behind a table with a map spread out on it. Five officers, three of them Brigadier Generals, are leaning over the table examining the map. Major Cleaves is standing behind the General. He sees us enter and whispers to the General. The General looks up, nods to us and says something to the officers bending over the map. They glance our way and go on studying the map. The General and Major Cleaves come around the table.

"What can I do for you?" the General asks.

"Sir, we'd like to leave these with you by way of thanks. I know the First Sergeant would want us to give you these." I hold out the bottles of gin and the cuffband.

"Gin, is it?"

"Dutch, sir," I say.

"I might be able to use this," the General says. "Paul, take these bottles and hang onto them." As Major Cleaves takes the bottles from me he winks and nods, as though to tell me we have done the right thing.

I hand the General the cuffband and say, "Sorry it's soiled, sir."

"Gin and a cuff band, hey? Trust First Sergeant Reardon. He take these himself?"

"I don't think so, sir." I don't tell him about Sergeant Symms' collection of military memorabilia. The General holds the cuffband up, reads the Gothic script. "'Das Reich,'" he says. "Those murderous bastards. Who took this?"

"Not us, sir," I say. "Someone in the Battalion took it, though. Last November, down in France."

"I'll keep this," the General says. "To remind me what we're about here. You know these bastards killed damn near everyone in a town in southwest France last summer?"

"I heard about that, sir."

"Well, I'm glad to have this. And I'm glad whoever wore it bled all over it. I hope he bled to death. I'm going to hang this up on the wall here behind the map table so every man who comes in here will understand what we're doing here. Many thanks. For the gin, and for this." He holds up the cuffband.

"Thank for your hospitality, sir," I say. Rutherford thanks the General, too. We salute, turn and go out of the tent. Major Cleaves follows us out, carrying the two square bottles of Dutch gin by their short necks.

"Good going," the Major says. He gestures with the bottles. "You two must be the doctor, because this is what the doctor ordered."

"We were going to leave it in the mess, Major," Rutherford says. "But Sergeant Harry said it would be better to bring it over here ourselves."

"Sergeant Harry, hey? Now maybe we can get the General to take a drink and take it a little easy. We'll remind him where this came from and mention your First Sergeant, what was his name?"

"Reardon, sir. First Sergeant William Reardon. William S. Reardon."

"Got it," the Major says.

"We ought to give you a bottle too, Major," I say.

"Yeah," Rutherford says. "That a good idea. Something else too, maybe."

"I'll sponge off the General," the Major says. But Rutherford has turned and is hustling toward the weapons carrier. He steps up into the back. In a moment he is back, a bottle of Dutch gin in his right fist, a Walther semi-automatic pistol in his left. Major Cleaves sets the two bottles of gin he is carrying on the ground at his feet. Rutherford hands the Major the third bottle of gin. "Sorry we ain't got the holster for this here," Rutherford says as he gives Major Cleaves the Walther. "But you can wear it in your belt. That's the way I do it in Kay See."

"You do? Kay See?"

"He means Kansas City," I tell the Major. "But I'll tell you, Major: he doesn't carry a Walther in his belt in Kansas City."

"I'm happy to know that," the Major says.

"More likely," I tell the Major, "it's a thirty-eight Smith & Wesson, with a gutting knife on the other side."

The Major looks at me, looks at Rutherford. When he looks back at me I wink. The Major laughs, his laughing voice rising loud enough to penetrate the olive drab walls of the operations tent behind him. "Glad you're joking," the Major says when he stops laughing. Rutherford doesn't seem to see the humor: he frowns at me as though I've slandered him. "I passed through Kansas City a couple of times on the way to Fort Leavenworth. I'd hate to think every other man was packing. Well, look, thanks." He lifts the bottle in his left hand and nods at the two beside his feet. "Now I can have a martini every time the General has two. If there's anything I can do for you, get in touch. And if there's anything we can do for you, get in touch and I'll talk to the General."

"We'll be going off now, Major," I say. "Got to get down to Nancy and get those supplies."

The Major tucks the bottle of gin under his arm, pulls back the Walther's slide an inch, checks the chamber and clip, lets the slide snap forward and sticks the Walther in his belt. He opens and closes his hand, working his fingers against his palm. "Feels tacky," he says.

"It might be the blood wasn't all wiped off, sir," I tell him. The Major looks at me, glances down at the pistol in his belt. "Just blood," I tell the Major. "It'll come off with a little water."

"Right," Major Cleaves says. "A little water." I recall holding Tom Holcomb's guts into the cavity between his breast bone and crotch as I lifted him part way out of Big Sam's driver's hatch so that First Sergeant Reardon could take half the weight of his body.

"Yes, sir," I say. "A little water. Sorry, sir. I should have said it might be bloody."

"Doesn't matter," Major Cleaves says. He pulls the Walther out of his belt and hefts it. "Shouldn't surprise me, should it? Shouldn't surprise any of us."

"We got to go," Rutherford says. He looks as though he still doesn't understand why the Major laughed when I said he carried a gun and a knife in his belt in Kansas City.

"Rutherford's right, sir: time to leave."

The Major walks with us to the weapons carrier. As I start the engine he waves the bottle of gin at us and calls out, "Good luck." I nod. Rutherford waves. I put the weapons carrier in gear and we drive away.

When we are on the main road heading down into yet another valley toward the distant spires of Luxembourg City, Rutherford says, "I don't understand why the Major laughed when you said I went out with a revolver and a knife in Kay See."

"I winked at him to tell him I was joking."

"Joking about what?"

"About you carrying a gun and a knife back in Kansas City."

"But I did," Rutherford says.

I am watching the road and I don't understand what he has told me: a convoy of two hundred and forty millimeter howitzers towed by M6 tracked prime movers is approaching. The M6 tractor weighs thirteen tons more than a Sherman. It carries ten men and ammunition for the gun. It is twenty-one and a half feet long and ten feet wide and can pull fifty thousand pounds. I take care with my driving as the convoy of massive vehicles and massive guns approaches.

"You did what?" I ask Rutherford when the prime movers and guns have passed.

"Carry a gun in Kay See. .32 Colt. And a knife from the stockyards. Everybody in Kay See carry a gun. Told the General that in the latrine when he asked about this machinepistol I carry over here," Rutherford says. "I don't see nothing funny about it," Rutherford says as I begin to laugh: Major Cleaves will have a good story to tell, until the General tells him it is not a story, but the truth. "What's so funny?" Rutherford asks. He is aggrieved that Major Cleaves thought his pistol and gutting knife were a joke, and even more aggrieved that I go on laughing now and then until we have left Luxembourg and entered France.

Nine

ON A NEAT RECTANGLE of cardboard pinned to the door of the quonset hut deep in the supply dump at Nancy is printed: Lt. Col. D. S. Hollis, Commanding Officer. Below the Colonel's name is printed: 1st/Sgt. John Pettit Burch.

Rutherford and I have had difficulty finding the First Sergeant's office. The dump covers acres of roads, woods, and fields southeast of Nancy. I have a vague recollection, from November, of the terrain: I think we passed through this area on our way east. The dump is fenced, and it is camouflaged with netting rigged up on poles sunk in the ground. Long corridors of crates and boxes stacked on top of one another, the stacks twenty feet high, lead away in all directions. Beyond the perimeter of the dump antiaircraft guns point at the sky. MPs at the gates in the perimeter fence examine the papers handed down to them by drivers and direct the tank transporters, prime moves, trucks and halftracks this way and that. The vehicles drive here and there down the lanes between the high stacks of crates, their tires and tracks grinding ruts in the damp ground and throwing up blocks of damp earth.

Below First Sergeant John Pettit Burch's name is printed, in smaller letters: "Knock And Enter."

"Whole quonset hut for the Colonel and the First Sergeant?" Rutherford asks from behind my right shoulder.

As I say, "Looks like it," a flight of three P-47 Thunderbolts pounds low over the dump.

Before I can raise my fist to knock the door opens. An elderly Lieutenant Colonel stands in the doorway. His cheeks are pink and plump. I imagine his body is the same: his long years of service have shifted his weight up from his knees and down from his shoulders. I guess he is almost sixty years old. He is the oldest man I have seen in uniform in Europe. As he turns his face from me to Rutherford his cheeks quiver and his bright blue eyes twinkle. His coat is unbuttoned and I see that he wears on his uniform jacket all the ribbons he has earned in all the years he has served. He is all dressed up and ready to go out. But where can he go on this day, in this place, in this year?

"Men?" he asks us.

"We're ordered to see First Sergeant Burch, sir."

I reach for our orders but he waves his hand as though he's seen enough paper today, steps aside and says, "Sergeant Burch's right inside, men. Go right on in and check with his clerk. He'll take care of you."

"Thank you, sir," I say. Rutherford steps aside to let the elderly Colonel pass. The Colonel nods, his cheeks quivering as he does so, and steps down from the small stoop in front of the quonset hut. He gets into a Jeep, starts the engine and drives away beneath the camouflage netting rigged up above the supply dump.

"Little early to be leaving the office, ain't it?" Rutherford asks. I glance at my watch: eleven a.m. Rutherford is right. On the other hand, Lieutenant Colonel Hollis commands this facility and he gets to make his own rules.

I step through the doorway, Rutherford right behind me. The interior of the quonset hut in divided into side-by-side offices with flimsy wooden doors opening off a central corridor. At the far end is a duplicate of the door through which we have just passed. A murmur of voices and the clatter of typewriters drifts up from the offices toward the building's semi-circular roof.

A corporal sitting with his feet swung up on a desk in the space to the right inside the doorway glances up from the newspaper he is reading, looks us over and looks down at the paper again. It is not an Army paper. I cannot read the name of the paper, but I can see that part of the name of the paper is the word 'Atlanta'. Great, I think, as I hear an ostentatious exhalation behind my right shoulder. Rutherford too has seen the word 'Atlanta'. I am sure Rutherford wishes he had brought along his .32 Colt and his gutting knife from the packing houses in Kansas City. On the other hand, maybe he doesn't: he has his Wehrmacht machinepistol slung over his shoulder and his trench knife in a scabbard on his belt.

"What you all want?" the clerk asks.

"We're ordered here to pick up supplies, Corporal. We have orders for First Sergeant Burch." Behind and to the left of the Corporal's desk is a door. On the door is a hand-lettered wooden board which reads: 1st/Sgt. J. P. Burch.

"You can give them to me," the Corporal says. "I'll see he gets them. Come back in two three hours and check to see what's been decided."

"We were ordered to hand the orders to First Sergeant Burch, Corporal," I say.

"That's it, Corporal," Rutherford says from behind my shoulder.

"Oh, yeah?" the Corporal asks. "Well, the First Sergeant don't take no orders from people just walk in here. You leave them here and I'll see he gets them."

"We also have a letter from an old friend of First Sergeant Burch's," I say.

"A letter from an old friend of First Sergeant Burch's. Seems hard to believe, but you can leave that here too, if you all really got such a letter. I'll see he gets that right along with the orders. If there's anything when you come back, I'll tell you about it." He examines his paper. His examination is ostentatious. I wonder how well he can read.

"Corporal, our First Sergeant ordered us to deliver these orders and the letter directly to your First Sergeant. I wouldn't want to have to go back and tell our First Sergeant I couldn't deliver his letter to First Sergeant Burch."

"Oh, yeah?" the Corporal asks. He looks up from his newspaper. "You all pretty demanding, ain't you? What, you don't think we got work to do around here? You think this is the Army Post Office? What the hell you think this is?"

I know Rutherford is thinking over one or two undiplomatic answers to this question, so I say, "Supply, Corporal. Services of Supply. You're the ones who keep us in beans and bullets, like the paper says. Now look: top kicker here is a friend of our First Sergeant. As I said, all we want is to deliver this letter and these orders to First Sergeant Burch."

"As you said? College boy, are you?" The Corporal shows me a mean grin full of grey teeth and begins his conspicuous examination of his hometown paper once again.

"That's it," Rutherford says. For an instant I think he is telling me and the Corporal he has had enough of the Corporal. He hitches the Schmeisser up his back, the swivels at the ends of the strap clicking. I turn to prevent Rutherford from doing what he is going to do. But he is standing with the Schmeisser slung over his shoulder, staring at the unpainted plywood wall. I realize that when he said 'That's it,' he was confirming to the Corporal that I had attended college.

But the Corporal has heard the clicking of the swivels at the ends of the Schmeisser's sling, and he thinks he hears a threat. He grits his teeth, takes his feet down off the desk, slaps the newspaper down, stands up and raises his voice to tell us what to do next. "You leave those orders here. Then get the hell out of here like I told you. And come back in two or three hours like I told you. You people come in here making demands, I don't have to put up with it." He stands behind his desk. To show us he is serious, he puts his pale clerk's hands on his hips and tries to glare. Then he says: "And don't you all be bringing weapons in here. We all got an office to run." He seems to have forgotten about the war.

Before Rutherford can say something rude, I hear the scrape of a chair's legs against the floor of the office behind the Corporal's desk. The Corporal cocks his head just as a voice inside the office says, "What are you doing now, Corporal Forrest?" The voice speaks as though the man inside the office can see that the Corporal is doing something disgraceful or useless.

Corporal Forrest turns his head and raises his voice at the door behind him. "First Sergeant I got some men here won't leave they orders."

"Goddamn you Forrest," the voice from beyond the door says. "I heard every word you said and every word they said and you're lying Forrest Goddamn you."

"First Sergeant I asked them to leave they orders and come back and they said they were supposed to give them to you. That ain't the procedure, First Sergeant."

"Goddamn you Forrest," the voice says. "Are you going to make me come out there? You know what happens when I have to come out there, don't you? As if this fucking job isn't enough, I have to put up with you Goddamn you Forrest."

I turn my head and glance at Rutherford. His eyebrows are raised and his eyes rounded. He doesn't seem to like the sound of 1st/Sgt. J. P. Burch's voice. I agree with him: the First Sergeant sounds tired, annoyed, hung over and angry. He sounds as though he will soon become furious.

Corporal Forrest is feeling around among his thoughts, trying to think what to say when the voice inside the office says, "Forrest Goddamn you I hate liars. If I have to come out there I'm going to shoot you, Forrest. I'm going to kill you and put your body—without identification, Forrest Goddamn you—in a crate and ship the crate down to North Africa. And you know what, Goddamn you Forrest? No one will care. I'll take your dog tags and your uniform and you'll be nothing but dead in a box in North Africa. You think I can't do that Forrest? I can do that. And if I have to come out there I'm going to do it Forrest Goddamn you."

"But First Sergeant," Forrest begins. He stops when he hears the distinctive snap of the slide of an automatic pistol drawn back and released.

"I'm coming out there, Goddamn you Forrest. I'm coming out there and I'm going to kill you you sonofabitch. I told you before but you wouldn't listen. Now I'm going to make you listen Forrest Goddamn you."

"Should I send them in there, First Sergeant?" Forrest asks.

"What do you think you should do?" the voice from inside the office says. "You better think fast Goddamn you. You're not a civilian, Forrest. You're supposed to be a soldier. But you're not, Forrest. You're a clerk in a uniform. You're in the Services of Supply, Goddamn you Forrest."

"I'm sending them in," Forrest calls out. He sounds as though he has made a decision to put every available man—cooks, mechanics, MPs, clerks and the lawyers from the Judge Advocate General's office—up on the line for one final push against the Waffen SS. When he turns to us I can see he is angry. He doesn't like the First Sergeant bawling him out in front of the troops. Particularly, I guess, in front of these troops.

Corporal Forrest opens his mouth to tell us to go in when the voice says, "Who are they, Forrest? Did you ask who they are? You'd better have asked who they were before you tried to make them leave their orders and that letter they have for me Forrest."

"I didn't ask, First Sergeant," Forrest calls through the wall.

"Goddamn you Forrest," the voice says. "You better ask them. If you want to live you'd better ask them."

"We're with Service Company of the Seven Hundred and Sixty-First Tank Battalion," I tell Corporal Forrest.

"They're from Service Company of the Seven Hundred and Sixty-First Tank Battalion, First Sergeant," Forrest calls out.

"Are you sure, Forrest? Did you look at their orders? Did you check? How do you know they're not Germans dressed up like American soldiers? We had a memo about that, Forrest. About Germans dressed up like Americans. The memo came in January, Forrest," the voice says.

Behind me Rutherford grunts. Forrest looks us over, shaking his head. "They're Americans, First Sergeant." He holds out his hand and I hand him our orders.

"How do you know that, Forrest?" the First Sergeant says. "Did you check their documents, Goddamn you?"

Forrest glances at our orders, hands them back to me, and says, "I've checked their orders, First Sergeant. They're Americans all right."

"How do you know their documents aren't forged, Forrest? Did you check their identification?"

"No, First Sergeant."

"Goddamn you, Forrest. I'm coming out there. With my pistol. I used this pistol when I was with the 15th Infantry in Tientsin, Forrest. And if I used it there I can use it here in Nancy. On you, Forrest."

"First Sergeant I know they're Americans," Forrest says.

"Do you, Forrest?" the First Sergeant says. His voice is low but the sound penetrates the thin wall of his office. "I know they're Americans, Forrest. I know that. But how do you know?"

"Goddamnit First Sergeant," Forrest shouts, "I can tell."

"That's about the stupidest thing you're ever said, Forrest. The stupidest. But all right, Forrest: you're a civilian and I guess I'll have to handle this. Send them in here. Now, Forest Goddamn you."

Forrest jerks his head at us, jerks it toward the door. I walk around Forrest Goddamn you's desk, Rutherford right behind me. As I pass I note that the newspaper he has been reading is the Atlanta Constitution. I knock on 1st/Sgt J. P. Burch's door.

"Enter," the voice inside the First Sergeant's office says.

I open the door and Rutherford and I step inside. Rutherford closes the door behind him. 1st/Sgt. J. P. Burch is standing behind his desk, a cocked Colt .45 pistol in his right hand, the muzzle pointed at the floor. On the front edge of the desk is a foot-long triangular block of wood with '1st/Sgt. J. P. Burch' painted on it. This is the third time I have seen his rank and name since I stood on the front stoop.

I step up in front of his desk, come to attention, salute, introduce ourselves and say, "First Sergeant Reardon ordered us to report to you, First Sergeant." As I speak I look at 1st/Sgt. J. P. Burch. Once he must have been a well set up, broad-shouldered good-looking man. Now he is worn and emaciated: his uniform is tailored, but it hangs three sizes too big on his bony frame. His skin is pale yellow and his face is thin and lined and I can see the bones in his skull beneath his thinning hair. His eyes are bright, as though he is sick with fever, and when he looks at us his eyes flick at us and away. On the sleeves of his shirt are the chevrons, rockers and the lozenge of his rank. Pinned above the lefthand pocket of his shirt is the Combat Infantryman's Badge, a musket within a wreath on a blue enamel field. He wears no other decorations.

"Well?" he says. He does not seem to recognize First Sergeant Reardon's name.

I hand 1st/Sgt. J. P. Burch our orders, the requisition, and First Sergeant Reardon's letter. 1st/Sgt. J. P. Burch takes them with his left hand, glances at them, and drops them on the desk. He raises the pistol in his right hand and presses the button behind the bottom of the triggerguard on the left side of the pistol with his left thumb. The clip in the butt of the pistol drops onto the desk in front of him.

I recall First Sergeant Reardon in Captain Knowles's Jeep yesterday morning releasing the clip from the .45 Colt he gave me to carry in my belt as we drove back to give Willy Thorn all the justice he deserved; or at least all the justice he was going to get.

1st/Sgt. J. P. Burch pulls back the pistol's slide and the round in the chamber of the pistol leaps out of the breech onto the desk. He locks the slide open. He puts the pistol down, picks up the bullet and the clip, inserts the bullet in the clip, picks up the pistol and clicks down the latch above the triggerguard on the left side of the pistol just below the slide. The slide slams forward. 1st/Sgt. J. P. Burch eases the hammer down against the firing pin with the thumb of his right hand, slides the clip into the butt of the pistol until it clicks, snaps the pistol's safety up, opens the shallow center drawer of his desk, lays the pistol inside and closes the drawer.

He picks up our orders, glances at them and hands them back to me. He glances at the requisition, detaches the last copy and hands it to me. Then he shouts, "Forrest! Get in here, Goddamn you."

Forrest knocks and opens the door. "First Sergeant?" he says. He sounds nervous. I do not turn my head but I suspect that Forrest Goddamn you is looking to see if 1st/Sgt. J. P. Burch has put his pistol away.

"Take this requisition and get it together."

Forrest steps forward and takes the requisition. He reads it and says, "I'll get Private Kingway on this right away, First Sergeant."

1st/Sgt. J. P. Burch says, "No you won't. You'll do what I told you. You'll take that requisition and get every single thing on it personally and have it back here as fast as you can, Forrest. This may not be the Cavalry, Forrest. Or the Infantry or the Artillery. I know this is the Goddamn Services of Supply Goddamn you Forrest, but even here you'll do what I tell you. You see these chevrons? And the rockers and lozenge? Now get out of here and do what I told you."

"But First Sergeant," Forrest says, "this stuff is scattered all over the dump. Periscope blocks, radio parts, medical stuff. They're all in different places. First Sergeant, it'll take all day to get this here together."

"That's right, Forrest," the 1st/Sgt. says. "All day." He sounds like a judge handing down a sentence of death by hanging. "And it's cold out there, Forrest. And damp. All of eastern France is damp this time of year. And the way is muddy, Forrest. Every foot of the way between every stack of crates is muddy. Now take that list and get out of my office and out of this building and get it all, every last thing on that list, and bring it back here. Yourself. And soon, Forrest. Soon."

"But First Sergeant, I. . ." Forrest tilts our requisition this way and that.

"Forrest Goddamn you I told you to get out of here and do what I tell you."

"But First Sergeant. . ."

1st/Sgt. J. P. Burch opens the shallow middle drawer of his desk. Forrest looks up at the sound of the drawer opening and says, "All right, First Sergeant, I'm going. I just don't know why these people can't wait their turn like everyone else." He turns toward the door.

"Wait a minute, Forrest," the First Sergeant says. "You want to know why they can't wait? I'll tell you why. Because these men, Forrest," he says, raising his voice, "are fighting this war, Forrest Goddamn you. They're fighting this war for you, Forrest, you sorry-assed draftee corporal. You're back here sucking on a Coke bottle and drinking wine and fucking the locals and getting the clap and they're up there fighting so you don't have to risk your ass, Goddamn you." The First Sergeant looks Forrest over and whispers, "Go!"

Forrest closes the door with care as he goes out, but through the thin plywood walls I hear him muttering. A drawer slams shut. 1st/Sgt. J. P. Burch nods as he hears Forrest muttering, nods again at the slam of the drawer and says, "Fucking draftee. In Tientsin, in China, we would have killed Forrest and eaten him."

"First Sergeant," I say, "Rutherford and I aren't in a tank company. We're maintenance. We're in Service Company."

"You think I don't know that?" he asks. His eyes glitter in his bony face. "Let me tell you: I know that. You think I don't know Bill Reardon? Think I think Bill Reardon would send a couple of tankers down here on a supply run? When you're short of tankers? When everyone's short of tankers? When the fucking Army can't find enough bodies to sit in all these Shermans I've got here? You think I need you to tell me to wipe snot off my upper lip?"

"No, First Sergeant." Nor, I guess, do I need to tell him his voice quavers when he shouts, or that his eyes glitter with fever and, perhaps, memory.

"But don't worry," 1st/Sgt. J. P. Burch says. "You'll get your chance. This war's going to go on long enough you'll get the chance. You won't be in Service Company forever. They'll make tankers out of you yet, because the Army can't find replacements." He points a bony finger at us and says, "And the Army can't find replacements for the Seven Six One more than it can't find replacements for other tank battalions. So pretty soon, they're going to cram the two of you into a Sherman, and then God help you both."

"He's been out a couple of times as a loader, First Sergeant," Rutherford says, gesturing at me. I recall Rutherford told General Hillman the same thing. I wish he would shut up.

"Couple of times as a loader, hey?" The First Sergeant rubs his bristly chin. "That's something, I suppose. Better than nothing, at least. But you ask Bill Reardon about tanks. He'll tell you rolling around in a Sherman and banging away from two thousand yards is nothing—you hear me? nothing," he shouts, "—compared to being an infantryman." He whispers the last word as though the reduction in volume will persuade me.

"Yes, First Sergeant."

"You bet your ass yes," he roars, as though I have disagreed. He looks from me to Rutherford to me and says, "Why're you two standing up? I thought I told you to sit down. At ease. Rest. Smoke 'em if you got 'em. And if you don't got 'em, I'll send that Goddamn Forrest out to get a couple hundred cartons of Lucky Strikes."

"Ah, yes, First Sergeant," I say as I sit down. Rutherford swings his machinepistol around in front of himself and sits in the chair beside me. He offers the First Sergeant and me a package of cigarettes. I take one. The First Sergeant waves the package away. "Keep 'em," he says. "I got plenty." He gestures at the wall behind him. "Got every damned thing you'd think anyone could use. Gasoline, bombs, trucks. Hell, you want to go home in a Sherman? I got a couple hundred Shermans here. Send you back in one if you want."

"Ah, thank you, First Sergeant."

"Don't mention it." He takes a crumpled package of cigarettes out of his breast pocket, puts one between his lips, lights it with a kitchen match and sits down. He opens the righthand drawer of the desk and takes out a German dagger with a fancy black and silver handle.

Rutherford shifts in the chair beside me: he doesn't like it when 1st/Sgt. J. P. Burch handles weapons. 1st/Sgt. J. P. Burch glances at him, picks up First Sergeant Reardon's letter, slits open the flap with the dagger, extracts First Sergeant Reardon's letter from the envelope, peers into the envelope to be sure it is empty, shoves the envelope into the righthand pocket of his shirt, and unfolds the letter.

"Lemme read this here," 1st/Sgt. J. P. Burch says, as though Rutherford and I were considering interrupting him. As he reads he says, "Uh-huh, uh-huh." Once he glances up at me and nods.

As he folds the letter and places it in the pocket of his shirt with the envelope, I say, "The First Sergeant had us bring some things down for you, First Sergeant. A case of gin and some souvenirs." I do not mention Sergeant Symms's second case of Genever.

"We had two cases gin," Rutherford says. "But we gave away six the bottles of gin from one case and a couple the souvenirs." Maybe the First Sergeant will understand.

1st/Sgt. J. P. Burch looks across the desk as though he is deciding whether to send us for court martial and a term in the stockade, and says, "You gave away my gin? That Bill Reardon sent down to me? And my souvenirs that he sent?"

"A general took us into his Headquarters for the night last night, First Sergeant," I tell him. "We gave the kitchen staff and the General and his aide some of the gin. And we gave the General and his aide each a souvenir."

"You gave a general and his aide my souvenirs that Bill Reardon sent me?" 1st/Sgt. J. P. Burch asks. His voice is full of menace. "You gave cooks my gin? Don't you know all cooks are drunkards?"

"Well, First Sergeant," I say, "the general took us in off the road into his mess. General Hillman and First Sergeant Reardon served together, and we thought we ought to give him something. On behalf of the First Sergeant."

"General Hillman," 1st/Sgt. Burch says. As he says General Hillman's name he relaxes. "I know Art Hillman. You know about Bill Reardon and Hillman's son?"

"You know the General, First Sergeant?" I ask.

"General Hillman served with Bill Reardon in the 24th," 1st/Sgt. J. P. Burch says. I consider the pre-war Army, in which an officer served with his First Sergeant. "I was at Benning then. That was years before I went to Tientsin with the 15th. And before I joined the Pineapple Army in Hawaii, where I saw all this shit begin. You know about the General's son?"

"That he was killed in Sicily?" I ask. "Yes."

"Killed in Sicily? Jesus Christ, no, I didn't know that. Killed?" 1st/Sgt. J. P. Burch seems surprised that the Germans would kill a general's son as they would any other young man. He shakes his head and says, "Jesus Christ. I didn't know. Hillman's wife died when the boy was three and Hillman and Bill Reardon brought him up together, sort of. Damnedest thing you ever saw, the three of them riding together, the kid on a pony. Bill Reardon was as close to being the boy's godfather as you could get. General Hillman and Bill Reardon brought that boy up. And now he's dead."

"Yes, First Sergeant. The General's cook said the General's son was killed in a Sherman. He was the gunner."

"Jesus Christ," 1st/Sgt. J. P. Burch says. "What a fucking mess. The kid dead. Jesus Christ Almighty." The First Sergeant looks as though he has discovered that a close friend has betrayed him. I wonder why? I cannot think why a General's son ought not to die in this war. But First Sergeant Burch disagrees: he roars and pounds his fist on the desk. "It isn't right

Goddamnit," he shouts, as though we are a distant part of a large audience. "Goddamnit all it isn't right!" he yells, his voice reaching for the last row in the balcony.

I agree with him. It isn't right. But neither he nor I can do anything about it. Like Sam Taylor and the four men in his crew and like Tommy Quineau, General Hillman's son is dead. His father grieves, and First Sergeant Reardon will grieve when he hears the boy is gone. But still: none of us can do anything about it.

"I suppose you two think I'm sentimental," 1st/Sgt. J. P. Burch says. This is an accusation, although I agree with him: he is sentimental. Who can mourn a single death among so many? Millions have died: why single out a single tank gunner? "Well," 1st/Sgt. J. P. Burch says, "I am sentimental. I get that way when I remember." 1st/Sgt. J. P. Burch is not shouting now. Perhaps he recalls that no matter how much he shouts, the General's son won't hear him. "And in this job," 1st/Sgt. J. P. Burch says, "I have a lot of time to remember. I sit and sign papers. And say hello to Colonel Hollis before he goes out to lunch and doesn't come back till ten thirty the next morning. And yell at Forrest, that useless Goddamned draftee."

"Can't do anything about the General's boy, First Sergeant," Rutherford says. "Too bad, but nothing anyone can do about it. Not you, not us, not the Lord Himself." I wonder if Rutherford can read my mind.

"Piss on that noise," 1st/Sgt. J. P. Burch says. "I know no one's going to do anything about it. No one's going to do anything about the General's kid, or any of the rest of them. But Goddamnit I don't like it. You understand that? You understand I don't like it?"

"Yes, First Sergeant," I say. What else can I say?

"You should have seen that boy up on his pony, Hillman and Reardon riding behind to make sure he was all right. Bill Reardon was as close to that boy as his own uncle. Closer, Goddamnit. And you should have seen them on the Canal, Goddamnit. I bagged a lot of them. Shelter halves and ponchos pulled up over their faces. Knew every Goddamned one of them that got shot dead or blown up. I knew Hillman when he was a Captain and his boy was seven. Jesus Christ."

"Sorry, First Sergeant," Rutherford says.

"Sorry? About what? What do you think you're here for? Think this is some fucking game? Part of what this is about is: some die and others don't. You know that? Most these draftees don't realize that, not until they're in too deep to know what the hell they're doing."

"We know that, First Sergeant."

"I hope you do, Goddamn it. Someone's got to. All the ones I know who know it are dead or sick. Everyone else is in the Services of Supply, passing out tanks, condoms, Spam and ammunition." I wonder if 1st/Sgt. J. P. Burch has been drinking. As he says, it's pretty boring sitting around signing papers and shouting at Forrest Goddamn you. Maybe he keeps a bottle in his desk and takes a drink now and then during the slow parts of the day. Say, every fifteen minutes or so.

"Okay, then," 1st/Sgt. J. P. Burch says, as though he is willing to put the General and the General's son and even the still sacks of his dead men on Guadalcanal behind him. "What are you guys down here for?"

"First Sergeant," Rutherford says, "the First Sergeant sent us down with that requisition."

"Sure. Periscope blocks. Radio parts. You guys." 1st/Sgt. J. P. Burch shakes his head. "Next you'll ask me if we got a bowling alley and a soda machine. What do you think I am? I know where every periscope block in Europe is, and I know damn well there's a enough of them up in Belgium for two armies at least. But you're down here in France. In Nancy, France. For periscope blocks."

"First Sergeant ordered us down here, First Sergeant. You know him, you know how he is: he orders, we go."

1st/Sgt. J. P. Burch gives us as sunny and as handsome a smile as he can with his bony yellow face and says, "Hasn't changed, has he? At least that's something. No one's going to change Bill Reardon." It sounds odd and unseemly to hear the contraction of the First Sergeant's name.

1st/Sgt. J. P. Burch stands up, rubs his hands together and sways as though he is going to fall. He catches himself, leans against his desk with one hand and says, "Goddamn fever. Bad as Forrest out there hanging around with his fucking newspaper."

For the first time I note that 1st/Sgt. J. P. Burch's shirt is damp with sweat in the armpits and down the sides of his chest; and now he is standing up I see dark patches on his thighs and beneath his belt cinched around his narrow waist. I think of him back in the whispering jungle on the Canal, sweating and killing Japanese and smelling them dead. And smelling himself stinking of dead Japanese. Europe is better: the stench of the dead must be worse near the Equator.

But as 1st/Sgt. J. P. Burch says: we'll get our chance, and when the war ends in Europe, I'm sure they'll ship us east to fight the Japanese. Particularly us. No doubt they believe we stand the heat better. Even those of us like myself, from windy Chicago.

"Glad you guys are in this," 1st/Sgt. J. P. Burch says. I don't know what he means. "Even if you are mechanics in Service Company. But like I said: don't worry. Even if you don't get your chance in this war, there'll be another war come along. So don't worry: you'll get your chance." He is trying to reassure us that we won't be left out. I am not encouraged: what 1st/Sgt. J. P. Burch says depresses me. I want to return to college and, as my father, who has spent his life in the Chicago Police Department and doesn't think much of criminals or the police, has suggested, make something of myself.

"But you still haven't told me why you were sent down here," 1st/Sgt. J. P. Burch says.

I shift in my seat. So does Rutherford. 1st/Sgt. J. P. Burch has asked this question before, and we answered him: what else can we say? We are here because First Sergeant Reardon ordered us to be here.

"I'll tell you why you're down here," 1st/Sgt. J. P. Burch says. He pulls the First Sergeant's letter by one corner from his pocket and waves it at us. "Bill Reardon needs some stuff, and you're going to take it to him. You two and Forrest Goddamn him and a bunch of men I got hanging around here somewhere stacking boxes and unstacking them and going into Nancy to get drunk and worse."

"First Sergeant?" I ask.

"General Marshall likes us to do business without a lot of long written orders," 1st/Sgt. J. P. Burch says. "That's what he taught everyone at the Infantry School at Benning. And I agree with him. Besides, he's Chief of Staff of the Army, and he ought to know."

"Sit on the Combined Chiefs of Staff, too," Rutherford says, as though he has a keen interest in command activities back in Washington.

"Sure," 1st/Sgt. J. P. Burch says. "But that's all something else. Talking with the squids in the Navy, talking to Congressmen. Who cares? I can't remember the last time the Navy did anything."

"Battle of Midway," Rutherford tells him. I recall the satisfaction I felt when the Japanese, who had been inscrutable, terrifying and, it seemed, invincible, lost four aircraft carriers in an afternoon.

1st/Sgt. J. P. Burch looks at Rutherford as though Rutherford has spent all his life without shoes, the mud of the bayous oozing between his splayed toes. "You call that a battle? That was 1942. June, 1942, if I remember my naval history. This is March, 1945, and you will note that the Japanese are still fighting like the little bastards they are. I remember them: their compound in Tientsin was right down the street from us. Hard little bastards. Sergeants beat the men with their fists. Hah! I'd like to see that Goddamn Forrest in the Japanese army."

But I am sure the battle of Midway was a good thing: President Roosevelt said it was. Still, I share 1st/Sgt. J. P. Burch's opinion of the Navy: if I start right now, it will be fifty years before I command a naval vessel. Still I recall reading of four mess men in round white hats manning an antiaircraft gun on some ship. It was in *Yank.* They fired at a Japanese aircraft piloted by an insane Japanese right up to the instant the Japanese pilot, not recognizing the subtle differences between Americans, crashed his stricken aircraft right into the circular steel emplacement from which they went on firing their gun right up to the instant all four of them were killed. But still: the Army is different. As 1st/Sgt. J. P. Burch says, in the Army everyone gets a chance in the end. We, for example, are getting our chance right here, and right now; and if the Seven Six One has two more casualties, I am sure we will be given what the officers, and First Sergeant Reardon, will call 'the opportunity' to move up from Service Company to one of the tank companies. It will be an offer we can reject. It will also be an offer neither I nor Rutherford will have the nerve to refuse. Not with First Sergeant Reardon looking out from under the brim of his campaign hat at us.

1st/Sgt. J. P. Burch is another matter: I'm not sure I would serve in a Sherman's crew just because 1st/Sgt. J. P. Burch suggested it would be a move up the chain of command—from mechanic to loader, say. 1st/Sgt. J. P. Burch may once have had the commanding presence of a First Sergeant; but the war in the Pacific, the fever that has racked his body and, I guess, almost thirty years in the Army, seem to have leached the hard, decisive manner out of him, leaving behind nothing but abrupt shouting. 1st/Sgt. J. P. Burch has been between the stones in the mill too long. Energy, presence, fat and muscle have been ground out of him, leaving nothing but the husk.

"Uh," I say to 1st/Sgt. J. P. Burch. "What's First Sergeant Reardon want us to do down here, then, First Sergeant?"

"You?" 1st/Sgt. J. P. Burch asks. He stares at me. "He doesn't want you to do anything except ride along with a few trucks and such up to where he's going to be. I order the stuff up for you and you go back with it. That's all. You don't have to do anything."

"Okay," I tell 1st/Sgt. J. P. Burch. I don't mind: I don't want command. I'd be happy to be the boiler orderly.

"Don't want to be in charge, do you? Well, you will be. In charge. You think I'm going to drive all the way up east of here with this stuff? By God you'd better know different. I want you to remember this: if the last officer and the last non-commissioned officer is killed, you're in charge, and you're to go on. Are you listening to me?"

I have heard this before. In a movie theater in Chicago, near the University. It was a short film about democracy in the armed forces. I still don't like to remember the part where the smooth neutral voice talked about all the officers getting killed and the men going forward. Even then I knew each officer commanded a lot of men. I also knew that if all the officers were killed, a lot of men had been killed along with them.

"I guess we can get a couple of trucks up to wherever the Battalion is," I tell 1st/Sgt. J. P. Burch.

"Good," he says. "Very good." 1st/Sgt. J. P. Burch sounds pleased. "All right then. Let's get down to this. I know I've got a little fever and I know I'm so fucking sick of this depot I could puke. But we do some serious work here. It's a shit job so long as everything's running smooth. But when someone runs out of the right stuff a lot of uncomfortable things happen. People die if they don't have the right stuff when they need it. Bill Reardon knows this. That's why he sent you down here with this letter." He holds up First Sergeant Reardon's letter and grins. When he grins a death's head of skull and teeth leaps from beneath his pale yellow skin.

When 1st/Sgt. J. P. Burch grins and shows me his skull behind his grin I understand: First Sergeant Reardon and 1st/Sgt. J. P. Burch have conspired by mail to achieve a purpose neither our Colonel, nor 1st/Sgt. Burch's commanding officer, intends, and Rutherford and I will be the instruments with which they will perform their conspiracy. I think of Ft. Leavenworth, which First Sergeant Reardon has mentioned on occasion. I do not recall him mentioning the Army prison at Leavenworth, or the bleak view of Kansas in the winter. I will have to ask Rutherford to fill me in.

"What we gone have do?" Rutherford asks. Since we arrived in 1st/Sgt. J. P. Burch's office Rutherford grammar and diction have been exemplary. Now they are deteriorating, retreating into the crabbed, careful, broken language he uses when he addresses officers and sergeants in the Seven Six One, or anyone outside it. Now he speaks as though he is addressing a foreigner and knows he must use as few words as possible.

"Nothing," 1st/Sgt. J. P. Burch says. Once again his death's head leaps out at us. "You ever been involved with a First Sergeant in charge of a supply depot in the middle of a war?"

I am about to tell him I have not when he raises his face to the curved ceiling of the quonset hut and shouts, "Wallace!"

Rutherford rolls his eyes at the ceiling, slides them toward me, raises his eyebrows until his forehead shows me six rows of wrinkles.

My face is smooth and empty. I have arranged it so, for I see 1st/Sgt. J. P. Burch's eyes darting this way and that, full of fever, cunning, anger and suspicion.

A master sergeant opens the door and steps into 1st/Sgt. J. P. Burch's office. The master sergeant is six feet tall. His uniform is immaculate and he wears a tie. He is blond and muscular, as though he has played a lot of sports and has never been injured. When he glances at us Rutherford and I stand up. "Manners," the sergeant says. "You guys sit down." We sit. "You all right, John?" he asks 1st/Sgt. J. P. Burch.

"I'm okay," 1st/Sgt. John Pettit Burch says.

"Uh-huh," Sergeant Wallace says. "Still, you look a little feverish still."

"I am, Joe," 1st/Sgt. John Pettit Burch says. "And a little hung over." He pauses, as though he is trying to figure out where he spent last night. "Joe," he says, "these men are in the Seven Six One."

"I can see that, John," Sergeant Wallace says. Sergeant Wallace smiles. "I see the shoulder patch." I recall Willy Thorn refusing to give his patch up to the knife in First Sergeant Reardon's hand. I also recall First Sergeant Reardon's back shuddering as he stood over his clerk's typewriter, his head bent, his face turned away. This office is a long way from the Seven Six One's Headquarters track.

"I served with their First Sergeant at Benning," 1st/Sgt. John Pettit Burch says, as though this will explain everything to Sergeant Wallace.

"That's good to know, John," Sergeant Wallace says. "Was that when General Marshall was attached to the 24th Infantry?"

1st/Sgt. John Pettit Burch wags a finger at Sergeant Wallace. He puts his elbows on his desk. "Seven Six One got an equipment problem, Joe. Got a letter right here from their First Sergeant. They need some punch up front. And some souped-up ammunition."

"Uh-oh," Sergeant Wallace says. "How much punch up front and how many rounds of souped-up ammunition are we talking about, John? Got a real demand for Jumbos and HVAP, John."

"What the hell does that matter?" 1st/Sgt. John Pettit Burch asks. "Whatever the demand, we have a problem here needs solving right now."

"John, John," Sergeant Wallace says. "I know Danny is pretty loose. Hell, sometimes I think the guy's going to settle in Nancy after the war. But you're talking about stuff everybody wants."

"Who Danny?" Rutherford asks. His grammar and diction may be regressing, but he is following the conversation with care.

"Lieutenant Colonel Daniel S. Hollis, our commanding officer," Sergeant Wallace says.

"Commanding officer," 1st/Sgt. John Pettit Burch says. "Couldn't command a Dump Truck Company."

"Met on the stoop," Rutherford says. "Elderly. Pink. Wobbly cheeks. Like that."

"He's all right," Sergeant Wallace says. "He just didn't make the right cuts after the first war."

"The first war," 1st/Sgt. John Pettit Burch says, as though he was there with Pershing.

"You all right, John?" Sergeant Wallace asks.

"You asked me that, Joe," 1st/Sgt. John Pettit Burch says. But he does not answer Sergeant Wallace's question.

"What's on the list this time, John?" Sergeant Wallace asks. He sounds like a reasonable man, as though he can be persuaded. He doesn't sound as though he loses many negotiations, though.

"Few things," 1st/Sgt. John Pettit Burch says.

"Uh-huh," Sergeant Wallace says. He sounds like the Colonel standing up in the back of the Headquarters track listening to First Sergeant Reardon explain about the stay behind sniper who shot Willy Thorn dead and couldn't be found by all the men in Service Company, no matter how hard they looked. "Like, what few things, John?"

"Joe, for Christ's sake. You're in charge of armor resupply. I'm not asking much. You get enough tanks and tracks and prime movers and parts and ammunition through here every day to supply an Army Corps. And the war's almost over, Joe."

"It is?" Sergeant Wallace says. "I thought it might go on some. And then there are the Japanese. And you know, John, well as I do: when it's over they'll add up the numbers in the books. I don't want them calling me up in Baltimore and asking me a lot of questions about numbers, John."

"Used to be," 1st/Sgt. John Pettit Burch says, "one sergeant asked another sergeant for a favor, the other sergeant came through."

"That's used to be, John," Sergeant Wallace says. "This is right now. Some of these machines I think you're talking about are expensive items. You're not talking about spare parts here, John."

1st/Sgt. John Pettit Burch grimaces, as though he doesn't like to have to explain to another sergeant.

"But all right, John: give me the list and I'll see. I'm not promising, now. You understand? You just show me what you're thinking about, and I'll see."

"Like I said, Joe: all this stuff they want is going up to the line. Nobody's making anything off this."

"I know, John. Nobody makes anything off anything you do."

"Or off you, Joe."

"Glad nobody making nothing," Rutherford says. "Ain't you?" he asks me.

I risk a nod.

"You want a favor, fella?" Sergeant Wallace asks Rutherford. "If you do, shut the fuck up. Danny isn't going to ask you about where something went. Neither are the auditors. They'll ask me. And John here. So shut up the fuck up while the First Sergeant and I deal with this."

"I don't know what's being asked for here," Rutherford says.

"This isn't for you guys?" Sergeant Wallace asks. "What's going on, John?" he asks 1st/Sgt. John Pettit Burch. "I thought you said this was for them."

"It is," 1st/Sgt. John Pettit Burch says. "They just don't know it." He picks up the letter on his desk. "They're the messengers. This is the message."

"Great," Sergeant Wallace says. "Now we're doing mail order." He backs up and leans against 1st/Sgt. John Pettit Burch's thin plywood wall, lifts a single cigarette and a Zippo lighter out of his left shirt pocket. He puts the cigarette between his lips and lights it.

"We can do the papers right here right now," 1st/Sgt. John Pettit Burch says.

"Sure we can do the papers. And who's going to sign?"

"This one here," 1st/Sgt. John Pettit Burch says, waving his hand at me. "His First Sergeant says he can sign for everything."

"Sign what?" Rutherford says.

"You want a sparkplug?" Sergeant Wallace asks. "You hand me a requisition and I'll give you a sparkplug," Sergeant Wallace says. "And the requisition I'm talking about? It's gotta be signed by someone who's accountable. Or no sparkplug."

Rutherford picks out the important word and asks me, "You accountable?"

I consider the question. The First Sergeant has written 1st/Sgt. John Pettit Burch for help. I know why he wants HVAP rounds and Jumbos—uparmored M4A3s designated M4A3E2s. First Sergeant Reardon wants them so that he and I will not have to go down into the pungent, slippery darkness inside a shot-down Sherman, rubber boots on our feet, rubber gantlets on our hands, shovels in our fists.

"Sure, I'm accountable," I say, as though I am giving the police my name.

"You got a willing one here, John," Sergeant Wallace says.

"That help, Joe?" 1st/Sgt. John Pettit Burch asks.

"You know me, John," Sergeant Wallace says. "If I got an accountable signature on the paper, I'm clean. And Danny agrees with me about accountable signatures. So does the Inspector General. If I can show the IG an accountable signature, I'll give these guys here a B-29 and they can fly back to where they came from."

"If they can find a ten man crew," 1st/Sgt. John Pettit Burch says.

"Har, har," Sergeant Wallace says. He is not smiling: he is thinking. I can see he is thinking about where to get what 1st/Sgt. John Pettit Burch wants. He is also thinking about the details: paper, fuel, machinery, orders, men. And explanations: for Colonel Hollis, and the IG's investigators. "All right," Sergeant Wallace says. "You got a list, John?"

"Right here," 1st/Sgt. John Pettit Burch says. He passes First Sergeant Reardon's letter across his desk.

"Hand written," Sergeant Wallace says, glancing at the letter. "No typewriter in your outfit?" he asks Rutherford and me. "Or maybe this here list was drawn up in the heat of battle, when there wasn't time to get to no typewriter?"

I consider what to say, but before I can find an answer Sergeant Wallace says, "Okay, okay. Forget it. Let me take a look here." He reads the letter. "Uh-huh," he says. "Uh-huh, uh-huh." When he finishes reading he looks at 1st/Sgt. John Pettit Burch. Then he looks at us, and says, "Your First Sergeant is a pretty ambitious guy. What's he planning, a single Battalion thrust right through to Prague?" He looks at Burch and says, "John, I swear. You sure this isn't a joke?"

"They need an edge in the Seven Six One, Joe."

"An edge? You call this an edge? General Patton would be happy to have an edge like this." Sergeant Wallace glances down at the letter. "Lemme put aside the stuff you got Forrest out rounding up—oh, yeah, I heard you, who didn't hear you in this tacked together building?—and go through what you got here on this list. What you got here, John, is what most armor Battalions would like to have a part of. Let's see, here," he says, reading from First Sergeant Reardon's letter, "four Jumbos, two thousand rounds 76 millimeter HVAP, four M3 halftrack-mounted quad fifties, four M7 self-propelled 105 millimeter howitzers 'with ammunition' and four 105 assault gun Shermans, also 'with ammunition'." Sergeant Wallace looks up at 1st/Sgt. John Pettit Burch and says, "You got any idea what 'with ammunition' means, John? That mean one full combat load, or does your friend here want three dozen trucks full of ammunition to go along with the 105 howitzers and 105 Shermans? In case they run short? No,"

Sergeant Wallace says, "you don't need to answer that right now. Let me get down to the end here first. I want to read it all out, to get a feel for it before we get into the details. Don't worry, though: seems there's only one more entry here. Let's see here. Oh, yeah: four Fireflies, and here's that 'with ammunition' again."

Sergeant Wallace places First Sergeant Reardon's letter on 1st/Sgt. John Pettit Burch's desk and leans back against the plywood wall. "You're got a pretty ambitious friend there, John. Man ought to be an officer, ought to be in command of at least an armored division, maybe an Army Corps. Pretty clear he thinks about the big picture."

"They need this stuff, Joe. We can't know what they're going to be doing next. Who knows, maybe they're going to have to break into the Siegfried Line."

"Everybody's going to have to break into the Siegfried Line, John. How else are we going to get into Germany? All right, though. Let me tell you a couple of things right now," Sergeant Wallace says. "No Fireflies: we don't have any. Thinking is, the M10 is just as good. M10's ninety millimeter gun is supposed to be able to take care of anything that comes along, just like the seventeen pounder in the Firefly. No, don't tell me: I know the M10 isn't up there with the Firefly, and I know the thinking about what ought to be able to handle German armor is fucked up. But there it is: we don't have any Fireflies. British just can't produce them fast enough."

"No Fireflies?" 1st/Sgt. John Pettit Burch asks, as though Sergeant Wallace has not been restocking the shelves. "Jesus, Joe, I thought we were the main supply facility for Third Army. And you tell me we don't have any Fireflies—not even four of them—for these guys?"

"There aren't any, John. Not here, and I bet not south of Holland. The Brits have them all."

"Joe, there's a war going on up east of here." 1st/Sgt. John Pettit Burch raises his eyebrows, as though Sergeant Wallace may not have heard about the war going on up east of here.

"John, let's not start with that shit," Sergeant Wallace says. "Some of this stuff I can deal with in one way or another and we can talk about the amounts. But there aren't any Fireflies."

"All right," 1st/Sgt. John Pettit Burch says. "If you don't have any Fireflies, we'll have to live with that. But what do you mean, we can talk about amounts? You're not trying to negotiate with me, are you, Joe?"

"John, John," Sergeant Wallace says. "I can swing maybe less than half of this stuff. Not all of it. There's no way I can get it all to these guys. Not in—how long are you guys here?"

"Tomorrow morning we're supposed to find out where the Seven Six One is and go up to meet them if we can get finished here by then."

"That gives us this afternoon and maybe part of tomorrow. John, this isn't a department store where you walk in and buy what you want. I couldn't produce all this stuff to the general in command of a division in a week. And you want it all in less than a day?"

"All this stuff ought to be on the ready-for-issue line," 1st/Sgt. John Pettit Burch says. He pounds his fist on the desk and shouts, "Goddamnit, Joe, this is Supply here. If the stuff isn't ready to go when it needs to go, what the hell are we doing here?"

"You know the answer to that, John. We're moving paper and equipment. When we have the right paper, we move the equipment. But we can't pass out all the armor we got to one unit and leave another dry. You remember the word 'allocation', John? And don't give me that talk of yours about the man with the rifle up at the front don't understand allocation when he runs out of ammunition."

"You got to help out here, Joe," 1st/Sgt. John Pettit Burch says. "Without this equipment this Battalion gonna be damned near defenseless."

"Oh, yeah?" Sergeant Wallace says. "You guys got your Table of Equipment, don't you?" he asks me.

"I don't know, Sergeant," I say. "I think we're short in men and equipment."

"You see, Joe?" 1st/Sgt. John Pettit Burch asks. "You see what I told you? They're short."

"If they're short in men how they going to crew all these machines you want them to have?"

"Discard what they got and use the crews on these here," 1st/Sgt. John P. Burch says. "What else?"

"You mean they're just going to junk what they got? How's that give them this edge you were telling me about?"

"Joe, Joe," 1st/Sgt. John Pettit Burch says. "This here is war. Adaptation, Joe. Change: that's what it's about. They junk a worn out Sherman for a new Jumbo, who can complain?"

"The battalion that's short of Shermans, that's who," Sergeant Wallace says.

"Joe," 1st/Sgt. John Pettit Burch says, "let's get down to this. What can you give these guys to take up to the Seven Six One?"

"Less than half of what they're asking, John. What their First Sergeant—your old buddy—is asking. Maybe less than less than half."

"Half?" 1st/Sgt. John Pettit Burch asks. He stares at Sergeant Wallace. "Half?" 1st/Sgt. John Pettit Burch shouts. "That's it? Half?"

"Less than half," Sergeant Wallace says. "Or less. Like I told you, this isn't a department store. Even Danny is going to notice this amount of stuff. And he won't let it by, John. Even if he has to put off going into Nancy for lunch, he won't let this slide past."

"Half," 1st/Sgt. John Pettit Burch says, as though he has been told he is dying.

"Less than half," Sergeant Wallace says. Sergeant Wallace is implacable.

"But maybe half," 1st/Sgt. John Pettit Burch says. "Goddamnit, Joe. That's the best we can do? Half? What if the Germans mount another offensive and it comes right through here to Nancy because these guys got half?"

"Less than half," Sergeant Wallace says. "Not half. Less than half. Or even less."

"Goddamnit, Joe." 1st/Sgt. John Pettit Burch stands up, sweating, flicking eyes bright with fever, teeth clenched.

"No more than half," Sergeant Wallace says before 1st/Sgt. John Pettit Burch can speak. "And probably less, John."

"Goddamnit. You want these men to go back to their First Sergeant empty-handed? How's that going to look, Joe? How am I going to look? I've known their First Sergeant twenty years. And if he says his Battalion needs this stuff—and I don't mean half of it, Joe, or less than half—then they need it. First Sergeant Reardon isn't going to ask me for a pencil he doesn't need it."

"Sure, John," Sergeant Wallace says. He stands with his back against the wall, arms crossed. "I understand you know the guy. But the answer is still no more than half and maybe less, depending."

"Depending? Depending?" 1st/Sgt. John Pettit Burch asks. "Depending on what?"

"Come on, John. Depending on what other demands we got. Depending on who got in line first. Depending on losses in this corps sector. Depending on all that."

"And that's it?" 1st/Sgt. John Pettit Burch asks. "That's the best you can do?"

"Maybe half and more likely less than half is the best I can do. And you know me, John: if I say half or less, that's all there is."

"I know," 1st/Sgt. John Pettit Burch says. He sits down and rests his forearms on his desk. "I know that, Joe." He glances at me, then at Rutherford. "Still, these guys are going to have to go up there with whatever we let them have, and what if it's not enough? What if they go in and they get into a lot of shit because they're short of equipment?"

"Right now they've got all their entitled to, John," Sergeant Wallace says. "Isn't that right?" he asks me.

"I don't know, Sergeant. But I don't think so. We've had a lot of casualties and not many trained replacements. And we've lost a lot of equipment."

"These guys have been in the line since November," 1st/Sgt. John Pettit Burch shouts. "Since November, Joe. Without relief, and without time out except for travel."

"I read that there in the last part of the letter," Sergeant Wallace says. He nods at First Sergeant Reardon's letter lying on the desk. "So what? Lots of tank battalions been fighting that long and longer without relief. Aren't any vacations out here, John."

"Except here in Nancy," 1st/Sgt. John Pettit Burch. "At this supply dump. All right, then, Joe, Goddamnit. Give me the details. Tell me—tell us—what half means."

"Or less than half, if I check and it can't come up to half. And I got to check, John, before I can give you a definite answer. But right now I think I can come up with two Jumbos, maybe eight hundred rounds of HVAP, and two 105 assault Shermans. That's it."

"That's it?" 1st/Sgt. John Pettit Burch asks. "You call that half? That ain't half. That ain't even less than half, Joe. You already cut out the Fireflies. Now you cut out any mention of the quad fifties on the M3 halftracks and the self-propelled howitzers. What the hell is this?"

"Quad fifties are for anti-aircraft units, John. You know that. There's no chance you're going to get those. And SP howitzers are short right now. Besides, these guys: what do they know about using them? Or maintaining them? These guys are tankers, John. They don't know how to maintenance quad fifties and SP howitzers."

"They can figure it out," 1st/Sgt. John Pettit Burch says. He turns to us and says, "You can figure it out, can't you?"

"Yes, First Sergeant," I say.

Rutherford nods and says, "Sure, First Sergeant. Figure out how to do anything if we have to."

"I don't care whether they can figure out how to re-equip their Battalion with Tiger tanks, John. Quad-fifties are for antiaircraft units, and these guys don't need them and won't get them. And self-propelled howitzers go to division artillery mostly. Besides, if they had quad-fifties, where'd they get the ammunition? Those things eat up fifty caliber ammunition, John. And you know as well as I do the supply people in the division trains of the division they're attached to are going to want to know where the hell all that ammunition is going. Someone'll check and the next thing you know they'll lose their quad-fifties. And they'll ask me how they got them in the first place."

"That's bullshit, Joe. You know that's bullshit. They'll find the ammunition. Everybody's got ammunition. That's the one thing we got enough of. Right here in Nancy we got enough ammunition for two corps areas. And more coming in all day every day."

"John: no quad-fifties," Sergeant Wallace says. "And they'll have to find the ammunition for the 105 Shermans themselves. I can't go along with that language you're buddy put in, that 'with ammunition' there."

"At least you can give them something, Joe. At least a set number of rounds. Where they going to find 105 millimeter rounds?"

"John," Sergeant Wallace, "this is a tank battalion we're talking about here. They got assault guns, don't they? 105 millimeter assault guns? Same thing as they're asking for here: Shermans with a 105 piece in the turret instead of a 76 millimeter. They get the ammunition for these 105 Shermans the same place they get the ammunition for the 105 Shermans they already got."

"Goddamnit, Joe, you're talking about nickels and dimes here. We got—what did the last inventory show?—how many thousands of tons of ammunition available for these weapons? I wish to Christ we'd had a hundredth part of it on Guadalcanal. And now you're telling me: no ammunition, they'll have to get it out of division trains."

"That's what I'm telling you," Sergeant Wallace says. "Come on, John. I'm giving you everything I can here. Even now there's going to be questions. Like, what's a battalion doing coming back here and indenting for supplies? They're supposed to go to division, and then corps, and corps is supposed to come to us. But they've come directly, and that's going to raise some questions."

"Not if we got the right paper," 1st/Sgt. John Pettit Burch says. "And we're going to have the right paper. He's going to sign where we say to sign," he says, pointing a bony quivering finger at my chest.

"Good for him," Sergeant Wallace says. "Anyhow, I've told you what I can come up with. It's more than I'd come up with for anyone else, John. If anyone else came in here and asked me for this stuff I'd tell them to get the hell out of my office. You know that."

"I know that," 1st/Sgt. John Pettit Burch says. "I know that. I know you're doing the best you can, Joe. But think about this: if you can find anything more than you can right now, I'd be grateful. So would First Sergeant Reardon and these guys here."

"Gee, John. Thanks. Your gratitude and theirs sets me up for the rest of the whole Goddamned day."

"Goddamnit, Joe, that's no way to talk," 1st/Sgt. John Pettit Burch says. "These guys and a lot of others are up there fighting while we're sitting back here doing nothing."

"I did my time, John. You know that."

"I know that. Did I say I didn't know that? I know it. I know about down there in Tunisia. But that's the past, like me on the Canal. That's finished, and now we got to do what we can to get these men through whatever they have to go through."

"Yeah, yeah," Wallace says. "I know all that, John. I knew it before I met you, too. Look, I gotta get out of here and do some things. I'll check back with you this afternoon, see what I've come up with. But I'm telling you: two Jumbos and two 105 assault Shermans and some HVAP is about the limit."

"I can't ask more than you try, Joe" 1st/Sgt. John Pettit Burch says. He still sounds aggrieved that Wallace hasn't done everything he can, but he grins to show he will get over it.

"All right," Wallace says. He pushes himself away from the wall. "Take it easy, you guys," he tells Rutherford and me. "John? Take care of yourself. You ought to lie down some: you look like hell." Sergeant Wallace is right: 1st/Sgt. John Pettit Burch does look like hell. His lips are gray, his face is flushed and his hands are shaking. The sweat-stained patches beneath his arms are spreading down toward the patches rising from his belt cinched tight around his waist.

"Get the hell out of here, Joe. I'll take care of myself. You take care of these guys and bring them what they want and I'll take care of myself."

"I'll do what I can," Sergeant Wallace says. "Within the limits we talked about. But I'll do what I can."

"I know you will, Joe. Just try as hard as you can."

"What else?" Sergeant Wallace nods at us and leaves 1st/Sgt. John Pettit Burch's office.

"You guys ought to be satisfied. Don't worry: Joe'll get everything Bill Reardon wants."

"Didn't sound so to me," Rutherford says. "Sergeant Wallace sound reluctant." I know Rutherford is thinking what I am thinking: that First Sergeant Reardon is going to be unhappy when we return without every last item on the list he has sent 1st/Sgt. John Pettit Burch.

"You guys don't seem to know Bill Reardon too well. How long you been in the Seven Six One?"

"Since the beginning, First Sergeant," I say.

"Took some time for them to turn you loose and let you get into this, didn't it?" I nod. "But they're making up for it now. I know you been in the line non-stop since November, except for motoring one place to the next. So do a lot of other people, from what I hear. You did good work there at the beginning when you were in Third Army. People remember that."

"Hope they remember it when this here war long gone," Rutherford says. I hope as much as Rutherford, but I am not optimistic.

"They'll remember. At least, here in the Army they'll remember. And a lot of people who're here are civilians. They're going to be out there somewhere when the war's over. Don't worry: even Forrest Goddamn him back in Atlanta is going to remember you came in this office out of the line. Lemme go back, though: you don't seem to know Bill Reardon too well." 1st/Sgt. John Pettit Burch looks from me to Rutherford. He seems to ignore the fact that not even the Colonel knows First Sergeant Reardon too well.

"Well, First Sergeant," I say, "he's the First Sergeant, and he's a reserved man." I recall First Sergeant Reardon pulling on the rubber gantlets and looking me over for signs of disgust and fear as he said, 'You want a see gar?'

"Keep your eye on him," 1st/Sgt. John Pettit Burch says. "You can learn a lot from a guy like Bill Reardon. For example, you can learn something right here from this letter. You think he wants all this stuff?"

"I hope not, First Sergeant," I say. "But I'm afraid he might."

"You're wrong. Bill Reardon wants forty percent. Standard rule: ask for two and a half times what you want. Then when supply cuts you back, you're happy. All Bill wants is two Jumbos and two 105 Shermans and three four hundred rounds of HVAP if he can get it. He knows as well as I do he isn't going to get no quad fifties and 105 millimeter SP howitzers."

"How you know that, First Sergeant?" Rutherford asks.

1st/Sgt. John Pettit Burch pulls the envelope in which First Sergeant Reardon's letter was contained from his pocket and flips it across the desk. "Take a look." I pick up the envelope, look at it, turn it over. Nothing is written on it except 1st/Sgt. John Pettit Burch's name.

"Nothing," I say.

"Better look inside," Rutherford says.

I open the envelope. I see writing inside. I turn the envelope upside down and, as Rutherford leans over my shoulder, read: 'John. I need 2 Jumbos, 2 105 Shermans and 3 - 400 HVAP. Bill.'

"See what I mean?" 1st/Sgt. John Pettit Burch asks.

"Looks like you got to keep your eye on the First Sergeant," I say.

"Ain't half of it," Rutherford says. "Seem like the First Sergeant more crafty than I thought. A lot more crafty." Rutherford speaks as though he sees that First Sergeant Reardon would be a man to watch in and around Kay See.

"Bill Reardon," 1st/Sgt. John Pettit Burch says, "been around long enough to know how to jerk the Services of Supply any way he wants. Particularly if he's got an old friend helping him pull on the rope."

"What about Wallace?"

"Wallace knows maybe there's something more than the letter. Phone call, maybe. But for sure he knows there's something more than the letter. Wallace is a smart guy. But he doesn't know what's in the envelope. And he wouldn't care, either, if he knew about it."

Rutherford nods at me and says, "Because this man here gonna sign."

"That's it," 1st/Sgt. John Pettit Burch says. "He's the responsible man."

Ten

In November, from the summit of this low hill in Moselle near Morville-les-Vic, I watched through fieldglasses as Sam Turley stood up against the night.

Now on this cold, clear March morning Rutherford and I have returned to look down on this terrible place again.

The sky above us is full of the distant growl of four-engined bombers. They are flying east, at altitude, drawing contrails behind them. I wonder what it is like to breathe oxygen from a steel bottle through a rubber tube and watch bomb bursts flower black and gray against the distant earth. Who knows? It is an experience Rutherford and I will never have to endure.

As we look down into the valley three P-47s—blunt, heavy aircraft with a single huge propeller—pound forward above the crest of the hill. The cowlings over the engines of these Thunderbolts are painted with a yellow and black checkerboard. Rockets and bombs are slung under the wings. Rutherford and I glance up at them without curiosity: pilots fly and fight a different, cleaner, faster war than we. They are all officers. Worse, they are technicians who could not function within the cooperative, stratified organism of a tank battalion. They fly in accordance with detailed plans. They have precise missions, a particular duty they repeat four or five times a day. We pursue only the most general instructions: to proceed along an easterly bearing until the war is finished.

"Down there, wasn't it?" Rutherford asks.

"Yes," I say. "See the tank trap? And the bunkers beyond?"

"Trap has weathered some, hasn't it?" Rutherford sounds as though he thought the tank trap would be preserved. As a memorial, perhaps, or a lesson. He is wrong: whoever owns this field will fill in the tank trap, and in twenty years no one will know what happened here.

Rutherford is right about the condition of the tank trap, though. The winter has softened its edges and it is crumbling in upon itself. Beyond it on rising ground the bunkers in which the Germans waited for the Shermans of C Company of the Seven Six One to come on have been shattered by charges blown by engineers who followed up our advance in support of the 26th Infantry Division.

The hedges along the road at the edge of the field are where they were in November, though; as are the woods on the lower slope opposite and the road leading to Morville-les-Vic. The shape of the low hills rolling east to the horizon is the same; and in less than seven months the sun will be in the same place in the sky in which it stood when Sam Turley and the rest of them began their short, disastrous trip across this field and into the night.

A cold autumn day: Thursday, November 9, 1944. Snow had fallen during the night and camouflaged the tank trap that extended across the foot of the far slope to the road leading to Morville-les-Vic. The snow had also camouflaged the pillboxes and antitank guns on the slope beyond the tank trap, and the eighty-eights in the woods farther up the slope.

By the morning of the 9th, the Battalion was uneasy. The Colonel had been wounded on the night of the 7th, and his evacuation set off a ripple of agitation and rumor that ricocheted through the Battalion. We had trusted the Colonel to make the right moves and we believed he would not make mistakes. We did not know his stand-in.

Worse, five men in a Sherman, the whole crew—Harvey Woodard, of Howard, Georgia, the commander; Carlton Chapman, of Pembroke, Virginia, the gunner; Claude Mann, of my home town, Chicago, the driver; Nathaniel Simmons, of Beaufort, South Carolina, the assistant driver and bow gunner; and L. C. Byrd, of Tuscaloosa, Alabama, the loader—had all been killed as they sat in their seats, though no projectile had struck their tank, and none of them had been wounded. Their deaths were mysterious and troubling, and no one has yet been able to explain how they died. The best guess is that concussion killed them all.

Worst of all, the Battalion's executive officer, whose name I have taught myself to forget, was evacuated on Friday, November 8 for what was called 'battle fatigue'. In the Battalion men muttered that the motherfucker had gone and left us to fight it out by ourselves, and that after all his talk at Camp Claiborne and Camp Hood: talk that was insult and innuendo; talk which led nowhere, for we were enlisted and he was an officer. I agreed with their mutters. It is a pity General Patton, in whose Army we were fighting in November, did not have the chance to visit the Battalion's 'battle fatigued' exec in hospital, to show the exec his gloves; or better yet, his revolvers with the ivory grips.

Thus we were nervous because we had lost our commander, whom we respected and who, thank Christ, has now come back to us and stands in the Headquarters track and listens to First Sergeant Reardon and says, "Uh-huh, Uh-huh"; nervous because our executive officer was the only despised color in Europe this year—yellow; more nervous because Woodard, Chapman, Mann, Simmons and Byrd had died such enigmatic deaths, leaving no one behind to explain what killed them; and most nervous of all about how we would perform that first time the bell rang and we came out of our corner.

Tense, expectant and dreading the fight ahead, our substitute colonel handing out the orders, the crews of C Company's Shermans advanced from the ground on which Rutherford and I loiter. Then I watched the M4A3s slide down the mild slope and reach the field, deploying as they moved forward toward Morville-les-Vic, trundling and jouncing, threatening the distance with the bobbing muzzles of their guns, tank commanders' heads stuck up out of the hatches, radio aerials whipping the chilly air, tracks chewing the snow and throwing up muddy clods.

Seeing the ground ripped up by the Shermans' passage, I thought of the damage with which the farmer who owned this field would have to cope. As I thought of the damaged ground, I heard the sound of the Shermans' engines alter as they discovered the tank trap.

Then I heard the first German antitank gun fire from the woods to the east.

Down the slope gray smoke rushed up out of a halted Sherman's commander's hatch. A man climbed up through the smoke, pulling himself up with his right hand, gripping an M3 Grease Gun in his left fist. Neither the gunner nor the loader followed him out of the smoke. I saw sergeant's stripes on the survivor's sleeve and thought: tank commander. The sergeant rolled from the turret onto the rear deck of the Sherman and fell into the snow and mud behind the tank, scrabbled up behind the cleats of the right track and pointed the submachinegun toward our enemy. As he pointed the weapon the driver and the bow gunner slithered up out of their hatches into the rising rattle of small arms fire from the camouflaged bunkers beyond the tank trap. The driver and bowgunner rolled from the Sherman. For an instant the bow gunner crouched in the muddy snow close to the right front drive sprocket. Bullets hammered the Sherman's armor above his head and he began crawling past the wishbone suspension assemblies, squirmed past his tank commander and knelt in the shelter behind the tank, panting, chest heaving, staring right and left. An instant later the driver crept around the left rear of the tank, got up on his knees and braced himself, one filthy hand against the lefthand air cleaner, mud all down the front of his uniform, staring and shouting at the tank commander, his shouted words lost in the rising roar of the machineguns, rifles and antitank weapons firing from beyond the tank trap.

In the instants in which the three survivors from the shot-down Sherman scrabbled and squirmed through the snow and mud, crouching and ducking as they slithered toward the protection at the rear of the Sherman, the surviving C Company Shermans began firing across the tank trap. But the Germans were not firing tracer from their camouflaged positions and they shot down five more Shermans as I watched, striking them with the peculiar rushing roar I learned, that day, not to forget: the roar of shot flung from an eighty-eight millimeter gun that rips the sky, and steel, apart.

As the tankers scrabbled up out of the Shermans and slid in the mud, crawling into shelter behind their tanks, I looked from one shot down Sherman to the next, counting the men as they came out. Not all of them made it: two Shermans were burning, flame flickering up through smoke streaming from their hatches and out the muzzles of their guns. Beside me Williston, who never cursed, shouted out one curse and another as I swept the glasses back across the field, counting the wounded who had escaped the disaster.

As I heard the air torn apart slap together as the antitank guns kept up their methodical fire, I examined the tank trap: camouflaged by the terrain and the fresh snow, C Company's Shermans had not seen it soon enough. Halted before the trap, bogged down at the edge of confusion, six of its tanks shot down by the Germans, C Company teetered in disarray, men scrabbling in the mud signalling with their arms, tanks backing and firing, the orderly precision learned at Camp Claiborne and Camp Hood shredded by the crack of the antitank guns firing from the bunkers beyond the tank trap and the woods beyond the bunkers.

Unable to identify targets, the fire from the Shermans that had survived the shock of the ambush diminished. No hope, I thought: three or four Shermans still fired, but C Company was broken, scattered in disorder across the muddy field.

I counted as Williston cursed beside me: six Shermans shot down, two burning, one smoldering. Those who had escaped the fires crouched behind their vehicles or lay wounded in the field, waiting, if they lived, for rescue.

Through my fieldglasses I examined the wreckage. Confusion and disaster. A corpse hung from the bowgunner's hatch of an M4A3, its face a scarlet pulp, the barrel of the seventy-six millimeter gun above the corpse shredded. A tanker lay dead in the mud, his left leg cut away below the knee. White smoke flowed from two neat ovals punched in the armor of a Sherman's turret. The bow machinegun of a disabled Sherman rattled, tracer weaving across the tank ditch, striking the bunkers and pillboxes beyond. The muzzles of the weapons concealed in the Germans' positions flashed, and when they flashed, shot struck the Shermans' armor again, and again. A tanker with a clean white compress in his filthy hand knelt behind a Sherman above the heaving, naked, bloody chest of a man lying on his back, his face turned to the side, his cheek pressed against the mud.

Destruction, death and failure. But worse than these, I knew, would be the smug whispers about incompetence, dereliction, and worse.

'Who's that?' Williston shouted. 'Who the fuck is it?' Williston shouted.

I lowered the fieldglasses. To the right, two hundred yards away, four hundred from the ragged line of destroyed Shermans, its wheels bouncing against the snow, the tracks at the rear flinging up snow and mud, a halftrack pulling a trailer jounced right to left across the slope beneath us. I raised the fieldglasses. The bed of the track was full of crates of 76 millimeter shells and metal boxes of machinegun ammunition.

'Just one man in there,' Williston shouted, as though I were standing a hundred feet away. I nodded and watched the single man wrestle the wheel of the halftrack.

'Who the hell is it?' Williston shouted, as though I knew, but hadn't disclosed, the track driver's name. 'Man's got to be crazy to go on up there.'

'Hold it,' I said as I examined the track bouncing and sliding left to right down the slope. 'Looks like Thorn,' I said. 'Willy Thorn.' As I spoke, Thorn halted the halftrack, set the brake, wriggled up out of the driver's seat and stood behind the machinegun mounted on a pintle at the front of the track's bed. Through the glasses I saw his furious face as he cocked the gun and pointed its muzzle down the slope and began firing. Long strands of tracer curved over the Shermans stalled and shot down in front of the tank trap. Willy Thorn, slick Willy who moved his hands when he talked and knew he was right, danced this way and that in the bed of the halftrack as he shifted the muzzle of the gun, adding the insignificance of a single machinegun's hammering to the roaring crash of German antitank weapons, rifles and machineguns.

'That man's fucking crazy,' Williston shouted.

'He's taking a hell of a chance standing up in all that ammunition,' I said.

'No kidding?' Williston shouted.

I nodded and raised the fieldglasses. Beyond Willy Thorn firing his weapon from the bed of the halftrack jumbled with crates of 76 millimeter shells and steel boxes of .50 and .30 caliber machinegun ammunition, a man climbed up out of the commander's hatch of a disabled Shermans, pulling himself up with his right hand, holding an M3 Grease Gun in his left. As he swung up out of the hatch, I saw the chevrons and rockers on the left sleeve of his tanker's jacket and identified him: Samuel J. Turley, 1st/Sgt. of C Company, a large, friendly man, respected, capable and calm.

Through the fieldglasses I watched Turley climb up out of the turret and down onto the rear deck as his men followed him out of the Sherman's hatches. Turley crouched at the rear of the Sherman's turret while his crew slid down into the mud and snow and crawled to the rear of the tank. Turley was still, and for a moment I thought he had been killed. Machinegun bullets struck the turret, gouging silver streaks from the steel beneath the olive drab paint. At last Turley moved and I realized he had loitered behind the turret to observe the field, to identify the enemy and to mark their positions. Turley slid and jumped down from the rear of the Sherman into the mud and snow. His knees buckled, but he steadied himself, the Grease Gun in his right hand.

As he stood behind the Sherman the German antitank guns' fire ceased. The racket of German machinegun and rifle fire increased. C Company's tankers knew what this meant: Germans infantry would now assault the shocked, dismounted remnants of this tank company.

Turley glanced from one crouched, shouting member of his crew to the next, spoke to them until they listened. Then he looked to his left toward the two burning Shermans and the one dribbling smoke from its hatches. He shouted and shifted the muzzle of the submachinegun he held in his left hand, gesturing with it: toward the tank trap. The forefinger of his right hand extended from his clenched right fist pointed the same way. Uninjured men kneeling behind the disabled tanks turned their heads toward Turley shouting instructions and pointing forward. Some of them nodded. Others waved.

Turley turned to his right, called to the survivors of the other disabled Shermans, pointed forward and, hefting the submachinegun in both hands, gestured with its muzzle toward the tank trap. Beyond the ditch Germans darted from one place to the next, crouching as they ran forward and lying prone in the snow and dirt to fire at C Company's dismounted tankers huddled behind their disabled Shermans looked at Turley shouting as he gestured with his weapon. The men hesitated, as though they could not quite figure what he meant.

Sam Turley looked away from his men, east across the tank trap toward the indistinct darting shapes coming on. He did not gesture or call out to his men again. Perhaps he realized how little time was left before the Germans arrived. Or perhaps he remembered the lecture on leadership and the reasons they gave him the chevrons and the rockers that enclosed the symbol of his first sergeancy. Or perhaps he remembered First Sergeant Reardon looking over the Battalion's assembled sergeants the first time he addressed them at Camp Claiborne and saying, 'Know this: there aren't no bad soldiers. There're bad officers, and bad sergeants, but there aren't no bad soldiers.' Or perhaps Sam Turley was no longer his sunny, friendly self: perhaps he was angry that the sonsofbitches had done so much right here the first day the Seven Six One had come out; and so perhaps he decided to teach the gray uniformed men coming forward beyond the tank trap the first lesson: where to get on, and where to get off.

Beside me Williston whispered his usual sermon—'Jesus Christ!'—as Turley stepped out from behind the Sherman he had commanded and began to fire his weapon, leaning forward into the recoil as he fired at the darting shapes of the Germans dashing from one piece of cover to the next beyond the tank trap. Turley's body trembled each time he fired the gun, and he leaned into the weapon's recoil as though he were leaning into a strong wind as he stepped forward toward the tank trap angled across the field. Beyond the tank trap a German soldier knelt and fired at Turley with a rifle. The rounds pounding from the muzzle of the submachinegun in Turley's hands threw the kneeling rifleman back and down into the mud. Hunched over the submachinegun, Turley shuffled toward the tank trap, sliding his left foot forward and then his right, firing as he went on.

Turley did not look back to see whether his crew, or the survivors from the crews in the other tanks, were coming on behind him, but the tankers clustered behind the wrecked Shermans watched Turley for no more than three moments before they got up shouting and shaking their fists at one another and stepped out from behind their disabled M4A3s and crouched as though they were stepping out of shelter into a heavy rain and rushed forward, firing as they went, each of them hunched over their submachineguns as Sam Turley was hunched over his. Not elegant. But good enough.

Down the slope in front of us Willy Thorn stood up at the front of the bed of the halftrack full of ammunition, firing the .30 caliber machinegun without a pause. A mistake: I knew he would burn out the machinegun's barrel or jam the mechanism if he went on firing. But his anger was terrific, and nothing but a jam or the expenditure of the last round in the belt of ammunition in the box magazine attached to the gun would stop him.

Beside me Williston shouted, 'See them go on!'

I nodded as Sam Turley and his men went on and the Germans began to retreat, rushing back from one bit of cover to the next, leaving still dead men and writhing wounded ones in the mud and snow behind them. The tankers tending the wounded behind the two burning Shermans and the one that smoldered but had not begun to burn saw the Germans retreating too, and saw Sam Turley turn toward them and gesture with his left arm, urging them forward toward the tank trap.

Taking the chance, gauging the moment between the German infantry's retreat and the inevitable arrival of the Germans' artillery, the unwounded men lifted the wounded and carried and dragged them forward across the snow-covered muddy ground to and down into the tank trap.

As our refugees straggled away along the muddy ditch, German artillery arrived, a careful mixture of mortars and the sudden slamming crash of eighty-eights firing high explosive.

In training at Camp Hood the British Major from the Royal Tank Regiment who lectured us had brought along an eighty-eight millimeter shell to show us what we would have to face. The projectile was the quintessence of menace. I can still recall the markings on the projectile—'92'—and on the shell casing: '8.8cm KwK 43 Pak 43/1/2/3'. The British Major did not know what the markings meant, 'except,' he said, 'the 8.8 centimeter thing there. That's all you need to know about the eighty-eight. Note that this is the antitank round. The high explosive round has different markings.' We learned that when this particular type of round was fired down the long tapered barrel of the eighty-eight millimeter gun, the projectile fled toward its target at almost two thousand seven hundred feet a second. Coupled with the Germans' optics, the high level of education of their populace and the muscular, detailed training and retraining of their gun crews, the weapon was lethal.

As I watched Sam Turley and his men ducking among the leaping explosions, I knew that everything the British Major said about the eight-eight was correct to the nearest millimeter. As the Germans fired high explosive rounds down the long elegant barrels from the protection of the woods, smoke and mud leapt up: an instant more, and Williston and I heard the vicious cracking rip of air torn apart and slammed together.

'Jesus Christ,' Williston shouted.

'Yes,' I said as I watched the quick springing eruptions of mud and smoke as the eighty-eight millimeter rounds hammered the earth among the disabled Shermans.

Standing up among the explosions Sam Turley held his submachinegun in his left hand and swept his right up and back, directing his small force back from the edge of the tank trap, back from the night, back toward the safety of the shadows behind the steel sides of the shot-down Shermans. Crouching and flinching, crabbing and ducking and shouting at one another, the tankers rushed this way and that among the springing shell bursts, retreating toward cover. One fell, another reached, grasped the fallen man's wrist, dragged him by the arm with one hand, hanging onto his M3 Grease Gun with the other, pulling and hauling at the weight of the wounded man down in the snow and mud. The man hauling and hanging onto his submachinegun shouted as he struggled with the wounded man he was hauling and hanging onto and kept on shouting as he dragged the wounded sliding tanker behind a shot up Sherman and hauled and shoved him between the treads beneath the tank's belly.

The eighty-eights went on firing diligent, spaced shots that demonstrated the scrupulous training of the gun crews. The fucking precision of the Germans, I thought as I watched the explosions spring from the muddy ground and watched Sam Turley's men seeking cover.

Crouching like the rest of them, carrying his weapon in his right hand now, Turley turned and ran among the leaping explosions, veering this way and that, but slowing as he ran, like a man tiring of a task he has set himself. He should throw the submachinegun away, I thought. But Turley hung on to his weapon and slogged on through the mud toward safety in the shadows behind the tanks.

A pillar of flame and smoke leapt from Sam Turley's feet. The submachinegun he would not abandon flicked end over end, flicked across the muddy field. Smoke rose toward the low grey sky, drifting east on the faint cold breeze. When it cleared Turley was gone, his body quartered, the quarters sliced to bits by steel shards and the rush of expanding gasses of the round that killed him, the bits of his body reduced to scraps squeezed to liquid.

A machinegun rattled. Rifles fired from beyond the tank trap. The uneasy firing tapered off. An eighty-eight fired one more round: a vicious final tearing howl ripping the sky in half, a final ringing explosion against the angled bow of the Sherman nearest the place where Sam Turley last loped toward the light and where, in mid stride, he disappeared.

I glanced down the slope: Willy Thorn stood in the bed of the ammunition track, pounding his fist against the breech of the jammed weapon he had fired and fired, ignoring the routine necessary to the proper operation in the field of the .30 caliber machinegun. Down in front of the tank trap two Shermans were backing from the disaster that had overtaken this segment of C Company. Their movements were cautious, as though they hesitated to leave. They fired now and then as they backed; but the enemy that had so damaged C Company was filtering away, preparing to defend other prepared defenses farther back.

Beside me Williston whispered 'Jesus Christ' just as our artillery began to arrive. A few shells fell here and there beyond the tank trap as the Germans, who knew a forward artillery observer was directing the fire and knew that the number of shells would increase, and increase again as the artillery observer informed the guns they had found the right map reference, withdrew.

But though I could see the German infantry sifting back from the bunkers and pillboxes beyond the tank trap, I could not see the long, elegant barrels of the eighty-eights that had fired from the woods farther back and shot down this part of C Company and killed Sam Turley and half a dozen others who lay out on the muddy ground and inside the destroyed M4A3s.

As I listened to our artillery pounding the empty ground beyond the tank trap, help began to arrive. Shermans eased down the slope to our left and right. As they came on they fired over the destroyed tanks and the tankers crouching behind them, the 76 millimeter shells ploughing over the ground ploughed by our artillery. It was impressive and useless. The Germans were gone. They had done their work, and withdrawn to prepare to do it again farther east.

Our artillery fired and fired, and then stopped firing: the forward artillery observer must have seen the Germans departing. The tanks trundling forward fired a few more rounds over the wreckage of Shermans and men; and then they too ceased firing.

'Let's go down,' I said to Williston. He started the Jeep's engine and we coasted down the slope through the thin cover of snow. We passed Willy Thorn still standing up behind his useless gun. He did not look at us as we drove past. I glanced across at him: his face was full of grief and fury.

At the foot of the slope small groups of tankers huddled near their destroyed machines, holding cigarettes in their filthy hands and watching the cavalry arrive. The Shermans that had reversed away from the tank trap and the antitank guns squatted in the mud, engines idling, hatches open, their crews peering at the devastation.

Smoke drifted east across the tank trap toward the positions from which the Germans had destroyed this part of the Seven Six One in detail before withdrawing in good order. A man climbed up out of the mud onto the Sherman behind which he had been hiding and peered down through the commander's hatch. I wondered what he saw. Whatever it was, he could not help: shaking his head, he climbed down from the Sherman as machinegun ammunition began to detonate inside one of the burning tanks beyond, rattling against the steel walls like gravel shaken in a can.

'Mud pretty deep in here,' Williston said as he put the Jeep in four-wheel drive and shifted down into second gear. We ground and slithered forward. Shermans, weapons carriers, halftracks and a 105 millimeter assault gun eased forward with us, advancing toward the shot-down M4A3s still threatening the distance with their 76 millimeter guns. As we drove toward the dead sprawled in the mud, Williston made a sound in his throat.

I glanced back up the slope down which C Company had approached its calvary and from the top of which Williston and I had watched this fight. The slope seemed less steep once we were at its foot among the shot-down Shermans and the shocked tankers standing in the mud close to their destroyed machines. As I looked back I saw Willy Thorn driving the halftrack full of ammunition across the slope. I wondered why he did not come down. Perhaps he had been ordered elsewhere with his jumbled load of 76 millimeter and .30 and .50 caliber ammunition. Or perhaps he did not wish to see the dead men and destroyed vehicles at the foot of the slope.

I knew Williston did not want to look at the dead. 'Jesus,' he said as he braked the Jeep twenty feet short of a corpse lying face down in the dirty snow.

C Company's commander arrived with the rest of the help, standing up in the turret of a Headquarters platoon Sherman, speaking into a microphone in his right hand, calling for Doc Turner and his medics, calling for maintenance tracks and recovery vehicles.

Behind the first wave of assistance but in front of Doc Turner's ambulance halftrack and Service Company's maintenance and heavy recovery vehicles came First Sergeant Reardon, driving forward alone in his Jeep. His uniform and hands and face were dirty and his '03 Springfield lying on the right front seat was crusted with mud. Half the pouches in his antique bandoleer were empty. He surveyed the wreckage as he drove forward across the snow cover torn up by wheels, tank tracks, explosions and scrabbling men. As he got down from his Jeep and surveyed the survivors of Sam Turley's impromptu assault force, I noted that he had prepared himself for the mud: he wore coveralls and knee-high rubber boots. He listened as the tankers told him what had happened, looked from one speaker to the next from under the flat round brim of his antique campaign hat. When they finished telling him about the bits and pieces of the fight they had seen, the First Sergeant ordered them into a halftrack from C Company's Headquarters platoon, walked to the Sherman in which C Company's commander still muttered instructions into the microphone in front of his lips, and spoke to the Captain. The Captain nodded and the First Sergeant waved the halftrack full of survivors away to the rear.

The First Sergeant glanced our way, watched as I got down from the Jeep and approached the corpse lying twenty feet away face down in the mud. The corpse's arms were stretched out beyond the head, the fists clenched. I reached down, gripped this dead tanker's right shoulder and pulled, my feet sliding in the sucking squelching mud as I eased the man over onto his back. I could not identify him: his jaw and face and forehead had been shot away. As I looked at what he had become, I knew that, except for the mud, I would have seen the terrible secret detail of this dead soldier's brain, throat and trachea.

I unbuttoned the corpse's muddy tanker's jacket, unbuttoned his shirt beneath, reached under his olive drab undershirt and removed his dogtags. Each dogtag is notched. The notch is necessary to the operation of the stamping machine that imprints the tags. Yet this notch is useful: it can be wedged between the two front teeth in the upper jaw of a corpse and then hammered tight between the teeth. But this soldier had no teeth, and no jaws. I buttoned one tag into the breast pocket of his shirt and held the other up to read it. The tag identified the corpse: Thomas A. Carnes. I remembered him leaning against the bar in a pub at Wimbourne, in England, chatting with the middle-aged barman about New Jersey.

'You got his tag,' the First Sergeant asked as he stepped up and looked down at what Thomas A. Carnes had become. I hand the tag to the First Sergeant. 'I need some help here,' he said.

'I know,' I said.

'In my Jeep. Boots like these here, coveralls too. Two pairs of rubber gloves. Get into the coveralls and boots and bring the gloves. And those mattress covers. And bring the shovels, too.'

'We're going to bury them here?'

'No,' the First Sergeant said. 'That isn't what the shovels are for. Go on and get dressed now. We've got to do this and get on. I'll show you what to do.'

'Yes.'

Our first task was to collect as many of Sam Turley's pieces as we could find: a slice each of rib cage, leg, and arm. We did not find his tags. It didn't matter: this was Sam Turley. I saw the explosion that killed him and I saw him disappear. As we collected the bits of 1st/Sgt. Samuel J. Turley that the eighty-eight millimeter round had left behind and placed them in a mattress cover, I told the First Sergeant about the last moments of Sam Turley's life.

'He deserves the medal for this,' I said.

'You're right,' the First Sergeant said. 'No officer saw him, though. Lieutenant Coleman was killed over on the other side leading some of his crew up.' The First Sergeant pointed to the left. I did not see Lieutenant Coleman go, and I did not see him die: I was watching Sam Turley standing up against it. 'Lieutenant Coleman's Sherman got shot down and he dismounted, got down in the mud and led his dismounted crew up against some bunkers up in front and drove them out. They killed the Lieutenant while he was going forward.'

'Turley deserves it, though,' I said.

'Sure he does. But let me tell you so you'll know from here on: even if the Colonel had been standing right here when Turley went up there, and seen what he did, and recommended him, there wouldn't be no medal. Not in this Battalion, and not in this here war.' First Sergeant Reardon looked at me and away at the destroyed and damaged Shermans, the barrels of their guns angled this way and that, and said, 'Man like Turley here is gonna have to wait till the next war, or maybe the one after that, to get the medal. Wouldn't want it myself: more than half of them are given to the boy's parents. You know what I mean?'

'I know,' I told him.

'Maybe a Silver Star,' the First Sergeant said. 'Too long a shot for a DSC. Most likely a Silver Star, or if the man on the other end of the recommendation is backward, a Bronze. Or maybe nothing. But the Colonel will listen to what you and the others tell him. Turley'll get a Bronze at least.'

'That's it?' I said. 'But Jesus Christ. . . .'

First Sergeant Reardon looked at me from beneath the brim of his campaign hat and said, 'Don't be cursing over a man died like this here.' He gestured toward the space between the destroyed and damaged Shermans and the tank trap as though Sam Turley's corpse lay, neat, whole and identifiable on the ground over which he had fought. But I knew no single gesture could point out all the scattered bits of Sam Turley. The First Sergeant looked at me dressed like a clown in oversize rubber boots and oversize rubber gloves and baggy coveralls, 'Listen to what I'm saying. What he gets for this here ain't the important part. You and the rest of them here going to see a lot more like this in the next six months or a year. So it's time you figured out that the important part is what someone like

Turley does. What people think about it don't mean anything. Take a man alone nobody sees him do the right thing. He ain't any the less, is he? Or any the more if he's alone and run instead of stand?'

'No,' I said.

'Take a man like Turley here, does something when they ain't no officer telling him or looking. What he did isn't no different, is it, because there wasn't no officer to see?'

'No,' I said.

'And if no one give him a medal for their own reason, that don't make any difference, does it?'

'No.'

'Then you know,' he said.

'He still ought to have the medal,' I said.

'He ought,' the First Sergeant said. 'But he ain't going get it. He's going to get maybe a Silver, but more likely a Bronze. Though might be he may not get anything. But that isn't the important part: learn that right now. Important part is what he done here. You saw it from up behind and you're going to be one of the few can remember whole what happened here. Rest of these men will remember it every which way because they were down here in it. That's the way. So you remember it. When you're an old man, remember this fight and Turley here in pieces in this here mattress cover. If you come through this, remember.'

'All right, First Sergeant.'

'Don't call me First Sergeant while we're doing this,' he said.

'All right.' But I did not know what to call him.

The First Sergeant knotted the end of the mattress cover on itself. 'Take this man over next to the Jeep. You'll find a marking pencil in the back of the Jeep in an ammunition box. Write Turley's rank and name on the mattress cover so Doc Turner will know. Then come back. We got to get into these Shermans and get to work.'

I lifted the sack containing what was left of Sam Turley and slogged through the mud and filthy snow to the First Sergeant's Jeep. On the way I passed Williston sitting behind the wheel of the Jeep. Williston nodded as I passed, but he did not speak and he did not look at the mattress cover I carried.

I set the sack containing Sam Turley's remains on the snow beside the First Sergeant's Jeep, found the marking pencil and wrote '1st/Sgt. Samuel J. Turley' on the mattress cover in large black letters. Hearing the engine of a halftrack, I looked up and saw Doc Turner's people coming forward down the slope. I waved and the driver of the ambulance halftrack angled toward me. I pointed at the mattress cover on the snow beside the First Sergeant's Jeep. The man beside the halftrack's driver nodded as though he knew what was in the mattress cover. I turned away and started back toward First Sergeant Reardon climbing up the front of one of the incinerated Shermans.

So I began my second career in the Seven Six One, serving as the First Sergeant's acolyte during the private ceremonies he conducted for the torn-up, incinerated men who died in shot-down Shermans.

"You want to go on down?" Rutherford asks me.

"No. It's gone. They've even hauled the wrecks away. And I remember it."

"Okay," Rutherford says. "Go on back, then?"

"Might as well. Burch said to come back around two. Said Wallace ought to have First Sergeant Reardon's machines and ammunition together by then. And we might be able to get back up to the Seven Six One no later than tonight, if Burch knows where they are and they're not too far away."

"I know," Rutherford says. He looks down the slope toward the place where Sam Turley and eight other men were killed. "Seem like it all happened years ago, don't it?"

"Yes," I tell him.

ELEVEN

AS WE RETURN TO the weapons carrier at the top of the slope I think again of Sam Turley dismounting from his tank and getting down in the mud and rallying his crew and the crews of other disabled Shermans and going forward, taking the chance. I also think of the British Major who in the late summer of 1944 addressed us at Camp Hood. The Battalion executive officer, who was not then yet suffering from 'combat fatigue', announced, in his twangy deep south introduction, that the British Major was an expert on armored warfare in Africa, in Italy and in northern Europe, and that the subject of his talk would be the use of armor in support of infantry.

Yet though the British Major spoke of lines of approach, hull down positions, expenditure of ammunition and wireless control, the gist of his talk concerned chemistry, steel, mathematics and chance.

Before the war the British Major must have been a slim engaging man. By the late summer of 1944 he was haggard. His face was narrow and bony and his bright blue eyes flicked and glittered. His skin was gray and pitted, as though they had made him stand out in the desert wind full of grit and sand. His thoughts darted and his voice trembled when he spoke, his long sandy hair swinging across his forehead. When he stood, he stood up straight; but when he walked he hunched his right shoulder forward and dragged his left leg as though it had been taken away from him, rebuilt according to a set of inaccurate plans, and reattached to his hip. Unlike some of our officers, he was an egalitarian: he ate with the officers or the enlisted men as he chose and he drank in the enlisted men's club when he pleased. Drinking one glass of beer after another, he chatted with anyone standing within the range of his voice and he did not seem to notice, or misunderstand, the different accents we brought to the Battalion from all parts of the country.

I could tell, as all of us could tell, that he had been in too many dangerous, terrifying and disgusting situations and that he was doing a lecture tour in Texas because he had used up the fund of courage he had brought to the war with him. It seemed he remembered friends he had left behind in the desert, and in Italy and in northern France. We thought he was a little crazy, but we knew he had the right; and as he had taken the trip we were going to take, and knew the price of the ticket, every one of us listened with care and watched his face while he spoke about even the most insignificant detail of armored warfare.

'And don't,' he said during one of the three evenings he spent in Texas, 'sleep under your tank. Remember: a tank weighs a lot. The Sherman is what? Thirty tons and a bit. That's more than sixty thousand pounds. And there's gravity, you see. In the early days, in Libya, we had a crew who took refuge from the cold and the wind and the wet under their tank. Rain softened the ground while they slept. As the night wore on and they slept out of the storm, the tank sank down into the ground. By morning it had sunk down to the top of the bogeys, belly plate right down in the muck. Naturally the crew was crushed into the muck by all that steel. All of them—the tank was a cruiser, smaller crew, decent engine, gun wasn't worth a shit—were pressed into the mud. They suffocated. A piece of shit as a tank, the cruiser, but it was heavy enough to suffocate its crew. An order was issued forbidding anyone sleeping under a tank. Useless waste of paper, of course: no one needed to be told about sleeping under tanks, not after that. I suppose they cried out for help. But no one noticed, what with the noise of the storm. And of course we'd learned to park for the night with the tanks well spread out—wouldn't want a single shell to hammer more than one machine, would we? Hell of a job trying to dig them out. Actually we had to get on, so we had to give up digging and drive the Cruiser out. Tore them apart, but they were dead so it didn't matter.' The British Major glanced around at us and said, 'So: no sleeping under tanks. Better to be wet and uncomfortable. I'll add that you can't see a damned thing if you're under the tank. For that matter, you can't see a damned thing if the whole crew is asleep. And you have to see. You have to keep guard.'

'Crushed?' a corporal named Mallon asked. 'Suffocated? Jesus Christ.'

The British Major nodded and said, 'Jesus Christ: I agree. Unfortunately even he wasn't much help. Still, quite a number of the men standing around looking at the tank with the dead crew underneath were saying 'Jesus Christ' over and over again. But the men were dead and couldn't hear them.' The Major raised the glass of beer in his hand and poured half of it down his throat as though he were just in from ten days in the Libyan desert and had not had enough water since the end of the first afternoon.

Rutherford gets behind the wheel of the weapons carrier and starts the engine. I walk around and get into the passenger's seat. "You thinking about Sergeant Turley?" he asks.

"Some. More about that British Major who came to Camp Hood. Remember him?"

"Remember him? I won't never forget that man. He put the fear of God Himself into me. Particularly when he talk about the Sherman and how it was *all right* he said, but that it was *after all* a medium tank, he said, and *the gun* wasn't good enough or the *armor* thick enough, he said. I felt sick like I was going to puke. I knew this wasn't going be no picnic; and I knew I was in maintenance. But I thought at least we would be pretty much equal. When he said all that about the Sherman I started to think about the fucking Germans shooting up the tank companies and sweeping them aside and coming right through to Service Company. And I *knew* they weren't gonna take any prisoners. Not from the Seven Six One. Listened to that British Major talk about the fucking Germans and what they think, I knew it was worse than Misssippi over here. At least I thought it was like that. Until Prettyman came back."

"Prettyman," I say. I laugh. Prettyman still can't figure it out. "Now there's a lucky man."

"Lucky, shit: when I play poker I want him to stand behind my chair with his right hand on my shoulder. Lucky? That man the luckiest man ever lived."

On Thanksgiving Day, 1944, south of Sarre Union, Prettyman turned up a lane in a two-and-a-half ton truck full of cases of rations, cigarettes and miscellaneous equipment and drove up between minefields and wire entanglements in the fields on either side of the road, past a series of bunkers, pillboxes, foxholes, strongpoints, camouflaged antitank guns and then farther back through heavier antitank positions and then even farther back past dug-in artillery pieces and back farther still until he arrived at a Headquarters at the edge of a small woods, parked his truck, got down with his orders in his hand and sauntered up to the Headquarters tent which he himself later admitted was 'gray and patterned, like, you know? Not like the tents we all got. And there weren't no guard.'

When he stepped into the tent the Wehrmacht Colonel and the two Wehrmacht Captains and the three Wehrmacht Sergeants bending over a map spread out on a table looked up at Prettyman. The Captains stood up straight, the non-commissioned officers looked at the Colonel, and the Colonel began laughing, rubbing his sides through the grey cloth of his uniform jacket.

Prettyman has refused ever since to tell anyone, even the Colonel standing in the Headquarters halftrack saying 'Uh-huh', 'uh-huh', even the First Sergeant eying Prettyman from beneath the tilted brim of his campaign hat, what he answered when the Wehrmacht Colonel stopped laughing and said, 'Well, Private, how can I assist you?' in good American English before he lost control and began laughing again. Prettyman said that until the Colonel got control of himself again the Wehrmacht Sergeants looked solemn and the Captains looked confused. Finally the Colonel said, 'All right, all right, Private. You hiked all this way? No, you must have driven: I heard an engine.'

Prettyman told the Wehrmacht Colonel about the truck full of rations, cigarettes and equipment. 'What was I supposed to tell him?' Prettyman later asked any of us who would listen. 'Truck was right outside the door, the paper there in my hand. What was I supposed to tell him else?'

'Ah, cigarettes,' the Wehrmacht Colonel said. 'Usually I smoke cigars. Every day, three enormous cigars. But we lack cigars these days, and so I must smoke American cigarettes. I trust you have my brand?'

'All kinds,' Prettyman told him. Later he explained that they would look in the truck and take everything in it anyway so why shouldn't he tell them?

'Good,' the Wehrmacht Colonel said. 'We have a great need of tobacco. Your arrival is most fortuitous. Many thanks.' Even though he laughed in the middle and at the end of every sentence, Prettyman said the Wehrmacht Colonel seemed to be a gentleman even if he was a German Colonel here in the middle of the war. 'As for you, Private,' the Wehrmacht Colonel said, 'I'm afraid we can't keep you. We don't have a lot of time here to deal with prisoners. And I doubt you'd like the accommodations farther back. You'd be unique, of course, but I regret to say that, given some of my countrymen's attitudes, I doubt you'd find being a prisoner-of-war very congenial.'

Prettyman said when he heard the Wehrmacht Colonel say he wasn't going to make him a prisoner-of-war, he knew what was going to happen. The Wehrmacht Colonel must have seen the look on Prettyman's face because Prettyman said the Colonel said, 'Oh, no, Private. Not that. I'm sending you back where you came from. You and the truck. As sturdy as they are, we don't have the parts for your trucks. But I'm afraid we'll have to keep the contents. I assume you have more of everything in your supply service?'

Prettyman reported later that he said, 'Yessir,' because he knew the Wehrmacht Colonel knew how well supplied we were.

'Good,' the Wehrmacht Colonel said. 'Then you won't miss this one load.' Prettyman said the Wehrmacht Colonel gave him a big smile as though he were already opening a pack of Chesterfields.

Then, Prettyman later said, he told the Wehrmacht Colonel, 'If I go back with the truck and no load and no receipt, sir, they'll say I sold it to the French.'

'Oh,' the Wehrmacht Colonel said, waving his hand as though he were brushing away an insect, 'don't worry about that, Private. I'll give you a note for your commanding officer.'

'Thank you, sir,' Prettyman said he said. 'But how come you doing this, sir? I know you could keep me prisoner here.'

'I don't want you on my conscience, Private. I spent an enjoyable year in Boston in 1933 -'34. I was a student. I studied law. And you were against us near Morville-les-Vic. We shot down some of your tanks but you had a sergeant who did very well getting his men together and driving off our infantry. I would have been happy to have him among my men. I saw him killed by a shell. Perhaps I feel I owe you something. But whether it's my memory of that sergeant of yours who came forward, or my memories of Boston, Private, you're going back. As I said, I don't want you on my conscience.'

So the Wehrmacht Colonel sat down, wrote out a note, put it into an envelope, sealed the envelope, handed it to Prettyman, gave one of the sergeants standing beside the table orders and said, 'Now, Private, the Sergeant here will blindfold you and drive the truck and you back to a place that is reasonably safe for both of you. Then he'll turn the truck over to you and away you go. Please give my compliments to your commanding officer when you return. And tell him I'm most grateful for the cigarettes and rations.'

Prettyman said he thanked the Wehrmacht Colonel and went out of the tent, the Colonel's laughter following him out. The Sergeant, a man maybe forty years old with a narrow unshaven face with a white scar in the stubble on his cheek, walked beside Prettyman hanging onto Prettyman's arm and snorting and laughing as he walked along, reeling now and then as though he were drunk and needed to hang on to Prettyman for support. Men in uniforms were unloading the truck. When they saw the laughing German Sergeant coming forward hanging onto Prettyman their bantering conversation became titters, laughter, guffaws.

'They was making fun of me,' Prettyman later told anyone who would listen. 'And you all think it's funny, too, don't you?'

'How can you tell, Prettyman?' whoever was listening to Prettyman would try to say before they doubled over laughing and beating their knees.

So Prettyman and the German Sergeant laughing and hanging on to Prettyman's arm watched the rest of the Germans unload the truck, laughing and lifting down cases of rations and tossing down cases of cigarettes and calling remarks to Prettyman that he didn't understand until one of the Captains came out of the Wehrmacht Colonel's tent and ordered the men to get on with it and they stopped laughing but went on giggling and snorting. When the truck was empty the German Sergeant glanced at the equipment piled on the ground, selected a new musette bag, gestured Prettyman up into the cab under the wheel and across the seat and climbed up after him. Instead of blindfolding Prettyman with a handkerchief the German Sergeant unbuckled the two straps on the musette bag, handed the open bag to Prettyman and gestured that he should put it over his head.

Prettyman put the bag over his head. The Sergeant started the truck's engine and drove off. The German soldiers were laughing and calling out as they drove away. All the time the German Sergeant was driving the two-and-a-half ton truck he was laughing just, Prettyman said, 'like it were some kind of great big joke that I took a wrong turn somewhere.' Prettyman said later he could not understand why the Germans thought it was so funny and tried to get his friends in Service Company to agree with him that it wasn't funny that he had driven right through the Germans' thick, neat defenses and had been driven back through them with a musette bag over his head and a note from teacher in his pocket for the Colonel.

When the German Sergeant pulled the bag off Prettyman's head he grinned at Prettyman, pointed through the windshield down the lane, and stuck out his hand. As they shook hands the Sergeant tried not to laugh. He did not succeed. To make amends the Sergeant introduced himself, saying: 'Friedrich Oberstadt.' When asked what he said in response, Prettyman said, 'I told him my name. What the hell else you think I tell him?' The German nodded when he heard Prettyman's name, said, 'Good trip,' got down from the truck, waved and walked back up the lane. Laughing as he went, Prettyman said, shaking his head as though the German Sergeant had been crazy and no one could see anything funny in what had happened and everyone in the Battalion, or at least his close friends in Service Company, would agree with him.

He was wrong. Even his close friends in Service Company laughed about Prettyman's 'trip', as it was called. Lucky Prettyman, everyone thought. No one could be luckier than Prettyman. They believed he was lucky because they did not believe Prettyman's luck would be repeated. Everyone knew enough about the Germans and their ideas to know Prettyman was the luckiest man in the world to come across a Wehrmacht Colonel with a sense of humor and a year in Boston behind him instead of, say, a Standartenführer in the SS who had put in three years in Poland and Russia.

The Wehrmacht Colonel's note to the Colonel was signed Burkhardt Meister-Richter, M.A., Harvard Law School, 1934. 'Uh-huh,' the Colonel said as he folded the note and handed it back to Prettyman. 'Uh-huh,' the Colonel said as the First Sergeant looked out from under the flat brim of his campaign hat at Prettyman as though he were examining Prettyman through the telescopic sight of a sniper's rifle.

Prettyman carries the note with him in his wallet everywhere he goes, and I know he will show it to his great-grandchildren when this war is as much part of history as is the Philippine Insurrection. He will also try to tell his great-grandchildren it was all a mistake and no one ought to think there was anything funny about it.

"That Prettyman," Rutherford says as he drives away from the top of the slope along the edge of the woods toward the road. I know that speaking of Prettyman lets Rutherford try to force aside my memories of Sam Turley standing up in the last of the light, facing the darkness. "If I see him in the street in Kansas City when I'm seventy-five years old I'll still break down. And he'll still look offended, like he knew exactly what he was doing driving right back up through all those guns and Germans and right up to that German Colonel's Headquarters."

"He was lucky that Colonel saw Sam Turley coming on, wasn't he? That made him decide to turn Prettyman loose, you know? That, and his time in Boston."

"I know," Rutherford says. "Shit, you and Williston and that German Colonel must be the only people on earth who saw the whole thing. Saw Turley get up and go on up and saw him killed coming back. You know?"

"Yes."

"What Turley did, though, and Coleman and the others, too," Rutherford says. He shakes his head. "After the Colonel was wounded and that fucking exec turned yellow and Byrd, Simmons, Mann, Chapman and Woodard died all together like that, I think everyone wondered whether we would come out at all when the bell rang."

"Every one always wonders that. Not just in this Battalion."

"Sure they do," Rutherford says as he eases the weapons carrier up onto the road. "But like everyone knows, we got a special something to do out here."

"Out here it's the armor that counts, and the fighting. That doesn't change from one Battalion to another."

"Bullshit it don't," Rutherford says, shifting up and accelerating. "Some units do all right, others don't. You can't get around that. We're doing all right now. But I wondered and I think everybody else too wondered, right up until Sam Turley went up like that, how we'd do. Turley and Lieutenant Coleman and the rest of them, I mean."

"I didn't see Coleman. He must have died over on the other side."

"Them two and seven others. But it's Turley who sticks in my mind," Rutherford says. "Bringing his weapon down, getting the others to follow him, and then going up against them. Prettyman's German Colonel was right to say Turley did all right. After Turley did that, we come out all right every time after. I guess everybody thought that after Turley, whatever came along we could face up to it."

"Yes," I say.

"You think 1st/Sgt. Burch going to have all that stuff together when we get back?"

"All that and more, I'd guess. He's got that manner that people who were in the Army before the war have. You know, like they know how to do everything better than anybody else, from cleaning a rifle to fiddling orders."

"And they do," Rutherford says. "I'll bet even with that fever and worn down as he is Burch can do all that and more."

"I hope he can," I say. "If you're right, we ought to get the Jumbos First Sergeant Reardon wants." The M4A3E2, nicknamed the Jumbo for its plump appearance, is an up-armored Sherman. It weighs eighty-four thousand pounds, tons more than the M4A3, and almost all of that additional weight is armor. The Jumbo's extra weight is supported by broader tracks and a different suspension system. The Jumbo is supposed to be the answer to German antitank fire, particularly to the fire of the Germans' eighty-eight millimeter gun. Everyone knows the Jumbo is not going to be up to that particular job, but the Jumbo is better than what we have, and the Germans are growing weaker now. However many guns they have, they will not have enough; and however elegant and vicious their tanks and self-propelled tank destroyers, they have lost too many of them to artillery, tactical air and the Russians, and too many of their manufacturing facilities to the bomber offensive.

"Sound to me like Wallace will come through with the Jumbos and the assault Shermans and some of the HVAP ammunition," Rutherford says. "I hope to Christ he does: I still remember that British Major telling us how the Sherman wasn't big enough."

"He was right."

"You remember what he said about the fighting just after the invasion last June? That the Sherman's shells bounced off the German armor?"

"I remember," I say. The British Major told us we would have to fight on what he called an 'uneasy footing.' When he said this he was standing on a low stage. Beside him, resting on its butt, was the eighty-eight millimeter shell he had brought along to show us. The menacing tip of the shell rose to the Major's waist. 'This is what they will fire at you,' he said. 'Of course, they have five different types of rounds,' he said. 'In addition to this one, which I brought along to show you, which is called Armor Piercing Capped, they have Armor Piercing Composite Rigid, which is lighter, but faster than APC. Then they have high explosive antitank, which is slower than APC or APCR but which is very effective at shorter ranges—say, out to two thousand yards. In addition, they have two types of high explosive round: percussion and time.'

Beside the eighty-eight millimeter round the Major had brought along stood the round fired from a Sherman's 76 millimeter gun. The 76 millimeter round looked puny. 'You'll note the difference in size,' the Major said, 'between this round and the one you're firing. It's a pity, I know, but there it is and there's nothing to do except make the best of it.'

Someone in the middle of the seated audience whispered, 'What the fuck he mean make the best of it?'

The British Major may have limped, but his hearing was acute. He surveyed the audience and said, 'Good question. I'll tell you what the fuck I mean by make the best of it. Bearing in mind that the frontal armor on a Sherman is less than half as thick as the frontal armor on a Tiger, and that the Tiger's gun will pierce the frontal armor of a Tiger, you have to do the other thing. What you have with the Sherman is numbers, mechanical reliability and, right at the other end of the radio in the turret with you, air and artillery support. We'd still be a mile from Gold Beach without tactical air and artillery. But you know that. What you want to know is what you do when you find you're up against a Panther with a 75 millimeter gun, a Tiger or a Hunting Panther with an eighty-eight, or God help you a Hunting Tiger with the biggest damned eighty-eight you've ever seen. The clever answer is: don't get yourself into that kind of situation. You're not required to provide targets for German gunners. Go to their flanks. By-pass them. Call in artillery. Be sure you're hull down if you have to fire at one of them. And when you've fired, move. Keep moving, and keep firing. And while you're firing and moving, call the cab rank. The cab rank? Oh, I see. The cab rank is on-call tactical air.

Typhoons and Thunderbolts armed with bombs, rockets and cannon. They do an excellent job on tanks. Be sure you establish your position with care when you call them in, though. They're awfully good pilots but they have been known to mistake a Sherman for a Tiger. Can't for the life of me think why. The length of the Tiger's gun alone ought to be clear to anyone, even a pilot. Can't mistake the twenty foot barrel of a Tiger for the stub mounted on the Sherman. As I have no doubt all of you will find out a lot sooner than you'd like. Any questions?'

Harry Herndon, a diligent, careful corporal with a fountain pen and three pencils in his left breast pocket and rimless glasses on his nose, stood up and said, 'Sir, what about hatches? Should we keep them open, do you think? Or closed? When we're in contact with the enemy, I mean.' Herndon believed that if he studied enough, he would be all right.

In training, hatches were a matter of intense concern and detailed debate. One faction argued that all hatches, with the exception of the commander's, should be closed at all times when the Sherman was in contact with the enemy. The other faction argued that hatches should be open at all times, to permit examination of the surrounding terrain, in which enemy infantry armed with hand-held antitank weapons tipped with hollow charges might be lurking.

Harry Herndon had asked the question to which he and everyone else in the audience knew the experienced British Major would provide a definitive answer.

'A good question,' the British Major said. 'Unfortunately, I don't think I have an answer for you. It's a matter of judgment, you see. It depends.' The British Major became silent. He looked out over the audience, placed his right elbow in his left hand and moved his lower jaw left and right with the thumb and forefinger of his right hand while Harry Herndon stood up in the middle of the audience, waiting to be given the answer. 'Well, ah, it's difficult,' the Major said, taking his hand down from his jaw. 'On the one hand, you want the hatches closed against smallarms fire. And against mortars and artillery, of course. Against any kind of plunging fire, for that matter. On the other hand, a closed hatch can be bloody dangerous if they're firing antitank weapons. Particularly large caliber antitank weapons, like the eighty-eight, or solid shot fired line-of-sight by artillery. The problem isn't the penetration of the round. If it strikes, it will penetrate. The problem is that when shot slams into armor it strikes with such force that it makes the target—ah, that's the Sherman you're in—jump. I don't mean it pushes at it, or makes it lean on its suspension. I mean it makes the whole machine jump as the armor piercing round strikes the target's armor. That shouldn't surprise you. After all, with one type of the eighty-eight's rounds, you're got a heavy, compact mass of hardened steel moving about three thousand two hundred feet a second. Now, when it strikes its target—that's the Sherman—the energy of the round is transferred to the target. That's a lot of energy. Along with everything else, that amount of energy distorts metal. The hatches are metal. If they are bent and distorted by the energy of the antitank round, they stick.'

'Stick?' Herndon asked from the middle of the audience. His question, like Prettyman's journey through German lines to visit the Wehrmacht Colonel, became part of the lore of our Battalion.

'Stick,' the Major said. 'As in: won't open. And naturally you want to be able to open them when the Sherman is struck by an eighty-eight. You want to get out. If the hatches are jammed, you can't get out.'

'But how do you know when to keep the hatches closed, and when to keep them open?' Herndon asked.

'Ah,' the Major said. 'That's the question, isn't it? I'm afraid I don't have any fixed rule for you. You see, it's a matter of judgment, Corporal,' the Major said. 'You learn as you go along and hope you learn enough soon enough. Suppose you glance out and see infantry lurking near at hand. You could close the hatches, since you might be shot if you didn't. On the other hand, if you don't see infantry near, they may be farther back in a screen in front of the antitank weapons and the tanks and self-propelled guns, and you'd want the hatches open. On the other hand, if you don't see infantry, they might still be near at hand. Behind the next bush, say. And they may not be alone. As I said, they may be protecting antitank weapons. But the antitank weapons may not be farther back, as in the situation I just described: they may be camouflaged, and right at hand. Note that I haven't discussed the situation in which you're under artillery fire, and enemy infantry and antitank guns are near at hand.'

'But what are we supposed to do, Major?' Herndon asked. Only a single man in the audience laughed: a single guffaw.

'That's the central question, isn't it, Corporal? I'm afraid it's one of these on the one hand on the other hand on the third hand situations. You find them all the time in this war. Simplest problem of this sort I can think of is: when to have a spade.'

Herndon, who had become the Battalion's spokesman, asked, 'A spade, sir?'

'Oh, sorry. Another expression. It means: evacuating your bowels.' The Major looked at Herndon's enquiring face. 'Taking a shit, Corporal.'

'Oh,' Herndon said. 'Yes, sir.' On the low stage behind the Major the executive officer who would become a coward on the day after the Colonel was wounded nodded as though the Major were giving us all valuable information about hygiene in the field.

'Decision on when to take a shit in the field can be important. If you're in thickly wooded country—as in Normandy, say—and you're worried the enemy may be near at hand and one of your crew finds he has to take a shit, fire a round from the main armament and have him use the shell casing. And when he's finished, pass the casing around and have everyone in the crew urinate or defecate into it as they feel the need. I mean, you can't go firing off round after round of valuable ammunition just to satisfy every man's urge when he gets the urge. Who knows? The round you fired so that the man who needed to take a shit would have a convenient receptacle might be the one round you'll need to keep yourself from being shot down. Or brewed up, as we say. It's the Germans who say 'shot down'. Best advice about this is: be sure everyone in the crew defecates and urinates before mounting up. Shits and pisses, I mean.'

'That's it, sir?' Herndon asked. 'About the hatches? You can't tell us when they ought to be closed and when we should keep them open?'

'I'm afraid not. General advice, of course. But your best bet is to rely on your own judgment. Consider your circumstances and act on what you think best. Don't let doctrine get in your way. Don't make rules for yourself. Rely on what you see and what you think you ought to do. And don't be afraid to run, or to waste ammunition, or to call for help. Use everything you've got, in whatever order you think best. But one thing: don't go up against bad odds. I'm telling all of you that, and I'm speaking particularly to the officers about that. You're the responsible parties, after all.'

Coughing and glances from the officers in the front row and on the stage.

'I can't emphasize that enough,' the Major said. 'Don't waste your capability.' He looked about at the officers as he spoke to them. 'By capability I mean your men and your machines. Remember your lessons. Go to the flanks. Go around the other way. Retire if you must and call in artillery and air to do the job. You're not trying to prove anything up there, after all: you don't work for the Sherman's manufacturers. You're trying to get through and out the other side, and if you can do it in the same tank, you're good, and lucky.' The Major glanced here and there at the men in the audience. 'I'm sorry,' he said. 'As I said, it's a question of judgment. Most of it is. I wish I could encourage you to believe that there is some magic formula. But there isn't. It's all a fog, you see. One thing happens, and then the next. The plans get fucked up, you see. The maps aren't right. And the Germans are good. I'll give them that: they're very good. A lot better than we are, I'm afraid.' The Major stopped talking. He stared over the heads of the men in his audience as though he were in Egypt, staring across Libya, trying to see Tunisia.

Down in the middle of the audience Herndon sat down.

As we came out of the Major's lecture First Sergeant Reardon, who had been sitting at the back of the audience, nodded and nodded as we walked past, as though he sure in hell hoped we were listening to every word the British Major had said.

"I been thinking," Rutherford says as we drive along the narrow road. "You said you going to sign for all this here equipment 1st/Sgt. Burch and Sergeant Wallace getting together for us. What are you going to say if someone come later and says: why you sign?"

"I'll tell them I thought it was all right to sign. I'll tell them I was forced."

"What are you going to do if someone says: you signed, and you going to jail."

"I'll tell them I didn't know what I was signing. I'll tell them the sergeant told me to sign and I signed."

"What sergeant?"

"One of these here supply sergeants I can't remember his name. You know they all look the same."

"You think that'll keep you out of jail?"

"I'll shuffle and roll my eyes and say 'yes, sir, you is right sir."

"And you think that'll do it?" We are approaching a farm cart. The horse in the traces is glossy and brown. I wonder how the farmer up on the box of the cart could have kept this one horse so healthy throughout the war and the fighting that passed through here and on to the east in November of last year. Rutherford steers around the cart. The old man up on the seat of the cart nods as we drive past and waves his right hand.

"Come on," I say. "No one's going to ask any questions. Uncle's got more. You know that. Besides, when a piece of equipment leaves the United States, it's written off as though it's already been destroyed by enemy action. Hell, I might ship one of those Jumbos home for use after the war."

"You might be needing one, after the war."

"Things'll change," I tell Rutherford. But I am not so sure: I'm trying to sound optimistic, but I am not.

"Yeah? We going to march in a parade in New York? They going to let me join up with the VFW in Kansas City? What about where I got to piss? They going to let me piss where I want? They ain't like General Hillman. Or not many of them."

"That's going to depend on where you want to piss," I tell him. But I know what he means. So does everyone in the Seven Six One. I wonder what First Sergeant Reardon did about pissing when he was stationed at Fort Benning.

"Don't fuck with me," Rutherford says. "You know what I mean." He jams the gear shift from fourth down into third as we head up a low hill. Above the sound of the weapons carrier's engine I hear a roar of engines in the sky. I look up as we reach the top of the hill. Three fat P-47s pound toward us, gaining altitude, flying in line astern a thousand feet up. These are not the same three we saw before: the bright scheme painted on their noses is different. But they are loaded with the same mix of bombs and rockets. As I watch, the leader of the flight banks to the right and the other two follow him.

"I know what you mean," I tell Rutherford as the P-47s pound away, heading southeast. "What do you want me to do about it?"

"You got some education, at least. You ought to be able to do something." He sounds as though he and I are the last ones left and that I should be the volunteer.

"I'm trying," I tell him. "But right now I'm trying to get past the Germans. You guarantee me I'll make it to the end of the Germans and I'll start thinking about what I'm going to do next."

"That still don't tell me where I'm going to go after the war, what I'm going to do. Everybody else over here in Europe going to be a hero. What you think they going to remember about us when this shit finished? They'll deactivate the Battalion, we'll be sent home and that'll be the fucking end of it."

"You could re-up," I say. "The Army's gonna need men when the war's over. You heard General Hillman. A man like you, Rutherford, if you stayed in, why you could rise up to, say, Master Sergeant in fifteen, twenty years."

"Like 1st/Sgt. John P. Burch say: piss on that noise. I ain't staying in this here suit one minute longer than the Colonel says I have to. I'm getting out."

"What are you going to do?"

"I don't know. Who knows? Try to find a place, I guess. Some place I can be. Some thing I can do."

"You'll find it," I tell him. But I am not so sure: what place will there be for Rutherford and the rest of us? Where will we be permitted to go, what will we be given leave to do?

"I hope to Jesus you right," Rutherford says. "But I don't know how. Right now I can't figure it."

"It's just like that British Major said. Some things, there aren't any rules. You have to use your judgment and hope it works out."

"Hope it works out. That's the best we got to look forward to?"

"After all this, here in Europe, going home's going to be easy." But I wonder what I will feel when I see the docks in New York or Baltimore. I know home will be different after this war. But the question is: how different?

"Except you can't just shoot them back home," Rutherford says. He sounds as though he regrets that direct action won't be allowed. "Sometimes," Rutherford says, "this here seems a lot easier. You just shoot and see what happens next. All you got to worry about is dying or getting hurt. But aside from that, hell, it's no harder work than the stockyards in Kansas City."

"That's true. On the other hand, they can't just shoot you down back home either."

"That the way it work up to Chicago? I didn't notice that in Kay See. Seem like, in Kay See, they could shoot you anytime they wanted. And they did." And they did in Chicago, too. But I don't want to think about that now.

"All that's going to change," I tell Rutherford. If I repeat this, he may believe me. If I repeat it enough, I may believe me.

"I ain't sure I believe that. Seem more like it won't change at all. May be it get worse."

"People will see what we did over here, and in other places, and they'll remember."

"Bullshit. Ain't nobody gonna remember, nor give us nothing for it either even if they do remember."

"That isn't the point. Why do you think Turley did what he did here? Cause he thought he'd get something out of it? Cause he thought he might live through it and get a job when he was back home if he did what he did?"

"Don't ask me why he did it," Rutherford says. "I don't know why he did it. I bet he didn't know why he did it either."

"Maybe not. But that doesn't matter either. Sergeant Reardon's right about that: only thing that matters is that Turley did what he did, instead of something else."

"Maybe you're right. That still ain't going to get me a job back in Kansas City. Or carfare."

"Where are we?" I ask. The narrow country road down which Rutherford is driving passes through woods and between fields and up and down slopes. I cannot see a farm house or a village anywhere.

"Chateau Salins is straight ahead. Then we go left to Nancy. Not much traffic around here, you know?"

"Everything's passed on east."

"Peaceful around here. You wouldn't think there was a war on. Here come another of them carts."

Rutherford is right. Approaching from the west is a cart piled high with a load of hay. Up on the box the driver is flicking the reins against the horse's back. The driver and the horse are both old. As Rutherford pulls over to the right side of the road to give the cart room the driver of the cart raises his hat and calls out, "Bonjour." Rutherford and I wave as we pass on.

"Be all right if we could stop in around here and talk with these people," Rutherford says. "They don't seem to notice, you know?"

"I noticed that. But they're probably just being polite."

"You think? I wonder what they think in Morville-les-Vic."

"They probably don't think anything," I tell him. "They probably don't know we went through there. It was a hell of a fight that day right inside the town. They were all probably hiding in the cellars. Besides, us and the Germans beat up their town pretty bad: you can't expect to have them like us for it."

"Still," Rutherford says, "I wouldn't mind stopping."

"Can't," I tell him. I look at my watch. It is after noon. "We got a little more than an hour to get back to First Sergeant Burch's office. Besides, it's behind us."

"I know," Rutherford says. "We got to get back. And then get back on the road heading east. To wherever the Seven Six One's gotten to."

"That's it."

"Still like to stop somewhere around in here," Rutherford says. "Take it easy for a time, you know? Sit and look out and not have to think about what coming tomorrow."

"Come back in thirty years," I tell him. "Be a tourist. Then you can stop anywhere you want." But I agree with him: I'd like to sit, too. Without obligation or duty.

"Tourist," Rutherford says. "Humph. You think I'm going to find somewhere to make me enough money to come back over here and tour around through these places?"

"Sure," I say. "Take the train. See Nancy. They got a cathedral. The old and new cities. The kings of Lorraine are buried in Nancy. Didn't you read the guide book?"

"Fuck the kings of Lorraine," Rutherford says. "Right now I ain't interested in no kings of Lorraine."

"That's why you want to come back as a tourist in thirty years. You'll have the time then to be interested."

Rutherford glances at me, shakes his head, looks forward and says, "Here comes another of those carts."

I look ahead. Rutherford is right: here comes another cart, piled high with hay. The horse isn't as old as the second one we saw, or as well kept as the first. The driver is a woman. She wears a heavy coat against the cold and has tied a scarf over her head and under her chin beneath the man's blue cap she wears. I guess she is fifty or more, but it is hard to tell: her face is thin and bony, as though she has not had enough to eat since 1940. As we approach the cart I see her skin is not lined. Perhaps she is younger than fifty. Who knows? We have no time to stop and chat. The woman sees us coming and waves and waves, calling out to us as we approach. She waves and smiles, as though it were a bright summer day and the war had ended years ago. As Rutherford drives past her I hear her calling, "Merci, merci bien, mes amis. Au revoir. Merci bien. Au revoir. Merci, mes amis."

"What's that she yelling?" Rutherford asks.

"Thanks, many thanks, my friends. And: see you again. And: thanks, my friends." I turn in my seat and see the woman's waving arm stuck out beyond the load of hay.

"Humph," Rutherford says. "You suppose she recognized us?"

"What else?"

Rutherford snorts, snorts again and says, "I see what you mean."

"On the other hand," I say, "maybe she just saw the uniform wasn't German."

"Haw," Rutherford snorts. "That one thing about it. You right about that."

TWELVE

1ST/SGT. JOHN P. BURCH says: "Joe Wallace came through." He lolls behind his desk as though Joe Wallace has won the war. "Two Jumbos, two 105 assault Shermans and eight hundred rounds of HVAP."

"Everything First Sergeant Reardon need," Rutherford says. He doesn't sound happy about the Jumbos, the assault Shermans and the HVAP. I suppose he is thinking about sitting and looking out and not having to think about tomorrow.

1st/Sgt. John P. Burch looks at Rutherford as though he expected more enthusiasm. "You guys," he says. He shakes his head. "You got to watch Bill Reardon, you know. You'll find a lot of sonsofbitches in the Army and out of it. Bill Reardon isn't one of them. He's come a long way to right here, and this stuff he's getting out of me he's getting because he and I knew one another back when. I want the two of you to remember that. Besides, Bill's going to need all the help he can find getting through. You know?"

"I know, First Sergeant," I say. But I am not sure I do: I have never heard anyone call First Sergeant Reardon anything but First Sergeant Reardon. And here's 1st/Sgt. John P. Burch calling the First Sergeant Bill, like the First Sergeant was the guy next door. I had thought First Sergeant Reardon was a remote, inscrutable career soldier, as immutable and eternal as the Army itself.

"We'll be there," Rutherford says. "He one of us and we be there."

1st/Sgt. John P. Burch stands up and puts his bony knuckles on the desk and stares at Rutherford with the sweating bony face he brought back with him from Guadalcanal before they told him, Services of Supply or out. "Piss on that noise," he says. "Bill Reardon isn't one of you and you aren't one of him. You don't know what he is. After you put in thirty years and fight over the same ground twice and learn how to tell your idiot officers how to keep themselves and their men from getting killed, maybe you'll get a feel for what Bill Reardon is. Right now you might be able to feel for him, but you sure in hell can't reach him."

"Okay by me," Rutherford says. "Whatever you say, First Sergeant."

"Don't give me that whatever you say First Sergeant shit, Rutherford. I been in this man's Army for more years than you've been standing up to piss. I don't need you to tell me whatever you say First Sergeant."

"Yes, First Sergeant."

"I'm telling you this: I want you to be sure Bill Reardon makes it through and out the other side of all this shit. I want to know he's retired safe. You understand me?" 1st/Sgt. John P. Burch looks at us as though we have been holding back a written guarantee we should have handed over when we first entered his office.

"Yes, First Sergeant," I say.

1st/Sgt. John P. Burch pounds his fist on his desk and shouts, "What the fuck does that mean yes First Sergeant?" I stand in front of him, saying nothing at all: what can I say?

"We'll take care with the First Sergeant, First Sergeant," I say. First Sergeant, First Sergeant, I think: how many times have I said First Sergeant? How many times will I say it after the war?

1st/Sgt. John P. Burch looks at me as though he has forgotten who I am and is trying to figure out why his clerk, Goddamn you Forrest, has let me into his office. His eyes glitter with fever and suspicion and the rage he must feel at what he does in this office: signing papers and commanding a telephone and Forrest Goddamn you. Still I can't figure it out: yesterday he took us to lunch in Nancy and talked about China and Fort Benning and his job in the Services of Supply and a little about First Sergeant Reardon, although it was clear he thought too much personal talk about First Sergeant Reardon would be bad for discipline in the Seven Six One. But today his eyes glitter and he shouts, ordering us to do what we would do in any case.

"You all right, First Sergeant?" Rutherford asks. He sounds calm, as though he has just noticed 1st/Sgt. John P. Burch has turned a little pale.

"I'm better than either of you will ever be," 1st/Sgt. John P. Burch shouts. "When you guys were civilians, Bill Reardon and I were soldiers. You civilians got no idea what that means." He looks at us as though he wants us to speak right up. But before I can speak he raves on. "Bill Reardon and I served when the guns had metal tires and wooden wheels and bores shot through and the United States didn't give a shit what happened. We were there when a tank was a set of drawings at the Rock Island Arsenal and an antitank weapon was a big rifle and the cavalry was a bunch of horses. We saluted Pershing when he came down to the Infantry School. And now you're telling me I don't have to worry about Bill Reardon because you two are gonna take care? I ought to reach down your throats and rip your hearts out." His hands and his voice are trembling with fever and anger. Or perhaps this is just another turn in every First Sergeant's repertoire. Who knows? I wish Sergeant Wallace would arrive with the Jumbos and the 105 Shermans and the HVAP ammunition.

"You can count on us," Rutherford says. "We're gonna do whatever's needed."

"You are?" 1st/Sgt. John P. Burch asks as though Rutherford's answer surprises him. 1st/Sgt. John P. Burch sits down. When he speaks again his voice is calm. "All right. I suppose that's good enough. I knew I could rely on you guys."

Rutherford rolls his eyes at me. I agree: I also wonder what is going on.

"I got something else for you guys." Rutherford raises his eyebrows. "That's right," 1st/Sgt. John P. Burch says, as though he can see we have guessed what else he has for us. "Tank transporters and drivers. All you guys are going to have to do is ride along in your weapons carrier. And two trucks for the HVAP. Any overage of the HVAP will be loaded on the transporters."

"Thanks, First Sergeant," I say. I wonder if he expected the two of us to drive two Jumbos, two 105 millimeter assault Shermans and two trucks and the weapons carrier back to wherever we're going.

"First Sergeant," I say, "We've got to find out where we're supposed to meet up with the Seven Six One."

"I figured you'd need to know where to go," 1st/Sgt. John P. Burch says. "So I got that information for you too. Up east near a place called Nieffern. It's south of Bitche. Sound familiar?" I nod: we were on our way to Bitche in November. We never got there. "Got a map for you right here," 1st/Sgt. John P. Burch says. He opens the shallow middle drawer of his desk where he keeps his pistol and pulls out the map. He unfolds it and traces our route. We edge closer to his desk and follow his moving finger: "You stay on the main road, see it here? from Nancy to Luneville, through Sarrebourg, through Saverne. You'll follow the line of the railroad. See it there? Beyond Saverne just before Detwiller you turn north to Ingwiller. See it on the Mader River there? Okay, from Ingwiller, ask the MPs. Your outfit is somewhere south southeast of right there. See?" 1st/Sgt. John P. Burch's fingertip rests on a dot on the map. Another village in the rolling countryside of eastern France. In Bas-Rhin, I note: as far east as you can get in France before you enter Germany.

"I see," I say. But I see no indication on the map of the fortifications the Germans have been constructing for years along their side of the Franco-German border. The West Wall, they call it. Great.

1st/Sgt. John P. Burch is looking at me. "Yeah," he says. "You guys are going right up there and through into Germany and across the Rhine and across Germany to wherever they tell you to go. But first, you're going to have to get through the Siegfried Line. That's why Bill Reardon wants these Jumbos and assault Shermans and the HVAP. HVAP is great stuff on fortifications. This map doesn't show it, but the Germans have extended the fortifications right down into France, connected them up with the Maginot Line. They're all wired in and waiting in these villages and little towns east of here," 1st/Sgt. John P. Burch says.

"Great," Rutherford says. He sounds as sick about it as I feel.

"Don't worry about it," 1st/Sgt. John P. Burch says. "Someone's sure to have some idea about how you're going to get through. And remember: the Germans are a hell of a lot weaker now than they were last year. When they came through the Ardennes in December they used up a lot of muscle. Besides, they need everything they've got to try to stop the Russians. So I don't think it will be that bad. No worse than anything else you've done." 1st/Sgt. John P. Burch seems confident we will make it. He, on the other hand, will be sitting here in his office in the middle of his so-and-so many square miles of supplies near Nancy, waiting to get the news and sweating with fever and anger and cursing that he can't be up there with us. "And the Russians are pounding away at them in the east, so they've probably had to thin out their troops here in the west."

"On the other hand," I say, "maybe they've thinned out their troops in the east to stiffen their defenses here in the west."

"I don't think so," 1st/Sgt. John P. Burch says. The tone of his voice tells me he believes his estimate of the situation is superior to mine.

I glance at Rutherford. He is rolling his eyes to show me how much he relies on the fact that 1st/Sgt. John P. Burch doesn't think so, and I can almost hear Rutherford thinking, 'Great, a two week vacation in eastern France. Except for the Germans, that is, and their mines and tanks and antitank guns and artillery."

Sergeant Wallace enters 1st/Sgt. John P. Burch's office, nods at us and says, "They're ready, John. Got everything loaded, got the transporters and trucks and drivers. I did good work." Sergeant Wallace is carrying a file in his left hand.

"I know you did good work, Joe. You think you deserve something extra for doing your job?"

"For doing this job, John, I deserve two weeks in Paris. At least two weeks. We're flying pretty high here, John."

"You got a man here's willing to sign," 1st/Sgt. John P. Burch says.

"What more do you want?"

"A lawyer?" Sergeant Wallace says. "To check the papers and give me an opinion in writing before anybody signs anything?"

"Piss on that noise," 1st/Sgt. John P. Burch says. "And piss on lawyers. No one's going to ask any questions. We get a requisition, we fill it. That's what we're here for. What? You think we ought to hold all the stuff in this dump until the war's over?"

"No, John. But on the other hand, two Jumbos? There aren't that many of them anywhere in Europe. Aren't we supposed to distribute these things around on the orders of Army and corps supply?"

"Joe, we been all over this three times, and we still got a tank battalion here needs equipment. We got a requisition here. You think the Colonel's going to make trouble over a duly signed requisition?"

"I'm not worried about the Colonel," Sergeant Wallace says.

"I told you: don't worry about the Inspector General. He's got other things to worry about. Stealing: that's what he's got to worry about."

"I'll take your word for it, John. You and the willing man here are going to sign. It's immaterial to me, if you and he sign."

"We're signing. Gimme the papers so I can sign." Sergeant Wallace opens the file and places it in front of 1st/Sgt. John P. Burch. 1st/Sgt. John P. Burch picks up a pen and begins signing. When he is finished he turns the file around and puts it on the front edge of his desk and says to me, "Sign." I step up to the desk and take the pen. I smell gin on 1st/Sgt. John P. Burch's breath and when I take the pen I touch his fingers: they would be no more warm and damp were his office in Halmahera. 1st/Sgt. John P. Burch is a sick man and ought to be under a doctor's care. But perhaps part of what he is is his refusal to do what others do, or what others tell him to do.

I sign, and sign again and again. When I am finished 1st/Sgt. John P. Burch tells me, "Good work. You did a good job here." Sergeant Wallace leans forward, separates the documents into four sets, hands two sets to me, a third to 1st/Sgt. John P. Burch, puts the fourth set into the file, closes the file and slips it under his arm.

"You're pretty quick, Joe," 1st/Sgt. John P. Burch says. "You think someone's going to take your file and erase their signatures? Nobody here is trying to screw you, Joe. Or the Army."

"Uh-huh," Sergeant Wallace says. "You keep those papers handy," he says to me. "If anyone asks, show him the first set with First Sergeant Burch's signature on them. You give the gate guard the second set when you go out." He turns and goes to the door.

"See you later, Joe?" 1st/Sgt. John P. Burch says.

Sergeant Wallace stops in the doorway, his hand on the knob.

and says, "Dinner? Why not? About six out front here?"

"Sounds good to me," 1st/Sgt. John P. Burch says. "I could use a drink."

Sergeant Wallace nods, steps through the doorway and closes the door behind him.

1st/Sgt. John P. Burch stands up and says, "You guys are set. I'll go down with you." He takes his campaign hat down from a nail in one of the exposed risers in the wall and puts it on. He adjusts it as First Sergeant Reardon does, fitting it square on his head, the chinstrap behind, the brim tilted forward an inch. The hat makes him look like an old time soldier, but it can't hide the sweat marks under his arms and around his waist and down his thighs, and it can't thicken his wasted body or fill out his uniform. 1st/Sgt. John P. Burch is diminished, an outline of what he must have been. I wonder what I will say when First Sergeant Reardon asks me how 1st/Sgt. John P. Burch is doing. I will think of an easy lie, so that First Sergeant Reardon will not be troubled about his old friend. He has enough to think about: his private request for Jumbos, 105 assault Shermans and High Velocity Armor Piercing rounds for our 76 millimeter guns indicates that he knows what is going to happen, doesn't like what he knows, and wants an edge. Who wouldn't? We have heard enough about the Siegfried Line to know that the best course would be to have the Eighth Air Force's B-17s come over and pound the Germans' bunkers and minefields and obstacles and gun emplacements for twenty days before we go up.

We follow 1st/Sgt. John P. Burch out of his office. Forrest gets up as 1st/Sgt. Burch passes his desk. Forrest looks up as though he wants instructions. "Do some work, Forrest," 1st/Sgt. John P. Burch says as he walks past Forrest's desk. "Stop reading that Goddamned newspaper and do some work. I'll check when I get back, Forrest. You understand me? I'll check."

"Yes, First Sergeant," Forrest says. He does not look at us as we pass and we do not look at him. We pass out of the quonset hut. It is chilly and I am glad I am wearing my overcoat. 1st/Sgt. John P. Burch does not wear a coat: the faint sunlight in the clear sky seems to project all the heat his feverish body needs.

Rutherford glances around. He looks down the corridors between the stacked crates and boxes under the camouflage netting and telephone wire strung up on poles. "I don't see no Jumbos," he says. Rutherford doesn't believe we will get the Jumbos, or the HVAP, or the 105 millimeter Shermans. He doubts, and he is suspicious. I know this. After all, he has told me he carried a gun and a knife under his coat in Kansas City, and in France he carries his German machinepistol wherever he goes, and each time his doubts are confirmed, he shifts his Schmeisser this way and that in his hands to show he is ready.

"You think you could get a tank transporter in here, Rutherford? You think they bring 105 assault Shermans around here in front of my office?" 1st/Sgt. John P. Burch asks. "You think I want a load of highly volatile ammunition brought in here among all this valuable equipment and spare parts?"

"I guess not," Rutherford says, looking this way and that. "First Sergeant," he adds.

"They're over at armor resupply. Let's go. I don't have a lot of time. Got to get back here and sign papers. And after that, I got to sign more papers." He walks to our weapons carrier and gets up in the back. Rutherford starts the engine and drives through the lanes and roads and avenues in the dump, following 1st/Sgt. John P. Burch's directions. Soon we drive out of the rectangular lattice of lanes between parallel stacks of crates and cartons and begin driving between rows of guns stored under protective canvas.

"I don't see no ammunition," Rutherford says.

"Neither do I," 1st/Sgt. John P. Burch says. He sounds as though he might begin shouting again. "You think we should store ammunition next to these guns? What do you think would happen if some nazi dropped a bomb anywhere in here? We lose ammunition, we can get more. Replacing a bunch of fucked up 105 and 155 millimeter howitzers is more difficult. It's also more expensive. And you'll have noticed the Army's concerned about expense. Besides, Services of Supply's got a plan for every one of these dumps. Keep the ammunition one place, fuel another, machinery another, food another. Like that. Keep it spread out. You think about a fire? What if we have a fire in one of the fuel stores? You want it to spread to the ammunition or the rations? Or the cigarettes? Or the officers' supply of whisky?"

"No, First Sergeant," I say.

"No, First Sergeant," Rutherford says.

"You're a couple of polite guys," 1st/Sgt. John P. Burch says. "And now you understand how we do things here in the Services of Supply, I can tell you're smart, too. Turn right here."

Rutherford turns right. We drive down a lane between 155 millimeter guns and their tracked prime movers. "Lot of stuff in here," Rutherford says, by way of making conversation.

"Got enough stuff in here to blow up two cities," 1st/Sgt. John P. Burch says. "Any two of your choice. Go left."

Rutherford goes left. We roll down a lane between 105 millimeter self-propelled guns. "Left again," 1st/Sgt. John P. Burch says. Rutherford goes left again. Now we are driving between two ranks of M4A3 Shermans. Their guns are elevated, and the shadows of their barrels flick over us as we drive on.

"Getting there now," 1st/Sgt. John P. Burch says as we drive out into an open space several hundred yards wide. Perhaps it was a field last year. Whatever it was has been scraped away by bulldozers and rolled flat. At the far edge is the fence that has been erected around the dump. In the rain the surface of this huge empty place will be mud, and in the summer dust will puff from the heels of a man walking across it. Right now it is damp but not muddy. "Over near the gate to the left," 1st/Sgt. John P. Burch says. I glance that way as Rutherford steers left. Far away by the fence beneath a clump of trees left by the bulldozers four tank transporters and two two-and-a-half ton trucks are parked. I see the drivers and their assistants, their faces indistinct in the shadows.

So does Rutherford. "Some us," he says.

"Some of you?" 1st/Sgt. John P. Burch says. "These guys aren't some of you. They're in fucking supply. You guys are in Bill Reardon's Seven Six One. Even if you are just in maintenance. You don't see any difference there? No? Lemme tell you: you don't have anything in common with these guys. Or them with you. They're a bunch of fucking truckdrivers, and half of them got the clap. They steal and they sell what they steal and buy women in Nancy and half of them get the clap. Our doctors got no time, the work they have to put in pumping penicillin into these guys. Most of the time they're okay. But they haven't served in infantry, or tanks, or even the fucking artillery."

"Maybe they haven't had the chance," I say.

"Maybe not," 1st/Sgt. John P. Burch says. "I know some of them haven't. But since the Ardennes they can volunteer for infantry if they want. You see any of them volunteering?"

I look ahead at the drivers smoking and standing around. "No, First Sergeant," I say.

"Actually, we've had a lot of volunteers from this facility," 1st/Sgt. John P. Burch says. "They're training now, and they're going to go up for sure. They're going to go in platoons and companies to regular infantry divisions. General Eisenhower's got a shortage of men. But that on one side, let me give you two a piece of advice: don't give Bill Reardon that they haven't had a chance shit. If you're smart, you won't bring that up. Pull up there at the front of the first transporter."

Rutherford pulls up at the front of the first transporter. As we halt the drivers and assistant drivers put out their cigarettes and come forward. A sergeant in a Jeep parked near the gate gets out of the Jeep and saunters over to us with a clipboard in his hand and a cigar in his mouth. "John," he says. "You got your copy of the paper for me to see?"

"How's it going, Millard? Sure I got a copy for you. You think I'd drive all the way over here without paper just to see you?" 1st/Sgt. John P. Burch hands Millard the papers. Millard flips through them, checking the signatures.

"Everything okay, Millard?" 1st/Sgt. John P. Burch asks. "Or you want a living witness to my signature?"

"Looks okay to me. Joe Wallace was down here before. He said you were going to sign, and one of these guys." He looks at me and Rutherford.

"Me," I say.

"Okay," Millard says. He points a finger at me. "You. Anyhow, I need a witness, Wallace is it. All right. Let me tell you," he says, speaking to Rutherford and me, "about what you got here. The M4A3E2s and the 105 assault Shermans are all ready to go. Checked out, fueled, loaded. Got every single piece of equipment in them and on them the manual calls for. You can drive them right off the transporters and start in on the fucking Germans if you want. All this here HVAP you're getting tells me you're going to be doing something I don't want any part of. The HVAP is in the trucks and on the transporters in the usual crates, ammunition containers inside the crates, cardboard tube around each round. You got directions?"

"First Sergeant Burch gave us a map, Sergeant," I say.

"Okay. Wallace told me where you're going. Soon as you get up there, I want the tanks and the assault Shermans and the ammunition unloaded, and I want the transporters and trucks back here. You guys hear me?" he asks the twelve drivers and assistant drivers.

"We hear," one of them, a corporal, says. "Go there and straight back, like always."

"You got it, Jameson," Sergeant Millard says to the corporal. "Corporal Jameson is in command of this convoy. You understand? He's the responsible man," Sergeant Millard tells us, as though the other eleven are not. "So are these other guys responsible. They know their stuff, and they'll get you there. You know it ain't easy driving one of these transporters through some of these little towns they got over here. Not easy at all. You get a bad driver, he can knock down buildings, fuck things up, even halt a convoy. Transporter and the load puts the whole thing up there near twice a Sherman's weight. But these guys know what they're doing and you ought to be there late afternoon today."

"Thanks, Sergeant," I say.

"You'll be all right," 1st/Sgt. John P. Burch says. I'm sure he's right about the drive up. It's the part after the drive up that worries me.

1st/Sgt. John P. Burch takes an envelope out of his pocket and hands it to me. "Give this to First Sergeant Reardon when you see him."

"I will, First Sergeant," I tell him. I put the letter in the inside pocket of my coat next to General Hillman's letter. The First Sergeant is going to get a lot of mail.

"And give him my regards," 1st/Sgt. John P. Burch says.

"We'll do that," Rutherford says.

"Tell him I wish I were up there with him," 1st/Sgt. John P. Burch says.

"I'll do that, First Sergeant," I say. I can't imagine why he would want to be up there with First Sergeant Reardon. Mud, gunfire, mines, sullen civilians standing in front of their wrecked houses, and beyond all that, concrete obstacles, bunkers and pillboxes full of guns and determined Germans peering through the sights of their weapons at the range markers they set up in their fields of fire years ago.

"All right, then. You guys get out of here." He looks at his watch. "It's near two o'clock. You ought to be able to make Nieffern by four if you go now. Millard, you can drive me back."

"Right, John," Sergeant Millard says.

"You guys take it easy," 1st/Sgt. John P. Burch says to Rutherford and me.

"We will, First Sergeant," Rutherford says. I wonder if I should speak, but before I can decide 1st/Sgt. John P. Burch turns around and walks away to Sergeant Millard's Jeep and gets in.

"Jim," Sergeant Millard says to Corporal Jameson, "you take care of these guys on the way up there. All right?"

"Yes, Sergeant," Corporal Jameson says.

"And like I said, come right back. We got a lot of stuff to move tomorrow and I want you in charge. Gonna be a couple hundred trucks and transporters going up the same way you're going today. So note the route."

"Yes, Sergeant," Corporal Jameson says.

"All right, then," Sergeant Millard says. "You get on now. And you two: you stick with Corporal Jameson here. He knows this work better than most of the people around here, whatever rank they hold. If he tells you to do something, you do it."

"Yes, Sergeant," I say.

"All right, then," Sergeant Millard says. He nods, shoves the clipboard under his arm, turns away, and goes to his Jeep. He gets in beside 1st/Sgt.

John P. Burch, starts the engine and drives away across the huge open space between the fence and the lines of vehicles and guns.

"What this space between here and those guns there empty like this for?" Rutherford asks.

"It's a precautionary measure," Corporal Jameson says. "Against fire and such. And thieves. Or saboteurs."

"Saboteurs?" I ask.

"We found a couple of people in here six weeks ago fucking with a Sherman. Later we found they'd cut through the fence down behind there. Guard didn't see them come through. He was asleep when they found him."

"What happened to the guard?" I ask.

"He's been charged. Gonna get ninety days at least in the stockade. But that's okay: he's a useless motherfucker. Laid around, got drunk, got in fights, wouldn't do shit except complain all the time about how they were fucking him."

"Were they?" I ask.

"This here is the Army," Corporal Jameson says. "That's what the Army does, most of the time: fuck you. Or isn't it that way in the Seven Six One?"

"It that way," Rutherford says. "Though it seem to have some kind of purpose."

"This here's got a purpose, too," Corporal Jameson says. "What do you think would have happened if those two guys who were messing with that Sherman had fucked it up enough to make it break down, or blow up? Lot of ways to mess up a Sherman. Like you know. That asshole on guard? I hope they send him to the stockade for ever. We'd have some kind of trouble here if one of these here tanks blew up. We got enough fuel and explosives in this dump to blow up everything around here, and us with it. And that asshole went to sleep and let two guys come through the fence like that?"

"Were the two found in here Germans?"

"I don't know. Nobody knows. They were in civilian clothes. Man walking past heard something in among the Shermans. He reported in by phone from the gate here and First Sergeant Burch come with Sergeant Wallace in a Jeep. They both had Thompson guns. When the two guys come out the Sherman First Sergeant Burch called on them to surrender. They ran, right across this open place here. Both of them had revolvers, some kind of old six shooter. Not military weapons. Sergeant Burch killed the both of them. That's another reason for this here big open space: good field of fire across it."

"He killed them both?" I ask. This is something else to tell First Sergeant Reardon about his old buddy 1st/Sgt. John P. Burch.

"Both of them. One burst. He knows how to use that weapon, I can tell you that. We hear he's had a lot of practice."

"What they do to the Sherman?" Rutherford asks.

"Nobody could figure it out. Fucked with the gunsight. Seemed like they were trying to steal the sight. Had it part unbolted. Couldn't figure it out: who wants a sight from a Sherman? Nothing much secret about it. Maybe they just wanted a souvenir. I know they weren't thieves, though. If they'd been thieves, they'd of been over on the other side in among the cigarettes and the food and personal equipment and such."

"Killed them both," Rutherford says. "Huh. He ain't as sick as he looks."

"He's sick all right," Corporal Jameson says. "Got the jaundice, and malaria he picked up on one of those islands out in the Pacific somewheres. Acts crazy, too. But he isn't. I think he acts that way so most people will stay away from him. He don't like a lot of people much, you know? Has a poor opinion of people. But he's okay. One of the men here get in trouble and it isn't his fault, the First Sergeant's there to fix it right. He doesn't like anybody outside this outfit fucking with his men. Had some people in here making remarks a couple of times. First Sergeant come out with his pistol in a holster on his belt and his chevrons and rockers and his First Sergeant's lozenge and show them where to go. Call on their officer to give them a lesson in military courtesy. Officer almost say 'Yes, sir' to First Sergeant Burch. Time First Sergeant finished with this officer and his people, they don't have much about anything to say. They take their stuff and go. First Sergeant wouldn't let them have any drivers or trucks. They had to call for their own. First Sergeant stood right about here and looked their officer in the eye and said, 'We don't have any available transport for you, Captain.' Standing right here. You see all those trucks over there?" I turn and look: to the left, beyond the guns and tanks, stand rows of two-and-a-half ton trucks. "Back then we had even more, filled up half this here empty space you was interested in. But when First Sergeant Burch say, 'No trucks,' that Captain said, 'Okay, First Sergeant, I can see you got no trucks.'"

"Sound like First Sergeant Reardon," Rutherford says.

I recall First Sergeant Reardon standing in the bed of the Headquarters Company halftrack explaining to the Colonel about the stay behind sniper who killed Willy Thorn as the Colonel said, "Uh-huh, uh-huh." On the other hand, I had no doubt the Colonel was willing to believe. The Colonel is an intelligent man, and I doubt anything that happens in the Battalion gets past him.

"He's your top kicker?" Jameson asks.

"Headquarters Company First Sergeant," I tell him. "Top kick of the Battalion."

"He's like First Sergeant Burch, is he?" Corporal Jameson asks.

"Ain't nobody like First Sergeant Reardon," Rutherford says. "You can look everywhere and you ain't gonna find another one like him. They maybe sound a little the same, but the First Sergeant in the Seven Six One all by himself in a different category."

"So's First Sergeant Burch," Corporal Jameson says, as though he wants us to know that 1st/Sgt. John P. Burch is unique, too.

"I don't think we have the time to decide which one of them is more," I say.

"You're right," Corporal Jameson says. "We've got to get going. Which one of you wants to ride in the transporter?"

"I thought we were going to go in the weapons carrier and your guys were going in the transporters and trucks," I say.

"No," Corporal Jameson says. "I've got to go out front in the weapons carrier, and one of the two of you has to ride in the first transporter as assistant driver and gunner. Usually I have a Jeep, but they left that out because you have this weapons carrier. Either of you know how to fire the .50 caliber?"

"Sure," Rutherford says. "We both know. But why you got to ride in our weapons carrier?"

"I command this convoy. I know that sounds like a lot of shit, and maybe it is; but I'm in charge and if something gets fucked up First Sergeant Burch isn't going to call you up. He's going to jump on me. So I ride in the weapons carrier, or drive it if you want, to go ahead and see."

"Go ahead and see?" I ask. "See what?"

"You want one of these transporters to come around some curve in the road at forty miles an hour and find a wreck, or the road bombed out, or a convoy stalled? You know what it's like to stop one of these things? Or have to back it up and go around if the road is blocked?"

"I see," I say. "So we ride ahead. To see."

"That's it," Corporal Jameson says. "We ride four, five hundred yards in front. If there's trouble, we have time to flag down the convoy."

"We ain't got no flag," Rutherford says.

"I got a flag," Corporal Jameson says. "Right here in the first vehicle." He gestures at the huge prime mover.

"I'll ride in the transporter, if you want," I say.

"I know the gun better," Rutherford says. I nod. He is right: he knows a lot more about weapons than I do.

"You guys want to flip for it?" Corporal Jameson asks. He is not exasperated, but he wants to get on. I know he is thinking about the convoy he is going to have to lead tomorrow.

"I'll sit up with the driver," Rutherford says. "Which one is he?"

"Jones," Jameson says. Jones steps forward from among the loitering drivers and assistant drivers. He is a tall skinny kid with a long neck and a thin skull and a long thin torso. His uniform is long enough in the sleeves and legs, but it was cut for a man who weighs fifty pounds more than Jones, who looks as though he did not get enough to eat when he was growing up. No wonder, I think: the 1930s were a hungry time for everyone, and hungrier for some than others. "Stanley, this here is Rutherford. He's going to ride with you. Me and this guy here are going to be four five hundred yards out in front of you, looking. The usual."

"I'll keep my distance, Corporal," Stanley Jones says. His voice surprises me: it is the deep voice of a full grown man.

"I know you will, Stanley. Rutherford," Corporal Jameson says, "this man here knows how to ease this transporter around. You know what I mean? Knows his job, and does it. So you listen to him. If he want to slow down, everybody slows down. If he tells you to signal us up in the weapons carrier, you do it. All right?"

"All right by me," Rutherford says. "I'm here for the ride."

"With Jones here," Corporal Jameson says, "you gonna have a smooth, easy ride. Jones and me delivered more of these Shermans and 105 Shermans and crates of ammunition than anybody around here. And we delivered them on time."

"Okay," Rutherford says. "Don't worry, Corporal: I do what he say."

"All right then," Corporal Jameson says. "Let me get the flag and then let's get on out of here."

I wait beside the weapons carrier while Jameson, Rutherford and Jones and the other drivers and assistant drivers fan out. Jameson waits while Private Jones climbs up into the first prime mover and hands down a white flag.

"You want to drive?" Corporal Jameson asks when he comes back.

"If you want," I say.

"I'll drive," he says. He hands me the flag: a white rectangle on a bamboo stick. "You watch up ahead and behind too. If I say, you stand up and wave that flag, all right?"

"What's it mean?" I ask.

"We used to have a bunch of them: red, green, white. Now we use just the one. It means: slow up and be careful. All it's for is to attract the attention of the driver in the first vehicle in the convoy. When he sees it, he slows up and starts watching and thinking. Sound stupid, don't it? But on some of these long drives, you can go to sleep driving at thirty miles an hour. This here flag is to wake them up."

"I'll take care of it," I say. "You say and I'll wave."

"All right."

Jameson says, "Help me get this canvas off from over the front seats."

"Going to be cold with the wind," I say. The weapons carrier is cold enough without its canvas roof and plastic doors.

"Going to be tough to stand up and wave that flag if this canvas is up here," Corporal Jameson says.

"Right," I say. I go around the weapons carrier and work the grommet in the canvas off the steel peg at the top of the windshield while Jameson does the same on the driver's side.

"Better to take it off than let it hang down," Jameson says. "Give us a view through the back." We lift the grommets in the canvas off the metal pegs on the first of the three squared-off metal arches that support the canvas walls and roof of the bed. Jameson draws the canvas to himself, folds it into a neat bundle and stows it in the back behind his seat. "Won't flap around if it's folded," he explains.

Jameson gets into the weapons carrier and starts the engine. I get into the passenger seat. "You got the paper?" Jameson asks.

"Right here in my pocket," I tell him.

"Good. Better haul it out. Gate guard will want his copy. Other people along the way will want to see yours. Everybody wants to see the paper. You have the right paper, you can drive all the way to Rome and no one's gonna ask a question."

As Jameson drives to the gate I take out the two sets of papers Sergeant Wallace handed me in 1st/Sgt. John P. Burch's office. The gate guard has his rifle slung over his shoulder and his hand out. I hand him both sets of paper. He reads the description of the material that is leaving the dump and glances at each of the signatures. "This you?" he asks, his thumb on my signature.

"Yes," I say. "You want to see my identification?"

"No. If it was cigarettes or liquor or food or clothes, I'd want to see your identification and your tags. But ain't no one yet tried to steal no Jumbos nor no 76 millimeter ammunition nor no assault Shermans for private profit. Cigarettes, though, that's another matter. We got orders to be a lot more careful about all like that."

"We got to get on, Billy," Jameson says.

Billy nods and hands me one set of paper back. He folds the other set and puts it in his pocket. He turns around and says, "Open it up, Frank," to another private with another rifle slung over his shoulder. Frank swings the gate open and we drive through, the four transporters and the two trucks easing along after us, engines roaring, air brakes hissing. I see Rutherford standing up in the pulpit at the back of the prime mover's cab, checking the .50 caliber machinegun. He looks serious, as though there are Germans waiting for us in the bushes right outside the gate. When he sees me looking he grins as though he is having a good time riding half out of the roof of the huge vehicle Private Jones is steering after us.

"Don't they check what's in the trucks?" I ask Jameson.

"They should. But they don't. They know me, and they saw First Sergeant Burch and Sergeant Millard. They know everything's all right."

"We could have cases of cigarettes and crates of booze in those trucks," I say.

Jameson glances at me, grins and says, "We do. That's why First Sergeant Burch come all the way down to the gate. Sergeant Millard told me to tell you when we're out the gate. You're supposed to turn them over to this here First Sergeant of yours. Reardon? He and Burch must go way back: Burch doesn't give anything away without a piece of paper and he don't get involved in any of the thieving that goes on in this supply dump."

"Cigarettes and booze," I say. "First Sergeant Burch must know we have something coming up."

"Know? Sure he knows. Every piece of paper in this place goes across his desk, and he knows where everything's going: vehicles, ammunition, explosives, guns, tanks, food. Germans would pay high to get their hands on the information he has. I mean, if he sign a paper to send two hundred thousand rations up one place instead of another, and it list the units that are supposed to get the rations, you know right away where we got men and where we don't. Same with guns. With bombs and aircraft parts, you know right away where the airfields are. 'Course the First Sergeant don't see much of the paper on the Air Force: they got their own dump here, attached to ours over on the other side. But they need trucks and movers and trailers and the First Sergeant and the Air Force First Sergeant have to get together and decide things. So Burch knows."

"I never thought of it that way."

"Neither did I, till I got here. You watching?"

I look up the road. It runs straight east. Far in the distance it disappears into a woods. "I'm watching," I say. It seems odd: what—who—could be waiting for us? "What am I looking for?"

"Anything. People in funny places. Accidents. Trouble with the road itself. Things blocking the road. Some of these villages and towns we go through, buildings been beat up months ago they all of a sudden fall down in the street. Then there's the Germans. You'd be surprised how many Germans still wandering around out in the country here, trying to make their way east. It's getting better now. But last fall, and through the winter, there were problems. Fucking Germans don't quit, you know."

"Germans?" I say. "Back here?" I had not realized.

"Yeah. Stanley Jones back there driving your buddy Rutherford had his assistant driver killed about two months ago, late January, up near Belgium. They were coming back alone from Third Army. Assistant driver was standing up in the pulpit and got shot through the chest. Stanley stopped the transporter, got up in the pulpit and sprayed the woods with the gun. Then he got down with an M3 and went into the woods and found one German dead from the machinegun fire. Killed the other one with the submachinegun. Two MPs come along in a Jeep to complain about the transporter standing in the road. When Stanley came out of the woods and told them what had happened, they went in and looked. First Sergeant Burch got a report on it and had Stanley in for a talk. Recommended him for an award. It didn't come through. So the First Sergeant gave him a week in Paris. He went down with a group and spent a week there. Said it's real nice. Me, I haven't seen it."

"Pretty nervy," I say, "getting out alone and going into a woods."

"That's what I told Stanley. All he'd say was: 'They killed Jimmy.' Jimmy was Stanley's buddy. Too bad: Jimmy was a good guy, always easy, willing to work, willing to stand up there in the pulpit hour on hour to see if anything was going to happen. Nothing much ever happened. Until, that is."

We drive on. I glance behind. Stanley is coming on four hundred yards behind, peering through the prime mover's windshield. Rutherford has climbed down from the pulpit and sits beside him. They are talking to one another.

When we arrive at the main road to Luneville, an MP waves us down even though the road is clear. Another MP sits in a Jeep at the side of the road: he is talking into a radio. The MP standing in the road turns his back to us and waits at ease in the middle of the empty road to Luneville. He is as officious as the German military policeman we once captured. The German MP wore a chain around his neck, a plate swinging against his chest. Even in captivity he was certain about the rules: it seemed he had studied prisoner's rights in detail, and could quote the Geneva Convention in bad English. I was surprised at his knowledge of law: I had not thought German military policemen were much interested in law. Even though the road is clear this MP waits until a convoy of truck appears, holds us up until it has passed, and then waves us on to the south with vigorous, precise movements of his hands, as though we aren't moving out fast enough to suit him.

"Dumb fucker," I say.

"May be," Jameson says. "On the other hand, he might have had orders to keep the road open no matter what for those trucks. Who knows? I just follow their instructions. It's easier to follow their instructions than to get into some kind of debate with them. Sometimes some things got to get up front right now and everybody else has to wait."

"Where you from, Jameson?"

"Alexandria, Virginia," he says.

"Where's that?"

"Right down the river from Washington, D.C."

"No kidding?" I say. I have never been to Washington, D.C. "I've never been there. I'm from Chicago."

"Cold, right?"

"In the winter. In the summer it's hot."

"Sound like Alexandria. Bitch both ways. But the spring and fall are nice."

I think of Chicago: I suppose the weather is all right in the spring and fall.

"You get a lot of trouble in Alexandria?"

"No, it isn't bad. Usual stuff. And this is Virginia I'm talking. Everyone there still thinks they remember the Civil War. But when I went off to join the Army they were pretty nice about it."

"Everybody seems to like a soldier."

"Sure. You ever wonder how they're going to feel when we aren't wearing these here olive drab clothes any more?"

"We'll have to see," I say. What else can I say? I try not to be optimistic or pessimistic about the future. But I am cynical. My mother says I was a cynical small boy.

"Just like this road," Jameson says. "You got to look out, to figure out what's coming along, and be ready."

I glance behind. Stanley Jones is holding his tank transporter four hundred yards behind us. Rutherford is standing up in the pulpit again, his right hand on the machinegun, his left on the rim of the hatch. The other three transporters follow at one hundred yard intervals. The trucks are farther back, the first one two hundred yards behind the fourth transporter, the second one two hundred yards behind the first truck.

"The two trucks are farther back," I tell Jameson. "Maybe two hundred yards apart."

"Right," he says.

"They shouldn't close up any?"

"They're too close right now. They ought to be another hundred yards back and another hundred yards apart. First time we stop I'll tell them to stay back more."

I look at Jameson. "Why?" I ask.

"They're loaded with ammunition. Something happen to either truck, there going to be a hell of a bang. Better it happen back farther. We don't ever put ammunition trucks in the middle of a convoy. Put them at the back, with a good gap between the end of the front part of the convoy and the ammunition trucks."

"You had any accidents?"

"Sure. Lot of men been killed driving these trucks. Accidents and German planes back last summer and into the fall. Not many planes now. Accidents the worst. And if you have an accident with a truck full of artillery rounds, you got all the pieces to make a lot of trouble. 'Course, this stuff we have here is pretty safe."

"You lost any people like that?"

"Ten, in all kinds of accidents. Lost four of them to explosions."

"What happens?"

Jameson looks at me, his eyebrows raised. "What happens? You ever seen a truckload of artillery ammunition go up? Lemme tell you: it isn't pretty. Rounds flying every which way, explosions here and there, trees chopped down, surface of the road chewed up."

"I meant, why does it happen?"

"Why? No one knows. Ammunition isn't supposed to detonate like that, and secure in the crates with the cap protected it ought to be all right. That's what they say. But it isn't true."

"Do they investigate?"

"Sure. Send people out, ordnance people. They pick around, examine one thing and another, look at this and that, collect some of the unexploded rounds, talk to everybody. But usually there isn't a lot left. No truck, no crates, and no men. Most of all no men. Piece of the skulls, maybe. Some teeth. Hip bones. Boots with feet in them and part of the shin. Funny how the boots don't seem to be destroyed in these explosions. Flexible, I guess. Torn up a little. But still there, with the foot inside at least some of the times."

"Not much left, then." I think of Big Sam shot down and burned up, all within it that could burn, burned.

"Not much. 'Course the damage isn't just to the truck full of ammunition. Every other truck and piece of machinery anywhere nearby is damaged. Windshields gone, tires flat, loads dislodged. Some of them, when it's a load of shells go up, take a round. 'Course it doesn't strike like it come out of a gunbarrel. Some time they come end over end when the propellant doesn't explode. Some time the propellant fires and they sort of lob out like they'd been fired. But all of them are out of control and nobody knows where the fuck they're going to land or what kind of damage they're going to do. But shells aren't the worst. The worst is engineer supplies. They use all these explosives and such. Dynamite, plastic explosive, guncotton. Like that. When it goes, the whole load, every last bit of it, goes up, and the truck and the drivers go with it. Nothing left but the engine block. Blast is something. Blast in an explosion like that can pick a Sherman right off a transporter two hundred yards away and drop the Sherman on its side. Two of the four men we lost to explosions went with a load of 155 millimeter shells. The other two disappeared when a truckload of engineer supplies blew up."

"Dangerous job you got here," I say. Corporal Jameson is examining the road ahead as though he thinks it might be mined. But he nods: he does not seem appalled that ten of the men in his outfit have been killed. Perhaps he is inured to deaths. But ten men, I think. We have not yet lost thirty killed out of our Battalion, though the number of wounded has been many times the number killed. On the other hand, perhaps Jameson knows that if he takes enough care and is quick enough, he will not die or be injured. Not, that is, unless some bored hungover worker back in Akron or Detroit or Fort Worth didn't quite get the pieces installed in the right order in the nose of a 155 millimeter artillery shell, or mismeasured the proportions of the chemicals in the charges he prepared.

"At least you got a name in the Seven Six One," Jameson says. "Back here, we're just a bunch of truck drivers and clerks and such. Even if we do handle enough stuff to blow us all up with."

"The name doesn't mean much. We wouldn't be up there at all without this kind of work back here." This is the best I can do. I know Jameson is good at what he does, and I suppose a lot of men in supply have died. But almost all of them, I am sure, have died in accidents, by their own negligence or someone else's. But none I know of have died because the crew of a JagdPanther picked them as the target for the next ten kilogram shell plucked from the ready rack in the rear of the hull. And none I know of have had to make the hard last choice Sam Turley made when he stood up against the night and came out fighting.

Rutherford is right: I wonder what the Seven Six One would be had Sam Turley not rallied the shocked, disoriented men around him and led them forward to a kind of victory, his own death and, for him at least, and so perhaps for us, a kind of immortality.

Jameson smiles and shakes his head, as though he has been listening to me think. "I know you wouldn't be up there if we weren't back here hauling crates and boxes. But that isn't the way anybody looks at it. And they're right. After all, anybody who dies back here, now at least, dies cause they make a mistake or someone else make a mistake. While you up in the tanks and even more maybe in the infantry got to go out and let them try to shoot you if they can. Particularly the infantry. I don't know how anybody can stand that. Nothing but a shirt between them and a bullet, and nothing but the soles of their boots between them and a mine. At least in tanks you got some steel to get behind."

"Yeah," I say. "Some steel. Sometimes it seems like a piece of dirty cloth when you're behind it and you know they're out there somewhere with one of those AT guns."

"Question of choice, I suppose. I think I could go in a Sherman. But I couldn't be an infantryman."

"You could transfer up if you wanted."

Jameson shakes his head and says, "No I can't. I tried. Tried for the Seven Six One and for the Six One Four, the tank destroyers. But they wouldn't let me go. Made me a corporal and said they needed me here. Said I had responsibility and could run a convoy for them. Without supervision, they said. That's the important thing, Jameson, they said: you can take a convoy where it has to go and get it there without a vehicle, a man or a sock lost along the way. So, they said, here's a corporal's rank and you're staying here supervising the convoys to where they got to go."

"You're lucky," I tell him. "I'm just in maintenance. I went a couple of times as a loader in a Sherman when they were short-handed, but that's nothing. I spend my time fixing up whatever we can fix up without sending the machine back to a field maintenance workshop. But I haven't seen a lot of fighting." This is imprecise: I have seen a lot of fighting—more, perhaps, than many of the men who go up in the Sherman and Stuarts—but I have not done a lot of fighting.

"Maybe you'll get the chance to move up to the Shermans, what with the casualties you've had."

I look at him: I wonder how Jameson knows about our casualties. He sees me looking and says, "Oh, we know. We keep a close eye on you. It's in the papers we get from home, a little bit, though they can't print the numbers. Mostly we hear when we drive up, or talk to people who come through. I talked to an infantry corporal maybe two weeks ago who was alongside you all east of here last fall. He had a lot to say about you, and all of it good. He got shot in the leg and face out in some field and said a driver from a Sherman got out of his hatch and off the tank, Germans shooting all the time, and came out and pulled him and two others behind the Sherman and gave them first aid until they could be brought back. He was grateful. An Iowa boy, from a farm near Des Moines, had a Swedish name if I remember. Looked like a Swede, at least: hair blond almost white, blue eyes, skin pale like he was sick. Scar on his face. I don't know, though: maybe he was sick, too, given he'd been in hospital up to England for almost three months before they rotated him back through."

I give him the usual question: "How'd this Swede from Iowa know this here tank driver that pulled him out of the field was from the Seven Six One? Given we all wearin' the same uniform here, officers and men alike, generals, even?"

Jameson looks at me. He sees my grin and says, "Had me going there."

"At least they can tell who did what. Without looking at the shoulder patch."

Jameson nods. "That part of what makes you go, I guess."

He is right. The Seven Six One has never been just another tank battalion, and the better we go the more likely it becomes there will never be another tank battalion like the Seven Six One. We are an experiment. Since we were ordered to Europe, and more particularly since the day on which Sam Turley made his stand, we have done our best to prove that General McNair was right, that we have given the Green Hornet himself better reason than he hoped not to care what we are, and that the sonsofbitches were wrong.

Yet like all experiments, we've had a couple of problems—like Johnny White and Willy Thorn—for the sonsofbitches to nod over and say, "Seed that, did you? I tolt you about them, dint I?" Except that the sonsofbitches will never know of Johnny White, who refused to get into his Sherman, and paid; or Willy Thorn, who raped and cut, and paid. First Sergeant Reardon manages this experiment for General McNair dead in Normandy and for the Colonel and the Colonel's officers, and for us, and he has made sure Johnny White's cowardice, and Willy Thorn's crime, will not be said to have spoiled the experiment.

"That's it," I tell Jameson. "That's what makes us go. I guess." There is more to it than that, but I cannot explain it.

"Only thing makes us go is to get things where they got to be and get them there on time."

"Same thing," I tell him, though I know I lie and know he knows I lie.

"Bullshit," Jameson says. "That's not the thing to say. If you aren't more than a bunch of truckdrivers like us, then we aren't anything at all."

"All right," I say. "But it's not that big a difference, Jameson."

"Call me Jim."

"Okay. It's not a big thing, Jim: it's a job, like almost any. . . ."

"Something coming," Jameson says. He is staring through the windshield. I see nothing ahead. "Get up with the flag and slow them down."

I get up and kneel on the seat, facing backward. I grip the bamboo pole and wave the flag above the weapons carrier's plump swaying canvas roof. Jones has seen the flag even as I raised it above the level of the roof. I see him nod three times at me through the windshield of the prime mover. As he nods he brakes and shifts down. Rutherford, taking the air up in the pulpit, is looking to the right when Jones brakes. Rutherford's head swings to the front, his waist strikes the rim of the pulpit and his torso bends forward, his hands scrabbling for a hold. Rutherford pushes himself upright, braces himself with one hand and waves and grins. He is lucky he locked the machinegun's mount: unlocked, it might have swung and injured him. It is a heavy .50 caliber weapon. I recall the sound of machinegun fire as Sam Turley walked forward to fight our enemies, and to show them, waiting beyond the tank trap in front of Morville-les-Vic, who they were fighting.

"What is it?" I ask Jameson. I do not turn around. I wave the flag and watch as Jones nods and nods at me, as though his neck is a spring.

"Some guy's dropped his two-and-a-half in the ditch," Jameson says. He is decelerating, shifting down through the weapons carrier's gears. "They seen you?"

"Yes," I tell him, still waving the flag.

"Soon as they see the flag you can get down." I get down and sit down in the seat. I tuck the flag into the space between the seat and the sill of the door. Once we had doors of canvas stretched over a tubular metal frame. They have been discarded: who wants to fiddle with a latch if one has to get out?

I look up: I still see nothing in the road. We come around a curve. A hundred yards in front of us a truck lies on its side in the ditch to the right of the road, crates spilled out of the back. Two men are getting up from the gravel verge.

"How'd you know there was an accident before we came around the curve?" I ask him.

"Saw the skid marks on the road. Road was damp, marks were dry."

"Pretty sharp."

"You get used to it."

Jameson looks in the rear view mirror and brakes the weapons carrier to a halt. "What's going on, Brand?" he asks the two privates standing by the road.

"It skidded off the road," the taller of the two privates says.

"It skidded? Horseshit," Jameson says. "You were going too fast, Brand. And you weren't looking. Haven't I talked to you about that?"

"Sure," Brand says. "But I was looking."

"Bullshit." Brand doesn't answer. "What are you hauling?"

"Rations."

"You ought to have the fire extinguisher out on the road, Brand. In case of fire. But okay. Stay here with the truck and I'll tell the next control point. And get the fire extinguisher out on the road. Somebody will be pissed if they don't see it when they come to get you."

"We'll get it out, Corporal."

"You'd better, Brand." Jameson pushes the clutch to the floor with his left foot and puts the gearshift into first. "And Brand. When I get back I'll ask to see if you got that extinguisher out of the truck."

Jameson lets in the clutch and we move off.

The pace of the rest of our trip—through Luneville to Sarrebourg and on through Saverne along the railroad to the turning beyond Saverne where we bear north before we reach Detwiller and drive to Ingwiller—which is, as 1st/Sgt. John P. Burch said, on the Mader River, right where it is on the map—is a trundle at twenty miles an hour, punctuated by stops at control points and crossroads. We stop four times to permit the crews to tighten the chains that secure the Jumbos and the 105 Shermans to the trailers. At the first stop Jameson gets out and tells the drivers of the ammunition trucks to leave more space between them and the transporters, and between one another. At Jameson's direction I get up and wave the flag three more times when we come upon two halted convoys and another ditched truck. Each time I wave the flag Stanley Jones nods through the broad slanted windshield of the prime mover, though the hissing of the huge vehicle's brakes and the revving of its engine as he downshifts tells me as well as his head nodding on his thin neck that he has seen the swinging white cloth on the bamboo stick in my hand.

At Ingwiller a short MP with glasses looks us over and directs us to the southeast, pointing out the route on my map. We pass unlimbered artillery pieces, armored infantry battalions in halftracks parked among the trees along the road and companies of Shermans parked and rearming and refuelling beyond the crushed hedges at the borders of the fields. The infantrymen wear the shoulder patch of the 103rd Infantry Division. I am looking at the map, repeating the MP's directions to myself, when Jameson says, "Six Hundred Fourteenth in along here."

I look up. In the fields on either side of the road American soldiers are working at halftracks and three inch towed antitank guns, cleaning them and preparing them for use. Now I see them working I recall that all the units we have passed in the last fifteen minutes have been preparing: the tankers loading fuel and ammunition, the infantry cleaning their rifles and loading equipment, ammunition and food into the tracks, the artillerymen shifting crates of shells and swabbing out the barrels of their howitzers.

"You going to ask me how I know this is the Six One Four?" Jameson asks. As he asks me the question he turns his head and grins at me.

"No," I say. I examine the halftracks and three inch guns of the 614th Tank Destroyer Battalion (Towed). A towed tank destroyer battalion is not a flashy outfit. It is not the Air Force, or Third Army, and newspaper reporters do not spend a lot of time with towed tank destroyer battalions. The parenthesized word 'Towed' implies that the Six One Four is not up to the higher standard required of a tank destroyer battalion equipped with the M10, which is a modified Sherman fitted with an open turret mounting a ninety millimeter gun. Still the Six One Four won a reputation in this part of France last December. Then they were northeast of where we are now, supporting the assault of the 411th Infantry Regiment of the 103rd Infantry Division on Climbach.

"What do they call them?" I ask.

"You mean," Jameson says, "what's their battalion motto? I don't know. But I know what it ought to be: 'I got to get on.' Because of Harris."

"Who's Harris?"

"Robert W. Harris. He was a truck driver supplying 3rd Platoon of the Six One Four's C Company. 3rd Platoon was split off and made part of a task force that was supposed to take Climbach, up east northeast of here, in December. The Platoon set up their guns on a slope leading up to a ridge in front of Climbach. The rest of the task force was supposed to go around by the flank. The Germans were firing down from the top of the ridge with mortars, machineguns, artillery, every damned thing, on 3rd Platoon's guns. The Platoon lost two half-tracks, three of their guns destroyed and half the men as casualties. During the fight they got down to one gun left firing, and that one was running out of ammunition. So Harris gets into his truck and drives back across the field through the German fire and down the roads through the German fire and loads his truck with cases of shells and drives forward. He was half way back to the one gun in 3rd Platoon still firing when the task force commander standing by the road stopped him and told him the German fire was too heavy for him to go forward. Harris said, "I got to get on," let in the clutch and drove on up the roads, Germans shooting at him all the way up, and out into the field, Germans still shooting at him, to within twenty-five yards of the one last 3rd Platoon gun that was firing. All the time he was driving up there and out into the field the Germans were firing everything they had—rifles, machineguns, mortars, artillery—trying to nail the last gun crew and Harris in his truck. When Harris arrives behind the last gun, he gets down and starts carrying the ammunition boxes—fifty-four pounds each, heavy bastards—up to the gun. They kept on firing until the rest of the task force could get forward on the flank and get the Germans out of Climbach. 3rd Platoon fought for four hours up there and got a Distinguished Unit Citation for what they did. And now they're going back up."

"They were all alone up there?" I ask.

"No. Three men with Browning Automatic Rifles from the 411th Infantry Regiment volunteered to go up there with them and provide security on their flanks."

"Volunteered, did they?" I wish I knew their names.

"Yeah. Surprising, isn't it?"

"I don't know. This is different from back home. No one has time for that shit up here."

"Yeah," Jameson says. "They'll put it off till later, when the war's over."

"Maybe," I say. "On the other hand, maybe not. Maybe they'll remember Harris." But I am not sure about that. After all, we have been there in every other one of America's wars, and after every one of those wars, nothing changed. But perhaps it will be different this time. What else can one hope for? Still I remember my ancestor, murdered at the Crater so long ago.

"Maybe you're right," Jameson says, "maybe things will be different. Anyhow, the Seven Six One ought to be down along in here somewhere."

"Well," I say, "the Six One Four is still attached to the 103rd Infantry Division. That says something, at least. If they didn't want them, they would have wangled some way to get them transferred to another outfit. And they wouldn't have gotten the Unit Citation if the 103rd hadn't thought they did all right."

"There's that," Jameson says. He doesn't sound convinced that the Distinguished Unit Citation awarded to the 3rd Platoon of C Company of the 614th Tank Destroyer Battalion (Towed) will mean much when the war is over.

"Whatever's going to happen," I say, "we'll just have to wait and see."

"You're right about that," Jameson says. "Like I said, it's like driving these roads."

We drive on. We stop to ask a military policeman for directions: he tells us the Seven Six One is right up ahead. Can't miss 'em, he says. He is right: five hundred yards on I see the familiar outlines of the Seven Six One's Shermans in the fields on either side of the road. Their crews and the men in the maintenance tracks and supply trucks are working on the tanks' engines and loading them with ammunition. They will have to remove some of the 76 millimeter rounds they are loading as soon as First Sergeant Reardon distributes his supply of High Velocity Armor Piercing.

As we pass along the road, I wonder how the French farmers who work these fields will deal with the hedges destroyed and the ground chewed up by the tanks' tracks when we have moved on. I dismiss the farmers' problems: four seasons on, the marks of our passage and the damage we have done, like the tank trap at Morville-les-Vic, will have been repaired, and a decade from now all evidence that we passed this way will be gone. In thirty years no one except those of us who still live will remember we came this way.

I look ahead. Headquarters Company is parked among the trees in an orchard to the right of the road. I see First Sergeant Reardon's campaign hat. He is standing where I left him, up in the back of the Headquarters halftrack. The Colonel is with him. They are both looking toward the road and the approaching sound of the engines of the prime movers. I see the brim of the First Sergeant's campaign hat dip and dip again as he nods and says something to the Colonel. The Colonel nods and I imagine him saying, "Uh-huh, uh-huh."

A Sherman has crashed through the hedge surrounding the field, making a gate for the rest of Headquarters Company's vehicles. Looking across the field at the Headquarters track, I know First Sergeant Reardon and the Colonel will be happy to have two more 105 assault Shermans in the Seven Six One. They will be even happier to have the two Jumbos, and happiest of all to have eight hundred rounds of HVAP, for HVAP will give us superiority over all the Germans' tanks and self-propelled guns except the Panther and Tiger, and the JagdPanther and JagdTiger. But even against those monstrous machines, HVAP will give us an edge against their flanks. If we can maneuver to their flanks.

"We aren't driving the transporters or the trucks down into that field," Jameson says. "They'll stay here on the road. Get up and wave them down."

I get up on the seat and wave the flag at Stanley Jones, drop the flag in the bed of the weapons carrier and move my arm across my throat. Stanley Jones nods, brakes the prime mover to a halt fifty feet behind us, sets the brake and turns off the engine. Rutherford scissors his arms above his head at the following vehicles, ducks out of the pulpit, jumps down from the prime mover's cab and walks forward to the weapons carrier. "I'll tell you," he says. "That thing is something to ride in. Make a Sherman seem puny. And up there behind the gun you can see all around for miles."

"I told you you ought to come here as a tourist."

"I will," Rutherford says. "If I can tour around in through here in a prime mover."

"First Sergeant's waiting for us. Get in." Rutherford gets in and Jameson drives through the hole in the hedge and across the field to the Headquarters halftrack. He does not need to be told where to go: he sees First Sergeant Reardon's campaign hat.

When Rutherford and I get out of the weapons carrier, Jameson stays behind the wheel. I tell him to come with us. He gets down and the three of us step up into the bed of the Headquarters halftrack. We stand to attention but the Colonel says, "We're not saluting up here. Stand easy." He smiles. "It looks like you brought us something."

"Yes, sir," I say. I hand the papers to the First Sergeant. He glances through them.

"Get everything you wanted, First Sergeant?" the Colonel asks.

"Got most everything we need, sir," the First Sergeant says. He is still looking through the papers. He seems to think something is missing. He looks up at me and raises his eyebrows.

"There's a couple of things in the trucks that aren't down there, First Sergeant."

"John came through, then," the First Sergeant says.

"Uh-huh," the Colonel says. "Sergeants working together, cooperating for the greater good of this particular Battalion among so many others. What couple of things?" he asks me.

"First Sergeant Burch put in some whisky and cigarettes, sir." I wonder why 1st/Sgt. John P. Burch did not mention the whisky and cigarettes to us. Perhaps he did not want us to thank him.

First Sergeant Reardon's eyebrows are still raised. "Oh," I say. "And he gave me a letter for you, First Sergeant." As I reach for the letter I feel General Hillman's letter tucked beside 1st/Sgt. John P. Burch's. "So did General Hillman, First Sergeant. He came across us on the road. Had us into his mess for the night." I hand the First Sergeant both letters. He does not seem surprised that we came across General Hillman. I wonder if he knows the General's son is dead. Whether the First Sergeant does or not, I decide I will not mention it to him. First Sergeant Reardon puts the General's letter in the pocket of his overcoat, opens 1st/Sgt. John P. Burch's letter, takes two sheets of paper out of the envelope and reads.

"Says here, Colonel, that the liquor and cigarettes he sent are surplus."

The Colonel says: "I've never heard of surplus cigarettes or surplus liquor, First Sergeant."

"Neither have I, sir, but if First Sergeant Burch says they're surplus, they must be surplus."

"Which means no one's going to ask any questions," the Colonel says. "Which in turns mean we aren't going to jail."

"That's it, sir," the First Sergeant says.

"What about the rest of it, First Sergeant?" the Colonel asks.

"The rest of it, sir? You mean these two Jumbos, the two 105 Shermans and the eight hundred rounds of HVAP?"

"Is this First Sergeant Burch your brother, First Sergeant?" the Colonel asks. "We've been trying—everybody's been trying—to get a decent supply of HVAP and we've struck out. Now we're hitting them over the fences. Now you're hitting them over the fences, that is, First Sergeant."

"1st/Sgt. John P. Burch and I go back a little, sir. To Fort Benning in the twenties."

"Uh-huh. Know General Marshall there, did you?" the Colonel asks.

"Yes, sir," First Sergeant Reardon says.

The Colonel raises his eyes, and then his face, to the sky. He shakes his head and says, "All right then." He lowers his eyes from the sky and says to me, "You did well. And you, Rutherford. A good trip."

"Thank you, sir. We got here safe today mainly because of Corporal Jameson here."

"I want to thank you, Corporal," the Colonel tells Jameson. "If this man says these, ah, items got here because of you, it's the truth."

"Thank you, sir," Jameson says. He is pleased that the Colonel of the Seven Six One has noticed the work he and his men have done.

"We're going to be able to put this stuff to use, Corporal. You tell First Sergeant Burch that when you get back. Particularly the Jumbos. And the HVAP, although I hope we don't find a lot of things we have to use it on." I know what the Colonel means: HVAP is the only thing we have that can penetrate the thick, tempered steel of the Germans' tanks and self-propelled guns. But even HVAP is potent only if it is fired when the target fills the sights: HVAP moves at 3400 feet per second, but to penetrate a

Panther's frontal armor, the gun that fires the HVAP must fire from less than three hundred yards from the Panther. Penetration of the frontal armor of the Tiger is not possible, though it is said that a gunner with enough ability and nerve can, if he is firing against the King Tiger with the Porsche turret with its rounded front, cause the 76 millimeter round to ricochet from the lower arc of the front of the turret down through the thin armor above the driver and bowgunner. It is also said that a 76 millimeter round, if fired with sufficient precision, can be bounced off hard ground up into the belly of the Tiger. No one in the Seven Six One has attempted this. Even with HVAP, approaching close enough to the target to gain penetration, if the target is a Panther—or worse, a Tiger—means danger and probable death.

General Eisenhower is said to have been surprised that the Germans' tanks and self-propelled guns were bigger than ours. He is said to have become angry when he discovered that the Sherman's 76 millimeter gun wouldn't shoot down any tank in the German arsenal except, with expertise no one going up to the line for the first time possesses, the PanzerKampfWagen IV. The Ordnance Department and the Armored Board had promised General Eisenhower that the 76 millimeter gun was up to the job. Now it seems they were mistaken.

I sympathize with the General, and I don't doubt that tankers who fought through the summer of 1944 in northern Europe were just as concerned about the disparity between our armor and the Germans' as the General was. After all, the Shermans' crews found out just how wrong the Armored Board had been the first time a ten kilogram shell fired from an eighty-eight shouldered through the Sherman's armor. I wonder how many of the survivors of such a strike had the chance to write up a report about their estimates of the 'viability', as the designers refer to it, of the 76 millimeter Sherman gun-on-gun against one of the fearsome, angular demons in which the Germans fight.

We can't complain, though. We arrived in Europe last November, long after the vicious tank battles on the plains of France in the summer of 1944, and we were warned about the angles and the chances long before we pitched out of the bow doors of the LSTs that transported us to Normandy and clattered up the sand hills over which so many others had preceded us. Last summer we heard the British Major lecture us about our tanks and their tanks. A matter of judgment, luck and the balance between our equipment and theirs, he said: our engineers and theirs, our mechanics and theirs. We have more, he said. But they have better. The British Major was right: the charred, crouched parcels left behind when the JagdPanther struck down Big Sam Taylor and his crew and Tommy Quineau are the manifest evidence of the truth he spoke.

"All right," First Sergeant Reardon says. He holds 1st/Sgt. John P. Burch's letter in his hand. The two sheets of paper flutter in the cold wind. "You did all right," he tells us. "And you, Corporal," he tells Jameson. "Good of you to get these two men and this equipment back up here in good shape."

The Colonel nods agreement. So do we. "You have the Battalion's gratitude," the Colonel tells Jameson. "I would appreciate it if you would pass that along to the men in your convoy."

"I will, Colonel. And thank you, First Sergeant."

"How is First Sergeant Burch, Corporal?" First Sergeant Reardon asks Jameson.

"Sir, he has the fever, but he is fine."

"Keeps you moving, does he?" This is as close to jocularity as First Sergeant Reardon will permit himself.

"He does, First Sergeant. In fact, we have to get back now: we have another convoy tomorrow."

"You and your men can eat here, Corporal," the First Sergeant says.

"Thank you, First Sergeant," Jameson says. "But we have rations in the transporters and we have to get back."

The First Sergeant nods and the Colonel says, "Keep up the good work, Corporal."

Jameson says, "Yes, sir."

Sergeant Reardon says, "You two go on now. Drive Corporal Jameson back to the road." The Colonel nods and nods, to show he agrees with the First Sergeant.

Rutherford and I nod and step down from the halftrack. As we do so, First Sergeant Reardon says, "You two." We stand with Jameson beside the track in the field under the trees and look up at the First Sergeant and the Colonel. "You did well," the First Sergeant says.

These words mean a lot. I do not recall the First Sergeant giving more praise to anyone except those who have died facing our enemies: anyone who lives has done his duty. I wonder why he tells us we have done well when we have done nothing except bring back four armored fighting vehicles, a supply of HVAP, and some booze and cigarettes. Then he tells us: "One more thing, though," he says. "We're going up"—all of us know what 'going up' means; even in maintenance we know what it means—"and we're short men for these two up-armored Shermans you brought. One of you can go as a loader, the other as a bowgunner. If you want." He looks at us. He has complimented us and made us an offer. Our career as maintenance personnel seems to have ended, for neither Rutherford nor I—nor the Colonel himself, nor General Hillman, I imagine—can say no to the First Sergeant.

"In the same Sherman?" Rutherford asks.

"No," First Sergeant Reardon says. "We're short a loader in one Jumbo, and a bowgunner in the other. Both going to be assigned to B Company, though." I guess: B Company needs the help. Sam Taylor and his crew were in B Company. So was Tommy Quineau. So were a lot of others who are gone, killed and wound in shelter halves and sent back, or wounded and sent back drugged or shouting to Doc Turner, and further back, to England, and then home. Home: what a place. Better, maybe, to die here as Sam Taylor died here. Or, if one can manage it, as Sam Turley died here.

"How'd you know to get crews for these here Jumbos we brought along, First Sergeant?" Rutherford asks. Rutherford is taking the bit in his teeth: no one asks the First Sergeant why or how. "You got crews for them before you knew you'd get them?"

Like Rutherford, I wonder how the First Sergeant knew we would bring two Jumbos and two 105 assault Shermans back with us when we returned from Nancy. I can't figure it out; but perhaps, as 1st/Sgt. John P. Burch said, the First Sergeant and 1st/Sgt. John P. Burch go back a long way.

"Sure I got crews," the First Sergeant says. "And sure I knew you were coming back with these here M4A3E2s and the rest. You think John Burch would let me go without these here machines? But what I'm telling you, Rutherford, is: I'm short a loader in one and a bowgunner in the other of these two Jumbos. You want to go on up? Or you want to go back to maintenance?"

What can we say? Jameson is looking at us, and we are not going to stand here in front of a driver from the Services of Supply and tell the First Sergeant we want to go back to maintenance. Besides, the First Sergeant has not given us a choice. He has told us what we must do next if we are to go on climbing the endless shaky ladder he has leaned up against the dangerous tall face of this war.

"We go," Rutherford answers for us both, "in the Shermans."

Thirteen

Between the ranks of burning pines along the narrow winter road, terrorized horses plunge in their polished leather traces, screaming and squealing like pigs. Their hooves scrabble at the muddy surface of the road and kick at the smashed wagons among which they lunge and screech. I stand up in the cold night air behind the Jumbo's turret, firing the .50 caliber machinegun mounted on a pintle behind and between the commander's hatch to the right and the loader's oval hatch to the left, shooting the horses I have wounded, praying I will kill them all and stop their screaming. Horses whicker and snort: they should not scream.

McCarthy, my Jumbo's tank commander, stands up in the tank commander's hatch and speaks into the microphone. As he speaks the Jumbo lurches and slides forward, shouldering wagons and carts onto the verge, crushing carcasses and screaming horses beneath its treads, making way for the column of tanks and halftracks behind us which an optimist on the staff of the 103rd Infantry Division has dubbed 'Task Force Rhine'. To brace myself against the thick lurch and sway of the Jumbo's bulk, I press my hips and thighs against the turret's bustle. As I hang swinging from the swinging heavy machinegun I see a horse in the tank's path. It is standing on three legs, its long triangular face turned toward me. Leather harness hangs from its flanks, and a thick, padded leather collar is askew around its neck. Its right front leg is drawn up, the hoof and foreleg tangled in its entrails swinging from its eviscerated belly. The horse stares at me; or perhaps it stares at the M4A3E2, all 84,000 pounds of up-armored Sherman sliding forward like a huge dun predator in a horse's nightmare.

"For Christ's sake get over it, Yates," I shout into the microphone. At my command, Yates works the clutch and accelerator and the steering levers, shifts the Jumbo's bulk to the right, and crushes the screaming horse beneath the tank's broad left tread. "Goddamnit to hell," I shout.

"Take it easy," McCarthy mutters down the intercom. I cannot see his face, but I know he is frowning as though I have been rude. He is the tank commander, but he does not order us. He suggests and persuades.

"I don't like it," I tell him. "I don't like this shit."

"Neither do I," McCarthy says. "But there ain't anything I can do about it so goddamn it take it easy. You're new to this here," he tells me. "But let me tell you: we seen dead animals in the road since November. So have you, coming on in maintenance. And there's nothing either one of us can do about it. So take it easy, will you?"

"All right," I say. "Goddamnit all right then."

As I say the last word Jackson, the gunner, says, "Stop!" The Jumbo jerks to a halt as Yates throws out the levers. The turret rotates and the breech is depressed as the gunmuzzle rises. Two seconds later Jackson moves his foot against the trigger and fires the Jumbo's 76 millimeter main armament. The cracking concussion of the round departing the muzzle presses against my face and shoulders and the bright muzzleflash of the gun firing fills my eyes with light as I leave the machinegun, scrabble up and over the turret's bustle and wriggle down through the loader's hatch—my hatch—as Jackson says, "Load HVAP. And cut out the conversation, will you, guys? Take a look four hundred yards down the road." Jackson speaks in the flat, factual manner of his home state of Virginia, his accent neither north nor south. I lift a shell from the ready rack, thrust it into the breech of the gun, shout "Loaded," and stick my head up out of the loader's hatch. Down the road beyond the two lines of burning pinetrees I see a clutter of waist-high concrete obstacles. Beyond the dragon's teeth something lurks in the dark at the verge of the road, just at the edge of the light from the moaning fire leaping through the pines. I jerk my head back inside the tank in the instant the lurking something fires its gun. The bulk of the Jumbo cowers backward from the tremendous strike of the shot against the Jumbo's sloped front. I hear the whirring hum of the round flicking away and up through the trees. A ricochet: we are lucky.

"Jesus Christ," Brown says from the machinegunner's position low in the right hand front of the hull. I know what he means: such a strike makes the armor glow dull red at the point where the energy of the round is transferred to the steel it has struck.

"Be a Pee Zee Kay Double U Four," Jackson estimates. I understand what he means: if the gun in the German vehicle were any bigger than the gun in the PanzerKampfWagen IV, the shell would have penetrated our plump Sherman's hull—no matter the praise the Armored Board has lavished on the Jumbo—and some of us, at least, would be dead or panting our way through our last four breaths. Through the intercom I listen as Jackson breathes. I watch as he shifts the turret two degrees to the right, then one degree more. The breech of the gun rises two inches as he depresses the muzzle of the 76 millimeter weapon. I watch Jackson's face across the gun's breech caged inside the gunshield: he stares through the gunsight, his forehead against the rubber bumper above the eyepiece. His mouth is open and I see his tongue slide across his upper lip. He depresses the footpedal trigger: the 76 millimeter gun fires and recoils, the breech opening as it is thrown back. The smoking shell casing rattles out of the framework guard fitted over the breech. I throw another round of HVAP into the smoking butt of the gun and bend to pick up the hot shell casing. As I fling the casing up and out of the loader's hatch above me I glance up and see smoke and flames rushing up among the tall pines, whispering and crackling as they rise, flinging sparks upward.

Jackson says, "Got part of him." I poke my head out into the flickering light from the blazing trees. As I do so the Jumbo jerks and shifts forward again, edging to the right, keeping its front to the German tank. Move and fire, the British Major said: as lame as he was and as crazy as he seemed, he knew what he was talking about. "One more," Jackson says. "Stop." Yates stops the slide of the Jumbo's tracks. Jackson depresses the footpedal trigger again, firing the main armament a third time. I catch the hot shell casing as it falls from the framework around the gun's breech. As I fling it up and out into the night I hear a wounded animal screaming: yet another maimed horse barking and coughing with pain and incomprehension. "Get on, Yates," McCarthy says from the commander's seat. "Brown," he tells the bowgunner, "kill that animal." I select another round of HVAP from the ready-rack and load the 76 millimeter gun as Brown fires the .30 caliber machinegun in the ball mounting embedded in the sloped steel glacis at the right front of the Sherman: a short burst, three or four rounds. Not enough to terrify infantry, but more than enough to kill a terrorized horse hobbling in the road, its gut torn open.

I peek out of my hatch, my chin at the level of the flat surface of the turret, as Yates drives the Jumbo forward. Down the road the dark has grown light: the German tank that lurked in the shadows and fired at us from the dark is burning.

"He's burning," I say into the intercom. I see a crouched man jump down from the burning PzKW IV onto the road. Holding his left arm with his right, the man limps into the woods to the right of the road. No one else climbs out of the German tank.

"Anyone see that guy get out?" McCarthy asks.

"Not me," Brown says from the bowgunner's position.

"Me neither," Jackson says.

Perhaps Jackson and Brown are telling the truth. On the other hand, they may not have seen the wounded German escape because they may not have wanted to kill a wounded tanker. We are reluctant to kill wounded tankers: when we see them dead, they remind us of what we may become.

"Doesn't matter," McCarthy says. "Looks like just one of them got out. I saw him: wounded in the arm and leg both it looked like. Went off into the woods to the right. He ain't going to do no more fighting. Billy," McCarthy tells Jackson, "you did a job on that Panzer."

"HVAP do the job every time," Jackson says, as though he is promoting High Velocity Armor Piercing to housewives.

"Almost every time," McCarthy says. "I don't want to try no HVAP, nor nothing else, on no Panther nor on no Tiger neither."

"Amen, brother," Jackson says.

"That makes three for you, Billy," McCarthy says. Three, I wonder? It seems they have done this twice before. "You're getting to be a regular ace tank gunner."

"I'd rather be home in Richmond," Jackson says. "Fuck being an ace tank gunner."

"How about being an ace tank gunner in Richmond?" Yates asks as we slide forward toward the burning PzKW IV.

"When I get home," Jackson says, "I don't care about this anymore. Used to go hunting in the fall. Not any more. Not ever again."

"Coming up, two hundred yards to the dragon's teeth," Brown says. Now that we are sliding closer, I see in the flickering light from the burning Panzer that the concrete obstacles embedded in the road are camouflaged with streaks of green and brown and gray paint.

"I see them," McCarthy says. "Billy, stop here?"

"Two hundred yards? Seems about right," Jackson says.

"I count maybe three you'll have to get out the way," McCarthy says.

"Okay," Jackson says. As he touches the controls the turret shifts and the breech of the gun rises.

"Everybody button up now," McCarthy says as he slips his shoulders and head down inside the Jumbo's turret and swings the commander's hatch closed above him. I close the loader's hatch. I know what McCarthy means: concrete shattered by gunfire throws off heavy, jagged projectiles that fly out from the center of the explosion along unpredictable trajectories. In addition, the ammunition inside the burning Panzer Four may begin to explode, and if it does, some of the racked shells may be flung out through the open hatches into the night.

"The one on the right," Jackson says. I stare through my periscope: in the lower half of my periscope's field I see the camouflaged concrete tetrahedrons that block the road. Beyond them the height of the flames rising from the Panzer is diminishing.

"Looks like the fire in the Panzer's burning out," I say. I hope I am right: I don't like to think about fire reaching the ammunition inside the tank Jackson has destroyed.

I am staring through the periscope when Jackson fires the 76 millimeter gun. I sense the breech of the gun close to my right shoulder flick backward and throw out the shell casing. As I hear the shell rattle from the gun's breech I see the precise geometry of the concrete tetrahedron at the right edge of the road bulge and shatter. Chunks of concrete are flung away into the trees. I turn from the periscope and bend to extract a shell from the ammunition stowage beneath the floor of the basket in which McCarthy, Jackson and I work. I hear thumps and clangs against the armor of the Jumbo as chunks of concrete strike our thick steel hide. The British Major was right: when to close hatches is a matter of judgment. We are fortunate that McCarthy, this Jumbo's commander, has learned a lot about judgment in the near five months since we came ashore in Normandy.

I slide a fresh round into the gun's breech as Jackson rotates the turret and adjusts the gun. He fires again. I do not need to look through the periscope to know that he has destroyed the second dragon's tooth, for McCarthy says, "Um-hmm, Mr. Jackson, um-hmm, that's two out of two. That shooting. You gone win yourself a prize if you get the third one with just one more shot."

"What prize?" Jackson asks as I slide a third shell into the breech. I cough: the turret and the basket beneath it are full of smoke and the bitter stench of the propellant in the 76 millimeter shells. The extractors in the roof of the Jumbo are no better than they are in the M4A3: it is as though some idiot has set off fireworks in the livingroom.

"Going to get a ticket right back to Richmond when this here war is over, Mr. Jackson," McCarthy says, "if you get the third one there with your next shot."

"Ticket back to Richmond," Jackson says. "Like I thought: that ain't no prize, McCarthy. That ain't no prize at all."

"That prize, Mr. Jackson, a whole lot better than the other thing," McCarthy says. No one acknowledges what McCarthy has said, because no one wants to acknowledge the other thing: for the other thing will cancel all tickets to Richmond in less than a third of a second. Each one of us knows the other thing well: it sat on its brass base on the low stage beside the civil British Major who, limping and gray in his lined face, considered his audience untutored soldiers and nothing more; and nothing less.

I heard less than half the advice the British Major gave us: I lost every other word he spoke in the glitter of the polished brass butt of the shellcasing and the perfect black of the pointed tip of the shell that waited beside him like a teaching assistant who, impatient with the professor's generalities, wants to get down to the gritty details of the lessons that need to be learned by repetition and example. The fucking thing was murderous, heavy, a wonder of engineering and chemistry and ballistics: penetration, violation and death in a slim, elegant package. "Sorry I couldn't bring along the gun that fires this," the British Major said. "But the size of the shell will give you an idea of what the eighty-eight can do. If you've any questions, remember this: the eighty-eight can shoot down one of your B-17s—or one of our Lancasters, for that matter—at thirty thousand feet. Of course, I don't think the Lancaster flies that high. But I'm sure the RAF are willing to leave German antiaircraft tests to the Americans. Haha." None of us asked the British Major what the eighty-eight would do to a Sherman. We knew: the eighty-eight would do the other thing. It would cancel the tickets, turn out the lights and send us for temporary burial before disinterment at the end of the war. Rutherford calls the eighty-eight the thick razor: because it slices through steel as a blade carves flesh. This is a sound analogy, for the eighty-eight millimeter gun and its ammunition and the steel in the best razors are made by the same reputable firm in the Ruhr valley.

Jackson adjusts gun and turret and fires the 76 millimeter gun a third time, and the third camouflaged tetrahedron explodes in a rising cone of debris that pounds and clicks against the steel walls and roof of the Jumbo inside which we crouch, doing our job, working the late shift. I glance at my watch: one-thirty in the morning.

"Prize, shit," Jackson says. "I get back to Richmond, I'm going to put all this here behind me and not tell anyone ever what I did in this war."

"You ain't going to join the Vets?" McCarthy asks, as though he has been soliciting us for prepayment of our dues and we've turned him down flat.

"Fuck the Vets," Jackson says. He has taken his face from the sight and turned around in his seat to look back and up at McCarthy sitting behind him. "I don't want nothing to do with any of this shit when this war is over."

"Yates," McCarthy says, "move us on up and over that mess of broke-up concrete and past that Panzer Four. Fast as you can, now: look like that tank ain't going to explode, but you never know."

Yates chuckles and says, "But you never know." Still chuckling, he revs the Jumbo's engine as we slide forward, working his way up through the gears. On a surface like this, we can move almost twenty-five miles an hour. Not fast enough, if the Panzer Four explodes when we are abreast of it. But we must pass the smoldering menace of this German armored fighting vehicle, and it is better to pass it going twenty-five miles an hour than a single mile an hour less.

"Something there," Brown says, "left of the road in the woods."

As he speaks the last word Brown begins to fire long sweeping bursts from the .30 caliber machinegun in the slanted right front of the Jumbo's hull. I rotate the periscope in front of my eyes half left. In the dull light flickering from the fire within the PzKW IV I see shadows shifting among the pines at the edge of the road. As I watch, the solid line of red fire from Brown's machinegun—every third round is tracer—passes across the shadows. The shadows fold upon themselves.

"What the fuck was that?" McCarthy asks.

"I don't know," Brown says. "But I'm not waiting to ask whoever out there howdy how you today? Maybe they lurking there, got some of them Panzerfaust. Or maybe some of them Panzerschreck, maybe." So Brown identifies the handheld rocket projectile tipped with a hollow charge, and its larger successor, which can, if the operator has nerve enough to wait until a Sherman is close enough, destroy the tank at which he fires and kill the crew within.

"Go on and fire, then," McCarthy says.

Brown hammers out strands of red fire one after the other, pausing every eight or ten rounds as he has been taught. The red strands float into the woods and flick this way and that from the stony earth in which the pinetrees are rooted. The shadows that moved among the trees are still.

"That's enough maybe," McCarthy says. "I don't see anything now. You sure you saw something?"

"I saw something," Brown says. He sounds angry, as though McCarthy has suggested that he is not telling the truth.

Yates has his foot to the floor. The usual mutter of the Jumbo's engine is a low roar. We pound forward, slithering toward the stumps of the shattered camouflaged concrete tetrahedrons that were supposed to bar our way farther into Germany.

"Get on," McCarthy says. "Go right on over them and down the road. Everybody hold on, now."

I ask: "McCarthy, you want me to look out up top?"

"Jesus Christ no," McCarthy says. "You want to get shot? You keep that hatch closed up till I tell you. Head sticking up out of a hatch like that is an invitation to get shot. Could be they're snipers all around in here."

"Okay," I say.

"You bet okay," Jackson says. I look at him: he is grinning at me across the breech of the gun and shaking his head. But I am not insulted by their critical remarks. I am untutored and they are educated, and they do not have a lot of time for subtle instruction: the precise lessons they give me are set out in gruff declarative sentences in which every third word is profane.

"Keep watch," Yates says. "Everybody watch a different way like always." I turn the periscope before my eyes from straight along the line of the Jumbo's sliding progress ninety degrees to the left. Yates, Brown and Jackson examine the way ahead. McCarthy observes the area from straight ahead of the Sherman ninety degrees to the right. McCarthy told me of this drill when I joined this crew, and I have not forgotten the importance of watching. We watch for infantry creeping in the woods or in the ditches along the verges of the road: the German infantry's antitank rockets will burn a hole through many, many millimeters of hardened steel. We hate this weapon as much as the infantrymen who carry it hate us. We shoot them as they try to creep close and closer so that they can shoot down our vehicle and kill us with rifles and machinepistols as we get out. If we get out.

As more than one of us has said, Christ what shit this here is.

"Something to the left front," Yates calls up, his voice rising up the intercom and up his throat as he shifts down and the Jumbo rises as its tracks scrabble and slither, grinding over the ragged stump of the first of the three dragon's teeth Jackson shattered with our 76 millimeter gun.

I rotate the periscope in the turret's roof. Fifty feet to the left in the flickering light of the smoldering fire in the PzKW IV to our right front, I see four bodies lying at the edge of the treeline. These are the shadows Brown saw and at which he fired. The corpses seem small. Perhaps it is the perspective I have of them through the periscope that reduces their size. Or perhaps, as everyone says, death has reduced them.

Yates horses the Jumbo's tons and tons of steel, machinery, weapons and ammunition over the echeloned stumps of the second and third dragon's teeth Jackson reduced to rubble with his gun. As the Sherman tilts to the left I grab handholds and brace myself, staring and staring through the periscope. The four bodies do not seem small: they are small. They are children dressed in uniforms. I wonder what they were supposed to do here. Whatever it was, they failed and we succeeded: we killed them all. The cuffs of their uniform pants are folded up, the skirts of their coats descend to their ankles. Germany is collapsing upon itself. All the tailors are dead or incapacitated or sewing whitesilver braid and ornate tabs on the shoulders and collars of generals' uniforms. They do not have time to cut a man's uniform to fit a child.

I cannot, for which I thank God, see their faces among the shadows in which they lie.

I open my mouth to announce what we have done as the Jumbo rocks over the stump of the last concrete tetrahedron. But I think of Brown sitting behind his machinegun, worrying what might be in front of us in the dark along this damp road, and I close my mouth: Brown does not need to know what he has done, and I do not want to start him thinking. Perhaps I will tell him when we have our tickets in hand and are waiting to board ship for home, where, before the war, we wore our elder brothers' pants shortened by our mothers.

"What was it?" McCarthy asks me through the intercom. I take my face from the periscope and look across the gun and up to the right at McCarthy.

"Four infantrymen," I tell him. I am at least part right: they were infantry, though they were not old enough to be out of school.

"Good work, Brown," McCarthy says. "You go on like that, you get a ticket home too."

"Fuck it," Brown says. "I don't want no ticket. I want this shit to stop and the sun to come out."

"Going into the dark," Yates says as he shifts up again. Through the periscope I see he is right: the road ahead is dark, the fire from the burning pinetrees and the smoldering PzKW IV behind us.

"Slow up a little in along here," McCarthy says. His face is pressed to his periscope. I know he is searching the dark, wondering what might be lurking, waiting for us to come on: gunmuzzles, whispered orders, the slick clink of an antitank round slid into the breech of a gun, the whisper of canvas as a grenadier hefts an antitank mine, the wooden handle in his trembling fist. "Open up, loader," McCarthy says. "Get your head out and look."

I fling open the hatch: this is no time for equivocation or questions. McCarthy made it clear the day I joined this crew that Timmy Smith, the former loader, had been a good man who followed every single order right up to the moment a bullet shattered the left half of his skull. Telling me the details of Timmy Smith's death, McCarthy also told me he expected me to follow every single order, and quick like, just like Timmy Smith had.

The bitter stink of cordite and the fug of oil and sweat inside the Jumbo rushes up out of the hatch around me. I thrust half my head out into the cold damp night. I hear the crackling of flames and the roar of engines behind us: Task Force Rhine is coming on in our wake, pounding along this anonymous road into Germany. I glance behind. Three vehicles back, against the glow of the burning trees three hundred yards behind, I see the outline of the Headquarters track. I also see, above the track's armored bed, the flat tilted brim of First Sergeant Reardon's campaign hat angling this way and that as he turns his head. I see the silhouette of a rifle's muzzle beside the silhouette of his face beneath his hat. This is the First Sergeant's private '03 Springfield, which I suppose he carries to encourage us, since a single antique rifle will add nothing to our firepower.

"Anything?" McCarthy asks.

"Looking," I tell him, jerking my face to the front.

"Look faster," McCarthy says. "Don't stay up there like that. This ain't no tour bus. Look and duck back in. Look again and duck back in. Didn't I tell you that for Christ's sake?" I hear an angry plea in the tone of McCarthy's voice: he saw Timmy Smith killed and he does not want to have to see another loader killed the same way.

"Yeah," Jackson says. "What the fuck you doing like that? Look like a turkey up there, neck stretched out so you can see."

"Don't forget," Yates says, as though he is narrating a training film. "If you can see them, they can see you. And they're out there: you don't have to worry they're not out there."

I wait for a comment from Brown. But he does not speak, and I worry that he noted the youth of the four infantrymen even as he killed them.

"I don't see anything to the front," I say. "See the First Sergeant standing up in the track behind."

"I hate killing those horses," Brown says. "Worse than killing people."

"That's the way it is," McCarthy says, "here in, uh, Task Force Rhine did they call it?"

"That's us," Yates says. "Task Force Rhine."

"Shit," Brown says.

I stick my head up through the hatch and glance around.

"Doughs coming on behind?" McCarthy asks.

I look straight back along the line of vehicles behind me. I see the halftracks of the armored infantry passing one after another between the ranks of burning pines trees. "They're coming," I say.

The armored infantry component of Task Force Rhine is the 2d Battalion of the 409th Infantry Regiment of the 103rd Infantry Division. The Seven Six One and the 614th Tank Destroyer Battalion (Towed) have been in support of the 103rd Infantry since March 15, when we began this attack. We fought at Kindwiller, where the 614th formed, from its

Headquarters platoon under the command of Captain Beauregard King, an infantry force to attack the town. When Captain King was wounded, he told his sergeant, 'Don't stop for me—finish the job!' Or at least that's what the press said Captain King said. I suspect he told his sergeant, 'Get the fuck on out of here and shoot that fucking dump up 'till they hand over or you drive them out or kill every fucking one of them.' Whatever, Sergeant Charles E. Parks took command of Captain King's scratch force and captured Kindwiller. At Bischoltz, the 1st and 2nd Reconnaissance Platoons of the 614th under the Battalion's Commander, Lt. Col. Frank S. Pritchard, raided the town and took forty-one prisoners. To the northeast, at Niederschlettenbach, a platoon of the Seven Six One's Company C killed thirty-five of the enemy and destroyed two dozen pillboxes and machinegun positions. Farther to the northeast, at Reisdorf, another of C Company's platoons, in support of the 409th Infantry Regiment, destroyed six pillboxes, killed eight enemy, took forty prisoners and opened a chink in the Siegfried Line through which the 103rd Infantry could pass. Northeast of Reisdorf, at Birkenhördt, infantry of the 409th rode the Seven Six One's tanks as Task Force Rhine fought through the town behind a rolling barrage of corps artillery.

Now it is March 23 and we have left Silz, where a house full of ammunition exploded and blocked the road, and Münchweiler, where we drove the crews from their antitank guns, behind, and are on our way northeast to Klingenmünster.

As I pull my head back inside the hatch McCarthy is saying, "Yes, Colonel. Yes, sir," into the microphone. The Colonel is with the First Sergeant three vehicles back. He is the commander of Task Force Rhine and he is doing a job good enough to have them make him a general. When we are not on the move, he walks the column, chatting with the men of the task force, telling them to stay awake. Staying awake is hard: we are all tired. We have been on the go for eleven days, and every step of the way we have fought or worried or listened to the enemy's gunfire and our own and heard the strike of shot against steel.

"Colonel's ordered us to drop back behind the Headquarters track," McCarthy says. "Says we been up here long enough, Lattimore going to take up this job."

"Good for Lattimore," Yates says. "You want me to pull to the side and let him by?"

"Be my guest," McCarthy says. Yates eases the Jumbo to the right onto the verge. Lattimore's M4A3 slides past us. Behind it comes the second M4A3E2 Rutherford and I brought from Nancy. As it begins to ease past us idling by the edge of the road I stick my head out of the loader's hatch and note that the bow machinegun of the other Jumbo is moving up and down and back and forth. I wave back: I hope Rutherford, sitting behind the machinegun peering out through the periscope built into the rotatable plate in the hatch above his head, sees me wave.

"Be all right not to be out front like this," Jackson says as Lattimore's Sherman and the Jumbo in which Rutherford rides trundle past. "I'm getting tired of looking and looking."

"Yeah," Brown says. "I'm tired of that, and the rest of it."

"Colonel said he thought we needed a break," McCarthy says. "So Ervin's taking over the lead. Fine by me. This one time, I agree with the Colonel: I'd like to take a three day weekend right now. Go anywhere, even the beach."

I know what they mean: beneath our physical exhaustion the nervous strain of watching and waiting for the next crisis can expand in an instant into fear and beyond, to the edge of panic, particularly if the transition occurs in an instant—as, say, when a burning round of tungsten-cored steel strikes the armor behind which we cower, waiting for a death worse than any we could have imagined in 1940.

Still I wonder why Lattimore's M4A3 is out front, and the second Jumbo 1st/Sgt. John P. Burch gave us in Nancy, and in which Rutherford rides, trails behind. Who can figure these decisions? Perhaps the Colonel knows Lattimore's crew and trusts them. Perhaps Lattimore's gunner is cooler and quicker than the gunner in the Jumbo in which Rutherford rides toward Klingenmünster. Or perhaps the Jumbo is low on ammunition, or has a mechanical or an electrical problem. Who knows? Who the fuck knows why anything happens one way and not another in this shit war?

The Colonel's Headquarters halftrack jounces past, the thick tires at the front skidding over the damp road, the tracks clattering against the asphalt. Looking from the loader's hatch I see the Colonel and the First Sergeant in the bed of the Headquarters halftrack, both of them standing up surveying the column in front and behind, checking as our column goes on through trouble and more trouble still. The Colonel and the First Sergeant nod at one another, as though they are satisfied. At least the Colonel is not muttering orders into a microphone in his fist and the First Sergeant is not jogging from one end of the column to the other, pounding his fist against the sides of Shermans and calling orders to the tank commanders peeking from their hatches.

The halftrack full of armored doughs from the 409th Infantry Regiment rocking along behind the Colonel's Headquarters track halts to permit us to enter the column. The sergeant in the right front seat sticks his arm from the cab and waves us on, the palm of his hand a pale oval in the dark. As Yates revs the Jumbo's engine and manipulates his levers and pedals and shifts us forward into the line of vehicles, I glance back. The bearded faces of the infantrymen from the 409th sitting in the back of the halftrack are pale beneath the rims of their drab steel helmets.

Like us in the Seven Six One, and like the men in the 614th Tank Destroyer Battalion (Towed), the men in the 409th have seen a lot more than any of them could have wished. They and we stand shoulder to shoulder here, faces turned to the east, the darkness, the enemy and, in a month or six weeks, dawn. Perhaps one day some of us in the Seven Six One—those of us this war leaves alive—will have a reunion with the men from the 409th. Not, I know, the year after this war is over. Not even, I know, in any one of the twenty years that follow. But perhaps one day, when things are easier and the ground is not so muddy and rough, when we are thirty years older than we are now or, if things do not go right, forty years older than we are now, we will jostle together on a lawn and remind one another of these days and nights when, recalling the example Sam Turley set us, we stood up against the night.

Yates drives the Jumbo along behind the Headquarters halftrack. We trundle along, the Colonel and the First Sergeant standing up in the halftrack swaying, the Colonel speaking into a microphone, the First Sergeant holding his '03 Springfield under his right arm as though he is preparing to shoot competition on the range at Benning.

We know that Klingenmünster is defended by fixed fortifications which the Germans have been building since 1937. Aerial reconnaissance tells us that the Germans have expended a lot of method and sweat to make these defenses tough and resilient. Not one of us likes to think of the overlapping fields of fire, the machineguns in bunkers and the artillery and antitank weapons in concrete emplacements, all the men serving the weapons rested and ready to defend this bit of Germany.

But we will get through them. Our Task Force has taken hundreds of prisoners in the last ten days. We have also destroyed hundreds of vehicles, guns, pillboxes, machinegun emplacements, antitank weapons and a couple of self-propelled guns. We have also killed two hundred enemy soldiers and expended almost fifty tons of ammunition. After the war, the construction business will boom in the parts of France and Germany through which we have passed in the last ten days. I ought to worry whether they can find the money to pay the bricklayers, but I don't:

Europe is an odd place full of odd people. The French have been standoffish, and their disdain is general: men in the 409th and 411th Infantry Regiments have received the same cold treatment as we. The Germans, on the other hand, have been more than standoffish: they have fought us for every foot of ground on which the priggish, surly French stood and muttered to one another, and have fought us again for every inch of Germany since we left France behind.

But the attitudes of the French don't matter: only the Germans matter right now, and they matter more than anyone any one of us have ever met. They matter more than our parents, our friends at home, our teachers. They matter more than the President. And the Germans up ahead in Klingenmünster matter more than all the other Germans, just as, four hours ago, the Germans in Münchweiler were the most important Germans in Europe.

"See something up there," McCarthy says. He is sitting on his seat fixed to the wall of the turret behind Jackson, bracing himself against the slide and sway of the M4A3E2 pounding forward, head out of his hatch.

"What are you doing up there, McCarthy?" Jackson asks. "I thought you told this here new loader of ours to stick his head out, look, and get back in. Now you sitting up there like this some tour bus up to Washington, D.C."

"You're from Richmond," McCarthy says, as though Jackson can't know about tour busses in Washington, D.C.

"I say," Jackson says as he reaches back and up from his seat and yanks at the hem of McCarthy's overcoat, "get the fuck down from there."

"I'm coming," McCarthy says. Jackson does not stop pulling on his coat until McCarthy is back inside the Jumbo's turret. "Klingenmünster up ahead there," he tells us. "I don't like the look of it."

"Do tell," Yates says.

"Getting late," McCarthy says. "Still, it's better going through here at night than in the day."

"Quarter to two in the morning," Yates says. "We go on like this, Colonel going to have breakfast in Klingenmünster."

As Yates speaks I hear McCarthy whispering into his microphone, speaking to the Colonel. "Yes, sir," McCarthy says: "go right on, fire everything." The answers McCarthy gives the Colonel are casual, as though the Colonel were not ordering us to carry out a night attack on the solid defenses of Klingenmünster. Still, we have become confident about this type of action and when McCarthy gives us the word, we begin. As we drive forward Jackson calls for high explosive and rotates the turret until our gun points to the right of our line of advance. I load the gun and check the belt in the coaxial .30 caliber machinegun. Then I stand up, stretch out of the turret hatch from the waist up and change the box magazine of the .50 caliber machinegun mounted at the rear of the turret. I descend through the turret hatch once more and take one round of 76 millimeter ammunition after another out of the ammunition stowage beneath the floor and fit them into the ready rack at the back of the basket.

"I can't see a thing," McCarthy says.

"You'll see okay once they start," Brown says. We have an advantage at night: we wait for the Germans's antitank guns to fire at us. Then we fire at the flashes of the gunmuzzles. If they miss with their first shot, we shoot them down. It is our bad luck that the Germans aren't stupid: they have learned to fire mortars and machineguns at us, to try to provoke us into firing our 76 millimeter guns at them, so that their antitank weapons can go to work on us. It's complicated: as the British Major said, if you fight in tanks you require good judgment, and good judgment about fighting in tanks is acquired only after you've spent time fighting in tanks.

"Lattimore's going up," McCarthy says. I look through the periscope. Lattimore's M4A3 is accelerating, sliding forward, the driver shifting up through the gears, his foot to the floor. "Look at him go," McCarthy says. Lattimore's turret is rotated thirty degrees to the right. I wonder what it is like to live in one's own house in one's own town and to have armored fighting vehicles appear across the fields, turrets swiveling, guns pointing.

I watch as Lattimore's Sherman leaves the rest of us behind. When Lattimore is three hundred yards in front of the sluggish Jumbo in which Rutherford serves as bowgunner, Lattimore's gunner fires his coaxial machinegun toward the dark, humped shape of Klingenmünster. Then he fires his 76 millimeter gun. A vicious tearing separation of the air, a clap as the ragged halves slap together. An instant more and Lattimore's gunner fires a second time. "He's a comer, all right," McCarthy says.

Behind us the Seven Six One's tanks and the 409th's armored doughs are firing everything they have at Klingenmünster. I see rifle and machinegun fire and the discharge of 76 millimeter tank weapons. The 409th's men are jumping down from their halftracks and spreading out in the darkness. Seconds pass. From the center of the column behind us I see the big bright flashes of the 614th Tank Destroyer Battalion (Towed)'s three inch anti-tank weapons firing on Klingenmünster. I can see nothing but the flashes of the muzzles of their guns; but I know they stand behind and beside their weapons, aiming the pieces, flinging the rounds into the smoking butts of the guns, breaking open ammunition cases, the gun captains speaking into radios and calling out orders. Theirs is a chilling job: they stand up behind the flimsy gunshield behind the bright flash of the gunmuzzle, exposed to the rain and whatever else comes their way. Here, as at Climbach last year, the Six One Four earns yet again the reputation we will recall during hard times back home.

I don't like being Jackson's loader: it is claustrophobic, sweaty work. Still, I'd rather be crouching behind this Jumbo's thick armored walls, plugged into the intercom and the Battalion radio net, faint heat seeping back from the transmission, than standing out there in the dark feeding a monster gun, adjusting it, shifting it. I cannot imagine standing with the Six One Four's gunners in the dirt and mud behind a three inch piece, the wind whistling through the dark night over the stubble in a muddy winter field, waiting for counter-battery fire, waiting for machinegun fire, sweating in the cold night air, listening for shouted changes of angle and elevation, waiting and waiting for the flash in the dark in the distance and the strike of a high explosive round, the blinding light and mounting pressure thrust up from the muddy ground, sucking breath from the faithful men standing behind their piece, firing on orders into the darkness.

"Pretty good cooking up in along here they're doing," McCarthy says as we roll forward. Yates gives the Sherman gas and we trundle and jounce along behind the accelerating Headquarters track. Far ahead, Lattimore's Sherman is pushing forward firing its main armament and all three machineguns. I take my eyes from the periscope, stick my head up out of the hatch: Lattimore is standing on the rear deck of his M4A3, firing the .50 caliber machinegun across the turret into the night, the sliding strands of tracer weaving toward Klingenmünster. As I watch, the Jumbo in which Rutherford rides as bowgunner begins firing too. In the flash of its gun bright as summer lightning I see First Sergeant Reardon standing behind the steel wall of the Headquarters halftrack, campaign hat set straight on his head, making a gesture: he is firing his '03 Springfield. At least he is firing with method, aiming each shot. The Colonel is standing up beside the First Sergeant, firing a .45 caliber pistol into the night at the shadows in front of Klingenmünster.

I wonder why Lattimore rushed ahead and began this fight. But who knows? Perhaps he saw a menace we did not. A masked weapon might have fired on him, the flash from its muzzle invisible to us but apparent and therefore fearsome to Lattimore and his crew. As the British Major said, it's all a question of angles and instants. And judgment, of course: judgment more than all else, he said. When to stay, when to go, which angle and instant to choose. Do you understand me, gentlemen?

No one had ever called any one of us a gentleman before.

Lattimore's gunner fires his 76 millimeter weapon again, and an instant later he fires it again. I imagine my counterpart standing to the left of the gun in Lattimore's Sherman, flinging shells into the breech, the smoking hot shell casings cluttering the floor of the fighting compartment.

"Firing on the go like that," McCarthy says. He sounds as though he doesn't think much of Lattimore's gunner's method. "I don't know about that." No gunner can hit anything when his Sherman is underway. The 76 millimeter gun may be stabilized in the vertical plane, but the stabilizer equipment is notorious for its unreliability, and even if it worked every time, the gunner would still have to compensate for the other two dimensions in which he must work if the shot from his weapon is to strike the target.

Still, this is a night attack against the stout, prepared defenses of a town, and Lattimore and his gunner are doing the right thing. Though his gunner may hit nothing, the noise of the gun firing and the shells exploding somewhere near the defenders may unnerve them.

I see shadows move and shift against the dark ground three hundred yards away in front of Klingenmünster. Now I know what the First Sergeant and the Colonel are shooting at: German infantry. As I open my mouth to speak McCarthy shouts, "Fire! Everybody work out!" Yates hauls at his levers and the Jumbo turns to the right, lurches off the road. Jackson fires the coaxial machinegun, tracer flicking away. He shifts the turret as Brown fires the bow machinegun. Then Jackson fires the 76 millimeter gun. A flash of light, the crack of the gun. An instant, and the high explosive round detonates close to the shifting shadows three hundred yards away. In the flash of light of the exploding shell I see the infantrymen scuttling in jerky rushes this way and that, retiring toward the buildings at the edge of Klingenmünster.

"Load," Jackson shouts. I jerk my head inside the hatchway. Jackson's face is pressed to the sight: I know he sees the scuttling German troops. I imagine his foot dancing on the trigger of the .30 caliber coaxial machinegun firing irregular bursts. Jackson takes his face from the sight, looks across the shielded breech of the gun at me, places his eyes back against the sight, and says, "Load, I said: load HE."

I bend and reach into the ammunition stowage, extract a high explosive shell and slip it into the breech of the gun. "Loaded," I say into the intercom.

"Keep it coming till I tell you stop," Jackson says. As he speaks he presses the footpedal trigger of the 76 millimeter gun and the gun roars and recoils, the breech flicking open, the shell casing rattling out of the framework shield around the breech. I kick the smoking casing to one side as I ease another round of HE into the breech, tell Jackson the gun is loaded, and bend to take another round from the ammunition stowage. As I lift the cold, smooth, pointed cylinder Jackson fires the gun again. I glance around in the dim light inside the Sherman's fighting compartment as I load the 76 millimeter gun again. McCarthy's feet are disappearing upward out of the commander's hatch, the intercom wire trailing behind him as he scrambles up out of the small safe space inside the turret. As I tell Jackson the gun is loaded, the .50 caliber machinegun mounted on the pintle at the rear of the turret begins to fire. Through the open loader's hatch above my head I feel the concussion of each heavy round hammer from the machinegun's muzzle. The bright flashing white light at the machinegun's muzzle illuminates the inside of the fighting compartment. In the flickering light, I see Jackson leaning forward against the 76 millimeter gun's sight. He shifts the turret, lowers the muzzle of the gun and fires another round of high explosive at the ducking scrambling Germans in front of Klingenmünster.

As I fit another round of 76 millimeter ammunition into the breech of Jackson's gun I listen to the crashing roar of the firing all up and down the line of Task Force Rhine's vehicles. The 409th's armored doughs are tuning up: a steady crackling rattle of machinegun, rifle and Browning Automatic Rifle fire has begun. From farther back the 614th's three inch antitank guns are firing round after round, as though the gun crews have wagered which crew will fire the most rounds in the shortest time. Glancing away from Jackson's calm face pressed to the periscopic sight, I hear the hissing rush of 2.75 inch rockets overhead: each of the armored doughs' halftracks carries a bazooka, and though the bazooka's effect on a German armored fighting vehicle is a well-known joke in northwestern Europe, the 2.75 inch rocket seems to have been designed to demolish buildings and bunkers.

Jackson fires the gun again. I load and as he aims I hear a new, distinctive sound among the crash and roar of weapons firing in the night: the high cracking sound of Germany antitank guns firing and the moan of German artillery shells arching through the sky.

The .50 caliber machinegun mounted at the back of the turret above my head stops firing. A second later Jackson tumbles through the commander's hatch. He pulls the hatch down over his head and shouts down the intercom, "Button up. Everybody close up now. Artillery coming in. Yates, get us moving. Get forward into this field here. Gunner, go on and fire. You too, Brown. Look for the muzzleflashes from those fucking AT guns." McCarthy sounds a little nervous. I understand why: no one can be calm about artillery and antitank guns. The guns protecting Klingenmünster are emplaced in fortified bunkers, the guncrews are rested, and their officers have had a lot more time than they need to sort out the likely approaches to Klingenmünster and set out aiming stakes for their gunners.

Yates zigs the Jumbo to the right, to the left. He throws out both the levers, puts the Jumbo in reverse and backs, zagging to the left, zigging to the right before he throws out both levers again, shifts into first and edges the uparmored Sherman forward to the right, to the left, to the right. The Jumbo moves like a huge hound hunting this way and that across the ground.

As Yates drives the M4A3E2 forward, altering speed and direction, Jackson elevates and depresses the muzzle of the 76 millimeter gun and rotates the turret degree by degree, holding the muzzle of the weapon on the target at which he stares through the sight. I wonder how he can identify and select targets in the dark night full of whipping tracer and exploding shells. As I wonder he fires the gun and tells his target, "Got you." I wonder who or what he has destroyed. He answers my thought: "Antitank gun in a bunker. Saw the barrel parallel to the ground."

"Good shooting," McCarthy shouts down the intercom. He reaches forward and down from where he sits behind and a little to the right of Jackson and slaps him on the right shoulder. "Real good shooting. You definitely going to win that prize, Jackson."

I lean back against the curved wall of the basket beneath the turret rotated forty-five degrees to the right as Jackson turns his head to look back and up at McCarthy. I look across the small fighting compartment of the Jumbo, across the breech of the 76 millimeter gun. I wait to hear what Jackson has to say about the prize McCarthy holds out to him.

A huge hammer strikes the far wall of the turret. The Jumbo lurches away from the vicious blow. Where the hammer struck, the Jumbo's thick carapace glows red. I see the glowing red steel turn white and spatter as I hear the moaning roar of the antitank round enter the Jumbo's fighting compartment. Bellowing and hissing, the shot flings shrieking chips and burning dribbles of its ricocheting self and the Sherman's armor slicing and carving this way and that through the fighting compartment.

Jackson's head leaps from his shoulders, propelled upward and forward by the thick thrust from his neck of blood under pressure. I smell burning blood and in the instant that I smell it McCarthy is cut in half as though a giant wielding a broadsword has entered the M4A3E2's turret and set to work with a fifteen pound blade. Severed at the waist, McCarthy's hips and legs leap down from his seat as his torso flings itself forward across Jackson's headless corpse, as though to shield the stump of Jackson's neck. In the instant they are killed the roaring antitank round hammers against the bloody breech of the 76 millimeter and flashes up through the thin armor of the turret's roof into the night full of glittering yellow and gold tracer and invisible shrieking shot.

I feel a stinging in my right leg and gulp and gulp again as my heart beats like a fist against my breastbone. Have I? Must I too now?

"What's. . . ?" Yates mutters up the intercom. The Jumbo lurches and slides forward, to the right, to the left.

I slide my right hand to my thigh, wriggle my toes inside my boot. My leg stings, but my toes move. In the faint light thrown by the small lamp I see flecks of blood on my trousers: but is it my blood, or Jackson's? Or McCarthy's?

"We're hit," I say.

"Fire?" Brown asks.

"Jackson's killed. So's McCarthy. And the gun's hammered," I say.

Brown says, "Are we burning?"

"No," I tell him. "No: the round exited through the roof above the gun. Nothing's burning. Didn't touch anything combustible." Not counting McCarthy or Jackson, I think. But I do not mention how they died: it will not help to describe McCarthy's upper half sprawled across six sevenths of Jackson.

"I better get us back out of here," Yates says. The Jumbo drives straight backward away from the defenses in Klingenmünster. I hope the armored doughs from the 409th infantry are not loitering behind us.

"Fast as you can," Brown tells Yates.

"Loader, look out if you can and tell me how I'm going," Yates says.

"Fuck don't turn side on to them," Brown shouts, as though Yates has begun to turn the Jumbo broadside on to the antitank gun.

"I ain't," Yates says. "You all right?" I know he is speaking to me.

"All right, I think," I tell him. "Nicked in the leg, that's all."

"You're sure McCarthy and Jackson are dead?" Brown asks.

"Sure?" I ask. Brown has asked a world record of a stupid question. Then I remember that he cannot, with the turret rotated forty-five degrees to the right, see the horror of this tank's gunner beheaded and its commander chopped in half.

"Did you check them?" Brown asks. "To be sure?"

"I'm sure," I say.

Brown is insistent: "Yeah," he says, "but did you check them?"

"I don't have to," I tell him.

"Be better if. . ," Brown says.

"Shut up, Johnny," Yates says. "If he don't have to check them he don't."

"Both dead," Brown says. "Goddamnit!" he says. Then he says it again, and again and again through the intercom until I tell him to shut up and he shuts up.

I stick my head up out of the loader's oval hatch just as an antitank round travelling three times the speed of sound rips apart the air above me. The halves of the air torn apart slap together with the sound of a steel door slamming shut.

"Still shooting at us," Yates says. "Motherfucker."

"Why not?" I ask him. "He has a hit. This is his chance for a kill." I force myself to sound realistic and tough. If I do not I may lose control of myself and begin to whimper.

"Motherfuckers," Brown shouts. He fires the bow machinegun.

"Cut that out," I tell him. "There's vehicles and infantry all around in here." Brown stops firing but he shouts 'motherfuckers' again and again until Yates tells him, "Better be quiet now, Johnny."

"We coming back up on the road," I tell Yates. "Go straight back up the edge and I'll tell you when to turn back left."

"I hear you," Yates says. When the rear of the Jumbo jounces up over the edge of the road between two trees I tell him to turn left and with a precise movement of his controls he backs our 84,000 pound up-armored M4A3 onto the road.

I look forward: the barrel of the 76 millimeter gun has been bent in its mounting. I wonder how: the shot entered the side of the turret and exited through the roof. Then I remember the round striking the gun's breech and ricocheting upward.

I recall the British Major telling us that an eighty-eight's shot makes a Sherman jump. I did not feel us jump, but it seems we are still not big enough. I wonder what the Armored Board and the engineers at the Rock Island Arsenal will come up with next. Whatever it is, they'd better hurry: not much of this war is left, but we still have time enough for a lot more men to be killed inside their flimsy thirty ton Shermans.

I look toward Klingenmünster. The vehicles of our task force are withdrawing. The attack has failed. I suppose it does not matter: we will attack again, and again, until Klingenmünster falls. We have tried surprise and movement. Now I expect we will bombard the town with everything we have, and call down corps artillery, too, to help us pulverize the fortifications and gun emplacements that have stalled this attack.

"They're coming back," I say. As I speak, the firing, ours and the Germans', tapers off. This fight is over. The battle will continue until dawn if need be, and through tomorrow, if need be.

"Shit," Brown says. "Shit and shit."

"Radio working?" Yates asks.

I reach to the radio fitted in the turret's bustle. The usual lights glow. Remarkable: one man beheaded, another hacked in half, and the delicate vacuum tubes of the radio are still whole. I flick the switch from intercom to the external channel and speak, calling for our platoon commander. No one answers. I call again, giving cursory details of the disaster we have suffered. A voice comes up. It is the Colonel. He listens as I give him the details of damage and death. He does not say, "Uh-huh." I imagine First Sergeant Reardon standing in the Headquarters track by the Colonel's side, listening. The Colonel tells me he is coming back with everyone else and to hang on. He asks me if we are burning. I tell him we are not. He does not have to tell me to stay in the Jumbo until the desultory firing ends, but just to be sure he tells me and the other two survivors not to leave the protection, such as it has been, of the Jumbo's armor until things are quiet. He also tells me he will have medics and maintenance come up the column. I tell him we will not need medics, except for a scratch or two on my leg. But the Colonel is in charge, and he is decisive, and he tells me that the medics will come up. He asks me if I have anything more. I tell him I don't and he signs off.

I switch back to intercom and tell Yates and Brown what is going to happen. They listen, and when I finish speaking they say, "Okay." They are unhappy about staying inside the Jumbo, but the occasional burst of machinegun fire sliding toward us, and the occasional antitank round tearing apart the air above us, persuade them that the steel walls of the Jumbo, no matter that we must share their protection with the corpses of McCarthy and Jackson, keep us safer than we would be were we to dismount.

"Like to get out of here even though," Yates says.

"Me too," Brown says.

"Better stay inside," I tell them. I know why they wish to leave the armored walls of the Jumbo: they thought it was a fortress and have discovered it may be a trap. Or perhaps they wish to get out into the night away from the pieces of McCarthy and Jackson strewn on top of one another on the floor to the right of the gun. But that can't be it: they cannot, from where they sit, see the indignity death has inflicted on their friends.

I stick my head up out of the hatch and listen: this attack is over. The desultory firing on both sides ceases. We, and the Germans, are conserving ammunition for the next go-round. That is our certainty: that we will fight again.

As I duck down inside the Jumbo, I understand why Yates and Brown, who cannot see McCarthy's corpse, or Jackson's, would rather dismount from our damaged tank: the inside of the Jumbo reeks. I had not noticed the thick mixture of scents inside the Sherman: now I smell excrement, burned metal, seared flesh, burned blood, singed hair.

"It's quiet," I say. "Let's get out," I say. I scrabble up out of the loader's hatch. As I swing over the side of the turret and drop to the ground Yates and Brown hoist themselves up out of their hatches in front of the turret and slide down the sloped armored front of the Jumbo.

"Jesus Christ," Brown says as he comes around the Jumbo and stands in its lee beside me in the cold dark night. I hold my watch up to my right eye: the glowing hands tell me it is 0215. I think of McCarthy and Jackson dying, think of Sam Taylor and his crew in Big Sam heading down into the valley.

"Jesus Christ is right," Yates says. He is panting as though he has been on a twenty mile march.

"You two all right?" I ask.

"Yeah. All right. Okay. You?"

"Couple of nicks in the right leg. But all right."

"Christ what a thing," Brown says. "I had a lot of confidence in this here Sherman, with the extra armor and all. And now? Jesus Christ."

"What was it?" Yates asks. I wonder what he means. Then I understand.

"AT gun," I tell him. "An eighty-eight, I think. Remember that shell that British Major showed us?"

"Remember it?" Yates said. "I ain't forgot it one moment since October."

"An eighty-eight," Brown says. "I mean Jesus Christ." He sounds as though he thinks the Germans have not played fair.

"Yes," I say. What else? I could tell him I wish the Germans didn't have the eighty-eight millimeter gun, or that we had a tank big enough to take the punishment the eighty-eight inflicts. But that would be useless: we are here, and the best we have is the M4A3E2 Jumbo, and now we know it is not big enough.

I hear the sound of an engine: an M3 halftrack is approaching. The Colonel. Against the pale light of the stars I see the angle of the First Sergeant's campaign hat. The Colonel's track eases up onto the road and slides up to us. The Colonel and the First Sergeant get down and walk over.

"Are you all right?" the Colonel asks us.

"Yes," I say. "McCarthy and Jackson are dead."

"You're sure?" First Sergeant Reardon asks.

"Never more sure about anything," I say.

"Do you think the First Sergeant should take a look?" the Colonel asks me.

"There's no need, sir. McCarthy was cut in half. Jackson was decapitated. One round."

"That gun firing from the right," the Colonel tells the First Sergeant. "I knew it."

"I don't know, sir," I say. "I didn't see. I was inside." The First Sergeant looks at me as though he wonders how I could have escaped the disaster.

"You're all right?" he asks.

"Yes, First Sergeant. Some bits of something in my the right thigh. Nicks. But I'm all right."

"You want to go back?" the First Sergeant asks. "Colonel called Doc Turner's people. You can go back with them if you want."

I wonder why he tells me this: he knows as well as I that I will not go back. "No," I tell him. "I'm all right. They can check the nicks, take out the bits. But they're nothing."

"I don't want you inside this here Sherman," the First Sergeant says.

"First Sergeant?"

"I know you'd go in, but not this time. There's a risk of infection." The First Sergeant sounds as though he's been studying bacteria for the last six months. "I'll handle this here, Colonel," he says to the Colonel. "Yates and Brown here and I will do it."

The Colonel nods and nods. "All right," he says. "You want me to take that rifle from you, First Sergeant?" he asks. The First Sergeant passes the Colonel his '03 Springfield. The Colonel tucks the First Sergeant's rifle in the crook of his right arm and puts his right hand in his coat pocket. The rifle's muzzle points at the ground.

"You'll be all right?" the Colonel asks the First Sergeant.

"Brown and Yates and I will be all right," the First Sergeant says. "You take it easy in the Headquarters track till the medics get here," he tells me. "Brown, Yates. There's two pair rubber boots and two pair rubber gloves in the rearmost storage box under the rear lefthand seat in the Headquarters track. Get them." He looks at me. In the darkness I cannot see his face: all I can see against the faint starlight is the dark tilted brim of his campaign hat. "We need a shovel?" he asks me.

I think about it. "No," I say. "No fire. But there's a lot of blood."

"We've got the boots," the First Sergeant says. "And the gloves. Leg smarts some, does it?"

"Yes, First Sergeant."

"That's good. If you'd been shot bad you wouldn't have felt much. In the beginning, at least." I wonder how he knows. Then I remember the wound stripes on his overcoat sleeve which he won in the first war. If 'won' is the right word.

"Get in the Headquarters track now and take it easy till the medics come up," the First Sergeant orders.

"Right," the Colonel says.

"What time we going up again?" First Sergeant Reardon asks the Colonel.

"I'm not sure yet," the Colonel says. "A couple of hours, I'd guess. I don't want any more of this. These two men dead in this crew. Lattimore wounded at Münchweiler. And others during this attack. We're going to prepare Klingenmünster before we go in again."

I know what the Colonel means by 'prepare'. I hope all the civilians have left Klingenmünster, or are hiding in the cellars.

I walk to the Colonel's halftrack and climb up. My leg is stiff and I can feel sticky drying blood tacky on my skin. Not too bad: I could have been the gunner, or the tank commander. But I was lucky: I saw the heavy, streaking devil round redden the steel of the Jumbo's turret even as I saw it butt through the softening armor and slash into the fighting compartment. I wonder why I lived. I can't figure it out and I tell myself not to think about it. But still I wonder why I lived and McCarthy and Jackson were killed. Something in the shape of the turret where the AT round struck, perhaps. Or a glint of light or a bead of sweat in the AT gunner's eye. Or a lurch of the Jumbo, a change of the attitude of its thick carapace against the angle and elevation of the muzzle of the eighty-eight that killed McCarthy and Jackson.

Who knows? Who can know?

Doc Turner arrives. I am helped down from the Headquarters track and up and through the rear doors of the ambulance halftrack. A medic closes the doors. Another adjusts the curtains over the windows and turns on the lights. Doc Turner tells me to get my pants down. I drop them around my ankles. He looks at my bleeding right thigh and says, "You don't need a doctor. You need a medic and a day riding with your leg up. I got other things to do. Matthews, Adams," he tells the medics standing by, "clean out these nicks. He doesn't need any anesthetic. Wash those wounds out. Give him a shot of penicillin and another of tetanus, bandage him up and get his pants back up. And have him come back once a day for four days for more penicillin. I don't want that leg infected: pissant wounds like that?" Doc Turner shakes his head and dismounts the halftrack ambulance. Matthews uses a probe and tweezers while Adams holds an enameled bowl. Matthews asks me if I want the slivers of steel he harvests from my thigh. I shake my head. He is fastidious: he drops each sliver into the bowl along with the gauze he uses to dab away my blood. When he has finished his excavations, he disinfects the nicks, tapes two two-by-four inch patches of gauze over my thigh, gives me the injections Doc Turner prescribed, tells me to come back each day at dusk for four days for a shot, tells me to get my pants up, hands me a blanket and says I can go.

As I get out of the ambulance halftrack I see First Sergeant Reardon, Yates and Brown lifting a stretcher into the back of a second medical halftrack parked close by the Jumbo in which I rode. The shapes of the four blanketed bundles on the stretcher are odd, but I recognize them: they are the four unequal parts into which the eighty-eight millimeter round divided McCarthy and Jackson.

I sit in the Colonel's halftrack, listening to him and his officers and sergeants and corporals working the radios, giving orders and passing the Colonel comments from the rest of the task force. From the radio traffic I understand that either the 36th Infantry Division or the 14th Armored Division is to rendezvous with us at Klingenmünster. But time passes and we see no sign of them, and do not hear a whisper from them over the radio. At 0400 the Colonel orders his task force to attack Klingenmünster again. This time the Colonel leaves the Headquarters halftrack and goes in with the attack in a 105 assault Sherman. This attack reaches the first streets on the outskirts of Klingenmünster before it is driven out. The Colonel mounts a third attack. Sitting in the bed of the Headquarters halftrack, my leg elevated and laid out on the seat along the right side of the bed of the track, the blanket the medic handed me wrapped around my shoulders, I watch the 105 assault Shermans, the Shermans, the plump Jumbo in which Rutherford serves as bowgunner, and the 614th's three inch antitank weapons go to work. Houses in Klingenmünster begin to burn. The Shermans trundle forward, the 614th's lethal fire exploding pillboxes and bunkers in front of them. The armored doughs of the 409th ride along behind the Shermans in their halftracks, boxes and bundles roped to the sides. Something in a building inside Klingenmünster explodes with a shuddering rumble. Flame rises from the town. Perhaps Klingenmünster will burn to the ground. Perhaps not. I do not care: I think of the throbbing in my leg and recall McCarthy and Jackson. Once I turn my head and see, a dozen vehicles back, German prisoners sitting up on the gasoline trucks. I wonder what they are thinking. It must be tough to sit up on a tanktruck full of gasoline and see one of your towns burning. On the other hand, I think as I turn my back on them, they once sat in their halftracks and watched towns burning and turned their backs on their disarmed prisoners.

As dawn arrives, the Headquarters track shifts across the field into Klingenmünster. Each jounce of the halftrack makes my leg ache, but someone mentions mines in the road leading to Klingenmünster and I put up with the pain. In Klingenmünster's streets Shermans and halftracks loiter. Unkempt prisoners stand and sit in a sloppy group against the wall of a large gray building. As we drive past them they stare at us: I suspect most of them have never seen anything like us before. The Colonel's driver parks in Klingenmünster's main square. As he does so, the Colonel climbs out of the turret of a 105 millimeter assault Sherman. He climbs up into the Headquarters track and nods at me. He is tired: he spent last night and the one before without sleep. I note the .45 Colt automatic in the holster on his hip: the slide is locked back on the empty clip in the butt of the weapon.

I wonder where First Sergeant Reardon is: it has been more than four hours since I saw him, and Yates and Brown, carrying the stretcher on which the four pieces of McCarthy and Jackson lay inside four folded blankets.

As the sun comes up it grows colder. Klingenmünster was a solid dull town of stone and plaster. It has been torn apart. Fires smolder three and four cobbled streets away. I see no civilians. The map indicates that an abbey lies in the southeastern quarter of the town. I wonder if it has been damaged: I hope not. I wrap the blanket around my shoulders and draw it across my chest and thighs. The sting of the insignificant wounds in my right thigh has tapered off to a persistent annoying throb. I listen to the Colonel and his staff conversing over the radios. They listen to the voices speaking to them through the ether and repeat the statistics they are given to Corporal Stuart, the First Sergeant's clerk. Corporal Stuart sits at attention at his typewriter, his tapping fingertips the center of the post-battle activity in the Headquarters halftrack. When the radios fall silent, the Colonel tells Corporal Stuart to total the results of Task Force Rhine's trip from France to Klingenmünster. Corporal Stuart must have been a dutiful student in high school: he rolls the paper out of the typewriter, shuffles it into a sheaf of other papers, plucks a sharp pencil from the side pocket of a musette bag on the seat to the right of the typewriter, and begins to add. When he looks up at the Colonel and clears his throat, I know he is going to give us the totals. I listen as he fills in the boxes on our scorecard: in the eight days since Task Force Rhine began its passage through the Siegfried line, we have killed one hundred and twenty of the enemy's soldiers and taken one thousand two hundred prisoner. We have destroyed dozens of bunkers and pillboxes, tens of trucks, fives of antitank weapons, a handful of self-propelled guns and a couple of tanks.

Corporal Stuart does not mention McCarthy or Jackson. His scorecard contains no box in which he can enter the number of pieces these two solid men have become, no line on which he can write out the details of their deaths.

I glance across the town square: armored doughs from the 409th are herding more prisoners together in front of what I guess is the town hall. These Germans are shocked: they huddle beneath the shattered cornices and broken windows of the mayor's offices and stare this way and that. They cannot believe they are prisoners. More, they cannot believe we have taken them prisoner. The armored doughs from the 409th note the Germans' confusion. A corporal from the 409th calls out to us: "Take a look at these guys. They ain't been around nowhere." We nod: we understand the corporal's compliment, and we understand the Germans' confusion. They thought they were invincible: now, huddled together, streaked with mud, unkempt and nervous, they know they aren't. I don't like looking at them.

I stop looking at the German prisoners we have taken—thirty and thirty-five year old men with hard, neutral faces and beardless, scared children—and listen as more information pours through the filters and tubes of the radios. It now seems the 14th Armored Division will pass through our task force and that we will then be detached from the 103rd Infantry Division and sent north to join the 71st Infantry Division in General Patton's Third Army on March 28th. We are to arrive at Lengenselbold, Germany on 1 April 1945. The road march to Lengenselbold will be about one hundred and forty miles. The 71st is composed of the 5th, 14th and 66th Infantry Regiments. I wonder if General Patton will visit us again. I doubt it: we have gone up there and killed the sonsofbitches as he told us to, and I guess the General will figure that is compliment enough. Besides, I doubt we would fit in well at Third Army reunions. Wrong cut to the uniform. Enlisted, most of us. And the officers? Wrong backgrounds. It doesn't matter: one day one of us will be a three star general, and I do not doubt that he too will be a hard driving sonofabitch with someone else's blood on his teeth.

An infantry major approaches the Headquarters track. His uniform and his face and hands are dirty. I don't wonder: he is an armored dough, and armored doughs have a lot of trouble staying alive, let alone clean. He stands in the mud beside the track and salutes the Colonel—an uncharacteristic gesture which any decent sniper would note through his telescopic sight. The Colonel nods at him. The Major introduces himself as executive officer of the 2nd Battalion of the 409th Infantry Regiment. The Major has a soft southern accent from somewhere near the border: Kentucky, I guess, or Tennessee. We ignore his accent and listen as he tells us his Colonel could not come over himself and gives the Colonel his Colonel's apologies. "Uh-huh," the Colonel says. "What can I do for you, Major?"

"Sir, the Colonel wants to write up letter of a commendation for your Battalion and he wants to know the name of the commander of the lead Sherman coming in here to Klingenmünster. He did more than his share, the Colonel says, and the Colonel wants to inform the division commander about him."

"You agree with the Colonel, Major?" the Colonel asks him.

"Yes, Colonel," the Major says. "That man did a lot. So did the rest of your men, sir."

"Sergeant Ervin Lattimore is the man's name," the Colonel says.

"Is he here, sir?"

"Why?" the Colonel asks.

"I wanted to compliment him myself."

The Colonel raises his eyebrows. Then he says, "Sgt. Lattimore was wounded outside Münchweiler. He stayed on in his Sherman until this morning. He's with the medics now. But I'll give him your regards, Major. You can look him up later, if you want. Or after the war."

"I'll do that, Colonel. Where is he from?" The Colonel's eyebrows rise another notch.

The Colonel turns and looks at Corporal Stuart sitting at attention at his typewriter. Corporal Stuart speaks the name of Sergeant Lattimore's home town.

"I know it," the Major says.

"Is that it, Major?" the Colonel asks. He's glad to have the 409th's 2nd Battalion's compliments, but he has a lot to do before the 14th Armored Division arrives and passes through us.

"Yes, sir. I hope you'll pass the Colonel's compliments—and mine—on to Sergeant Lattimore and your men, sir."

"I'll do that, Major.

The Major salutes, the Colonel nods, the Major turns and walks away. The Colonel looks around at the men in the bed of the Headquarters track. "You men tell everyone about the Major and what he said." We say yes, sir, we will. And we will. We are not the 827th Tank Destroyer Battalion, most of whose officers and men fucked up and fucked up from November, 1944 until they were withdrawn in January, 1945. Officers hiding in bunkers, men refusing orders, missions aborted, molesting civilians, jobs left undone. Some say they had too many changes of officers and their sergeants were no good. Whatever, their dishonor angers us, and our need to take up their slack, to show the Kentucky or maybe Tennessee Major we are not them, angers us even more.

The radio squeaks. A voice tells us it has found four German infantrymen fallen on top of one another, each of them shot once through the breast. The Colonel takes the radio's microphone in one hand and holds the headset up to his ear with the other. He listens and speaks, checking the location of the corpses. He looks at me over the bent backs of the Headquarters crew working the radios. Four shot once each through the chest with a rifle? he asks. He nods at me, as though he and I know the rifleman.

I recall First Sergeant Reardon standing up in the roaring night, head stuck up, it seemed, into the weave of streaming tracer, back straight, arms and body still and ominous, firing his '03 Springfield over the steel wall of the Headquarters halftrack at the scrambling German infantry. I thought when I saw him firing at our enemies that his firm stance and steady, spaced rifle fire were gestures, to encourage those who saw him. Now I see the Colonel nod at me again, and as I nod back at the Colonel and pull the blanket tight and tighter around my shoulders, I recall that the First Sergeant does not favor gestures.

Fourteen

When the Seven Six One crosses the Rhine, Rutherford and I ride once again in the maintenance halftrack: the Battalion has not received sufficient replacements to make up tank crews in which we could serve.

"Still," First Sergeant Reardon said as he told us we were back in maintenance, "if there's a need, I'll call on you two first. You both did all right at Klingenmünster." I know this is a compliment, but I am not sure I want him to call on me if a loader in one of the Shermans is injured or killed; for I remember the instant when the Jumbo's steel glowed red and then white and spat liquid silver slivers of steel as the eighty-eight millimeter shell shouldered into the fighting compartment and hacked McCarthy and Jackson to pieces.

On the other hand, the First Sergeant also told us he didn't think the need for Rutherford and me to go in the Shermans would arise. "This war is winding down," he said, as though he was sure we would have a short breathing space before the next one began.

Looking at Germany as we drive down and across the Rhine tells me the First Sergeant is right about the war coming to an end. Germany is not quaint or pretty: the structures in the town of Oppenheim, and in the cluster of houses across the wide, deep Rhine from Oppenheim, are like most of the buildings we have seen since we drove north and west from Klingenmünster and then northeast to Lengenselbold, and then on to the Rhine: the buildings are shattered, their solid shapes bent or churned to rubble by bombs and artillery fire. Beams and plastered lengths of lath stick through the chinks between stones dislodged from the walls. Shattered doors lie on the cobbles. The panes have been blown from every window and the frames are askew. No civilians walk the streets. The pontoon bridge over which we drive is the only shape I see that is not damaged.

As we roll onto the pontoon bridge twelve B-26s—vicious high-winged twin-engined aircraft thick in the body that are rumored to be dangerous to handle—each of them armed with bombs, rockets and machineguns packaged in their noses and in sponsons on their sides, pound low across the river, heading east. Men sitting up in the hatches of tanks and armored cars and in the beds of half-tracks and trucks cheer and wave and point the way east. All of us know the Air Force is as valuable to us as a deep hole in which we can hide. The Air Force is also clean and remote: I have never met a man who flies a plane, or services one, or guards an airbase; but the Air Force has, since June, 1944, destroyed more tanks and self-propelled guns and antitank weapons in factories and on railroad sidings and on the battlefield than the Army has. We are lucky the Air Force controls the sky and looks down on the ruin they have built in Germany and over which they now fly with impunity. I would hate to try to cross this river if the air hummed with the sound of Daimler-Benz engines and aircraft with stiff black crosses on their wings were slanting toward this thin string of floats and pontoons which only the engineers who erected it would call a bridge.

When Williston drives the maintenance halftrack up off the pontoon bridge onto the east bank of the Rhine, the wheels judder and bounce and the tracks grind. An impatient MP waves us on, jerking his right arm, as though he doesn't think much of Williston's ability behind the wheel. Williston grins at the MP and curses him under his breath. I ignore the MP and Williston: I am glad to be off the water. No one in an armored battalion wants to be inside a heavy vehicle on a shaky bridge designed by Army engineers who learned their calculations in the academy of expedience and therefore build structures for a use so temporary the weather and this broad river's waves may tear it apart before sufficient forces can cross into the bridgehead on the east bank.

The nameless village on the east bank of the Rhine is devastated. It has been bombed and shelled in detail. Every building I see as we drive up from the river displays fresh scars. The streets are full of chipped bricks, cracked chunks of masonry, rock dust, unidentifiable shards of wood, broken furniture, clothing, disabled wagons, dead farm animals pointing their hooves at the sky, their bellies burst open by the pressure of corpsegas and, here and there, the corpses of humans dressed in warm clothing. The cold windy air of this day on the border between winter and spring is full of swirling ashes, the bitter smell of burned wood and the stench of rotting flesh.

The condition of this nameless village tells me that Germany is in distress. If we have so battered this small community, what have we done to Düsseldorf and Hamburg? Yet still the sharp, dangerous part of Germany fights on with determination: with the sort of determination with which I suspect my great-grandfather fought at the Crater. The press tells us the Germans are fighting 'like cornered rats.' The press is mistaken: the Germans do not fight like cornered rats. They are men, and desperate, and they fight like desperate men. We and the British have bombed them for years to encourage them to end this war, but even as we bombed them we told them the single term we would accept in the instrument that concluded hostilities would be unconditional surrender. This policy seems illogical to me, but I have no say: only Washington and London have a say. I am relegated to a maintenance halftrack in the Seven Six One, and I can do nothing but tour onward through one nameless town and the next east of the Rhine and note, with distress and disgust, the higher price Germany will pay each day until The End.

We drive away from the Rhine on a track that will lead us northeast of Frankfurt. The road is pitted with shell craters, ploughed to rubble by bombs. Far across the fields tiny figures dressed in civilian clothes walk or stand. None of them work: they walk and stand. I suppose they are wondering whether they will be able to avoid the violence approaching from the west. And the violence behind them: their military, or their police, are enforcing bitter, fearsome decisions against them now. Driving northeast of Frankfurt we see the swinging corpse of a man who has been hanged from a tree beside the road.

Williston draws in his breath when he sees the hanged man. "Jesus Christ," Rutherford says from the back of the track.

"Amen," Simpson says, as though he is mourning the death of a member of his family.

The executioners have pinned a square of cardboard to the hanged man's chest, and written on the cardboard in ornate, angular script. I cannot read German, but I recognize the word Ich and I can guess what the words say: the usual. 'I am a traitor,' 'I am a blackmarketeer,' 'I am a defeatist', 'I spoke ill of the Leader.'

"Bastards," someone says from the back of the track.

"What else?" Simpson asks. "Motherless sons, every last one of them."

"Got to be some decent people in around here somewhere," Rutherford says.

"Why?" Franklin asks.

"They always some decent people anywhere," Rutherford says.

"In Misssippi?" Williston asks. This gets a laugh from the congregation.

"Well," Rutherford says, in exchange for one more laugh, "maybe not Misssippi. But you know what I mean."

"I know what you mean," Simpson says. I turn and look at him. He is looking back over the steel wall at the rear of the halftrack. I know what he is looking at: I too can still see the hanged man. "I know what you mean," Simpson says again. "But I got to doubt it when I see something like that."

"What?" Rutherford says. "You ain't heard of no hangings back home, Simpson?"

"Sure I have," Simpson said. "Even waaay up in Ohio we hear about hangings. But that's different. Here they're hanging their own people, and for what? Back home, they only hang people they don't credit being the same as they are."

"Doesn't make a difference," Fellows says, "to the one at the end of the rope." Fellows has the steady, solid manner of a judge who does not doubt his ability to weigh and decide.

"No kidding?" Franklin asks.

"That's it," Fellows says. He nods and says, "Doesn't make a difference to the one at the end of the rope." Fellows reminds me of a bulldozer easing into a pile of sand.

The four of them in the back banter back and forth as Williston drives us forward. The bantering relaxes them, and erases part of the memory of the hanged men. Then I see men in the vehicles ahead pointing. One man sitting up out of the commander's hatch of an M4A3 pounds his fist against the steel turret. Soon we see what those ahead of us have seen: a woman hanged from a tree in a village square. The hanged woman is fearsome. The shoes have fallen from her feet. Her toes point toward one another. Her ungloved fingers are puffy and blue, suffused with rotting blood. Her face is livid, her chin jutting upward, her jaws wrenched open, her tongue hanging from the side of her mouth.

"Jesus Christ," Williston says.

Withers, who sits between me and Williston, shudders and says, "Oh, my God." Withers has not spoken much since we crossed the Rhine, and he glances this way and that as we motor on, as though he cannot understand why Germany has become what it is.

We drive on, Frankfurt to the northwest. Ahead and behind us the Seven Six One's vehicles trundle forward, part of the broad, northeasterly sweep of Third Army. I wonder how far east we will go. Who knows? Grand strategy and the movement of armies is not one of my specialties. My specialties are the maintenance of the M4A3 tank and the disposition of the dead First Sergeant Reardon and I find within Shermans shot down or burned up.

Near noon the word comes through the radio that the Battalion will stop beside the road to eat lunch. "Like working in the stockyards," Rutherford says. "Lunchbreak." I do not recall the Seven Six One stopping all together to eat lunch since we landed in Normandy last November.

As I look along the line of vehicles parked beside the road, I wonder what the Colonel could be thinking. One German fighter-bomber could do a job on us were it to fly low along this road firing its cannon and dropping bombs.

But that, I know, will not be a problem: the air is full of P-51 Mustangs and P-47 Thunderbolts, twin-engined B-25 and B-26 bombers ranging here and there across the countryside in front of us, hunting for targets. Higher up, ignoring the ground-attack aircraft and the plodding military far below, B-17s and B-24s fly east in silvery formations, filling the air with a bass humming.

From what I have seen on this side of the Rhine, finding a target must be difficult work for the pilot of a fighter-bomber: everything seems to have been bombed yesterday, and the day before, and the day before that.

"Look at this place here," Williston says. He is eating from a can of rations and looking out of the cab of the maintenance track across the fields. "Not going to be any plowing this spring, it looks like. At least not this week. And what're they going to do this fall and winter when it comes time to eat?"

"They'll go hungry," Fellows says. Just like a judge, I think: solid reasoning based on the relevant facts.

"No they won't," Simpson says. Simpson is thin and lively. When he talks he moves his hands. When he talks to Fellows his hands flick this way and that. As he turns and listens to Simpson, Fellows becomes still and solid, his face motionless, his unblinking eyes fixed on Simpson. "We'll ship in food for them," Simpson says, as though he expects Fellows to agree with him.

"No, we won't," Fellows says, as though he has been consulting with General Marshall and the President about the distribution of grain in Europe after the war.

"Oh, yes we will," Simpson says. Simpson and Fellows have been debating since Camp Claiborne. They used to debate the riots there, and in Houston, and the troubles in Arkansas. Then they debated the utility of the Seven Six One's Table of Organization. Then they debated the Sherman versus the Tiger: the single most useless debate they or anyone else has ever had. Now they debate the post-war fate of the Germans. I wonder why they go on talking: they have debated for more than two years, and have resolved nothing. Still, they have amused us and taken our minds off ballistics and rising temperatures, trauma and decapitation. And it may be that I see civilization in their debate. Who knows? But I worry that I, like the Germans, will find out about sustenance when it arrives, and not before.

"Look at that fucking guy fly," Williston shouts from the driver's seat beyond Withers sitting to my left. I glance up to the right, to the left. This must be something to see, for this is the third time Williston has cursed in six months: Williston has told me, in confidence, that his father is a minister and disapproves of soldiers and their ways. His mother disapproves too, but told him to go. So he went. So he sits three feet to my left.

Far up and to the left of the road where we loll in our tracks and tanks and trucks eating greasy food from tins, munching crackers, eating chocolate and smoking cigarettes, a single German plane—an FW 190D, the 'Dora', the Germans call it—whips up into a ripping turn to starboard, rolls and dives straight toward the earth, three P-51 Mustangs diving after it. The P-51 is the abler aircraft, but the pilots of these three Mustangs are not in the same class with this German, who flies so well I think he must have survived the dogfights over England in the summer of 1940. The German pilot pulls out of his dive a hundred feet above farmland and villages and jinks this way and that. I wonder what he is doing down here: I have read in the Army newspaper that the FW 190D was designed to fly at high altitudes and shoot down B-17s and B-24s.

The Mustangs pull out of their dives and follow the German. Their formation is a ragged arrowhead. They fire their guns at the German: tracer glitters against the blue sky. But they are too far away to hit him. The German flies over a town, raises his left wing to avoid the spire of a church and flees on, heading left to right, west to east across my field of vision, flicking over the slate roofs below and then over the fields beyond the town. I guess he and the Mustangs going after him are three miles away.

From up the line of vehicles I hear a voice shout, "Everybody in the trucks and tracks get down." It is the First Sergeant's voice. All along the line men are leaping down from trucks and tracks and getting into the ditch along the side of the road away from the FW 190D and the Mustangs sliding after it.

As I hear the First Sergeant commanding that part of the Battalion that travels in soft vehicles to get down the German pilot yanks his aircraft to starboard: now he is flying straight toward us over the fields, and though he is three miles away he is moving more than four hundred miles an hour. Withers scrabbles up from where he sits beside me and stands up behind the machinegun mounted in the front of the bed of the halftrack. "You guys get the hell out of here," he says.

"Get down," the First Sergeant shouts. He is on the road, walking the line of the Battalion's vehicles. "Everybody not in armor get down." The Colonel's voice speaks over the radio. He too is telling everyone to get down out of the soft vehicles. He sounds tense and annoyed, as though someone told him the tough fighting was finished and he has found out they lied. Fellows and Simpson have suspended their debate: they are leaping over the steel side of the track, Rutherford and Franklin right behind them.

"What the hell you doing up there with that gun, Withers?" The First Sergeant's voice is piercing. It carries two hundred yards without apparent effort, and I think that the First Sergeant should be a politician: he would be a great stump speaker.

He is walking in the road on the side of the column exposed to the guns of the on-coming aircraft. He is carrying his Springfield rifle under his arm as though he is out bird shooting and he has his antique bandoleer slung over his shoulder. From a hundred feet away his voice says, "Didn't you hear me, Withers? I know you, Withers. Lot of guns coming this way and these air corps pilots, German or American, don't care what they shoot. You get down from there before I take your name, Withers." The First Sergeant comes on, pacing as though he is back in the infantry and on the march. He passes our track shouting out orders to others far down the road: he does not look to see whether Withers has gotten down. He does not need to look: no one disobeys the First Sergeant.

As the sound of aircraft engines rises, Williston and I scramble out of the track through the door in the right side of the cab. Withers slips around the gun, down through the cab and out. We get down in the ditch with Fellows, Simpson, Franklin and Rutherford. No one has unslung his weapon: we can do nothing against the two machineguns and two cannon mounted in the nose and wings of FW 190D—or against the .50 caliber machineguns in the wings of the three P-51 Mustangs coming on behind, swinging this way and that in the sky. Rutherford, who I figure might unsling his Schmeisser machinepistol and try to get a piece of the fearsome German aircraft bearing down on us, hunches his shoulders and gets his head down below the edge of the ditch. Perhaps he hears the First Sergeant still calling, "I said get down in that ditch!"

Just as I wonder when the First Sergeant will follow his own orders, a voice to our left shouts up out of the ditch, "Goddamnit, First Sergeant, you get down." I glance toward the voice: it is Lieutenant Shaw. He must not be thinking: no one shouts at the First Sergeant. General Eisenhower himself would not shout at the First Sergeant.

"I'm coming, Lieutenant," the First Sergeant calls as the roar of the four approaching aircraft engines mounts. I see the First Sergeant emerge from between the rear of a halftrack and the front of a Sherman. He is walking, his rifle fitted in the crook of his arm. He steps off the road and down into the ditch. Lieutenant Shaw says something to him. I do not think he is apologizing for shouting at the First Sergeant: the Lieutenant's thin face beneath the rim of his helmet is frowning and he is shaking his right forefinger at the First Sergeant. The First Sergeant nods and nods as the Lieutenant speaks, but he is looking toward the four aircraft screaming toward us, flying just above the ground.

When the Mustangs begin to fire their guns, the Lieutenant stops scolding the First Sergeant and they both hunker down in the ditch. The sound of the four aircraft engines and the Mustangs' machineguns hammering .50 caliber slugs through the air is a single extended crash. I hear the heavy slugs crackle in the air above us and strike the sides of the vehicles parked along the road in front of us.

I look up as the FW 190 Dora flashes over us. Two seconds, and the three Mustangs leap across the road and the Battalion's vehicles, fleeing after the long-nosed Focke-Wulf. They are still firing all their guns when the German flicks his aircraft up and up and over onto his left wingtip, gaining altitude and sliding to the left. The Mustangs' tracer rushes past the Dora's sliding tail. The German gains what must be enough altitude and then rolls his aircraft onto its back, points the nose at the earth and dives, pulling up as he does so, swinging down through an elegant curve that leaves him flying fifty feet off the ground straight back the way he came: straight back toward us crouching in the ditch. The three Mustangs cannot follow him. One tries: he gains altitude, just as the German did, rolls his Mustang onto its back, just as the German did, and tries to fly through the same elegant curve through which the German flew. He tries hard, but he is not as deft as the German and he fails. His failure is spectacular: he flies his Mustang straight into the ground in front of a woods at four hundred miles an hour. The sound of the crash a mile and more away arrives an instant after the bright flash of the Mustang exploding. The other two Mustangs jerk away right and left, wings angling this way and that in the sunlight. They do not follow the FW 190D.

The German beneath the humped canopy of the Dora must have strong nerves: he is flying no more than fifty feet above the ground, and as he whips toward us hiding down in the ditch in front of the line of Seven Six One's vehicles, he waggles his wings and shimmies his aircraft side-to-side. He does not, however, fire his guns at us. Perhaps he is out of ammunition.

Or perhaps he flew today only to strut his stuff; and having done so will now fly home.

The shadow of the Focke-Wulf flicks across our faces, across our vehicles and the road and flees on across the field beyond. As the German flies away he gains altitude and turns northeast. Soon the roar of the Dora's engine fades.

We look over our shoulders: the two Mustangs circle and circle around the greasy black smoke rising from their comrade's crashed Mustang. Then they figure out they can do nothing for him. One forms up on the other and they fly away northwest.

"Anybody get their number?" Withers asks. "Those bastards could have killed the lot of us, shooting that way all three of them together."

"No shit?" Franklin says as he gets up out of the ditch. The knees and thighs of his pants and the skirt of his coat are muddy. Franklin bends down and picks up a brass cartridge case. Fifty caliber. The road is littered with them. The three Mustangs tried hard, but they failed, and one of the three of them found out what failure means.

"You think somebody ought to go on over there?" Fellows asks. It is unusual to hear Fellows ask a question: his ordinary method of conversation is to assert, and to back up his first assertion with another.

"I can't see why," I say. It is the traditional thing to do: to go, to look, to see the wreckage and the pieces of the corpse. But this pilot's corpse is not going to be pretty, and I have seen enough ugly corpses.

"Someone ought to go on over there," Fellows asserts.

"You want to go?" Rutherford says. "More than a mile over muddy ground. I know about muddy ground."

"What you know about muddy ground?" Franklin asks. "You're from Kansas City. You don't know nothing about muddy ground."

"I know muddy ground from Louisiana and Texas. And from here in Europe."

"That isn't muddy ground," Franklin says. "You got to work a farm before you talk about muddy ground."

"Is someone going over there or not?" Simpson asks.

"First Sergeant coming," Withers says.

Withers is right: the First Sergeant is walking along the line of men getting up out of the ditch. He walks up to us and says, "What did you think you were going to do, Withers? Shoot that German down?"

"I thought I might try, First Sergeant," Withers says. He is standing at attention.

"Don't stand at attention, Withers. You don't stand at attention in the field." He looks at Withers from under the brim of his campaign hat. Then he looks at us. He shifts his rifle from the crook of his right arm and grounds the butt on the toe of his boot to keep it up out of the mud. "I don't want to have to write your mother a letter, Withers. What would I say? That you thought you might try? That you were going to go one-on-one with a Focke-Wulf 190D armed with two cannon and two machineguns? Not to mention three Air Corps pilots jinking all over shooting .50 caliber machineguns at you?"

"No, First Sergeant."

"What do you mean no First Sergeant?" the First Sergeant asks.

"I mean, yes, First Sergeant."

The First Sergeant stares at Withers. "You don't know what you mean. But let me tell you this, Withers: you do anything like that again and you're going to be digging latrines for the whole gud-damned Battalion. Six feet deep, corners squared-off. You understand what I'm saying?"

"Yes, First Sergeant," Withers says.

"You men take this track and drive over there and see," he says. He points with his left arm at the Mustang pilot's funeral pyre. "I'll call in and one of the ambulance halftracks will meet you. Look for personal effects and identification." He glances at us and looks away at the smoke rising from the bits and pieces of the broken P-51. "I don't have to tell you what to look for," he says. "You know what to do. Except maybe you, Withers. Go on, now."

The First Sergeant walks away up the line of parked vehicles. Men in other trucks and tracks near us are picking up the utensils and cans and boxes of rations they threw down when the planes appeared. We get up in the halftrack and Williston starts the engine, maneuvers us out of line and over the verge of the road and over the ditch in which we hid and drives out into the field.

"Almost springtime, ain't it?" Rutherford says. No one answers him. We are looking ahead at the pall of smoke rising straight up into the sky from the crashed Mustang. I wonder how old the pilot was. Not old: pilots are young. And this one was younger than most. Or more foolish: he tried something he shouldn't have tried, and he paid for it.

Far up the column a halftrack ambulance lurches from the road into the field and trundles forward, heading toward the same rising smoke toward which we drive, angling toward us as it comes on. I see Doc Turner in the righthand front seat. He doesn't look happy. I know why Doc Turner doesn't look happy. The Mustang is no longer an aircraft: it is a scattered group of disassembled, twisted parts, none of them identifiable, all of them burned. I wonder, as Doc Turner must, how many pieces of the pilot we will find.

I know the answer to that. I have a lot of experience with this kind of thing. The answer is: not many, and each one charred.

"Stop short?" Williston asks.

"Say fifty feet from the nearest piece you see," I say.

"That's right here," Williston tells me. He brakes the track and turns off the engine. In the woods beyond the wreckage of the Mustang maples and oaks rustle against the wind.

"Stay with the track," I tell Williston. "Monitor the radio."

"All right by me," Williston says. He climbs up past the machinegun into the bed of the track.

As we get down, Fellows says, "You don't suppose this guy could be from the 99th, do you?"

"Fellows," Rutherford says, hitching his machinepistol around from his lower back in front of him, "you're something. You'd ask if maybe the Lord Jesus might have been flying this here machine."

"It's a reasonable question," Fellows says. "The 99th is flying over here somewhere."

"That's bullshit," Simpson says. "That this guy might have been from the 99th. What are the odds?"

"I agree," Withers said.

"So do I," Franklin says.

"It's a reasonable question," Fellows says.

"No, it ain't," Rutherford says. "You know, Fellows, you ain't worth a pinch of shit sometimes. That ain't a reasonable question. It ain't a reasonable question at all." Rutherford tries with his grammar, but the details escape him. But his grammar doesn't matter: he does all right here in the track, and he went up as machinegunner in the other Jumbo when we fought in front of Klingenmünster.

"I say it's a reasonable question," Fellows says. "There's nothing unreasonable about it."

"Yes, there is," Withers says.

"What?" Fellows asks. This is another debating tactic: Fellows prefers to let the other man talk.

"I'll tell you what," Withers says. Thin and taciturn, the helmet heavy on his head and bigger than it ought to be, Withers looks around at each one of us and says, "I'll tell you why: because no one in the 99th a stupid enough fuck to try some stupid trick like this guy here tried. Pilot in the 99th see that German, they know he's good. They know he's better. And they ain't going to try following him through some loop like that. And most of all, they ain't going to waste ammunition like that. Last of all, they ain't going to shoot up the Seven Six One."

I have a number of comments about this. The 99th's pilots are known for their flair: they sank a destroyer off Sicily and flew right down on the deck in Sicily to shoot up Tiger tanks and shepherded B-24s and B-17s over Germany without a loss. But they're pilots and they've got to be arrogant: all pilots are arrogant. Furthermore, like every single one of the rest of us in Uncle's service, they'll shoot more rather than less: everyone—in a tank battalion or in the Air Force—believes twenty tons of explosive laid on a village quiets things down before anyone waiting there can think about getting his razor out and starting something.

I assume Fellows is going to make all these points for me, so I do not speak. But Fellows says, "I think you're right, Withers." This is a first: Fellows does not think anyone is right, and if he does he won't admit it.

Rutherford confirms what I think: "Fellows, you came through. I knew you could do it: not say no for once."

"I'd say fuck you, Rutherford," Fellows says, "but that's too categorical."

"'Categorical,'" Rutherford says. "Okay, Fellows. Whatever you want: categorical's okay if you want. What say we spread out and start looking around?"

"That's it," I tell them. "Spread out and start looking around. Forget the Mustang. Look for pieces of the man. Clothing. Wallet. Identification."

"What are we doing this for?" Franklin asks. His tone is plaintive, and he looks a little green. He is looking for a way out before we begin sorting through the burned bits. "His two buddies in those other two planes saw him go down, and they know he's dead. They know who he is. What we searching for? And why?"

"Because the First Sergeant told us to," Withers says. This is the right answer, and a sound reason to look, and to go on looking until we find something.

"That's part of it," I tell them. "The other part is: the First Sergeant wants the Battalion to be able to report to the Air Force that we looked. He also wants the Battalion to be able to report that the Battalion found something. He wants the man's identification, and whatever personal effects we can find. And I get the feeling he's not going to be his same happy self if we come back and say, 'First Sergeant, ain't nothing but bent 'luminum and a burned up pilot over there. We all didn't find nuffin.'"

"I see you," Fellows tells me. "And I mark you."

"Get looking, Fellows," I tell him. "Looks for pieces. Look for leather from his jacket. Or fresh tanned if you want. But look. And the rest of you," I tell the rest of them.

I leave them standing and walk across the field toward the wreckage. Mud and debris. An expensive airplane in bits. And somewhere among the bits, bits of the pilot. A kneecap here, a shoulder over there, a curved piece of skull in another place.

Doc Turner and his men are dismounting from the ambulance track and walking toward us looking this way and that. None of us have dealt with a crashed airplane before: in a Sherman we know we'll find what we're looking for right under the hatches. But here everything is outside and in the light, while the inside of a Sherman is dark, even with the hatches open. Here I smell nothing except burned gasoline and seared metal, while in a Sherman the stench of roasted meat is strong.

I walk on. Plexiglass glitters, twisted aluminum shines. But I see no pilot. I do not see even a piece of pilot. But having ordered the others, I glance and glance this way and that, looking for some trace of the man who flew this Mustang. I go on looking at the scattered bits of aircraft until I hear Franklin say, "Lord have mercy."

I turn and look at Franklin standing with his head tilted back. His mouth is open and he is staring up at the trees in the stand of woods close by the site of the crash. I follow the line of his gaze. Forty feet up an oak tree the pilot waits for us. The first thing I notice is that he does not fly with the 99th, for I can see his forehead between the rim of his leather flying helmet and his oxygen mask. The second thing I notice is the four-inch thick branch thrust through his back and out his chest. As Franklin said, Lord have mercy. But we have some luck: the flying helmet and oxygen mask are still in place and they obscure most of his face. Only his pale, unlacerated forehead is visible.

"Jesus Christ," Rutherford says.

"Amen," Fellows says.

Doc Turner, his medics and we converge on the oak tree. We look up.

"Got to get him down out of there," Doc Turner says.

"Not going to be easy," one of the medics says.

"Nothing is," Doc Turner says. "Get some rope and such out of the track." The medic nods and goes off to the ambulance halftrack.

"We're going to need a saw to get him off that limb," Fellows says.

"You mean," Rutherford says, "to get the limb, and him with it, off the tree."

"Like I said," Fellows said.

"Rutherford's got a point," Doc Turner tells me.

"We have hacksaws in the track," I say. "Withers, go get a hacksaw and bring it."

"Be slow, cutting it with a hacksaw," Doc Turner says. "That's all you've got?" He sounds as though he thought we carried a selection of saws in the track.

"Yes, sir," I tell him.

"Who wants to go up?" he asks. He looks at his medics and at us.

"I'll go," Rutherford says. "I been up trees before."

"Regular Paul Bunyan," Franklin says.

"That's me."

The medic comes back with a coil of rope slung over his shoulder. "Hundred feet of rope here," he says. "Ought to be about right." I wonder why the medics carry a hundred feet of rope.

When Withers returns with a hacksaw, Rutherford hands me his machinepistol and takes the saw from Withers. I sling the machinepistol over my shoulder. Rutherford unbuckles his belt, threads it through the handle of the saw and buckles the belt. Then he takes the coil of rope from the medic and fits the coil of rope over his head and under his left arm. He seems to know what he's doing. Fellows and Simpson and Rutherford walk to the foot of the oak tree. Fellows and Simpson each grip one of Rutherford's legs and lift him up off the ground so he can reach the lowest branch. Rutherford hoists himself up as they push. Then he begins to climb up among the tree's branches. Soon we hear the sound of sawing high above the ground and a fine, steady fall of sawdust filters down through the branches shifting in the breeze. I step back from the tree and look up. Rutherford is doing a workmanlike job of it: he saws notches in the butt of the branch and ties the rope around the branch and through the notches, so that when he cuts the branch the rope will not slip and let the branch and the pilot plummet to the ground. Rutherford flips the free end of the rope over an adjacent branch and lets it fall to the ground. His plan is a good one: we will take up a strain on the rope as he cuts through the branch and then we will lower branch and body to the ground.

Rutherford saws and saws. The wood is hard. I can see the sweat on his face: he is lucky this is a cool breezy day in early April.

"About through," he calls down. Withers, Franklin and Fellows take up a strain on the rope. I stand with Doc Turner and watch. Doc Turner's medics wait off-stage, holding a stretcher and a mattress cover.

"It's going," Rutherford calls. I see the limb, and the pilot through whose chest the limb extends, ease down, the weight of wood and dead man expanding the narrow cut Rutherford has made with the slim saw. The limb trembles and the pilot's hands at his sides flutter like leaves. "Hang on to the rope, now," Rutherford calls down as he begins sawing again. I listen to the quick singing passage of the narrow blade through the twisted wood at the bottom of the cut. The sun is high up in the sky. More sawdust drifts down and is blown away. I hear a bird call and listen to the medics chatting. A quiet place. Even here in the devil's Germany, quiet places are just off the roads jammed with tracked vehicles and guns.

"Excuse me, please," says a voice from the woods beyond the trunk of the tree. "We wish to surrender."

I take my eyes from Rutherford sawing high up in the tree and look into the shadows beneath the leafless trees in the woods. Three old men in German uniforms stand twenty feet beyond the tree up which Rutherford has climbed. One is tall and heavy. The other two are wiry men of medium height. All three have their hands up. They are not carrying weapons.

"What the hell's this, then?" Doc Turner says, as though a filthy madman had appeared in his operating theater.

"Prisoners," I tell him. "Old prisoners."

"Ja, prisoners," one of the shorter thin ones says, picking up on the word. The tall heavy one eyes the Schmeisser machinepistol slung over my shoulder.

"Okay," I tell them. "Prisoners. Right now we're a little busy."

"We heard you establishing a sniper position in the tree," the German says. His English is good: better than the English most of us speak each day. He has a faint English accent, too. This war is as curious as it is violent.

"It's not a sniper position," I tell him. "Come on over here. You have any weapons?"

"In the woods. We left them there. Three rifles and a revolver. Mausers from the First War. An old British revolver."

"Home guard, are you?" I ask them. I glance up into the tree: Rutherford is still sawing. The wind has dropped. The sawdust is collecting like snow on the dead pilot's flying helmet.

"Yes," the German says. "Home Guard. All three of us. You aren't looking for us?"

"Not today," I tell him. "You didn't hear the aircraft crash?"

"We heard. Then we heard your vehicles coming. We thought you were coming for us."

I nod toward the three men standing beneath the tree holding onto the rope and nod again, upward, toward Rutherford sawing high in the oak tree. Toward the pilot with the branch plunged through his back and out his chest.

The German looks up, examines Rutherford, the pilot, the men holding the rope. "I see," he says. "I'm sorry." But he does not sound sorry: he sounds as though he has seen corpses in trees so often that he no longer wonders how they got up there.

"What the hell's going on here?" Doc Turner asks. He glares at me and glares at the old German. "This man and the other two are Germans. You're supposed to take them prisoner," he tells me. "You're not supposed to stand around chatting with them."

"They're old men," I say. Doc Turner eyes the Germans. Doc Turner seems more comfortable with the dead and the injured than with old men in uniform.

"Old men who learned a hell of a lot in the last war and this one, you mean," Doc Turner says.

"This is true," the German sergeant says.

"What the hell's going on down there?" Rutherford shouts down from high up in the tree. He sounds peeved, as though he has done all the work and no one has taken the time to thank him.

"Three prisoners came out of the woods," I call up to him. "Everything's all right."

"Down there it's all right," he shouts. "Up here it's shit and hard work. Take a strain on that rope, now. I'm almost there."

I nod. I glance at the Germans. Whatever they were once, in 1914 or 1915, or in '16, '17 or even 1918, they are old men now. This is their last war for sure. Unless someone comes stamping into their houses in ten years and orders them to get ready. "Tell your friends to get the weapons," I tell the English speaker. The German speaks to his two old buddies. They nod and walk away into the woods.

"Name?" I ask him.

"Herman. I was a sergeant in the first war. Then I worked for a building company."

"Construction? Where?" Doc Turner asks, as though he has spent his life throwing up barns and houses instead of, as they say in the Seven Six One, looking down throats and up the other end.

"In Dresden," Sergeant Herman says. As he names the place I see his old, pale blue eyes glitter. We've heard rumors about this city: gingerbread houses, a river, museums, the rumors said. And then, February of this year, something happened: something worse than the bad that happened elsewhere in Germany. Something horrific and fearsome. Something even those who arranged it did not believe.

"Pretty bad, was it?" Doc Turner asks. Doc Turner has heard about Dresden too.

"Unnameable," Sergeant Herman says. "The devil's furnace. Worse than the devil's furnace."

"Sorry," I say. What else can I say? I don't know Dresden. I know the inside of Big Sam and the incinerated corpses of Sam Taylor and his men. I know McCarthy and Jackson chopped in half and thrown away into indignity and darkness by an eighty-eight millimeter shell. I know Sam Turley standing up against the cold dark wind that blew across Morville-les-Vic and the tank trap before which he died. But Dresden is far away: a place beyond the horizon, an alien place full of people who seem to have let all this shit happen. Whatever happened to them there, happened there. Our hurts are greater than theirs. At least, that is, until the war is finished. Perhaps I will one day read about what happened at Dresden and comprehend how small we were, how slight our wounds, how minor our losses. But right now, the boy dead up the tree with a limb thrust like a crooked spear through his back and broken spine and out his chest is more important. So is Rutherford cursing as he saws at the hard twisted fiber that binds the last bit of the butt of the branch to the tree. So are Withers, Franklin and Fellows straining at the rope, and Simpson and Doc Turner and his medics waiting with their stretcher to package this pilot and send him home.

"What're the names of the two with you?" Doc Turner asks. The Doc has a lot of delicacy, and he wants to stop Sergeant Herman thinking about Dresden, where the sergeant put up buildings and then watched them burn down. Every last one of them, the rumors say, and every last person in every last one of them. What a February night it must have been: the roaring wind fleeing toward the flames, the fires leaping like giants across the cracking slate roofs, the rising heat working fissures in the paving stones, the heated winter air full of sparks, poisonous gasses, bombs plummeting from the illuminated night sky, and people fleeing from death in one place to die in another.

"Corporal Haffitz," Sergeant Herman says. "And Corporal Stahlmann."

"It's going," Rutherford calls. I look: Withers, Franklin and Fellows are digging their heels into the soft ground, holding onto the rope as they lean away from Rutherford's voice calling down that they should hang on.

The pilot's body and the branch which transfixes it swing and bump from one branch to the next one below as Fellows, Withers and Franklin do their best to let this boy down easy. Rutherford drops the saw to the ground and swings down through the branches of the oak tree, maneuvering branch and pilot through the gaps between the larger limbs lower down the tree's trunk. At last the boy and his branch are lowered to the ground. The medics pick up their stretcher and their mattress cover and their blankets and move forward. Doc Turner goes with them. Simpson, Sergeant Herman and I let the medical professionals go forward to do their job.

Corporal Haffitz and Corporal Stahlmann come out of the woods carrying the three rifles and the pistol. One of them is carrying two of the rifles in his arms as he might carry two logs into his house. The other holds the third rifle as he would a walking stick, gripping the forepiece behind the sight. He also holds the revolver in his left hand, by the barrel, the cylinder swung open. These two old men are not taking any chances.

"This is Corporal Haffitz and this is Corporal Stahlmann," Sergeant Herman says, indicating one and then the other. They stand at attention and nod.

"Ask them to give Simpson here the rifles. I'll take the revolver." The two elderly Germans hand the weapons to Simpson and me. "Spell Williston on the radio, Simpson," I tell him. "Both of you stay in the track." Simpson nods and walks away, cradling the three antique rifles in his arms. I look at the revolver. It is an antique too: at least as old as these old Germans called back into service. It is, as the Sergeant said, an antique, and British.

"A souvenir," Sergeant Herman explains. "From the first war."

"Give me your address," I say, "and I'll send it back to you after the war."

"I don't have an address any longer," Sergeant Herman says. He gestures at the revolver. "And that's all finished now. You keep it. Take it home with you."

"You're sure?" I ask him. I heft the revolver. What will I do with an old revolver in Chicago?

"I give it to you." I nod and stick the weapon in my belt.

"You want to come over here," Doc Turner calls to me from where he and Withers, Franklin and Fellows and the medics are standing around the pilot impaled by the branch, "and see if you can figure something out here."

"Do you wish me to accompany you?" Sergeant Herman asks.

"If you like," I say.

Herman says something to Haffitz and Stahlmann. They nod. Sergeant Herman and I walk to where Doc Turner and the rest of them are standing around looking at one another and at the impaled pilot in his flight jacket, helmet and oxygen mask. I unsling the MP-40 machinepistol and hand it to Rutherford.

"I don't know," Doc Turner says as I come up. "I just don't know. This is different, somehow, and I don't like the idea of messing with him." I see what the Doc's problem is: the pilot lies on his side on the ground. The branch driven through his chest is four or five inches in diameter and eight or ten feet long. Through his torn flight jacket I can see the jagged ends of his broken ribs. "I don't know," Doc Turner says. "I just don't want to work it out of him. It'll tear him up something bad." I'm surprised the Doc is squeamish about this: after dealing with the corpses that the First Sergeant and I brought out of the Shermans and collected in the field in front of the tank trap at Morville-les-Vic, I wouldn't have thought anything would make Doc Turner hesitate. But it is near the end of the war, and every one of us has had enough.

"Can I help?" Sergeant Herman asks.

We look at him.

"I have dealt with this sort of thing before," Sergeant Herman says. "If you would like me to deal with this?" He sounds as though he is offering to wash the dishes or wipe the table.

"All right," I say. Doc Turner nods: it is okay by Doc Turner if someone else does this one. "You want help?" I ask Sergeant Herman.

"No," Sergeant Herman says. "Corporal Haffitz will help. He and I have worked together with this sort of thing before."

He calls Haffitz over. Haffitz looks at the young pilot's body and nods. "*Wie die Pforte,*" he says.

"What's that mean?" Doc Turner asks.

"He said, 'Like the gate,'" Sergeant Herman says.

"Gate?" Withers asks. "What gate?"

"A gate of spiked cast iron pilings," Sergeant Herman says. "On the morning of the 14th of February this year, we had to remove it from a young woman's body."

"Jesus Christ," Rutherford says.

"Precisely," Sergeant Herman says. He walks a step closer the pilot's body and stops. He looks at us and says, "You may wish to take a break, gentlemen. Or look the other way. It is not pretty."

I can guess.

"Let's us walk on over here," Doc Turner says. We shuffle away. "I feel bad about this," Doc Turner says. "We ought to do whatever's necessary about this. I don't like letting them do it."

"They've got experience," I tell him. "And you've done enough, Doc." Doc Turner doesn't mind if we don't address him by his rank. He is much more than half civilian.

"Besides," Withers says, "that pilot ain't one of us."

Doc Turner looks at Withers and says, "You're wrong, Withers. He is one of us. Just like you and me. I don't want to hear you say that about any man dead ever again. Or living, for that matter. You hear me?"

"Yes," Withers says.

"Yes, what?" Doc Turner asks.

"Yes, sir," Withers says.

"Don't forget it, Withers. Every man in the uniform's just the same as the next one." He draws a deep breath and shouts, "What the fuck you think we're over here for, anyhow? Goddamnit, man, think about it before you start talking. And the rest of you, too," the Doc says, looking at each one of us in turn.

"I didn't mean anything, sir," Withers says.

"I know, I know," Doc Turner says. "Forget it. I shouldn't have blown up like that. It's just that. . ," he says. Lips pressed together, he shakes his head, shakes it again. He takes out a pack of cigarettes, takes a single cigarette out and hands me the pack. "Pass them around," he says. He sticks the cigarette in his lips but he does not light it. He shakes his head again and says, "It's just that. . . ." But he can't think of what to say next: he shakes his head again and turns and walks off toward the ambulance track.

I pass out Doc Turner's cigarettes and all of us smoke and examine the fantastic disarray of the Mustang's debris. I try not to listen to Sergeant Herman and Corporal Haffitz as they go to work. They speak to one another without urgency, the sergeant instructing, Haffitz murmuring answers and suggestions. I sense that one of them lifts the pilot while the other does what he must to extract the limb thrust through the boy's back and chest. I hear a squelching sound and a sound of wood creaking as it flexes. Haffitz murmurs and Sergeant Herman says, "*Ja, Willi, er kommt. Ziehen.*" I understand this much German, and therefore I understand that Sergeant Herman is holding the boy in his arms while Corporal Haffitz works the branch out of the boy's body. Then I hear one of them walk off toward the woods. I glance over my shoulder. Corporal Haffitz is carrying the limb. He walks fifty feet into the woods, drops the limb, comes back and stands beside Sergeant Herman kneeling beside the boy.

"All finished," I say. Doc Turner's medics stop examining the interesting bits and pieces of the P-51 scattered over the field and walk with me to where Sergeant Herman is kneeling in the field beside the boy. Sergeant Herman has removed the boy's oxygen mask and leather helmet and laid them on his chest. They cover the fearsome wound the boy suffered. As we walk up, Sergeant Herman folds the boy's hands across his stomach below the helmet and oxygen mask. I'm about to thank Sergeant Herman when he reaches up and places the tips of the fore and middle fingers of his right hand on the pilot's eyebrows and eases the fingertips down, closing the boy's eyes.

We stop a discreet distance from Sergeant Herman as he takes a blanket from the stretcher, unfolds it, shakes it out and spreads it across the boy's legs. He draws the blanket up over the boy's hands, farther up over his oxygen mask and flying helmet and farther up still over the boy's pale, bloodless face.

Sergeant Herman crosses himself and stands up.

"Catholic?" I ask.

"I am," Sergeant Herman says. "So is he. He was wearing a medal on a cord around his neck along with his identification tags. Note the 'C' on the tag." The sergeant hands me one of the boy's tags and the medal. "I placed the other tag in the breast pocket of his shirt," Sergeant Herman says. "I didn't go through his pockets," Sergeant Herman says.

"That's all right. Doc Turner can handle that." I glance at the tags: Lovejoy, Donald R. I glance at the serial number and note the 'C' stamped in the metal that indicates Donald R. Lovejoy was a Catholic. I feel the notch in the end of the tag with the tip of my thumb. I know what the drill is, but I am not going to take the blanket away from this boy's face, open his mouth, and work the notch in the tag between the two teeth in the middle of his upper jaw. I'm not going to do that, and I will wager Doc Turner isn't going to do it either. We know his name, and Doc Turner will take care of the paper that will identify him.

"Thank you, Sergeant Herman," I say. "And thank Corporal Haffitz for me." The sergeant passes on my thanks as I take out a package of cigarettes and offer it to Sergeant Herman. Beside me, Rutherford pulls a package of cigarettes out of the right slash pocket of his coveralls and hands it to Corporal Haffitz. "*Danke*," Corporal Haffitz says.

"Yes," Sergeant Herman says, "Many thanks for the tobacco." He and Haffitz light cigarettes. As they do so I notice dried blood on Sergeant Herman's hands.

"Doc Turner's seen too much of this sort of thing," I explain. "It was good of you two to step in and help."

"We've all seen too much," Sergeant Herman says. "Too much of this sort of thing, too much of other things. Thank Christ the war's coming to an end."

"Amen," Fellows says.

We watch the medics shift Lieutenant Lovejoy's body onto the stretcher. They place the other folded blanket and the folded mattress cover on

Lieutenant Lovejoy's thighs and lift the stretcher and walk off toward the ambulance halftrack.

"Time to go," I say.

"It will be strange, being a prisoner again," Sergeant Herman says. "I was a prisoner in England from the middle of 1918 to the end of the war and beyond."

"You'll be well treated," I tell him.

"I know," he says. "I was the last time."

We walk to the maintenance halftrack. Rutherford, Franklin, Withers and Fellows get up in the back with the two German corporals. Simpson eyes the crowd coming up into the track. With seven men in the back it is a tight fit, and Rutherford and Withers stand up against the rear door of the track. I motion Sergeant Herman into the cab. He gets in and sits between Williston and me. Williston steers a wide turn across the field. Doc Turner's ambulance halftrack is underway, angling away from us toward the line of the Seven Six One's vehicles parked along the road.

"First Sergeant wants to know what we've been doing," Simpson says from the back. I glance over my shoulder. Simpson is wearing a headset and holding a microphone up in front of his lips. "He doesn't sound happy."

"Tell him we're on our way. Tell him we had some difficulty getting the pilot's body ready. Tell him we have three prisoners."

Simpson mutters into the microphone.

"I fought against you in the last war," Sergeant Herman says. "You were with the French then, in the south. The 369th Infantry."

"Our First Sergeant was in the 369th."

"You didn't fight with the rest of your army then," Sergeant Herman says. "You fought with the French."

"Times change," I tell him.

"I know. At the time we thought it was strange that you weren't with your own army."

"So did the 369th."

"They made a good showing. Not highly professional, you understand. But they were willing. I lost several men to them. And of course they weren't at fault for their shortcomings. Shortcomings are the result of bad officers and lazy sergeants."

"I see," I say. I wonder if Sergeant Herman and First Sergeant Reardon trained together. I also wonder what Sergeant Herman thinks of his officers in this war. Not much, I guess, given the shortcomings he has seen all around him, and sees all around him now we are east of Frankfurt and heading farther east.

"Whatever," Sergeant Herman says. "It will be over soon."

"Let's hope to Christ you're right," Williston says as he steers across the field.

The First Sergeant is waiting for us, standing in the empty space in the line of the Seven Six One's vehicles in which our track stood before we set out to get Lieutenant Lovejoy down from his tree. The First Sergeant listens as I explain about the pilot and how we took three prisoners. He glances at Sergeant Herman when I tell him about Sergeant Herman's and Corporal Haffitz's assistance.

When I finish he looks up at Rutherford and says, "Up a tree with a saw, Rutherford? Is that it? And three men come out of the woods and surrender and they're your prisoners, hey?" he says to me. He shakes his head as though he cannot figure what to do with us. Then he looks at the three old men as though he has not been able, since 1917, to figure out what to do with three aged, willing prisoners who want nothing more than a guarded fence around them until the shooting stops. "This isn't a war anymore," he says. "This here is becoming a drive in the country. But I catch anybody not looking I'll take their name. Because we're still going to find trouble up ahead. Word is the Germans going to fight around Coburg, east of here." He pauses, glances at Sergeant Herman. "Well," he tells me, "I suppose we'll find a place for your prisoners until we find some MPs. And they helped out, you say. You check them for weapons?"

"They handed over three rifles and a revolver." I pull the revolver out of my belt and show it to him.

"All right," the First Sergeant says. "Keep the revolver, if you want. They can ride with you."

"Going to be crowded," Fellows says. I doubt the First Sergeant needs to be told how crowded a maintenance track is if it is carrying ten men.

The First Sergeant turns and looks at Fellows. He looks at him with care, and then he looks at him some more. Then he turns back to me and says, "You caught them, you carry them. Until you find some MPs. Give them something to eat while we go on." He looks at Sergeant Herman and says, "Thanks for helping out with that boy."

"You are welcome, Sergeant."

"He fought the 369th in the first war," I tell the First Sergeant.

"That true?" the First Sergeant asks Sergeant Herman.

"Yes, Sergeant," Sergeant Herman says.

"That was better," the First Sergeant says. He is telling us the first war was better than this one.

Sergeant Herman nods and says, "Yes. Different. And you are right: better."

"And none of these damned kids everywhere driving around. We marched," he tells us. "You people today wouldn't know how to get from here down the road one mile if you didn't have tracks and wheels."

Sergeant Herman says, "You're right. We marched. Today they ride. Or they fly."

The First Sergeant nods at Sergeant Herman and tells us, "You listen to this man. This man knows what he's talking about."

It is true what they say about sergeants: they are all alike. They disparage everyone but sergeants. They disparage officers and enlisted men and civilians. They like to march, and they like everyone else to march as far as they do. Sergeants constitute a secret society with identical rules in every country. But we are a modern army, and we ride and we pretend not to care about how fast the old warhorse traveled when it was a colt.

The First Sergeant gives us orders: "Drive back along the column until you find MPs and leave these prisoners off. Be sure the MPs know about them helping out here so these three get a fair deal. Then come back. We're going on." I nod as he speaks and tell him we will come back right away. He extends his hand to Sergeant Herman. "Thanks again for helping these men out," the First Sergeant says.

"It was nothing," Sergeant Herman says, shaking the First Sergeant's hand. "A small thing."

"No," the First Sergeant says. "If you hadn't helped them out they'd probably still be standing around out in that field wondering how to get that boy out of the tree." This is a slander, and the First Sergeant knows it is; but it is polite, I suppose, for one sergeant to compliment another by disparaging his own men.

We drive back until we find MPs standing by the road near a Jeep and a weapons carrier. We explain about Sergeant Herman and Corporals Haffitz and Stahlmann and the pilot. The MPs nod and nod as though they understand. The MPs don't object when we hand Sergeant Herman and the corporals a crate of rations, three cartons of cigarettes and a bottle of brandy. They are grateful: I can tell they haven't been eating well the last few weeks. The MPs are tolerant. They gesture Sergeant Herman and the corporals with their food and drink up into the back of the weapons carrier. "We'll take care of them," the senior MP says. He is about twenty. Sergeant Herman is old enough to be this boy's father, or, except for the details, mine. "Pretty old for this kind of stuff," the MP tells me. His voice is quiet, as though he doesn't want to offend the three elderly Germans. He seems to sympathize with anyone more than twenty-five years old who has to put on a uniform.

Williston gets the track turned around and we drive off. As we go Sergeant Herman, Corporal Haffitz and Corporal Stahlmann wave. We wave back. Then Williston drives around a curve in the road and I can no longer see the three old Germans who helped get Lieutenant Donald R. Lovejoy ready for the trip home.

"Pretty decent guys to find here in the devil's country," Withers says. Of all of us, Withers dislikes being in Germany the most.

"They were pretty hungry," Rutherford says. "Things must be tougher here than we thought."

"They spent the whole war making weapons and such," Franklin says. "Now they're short of food. I don't know what they'll do next, the way things look around here." Franklin is right: dead animals litter the unploughed fields.

"We'll send them food when the war's over," Simpson says. He eyes Fellows. "Like I said before: we ain't going to go away and leave them starve." Fellows snorts and shakes his head.

"I don't know," Franklin says. Franklin is not yet prepared to cast his vote one way or the other.

"We'll send it," Simpson says. "What're we going to do, let them starve over here?"

"They're the enemy," Fellows says. "They are at our mercy. We'll send them nothing." Each word sounds like the strike of a heavy wooden mallet against a hard wooden stake.

"Fellows, that ain't right," Rutherford says. "We aren't like that: we don't do things like that. Others are different. But we don't do like that."

"You will see, Rutherford," Fellows says. "Wait until the war is ended. Then you will see."

"I'm telling you," Simpson says, "that when this here war's over, we're going to be feeding all these people in around here."

"No," Fellows says. "You're wrong about that. You'll see." Fellows is implacable. Simpson cannot defeat him, no matter how much he argues. Fellows is solid: a sound structure eight bricks thick. No one will pound his way through: nothing but explosives will shift Fellows.

"You guys stop arguing and start looking like the First Sergeant said," I say. "There're Germans all around in here."

"No shit?" Franklin says. "This here Germany. You got to expect to find a lot of Germans around here."

"This isn't a Sherman," I remind them, even though they came over the pierced metal matting at Omaha Beach in this track and have called it home since Texas.

"No shit?" Franklin says.

"It's walls are thinner than a Sherman's," I remind them, as though I am giving them their first lesson about the different types of vehicles in the Table of Equipment of an armored battalion.

"Man here's got a point," Franklin says. "One of them Panzerfausts do a bigger number on us than on a Sherman."

"I know that," Simpson says.

"But you forgot it," Fellows says. "You were talking about feeding all these people, and you forgot the sides of this track are about as worthless as a tin can."

"It'll stop a rifle bullet," Withers says. Withers has not spoken much since we crossed the Rhine: not when we saw the hanged civilians, not when we stopped for lunch, not when we got Lieutenant Lovejoy down out of the tree, and not to intervene in the irresolvable debate Simpson and Fellows have been waging against one another since Louisiana in 1943. "Just a rifle bullet," Withers says. "Nothing more."

"Withers got a point," Franklin says. I glance over my shoulder. I note that Franklin, Rutherford, Simpson and Withers bend forward a little: to get their heads down, to get the backs of their necks below the upper edge of the steel walls of the halftrack.

"Uh-huh," Williston says as he glances into the bed of the track. "Seems like you all remembering now about the Germans out there. Man in an upper window of any one of these houses in these little towns we pass through could do us. And this is the end for them. A few weeks, and all this shit is finished forever. But right now they're still fighting."

"Maybe you're right," Fellows says. "And maybe you're not. I think you're wrong." But he is still bent forward, forearms on his knees.

"You think everyone's wrong, Fellows," Rutherford says. "One day you're going to find yourself telling yourself you're wrong. What you going to do then?"

"Argue it out," Fellows says, as though he knows he'll win that argument too.

Withers holds up a hand and presses the earpiece of his headset against his right ear. He repeats what he has been told. Simpson scribbles down what Withers says in an order book. Withers stops talking, listens and says, "Yes, sir, Chi City." He puts the microphone down and says, "Seven Six One's on the move. Captain says they're going forward but Chi City's got something wrong with its engine." Chi City is a C Company Sherman with chronic engine problems: we have recommended more than once that the best course would be to pull Chi City's engine, install a new one and be done with it. But we have been on the move for almost eight weeks and we have had no time to pull engines. Chi City's commander, James Hilliard, is a fellow townsman of mine, and he has put at least part of Chicago's name on his tank. "It's broken down off the main road in this village they just went past," Withers says. He gives me the name of the village and I locate it on the map: it is six or seven miles on from where we stopped for lunch, half a mile off the main road.

"I got it," I say. "Ought to be there in twenty thirty minutes."

We go on, Williston driving on the lefthand side of the road to pass slower vehicles. All the traffic is moving in one direction: east. Now and then we pass groups of prisoners clustered by the side of the road, guarded by bored MPs. I suppose the MPs are waiting for transport for the prisoners. The First Sergeant would say that in this war even the prisoners ride. The prisoners look away when we glance at them.

I find the turn-off to the village where Chi City and its balky engine wait for us. Williston drives us along the narrow country road past stands of oak and maple. As we approach the outskirts of the village Williston says, "Look out now." Williston stops the track. I look up from the map to see what Williston is talking about.

A man is stepping away from a grey stone house beside the road. The house is prosperous: it has leaded windows and a slate roof and a garden to one side. The man is dressed in the black uniform of the SS. Pinned to his black tunic are wound badges and medals. At his neck is the Iron Cross. He is tall, emaciated, blond and dirty. He has lost his helmet. A machinepistol like Rutherford's hangs on its sling over his left shoulder. He holds an unfolded straight razor in his dirty right hand. He grins at us: a stiff clench of his jaws, a flash of grey teeth and glittering eyes.

This German stormtrooper looks like the devil incarnate. I wonder what he will do: he has a submachinegun slung over his shoulder and a razor in his right hand. But this isn't a dark street in south Chicago: Withers has armed the .30 caliber machinegun on the pintle in the front center of the halftrack's bed and is pointing the muzzle at this stormtrooper's chest. Rutherford has his Schmeisser aimed at the man, and everyone else has an M3 greasegun or a rifle pointed at him. I myself am standing up aiming a Thompson submachinegun at him over the windshield. The Thompsongun's selector is on autoload and a full magazine is shoved up into the breech. What can he do? If we fire we will tear him apart. What does he think he can do, except surrender?

He chooses not to surrender. He grins at us as though he knows he is going to escape. He lifts the razor, presses the blade against his throat, presses it into his flesh. Blood seeps and then leaps spurting from the wound. He jerks the blade from left to right across his throat above his adam's apple. As he falls to his knees in the dusty road he is still grinning at us above the pumping gushes of blood that stain his uniform and obscure the awards he has been given for courage and for the wounds that have been inflicted on him by a bigger enemy. He struggles to stay on his knees, and for three beats of his heart he succeeds. Three thick rushes of blood pumped from the severed artery in his throat describe a dark semicircle in the dirt in front of him as he moves his head left to right. His eyes seem to be clouding over: no wonder. The razor slips from his smeared fingers and as a fourth thick gout of blood leaps from the fearsome wound in his throat he falls forward onto his face. His fingertips press against the earth, his knuckles and the backs of his hands rising. Then his fingers curl into loose fists and he is still. And, I am sure, dead.

"What he do that for?" Rutherford asks. He hitches his machinepistol this way and that, as though he expects more madmen to come out into the road.

"How the fuck should I know?" Williston says.

"I know," Simpson says from the bed of the halftrack. "He didn't want to surrender. More, he didn't want to surrender to us."

"No kidding," Franklin says. Franklin looks down at the dead German in the road in front of our track. He frowns and I know he is disturbed by the shape of the door through which this German chose to let himself out of life.

"How you know that, Simpson?" Rutherford asks. Rutherford is aggrieved that this one man chose to die rather than give up. "That he didn't want to surrender to us? Lot of them have surrendered to us."

"Not lots of them like that guy," Simpson says. "Did you see his face? I'll bet he's been in Eastern Europe since August, 1939, and in Russia since the summer of 1941." Simpson has read every single issue of *Yank* and he has a scholar's interest in the distant, vicious fighting between the Russians and the Germans. "We didn't see any like that in France," Simpson says.

"Yes, we did," I say. "2nd SS Panzer was there. Das Reich, they call it. You remember them."

"Sure I remember them," Simpson says. "Of course I remember them. But this guy was. . ."

"I don't recall," I say. "Let's get on. Drive around him, Williston."

"Leave him there in the road?"

"You want to bury him?" I ask. "We don't have the time. We've got to get on up and deal with Chi City."

As we drive around the dead German I think about him grinning at us as he slit his own throat. As they say, they're different from us.

When we have gotten Chi City running again we drive out of the village the way we entered. The SS trooper's corpse is gone.

"The devil come for him," Withers says.

"That a bunch of shit, Withers," Rutherford says. "Someone drag him off the road is all."

We rattle past the neat, prosperous house and garden near which the grinning blond man in the black uniform killed himself. Chi City is close behind us. SS trooper or no, I am glad someone, whether it was the devil himself or one of the locals, removed his body from the road. Chi City's tracks would have chewed the corpse to shreds.

"This is working out to be some day," Williston tells me. "People hanged, that boy speared dead up a tree, one of these here SS they got killing himself like that."

I nod.

"Sure a different kind from that Sergeant Herman," Williston says.

"Yes," I say.

"Don't seem they can come from the same place, does it?"

"No," I say. "It doesn't seem so."

"But they do," Williston says. "Strange, isn't it?"

I nod. Strange is the right word. So are odd, fantastic, fearsome and unsettling the right words. I wonder what Sergeant Herman would say about this suicide with the glittering blade in his hand and the glittery look in his eye. Like us, I suppose he would shake his head and say he could not explain. As Williston says, this is working out to be some day. What next? I wonder, and worry that whatever comes next will be worse.

It is: west of Fulda, looking for yet another broken down Sherman, I hear Withers, who is standing in the bed of the track behind the gun looking this way and that, say, "What the fuck?"

I glance to see what has made Withers curse. I see nothing.

"Up ahead there?" Withers says. "Beside those trees?"

I look: I see the thin outline of a man drawn with an inflexible steel nib and gray ink. He stands beside a stand of trees. His clothes, like his face, are grey.

"Smoke gray," Rutherford says. This one time, Rutherford's visceral judgment is right: the man standing beneath the tree might disappear if a decent breeze comes up.

We are upon this wraith before he responds to the clatter of our tracks and the mutter of our track's engine. I guess his hearing and sight are deficient.

"Slow up and stop," I tell Williston.

"Okay," he says. He slows and stops fifty feet from the wraith, as though he is worried the man is diseased.

"You like to see me walk, Williston?"

"You want me to go closer?"

"Why not? Guy doesn't look like he's got a weapon, does he?"

"I was thinking about scabs and such. Typhus. The influenza."

"What? Drive on up to him, Williston," I say. Typhus? Influenza? Williston must have been reading something dread: another Army pamphlet stuffed with useless information.

Williston drives up the road fifty feet and stops near the trees. The wraith stands under the nearest tree, ten feet away from my right hand.

"Glad I'm here on this side," Williston says. I glance behind me: Rutherford, Simpson, Fellows, Franklin and Withers are staring at the wraith.

"Who the hell is he?" Franklin asks.

"Who knows?" I tell him. "Just one more of these people they got over here."

"He's one of those DPs," Fellows says. I'm not going to dispute this: Fellows is right. The wraith is a displaced person. The Army has told us to be on the lookout for them.

The wraith totters forward from beneath the tree. He stares at us. He opens his mouth and shows us dirty teeth. He makes a sound.

"What's he say?" Simpson asks.

"You need any help?" I ask the wraith. As soon as I speak I know this is a ridiculous question: this guy needs a field hospital, six months rest, a steady diet high in calories and protein, and three or four understanding people to talk to in his own language.

"He needs help," Fellows says.

"No kidding?" Simpson says.

"Shut the fuck up," I tell them. "You need any help?" I ask the wraith. I speak one word a second after the one before, to give him a chance.

The wraith coughs and totters forward. He makes the same sound he made before.

"Anybody here guess what he's saying?" Franklin asks.

"No," I say. "Give him a chance, will you?"

The wraith totters another two paces and opens his filthy mouth. He makes the same sound again, and then he speaks it: "America." He pronounces the word 'A*me*rica.'

"You hear that?" Rutherford asks. "Man here studied geography. Or he recognizes the uniform maybe. Or maybe he teaches history when he ain't standing out on this here road."

"How you think he knows we're Americans?" Franklin asks.

"Huh?" Rutherford asks him.

"Franklin," Fellows says, "that's about as stupid as it gets. As it can get," Fellows says.

"That ain't stupid," Simpson says. "That's dead above the jaw."

"Hey, fuck you motherfuckers," Franklin says. He is outraged, but without reason. "All I asked was how he knew we were Americans?"

"Where you from, Franklin?" Simpson says. "Canada?"

"Burma," Fellows says. "He's from Burma. He's a Burmese."

"Piss on Burma," says Rutherford, who listened with care when 1st/Sgt. John P. Burch spoke. "And Canada too. Franklin here from Alabama. That tells you the last thing you need to know about Franklin."

"How about some quiet, you guys?" I ask. "I can't hear this man here."

"You call that a man?" Withers asks.

Withers has a point: tottering and creaking across the ten feet between the tree and our halftrack, the wraith is a caricature of a man.

Rutherford is eying me from up in the bed of the track. "All right," he tells the rest of them on my behalf. "You heard the man. This here serious."

"That's it," I say, and the five of them up in the back nod and nod.

The wraith totters forward another two feet. He seems to have trouble walking. "A*me*rica," he says.

I turn around in my seat and say, "Simpson. Get on the horn. Bring up Headquarters and tell them we got a DP here needs medical attention. Ask them what to do."

"A DP?" Withers asks. "Look like a half dozen and more to me." I look. Tottering out of the woods behind the wraith are seven more. Some of them are dressed in striped jackets and pants, others in the grey stuff the wraith wears.

"Simpson," I say. "Call in and tell them eight DPs, and maybe more. Tell them we're going to need a truck up here and Doc Turner too."

Simpson calls. The wraith has made it all the way across the ten paces from the woods beside the road to the side of our track. He raises his left hand, but he hesitates to touch the halftrack. I wonder why. The others, coming on behind him, hesitate too. To see what we will do, I suppose. To try to determine whether we are going to hurt them.

"Break out some food for these guys," I say.

Rutherford and Fellows rummage in the back of the track. They break open a case of rations and get down from the back of the track. The DPs shuffling forward stop shuffling when they see Rutherford and Fellows coming toward them, rations in their hands. Rutherford and Fellows walk among them, passing out the oblong cartons full of what the Army calls nourishing food and everyone else calls every bad word they can think of.

The DPs take the waxy cartons and turn them in their hands.

"Don't seem to know what these here are for," Rutherford says.

"If they ain't seen these rations before, they're lucky," Withers calls down from where he stands behind the machinegun. Behind him Simpson is muttering into the radio.

Rutherford tears open one of the cartons. He takes out the cans and packets within, holds them up, and hands them to the DP nearest him. Then he holds up the can opener included in the ration package so the DPs can see it. He moves the can opener as though he is opening yet another can of delicious pressed meat. He hands the can opener to the DP. Then he opens and closes his jaws to demonstrate how to chew. Then he rubs his stomach.

"You lying to these poor people, Rutherford," Williston says. "It ain't edible and it don't taste good. Still, you're pretty good: I ever want to sell whiskey to the Indians I'm gonna bring you along to translate."

"Shut the fuck up, Williston," Rutherford says. Rutherford moves his hands, encouraging the DPs to open up their rations and dig in. They look at him, turning the ration cartons in their hands. Some of them slip the cartons beneath their clothes, as though they think Rutherford may try to take them back.

"Well, shit," Rutherford says. "I don't know."

"Maybe they want a drink," Withers says. He leaves the machinegun, steps to the rear of the track and hands two bottles of wine down over the high steel side. Rutherford takes the bottles and passes them to the two nearest DPs, moving his hands to demonstrate how to drink, and how to pass a bottle around. The DPs holding the bottles look at Rutherford. Then they look at the bottles. Then they look at Rutherford again. The other DPs look at the two holding the bottles.

"I swear I just don't know," Rutherford said.

"Neither do I," I tell him. I get down from the track. "Simpson? You got anything yet?"

"Hang on," Simpson says. "They're checking with Doc Turner. Hold it." He listens and says, "Yes, sir." He nods as he says it, as though the officer to whom he is speaking is standing in front of him. Simpson takes off the headset and says, "Doc Turner no more than four five minutes away. He's coming, and the Colonel's sending a truck on out here right now."

"Truck," Rutherford tells the DPs standing around holding the packages of rations. Rutherford moves his hands in front of him as though he is holding a steering wheel and driving a vehicle through a series of sharp descending turns on a mountain road. The DPs look at him. They don't seem to think much of his acting. Or maybe they've never seen a truck.

"You're doing all right, Rutherford," I say. I turn to the DPs who have edged closer together and closer to the track. "Anybody here speak English?" I ask. The DPs mutter and look at one another. "French?" I ask. I speak fifteen words of French, but fifteen words may be more useful than waving my hands. But the DPs know no French: they mutter and look at each other.

"They aren't speaking the same language," Fellows says.

"A*me*rica," the wraith who was standing by the road says.

"Right," I tell him. I nod at Rutherford and Fellows and point my thumb at my chest. "America," I say.

"Ross Velt," the wraith says. The other DPs nod.

"Right," I say. "Roosevelt."

"That's pronounced Roooooos Velt," Williston says from the driver's seat. The wraith looks at him. Williston gives him a big smile to show he is kidding. The wraith smiles too: when he smiles I see his translucent skin move across the bones in his face.

The wraith points at a DP standing close beside him and says, "*Polen.*" He points at another DP and says, "*Tschechoslowakei.*" Then he points at a second, a third and a fourth DP and says, "*Jugoslavien.*" He points at the last two DPs and says, "*Sowjetrussland.*" Then he looks at me and nods. Then he points at himself, looks at us as though he thinks we may speak English, and says, "Holland."

"He's telling us where they're from," Rutherford says.

"And mostly in German," Fellows says.

"What else?" I ask. "He knows none of us speak Polish, or Dutch."

The wraith nods his head twice as though we are getting somewhere and says, "*Polen.* Holland."

"Right. You want to eat?" I ask. "*Essen*?" I point at the box in his hands and repeat, "*Essen*?"

The wraith looks down at the waxed carton of rations in his hands. Then he looks up at me. I wonder what he is thinking. Whatever it is, a little food can't hurt. "Why don't you sit down and eat? *Sitzen* and *essen*?"

"Maybe they want to save it," Simpson says.

"What the fuck for?" Withers asks. "We got more."

"Maybe they don't know that."

"Maybe Simpson right just this once," Rutherford says. He gets up into the back of the track and lowers a case of rations over the side to Fellows. Fellows sets the case on the ground and opens it with the knife he carries in a scabbard on his belt. He and Rutherford hand out more packages of rations to the DPs. Those that have not done so slip one package inside their clothes. As the wraith puts one of his packages beneath his shirt he says something in what must be Polish, or German, and grimaces.

"Come on, now," I say. "Time to *essen.*"

The wraith nods. He squats beside the road and opens the waxy carton of rations with care, as though he may find the carton useful. I wish I could tell him it is good for nothing except burning. The other seven follow his example. They have trouble with the can openers. Rutherford, Fellows and I help them with the openers. They are grateful for our help. I am reminded of what it is like to help a child. When we have opened the cans, they begin to eat. They scoop the pressed meat out of the cans with their fingers and nibble at the hard crackers in the package. As they eat they glance at one another again and again. Rutherford sees them glancing and says, "Look like they afraid someone gone steal they food."

As I say, "Looks like it," one of the DPs heaves himself upright. He holds the open tin can of meat in one hand and the waxy carton with the rest of the ration in the other and walks off toward the woods.

"He all right?" Rutherford asks.

"How the hell should I know?" I ask. "Maybe he's got the gut."

As though to confirm what I have said, the wraith squatting by the road eating pressed meat nods and points at his stomach and shakes his head. The DP with the stomach walks twenty feet into the woods. He stops behind a tree four inches in diameter. He puts the open can of pressed meat and the waxy carton of rations on the ground, drops his filthy grey pants—he wears no underwear—and squats. A rush of bloody liquid belches out of his anus.

"Jesus Christ," Rutherford says. "That man sick."

"Doc Turner coming," Williston says. I think he is reassuring us that help is on the way; but then I hear motors approaching. Doc Turner's ambulance track and a two-and-a-half ton truck are coming top speed up the road. Doc Turner's driver drives right up behind our track and stops. Doc Turner gets down, takes one look at the DPs squatting like the beggars they are in a cluster close to the side of our track, says, "Well, Jesus Christ," and begins shouting orders. The DPs turn their faces toward the sound of his voice hectoring his medics out of the ambulance track. Four medics get out carrying medical satchels and two more get down out of the truck.

Doc Turner comes up and repeats himself, "Well, Jesus Christ."

"I agree," I tell him. "The one over there in the woods is sick. He's shitting blood."

"Goddamnit. This fucking Europe," Doc Turner says. It doesn't sound like the Doc is going to be coming over here touring after the war.

The medics examine one of the DPs after another, getting their jackets off so Doc Turner can use his stethoscope. Doc Turner gives us a running diagnosis: "All these men are malnourished. This one here's got an arrhythmic heartbeat. Fever in this one, and this one too, and this one. Rash on these two here, might be typhus or typhoid. Come from filth, fleas and lice. Stevens," he says to his head medic, "I want these two with the rash in the ambulance. And the one over there in the woods with the gut. Rest of them go in the truck. Jesus Christ almighty. This one here had some kind of accident, cut his leg and it wasn't sewed up at all. And that one over there—he goes in the track, too, Stevens—most likely got the same these here with the rash got." The Doc nods toward the woods where a medic is helping the DP who defecated blood and mucous. As the medic gets the man's filthy pants up and begins to lift him, the DP picks up the open tin of pressed meat and the ration carton and holds them against his filthy shirt as the medic helps him stagger back to the road.

"They going to be all right, Doc?" Rutherford asks. Fellows nods, to show he is interested in how this flock of the Doc's patients are going to make out.

"Oh, they'll be all right after a time. Get them fed up right, rest them, shots, treat these three here. Stevens, let me have my bag." Stevens hands the Doc a medical satchel. The Doc opens it, takes out a syringe and small bottle of medicine. He prepares the syringe and injects the medicine into the two DPs with rash, lifts the shirt of the one the medic has helped out of the woods, nods when he sees a rash on the man's chest and belly, injects him too and says, "This one goes in the track, too, Stevens." The DPs do not object when the Doc injects them: they watch the needle slide into themselves as though it is happening to someone else.

"Where do you think they came from, Doc?" I ask him. "I mean, this one here said they were from Poland and Czechoslovakia and Yugoslavia and Russia and Holland. But where do you think they came from that they got like this?"

"Where they come from?" he asks. "I'll tell you where they come from: they come from here in fucking Europe where they do this kind of thing to one another. That's where they come from." The Doc's low opinion of Europe is lower than I had thought. "Treat people this way," the Doc says. He seems to be forgetting the rickets and scurvy back home. But maybe he's right to forget back home, because back home, bad as it is, is different from what he sees as he stands among these squatting DPs with the syringe in his hand, looking at them as though he can't believe what he knows must have happened to these people. I'm surprised at Doc Turner's reaction: to me DPs are just another part of the war.

Doc Turner and his medics lead the DPs to the truck and the halftrack ambulance and get them in. The DPs clutch the rations and bottles of wine we gave them. They nod at us as they wait their turn to be helped up into the truck and the ambulance. The Dutch wraith who said "A*me*rica" nods and nods, as though everything is all right now. But I wonder what they will do now, and how they will get back to Holland, Poland, Czechoslovakia, Yugoslavia and Russia; and what they will do if they are able to find their ways back.

We drive on, and as we do we find more clumps of DPs. They cringe as we approach and shuffle forward when they see we are Americans. "They don't mistake where we're from," Fellows says.

None of the DPs we find are women, and none are children. They are all men; though it seems to us at least two thirds of the number the Germans processed like pork in a sausage factory must have been woman and children. I suppose the men have survived and the women and children have died for no reason other than that they were weaker.

We have been briefed about DPs: we had a memo, and the papers, and the Colonel told us to look out for them and take care. But no one told us what they would look like. Perhaps no one knew. They look like scarecrows, and they smell and demand and reach out, the frail flesh of their hands like milky glass that permits us to see the shape, but not the detail, of each bone of each finger and palm. They speak and are incomprehensible in languages we will never know and they are suspicious of one another and some of them steal from one another and hit one another.

We were told DPs were rounded up and made to work, and were killed or permitted to die when they could work no more.

Doc Turner is right: this fucking Europe. They hang women and work men to death. I suppose they just killed the children. I wonder how we would have fared had we been brought to Europe so long ago. I know the answer to that: we would be dead of malnutrition, or worse. But maybe we would not have gone where we were told, and died when we were told. We have too many Rutherfords for that; and enough William S. Reardons to show us the way.

I wonder about the answer to the most obvious question: why didn't they fight? Why didn't they take up a shotgun and fight? Or a knife, or their fists? Why did they do nothing? It is incomprehensible. The papers tell us how the Germans made them go. But none of us understand how they could walk away trusting, and do what they were told to do. Fellows has tried to explain this: "They thought they weren't different. They forgot, or they didn't know. They're not like us. We know what we are: so do they, back home. And if they come for us, they know it's going to cost them. So they aren't going to come. Of course," Fellows says, to grind the rough edges from what he has said, "they're different back home. Take a look at the Colonel. Long as we got the Colonel, we're okay."

"Colonel's all right," Rutherford says, as though he has the authority to decide on the Colonel.

"That's what I said, Rutherford," Fellows says.

Fellows may be right, but I still don't understand the DPs: they laid themselves down, closed their eyes, folded their hands across their chests, told their children to shush and permitted themselves and their wives and children to be slaughtered. And now the few of them who have survived hold out their hands to us. I wonder what they would have said to us had they come across us in Georgia, or my south Chicago, or Rutherford's Kansas City. I doubt they would have said anything: DPs or not, I doubt they're different from anyone back home, and their eyes would have slid away as though we were part of the landscape even though we were standing right there in front of them talking to them.

Still, Fellows is right: we are different from the DPs. Growing up, we were taught that we were not required to shush and die; and with the Colonel to read the maps and hand out directions and say 'Uh-huh' at the right times, and the First Sergeant to tell us how to do what the Colonel orders, and Sam Turley to show us the way toward dawn, we are big enough to stand up against the darkness until morning comes.

Fifteen

South and east of Coburg, where the Seven Six One assisted the 71st Infantry Division with the investment of the city while artillery and tactical air pounded Fortress Coburg into surrender and where, it now appears, we may have fought our last action, we rattle and sway down a country lane, following the First Sergeant driving ahead in his Jeep.

It is afternoon and the First Sergeant and I and the six men in the maintenance track are looking for suitable accommodations for the night for the Seven Six One's Headquarters Company. The weather is warm—it is late April—and the war has become an easy drive through the lengthening days of spring. The Seven Six One, which is edging south toward Austria along country roads that parallel the one down which we drive, is becoming a tank battalion in an army marching against a disintegrating enemy.

The First Sergeant drives his Jeep as though he is out for a drive in the country back home: his right arm lies across the back of the right front seat and he leans back, his left hand on the top of the steering wheel, glancing from side to side at the scenery. Everything seems peaceful. But the First Sergeant is a careful man, and from the elevated vantage of the halftrack's cab I see a Thompson submachinegun clipped in a bracket in the center of the Jeep's dash and his Springfield rifle in the back seat.

"Warm spring day," Williston says as I glance to our right across one field and the next, and the next, where a track full of armored doughs jounces along through the afternoon sunlight, angling away from our track.

"Yes," I say. "Pretty nice around here. Farms, little towns. And not beaten up much. For once."

"You think we're going to leave these people hungry this winter? Like Fellows says?" Williston has told us more than once that most of the farms we have seen in Germany have not been worked this spring. He is right: the unploughed fields are producing crops of grass and weeds. But we see few animals, and I suspect the grass and weeds will grow through the summer, and that the weeds will grow higher than the grass.

"No," I say. "Right now we might think about leaving them destitute. But when the war's over, we'll come back with help."

"I'm glad to hear you say that," Williston says. Williston seems more worried about the future of Germany than anyone else I know. I wonder why. Perhaps it has something to do with the fact that his father is a minister, and with the violence we have inflicted and had inflicted upon us.

"First Sergeant's pointing," Williston says.

He is right: the First Sergeant is now driving with his right hand on the wheel, pointing across a field with his left arm, the forefinger aimed at a barn. The walls of the barn are of stone eight feet high and then of weathered grey wood rising to the eaves. The pitch of the roof is steep. I think of the snow that will cover this steep roof in six or seven months.

"Looks like maybe the First Sergeant's found a place to stay," Withers says from the track's bed.

"Think he'll let us sleep in one of the stalls?" Rutherford asks. "If Headquarters take up the front of the barn, we ought to get a stall for helping find this here hotel."

The First Sergeant ordered us to accompany him on this search for real estate because we have little left to do. Travelling by road, the Shermans go a long way between maintenance checks, and we have not fought since Coburg. Only the Battalion's trucks are working hard: they are hauling prisoners back up the line. But we do not maintenance trucks. Finding us out of work, the First Sergeant pressed us into his service as house hunters for the Colonel and the Colonel's Headquarters.

"I don't know about cleaning out some stable," Simpson says.

"I thought you knew all about that," Franklin tells him. "I thought that was your specialty in this crew, Simpson."

"Franklin," Fellows says, "you know Simpson a motor specialist, with only a side specialty in barn cleaning and privy scouring and such."

"Piss on that noise," Simpson says. He has learned this phrase from Rutherford, who learned it from 1st/Sgt. John P. Burch at the supply dump near Nancy. Rutherford and Simpson seem to think that if they say 'piss on that noise' the necessary number of times, the troops will unbutton. And one day, if they stay in the Army for another twenty-five years and become top kickers, it may be that those who hear them give the order to micturate will be impressed. We are not: Franklin yawns and Fellows looks out over the side of the track as though he is riding in a bus back home.

Still, Rutherford's and Simpson's repetition of 1st/Sgt. John P. Burch's injunction spreads 1st/Sgt. John P. Burch's influence east and south from

Nancy. Soon we will be in Austria, and when they speak 1st/Sgt. John P. Burch's words, Rutherford and Simpson will remind me of 1st/Sgt. John P. Burch burning with fever and shouting at the walls of his office. Reminding me of him, the phrase will also remind me that 1st/Sgt. John P. Burch provided the up-armored M4A3E2 Jumbo in which I went up to Klingenmünster as loader. Had 1st/Sgt. John P. Burch not been so open-handed with the Army's equipment, and had I gone up to Klingenmünster in an M4A3, I might have died a death as brutal and fearsome as those which McCarthy and Jackson suffered; and so I think of 1st/Sgt. John P. Burch with fondness each time Rutherford or Simpson says 'piss on that noise'.

Ahead of us the First Sergeant steers one-handed into the side road leading to the barn. Williston follows. The road is humpy, and the halftrack tilts and rocks as we follow First Sergeant Reardon bucketing along through the rustling shade beneath the spring leaves on the trees between which we drive. Far to the right, fields and fields away, the single halftrack full of armored doughs from the 71st Infantry Division trundles along, shifting through Germany toward Austria. I figure they are a mile away. Perhaps they too are looking for a barn in which to pass the night. We are lucky: they are not near enough to compete with us for the barn the First Sergeant has chosen for Headquarters Company for this night's stay.

The First Sergeant stops at a gate beside the road. Beyond the gate, an uncertain, weedy track leads along the edge of the field and then up a slight incline to the barnyard and the barn. The First Sergeant gets down, unlatches the gate and opens it. Surely, I think, this war is finished now. Were it not, the First Sergeant would have gestured us forward and we would have flattened a section of the fence. Who in war can care about a farmer's fence, or take the time to open a farmer's gate?

The First Sergeant gets back into his Jeep and drives through the gate. He stops fifty feet up the dirt track inside the fence and looks back. Williston drives the track through the gate and stops. Franklin jumps down from the back of the track. As he closes the gate, the First Sergeant nods. Then he drives on, turns left and accelerates up the slight slope toward the barnyard as though he has just remembered he has an appointment.

Franklin climbs up into the back of track, calls out "Okay", and Williston drives us along the way beside the fence.

The First Sergeant has halted the Jeep in front of the barn two hundred yards ahead. He gets down, stretches, glances back at us and goes to the barn door as we clatter forward. I see him knock at the double doors of the barn. I note that the barn's double doorway is large enough to admit a tractor or a haybaler.

It is peculiar to see the First Sergeant knocking on a door. We have not knocked on a door since November. We have not needed to: most of the doors we have seen were shattered by explosives or cracked apart by soldiers' boots. Those that were whole were left unlocked by the departed inhabitants so that soldiers would not batter them down.

The First Sergeant knocks, shrugs, pulls the righthand half of the double door open, swings it back against the wall of the barn and looks into the dark interior. Looking from the bright late afternoon into the darkness, I doubt he can see much. Still, I see the First Sergeant nod at what he sees as we trundle forward. It seems the barn must be roomy enough, and clean. And if it is clean it will be satisfactory and we will stop here and radio back to Headquarters Company to come on.

"Seems like. . . ," Withers says from the track's bed. The clatter of the tracks is louder than it should be—we will have to tension them tomorrow, or the day after—and I turn in my seat to hear what Withers has to say. But as I turn to Withers standing up behind the .30 caliber machinegun an automatic weapon begins to fire, and the swift ripping detonations of the cartridges as they cycle from the magazine into the breach, the rounds hammering out the barrel, the shell casings flicking from behind the slide snapping back and forth, tells me it is a German automatic weapon.

Withers's mouth is open, but he does not speak. I turn and see the First Sergeant stumbling backward, his heels dragging in the dirt. As he falls something spurts from his back and something else leaps from his lower chest and stomach and splashes down his thighs. His campaign hat is flicked away. It rolls on its brim through a tightening half-circle and halts, rocking on its crown.

The First Sergeant lies on his back in the dirt. His right knee is drawn up. His right arm is flung out as though he is pointing the way. The palm of his left hand lies against his chest. His face is turned toward us and his eyes are open. I note, as I have before, that his hair is grey at the temples. He looks old: I had not thought of him as old before. I thought he was immortal. Now, I know, he is dead: gone into the valley.

"Kill the motherfucker!" Rutherford shouts.

I look: Rutherford's is standing up in the bed of the track, his lips drawn back from his teeth. Grimacing, he swings his Schmeisser up, his right hand scrabbling at the cocking handle, cursing under his breath. The muzzle of the machinepistol shifts this way and that, threatening the horizon, threatening Williston's back, threatening the smooth soft spot between my eyes. I open my mouth to tell Rutherford to take care. Rutherford jerks at the cocking handle, jerks at it again. "Shit!" he says. Rutherford curses again and again as though someone has fiddled with his weapon and jammed it while he wasn't watching. He presses the release and drops the long straight clip from the bottom of the breach, jams it into his left rear pocket, yanks the slide back until it locks, holds the weapon up and with his picking fingernails dislodges the round jammed in the breach. The slide snaps closed. Rutherford jams the clip back up into the breach and yanks the slide back: he is at last ready to go. We are lucky we are not relying on Rutherford for covering fire.

"Take it easy," I say. I am talking to all six men in my crew, and to myself. Withers is standing up behind the .30 caliber machinegun, shifting the weapon this way and that, the muzzle bobbing and weaving. If he fires with the muzzle dancing right and left and up and down he may kill Williston and me sitting in front of him in the cab. It is certain he won't kill the German inside the barn. Franklin, Fellows and Simpson are crouched behind the high steel wall of the halftrack, M3 submachineguns in their fists. Their eyes and the muzzles of their weapons peep over the steel wall of the track. They point their weapons this way and that. If a robin flutters up from the woods beyond the barn, they will fire until they have expended all the ammunition we have. And we do not have much: this is a maintenance halftrack, and we carry peaceable tools and utilitarian spares and little ammunition.

Even Williston, who has been steady all the way from Camp Hood, Texas, and who knows driving a track and curing balky fuel systems better than anyone in the Seven Six One, is holding an M3 submachinegun in both hands and shifting the muzzle this way and that as though his target is zigging and zagging across the barnyard.

"Put those weapons on safe," I tell them. "I don't see anything to shoot and I don't want you shooting up the First Sergeant any more than he is. Besides: a single weapon fired. I figure there's just one man out there. Anyone see where it came from?"

"Right out the fucking barn's door," Simpson says. "I saw the muzzleflashes back in the dark."

"Anyone else?" I ask.

"It came from the barn all right," Fellows says. "I saw it." He is as certain about this as he has been about everything else since 1942.

"I didn't see a Goddamned thing," Franklin says. He seems ashamed he did not see the muzzleflash of the weapon that killed First Sergeant Reardon.

"Rutherford?" I ask.

"Let's go on up there and kill that motherfucker," he shouts. He is furious: furious that we are wasting time while the man with the machinepistol may be creeping out the back of the barn; more furious that someone has killed the First Sergeant; and even more furious that the First Sergeant has been killed now we all thought the war was over.

"Easy now," I tell him. "Everybody take it easy." I am still speaking to all seven of us. We are tense, and we do not know how to do what we are going to have to do. We are not armored doughs from the 71st and we do not know how to assault a building with thick walls of stone and wood.

On the other hand, only one weapon fired.

On the other hand, the rest of the sonsofbitches may be waiting for us to come on up into the barnyard where the First Sergeant lies in the dirt.

On the other hand, we cannot leave First Sergeant Reardon lying dead in front of the open barn door. Every man in this track would rather lie dead in the dirt beside the First Sergeant than leave him there while we call for help.

"So?" Williston says. He is talking to me: he wants to cut through my aimless thoughts. "Tell us what we going to do. First Sergeant's lying up there, and you're the man now. So tell us."

On the other hand, we could call the Colonel. But I know that though the First Sergeant may be dead, he is looking at me, and I know that if I suggest we call the Colonel, the First Sergeant will lower the brim of his campaign hat and breathe through his nose until I think again.

"We're going up there," I say. "But we're going up there careful. I don't want anyone rushing up, or getting in front of that barn door." I wonder why the First Sergeant opened the door without considering whether someone inside the barn might try to kill him. Perhaps he too thought the war was over. "Williston is going to drive us up there and get the track up beside the stone wall of that barn. Simpson, Fellows, Withers, Franklin: when we get down, you go around back. Watch the back and the other side. Don't anyone shoot unless you see a German with a weapon in his hands. Or until I say."

"What if we don't hear you?" Simpson asks.

"We'll hear him," Fellows says.

"Goddamnit, you guys listen to me." I'm not going to let them wrangle: not with First Sergeant Reardon waiting for us to come up. "One way or another, you wait. If you hear someone shoot, then shoot if you see something. If you don't see anything, don't shoot. But if you see a German in a uniform, and with a weapon, kill him. Don't shoot at him: kill him.

But don't start shooting holes in the barn because you get nervous or hear something. You might kill one of us over on this side. You with me?"

I hear a doubtful affirmative mumble. At least I hear no objections.

Simpson says, "You want me to call in about this now?"

"No," I say. "We're going to do this without the Colonel telling us, or the Shermans backing and filling, or the gun boss who commands the 71st Infantry Division rattling up here in a track, or the walking boss in command at corps standing on a rise pointing toward the next hill, or the riding boss the fucking Army commander the Green Hornet himself yelling down the field telephone from an office. We don't need anyone to help us with this thing. We're going up there and we're going to get this sonofabitch, and we're going to do it ourselves. But hear me: we aren't going to kill him until we know who he is. And we aren't going to kill him at all if he comes out without a weapon and surrenders."

Rutherford starts to speak. But I know what he is going to say: he is going to quote 1st/Sgt. John P. Burch yet again. But this is not a supply dump in Nancy, or a jungle on Guadalcanal, or the old Army in which 1st/Sgt. John P. Burch and First Sergeant William S. Reardon served. This is here, and I am not going to kill anyone who is trying to surrender, for I know I will think about this late April afternoon as long as I live, and I know I do not want to recall that I arranged a lynching in Germany in April, 1945, even if I did not use a rope. I also know that if I assist in the murder of an unarmed man, I will see the First Sergeant's disapproving face each time I think of this barn and barnyard so far from home.

"No," I say before Rutherford can speak. "We're going to do this my way. Williston, drive up along this track here. Go wide to the right close to the fence so he can't shoot at us from inside the barn. All of you in the back get down."

Williston drives forward along the fence to our right. When we are opposite the middle of the long stone footing beneath the barn's timber wall, Williston turns hard left, drives straight toward the barn, swings the halftrack parallel to the stone wall, and stops. We are close enough so that I can reach out and touch the rough stones.

Simpson, Fellows, Withers and Franklin jump down hunched over out of the door at the rear of the halftrack and jog hunched over to the rear of the barn. They halt. Simpson peeks around the corner, draws his head back, looks over his shoulder and shows the three men with him, and Williston, Rutherford and me getting down from the track, his thumb stuck straight up from his balled fist.

The four of them disappear around the corner of the barn. Williston and Rutherford and I stand close against the armored side of the track away from the barn. Rutherford holds his Schmeisser in both hands. Williston and I carry M3 submachineguns slung over our shoulders.

"What we going to do now?" Rutherford whispers. He is impatient: he would rather have blasted the barn with Withers's .30 caliber machinegun and charged inside shooting. But I don't want anyone else killed, and I ignore his impatience. How would I explain another death to the Colonel, and Captain Knowles—and myself?

"Anyone know enough German to call out to whoever's in there?" Williston whispers. "I can't get my tongue around the words."

"I don't know any except that Kamerad they say," Rutherford says, "and we ain't got no time right now for no language lesson."

"It's worth a try," I say.

"What you know?" Rutherford asks. He eyes me. The tone of his voice is full of suspicion and menace, as though he thinks I may have been a German spy all along.

"Some," I say. "Few words. Worked the kitchen in a restaurant summers in Chicago. German restaurant. Picked up a few words."

"Yeah," Rutherford says. "Like Sauerkraut and Wiener Schnitzel."

"More like orders," I tell him. "Come, go, bring this, bring that. I was on the ordered side of the kitchen. Seems about right for this situation here: this man in the barn is on the ordered side now."

"Huh," Rutherford says. "I thought maybe you was the head waiter or something."

"Let's get on with this," Williston says. He cocks his head to one side as he whispers the last word and says, "Track coming. Long way off, though."

The three of us glance about. "There," Rutherford says. He points across the fields past a woods. A track is coming cross-country. I guess it is a mile away: fields, fences and streams separate it from us. As I watch, the track drives into a fence, stops, reverses, drives forward into the fence again. The fence sways but it does not break. I guess this is the track full of armored doughs I saw as we drove behind First Sergeant Reardon toward this barn. But they are not going to help us: they will not be here soon enough to help us with what we must do.

"Piss on them," Rutherford says. "I thought you said this here is something we're going to do?"

"It is," I tell him. "Even if all of Third Army's coming, we're going to do this before they get here."

"Then let's get on with it."

"All right," I say. "You two stay behind me. I'm going up to the end of the barn here and call out to whoever's inside there."

"What if he don't answer?" Rutherford asks. "What if he don't come out? What if he fire?"

"We'll deal with all that when it happens. But he can't get out the back now, and we're okay as long as we stay behind this stone wall." I nod beyond the halftrack at the eight-foot high stone wall on which the timber wall of the barn is built. The stones are morticed together and I guess this wall would stop a 76 millimeter round. For sure it is going to stop anything that comes out the barrel of an MP-40 machinepistol like the one in Rutherford's hands.

"And if he don't come out," Rutherford says, "then we go in and get him."

"No we don't," I say. "If he won't come out, I'm going to burn this fucking barn down on top of him. And if he comes out of the fire holding a weapon I'll kill him myself."

"That sounds simple enough," Williston says, as though I have just instructed him in the operation of a mace.

"No one's going into that barn," I tell them. "This guy's got three choices: surrender when I call out to him, burn, or get shot dead."

Rutherford and Williston look me over. I must sound pretty tough, but I worry that I may have to do what I say and burn this barn down. I worry even more that a man clutching a machinepistol may run out of the flame and smoke of the burning barn and I will have to shoot at him until I kill him.

"All right," Rutherford says. "Sound good enough to me."

"Burn the barn down?" Williston asks, as though he has now remembered that he wrote the insurance on the barn.

"That's it," Rutherford says. "Sound all right to me. I didn't think: I would have gone in there."

"And got killed," Williston says. "Still, burn down this here barn?"

"You want to stride on in there, Williston?" Rutherford asks. "Shit," he tells me, "I think we ought to skip your ten words of German and burn the fucking thing down right on top of this motherfucker right now and get it over with."

"If he comes out without a weapon, Rutherford, I don't want you shooting at him. You understand me?"

"I hear you."

"I know you hear me. What I want is for you to do what I tell you."

"All right," Rutherford says. "All fucking right."

"You two stay behind me, now," I say. I unsling the M3 submachinegun, cock it and put it on safe. I ease around the front of the halftrack and step up close to the rough stone wall. I creep forward to the corner of the barn and dart my head out and jerk it back. I saw nothing but a barnyard and the First Sergeant lying dead in the dirt, the uniform shirt over his lower chest and stomach and thighs soaked with blood, the grey dirt beneath him stained red. But the upper half of his chest is whole, and so is his face: thank Christ his face was not shot away.

Seeing him dead, I realize I will never again hear anyone call out, 'First Sergeant coming!' as I have heard them call out during the past two-and-a-half years. No matter who becomes the Seven Six One's top kicker now, I will recall William S. Reardon whenever anyone says, 'the First Sergeant'.

Behind me Rutherford is breathing and hitching his machinepistol this way and that. Williston stands beside him, waiting for me to do the next thing. I am surprised that Williston can be so relaxed.

"*Kommen aus,*" I say. It is almost German, and I hope whoever is inside the barn almost understands it.

I peek around the corner, and as I do I hear movement inside the barn. Footsteps and a snuffling sound. I am about to call out again when a machinepistol flicks out of the barn door into the light, cartwheeling over and over. Its frame stock strikes the ground and it clatters and slides in the dirt. Before I can see whether a clip is fitted into the weapon in front of the triggerguard, the clip comes flicking out of the barn, flying end over end.

The end, I think.

"That's it," Rutherford says. He pushes past me.

I grab him by the arm and say, "Get back." He turns his face and I see his what-you-grabbing-my-arm-for frown. "You certain," I ask him, "two more of them aren't waiting in there? Or that whoever threw out that weapon doesn't have a pistol in his hand?"

Rutherford looks at me and nods. As he nods his frown dissolves. He steps back and stands with Williston. Williston shakes his head as though he doesn't think much of Rutherford's judgment.

I listen. Whoever it is inside the barn is shuffling toward the door from within. He is making a peculiar snuffling sound with his mouth and nose. He sounds as though he has a bad headcold. Or is it an animal? No: I hear the chink of metal fastenings on an equipment harness. This is a man, and he is shuffling toward the open door of the barn.

"He's coming," I say. I gesture with my left arm at Williston and Rutherford to shift them left to cover the man when he steps out of the barn. I peek around the corner again. I see nothing: the feet are still shuffling forward, the peculiar snuffling approaching the doorway in front of which, ten feet away, the First Sergeant lies.

I glance up: across the barnyard to the right at the edge of the woods behind the sturdy fencing, Fellows kneels behind a tree. He is aiming his M3 Grease Gun toward the barn: toward me. Fellows has seen the machinepistol and the long black clip of 9 millimeter shells flick out into the sunlight and he is getting ready to fire at whoever comes out of the gloom inside the barn. I shake my head at Fellows and go on shaking it: if he fires his weapon, he may kill Williston, Rutherford, and me—and, if he is lucky, he will also kill the German shuffling and snuffling his way toward the barn door.

Fellows does not see me shaking my head. I wave my arm at him, and he notices me. I gesture that he should go where I told him to go: behind the barn. He shrugs, nods and eases back into the woods.

I step away from the side of the barn and point the M3 submachinegun in my hands around the corner of the barn at the space in front of the door. I snap the weapon's safety down. "No shooting now," I caution Rutherford and Williston without looking at them. If anyone is going to shoot someone, I will do it: shooting, as the First Sergeant once said, is my job.

As I speak a boy in a man's Wehrmacht uniform comes out of the doorway. His dirty hands are raised, his thin wrists stuck up out of the sleeves of the heavy cloth folded back and pinned up with safety pins. He is terrified: of what he has done, I hope; and of what he fears will now be done to him, I suppose. His eyes are squeezed shut, as though he cannot bear to watch what he knows we are going to do to him. His face is dirty and he is weeping. Tears run down his dirty cheeks. I wonder how old he can be: thirteen? fourteen?

I know what he will say: a mistake. A simple mistake. I didn't know, he'll say.

"Well Jesus lookit here," Williston says. He is as surprised as I am: we both expected a giant storm trooper to march out of the barn.

"Goddamnit all," Rutherford says, as though he has been denied something he thought he had coming to him.

I step out into the barnyard, but I stay away from the doorway in case this boy brought a friend along. "You," I say.

The boy forces himself to open his eyes, as though he knows what he will see and does not want to see it. Looking away from the needle sliding into his arm, I think.

I gesture with the submachinegun in my hands. He stares at me. I gesture again, and say, "*Komm* here." He shuffles toward me. I glance down: his boots are two sizes too large. His hands still up in the air, snuffling and weeping, he shuffles forward in the man's boots he won't need for six or seven years. Or ever, if he's lucky.

He is terrified: he thinks I am going to shoot him and kill him. He does not know the First Sergeant still stands behind me, watching what I do.

The boy steps around the corner of the barn and I gesture at him to stop. He stands with his back to the stone footing. I sling the submachinegun over my shoulder and step up to him. I raise my right hand: a hard slap across his face will not constitute a lynching. But I drop my hand when I hear the First Sergeant ask me what the hell I think I'm doing.

"Goddamnit to hell," Rutherford says. He steps up next to me and menaces the boy with the muzzle of his machinepistol, grimacing as though he knows he is not going to like the noise the weapon in his hands will make when he fires it.

"No," I tell him. "Put up that weapon."

"This son of a bitch," Rutherford says.

"Yes," I say. "But no shooting."

"Goddamnit," Rutherford says. "Goddamnit to hell." He throws his beloved Schmeisser down on the ground and stamps his right boot on it. Then he bends down and snatches it from the ground and wipes the dust and dirt from it.

"Easy," Williston tells him. "That's not going to help out here."

"Going to help me out," Rutherford shouts.

"Calm down till I ask him if he's got any friends," I say. I look at the boy, point at the barn behind the boy's back and say, "*Ist mann da?*"

He shakes his head and says, "*Nein. Nein, keiner.*"

"What's he say?" Williston asks.

"Says no one else is in the barn."

"You sure?" Rutherford asks. He is angry, and his anger makes him doubt my ability as a translator.

"No," I tell him, "I'm not sure." I know my German is what I said it was: ten words. I look the boy in the face and ask him once again, "*Ist mann da? Oder zwei oder drei mann?*"

"*Nein, nein,*" he says, and shakes his head. "*Keiner.*"

"He still says there's no one there," Williston says.

"That's it," I say. But who can know? "Williston, you hold him here while Rutherford and I take a look."

"Okay," Williston says.

"And, Williston: no shooting," I say.

"You think I'm going to shoot this child?" he asks me. "I'm not going to shoot him: I want him to remember what he's done until he's an old man, and I want him to live a long life."

"All right. Rutherford, you ready?"

"I been ready all Goddamn along," Rutherford says.

I step out from behind the protection of the stone footing of the barn and peek through the doorway into the shadows beyond. I see nothing. I dash through the doorway and duck into the shadows. Rutherford is right behind me. I sniff: the barn does not smell of animals, and I wonder when the farmer sold his last steer and his last horse.

"I don't hear nothing," Rutherford says from the shadows beside me.

I nod and listen: I hear nothing except Rutherford's breathing, and my own.

We edge down the length of the barn's interior past a farm cart, a harrow, farm implements hung on wooden pegs in the walls, a tractor with flat tires, rust eating through the paint on the fenders, a pump on a low concrete platform. We hear nothing.

"Spooky in here," Rutherford says. I look at him and raise my eyebrows. He grins: I knew his usual good humor would return.

At the back of the barn behind a stall in which leather bridles and collars and bits of linked chain hang on nails driven into the thick plank walls, we find the place from which the boy fired his weapon and killed the First Sergeant. Brass cartridge cases litter the packed earth floor of the barn. A small pack leans against the stall. It is not a soldier's pack: it is the kind of small pack in which a boy out for a hike would carry his lunch. Beside it is a gas mask container, a canteen and a small bundle of grey cloth. Rutherford opens the bundle and shows me the contents: four inches of hard stale sausage and two slices of stale bread.

"Holed up here," Rutherford says. "I wonder what he was waiting here for."

"The end of the war, I suppose. Let's check the loft."

"Check the ladder first," Rutherford says. He walks to a ladder leading from the floor of the barn to the loft. He examines the rungs. "Dust all over them ain't been disturbed," he says. "No one up there."

"You're sure?" I'm a city boy.

"Been working in barns around east Kansas since I was a boy. No one up there at all."

"Let's take his stuff and go out and call this in."

Rutherford slings his machinepistol. We walk to where the boy hid. Rutherford picks up the small pack, the canteen, the gas mask container and the bundle. It is not much of a load.

We go out of the barn. Williston stands with the boy, the strap of his submachinegun over his shoulder, the weapon's muzzle pointed at the ground in front of him, his right hand near the M3's pistol-grip just in case.

He has let the boy take his hands down. When the boy sees Rutherford and me he puts his hands back up. Williston says something to him, frowns and gestures for him to put his hands down.

"Found this stuff here," Rutherford tells Williston, showing him the things in his hands. "Nothing more. And no one else in the barn."

"That's one thing right, at least," Williston says. "What now?"

"Williston, call in to the Colonel. Tell the Colonel himself: no one else. Rutherford, leave that stuff here. Go call Fellows and the rest of them and then get some blankets and cover the First Sergeant up."

"What you going do?" Rutherford asks, as though he thinks my division of the work is unfair.

"Watch this boy here."

"He don't look like he need much watching," Rutherford says.

"He stays right here until this is sorted out. Until then he needs watching. I'll set Simpson and Fellows to guard him when they get here. Then I'll come over and help you get the First Sergeant ready."

"All right," Rutherford says. He sounds dispirited. "But I still say: Goddamnit." The boy recognizes the last word and looks troubled. As well he might: he seems to know what a stupid senseless thing he has done. I hope he remembers thirty years from now.

Rutherford and Williston walk to the halftrack. Williston gets up in the bed and makes the call while Rutherford walks on to the back of the barn. I can see Williston is troubled that he must tell the Colonel what has happened. I watch as he waits for the Colonel to come up on the radio. Then I watch as he explains. The Colonel does not interrupt him. Williston tells it all and then he listens. I can tell the Colonel does not say much: what is there to say?

Williston puts the microphone down and nods to me from the track as Rutherford, Fellows, Franklin, Simpson and Withers come around the back of the barn. Rutherford gets up in the back of the track: to get blankets to cover the First Sergeant's body.

Fellows, Franklin, Simpson and Withers walk toward us. As they come up they eye the boy who killed the First Sergeant. I expect them to comment, but it seems Rutherford has told them all they need to know. They look the boy over and shake their heads and turn away. When they turn their backs on him the boy looks at them and begins to weep.

"Those armored doughs coming," Williston calls down from the track.

Across the field beyond the fence the armored doughs' halftrack is approaching. A man crouches behind the machinegun in the front of the bed. He is bareheaded. As I look, he bends down, picks up a helmet and puts it on. I know what he is thinking: the fucking war has begun again. The armored visors are closed over the track's windshield, and the armored doughs in the back are crouched down behind the steel walls. These doughs have come a long way from the English Channel and they are not taking any chances now they are nearing Austria and the end of the war.

Wood creaks and splinters and the halftrack's engine roars as the halftrack's driver rams through the fence between the field and the barnyard. The track drives up the slight incline and stops. The doughs dismount as the Germans have taught them to: crouching, hurrying, but hurrying with care. The man who gets down from the passenger's side of the cab is a sergeant. He looks at us, speaks to his men and walks across. He is a tall, strong and he has not shaved for three days.

"Heard the shooting," he says. "Thought we ought to come on over."

"Everything's all right now," I tell him. The sergeant looks beyond me at the boy in the man's Wehrmacht uniform. Then he looks at the First Sergeant's body.

"Man killed?" I watch Rutherford get down from our track with two blankets over his right arm. He walks past us toward the First Sergeant lying out dead in the late afternoon sunlight.

"Our First Sergeant. Battalion Headquarters' First Sergeant."

"Sorry about that," the armored doughs' Sergeant says. "Regular, was he?" I suppose he has noted the grey hair at the First Sergeant's temples. Or perhaps he has heard a lifetime of service in the statutory regiments is necessary to acquire the rank of a first sergeant.

"Yes," I say.

"Shit," the Sergeant says. "Sorry," he says. I cannot tell if he is apologizing because he has cursed, or extending his sympathy again.

"It's all right," I tell him.

"Anything we can do?" the Sergeant asks.

"No," I say. "Thanks, but no."

"You'll be all right?"

"We'll take care of him."

"And the kid?" he gestures at the boy standing with his back to the wall of the barn, his dirty face bent toward the dirt in front of his feet. "You want us to take him?"

"No," I tell him. "We can handle him."

The sergeant looks at me. Then he looks away at his men clustered beside their halftrack. They are tired, pale and thin. They are disgusted that someone else has been killed, and for no reason. But they are bored, too: they wish more than anything—even more than they wish the First

Sergeant and everyone else dead had not been killed—that they were not here. They have had a bad war: worse, I know, than we have had. I doubt any of them will come back to Europe as tourists until they have grown old enough to persuade themselves that what they did over here was not that bad.

"We could deal with the little bastard if you want," the Sergeant says.

"We can get him to the MPs," I say.

"The MPs?" he asks. "I know you can get him to the MPs, if you want. I just thought maybe you'd like us to take him off your hands."

I am not sure what he is saying, but I say, "No. We'll turn him in to the MPs."

"That's it, then?" the Sergeant asks. He looks grim, as though the boy presents a problem the military police can't solve.

"That's it," I tell him. "We'll just put up with it. Like everybody's had to put up with all the rest of it over here."

"Amen, brother," the Sergeant says. "If there's anything you need, though?"

"We're all right. Colonel's coming. We can sort this out with him."

"Okay, then: your Colonel. Ours got killed in the Siegfried Line. That was a shitty day. So's this one, even though the sun's shining. All right, though: what the fuck? We'll take off. Look me up if you get to Cleveland. Dombrowski, Charles S. I'm in the book. Or I'll be in the book when they turn me loose of this suit and this place. You know my grandfather came from no more than three hundred miles northeast of here? Philly to Boston, about. No wonder he left: all this shit over here?"

"I know," I say. "Thanks for coming over, Sergeant."

"Nothing." Sergeant Dombrowski turns to his men standing around and as he walks to their track he calls out, "Everything's under control here. Let's take off." His men nod and mutter to one another. I cannot hear what they say, but I know they are pleased they have no work to do. They get up in the track. Dombrowski climbs up in the right hand front seat and waves as the driver gets the halftrack going and circles away from the barn and drives back through the gap he battered in the fence. Soon they are jouncing across the field beyond the fence, heading back the way they came.

Williston says, "Colonel's coming, like you told those doughs. Ten minutes, he said. Said to get the First Sergeant ready."

"We'll do that," I say. "Williston, you stay here and help me and Rutherford with the First Sergeant. The rest of you take that boy over to the track and watch him. Take his stuff, too. And be easy: this is finished, and we don't want to do anything we'll think about later."

Franklin, Withers and Simpson nod and walk off toward the boy standing against the stone wall of the barn. Fellows waits until they have walked up to the boy and picked up his pack and gas mask container and canteen and bundle and gestured him toward the track. Then Fellows says, "Sorry about creeping around in front of the barn like that."

"Glad I caught your eye," I say. I smile to show him no harm was done.

"So am I," he says. "I don't know what I was thinking."

"Neither did he, I guess." I nod at the boy trudging toward the track, Simpson, Withers and Franklin walking with him.

"He tell you why he shot?" Fellows asks.

"I can't talk to him. I guess he got scared when the First Sergeant opened the door, and he started shooting before he thought about it."

Fellows shakes his head as though he doesn't know what to say. He turns and walks away toward Franklin, Withers, Simpson and the boy getting up into the track.

"Go on over?" Williston asks. He nods toward Rutherford and the First Sergeant.

"Yes." Rutherford has straightened the First Sergeant's legs and bent the First Sergeant's right arm and placed the hand on his chest and covered him up to the collar with a blanket. As I watch, Rutherford shakes the other blanket out and spreads it on the ground beside the First Sergeant. "What about the boy?"

"Send him back," Williston says. "What else?"

"We'll send him back. Question is: is there anything else we ought to do?"

Williston thinks about it and says, "He ought to remember this."

"Yes."

"Give him dinner?" Williston says. "We'll be here for the night. Give him dinner and then take him on back."

"All right," I tell him. "Good thought."

"Easy," Williston says. "Be dinnertime soon, and we can stay here tonight."

"And the Colonel?" I ask. "We were looking for a place for Headquarters Company to stay the night."

"You tell him we're going to have this boy stay here with us for dinner, Colonel will find somewhere else for Headquarters Company tonight. We can rely the Colonel. As always."

"All right," I say.

Williston and I walk to where Rutherford waits with the First Sergeant. I walk four more steps and pick up the First Sergeant's campaign hat. I brush the dirt from the crown and turn it over. As I do so the acorns at the ends of the blue cord around the base of the crown brush the back of my right hand. I look at the leather band inside the hat. Inked in the leather is '1st/Sgt.' To the right of '1st/Sgt.', crossed out but still readable, is 'Sgt.', and to the right of 'Sgt.' is his name, William S. Reardon. I don't know what the 'S' stands for: now I will never know. I note that the First Sergeant has fitted folded paper between the leather band and the felt. I wonder whether the hat was too large when he bought it. Then I recall the grey hair at the First Sergeant's temples, and guess his hair has thinned since he made sergeant and bought this hat.

I hand the First Sergeant's hat to Rutherford and kneel on the blanket Rutherford spread beside the First Sergeant's body. The First Sergeant's eyes are open. His right cheek lies against the earth.

"I didn't want to touch his face," Rutherford says.

"It's all right," I say. I place my left hand beneath the First Sergeant's right cheek and my right hand on the left side of his head. As I touch him I recall the clammy feel of the rubber gloves on my right hand as I lifted Tom Holcomb's sliding guts from the floor of Big Sam and fitted them back inside the empty cavity between Holcomb's breastbone and groin. But I have no rubber gloves here, and I would not pull them on if I did.

The First Sergeant's skin is warm. I turn his head until he faces the clear blue sky. Then I close his eyes as Sergeant Herman closed Lieutenant Donald R. Lovejoy's eyes.

"Let me get the blanket down off him so you can get at his things," Williston says. I can do this myself, but Williston wants to help.

"It's bad," Rutherford says. I nod: I know he is talking about the First Sergeant's wounds. Williston eases the blanket down from the First Sergeant's collar to his waist and I see that Rutherford is right: the Schmeisser's 9 millimeter rounds have torn up the First Sergeant's lower chest and stomach. I see bone and muscle and coagulating blood. But the First Sergeant trained me to do this work, and I do not flinch. I feel the late afternoon sunlight warm on the back of my neck and remind myself as I look at the First Sergeant that this is what he is; that this is what we all are, and what we will become.

Rutherford squats beside me, the First Sergeant's campaign hat in his hands. I empty the First Sergeant's pockets into the hat. Keys, a box of wooden matches, a handkerchief. I roll the First Sergeant's hips toward me to reach the pocket knife he held in his hand when he told Willy Thorn he was going to cut Thorn's Battalion patch off Thorn's jacket. In his left front pocket are two coins: a French one Franc piece and a German one

Mark piece. Both of them are stamped with the same date: 1918. I show the coins to Williston and Rutherford. They nod but they do not speak. I roll the First Sergeant's hips away from me and take a worn wallet from his left hip pocket. I do not open it: I will leave that, and the rest of his gear, to the Colonel. When I have emptied his pockets I slide the chain of the First Sergeant's dogtags up over his head, remove one tag from the chain and button it in the right pocket of his uniform shirt. I place the other tag with the rest of his possessions in his campaign hat.

I unbuckle the webbing belt from which the First Sergeant's holstered .45 Bisley Colt revolver is suspended and pull the belt from beneath his waist. I wind the bloody belt around and around the holster and lay the compact bundle of belt, holster and revolver on the blanket just above the First Sergeant's knees. Rutherford reaches past me and places the First Sergeant's campaign hat on the blanket over the First Sergeant's legs above the revolver in the holster wound inside the bloody webbing belt.

Rutherford and I stand up. I cannot look at Williston, or Rutherford. I stare down at the First Sergeant's campaign hat filled with the contents of his pockets.

Williston draws the blanket up to the First Sergeant's collar. He hesitates, looks up at me and says, "Cover him all up?"

"Leave his face uncovered until the Colonel gets here. Let's move him onto the blanket. Williston, you take his feet. Rutherford, take his shoulders."

Rutherford and Williston squat at the First Sergeant's head and feet. I walk around Rutherford and kneel in the dirt and work my hands beneath the First Sergeant's lower back. I feel the sharp ends of broken bones, and the thick, sticky pulp the 9 millimeter rounds have made of his muscle and flesh. I nod and we lift the First Sergeant and shift him onto the blanket Rutherford shook out and spread on the ground beside him.

My hands are smeared with blood. Williston and Rutherford look at my hands and look away.

"Colonel's coming," Williston says. Yesterday Williston said, 'First Sergeant's coming.' Now it is the Colonel. I hear nothing. "I hear a Jeep. And a track coming behind." Williston hears approaching machines long before anyone else in the maintenance track.

"Doc Turner coming with him, I bet," Rutherford says.

"He'll be here," I say. What would we do if Doc Turner and his medics and their ambulance track did not come forward with the Colonel?

"I'm going over to the track," I say. I hold my hands in front of me. My uniform is dirty, but I do not want the First Sergeant's blood on me. "You two stay here with him."

I walk across the barnyard to the rear of the track. I open the external door of the rear left equipment bin, take out a canteen and pour water over my hands. The water flows pink from my fingers. When I finish washing, I look through the rear door of the track. The German boy is sitting on one of the seats in the righthand side of the bed, his elbows on his knees, his face in his hands. Withers, Franklin, Simpson and Fellows are sitting and standing, murmuring to one another and glancing at the boy. They look sad. I am surprised: none of them knew the First Sergeant. But perhaps I should not be surprised, for no one in the Seven Six One knew the First Sergeant. I suspect even the Colonel did not know him. We knew what he was: uniform, chevrons, rockers and lozenge, campaign hat, diligent manner and straight back. We also knew he was there, somewhere, watching; and we knew that when we had trouble, he dealt with it. Whatever it was—a vicious fight against the Germans, incinerated men inside a Sherman, Willy Thorn or Johnny White, indiscipline, low morale, or the disparagement of us by others in the Army—he dealt with it. He was our spine, and our goad and our support. Without him we would have been another thing.

Fellows sees me looking up into the track and says, "This boy's troubled. Can't get through to him, can't understand what he says and he isn't saying much. Can't talk to him at all."

This German boy may be lucky he knows no English. If he knew English he would have to listen to Fellows's categorical explanations; though I guess listening to Fellows would be no worse than listening to lectures in school: declaratory, consistent and insubstantial, explaining everything, explaining nothing.

"He'll get over it," I say.

"You warrant me on that?" Simpson asks.

"Yes," I say. "We'll get over it too."

"I don't know about that," Withers says. "Losing the First Sergeant?"

"That was the point about him," I tell him.

"What's that mean?" Franklin asks.

"The First Sergeant. That was the point about him."

"I don't know what you mean," Franklin says.

I hear the Colonel's Jeep and Doc Turner's track coming up the narrow way inside the fence. "You'll figure it out," I tell Franklin. He opens his mouth to object, or to ask another question about what I have said. But I have no time: the Colonel is coming and he will want to hear what happened. "Take care of the boy. Bring him down if I call you. And think about what we're going to have for dinner."

Franklin, Simpson, Withers and Fellows look at me. "We're keeping him here for dinner. Then we're going to take him back."

Franklin, Simpson, Withers and Fellows look at me. "What kind of dinner?" Withers asks.

"Whatever you can find, or make. I want to feed him before he goes back."

Fellows nods and says, "I see."

"I don't," Simpson says.

Franklin shakes his head. Then he nods. Then he shakes his head again.

As I get down the Colonel's Jeep comes up the last of the incline to the barnyard. The Colonel is alone, driving himself. Doc Turner's ambulance track follows. When the Colonel halts his Jeep and gets down, the ambulance track stops a discreet fifty feet behind.

I salute the Colonel and he salutes me. "What happened?" he asks. He sounds tired and he looks upset. I tell him what happened. He listens to every word I say. He nods now and then, but he does not say "Uh-huh."

When I finish, the Colonel shakes his head and says, "I don't know what I'm going to write his wife and son about this."

"I didn't know he was married, sir," I say.

"Married, son fourteen." The Colonel shakes his head. "Damnit all," he says. "And the one who killed him?"

"He's in the track, sir, with four of my men. You want me to get him out here?"

"What for? No, I don't want to look at him."

"He's all right," I say.

The Colonel looks at me. "What else?" he says. "Williston said you took him prisoner."

"More like he gave up, sir. But he's all right, except he's crying and sobbing every now and then."

"Tough. Come on, let's go on over there."

The Colonel and I walk to where the First Sergeant lies on his back on one brown Army blanket, the second one drawn up to his collar. Williston and Rutherford salute the Colonel and the Colonel salutes them.

"We put his effects in his hat, sir," Rutherford says. "And got his revolver off him."

"Good," the Colonel says. He nods and looks at the First Sergeant's face. "Damnit all. Damnit all to hell," he says. He does not raise his voice when he says this. He is not cursing: he is mourning. He shakes his head and says, "Thanks for getting him ready."

"Yes, sir," Williston says.

"We left his face uncovered, sir," Rutherford says. "So you could. . . ."

"I know," the Colonel says. "Thanks. But damnit it all to hell." He bends down and picks up the First Sergeant's campaign hat. He looks into it and nods.

"We put one tag in his hat, sir," Rutherford says. "The other's in the right pocket of his shirt."

"You did well. All three of you. All seven of you." The Colonel bends again and picks up the bloody webbing belt wound around the holster and the First Sergeant's holstered revolver. He weighs it in his hand. "Damnit it all to hell, though," the Colonel says.

I agree with the Colonel: the First Sergeant's death is senseless.

"Where's his rifle?" the Colonel asks me.

"I saw it in his Jeep, sir," Williston says.

"All right. I'll get it. That's his rifle, and this revolver is his. I want to take them back to his wife and son when the war's over and we go home," the Colonel explains. "And his cigar case: he always left that in his Jeep."

"Yes, sir," I say.

The Colonel nods and nods as he looks at the First Sergeant's face. Then he says, "Cover his face up."

I stoop and pull the blanket up over the First Sergeant's face. As I do so the knuckles of my right hand brush his forehead and the thinning tight curls of his hair. I think of the paper fitted between the felt and the leather band inside his campaign hat.

"All right," the Colonel says. He holds the First Sergeant's antique hat in his right hand and the First Sergeant's revolver in his left. He does not seem to notice the sticky blood on the webbing belt wrapped around the holster. "All right then," he says. His eyes glitter, but I know he won't weep: he is the Colonel, and he will no more weep over the First Sergeant's body than the First Sergeant wept over the bodies of Sam Taylor's crew waiting for us inside Big Sam. Still, the Colonel has lost a friend, and he is having difficulty controlling himself.

The Colonel turns and nods at Doc Turner. The Doc nods and starts forward, his men coming from behind the ambulance track carrying a stretcher. Williston, Rutherford, the Colonel and I step aside to let them work. Doc Turner does not speak while his men shift the blankets that contain the First Sergeant's body onto the stretcher. They get the stretcher up between them and Doc Turner nods at them and follows them back to their track.

"Damnit it all to hell," the Colonel says. He breathes and breathes again. As he breathes I note a tremor in his right arm and hand transmitted to the

First Sergeant's hat: the brim of the hat trembles as the Colonel's right hand trembles. "All right," the Colonel says. "All right, then. You men did well. All of you. Taking a prisoner without anyone getting hurt." Rutherford flicks his eyes at me and nods. "And to get the First Sergeant ready like this. You," he says to me, "walk over here to his Jeep with me. And you two," he says to Rutherford and Williston, "you did well. When I write his wife and son I'll mention every one of you in this crew."

I walk with the Colonel to the First Sergeant's Jeep. "One of you can drive the Jeep back," he says. "Tonight. Or tomorrow if you want to stay here." I glance over my shoulder. Doc Turner is standing by the open rear doors of the ambulance track watching his men slide the stretcher inside. "Bring his rifle," the Colonel says. He nods at the '03 Springfield laid across the back seat beside the antique bandoleer the First Sergeant wore over his shoulder and chest. "And the bandoleer and his cigar case down next to the seat."

"Yes, Colonel," I say. I take the First Sergeant's rifle and the bandoleer of ammunition clips from the back and fish his cigar case from beside the driver's seat. I follow the Colonel to his Jeep. He places the First Sergeant's campaign hat full of the contents of the First Sergeant's pockets on the right front seat and puts the First Sergeant's revolver on the back seat. The Colonel takes the bandoleer from me and lays it on the front seat in front of the First Sergeant's hat so that the hat will not shift during the drive back down the track and the country road. I lay the First Sergeant's rifle on the back seat of the Colonel's Jeep beside his holstered revolver and put the cigar case in the First Sergeant's hat with the rest of his things. Then I wait for the Colonel to tell me what to do next.

"A thing like this," the Colonel says. He looks at me. "You knew him."

"A little, sir. We did some work together." The Colonel nods: he knows the work I did with the First Sergeant.

"I want you to come back tonight, or tomorrow morning early, and get his things ready. Will you do that?"

I wonder why he doesn't do it himself, or have someone in Headquarters Company do it. But he is asking me, and I say, "Yes, sir. I'll come tonight after dinner. I'll come about seven, if that's all right."

"Fine. Any time you want. Come to the Headquarters track. That's where he kept his stuff. Get it and take it to my tent. You can sort it out there. I'll tell them you're coming."

"Yes, sir," I say.

"He was a good man," the Colonel says.

"Yes, Colonel."

"I don't know where I'd be if he hadn't been here."

"Yes, sir."

The Colonel nods and nods. "You did the right thing with the boy who killed him. Taking him prisoner, I mean."

"Thank you, sir."

"Hand him over to Doc Turner. He can ride back with the Doc. I don't want him in my Jeep. I don't want to talk to him or see him."

"Sir," I say, "we thought we would keep him here and feed him dinner and then bring him back."

The Colonel looks at me and looks away. I wonder what he thinks. Then he looks at me again and nods. "All right," he says. He looks at his watch. "About four-thirty now. You'll come at seven? We're about a mile back, in a field beside the turnoff to the road that leads here. You'll come at seven, to go through the First Sergeant's gear and get it ready?"

"Yes, sir," I say.

"All right, then," the Colonel says. He gets into his Jeep. Doc Turner is watching us. The Doc nods at his driver and the driver and Doc Turner get up into the ambulance halftrack. The rear doors are closed: the medics are inside in the dark with the First Sergeant.

The Colonel starts the engine of his Jeep. "About seven, then," he says.

"Yes, sir. Seven o'clock sharp. I'll be there. We'll hand the boy over to the MPs and then I'll come and do the First Sergeant's effects."

"I'll have the MPs there," the Colonel says. He puts the Jeep in gear but he does not let in the clutch. He looks up at me and salutes. Before I can return the salute he turns in his seat and salutes Rutherford and Williston standing in the barnyard. Then he salutes Franklin, Withers, Fellows and Simpson standing up in the maintenance halftrack watching us. We all salute him with a ragged, uncoordinated movement of our arms. He nods at us and lets in the clutch and the Jeep eases away. The Colonel steers with his left hand, steadying the First Sergeant's campaign hat with his right. The ambulance track follows the Colonel's Jeep. As it moves off Doc Turner raises his hand.

Rutherford, Williston and I walk to the track. Withers and Franklin are getting down, carrying their M3 submachineguns. Simpson and Fellows are peering over the side of the track.

"Where are you two going?" I ask Withers and Franklin.

"Take a look around," Franklin says. "Got to be a house nearby here. Maybe we'll find something to add to the rations."

I think about it. If there were other Germans nearby they have departed: the single ripping burst from the boy's submachinegun would have told them it was time to go. "Don't go far," I say. "And don't go in any houses." I don't want them opening any doors. They nod and go off.

"What now?" Rutherford asks.

"Dinner. Let's get ready."

"This boy here is upset as hell," Fellows says. He looks down at us from the track and shakes his head. "Won't stop crying, and he's all scrunched up there in the front of the track. I don't like to see that," he says.

"He'll be all right once he eats something," I say.

"May be," Simpson says. "Or not."

"There's a pump in the barn," I tell Fellows. "See if you can find a bowl. Get water and have him wash his face and hands."

"Good thought," Fellows says. He gets down from the track with a canteen in his right hand and goes off to the barn. Simpson and Williston begin lifting rations and cooking utensils out of the track's storage bins.

"Build a fire?" Rutherford asks.

"Yes. Let's get some wood. It's been dry the last week, it should start easy enough."

"If it don't, they's gasoline to help out."

"Williston, you and Simpson keep an eye on that boy."

"Don't seem he need much watching," Williston says.

"Watch him anyway."

Rutherford and I climb the fence in front of the woods where Fellows lurked. We walk among the trees collecting fallen sticks and breaking dry limbs over our knees. When we each have an arm full we climb back over the fence and walk toward the track. As we do, Fellows comes out of the barn with his canteen in one hand and a white enamelled bowl in the other. He walks with care, and I know he has found the pump and filled the bowl with water. He carries it to the track and calls to the boy sitting inside the four steel walls and gestures up through the track's rear door. He gestures again and the boy comes to the rear door of the track and gets down. Fellows sets the bowl on the sill of the rear door, climbs up into the track and hands the boy a towel and soap and makes washing movements with his hands. The boy looks at the towel in his right hand and the soap in his left. Fellows moves his hands again and the boy nods, drapes the towel over his shoulder and begins to wash his hands and face.

Withers and Franklin come around the rear of the barn. Withers carries a chicken in each hand. He holds the chickens by the feet. The chickens' heads swing and jerk at the ends of their broken necks. Withers grins and says: "They didn't resist, and they're not thin."

"Withers is pretty quick on his feet," Franklin says, "when it comes to chickens. 'Course I taught him near all he knows about chickens."

Withers holds up the birds. They are plump. I am surprised: I have not seen many plump farm animals, or for that matter plump people, in the last six months.

"Rutherford and I are doing the fire," I say. "Simpson and Williston are getting the rest of dinner ready. Fellows is tending the boy."

They glance at the boy washing his hands and face. Fellows stands over the boy as though he wants to be sure he washes behind his ears. Fellows, I note, is now holding the towel the boy draped over his shoulder. The boy finishes washing and Fellows hands him the towel and watches while he dries his hands and face. Then Fellows shoos him back up into the track. I note the .30 caliber machinegun swinging on the pintle at the front of the bed, but I know this boy is not going to do any more shooting. Not today; and if he is lucky, not ever again.

"And we're doing these chickens," Franklin says. He glances toward the front of the barn where the First Sergeant lay. "We'll clean them back of the barn," he says.

"You see a wood pile back there?" Rutherford asks. "We need two logs to rest the pot on."

"Wood pile, Mr. Rutherford? Sure there's a wood pile. Got all the logs you want back there."

Rutherford brings two sawn logs from behind the barn and he and I build a fire between them. Williston and Simpson bring our messkits and the pot we took last November from an abandoned farm house near Morhange far to the west in France. Our need, we reasoned, was greater than that of the departed farmer and his family; and the First Sergeant, we figured, would not call taking an old pot looting.

Williston and Simpson have filled the pot with water and the contents of what appear to be several Menus No. 1, 2, and 3. I look at the mess in the pot and am glad that Withers and Franklin found the chickens. We watch the fire burn and the water heat until Franklin and Withers come around the end of the barn, holding the gutted, bloody plucked birds in their hands. They go into the barn and I hear the pump screech. They come out of the barn, the chickens white and yellow in their hands. Williston, who has appointed himself chef, takes the two chickens and lowers them into the boiling water.

"Pretty soon now," Williston says. "Give it say fifteen minutes on the boil and then we'll see."

"We have water," I say. "Somebody want to bring some of that wine over here?" Rutherford walks to the track and steps up into the back and begins to rummage among the boxes and equipment in the bins as though he is looking through his cellar for just the right vintage.

I call to Fellows. He looks over the side of the track and then he bends down and says something to the boy. The two of them get down and walk toward us. Fellows holds the boy by the arm and speaks to him as they come on. Fellows looks as though he is telling the boy who we are before he introduces us. At a distance the boy's face seems strained, as though he is going to be interviewed for an important position. As he comes closer, I see the expression on his face is one of shame: of what he is and of what he has done.

"*Sitzen*," I say. The boy sits. Fellows sits beside him. Rutherford returns from the track with two bottles of wine and an extra messkit for the boy.

"You want *wasser*? *Wein*?" I ask the boy, using up two of my ten words of German.

"*Wasser*?" he repeats. "*Wein*?"

"See?" Rutherford tells me. "I told you you don't know no German. Give him some of both and see which one he take."

Withers pours the boy a cup of water and gives it to him. The boy drinks it and Withers pours him more. The boy nods and places the cup on the ground beside him. He is a good-looking boy with brown hair who will grow up to be a good-looking man. But right now he looks sad, ashamed and distressed, and I worry that he may begin to weep again. Fellows uncorks both bottles of wine, pours some into a second cup and hands it to the boy. As he does so, he says, "I don't know about a boy his age drinking."

"This is a special occasion," Williston says. The boy sips the wine. He does not grimace at the acid taste: it seems he is old enough to drink wine, too.

While we wait for the chickens and the rations to cook we speak of this and that. No one mentions the First Sergeant or the Colonel or Germany or the war. No one even speaks of conditions at home. Withers talks about the solid construction of the barn, but he does not mention what happened in the yard in front of it. Rutherford tells Withers and Franklin that cleaning chickens is nothing compared to working in the stockyards in Kay See. They don't dispute him, though Withers says, "Wait until you taste this chicken, Rutherford. Then you'll see." Williston talks about a place his parents took him on a trip in Connecticut when he was fourteen. He does not note that the boy sitting watching us talk is about fourteen—or less, I think, as I look at his face: he does not shave. Hearing about Williston's trip to the country, Simpson eyes Fellows and tries to begin a debate about different methods of transportation: he holds that the motorcar allows the traveller more scope than the train.

But Fellows does not respond on behalf of the railroad. He glances now and then at the boy beside him. He seems almost as uncertain and distressed about what has happened as does the boy.

When Withers, who has been watching the time, says, "These chickens are ready," Williston ladles chicken and a portion of Menus No. 1 to 3 into a canteen cup and hands the cup to me. I pass it to Franklin, who hands it to Fellows, who hands it to the boy. The boy begins to pass it on, to Simpson, but Fellows touches his arm and shakes his head. The boy whispers, "*Danke*" and holds it by the handle, glancing from one of us to the next. He does not eat: he is waiting until all of us have been served. It seems his parents taught him decent manners. I wish they had done a little more with other parts of his upbringing. Withers passes the boy a knife and fork and makes cutting and forking movements with his hands. When we are all holding canteen cups, the boy begins to eat, and as he does so I see tears in the inner corners of his eyes.

"Shush, now," Fellows says. The boy nods as though he understands, but still he weeps. Fellows motions to the boy to drink more of the wine. The boy nods and picks up the cup and drinks. "Simpson, pour him some more of that wine," Fellows says. Simpson pours, the boy drinks again and puts the cup down beside him. He wipes his eyes with the pinned back sleeve of his man's uniform.

It is after six when we finish dinner, if a mess of rations and looted chickens can be called dinner.

"Williston," I say, "we're going to take him back now, turn him in. We'll go in the track. Tomorrow morning one of us can drive the First Sergeant's Jeep back. Another thing: the Colonel wants me to go through the First Sergeant's gear and get it ready. So we'll be a while."

"I'm with you," Williston says.

"You mind cleaning up?" I ask, looking from Fellows to Franklin to Simpson to Withers to Rutherford.

"No mind at all," Rutherford says. "'Course you got to buy us all a beer when we get where we're going."

"I'll buy everybody I see a beer when we get where we're going," I say.

I get up and motion to the boy, but Fellows says, "Got to let him wash up before you go on with him. And get his pack. Got his stuff in there. Pictures and letters and such."

"All right," I say. I don't see why not: we have time.

Fellows takes the boy to the track and pours water from a canteen into the enamelled bowl and stands with the towel while the boy washes his hands and mouth. While the boy is drying his face, Fellows gets into the track and brings out the boy's pack and the machinepistol with which the boy killed the First Sergeant, and the gas mask container, and the boy's canteen and the cloth bundle in which the boy kept a piece of hard sausage and two pieces of old bread. Fellows hands the pack and the bundle and the canteen to the boy and holds up the Schmeisser and the gas mask container and says, "You want to take these along?" I note that the boy does not look at the weapon in Fellows's hand.

"No," I say. "We'll turn them in tomorrow."

Fellows nods and puts the machinepistol and the gas mask container down inside the track. When he and the boy come back to the fire, Simpson says, "That bundle he's got seem bigger than it was."

"I put in some rations for him," Fellows says. "We don't know where he's going from here."

Simpson nods and nods, but he does not speak.

"All right," I say. "We'll be back in a couple of hours. Everybody stay near the barn, and two of you stay on guard. We don't know who else might be out there."

"Right," Rutherford says. I notice he does not have his machinepistol near at hand. I wonder if he damaged it when he threw it to the ground.

The boy sits between Williston and me as we drive back. He holds his small pack and the plump bundle of rations Fellows prepared for him in his lap. His thin neck is bent and I cannot see his face. But as I glance at him as Williston drives down the road up which we followed the First Sergeant this afternoon, I see the tears that fall on his hands crossed on top of his hiker's pack.

Sixteen

Two MPs sitting in a Jeep watch us drive up to Headquarters Company's bivouac. They get down and throw down the cigarettes they are smoking and approach our halftrack. As they come forward I recall the Colonel saying he would have MPs standing by to take the boy along. Williston and the boy and I climb down from the maintenance track and wait for the MPs to come up. The boy slings his pack over his right shoulder and stands with the bundle of rations Fellows fixed for him under his left arm, his canteen in his right hand, waiting for us to tell him what to do next.

Beyond the MPs, the personnel of Headquarters Company glance toward us and away, as though they do not want to see the boy who killed the First Sergeant. One man—a corporal whose name I cannot remember—starts toward us. Another man says something to the corporal and the corporal stops, looks at us, turns and walks away.

"Captain told us to come up and take care of this kid," the ranking MP, a corporal, says when he comes up. "Your Colonel came out and said we were to treat him well."

"That's it," I say. "He's had a rough afternoon. We've all had a rough afternoon."

"Captain didn't say anything about that. Neither did your Colonel. They just said to take care of him, and that's what we'll do. They're setting up a place for kids like this. He'll be turned loose and sent home soon as the war's over." The corporal glances at the boy, shakes his head and says, "I swear I don't understand how they can put these kids in uniform. What have we seen, Herm, three four of them?" Herm nods. "This one doesn't look more than thirteen."

"Twelve, more like twelve," Williston says, as though he has spent three or four years gauging the ages of children brought in front of him. "I don't think he's felt a razor against his face one time."

"You got his name, any identification?" the Corporal asks.

"I didn't think to look," I say. The boy was not a soldier, and I did not think to take his name and number.

"It's okay," the Corporal says. "Herm here—Private Steinmetz, that is—speaks German perfect. From Seattle," the corporal explains, as though everyone in Seattle speaks fluent German. "Lives in Seattle," the corporal says. "Got the German from his parents, like. We'll get all we need on identification from the kid. He'll talk to Herm." The corporal has a lot of faith in Herm.

Private Steinmetz speaks to the boy in German. The boy looks up at Private Steinmetz. He is surprised to be addressed in his own language. Private Steinmetz listens and nods as the boy whispers to him.

"I didn't know," Private Steinmetz says. "We didn't know," he amends. "Your Colonel didn't tell us. This kid killed one of your men?"

"First Sergeant. A mistake. Boy didn't know what he was doing." Williston nods to confirm that I have told the truth.

The boy whispers and Private Steinmetz says, "He says he's sorry. Says he was scared and shot before he thought. Says he wishes he hadn't fired. Wishes he could bring your, ah, he says 'friend' back. Kid's all broken up about this," Private Steinmetz interpolates. "Also says: is there anything he can do? Says he knows there isn't, but if there's something?"

"Nothing," I say. "Just a mistake. Part of the war."

"There's one thing," Williston says. The MP corporal and Private Steinmetz look at Williston. So do I. "Tell him," Williston says, "to remember what he did. And tell him not to do it again ever."

"I'll tell him," Private Steinmetz says. He speaks German to the boy, explaining. Private Steinmetz is calm, and the German he speaks is quiet and expressive. I do not hear in the tone of his voice or in the words he speaks any of the past two decades of stamping boots and shouting men in uniforms, spittle at the corners of their mouths, blood in the whites of their eyes. Of course, Private Steinmetz was in Seattle most of those years and not down here south of Coburg, so his German may be a little out of touch.

As Private Steinmetz speaks to the boy, the boy nods and nods. When Private Steinmetz stops speaking the boy nods once more and begins to sob. Private Steinmetz pats him on the shoulder and speaks to him again. The boy sobs again as he nods and nods.

"Boy says he won't," Steinmetz says. "Ever again."

"What else did you tell him?" I am curious. I don't need to know German to know that Private Steinmetz told the boy a lot more than don't do it again.

"Told him: see the difference between us and what you've had over here? Asked him how he thought he would have fared if he'd been an American boy and shot a German sergeant by mistake. Asked him would he be standing here saying he won't do it again?"

"How come you told him all that?" I ask.

"We're supposed to start indoctrinating all these prisoners and civilians we meet up with," the Corporal says, "about democracy." The Corporal sounds bored with the idea of spreading democracy through central Germany.

"That," Private Steinmetz says. "I also said it because it's true. We don't shoot boys like this because of a mistake." I think of Sergeant Dombrowski and his track full of tired armored doughs, but I don't mention them. I also think of home, but I don't mention that either.

"That's true," I say.

"And even if it wasn't a mistake," Private Steinmetz says, "he surrendered, and we don't shoot soldiers who surrender." Private Steinmetz seems pretty certain about the way things work. I wish he'd been around in November when men in one of our tank companies were ordered to shoot two surly, shouting SS snipers we had taken prisoner. They had fired on us and then surrendered just as the Shermans were about to kill them. The two shouting legalistic SS troopers shouted about their rights, I guess, right up to the moment they were murdered.

But I say, "There's that."

"Anyhow," the Corporal says, "we got him and we'll see he's all right. You check his stuff?" The Corporal asks the question as though he thinks the boy might have three or four stick grenades stuck in his hiker's pack.

"We checked," Williston says. "It's all personal, and some food we gave him."

"Damn nice of you guys," the Corporal says.

"Yeah," Private Steinmetz says. He speaks to the boy and the boy answers him. "Boy says thanks for the food. And says he'll remember and won't do it again ever."

"Tell him okay," Williston says. Steinmetz nods and whispers at the nodding boy.

"Well," the Corporal says, "we got to get on."

"Take care of him," I say. "Enough going on we don't need a boy like this up against it."

"We'll take care of him," Private Steinmetz says. The three of them get up into the Jeep. The Corporal drives. Private Steinmetz speaks to the boy, takes the boy's pack and bundle, puts them in the back of the Jeep, climbs up into the back and gestures for the boy to sit in the right front seat. The boy gets in and the Corporal starts the engine. As the Corporal makes a wide turn into the field and back onto the road, the boy moves his hand, raising it a few inches, as though he is too embarrassed to wave.

"That takes care of that," Williston says as they drive away. I see the boy's face turn: he looks back at us. Private Steinmetz leans forward and speaks to him. The boy nods and waves at us. Then the Jeep drives around a bend in the road. I think of Sergeant Herman, Corporal Haffitz and Corporal Stahlmann waving as they departed the war for captivity southeast of Frankfurt.

"I hope he meets up with Sergeant Herman."

"Yeah," Williston says. "You know we didn't get his name?"

"Do you care?" I ask.

"I guess not. No, I don't care. Whatever, he's safe now. And all this is over."

"Except for the First Sergeant's stuff," I say.

"I know," Williston says. "I wasn't going to mention that. You be all right? You want any help with it?"

"No," I say. "Shouldn't take long to sort it out." But I worry about seeing the Sergeant's effects. I worry about knowing more about him.

"Why the Colonel ask you to go through it? I'm just asking, but we're in maintenance and all, and he's got these people here, sergeants and officers in Headquarters Company, to tell to do it."

"I don't know," I say. "I don't know why he asked me."

"I'll be here when you get back," Williston says.

"Right." I leave Williston and walk to the Headquarters track. The Colonel's tent is set up under a tree fifty feet away. A lantern glows within the tent: it is not quite night, but it will be soon. I wonder if the Colonel is waiting for me.

Corporal Stuart sits in front of his typewriter in the Headquarters track. He is not typing. When I step up into the track he looks at me and nods. He is as troubled as everyone else about the First Sergeant's death. I suppose he too thought the First Sergeant would come back every time.

"Hi," Stuart says. His voice is dull, as though he has been working hard all day and needs rest. "The Colonel said you were coming. Said for me to show you the First Sergeant's gear. Said you were to use his tent. He's gone off around the companies. Said he wouldn't be back for an hour or more. I don't think he wanted to be here when you went through the First Sergeant's stuff. Or when you brought that boy here who. . . ."

"That's all right," I say. "Show me the First Sergeant's gear and I'll take it over to the Colonel's tent and go through it and get it ready to go before he comes back. There much of it?"

"No. First Sergeant had a duffel and a musette bag. And his rifle and revolver. Colonel took the weapons to his tent. Just the duffel and the musette bag here in the track. Colonel said to hold them here for you." Just a duffel and a musette bag? I know the First Sergeant, being a first sergeant, could have brought with him to the war what he wanted in the way of personal effects. In fact, if he had brought along a baby grand piano and installed it in the Headquarters track the Colonel would have said no more than, 'Little crowded in here, First Sergeant. But I always knew you played the piano.'

Corporal Stuart shows me the First Sergeant's duffel and musette bag. Two pieces, and neither of them full. Not much at all.

"I don't know," Corporal Stuart says as he gestures at the First Sergeant's belongings. "I just don't know."

"Me too," I tell him.

I carry the duffel and the musette bag out of the track and walk to the Colonel's tent. The First Sergeant's rifle leans against a small table on which lie the First Sergeant's campaign hat and his holstered revolver. I set the duffel on the ground beside the Colonel's cot and lay the musette bag on the cot and turn up the lamp. The tent smells of mildew and creosote and its walls are creased. It has been packed away for months: I cannot recall when the Colonel used it last. Texas, maybe. Or Louisiana, before Texas.

I take the First Sergeant's effects one by one from the olive drab duffel bag and lay them on the cot. Everything in the duffel is Army issue except a box of cigars. I lift out shirts, pants, socks, an extra pair of polished boots buffed glossy, handkerchiefs, underwear, an olive drab sweater, an overcoat. The common clothes of the common soldier. I feel the pockets of his pants and shirts to be sure the First Sergeant has left nothing personal behind in the clothing issued him by the government. I know I will find nothing: the First Sergeant was a diligent soldier and a neat, careful man. Still I check each pocket to be sure, so that I can tell the Colonel that I looked and that I am sure.

I repack the duffel with the First Sergeant's handkerchiefs, underwear, socks, shirts, pants, boots, sweater, overcoat and cigars. I will suggest to the Colonel that he send the First Sergeant's duffel back to the First Sergeant's wife. I know Uncle won't miss these clothes and I am sure the Colonel can arrange to have the duffel sent home to the First Sergeant's family.

I unstrap the musette bag's two straps. The musette bag is divided into a single large compartment in front with a thinner one behind. The divider is two pieces of thick cloth sewn to the bag at the ends and sewn together in the middle of their vertical lengths to form two pockets twice as deep as they are wide. The bag is designed to hold handgrenades, ammunition clips, medical supplies or whatever the owner wants to haul.

I spread the contents of the large compartment of the musette bag on the Colonel's cot. It is not much for almost thirty years of service: the largest item is the .45 caliber automatic pistol the First Sergeant took from his belt beneath his coat as I drove him back to make Willy Thorn stand up against it. I open a small, oily metal box: it is packed with gun oil, solvent, patches, a rod and a wire bore brush. I note the figures stamped in the metal base of the brush that indicate its caliber: .45. I close the box. I count ten of the curious clips of ammunition the First Sergeant's '03 Springfield requires, three boxes of .45 ammunition for his .45 Bisley Colt revolver, and six loaded clips for the .45 Colt automatic. A small leather bag contains the First Sergeant's toothbrush, toothpowder, a plastic box with a bar of soap inside and a razor and blades.

We will return the toilet articles to his family. The First Sergeant is a noncommissioned officer, so the ammunition, like his uniforms, belongs to Uncle Sugar. Unless the Colonel says otherwise. I will encourage the Colonel to say otherwise. He has said he is going to take the First Sergeant's '03 Springfield and his antique revolver home to the First Sergeant's wife and child. The Colonel might as well take them the ammunition too. Who knows? They may need it.

I put the .45 automatic, the ammunition and the cleaning kit back into the musette bag and reach into the two compartments in the divider between the musette bag's large compartments. In one I find a neat stack of letters held together with rubber bands. In the other is a leather case as wide as a wallet and twice as tall. It is a combined notebook and picture frame with a strap around it.

In the thinner compartment at the back of the bag is a file of papers. I know when I touch them that they are the flimsy onion skin sheets the Army uses for copies. I leave the papers and open the leather case.

To the left beneath a rectangle of glass—how, I wonder, has a thin slice of glass survived our journeys from Texas to this crossroads in south central Germany?—in a frame with brass corners, is a photograph of a woman about forty years old. The woman is seated. A boy in a shirt with horizontal stripes stands beside her. The boy is nine or ten. The woman and the boy are smiling. I can see a corner of the photographic studio's seal embossed in the photograph's lower right hand corner. I slip the photo out of the frame: it slides out with ease and I can tell, because the leather is worn in the center of the edge of the slot in which the photograph fits, that the First Sergeant often took this photograph of his wife and son out of the frame to look at it. I turn the picture over. On the back the woman has written: "For my dearest Stanley, with all my love, Alice." Below this, the boy has printed in an uncertain hand, "I love you, Dad."

'Stanley.' Now I know First Sergeant William S. Reardon's middle name.

I replace the photograph and open the diary. The First Sergeant's neat handwriting on the plain unlined pages of good paper is a terse chronicle of the Seven Six One's journeys and battles since we arrived in Europe. The First Sergeant's handwriting is precise, his language full of gritty detail. The entries in the diary mention the names of this man and that in the Battalion whose performance the First Sergeant noted. I have no time to read it all: the Colonel will return soon, and I must hurry. I turn the pages to 9 November 1944, but I find no entry for 9 November 1944. But the First Sergeant wrote two pages of terse comment on 10 November 1944. I read snatches of it: 'tanks shot down', 'Morville-les-Vic', 'nine killed, among them Lt. Kenneth W. Coleman and 1st/Sgt. Samuel J. Turley, good men both. Their deaths and the deaths of the other men'—here the First Sergeant listed the names of the others—'are a loss to the Battalion, to the Army of the United States and to the United States of America.'

I am surprised he could write this down: 'to the Battalion, to the Army of the United States and to the United States of America'? It is too much to say of us, or of anyone. It is sentimental, and the First Sergeant was the least sentimental man I have known. Yet perhaps because he felt the grit beneath his fingernails and knew the smell of incinerated flesh and had seen lung and bowel, he had the right to think that when one of us died, an insignificant chip flicked this way and that on the world's raging sea, it was 'a loss to the Battalion, to the Army of the United States and to the United States of America.'

Wondering what he said about those he did not consider 'a loss to the Battalion, to the Army of the United States and to the United States of America,' I flip forward, looking for an entry for 17 November 1944, when the First Sergeant shot Johnny White for cowardice when White refused to get up and go as loader in his Sherman. The four others in his crew cursed White as the First Sergeant told him to mount up. They went on cursing him when White refused for the last time and the First Sergeant took White to the edge of the road. They stopped cursing him when the First Sergeant shot Johnny White in the chest and shoved his corpse into the filthy water in the muddy ditch beside the verge. They did not speak at all when the First Sergeant got into their Sherman and served as loader all that day and the next until the Colonel found a replacement. The First Sergeant's diary does not mention Johnny White's name on 17 November 1944, or on the 18th, the 19th or the 20th. So much, I think, for Johnny White.

I turn back to 10 November 1944. Toward the end of the entry I find my name, and the comment, 'Calm and decent. Will be good in tanks when I get him out of maintenance. Well brought up.' My parents would, I know, be happy about the first and last sentences. The second sentence would have made them a little queasy last fall had they read it: they followed the papers, and they knew about Shermans. Most of all they knew about the Seven Six One, whose fortunes they followed through the press, neighborhood gossip, and rumor. Therefore they knew of the Seven Six One's losses.

I turn the pages through November. More names, more deaths. Shocks, encounters, self-propelled guns, pillboxes, mines, wire entanglements, mortars, antitank guns. Travels north to Belgium in the snow in December, to fight in the Ardennes. Captain Williams wounded and gone from the Seven Six One. Names I do not remember: the wounded and killed, long gone from the Seven Six One, disappeared back to the alien nation of our birth. January and February. Bitter fights, lists of lost vehicles and men. The weather. More names of men, and names of places no one will remember, or visit, or wish to remember or visit.

I keep turning. March. The First Sergeant, I note, did not record the death of Willy Thorn. But he wrote out the names of Thomas S. Quineau, who was killed in Bayou Queen, and the names of the five men in Big Sam's crew killed by the JagdPanther: Samuel M. Taylor, John P. Thompson, Moses B. Smith, Thomas H. Holcomb and Simon L. Beane. Of Big Sam Taylor the First Sergeant wrote, 'would have made company 1st/Sgt. had he lived.' Of all six of them dead he wrote, as he had written of others who had died before, 'their deaths are a loss to the Battalion, to the Army of the United States and to the United States of America.'

At the end of the entry about the destruction of Big Sam and Bayou Queen, the First Sergeant wrote down my name and the comment: 'helped again with the men killed. Solid.'

Shadows slide across the page. I glance up and listen. A wind is rising, pushing against the walls of the tent, swinging the lantern hung by its handle to a hook fixed in the tent pole.

The diary continues through March, all the way to the screaming, kicking horses on the road to Klingenmünster. The First Sergeant did not write down the number of German infantrymen he killed with his rifle during the fight in front of Klingenmünster. The number of Germans killed, it seems, were not the important part either. Of the Colonel's performance before Klingenmünster the First Sergeant wrote: 'a fine officer who returned to the Battalion after being wounded in November. Led three attacks against the enemy before taking this town. We are proud of him, and the 409th and 411th Infantry Regiments have noted his performance, and ours.'

In April the First Sergeant wrote on successive days of our rapid passage northeast past Frankfurt to Fulda and then farther east, to Coburg. Of the day on which we brought Lieutenant Donald R. Lovejoy down from his tree, the First Sergeant wrote, 'Retrieved the body of a young American pilot. Three Germans surrendered to Doc Turner and to the crew of the maintenance track sent to retrieve the pilot's body. Old men, whose Sergeant fought against the 369th Infantry in the First War. All three of them, though old, were soldiers.'

The last entry concerns the Battalion's progress toward Austria. The First Sergeant wrote of problems of coordination among the tank companies and the infantry regiments of the 71st Infantry Division which we accompany to the southeast. The First Sergeant did not, of course, write an entry about today. I turn the blank pages of the rest of the diary. Nothing: a methodical man, the First Sergeant began at the beginning and marched through the pages of his diary one by one, filling them with his precise handwriting. I am about to close the diary and put it away, but to be sure—so that I can tell the Colonel I looked and am sure—I riffle the last pages of the diary to the back cover. I am glad I have done so. Inside the back cover the First Sergeant wrote: 'John N. White. Executed for cowardice in the face of the enemy.' Below that is a second entry: 'Wilton C. Thorn. Executed for rape and attempted murder.'

White and Thorn are where they belong, at the very end of what the First Sergeant wrote down about the Seven Six One.

I close the diary, glance once more at the First Sergeant's wife and child smiling from the frame to the left of the diary, and close the leather case. Little about his diary surprised me, except the First Sergeant's extravagant language about the death of a man in the Seven Six One being 'a loss to the Battalion, to the Army of the United States and to the United States of America.' I turn the leather case in my hands and recall that he did not mention any of the medals which the men in the Seven Six One received in exchange for their heroism, wounds and, in too many cases, deaths.

I replace the case in the musette bag and ease the bundle of letters from the other compartment in the divider. I will not read them, but I remove the rubber bands and glance at each envelope. All except one are addressed in the same handwriting. I glance at the return address: Dayton, Ohio. I wonder if the First Sergeant was born and brought up in Dayton, Ohio. Perhaps the Colonel will show me his file, and I will see the place of his birth. It seems the only letter he received which his wife did not write was written by General Hillman. I am curious, and would like to know what the General wrote to the First Sergeant. But I would not read this letter unless the First Sergeant asked me to do so, and he is not here to do so.

I shuffle the General's letter and the First Sergeant's wife's letters together and put the rubber bands around them and slide the packet back into the compartment in the divider in the musette bag where the First Sergeant kept it.

I take the last item—the file of flimsy papers—from the thinner compartment at the back of the bag. Company documents, I suppose: orders, requisitions, the paper detritus of a tank battalion at war. I open the file and find that the First Sergeant has kept copies of the citations which accompany the award of medals given to men in the Seven Six One. I read the first sheet of onion skin paper:

2 December 1944

Award of Silver Star Medal
The CITATION:

Sergeant WARREN G. H. CRECY, 18232347, Infantry, United States Army, for gallantry in action near __ and __ France, on 10 and 11 November 1944. During offensive operations near __ and __ Sergeant CRECY, a tank commander, lost his tank when it was knocked out by enemy antitank fire. He immediately dismounted, took command of another vehicle which carried only a .30 caliber machine gun and wiped out the enemy antitank gun and crew. On the next day of the offensive when his tank was bogged down in the mud, he fearlessly faced enemy antitank, artillery and machine gun fire by dismounting and attempting to extricate the vehicle from the mud. In the course of his work, he saw the advancing infantry units crossing open terrain under enemy machine gun fire and unhesitatingly manned the tank's antiaircraft gun from an exposed position, neutralized the enemy machine guns by direct fire, thereby aiding the infantry in its advance. Later in the day he again exposed himself by mounting his tank turret and destroyed enemy machine gun nests by direct fire and aided in silencing one enemy antitank gun. His brilliant display of leadership, courage and initiative reflects the highest credit upon Sergeant CRECY and the armed forces of the United States.

Crecy is from Galveston, Texas. His reputation is that of the toughest man in the Seven Six One. I wonder if he recalls three men my father told me about who played 'Will You Come To The Bower?' at San Jacinto. My father, whose father came from east Houston, spoke with particular pride of the drummer.

I turn Sergeant Crecy's citation face down on the lefthand side of the file and read the next sheet:

2 December 1944

Award of Silver Star Medal

The CITATION:

Staff Sergeant RUBEN RIVERS, 38063493, Infantry, United States Army, for gallantry in action near — France, on 7 November, 1944. During the daylight attack on — Staff Sergeant RIVERS, a tank platoon sergeant, was in the leading tank when a road block was encountered which held up the advance. With utter disregard for his personal safety, Staff Sergeant RIVERS courageously dismounted from his tank in the face of directed enemy small arms fire, attached a cable to the road block and had it moved off the road, thus permitting the combat team to proceed. His prompt action prevented a serious delay in this offensive operation and was instrumental in the successful assault and capture of the town. His brilliant display of initiative, courage and devotion to duty reflects the highest credit upon Staff Sergeant RIVERS and the armed forces of the United States.

Ruben Rivers: an Oklahoman, strong and slim. He boxed at Camp Claiborne. Wounded on November 18 when his Sherman ran over a mine, he refused evacuation and was killed the next day in front of Guebling when his tank was struck by antitank fire.

I leaf through the pages reading here and there, noting the names. Major Edwin W. Reynolds, the Bronze Star. Captain Garland N. Adamson, the Bronze Star. Last November, Doc Adamson crouched in a shell hole while artillery pounded the Seven Six One's bivouac and groped for, found, and caught with a hemostat the slippery, spurting end of a wounded man's artery.

I read on: Private Austin C. Jackson, the Bronze Star, and Technician Fourth Grade James I. Rollins, the Bronze Star, for going out into the storm of German artillery fire pounding the Seven Six One's bivouac and bringing back a wounded man. If I recall, the man they brought in was the same one whose artery Doc Adamson tied off. Whoever he was, he owes Jackson, Rollins and Doc Adamson everything he's got.

I read the whole of the next citation:

2 December 1944

Award of Bronze Star Medal
The CITATION:

> Private First Class FREDDIE C. REEDY, 35263504, Infantry, United States Army, for heroic achievement in connection with military operations against an armed enemy near ___ France, on 9 November 1944. Private First Class REEDY, a tank driver, while driving his tank near ___ saw some seriously wounded infantry soldiers lying in the open terrain. Utterly disregarding his personal safety, he dismounted his tank, moved across the open terrain under heavy enemy artillery and small arms fire, evacuated the wounded men to the shelter of a disabled tank and administered first aid to them. His courageous action and initiative was instrumental in saving the lives of three of the wounded. His display of courage, initiative and solicitude for his comrades reflects the highest credit upon Private First Class REEDY and the armed forces of the United States.

I read Freddie Reedy's citation again. I wonder what they would think of it in Misssippi. Whatever, I guess the men from Mississippi in the 26th Infantry will remember Reedy, even if they don't remember his name. They will remember him, and know what to call him twenty years from now.

Sergeant Moses Ballard, the Bronze Star, for dismounting from his disabled Sherman under heavy antitank and mortar fire and evacuating the wounded members of his crew.

Staff Sergeant Frank C. Cochrane, the Bronze Star, for dismounting under fire from his Sherman on 9 November and saving two men who might have died of their wounds had Cochrane not saved them. The names of the men Sergeant Cochrane saved are set out in the citation: Corporal Ernest Chatmon and Technician Fifth Grade George Collier. Sergeant Cochrane helped one up onto the rear of his Sherman and got the other inside and brought them to the rear. Chatmon and Collier owe Frank Cochrane as much as others owe Adamson, Jackson, Rollins and Reedy.

I read on. Corporal Dwight Simpson, the Bronze Star, for rescuing a wounded man on 9 November when C Company's Shermans were shot down before the tank trap near Morville-les-Vic. I think I remember Simpson: he was one of the men who helped the wounded into the tank trap when Sam Turley counterattacked the Germans.

I read the next citation: Sergeant Emery G. Thomas, the Bronze Star. On 22 November 1944, when his platoon leader's Sherman, and then his own, were shot down, Thomas got down, led some of his crew forward and rescued three wounded men lying out beside the platoon leader's tank. I read part of the citation: 'Utterly disregarding his personal safety, he courageously led a few men to the wounded men under heavy enemy mortar and machine gun fire, dragged the wounded men to a sheltered point and administered first aid to them. This done, he personally carried one of the men who required immediate treatment into *** to the aid station, then returned and evacuated the other wounded.' As the citation says, Sergeant Thomas's 'display of courage, initiative and solicitude for his wounded comrades reflect the highest credit upon Sergeant THOMAS and the armed forces of the United States.'

Sergeant James E. Stewart, the Bronze Star, for dismounting from his Sherman on 25 November 1944 under intense enemy fire and rescuing wounded men from the field.

I read every word of the next citation:

8 December 1944

Award of Silver Star Medal
The CITATION:

Second Lieutenant KENNETH W. COLEMAN, 0517590, Infantry (Armd.), United States Army, for gallantry in action near — France, on 9 November 1944, Lieutenant COLEMAN, a tank platoon leader, was leading his platoon in the attack on — when his tank was disabled by enemy antitank fire thereby halting the advance. He immediately dismounted and courageously led his crew on foot under the heavy artillery and small arms fire against a much larger enemy force, driving them from their positions and thus enabling his platoon to proceed on its mission. During the performance of this outstanding feat, Lieutenant COLEMAN was killed by enemy small arms fire. His brilliant display of leadership, initiative and devotion to duty exemplifies the highest traditions of the service and reflects the highest credit upon Lieutenant COLEMAN and the armed forces of the United States.

I turn Lieutenant Coleman's citation face down on the others lying face down on the left hand side of the file. The next citation is Sam Turley's. The words about him are less bright than my memory; but I can confirm what the citation says, and tell more if I am asked:

8 December 1944

Award of Silver Star Medal
The CITATION:

First Sergeant SAMUEL J. TURLEY, 37030404, Infantry, United States Army, for gallantry in action near — France, on 9 November 1944. During the attack in the vicinity of — France, on 9 November 1944 the tank of which First Sergeant TURLEY was acting as tank commander, was disabled by enemy antitank fire. He immediately dismounted and rapidly organized a dismounted combat group from the members of his own crew and the crews of two other tanks. Skillfully led by First Sergeant TURLEY, this group fought counter-attacking enemy troops to a standstill making it possible for the crew members of three other tanks to escape uninjured from their disabled tanks. During the fire fight, First Sergeant TURLEY was killed by enemy artillery fire. His initiative, his inspiring courage and his strong devotion to duty reflect the highest credit upon First Sergeant TURLEY and the armed forces of the United States.

I read on. Sergeant Joseph A. Tates, the Bronze Star, for a long day of intense fighting and selflessness in November, 1944.

Captain David J. Williams, the Silver Star, for gallantry in action in November, 1944, in France. Captain Williams swam a canal at the far edge of three hundred yards of open ground to determine whether the Shermans could wade the canal. A few days later he rescued two wounded men who had bailed out of their Sherman. And a few days after that he stood out in what more than one of us have called 'the fucking open', directing the fire of his Company's Shermans from covered positions against antitank guns that, having no Shermans to fire at, fired at Captain Williams. Captain Williams was wounded in January and evacuated.

I read more quickly: the Colonel will return soon, and I must have the First Sergeant's effects ready to go. As I flip through the pages of citations I note the names and the medals awarded for courage in the field: Captain Russell C. Geist, Jr., the Bronze Star and, later, when he became a Major, the Silver Star; First Lieutenant Charles A. Gates, the Bronze Star; Private First Class George Goines, the Bronze Star; Corporal Otis Johnson, the Bronze Star; First Lieutenant Harold Kingsley, the Bronze Star.

I stop turning the sheets of paper over when I find the citation awarding Sergeant Ervin Lattimore the Silver Star. I recall our Jumbo pulling over to let Lattimore's M4A3 pass and go on up to Klingenmünster. I read part of his citation: 'Although wounded, Sergeant LATIMORE refused to be evacuated. Upon reaching the outskirts of***, Germany, his tank was fired upon by enemy anti-tank guns. Locating the hostile emplacements by gun flashes, he overran the enemy positions. Sergeant LATIMORE's actions reflected the highest traditions of the military service.' It seems the typist misspelled the sergeant's name; or perhaps I do not remember how he spelled it.

First Lieutenant Thomas E. Bruce, the Bronze Star, for supporting infantry attacks during the third week in March.

First Sergeant William R. Burroughs, the Bronze Star, for heroic achievement in action during the same week in which First Lieutenant Bruce gained a reputation among the men of the 409th and 411th Infantry Regiments.

Sergeant Daniel Cardell, the Bronze Star, for supporting the 411th Infantry Regiment and evacuating casualties under mortar and artillery fire.

Second Lieutenant Moses E. Dade, the Bronze Star, for destroying thirteen pillboxes and an ammunition dump, capturing an anti-tank gun intact and killing what someone referred to no more than a month ago as 'a mess of Germans' while supporting the regiment of armored doughs to which he was attached.

Sergeant Louis M. Daniel, the Bronze Star, for destroying an antitank gun from a distance of eighty yards—eighty yards, I think: the mouth of the dragon—after he had gone up on foot and located the German weapon lurking in its camouflaged emplacement.

Technician Fourth Grade Ivery Fox, the Bronze Star, for getting back into his Sherman slashed through and through thrice by antitank fire and trying to get the Sherman off the road so that two others could maneuver past and out of the antitank gun's field of fire.

Technician Fourth Grade Otis Johnson, the Bronze Star, for dismounting from his Sherman and advancing two hundred yards under antitank and small arms fire to locate German gun positions, returning to A Company and leading the Company's mortar section leader forward and helping him direct the fire which silenced the German guns. Tech Four Otis Johnson's actions, I read, 'reflected the highest traditions of the military service.'

I turn the pages over from the right side of the file to the left. The Colonel will be here soon, and I must finish: Private Christopher P. Navarre, the Bronze Star; Technician Fourth Grade Isiah Parks, the Bronze Star. I pause to read Crawford Pegram's citation:

> 4 April 1945
>
> Award of Bronze Star Medal
> The CITATION:
>
> Private First Class CRAWFORD O. PEGRAM, Armored, Company D, 761st Tank Battalion. For heroism in action. On 24 March, 1945, near ***, Germany, Private Pegram's tank and three one-quarter ton trucks on reconnaissance were fired on by the enemy. The vulnerable trucks withdrew and Private PEGRAM moved his tank behind a wall, opened fire, killed the crews of two hostile machine guns and pinned down two bazooka teams and one antitank crew, permitting nearby infantrymen to capture the pinned down enemy. Moving forward, his tank was fired upon by an antitank gun. Private PEGRAM dismounted and located the hidden weapon but was cut off from his tank by small arms fire. Crawling to higher ground, he met a group of soldiers with a mortar, and quickly setting the mortar in position, he fired five rounds into the emplacement, forcing the enemy to abandon the gun. His actions reflected the highest traditions of the military service.

I glance through the last three citations for the Bronze Star: Private First Class Leonard Smith, for heroic achievement in action, in support of the 411th Infantry; First Lieutenant Harold B. Gary, for heroic achievement in action; Sergeant Buck A. Smith, for heroism in action.

I riffle through the citations again, noting that the authors of the ones written last fall and winter took care to replace, with dashes or asterisks, the names of the French and German towns near which the Seven Six One fought. Then the deletion was a reasonable security measure. Now it seems antique and unnecessary. But the deletions do not matter: I remember each small town and muddy field.

So far as I can tell, the First Sergeant placed in this file in my hand a copy of every citation written for each medal awarded a man in the Seven Six One. I remember him speaking of what Sam Turley might or might not be awarded for his courage and death before the tank trap at Morville-les-Vic. Then the First Sergeant seemed to disparage medals. Now it seems he valued the evidence of what his men—and we were his at least as much as we were the Colonel's, or General Patton's, or General Eisenhower's—accomplished.

As I return the file to the thin pocket at the back of the musette bag, my fingers touch an envelope in the bottom of the compartment. I take the envelope out. It is unsealed. I open it and examine the contents: a sheet of paper and two articles clipped from newspapers.

I unfold the sheet of paper and read the First Sergeant's handwritten description of an incident which occurred last November in France. Inside Morville-les-Vic, infantrymen of Company K of the 101st Infantry Regiment of the 26th Infantry Division attempted to extract the body of one of our tank commanders from his burning tank. They failed, but several of their own were killed in the attempt. At the end of this description, the First Sergeant wrote: 'The names of the men in Company K of the 101st Infantry who attempted to save the body of the Seven Six One's tank commander from his burning Sherman should be determined and the Colonel encouraged to commend them.' I am sure that, had he found the names of these Company K infantrymen, and passed them on to the Colonel with a recommendation that they should be commended, the Colonel would have been happy to do so. Who wants to be a Colonel with a cranky First Sergeant in the Headquarters track?

I fold the paper and return it to the envelope. I unfold the newspaper articles. One states that the 57th Ordnance Ammunition Company, a Services of Supply outfit, engaged sixty-five German troops at Peronne during the Allied sweep across France last summer, killing fifty and capturing fifteen of the sixty-five. Members of the 57th were awarded two Croix de Guerre, a Silver Star and a Bronze Star. The other article states that the 592nd Port Company went ashore in three groups in the fourth wave of the 5th Marine Division's landing on Iwo Jima. Everyone in the

Seven Six One—everyone in Europe—heard about Iwo Jima in February, and we all agreed at the time that we would rather fight the Das Reich three more times than fight the Japanese on Iwo Jima.

I fold the newspaper articles and place them in the envelope and replace the envelope behind the file of citations in the thin rear pocket of the First Sergeant's musette bag and strap the musette bag up.

I glance at the duffel and musette bag. As I thought before, it is not a lot of gear for a first sergeant.

I leave the duffel and musette bag, turn down the lamp and go out into the night. Two sergeants whose names I don't remember stand a little away from the Colonel's tent. As I walk past I note that one of them has an unlit cigar in his mouth. The other one says, "Y'all right?"

"All right," I say. The speaker and his companion with the cigar nod as I pass on.

Corporal Stuart is fretting in the Headquarters track when I step up into it. He seems nervous without someone to tell him what to do.

"How's it going?" I ask him.

"Colonel's supposed to be back. C Company called in, said he'd left and was coming back now. He ought to be here. But he isn't."

"All right if I wait for him here?"

"Sure, fine," Corporal Stuart says. "You, ah, finished up there in the Colonel's tent?"

"Yes. All finished."

"Everything okay?"

"Fine."

"You want anything? Got some brandy here, and some of this clear German liquor they have like gin."

"Why not? Colonel won't mind?"

"Tonight? No. I bet he'll have a couple with us when he comes. He's had a long, bad day like the rest of us. Almost as long and bad as the one you had. You want brandy? Or this other stuff?"

"Brandy would be fine," I say. "They were close?"

"Colonel and the First Sergeant? Yeah." Corporal Stuart takes a fat wool sock from an equipment bin in the side of the track, pulls a bottle from the sock and pours brandy into two canteen cups. He corks the bottle, sets it on the floor of the track and hands me one of the cups. "Here. Yeah, friendly. Formal like, officer to sergeant and all, but close. Like they understood one another. 'Course they had to. Had to rely on one another, you know? To figure out how to do the job and keep people from getting killed and hurt and such at the same time. And I suppose any two men run a battalion through all this last six months since we came to France get close. You know what I mean?"

"I know," I say. "I couldn't take the responsibility myself. Not for almost seven hundred men and all these vehicles. With the need to make a showing."

"I couldn't either. That's why we had the First Sergeant. And the Colonel. To take the responsibility and see that things went right. To be sure we made a showing. Colonel's coming," Corporal Stuart says. I hear the engine of a Jeep and see the faint glow from its slitted headlights. The Jeep stops and the Colonel gets down. Stuart and I stand up as the Colonel climbs up into the track.

The Colonel nods at me, turns to Corporal Stuart and says, "How's it going, Corporal? Anything?"

"No, sir. Everything's quiet. Nothing happening anywhere. Seems like the war is almost over."

"It is. What's that you two are drinking? Brandy? Got any more of that?"

"Yes, sir," Corporal Stuart says. "Here, sir, I haven't drunk any of this yet." He hands the Colonel his canteen cup. The Colonel sits down, raises the cup, waves it at me and drinks. Corporal Stuart rummages another cup out of the bin and pours himself a drink.

"Sit down, both of you," the Colonel says. "Long day, and the rule is: sit down when you can."

"Yes, sir," I say.

"You brought someone with you to drive?" the Colonel asks.

"Yes, sir."

"Then have another drink and let's go over to my tent. You left his stuff there?"

"Yes, sir," I say as I hold up my cup while Corporal Stuart pours more brandy for me. The Colonel holds out his cup and Corporal Stuart pours.

The Colonel stands up, says, "Hold the fort, Corporal," gets up and gets down from the track. I follow him.

"You went through it?" he asks as we walk to his tent.

"Yes, sir. It's all packed away in his duffel and musette bag in your tent, sir."

"Anything?"

"The duffel's packed with uniforms and such. Nothing in any of the pockets. The musette bag is, well. . . . Perhaps you'd like to look through it yourself, Colonel."

"Can't I just send it back to his wife and child?" I have never heard the Colonel ask anyone to help him with a decision.

"Sir, I think you should send it all back. Actually, I think you should write Mrs. Reardon that you are holding on to it and will bring it back with you. There's ammunition for his rifle and revolver in the musette bag, sir, and it might be stopped if you sent it back. But you said you were going to take the Springfield and the Colt back to her, so I thought you might want to take along the ammunition too."

"It's an idea," the Colonel says. "I could write her and ask her if she wants me to send the stuff, or bring it. Anything else?" We are at the flap of the Colonel's tent. He moves the flap aside and gestures me in. I enter and he follows me.

"Sir, the First Sergeant kept a diary."

"A diary? I didn't know he kept a diary." The Colonel sits down on a three-legged stool with a canvas seat.

"It's about the Seven Six One's activities since we came over here, sir. To Europe."

"Damned place," the Colonel says. He looks around at the creased, dun-colored walls of his tent as though he is surveying Europe. "Wish we were home. All of us out of Europe and back home."

"You might want to read the diary, sir. And there's a file of copies of the citations for the medals that have been given to men in the Battalion. Also, a note to you about men in the One Hundred and First Infantry at Morville-les-Vic. And a couple of newspaper articles. One about an Ordnance Company, the other about a Port Company in the Pacific."

"The Pacific?" the Colonel says. "Don't tell me about the Pacific. I worry they might send us out there."

"You think, sir?" This is an impertinent question, but I ask it before I think not to, which the Colonel will understand; and I want to know, which the Colonel will also understand.

"No, actually, I don't. I haven't hear a whisper about us going to the Pacific. I'll tell you: the Japanese have got to quit sometime. I don't care what you read about them all fighting to the death. They'll give up, and not too far from now. You said a story about a Port Company and an Ordnance Company in the Pacific?"

"No, sir. Two stories, sir. One about an Ordnance Company got in a fight near Peronne in France last summer and killed a bunch of Germans. Other one's about a Port Company went ashore on Iwo Jima early on. Fourth wave with the 5th Marines."

"Iwo Jima," the Colonel says. "Jesus Christ. Fourth wave. Better anything here than that. Anything else?"

"Yes, sir. There a .45 automatic in the musette bag too. And six magazines for it."

"Show it to me," the Colonel says.

I unstrap the musette bag and reach into the large front pocket and bring the .45 out. The Colonel takes it, weighs it in his right hand. I wonder if he is thinking about standing beside the First Sergeant in the back of the Headquarters track, firing his own pistol toward the German infantry in front of Klingenmünster. "I've got his rifle," the Colonel says. "And his revolver. They're his. I'll give them to his wife and child." He hefts the pistol in his hand and looks at the creased wall of his tent. Then he nods and says, "You keep the automatic." He looks up at me and says, "He wore it in his belt that day, didn't he?" I am not surprised the Colonel knows about Willy Thorn. I remember him standing in the Headquarters halftrack almost two months ago saying, "Uh-huh, uh-huh," as he listened to the First Sergeant explain about the stay-behind sniper who killed Willy Thorn. On the other hand, I am not going to say anything specific about that day, and if he asks I am going to tell him a sniper shot Willy Thorn from the nearest tree line twelve hundred yards away.

"Yes, sir," I say.

"Gave it to you, didn't he? To back him up?" I wonder how he knows this, but I am not going to ask.

"Yes, sir. He didn't need me to back him up, though."

"I know. Part of the lesson. You know, most of what he did was teach," the Colonel says. "Me, you, everyone else." The Colonel holds the pistol by the barrel and hands it to me. I hold it in my hand and remember the feel of it stuck in my belt when the First Sergeant and I walked up to the back of the truck and looked up at Willy Thorn inside in the dark under the canvas. "I'll have Stuart type up a note about this pistol. I'll sign it. You ought to be able to take it home with you when we get out of here. Or if you want, see me and I'll take it back in my gear and return it to you in the States."

"Thank you, sir.

"Don't thank me. You did a good job today. Damn good job. Getting that kid out of there. And getting the First Sergeant ready. And now, getting his stuff ready."

"You might want to read the diary, sir. And read over the citations."

"The diary. Yes, I'll read that. I've got my own set of the citations. There'll be more of them coming down, you know. Late this month, and early next. And then a bunch when the war's finished and there's time for everyone to sit down and think about what the hell happened and who did what."

"The First Sergeant's diary will help with that, sir. He noted down the names of a lot of men he thought did all right."

"If he thought they did all right," the Colonel says, "they probably did damn well. But whatever. All right, look: finish your drink and go on. And take themagazines for the pistol." I shove the pistol into my belt and reach into the musette bag and lift out the six magazines. "Prepared for anything, wasn't he?" the Colonel asks, nodding at the clips in my hands. The Colonel is right: it is a lot of ammunition to keep near at hand. On the other hand, the First Sergeant favored chance no more than he favored gestures.

As I distribute the magazines among my pockets the Colonel says, "I'll take a look at his diary. Then I'll write his wife. I wish I could have someone write this letter for me, but I can't. None of them—more than thirty, just for the men killed—have been easy. This one is going to be the toughest. He was the Seven Six One's First Sergeant, but he was my friend, too."

"I know, sir." The Colonel coughs and raises his hand to his face.

"Drink up," he says when he stops coughing. He raises his canteen cup, waves it at me and drinks. I raise my cup and pour the brandy down. I recall the First Sergeant offering me a drink after we finished inside Big Sam. The Colonel hands me his cup and says, "Ask Corporal Stuart to bring me over another slug of this, would you?"

"Yes, sir." I nod, a cup in either hand, and turn to go.

"And look," the Colonel says. I turn and face the Colonel. "Thanks for all this," he says. He gestures at the First Sergeant's gear. "For helping out today. Getting him ready, and going through his things. And for helping him out, before, with the men killed. And that other thing. He thought well of men who did the right thing, and he thought well of you."

"Thank you, sir."

"All right, then," he says. He nods and I leave his tent and walk toward the Headquarters track. The automatic nudges my belly and groin as it did when I took off my coat and helped Willy Thorn into it. The clips of .45 ammunition in the pockets of my coat swing against my hips. As I approach the Headquarters track, I glance back. The Colonel's bloated shadow bent at the waist shifts across the tent's canvas wall. The huge shadow arms descend and rise, the shadow hands holding a hard rectangular shadow: the First Sergeant's diary.

Seventeen

When the war ends we are in Steyr, Austria. Steyr lies between the Steyr and Enns rivers. Steyr is ancient: the castle that dominates the town was constructed, we are told, in the tenth century. Now soldiers walk the streets and loll in the cafes below the castle's walls as they walked and lolled a thousand years ago.

The Army tells us Steyr's population is 40,000. The Army also tells us that the iron and steel industry provides much of the work for the populace. The town is not pretty, but it is lucky: it has been bombed now and then, while the cities of Germany have been bombed and bombed, and then shelled and shelled.

We entered Steyr on 5 May 1945 and met Russian troops of the 1st Ukrainian Front at the Enns River the next day. We looked at the Russians and wondered and they looked at us and wondered too. We, and they, had come a long difficult way to a river bank in Austria to find no Germans separating us.

But though the war is over, work is not. Ten of our tanks are ordered to appear as part of the honor guard at General Lothar von Rundulic's surrender of German troops in Austria. Captain Knowles stands up in the bed of a halftrack and gives his maintenance and supply troops a vigorous speech about the need to brush up the ten M4A3s which will form a fragment of the American forces present at the surrender. "I want," Captain Knowles says, thick fists on his hips, "you men to clean these ten tanks up inside and out. Do it every which way. I want these Shermans looking and working like Packards just come out the factory. I want them to look better than they looked coming off the assembly line at Grand Blanc. And I'm telling you I'm gonna check every nut and bolt. I want the radios working, the ready racks and the ammunition stowages full. And I want every shell polished before you put it in. I'm gonna dig those shells out the bins and look, now. I want the engines and the engine compartments cleaned—washed, you hear me? and the tracks tensioned. I want the insides done right: clean everything up and then polish it. Then tell someone else to polish it again. I want every single one of the weapons in these tanks cleaned and oiled. And I want the 76 millimeter armament in each tank balanced. You never know what these officers going to look at," Captain Knowles says, as though he has never risen above the rank of private first class. "And I want the outsides polished. Touched up where necessary with paint. And then waxed. You understand me?"

"Where we going to get the wax to shine these tanks up with, Captain?" an anonymous voice calls from the crowd. Most of us laugh.

Captain Knowles looks us over and says, "Don't worry about wax. Sergeant Symms working on wax. Sergeant Symms going to have enough wax down here tomorrow morning early to make these machines shine under three coats. So start now on the rest of it. This honor guard our Shermans going to be part of is going to get together day after tomorrow in the late morning. So get to work, every last one of you. I want to see those elbows moving. And if one of these here Shermans breaks down or gets a bad comment from one of these officers at this surrender signing—even some motherfucking German officer, you hear me?—you all going to be in the worst trouble you seen since Louisiana. I couldn't give a half damn about whoever's there from our side, but I want these motherfucking Germans who're surrendering to know who they been fighting." Captain Knowles looks out over the crowd of near one hundred fifty men who have spent most of the war driving and maintaining and supplying and says, "I'm gonna inspect these vehicles. Every bolt and nut." Captain Knowles glances around and says, "This here's an important moment for the Seven Six One. We come a long way to this place, and I want us to go up looking good when this German General whoever the hell he is hands over his sword or pistol or whatever to the commander of the 71st Infantry Division or whoever it might be is gonna take it off him. So let me tell you: you heard this before, but I'll say it again: I don't expect nothing but the best on this job. So don't let yourselves down, and damnit all, don't let me down."

It is an echo of General Patton's vivid, high-pitched speech of welcome to the Seven Six One last autumn, before we went up and fought it out with them at Morville-les-Vic.

But Captain Knowles's rough paraphrase of General Patton is at least as encouraging as what the General shouted out to us: Captain Knowles's speech sets us working. We work through that afternoon and the night after and the next day and the next morning: near forty hours.

Near the end of the forty hours Captain Knowles calls me out of an

M4A3 in which Simpson and I are balancing the 76 millimeter gun, while Rutherford and Fellows adjust the engine, Withers and Franklin tighten the tracks and Williston tinkers with the fuel system. "Need a maintenance crew to go along as back-up for the Shermans going to this here surrender ceremony. I know everyone here putting their shoulder to the wheel and everything's looking good and they ain't going to be no trouble. But I want to be sure. So I want a track with anything they maybe going to need lurking nearby in case something break down or get out of whack. You're the track that's going. I asked the Colonel who to send and mentioned your name and he said send him and his men."

"Thanks, Captain," I say. "It'll be a nice outing."

"Don't thank me: you people done good work since we came to this damned Europe." He looks away down the line of ten Shermans shaping up for the ceremony. I wonder what he is thinking. Willy Thorn, maybe. Or Big Sam. Or all the rest of the machines, and the men who went to war in them, whom we left behind in the rough terrain between Nancy, in France, and this place in a valley in Austria. "What are you going to do after?" he asks. I'm surprised: I know Captain Knowles has never asked anyone in the Seven Six One a personal question.

"Go back to college, sir. I guess."

"You guess? Don't guess. Think about it: college. That's it. That's the thing to do. Me, I went two years and had to go to work. You finish it. Don't let anything stop you. Your hear me?" The three words of his last sentence rise from one to the next, each one full of menace. I guess he will check my transcript during the last two years of college: as my father will. "And go on after," he says. "Be a lawyer or an architect, maybe. Or an engineer: you got a good beginning here on engineering. But whatever you do: go on. You hear me?"

"Yes, sir."

"All right, then. Want you and your men to get cleaned up when you finish here. I've had some others doing your track so it'll look right if some one of these here Germans take a look at it. Or the 71st Infantry Division Commander. Or General Patton, if he comes down to glare at this here German Rundulic who's giving up today."

"Thanks, Captain."

"Like I said," Captain Knowles says, "don't thank me. Colonel said: send a track. I said how about this one here—mentioning you and your people. He said, yes, send them."

"Kind of him. And of you, sir. We'll keep them running. If any of them have any trouble, sir."

Captain Knowles shakes his head and says, "Won't be any trouble. Drive out a few miles on a road. Park. Stand up out of the hatches and look smart while the Generals drive by. Drive back, park, have a few beers in town. I'm sending you people because you did well over here. No medals, nothing they'll write about. But you did all right. First Sergeant Reardon. . . ," Captain Knowles says. He stops speaking and looks behind him, as though he thinks the First Sergeant may be standing behind his back, waiting for him to get on with it. "First Sergeant Reardon," he says, raising his voice a little, "thought you people did all right. Told me that personally. That you did the right thing. And I relied on him to know. So did every other officer here, right up to the Colonel. I'm no soldier. Manage the floor in an engineering company back home in Trenton. So I relied on the First Sergeant. Smartest thing I've done in this war."

"We all did, sir," I say. "Relied on him."

"I know." Captain Knowles shakes his head. "We're lucky this war ended when it did. War like this one here," the Captain says, as though he fought down the Mississippi to Vicksburg, against the Indians in Arizona, put down insurrectos in Luzon, went over the top in France in 1918 and slogged through the jungles of Central America in the twenties and thirties, "you need someone like First Sergeant Reardon. Knows the ropes, knows how things work."

"Yes, sir," I say.

"Other things about him, too," Captain Knowles says. "And the rest of them who're gone. But I don't want to talk about that now. You get ready to go up with these Shermans to see this German hand over. Get cleaned up. I had everything done. Uniforms been pressed, helmets polished, weapons cleaned. You check your men's fingernails. These officers always look at everyone's fingernails. Go on up with the Shermans, wait while the ceremony happens, then come on back."

"Yes, sir," I say.

Captain Knowles nods, glances up at Simpson climbing up out of the commander's hatch of the M4A3 we have been servicing, turns and walks away.

"What's going on?" Simpson asks.

"We're the maintenance detail for these ten Shermans. Going to see the surrender."

"Good thing Knowles got us going on these tanks," Simpson said. "I wouldn't have wanted them to go up there looking scruffy."

Neither would I: as Captain Knowles says, I want this German general to know who he's been fighting. And I don't want any glances from the general commanding the 71st Infantry Division. Or anyone else. Not even from General Patton, if he's there.

At the surrender no one misses a beat. Officers admire the condition of the Seven Six One's ten Shermans and our maintenance track. General von Rundulic glances our way and nods, as though he has heard about us. The general commanding the 71st Infantry Division, standing in front of a bevy of colonels, majors and captains, looks our way too. I whisper to Rutherford, Williston, Fellows, Franklin, Withers and Simpson to get ready to return his salute. But the general does not salute: he waves and smiles and nods at us and says something to his colonels, majors and captains. They nod and glance our way and smile. A captain at the back of the group seems to remember the Seven Six One's motto: he clenches his hands together high over his head.

We salute officers who pass by and they salute us. Some of them stop and admire our waxed Shermans. It is old home week: the 71st and the Seven Six One have come from the Rhine together, and we have functioned as their armored spearhead every mile of that long way. Still I wonder if we will be invited to 71st Infantry Division reunions when we are all back home and the war is far away and long ago.

Captain Knowles watches as the Shermans trundle past when we return from General von Rundulic's surrender of German forces in Austria. He waves our maintenance track down and gestures for me and Rutherford to get down. "Colonel wants you two up to Headquarters right now. Got a Jeep here. Go on now. I'll go on with the track."

"Sir?" I say.

"I don't know what it's about. Colonel radioed, said you were to come on soon as you got back. So you two go on. You can tell me about our turnout later. And about that German general and how he give up. Though I know there's not much to tell. We looked sharp and he looked like shit, right?"

"Yes, sir," I say.

We get into the Jeep as Captain Knowles gets up beside Withers and Williston in the maintenance track. Rutherford puts the Jeep in gear and we drive off toward Headquarters Company's bivouac. "What the fuck happening now?" Rutherford asks. "Forty hours of polishing and cleaning and tuning up these Shermans and now we going to see the Colonel. I wonder what for?"

"I don't know," I tell him. And I don't: I can't imagine why the Colonel wants to see the two of us. Unless it has something to do Rutherford and I traveling to Nancy, First Sergeant's orders, to visit with 1st/Sgt. John P.

Burch inside his eight square miles of supplies. I recall Rutherford nodding at me and saying, 'this man here gonna sign,' and 1st/Sgt. John P. Burch telling Rutherford, 'That's it. He's the responsible man.'

Rutherford, who has learned to read my mind, says, "You think maybe it's about that trip to Nancy and the two Jumbos and two 105 Shermans and the eight hundred rounds HVAP? When 1st/Sgt. Burch and Sergeant Wallace kept talking about the Inspector General and the auditors and such? You think maybe it's about that?"

"It better not be," I say. "I don't want to spend the next forty seasons in Kansas."

"Haw," Rutherford says. "That's right: you signed. But they said it was legal."

"Sure they did," I say. "But Sergeant Wallace was a little restrained, and 1st/Sgt. Burch had that crazy glint in his eye, and I didn't have time to talk to my lawyer before I signed."

Rutherford drives us through the fields in the valley of the Steyr river. Soon we approach Headquarters Company's bivouac. The Colonel's command post is an inn close to the river. As we drive up the lane leading to the inn I hear the rush of the river full of spring snow melt, and watch as a cool, dodging wind pushes against the green branches of the trees that line the river. Then we turn out of the lane into the grounds of the inn. I see a general's staff car standing in the drive, a red tin flag on the fender with three white stars on it, and I know why Rutherford and I have been called up to see the Colonel. I also know that what we will have to tell the general whose car this is will be more difficult than breaking rock at Leavenworth.

Rutherford knows this too. "Shit," he says, nodding at the staff car. "It's a general. And I know it the General, and I know he got hisself another star. Now I know why the Colonel call us on up here." He looks at me and says, "I don't want to do this, you know?"

"Neither do I," I tell him. "But we owe him: he gave us a place for the night and had us into his mess."

"And made me a place in that officers' latrine," Rutherford says. He sounds as though he wishes General Hillman had not come across us in the night when we were on the road to Nancy. "Okay, then. But I don't have to like it."

Rutherford parks behind General Hillman's staff car. The General's driver is civil: he nods at us as we get down and go into the entrance hall of the Colonel's Headquarters. Headquarters Company's officers and sergeants are sitting and standing in the inn's bar to the right of the entry hall. Until the Seven Six One departs Steyr, the bar will be the Colonel's communications center. But the war is over and the radios are quiet. The sergeants flip through files and the officers drink coffee. Some of them are chatting with a Major I have not seen before: one of the General's aides, I guess. I wonder why Major Cleaves is not here with the General.

When we enter the bar Sergeant Simmons gets up from his desk and comes to meet us. "Colonel wanted me to tell him when you came," he whispers. "General in there with him. Seem like you met him? Anyhow, you know what it's about. No one here been told, but we all know. You men ready to go in?" I note that the door to the Colonel's office at the end of the bar is closed.

"Yes, Sergeant," I say. Rutherford nods and stands up straight beside me.

"Okay," Sergeant Simmons whispers. He looks our uniforms over with a single slick glance, nods and says, "Come on with me."

The Headquarters Company officers and the Major I have not seen before and the sergeants sitting at their desks watch us follow Sergeant Simmons to the door. Sergeant Simmons knocks and a voice within calls out. Sergeant Simmons opens the door and says, "They're here, Colonel," as though the Colonel was not expecting anyone today except us. The Colonel is standing up behind his desk. I cannot see the General.

"Show them in," the Colonel says. Sergeant Simmons nods at us and stands back to let us pass through. We march into the Colonel's office and Sergeant Simmons closes the door behind us. As Rutherford and I step up in front of the Colonel's desk, stand at attention, salute and report, I see General Hillman standing close to the wall beside a fireplace to my right. I note the First Sergeant's diary on the Colonel's desk.

The Colonel salutes us and says, "You men know General Hillman."

"Yes, sir," Rutherford and I say. We turn and salute the General. He pushes himself away from the wall and salutes us. We saw him last eight weeks ago; but eight weeks have cut more criss-crossing lines in his face and bleached his gray hair white.

General Hillman steps away from the wall. His face is gaunt and strained. "Stand easy." Rutherford and I relax. "Good to see you," he says. Rutherford and I shake hands with the General. His hand is thin and dry, without flesh or muscle: all I feel is tendon and bone. "I heard about First Sergeant Reardon. I wanted to come down to see you." I wonder why he wants to see us: the First Sergeant is dead and gone. But perhaps the General wants to hear the sad details of the First Sergeant's passing.

"Yes, sir," I say.

"Your Colonel said you saw him killed."

"Yes, sir. I doubt he knew what was happening to him." I don't know whether this is true or not, but I am not going to tell the General anything else.

"Tell me about it."

"He opened the door of a barn and a German boy inside the barn shot him in the lower chest and stomach with a machinepistol, sir. MP-40. The First Sergeant fell back on the ground. He was killed instantly, General."

"Yes, sir," Rutherford says. "That's the way it happened."

"And you captured the boy who killed him."

"Yes, sir. Though it was more that he surrendered than we captured him. Threw the gun out of the barn. Then the clip. Then he came out. That was all there was to it, sir."

"I see," the General says. "A boy: my God."

"He was frightened, sir, when the First Sergeant opened the door," Rutherford says. "Thirteen years old, maybe, maybe less. Shot before he thought, I guess. Just a kid. Nothing like a soldier about him except the man's uniform. Cuffs folded back from his wrists and pinned up. Pants cuffs too."

The General shakes his head and says, "What a shame." I wonder whether he is speaking of the First Sergeant's death, or the boy being forced into a man's uniform.

"Yes, sir."

"And you men didn't shoot into the barn," the Colonel says. "Didn't fire a shot."

"There was no need, sir," I tell him. "He came out before we had to do anything."

"But you could have shot," the General says. "You didn't know it was a boy in there."

"No, sir," Rutherford says. "We didn't know. I and the rest of us were ready to fire, but he"—he gestures at me—"said don't shoot till we know."

I nod as though I had assessed the situation and taken charge of the tactics. But I didn't assess anything, and I didn't care about tactics: I told them not to shoot because I feared to see the First Sergeant's face shot away. He was dead and it would not have mattered had his dead face been shot away. The blanket drawn over him would have covered the savaged remains of his face as well as it did the wounds in his lower chest and stomach. But he had lost enough and I did not want to see him lose more.

I look among the creases and seams of the General's face and see him watching me. He presses his lips together, shakes his head and says, "Commendable. To think it through before you acted. I understand."

I wish I did. The General seems to be thinking of something, or someone. The Colonel coughs. We wait. Then we wait some more. Then Rutherford says, "General, how is Major Cleaves?"

"Killed in the Siegfried Line a week after you two came by," the General says. A sound comes up Rutherford's throat. I recall the Major easing our way into the General's mess and helping to explain Rutherford's problem to the General before breakfast. Rutherford liked the Major. So did I.

"I sure am sorry, General," Rutherford says.

"And I, sir," I say.

"Major Cleaves was a good man," the General says. His voice is without expression, but his eyes tell me he has lost a lot more in this war than he may be able to handle: a son, an aide, an old friend. The General looks this way and that and says, "I think about Cleaves. And the First Sergeant. And the rest of them." I wonder how high he must count before he reaches the number that equals 'the rest of them'.

"What happened to him, sir?" Rutherford asks.

"Something went wrong with the radios: the atmosphere, the weather, something. I sent him up with a message. He was coming back. Artillery killed him." The General's eyes glitter. "They brought him back to me in a track." The General shakes his head. "A lot of them are gone this time." He looks at the Colonel standing up behind his desk. "Isn't that right, Colonel? A lot of them are gone this time, aren't they?"

"Yes, sir," the Colonel says, as though he was there in the first war too. "Too many."

"And too many the last time," the General says. He looks from one of us to the next.

"Yes, sir," the Colonel says. The Colonel sounds uneasy: he knows no more about handling a Lieutenant General than do Rutherford and I.

"I think about them," the General tells us. "Reardon and Cleaves. Men in the divisions. Men from the last war. Ghosts." He smiles at us. "They visit me," he says. He smiles at us again. "I've thought a lot about the men from the first war during the last few months. I remember them all. A man named Holloway in the Three Sixty Ninth. A private. A machinegun took off his left arm right up against the shoulder." I recall Sergeant Herman and Corporal Haffitz working behind my back and hear again the crunch of gristle and the creak of wood flexing as they extract the tree's limb from Lieutenant Lovejoy's chest. I also recall Sergeant Herman telling me that he had fought against the 369th in the first war. Perhaps he was sitting behind the machinegun that took away Private Holloway's arm. "Couldn't put a tourniquet on him and the compresses were no good," the General says. "He bled to death in the trench. Lying in the mud." The General looks at us and says, "In the Goddamned mud. Bill Reardon and I were with him. He was conscious all the way down. He asked us if it would be all right. Bill Reardon and I told him yes, it would. He relied on us to tell him the truth. Maybe we did. Or not. I don't know. What else could we tell him? A boy, no more than nineteen, dying with his arm shot away? Bill Reardon held him and I held him. His blood was all down the front of my coat. It was cold. Christ it was cold. I hoped to Christ his blood would freeze and stop the bleeding. It didn't. But it froze on the front of my coat. We did what we could, Colonel," the General says, as though he thinks he must explain himself to the Colonel. "What else could we tell him?"

"Nothing, sir. There was nothing else to tell him." The Colonel sounds certain, but he is troubled: he glances and glances at the General, and at us. I wonder whether the Colonel will roll his eyes and flash the whites at us if the General goes on. The Colonel knows how, for sure: he's been in the Seven Six One long enough to know all about it.

"They die, though," the General says. "Whatever we tell them, they go over. Holloway. Cleaves, and Bill Reardon. Phillips. Thompson. Ravens and Connor: they died together, shot one after another by a rifleman. Samuels, Cobb, Morton. Fleming, Brown, Staskewicz. Olafson and Karl. The rest of them."

"Yes, sir," the Colonel says.

"And you say the First Sergeant didn't suffer?" the General asks me.

"Nosir," I say. "He died just like that. He might have felt something strike him but he didn't know what it was, sir. He had no time to know what it was."

The General nods. His white hair gleams. I wonder how long he will live, now the war is over and no one is shooting anyone else, at least for a time. The General looks at me. "Sometimes I wonder why one dies and another not," the General says. "Do you?"

I nod and say, "Yes, sir. Every single time. But I don't understand it."

"The man's right, General," the Colonel says. "No one can understand it." I'm not surprised the Colonel backs me up: with two exceptions, he has backed up every one of us since the Seven Six One—an experiment, they said, muttering that we might not be able to tell right from left, or change a sparkplug, let alone go up against the Germans—formed. We had a lot of aspirations then. Now we have fulfilled them. And now we know the price of their fulfillment. The Colonel, who still favors the leg where he was wounded last November, has paid a part of this price in person.

"Yes, perhaps he is," the General says. "Still I think of them." To be sure we remember the price paid for this trip's ticket, the General counts out more of the coin that has been handed over: "Hendricks, Wilton, Paul, Severins, Browning, Haltman, Stander, Perrine, Starkman," he says. "And others."

"Yes, sir," the Colonel says. "That's the way, it seems." The Colonel looks sad, and I guess he is thinking of his own, shorter list, of the men in the Seven Six One who have been killed.

"You think they thought it was worth it, Colonel? The ones gone, I mean." The General does not need to say this: we know he is talking about the dead. "You think they thought their deaths were worth it?"

"Yes, sir," the Colonel says. "Yes, I think they thought so, sir."

"I wonder," the General says. He looks at his hands and glances out the window. Then he looks at his hands again. I think of the numbers he is counting. First one number and then the next, and then the next. I hear the silence as the General counts and I wonder what to say to stop him counting. But I can think of nothing to say to him that will still his mind. I do not know what to do, even though I know the General would rather be dead alongside his son, Paul Cleaves and Bill Reardon than be here in the Colonel's office, counting one remembered face and then the next.

I glance at the Colonel as the General stands in silence in front of us, his shoulders slumped, his head bent down as he remembers each one gone. The Colonel cannot think of anything to say either: his face is rigid and without expression, but his eyes are wary, doubtful, concerned.

But Rutherford speaks right up. "General," he says, "it don't matter whether they thought it was worth it, or knew what it was going to cost them. What matters is they did what they had to do. They went up, General, every single one of them. They stood up. They dead now, but they went up and did the right thing, General. That's all there is to it. The First Sergeant and Major Cleaves, sir, and your son, sir: they did the right thing, and that's enough."

I am surprised: surprised that Rutherford would speak, surprised that he would mention the General's son, and surprised that, while neither I nor the Colonel knew what to say to stop the General counting one and then another, and then the next, Rutherford seems to have found the exact words the General needs. Rutherford's voice, and his words, raise the General's face and draw his shoulders back. The General nods and looks at the three of us and says, "Yes. They got up and went. Whatever they knew about the price. Got into the tracks, the tanks, stood up to their guns. Like the Six One Four. Stood up, didn't they? And here in the Seven Six One. You went up when you were supposed to. You're right, Rutherford."

The General nods as though Rutherford has won a battle. If this is what the General thinks, he is not wrong: some kind of a battle has been fought here in the Colonel's office. Neither the Colonel nor I knew it. But the General and Rutherford did, and Rutherford has won: he has driven the General's numbered ghosts away.

"All right, then," the General says. "Yes. Colonel, I want to thank you for showing me the First Sergeant's diary. I'd appreciate it if you'd ask Mrs. Reardon if she would let us make copies. It's a valuable document."

"I know, sir," the Colonel says. "I will."

"The First Sergeant was a good man," the General says. "And the rest of them." Somewhere among the rest of them, I know, is the General's son, yet another one of the many who went up and were killed, not quite understanding why, not knowing the purpose of their deaths. "As the First Sergeant wrote, every one of them dead is a loss to the Army," the General says. "And our country."

This is not a precise quote, and it is not as eloquent or as sentimental as what the First Sergeant wrote; but it is close enough, and good enough.

"Yes, sir," the Colonel answers for all three of us.

"Well," the General says, "I've got to get on." He takes his helmet from the mantel and puts it under his arm.

"Yes, sir," the Colonel says.

"You've done a good job, Colonel. And the Battalion. Every man in it has done well." I think of Johnny White and Willy Thorn; but I dismiss them. Wherever they are, they are not part of us now. The First Sergeant saw to that.

"Thank you, General. It's kind of you to say so."

"I'll try to do something," the General says. "I'd like to see you get a unit citation."

"Thank you, sir. But if it doesn't come through, sir, it doesn't matter."

"Oh, it matters," the General says. "But it's not important." I nod when the General says this: I remember the First Sergeant standing amid the litter of destroyed Shermans before the tank trap at Morville-les-Vic saying, 'That ain't the important part.'

"Yes, sir," the Colonel says.

"Well, I've got to get on now. I want to thank you, Colonel. And you two." He shakes hands with me, and with Rutherford. As he shakes Rutherford's hand he says, "Thank you, Rutherford. For what you said. And thanks for mentioning my son with the rest of them. You're the first person to mention my son to me since right after he was killed. I appreciate it."

"It's nothing, sir," Rutherford says. I glance at him. He has an uncharacteristic look on his face: he is embarrassed.

"No, it's a lot," the General says. "Anything else?" He looks at me, at the Colonel, at Rutherford.

"No, sir," the Colonel says. I can tell he is glad this meeting with the General is over.

"No, sir," I say.

But Rutherford says, "Sir, when we were up to your mess you said about those two men. Johnson and Roberts? You said you were going to write to the First Sergeant something about them, and we delivered the letter, sir. But the First Sergeant never said nothing about them. And I've been wondering, sir." I recall the General's letter among the letters from Mrs. Reardon.

"Henry Johnson and Needham Roberts," the General says. "The Three Six Nine. I remember them both: they were about your age, Rutherford. Decent men." He looks at me, at the Colonel, and at Rutherford, his eyes bright and piercing. "The First Sergeant wrote me back. Said the Seven Six One had made its own name and didn't need to have men in the infantry from the first war pointed out to them." I recall the First Sergeant sitting in Captain Knowles's Jeep, answering my question about his campaign hat and why he wore it with the strap behind; and I recall him saying, when Sergeant Herman spoke of the first war, 'You listen to this man', as though his experience as an infantryman, and Sergeant Herman's, were worth more than our experience in the Shermans. "The First Sergeant said you would learn about Johnson and Roberts yourselves. He thought that was good enough."

"Yes, sir," Rutherford says. "But no one's told us about them and I wondered."

"You were right to wonder, Rutherford," General Hillman says.

"Yes, sir. I just wanted to know, sir."

"I understand," the General says.

"You said they were important, General," Rutherford says. Rutherford is not going to let the General go until he finds out. "I just thought maybe we should know."

"I'll tell you about them later, Rutherford," the Colonel says. "Right now the General's got a lot to do, and he wants to get on."

"Yes," the General says. He still looks old and worn, but he looks as though he is looking ahead to whatever comes next, even if it wears him down some more. "A lot to do, but none of it's worth a damn. The war's over. Now it's reports to write, lessons to discuss. Soon they'll write the histories. Then they'll forget it, except for a few names and a few places. In forty years it will be as far in the past as the Civil War. Then the politicians will stand up and shout about it, as though they remember. But they won't: remember that, men, when they shout at you." The General looks at the Colonel, at me, at Rutherford. "Whatever," the General says. "You'll know what to do when they shout at you and tell you what to think." He nods. "Colonel, thanks for taking the time with me." He nods at me and says, "Good to see you, and thanks." To Rutherford he says, "Rutherford, thanks again for what you said about my son, and the First Sergeant and the rest of them. I'll remember it."

The Colonel and I mumble reassuring sounds at the General. Rutherford says, "Thank you, sir." But he looks concerned that he knows no more about Johnson and Roberts than he did when this conference began.

General Hillman goes to the door and opens it. The officers and sergeants standing in the bar stand at attention. The officers and sergeants who are seated stand up and stand at attention. The General says, "Rest," and the sergeants and officers relax, but those who were sitting do not sit back down. The General nods at his aide and they walk out of the bar and out of the inn. As the Colonel closes the door to his office I hear the engine of the Colonel's car start.

"Rutherford," the Colonel says, "you ought to know better than to keep asking a General the same question again and again. But all right. Now tell me: how come you want to know about Johnson and Roberts so much?"

"Sir, the General thought we ought to know about them. And the First Sergeant didn't tell us. They seem like something the First Sergeant left behind for us to find out about and think at, sir."

The Colonel looks at Rutherford. He starts to say something and stops. He nods as he sits down behind his desk. "Yes. All right. Now I think of it, you're right: that was the First Sergeant's way. To let you find out for yourselves. But to watch while you found out: to be sure the water wouldn't get too deep. I remember him watching me pretty closely now and then when the water was rising. All right. Henry Johnson and Needham Roberts were in a post out in front of the Three Sixty Ninth's trenches. 1918: long time ago. A German raiding party came at them. They killed and wounded twenty of the Germans and chased the rest of them off. They were both junior enlisted, you understand. No one to tell them what to do, no one to keep them there. They could have come back. They were an outpost, after all. On guard. They could have come back to the Three Sixty Ninth's lines. But they didn't. They stayed and showed the sonsofbitches. Maybe that was what the General was thinking about. And the First Sergeant, when he told the General the Seven Six One didn't need to be told about them."

I can see Rutherford thinking about it. I think about it too: two men on guard duty listening to the slither and rattle of the Germans coming forward. Killed and wounded twenty, I think. Sergeant Herman must not have liked that.

"Thank you, sir," Rutherford says, "for telling us. And for the rest of it."

"The rest of it?" the Colonel asks. He looks puzzled.

"Yes, sir."

"We'll be going, sir," I say before the Colonel can say, 'The rest of it?' again. "Unless you've got something more for us, sir?"

"No. Go on. The surrender went all right?"

"We looked better than anybody there, sir," Rutherford says. "Captain Knowles did a job: had everyone working the last day and a half and more. If General Patton'd been there, he would have wondered if those ten Shermans had ever fought anything."

"I don't think so, Rutherford," the Colonel says. "General Patton's had his eye on us. I've been told that. And he's damned pleased with what we've done. Pass that on."

"Yes, sir," Rutherford and I say.

"All right," the Colonel says. "Go on back. You did well here. Both of you. And you said the right thing, Rutherford. The General seemed to ease up a little after you spoke. What made you do that?" the Colonel asks. He seems interested that Rutherford would find the words when he and I could not.

"Seem like the right thing to say just then, Colonel. Man was troubled. Pierce him, I thought, let the trouble drain away."

"I see," the Colonel says. "Yes. You're right."

"We'll go now, sir," I say.

"Yes," the Colonel says. "Go on. And thanks for coming."

I do not remind the Colonel that he ordered us here.

We salute, turn and leave the Colonel's office. The sergeants and officers in the bar look at us. A few of them who are sitting stand up and look this way and that. Sergeant Simmons walks up to us and says, "Everything all right?"

"Yes, Sergeant," I say. "No problem."

"I'll walk you out," he says. Rutherford and I and Sergeant Simmons walk across the bar and out into the entry hall and out of the inn. "General seemed more relaxed when he came out than when he went in," Sergeant Simmons says. He is not fishing, but he has a line ready to put in the water.

"He seemed all right to me," I say. "Just wanted to know about the First Sergeant. They served together last time around."

"Last time around," Sergeant Simmons says. He shakes his head as though he worries that we may have to go around again. "Okay, though. Long as the Colonel's okay, everything's fine."

"That's it, Sergeant," I say. As we get into the Jeep I hear the wind rustling the trees along the river rushing full of the spring melt from the mountains.

"Whatever, you seem to have done all right. You two take it easy now," Sergeant Simmons says.

"What else?" Rutherford asks. He grins. "War's over, Sergeant Simmons. Time to take it easy."

"No it isn't," I say.

"This man's right, Rutherford," Sergeant Simmons says. "You listen to him. Things go on. War over, something else begins. No time to lie down and take it easy."

"You sure, Sergeant?" Rutherford asks.

"I'm sure. But for now get on out of here and go to town if you ain't got anything else to do. Get a couple of beers and unwind. I was listening to the General's aide talk. And then the General came out of the Colonel's office better than he went in, and you two had something to do with it. I don't know what, and the what don't matter. So go have a couple beers and relax. Peacetime, you going to have to pay hard to come over here and see this here castle they got, and these mountains up around in here."

"And if we come," Rutherford says, "they gonna look at us just like they do to home."

"Maybe so, Rutherford," Sergeant Simmons says. "But they gonna remember, too, however hard they look. But all right, get on out of here now." Sergeant Simmons waits in the drive as Rutherford drives us away from the inn.

We drive down the lane to the road. The wind blows, swirling through the trees, pushing the leafy branches this way and that. At the end of the lane Rutherford turns right toward our bivouac. As he shifts up from one gear to the next he says, "Seem like it wasn't that bad."

"You did all right in there," I tell him. "Bucked the General up. You said what he needed to hear."

"I just thought to speak up," Rutherford says. "Wasn't more than that."

"Yes it was," I tell him.

Rutherford nods but he does not speak again until Service Company's bivouac is in sight.

As he turns off the road into the bivouac full of Shermans and tracks, he says, "We did all right today at the surrender." I glance at the machines we have serviced and in which Rutherford and I fought just a little: now the war is over they seem diminished and antique.

"You're right: we did okay. What do you say we get the rest of them and go into town? Captain Knowles said when we got back from the Colonel's it would be okay to take off."

"Seem like the right idea to me," Rutherford says. "Pretty small town for a infantry division and the Seven Six One to find a place to sit, though. But sure, let's go on in, see what they got there. Have a couple of drinks, sit out in the sun and watch the river go by."

We find the maintenance track. Fellows, Simpson, Withers, Franklin and Williston are sitting on the ground in the sun talking and drinking coffee. Rutherford beeps the horn to tell them we are coming. They look up at us and wave. As they do I see Captain Knowles striding, thick short arms swinging, angling toward us.

"Captain coming," Rutherford says. "Wants to know what's going on."

"What else?" I ask.

We get down as the Captain comes up to the Jeep. He crosses his thick arms on his chest and stands with his small feet apart and says, "Everything all right with you two?"

"Fine, sir," I say. "General who served with the First Sergeant came up to Headquarters, wanted to hear about it. We told him. That was it." I skip over the General's ravaged, seamed face and the ghosts that reached out to touch his shoulder and grip him by the elbow.

"All right," the Captain says. "I thought maybe it was something wrong. You told this here General what he wanted to hear, did you?"

"Yes, Captain."

Captain Knowles nods. "Okay then." He uncrosses his arms and puts his hands on his hips. "Then what the hell you doing sitting around here taking the sun and getting down from this Jeep? Thought I told you, after the ceremony, you take a weapons carrier go into town get a few beers and come on back. You men don't listen to me anymore now the war's over? Go on, get the hell out of here. Couple of drinks, now," he says, wagging a thick forefinger at us. "Nothing more. And no chasing these here women: no fraternizing, they told us, and that means no fucking, in case you don't know what fraternizing means. I don't care if the war's over, you listen to me and take it easy. Besides, this here is a foreign country and they got diseases over here you ain't heard of at home. You seen the training films, so remember what I say. Now go on, the seven of you, get to hell out of here. Weapons carrier's right over there." Captain Knowles turns and points at a weapons carrier fifty feet away. I wonder why the Captain is so relaxed and cordial. I cannot figure it out. Perhaps the end of the war has helped him find some peace too.

In Steyr we drive down narrow streets full of soldiers. They glance at us and we glance at them. A few of them nod. A few wave. Williston drives this way and that as we look for a place to sit out. Most of the houses are shuttered and few Austrians are out in the streets. Of course: they have nothing to do, and they fear soldiers as they have since the castle was constructed a thousand years ago. That is why they were happy to see the castle built and suffered the presence of its garrison. None of them wanted the soldiers, but they were needed. Because of the other soldiers.

"Stop here?" Williston asks. I glance up. We are entering a square. Ancient buildings lie along three sides, the river rushes past the fourth. Three or four cafes have set tables out in the square. Soldiers slouch toward the tables and away, their hands in their pockets. Yet all the tables are full.

"Look like this the place," Rutherford says.

"Park out in the square," I tell Williston. He drives out into the square and parks the weapons carrier. We get down and look this way and that.

"Which one of these places you want to try?" Fellows asks. He sounds about as nervous as I feel: this is going to be a new experience, I guess, for all seven of us.

"Let's try this one over here," Rutherford says. "The one with the blue awning." He sounds enthusiastic, as though things in Kay See were different from what they were in Chicago.

"You think this is a good idea?" Williston asks. "War's over, you know."

"We're going into one of these places and have a beer," Withers says. He sounds determined, as though elements of the Das Reich are waiting for us beneath the cafes' awnings.

"Let's try the one with the blue awning that Rutherford likes," I say. I'm not going to stand around out here in the square looking this way and that as though I were standing in front of a bus station half way from Chicago to Mobile, trying to look innocent.

We drift across the square toward the cafe Rutherford has chosen for us. Bored soldiers slouch at tables outside the cafe. They are drinking beer and smoking cigars and cigarettes. The women who bring the beer are more than middle-aged, and they are nervous. The soldiers seem not to notice them. They drink and grimace as though the beer is bitter. No wonder: Austria has been at war as long as Germany, and I suppose decent beer is in short supply.

Beyond the tables outside, from within the cafe, a voice calls, "Hey, you guys."

We walk on toward the cafe: the soldiers sitting out in the sun and inside the cafe seem not to hear the voice.

"Hey, you guys," the voice calls again. I look into the cafe. A soldier is standing up behind a table waving. Another soldier sits beside him.

"That guy waving at us?" Simpson asks.

"Who knows?" Franklin says. "Who cares?"

"Hey, you guys. You guys in the Seven Six One. Hey, over here."

"He's calling us over," Williston says.

"I'm not sure about that," Fellows says. "There may be others from the Battalion here."

"What you talking about, Fellows?" Rutherford says. "I don't see no one from the Seven Six One around here. And I know how to tell the difference between us and everybody else over here in Europe."

"Hey, you guys," the soldier in the cafe calls out a third time. A few of the soldiers slouching at tables look at him, look at us, look into their beers.

"He's waving at us," Simpson says as we walk on toward the cafe. "Look at that guy's arm move."

"Maybe he's in the Signal Corps," Williston says.

"What's he waving like that for?" Franklin asks. "He's making a spectacle of himself waving like that."

"He wants us to come over," I tell Franklin.

"No!" Rutherford says. "And here I thought he was shooing us around to the back."

"Doesn't look like he's shooing us at all," Fellows says. "Looks like he's telling us: come on. That's what it looks like to me."

We walk among the tables set out in front of the cafe. Some of the soldiers sitting at the tables look at us. Others don't. Some of the ones who look up nod. Others don't. This is a good sign: we are not attracting attention. If the soldier who is no more than twenty feet away would stop waving his arms at us, everything might be all right.

As we enter the cafe, Rutherford mutters, "We're coming. Tall grass in through here, but we're coming."

"Come on over here and have a drink," the soldier calls. "Sergeant Miller here wants to ask you something. Come on, pull up a chair. I'm Jim Sparkman. This is Frank Miller." Miller is a sergeant, Sparkman a corporal. Miller nods at us. He looks at each one of us, first one and then the next. Miller is large and solid, with a broad face, a high forehead and blond hair. When he has looked at us he glances around the bar and out into the square. Only his eyes move. The rest of him is still. Sparkman is thin and tall, and he is in motion: he pushes chairs and drags a second table screeching across the stone floor to the table at which he and Sergeant Miller have been sitting. Men sitting at other tables glance at him as he arranges the furniture. Then they glance away.

As we sit, Miller lifts his arm and an elderly woman wearing an apron comes over and stands beside the two tables where all nine of us are sitting. I count three empty beer glasses and three empty brandy glasses on the table at which Miller and Sparkman are sitting. "Beer?" Sparkman asks. "You guys want beer?"

Everyone except Williston nods and says, "Beer." Williston says, "Brandy."

"Good choice," Sergeant Miller says. "You and me," he tells Williston, "are the only ones here with any taste. The brandy's all right. The beer tastes like horsepiss." I glance at him. Rutherford glances at him too. Sergeant Miller sees us glancing, nods and says, "On the other hand, Jim here's drunk three of them, so maybe they're all right. But I'll drink the brandy.

"*Sieben* beer," Sergeant Miller tells the waitress. He lifts one of the brandy glasses and shows it to the elderly woman and lifts two fingers. She nods and goes off.

"How are you guys?" Corporal Sparkman asks. He offers a package of cigarettes. I take one. Sparkman lights it: the wick of his lighter is long, the flame yellow, the smoke greasy black. It is a small replica of the burst of smoke and flame that lurched from the muzzle of the JagdPanther's eighty-eight millimeter gun in the instant before Big Sam Taylor and the four men in his crew were killed.

"We're doing all right," Williston says. "Long day today. Went up to the surrender ceremony with ten Shermans. We were in the maintenance track. In case one of the Shermans had trouble."

"Saw you there," Miller says. "We were down in the infantry company just across from your Shermans. Where'd you get those Shermans, anyway? Looked right off the line."

Withers, who spent hours waxing one of the M4A3s, snorts and says, "That's cause our Captain had us and everyone else in Service Company working on them almost two days without a break. Got wax and had us shine them up. And let me tell you: they take a lot of wax. Those things are a lot bigger than some Ford."

"Wax? Wax in Europe this month?" Sergeant Miller asks. "Your Captain must be able to fix things the way he wants."

"That's Sergeant Symms standing behind the Captain," Franklin says. "Anything you want, Sergeant Symms got two or three salted away waiting for a willing buyer."

I recall standing up in the gloom inside the two-and-a-half ton truck trying on the overcoat Sergeant Symms gave me after I had given mine to Willy Thorn to keep him warm on his journey.

"Ask them," Corporal Sparkman tells Sergeant Miller.

"Give it a chance, will you, Jimmy?"

The elderly waitress comes from behind the bar with seven glasses of beer and two brandies on a tray. She puts the glasses down on the table one by one. We are getting out our wallets and reaching into our pockets. Sergeant Miller takes a bill—a five dollar bill, not German currency, or scrip—from his pocket and hands it to the waitress. "This is on me," he says.

"We'll get the next round," Simpson says.

"No you won't," Sergeant Miller says.

"I don't get it," I say.

"Go on and ask them, Frank," Corporal Sparkman says.

"Jimmy?" Sergeant Miller tells Sparkman. "I'll handle this, all right?"

"Sure, Frank. I just thought you ought to ask them."

"I'm going to ask them. When it's time."

I glance at Rutherford. Rutherford is glancing at Withers, Withers at Fellows. Williston sees them glancing, drinks his brandy down and says, "You're right about the brandy, Sergeant."

Miller raises his brandy glass, waves it at Williston and drinks. "You and me," he says, "we'll let these other guys drink the horsepiss. We'll deal with the brandy." He raises his arm, the glass in his big pale fist, straight up into the air. The waitress comes with a bottle of brown liquid. She fills Miller's glass, and Williston's, and goes back behind the bar. I wonder what it feels like to be occupied. I ought to know: after all, I've heard the stories handed down from my great-great-grandparents. But tales of the past were all I knew. Here in Steyr I see: a waitress in a worn cafe terrified of her docile, quiet customers. I suppose she knows the numbers: sixteen thousand men in an infantry division, near seven hundred in a tank battalion, all of them tired of what they have had to do, each one prepared, and able, to lash out and destroy.

"I'll tell you guys," Sergeant Miller says. "Couple more drinks and I'll be ready. Have another beer." He raises his voice and says, "Ma'am?"

Ma'am? I wonder where Sergeant Miller was raised. The waitress seems not to have heard him. He raises one thick arm and waves and points at the beer glasses and nods at the waitress. She goes to work drawing mugs of beer and bringing them to the table.

"Where you from, Sergeant?" I ask.

"Here and there. Minneapolis. Pittsburgh. My parents are in Portsmouth, New Hampshire right now. I've never been there. Never been out of the Middle West before, except here. Went to Texas to train. Dad works in a shipyard up there in New Hampshire. Guess the work is finished now, though. A little more and the Japs will give up. Then it'll be all over and the shipyard will close and we'll have to find something in the Middle West."

"It gets worse after a war before it gets better," Fellows says.

"That's it," Sergeant Miller says. He looks us over and says, "None of you are the one."

"The one what?" Williston asks.

Sergeant Miller nods. He puts his glass down, stands up and removes his jacket. He unbuttons his olive drab shirt and pulls up his olive drab undershirt. Four inches along a line from his right shoulder to his solar plexus is a slick pink indentation half the size of the palm of my hand. Sergeant Miller nods at us, puts his right boot up on the table among the brandy glasses and pulls up his pantsleg. In the muscle of his calf six and eight inches below his knee are two circular pink indentations, each a half inch in diameter. Sergeant Miller nods at us again, shoves his pantleg down, lowers his undershirt, buttons his shirt, pulls on his jacket and sits down. "The two in the leg were nothing. Two through and throughs. Rifle bullets, the doctor said. Didn't hit an artery, didn't do much damage at all except core out some muscle, and muscle grows back. I didn't know that: that muscle grows back." Sergeant Miller taps his chest up near his right shoulder with his left forefinger. "This one was something else. Machine-gun bullet. Punctured the lung, cut some large vessels, but again: no artery. But I was bleeding inside, into my lung. Slow drowning, the doctor said. He explained it to me: blood fills up one lung, the one that's shot. When it fills up enough the blood pours over into the other, and bit by bit you drown. I'm lying out there in a field, see. Last November. The tenth of November, east of Nancy. I was in the Twenty-Sixth. A corporal then, like Sparkman here. Me and two guys, Slater and Henderson, were scouting the edge of a field. Didn't see a thing. Then the Germans opened up. Killed Henderson and Slater right off, just like that. Shot Henderson in the head, Slater three times through the chest. Got me here," Sergeant Miller says, raising his left hand once again to the spot near his right shoulder, "and here," he says, reaching down to touch his right leg. "I'm alive partly because I got thrown down into a low place in the ground. The Germans kept firing, trying to dig me out. They couldn't hit me and I couldn't move. Standoff. Except that I could feel myself bleeding inside and I was getting short of breath and coughing up blood and spitting it out: blood filling up the right lung, like the doc told me later."

Sergeant Miller pauses, drinks, puts the brandy glass down and says. "So I'm getting ready to die. Didn't have any question about that. It's afternoon, and you know how short the days are over here in fucking Europe in the fall and winter. The light's getting a little thin, and it's cold, and I'm drowning in my own blood. Every time I move the Germans try again, the same machinegun and a couple rifles hammering from the woods across the field. I knew I was gone. Then this truck drives out in the field. Regular two-and-a-quarter ton truck, one man driving, no one else. He drives the truck around till it's between me and the German machinegun. I can hear the bullets flicking through the canvas and hammering through the cab. Guy leaves the engine running, gets down, takes one look at Henderson and Slater, gets me up—the machinegun's firing all the time now, I hope the fucking gunner will burn the barrel out—and then here come mortars falling a little over, then a little under. The driver shoves me up in the cab, right across the floor, I'm pushing with my feet to help him push me past the gear shift. My face is down in the mud on the floorboards. Guy tells me, 'Stay down.' I take his advice. I'm coughing blood, what else can I do? Guy gets up in the cab behind the wheel, picks up a Grease Gun lying on the seat above my head, fires a magazine through the righthand window across the field, reloads, fires another clip, puts the gun down and drives off, mortars coming down here and there to the sides and in front. Guy does a U-turn in the field and drives back the way he came. I'm looking up from the floor at him. He held the wheel with his left knee, reloaded the Grease Gun and fired another magazine across the field, out his side this time. Couldn't have hit a thing. But he was a comer, you know? He drives us out of the field into a road and then on back. First guys in the 26th he comes to with a medic and a radio he stops, gives them the word. They get me down and make the call while the medic starts in on me. The guy gets back up in the truck. I can't talk, I'm coughing blood, but I want the guy's name. The sergeant with the platoon we came across gets up on the running board and says, 'What happened, what's your name?' The guy in the truck says, 'I don't have the time, Sergeant. I'll catch you later. Got some 76 millimeter rounds here I got to take on up to the Shermans.' I hear him say 76 millimeter rounds and right away I think about the mortars ranging on us in that field where he found me: if just one of them had hit had hit that truck, me and that guy would have been pieces the size of your hand. The sergeant bawls at him to hold on but the guy just says, "They're waiting." And he lets in the clutch and the truck starts to roll and the sergeant has to jump down. Truck goes off down the road. That's the last I saw of him. So: that's why Jimmy here called you guys over. I want to find this guy if I can. You know him, hear anything about someone doing something like that?"

"What was it made you think it was someone from the Seven Six One?" Simpson asks.

"Yeah," Rutherford says. "Did you see the Battalion patch?"

"Maybe the guy told you he was from the Seven Six One?" Withers asks Sergeant Miller.

"Maybe it was the number on the truck's bumper," Franklin says.

"I didn't see a patch and he didn't say nothing about the unit he was from and I didn't see any number on the truck's bumper," Sergeant Miller says. He looks from one of us to the next. "What? Are you guys kidding me?"

"They're kidding you," I say.

"Kidding me," Sergeant Miller says. He shakes his head. "You guys. But look: you heard anything about a guy like this?"

"You sure it was a truck?" Fellows asks. Simpson sighs: he is sure Fellows is going to begin one of his judicial enquiries. "We got a man named Reedy, a Sherman driver, got down and pulled three wounded infantrymen out of a field under fire. Just about that time, the ninth or tenth of November, I think. Sort of like what you described."

"No," Sergeant Miller says. He shakes his head to show us he remembers. "One man, in a two-and-a-quarter ton truck. No tank. A truck, carrying a load of ammunition like I said. Must have been from your outfit's Service Company. You guys said you were in maintenance. So you're in Service Company. You ought to know something about this."

"Maybe it was someone in division trains," Withers says.

"No," Sergeant Miller says. "I asked. And I had our lieutenant ask too. I wanted to find this man. So did the lieutenant. That was my first thought: that he was in division trains. But he wasn't: they don't send people up with ammunition to the tanks. They send it to the tank battalion's service company and the service company takes it on up. And let me tell you: the people in division trains asked around. If it was their man did it, they wanted to know. But no one in division trains went anywhere near where I was that day. And the Seven Six One was the only unit, ah, like yours, around there then. So it had to be someone driving a truck from your outfit. From your Service Company."

"I don't know," I say. "I didn't hear anything about it. And you know how people talk. If someone from the Seven Six One's Service Company pulled someone from the Twenty-Sixth out of a field under fire, we would have heard about it."

"You telling me something else happened?" Sergeant Miller asks. He looks grim, as though he does not like us questioning his word.

"No," Franklin says. "It's just we haven't heard anything. And a thing like that? Whoever did it would have reported back, told what he did. At least I think he would. Can't see a reason why he wouldn't."

"Unless he was wounded," Rutherford says. "Or killed."

"Hell," Sergeant Miller says. "Look, you guys do me a favor. Take my name. Sergeant Frank J. Miller. Here, let me write it down." He takes a pen and a notebook from his breast pocket and writes down his rank, name, serial number, company, battalion, regiment, division, and an address in Minneapolis. "That's my aunt's place. If you hear, write me, will you? And if you find out who this guy was before we leave here, or you leave here, get in touch with me, will you? I want to thank this guy. I owe."

I take the paper he holds out to me and fold it into my pocket. "We'll ask, Sergeant. Ask everyone. Maybe even get the Captain to make it a Company matter, have him make an announcement in front of a Company formation."

"We ain't had a Company formation since England," Rutherford tells me. He is wrong: we had one, in March, in Germany just east of the last southern piece of Holland. But Rutherford didn't attend that formation: he was helping Captain Knowles tell the recovery crew how to winch Bayou Queen up onto the Dragon Wagon's trailer while I was helping First Sergeant Reardon show Willy Thorn how to stand up against it.

"We'll ask," I say. "And we'll ask the Captain to ask. But we might not find anything."

"If you don't," Sergeant Miller says, "you don't. But I'd appreciate it if you guys would try. Or if you'd get in touch if you hear anything after."

"We'll try for certain," Williston says. The rest of us nod and Sergeant Miller looks like he thinks he's going to be able to rely on us.

We have a couple of more drinks apiece and talk about this and that: the war, and after the war, and before the war. Sergeant Miller is depressed about the after part: he thinks we will all have hard times once the economy slows up. I don't know about him, but I'm pretty sure if anyone has hard times, we'll have harder. At seven I look at my watch and say, "We've got to get on back."

"All right," Sergeant Miller says. "But first, you guys are going to have a brandy with Williston and me." He waves at the waitress, holds up his brandy glass, puts it down and holds up nine fingers. She nods and brings the bottle and seven brandy glasses on a tray.

Sergeant Miller holds up his full glass and says, "Here's to whoever he is." He drinks, and we drink with him.

As we get up, Sergeant Miller says, "You guys will ask, right?"

"Yes," I say. "We'll ask. Don't worry about that." But I doubt we will find out who brought Sergeant Miller in out of the field where he was bleeding to death. We have had a lot of casualties, and many of the men we started with in England last October have left the Seven Six One dead or wounded. And I have heard nothing about an incident like the one Sergeant Miller has described.

"That's all I ask," Sergeant Miller says. "That you try and find out who he was."

"We will," Fellows tells him. "Don't worry about that. We'll try."

"All right," Sergeant Miller says. He gets up and shakes hands with each of us and he and Sparkman walk out of the cafe into the square with us. They stop just beyond the last of the tables set out in front of the cafe. It is late evening but it is still light.

"Come on back and see us here," Corporal Sparkman says. "Me, I always find chairs and tables for anyone who comes by."

"We'll do that," Rutherford says. "Nice place you found here."

"Any time you're around," Sergeant Miller says. We nod and walk to the weapons carrier. As we drive away across the square I look back. Sergeant Miller sees me looking. He waves. When he waves, Corporal Sparkman waves too. I wave back.

"Who you think it might have been?" Williston asks.

"The guy who got Miller out of there?" I say. "I don't know. I didn't hear anything about it at the time."

"Hell of a lot going on then," Withers says from the back of the weapons carrier. "Bad bunch of days back there in November."

"You're not just kidding, brother," Franklin says. I turn and look at him. He looks grim. He has good reason: anyone in the Seven Six One who recalls last November has good reason to look grim.

"Still, we ought to be able to find out who he is?" Simpson says.

"I doubt that," Fellows says. "He would have come forward and explained himself. I think he was wounded. Or killed. Whoever he was."

"What you think," Rutherford asks from the back of the weapons carrier, "the First Sergeant would think about someone like that?"

"He would have asked why he was late coming with the 76 millimeter armor piercing for the Shermans," Withers says.

"No he wouldn't," Simpson said. "First Sergeant would have said he did all right. Then he would have asked why he was late coming with the armor piercing."

"Maybe," I say. "Maybe not." They listen as I speak: they think I have a special knowledge of the First Sergeant. Perhaps they are right. "If the guy lived through it, the First Sergeant would have said, 'You did all right up there. I'll talk to you later.'"

"What would he have said if the guy had died trying to get Miller out of that field?"

"He wouldn't have said anything," I tell them. "But in his diary he would have written, 'his death is a loss to the Battalion, to the Army of the United States, and to the United States of America.'"

"All that, for getting killed trying to save Sergeant Miller?" Williston asks. He shakes his head and puts the headlights on: the light is fading and infantrymen from the 71st Infantry Division are walking toward us along the verges of the road, heading for the quiet nightlife of Steyr. "I don't know. I'm not so sure we're going to count that much when they do the numbers after."

"You asked me what the First Sergeant would have written," I tell him. "I told you. You didn't ask me how they'll count when they run the numbers."

"I know what I asked," Williston says. He sounds tired and annoyed: perhaps it is the brandy he drank that makes him so. "The question I'm asking is," he says, "what do you think? You agree with the First Sergeant? That this guy, whoever he was, was all that? A loss to the Seven Six One, to the Army and the country? You'd say the same thing about him as the First Sergeant would have written?"

I think about it as Williston drives on between the small groups of infantrymen ambling toward Steyr. I think about it with care, for though I do not look over my shoulder, I know that Rutherford, Withers, Fellows, Simpson and Franklin are listening from the back of the weapons carrier for my answer to Williston's question.

What the First Sergeant wrote here and there in his diary about men killed in France, Belgium and Germany is a lot to say of anyone, even of our own in the Seven Six One. It may be more than one should say of a man whose name we may never know, and who did no more than the right thing when he rescued Sergeant Miller from the raging war in which he was about to drown. But perhaps it is not enough to say.

"Yes," I tell Williston and the others sitting behind me. "Yes. I'd say the same thing."

All these were honored in their generations
And were the glory of their times
There be of them
That have left a name behind them
That their praises might be reported
And some there be which have no memorial
Who are perished as though they had never been
And are become as though they had never been born
And their children after them
But these were merciful men
Whose righteousness hath not been forgotten
With their seed shall continually remain
A good inheritance
And their children are within the covenant
Their seed standeth fast
And their children for their sakes
Their seed shall remain for ever
And their glory shall not be blotted out
Their bodies are buried in peace
But their name liveth for evermore

Ecclesiasticus xliv